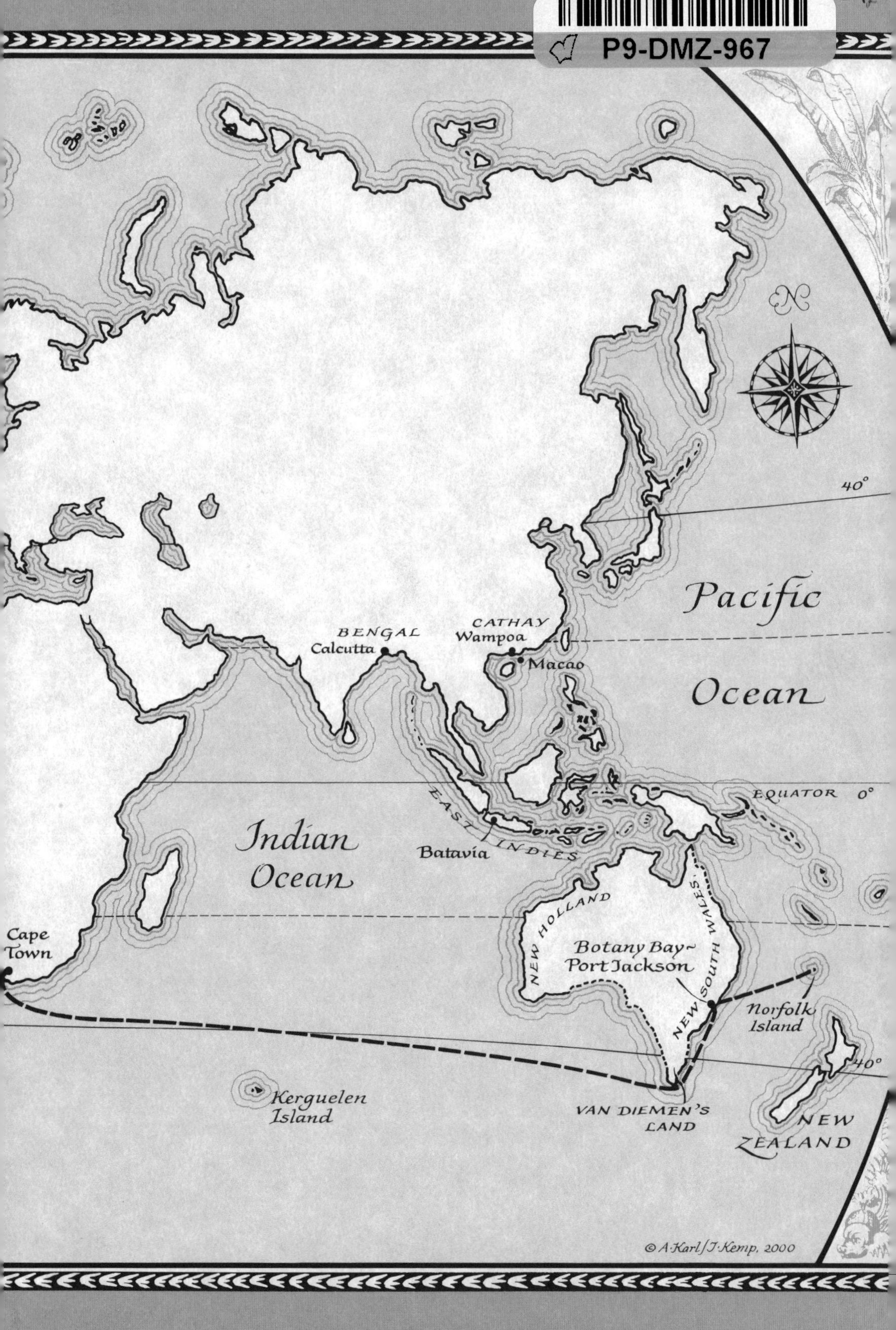
Pacific
Ocean
Indian
Ocean
BENGAL
Calcutta
CATHAY
Wampoa
Macao
EAST INDIES
Batavia
EQUATOR 0°
40°
Cape
Town
NEW HOLLAND
NEW SOUTH WALES
Botany Bay~
Port Jackson
Norfolk
Island
40°
Kerguelen
Island
VAN DIEMEN'S
LAND
NEW
ZEALAND
© A·Karl/J·Kemp, 2000

Also by Colleen McCullough

Roden Cutler, V. C. (biography)

The Song of Troy

Caesar: Let the Dice Fly

Caesar's Women

Fortune's Favorites

The Grass Crown

The First Man in Rome

The Ladies of Missalonghi

A Creed for the Third Millennium

An Indecent Obsession

The Thorn Birds

Tim

Colleen McCullough

Morgan's Run

Simon & Schuster

New York London Toronto Sydney Singapore

SIMON & SCHUSTER
Rockefeller Center, 1230 Avenue of the Americas, New York, NY 10020

This book is a work of fiction based upon eighteenth-century events and persons.

Designed by Brooke Koven
Illustration pages 141, 331, and 543 copyright © 2000 by David Cain
Maps copyright © 2000 by Anita Karl and Jim Kemp
Manufactured in the United States of America

3 5 7 9 10 8 6 4

Library of Congress Cataloging-in-Publication Data
McCullough, Colleen, date.
Morgan's run / Colleen McCullough.
p. cm.
1. Morgan, Richard, b. 1748?—Fiction.
2. Penal colonies—Fiction. 3. Australia—Fiction.
4. Convicts—Fiction. I. Title.
PR9619.3.M32 M67 2000
823'.914—dc21 00-041006
ISBN 0-684-85329-9

Permission to reproduce the art on part title pages is gratefully acknowledged: PART ONE: English School, Bristol Docks and Quay, early 18th century, City of Bristol Museum and Art Gallery/The Bridgeman Art Library. PART TWO: William Hogarth, "The Bench" c. 1753–58, oil on canvas backed onto wood, 17.4 x 18.1 cm, Fitzwilliam Museum, University of Cambridge. PART THREE: Edward Cooke, "York Prison-ship in Portsmouth Harbour," convicts going on board, etching, 16.2 x 23.7 cm, Rex Nan Kivell Collection, NK 4656, National Library of Australia. PART FOUR: George Raper, "Entrance to Rio de Janeiro (Brazil)," drawing No. 8, 1790, from the anchorage without, the Sugar Loaf bearing N.W. ½ N. off shore 2 miles, The Natural History Museum, London. PART FIVE: William Bradley, "Sydney Cove, Port Jackson, 1788," watercolour by William Bradley in *A Voyage to New South Wales: the journal of Lieutenant William Bradley RN of the* HMS *Sirius 1786–1792,* England c. 1795, Image Library, State Library of New South Wales. PART SIX: George Raper, "The Settlement on Norfolk Island, May 16, 1790," watercolour by George Raper, Image Library, State Library of New South Wales.

For Ric, Brother John, Wayde, Joe, Helen, and all the other many hundreds of people alive today who can trace their roots directly to Richard Morgan.

But most of all, this book is for my beloved Melinda, the five-times-great-granddaughter of Richard Morgan.

We are born owning many qualities; some we may never know we possess. It all depends what kind of run God gives us.

Morgan's Run

PART ONE

From August of 1775 until October of 1784

"We are at war!" cried Mr. James Thiſtlethwaite.

Every head save Richard Morgan's lifted and turned toward the door, where a bulky figure stood brandishing a sheet of flimsy. For a moment a pin might have been heard dropping, then a confused babble of exclamations erupted at every table in the tavern except for Richard Morgan's. Richard had paid the stirring announcement scant heed: what did war with the thirteen American colonies matter, compared to the fate of the child he held on his lap? Cousin James-the-druggist had inoculated the little fellow against the smallpox four days ago, and now Richard Morgan waited, agonized, to see if the inoculation would take.

"Come in, Jem, read it to us," said Dick Morgan, Mine Host and Richard's father, from behind his counter.

Though the noonday sun shone outside and light did diffuse through the bullioned panes of Crown glass in the windows of the Cooper's Arms, the large room was dim. So Mr. James Thistlethwaite strolled over to the counter and the rays of an oil lamp, the butt of a horse pistol protruding from each greatcoat pocket. Spectacles perched upon the end of his nose, he started to read aloud, voice rising and falling in dramatic cadences.

Some of what he said did penetrate the fog of Richard Morgan's worry—snatches, phrases only: " 'in open and avowed rebellion. . . . the utmost endeavors to suppress such rebellion, and bring the traitors to justice. . . .' "

Feeling the contempt in his father's gaze, Richard genuinely tried to concentrate. But surely the fever was beginning? *Was* it? If so, then the inoculation was definitely taking. And if it did take, would William Henry be one of those who suffered the full disease anyway? Died anyway? Dear God, no!

Mr. James Thistlethwaite was arriving at his peroration. " 'The die is now cast! The colonies must either submit or triumph!' " he thundered.

"What an odd way for the King to put it," said Mine Host.

"Odd?"

"It sounds as if the King deems a colonial triumph possible."

"Oh, I doubt that very much, Dick. His speech writer—some scurvy undersecretary to his bum boy Lord Bute, I hazard a guess—is fascinated with the balances of rhetoric—ah?" This last word was accompanied by a gesture, forefinger pointing to mouth.

Mine Host grinned and ran a measure of rum into a small pewter mug, then turned to chalk a slash on the slate fixed to his wall.

"Dick, Dick! My news merits one on the house!"

"No it does not. We would have heard sooner or later." Mine Host leaned his elbows on his counter in the place where they had worn two slight depressions and stared at the armed and greatcoated Mr. Thistlethwaite—mad as a March hare! The summer's day was sweltering. "Seriously, Jem, it is not exactly a bolt from the blue, but these are shocking tidings all the same."

No other voice attempted to participate in their conversation; Dick Morgan stood well with his patrons, and Jem Thistlethwaite had long enjoyed a reputation as one of Bristol's more eccentric intellectuals. The patrons were quite content to listen as they imbibed the tipple of their choice—rum, gin, beer, Bristol milk.

The two Morgan wives were there to move about, pick up the empties and return them to Dick for refilling—and more slashes on the slate. It was nearly dinner time; the smell of new bread Peg Morgan had just brought in from Jenkins the baker was stealing through the other odors natural to a tavern adjacent to the Bristol quays at low tide. Most of the mixture of men, women and children present would remain to avail themselves of that same new bread, a pat of butter, a hunk of Somerset cheese, a steaming pewter platter of beef and potatoes swimming in rich gravy.

His father was glaring at him. Miserably aware that Dick despised him for a milksop, Richard searched for something to say. "I suppose we hoped," he said vaguely, "that none of the other colonies would stand by Massachusetts, having warned it that it was going too far. And did they truly think that the King would stoop to read their letter? Or, even if he had, yield to their demands? They are Englishmen! The King is their king too."

"Nonsense, Richard!" said Mr. Thistlethwaite sharply. "This obsessive concern for your child is fast addling your thinking apparatus! The King and his sycophantic ministers are bent on plunging our sceptered isle into disaster! Eight *thousand* tons of Bristol shipping sent back unloaded from the thirteen colonies in less than a year! That serge manufactory in Redcliff gone out of business and the four hundred souls it employed thrown upon the parish! Not to mention that place near the Port Wall which makes painted canvas carpets for Carolina and Georgia! The pipe makers, the soap makers, the bottle makers, the sugar and rum makers—for God's sake, man! Most of our trade is across the Western Ocean, and no mean part of that with the thirteen colonies! To go to war against the thirteen colonies is commercial suicide!"

"I see," said Mine Host, picking up the sheet of flimsy to squint at it, "that Lord North has issued a—a 'Proclamation for Suppressing Armed Rebellion.' "

"It is a war we cannot win," said Mr. Thistlethwaite, holding out his empty mug to Mag Morgan, hovering.

Richard tried again. "Come now, Jem! We have beaten France after seven years of war—we are the greatest and bravest country in the world! The King of England does not lose his wars."

"Because he fights them in close proximity to England, or against heathens, or against ignorant savages whose own rulers sell them. But the men of the thirteen colonies are, as ye rightly said, Englishmen. They are civilized and conversant with our ways. They are of our blood." Mr. Thistlethwaite leaned back, sighed, wrinkled the nobly grog-blossomed contours of his bulbous nose. "They deem themselves held light, Richard. Put upon, spat upon, looked down upon. Englishmen, yes, yet never quite the bona fide article. And they are a very long way away, which is a nettle the King and his ministers have grasped in utter ignorance. You might say that our navy wins our wars—how long is it since we stood or fell by a land army outside our own isles? Yet how can we win a sea war against a foe who has no ships? We will have to fight on land. Thirteen different bits of land, scarcely interconnected. And against a foe not organized to conduct himself in proper military mode."

"Ye've just shot down your own argument, Jem," said Mine Host, smiling but not reaching for his chalk as he handed a fresh mug of rum to Mag. "Our armies are first rate. The colonists will not be able to stand against them."

"I agree, I agree!" cried Jem, lifting his gratis rum in a toast to the landlord, who was rarely generous. "The colonists probably will never win a battle. But they do not need to win battles, Dick. All they need to do is to *endure.* For it is their land we will be fighting in, and it is not England." His hand went to the left pocket of his greatcoat; out came the massive pistol, down it went on the table with a crash, while the tavern's other occupants squealed and shrieked in terror—and Richard, his infant son on his lap, pushed its muzzle sideways so quickly that no one saw him move. The pistol, as everybody knew, was loaded. Oblivious to the consternation he had caused, Mr. Thistlethwaite burrowed into the depths of the pocket and produced some folded pieces of flimsy paper. These he examined one by one, his spectacles enlarging his pale blue and bloodshot eyes, his dark and curling hair escaping from the ribbon with which he had carelessly tied it back—no wigs or queues for Mr. James Thistlethwaite.

"Ah!" he exclaimed finally, flourishing a London news sheet. "Seven and a half months ago, ladies and gentlemen of the Cooper's Arms, there was a great debate in the House of Lords, during which that grand old man, William Pitt the Earl of Chatham, gave what is said to be his greatest oration. In defense of the colonists. But it is not Chatham's words thrill me," continued Mr. Thistlethwaite, "it is the Duke of Richmond's, and I quote: 'You may spread fire and desolation, but that will not be government!' How true, how very true! Now comes the bit I judge one of the great philosophical truths, though the Lords snored as he said it: 'No people can ever be made to submit to a form of government they say they will not receive.' "

He stared about, nodding. "That is why *I* say that all the battles we will win can be of no use and can have little effect upon the outcome of the war. If the colonists endure, they *must* win." His eyes twinkled as he folded the paper, shoved the quire or so back into his pocket, and jammed the horse pistol on top of them. "You know too much about guns, Richard, that is your trouble. The child was not endangered, nor any of the other folk here." A rumble commenced in his throat and vibrated through his pursed lips. "I have lived in this stinking cesspool called Bristol for all of my life, and I have alleviated the monotony by making some of our festering Tory sores in government the object of my lampoons, from Quaker to Shaker to Kingmaker." He waved his battered tricorn hat at his audience and closed his eyes. "If the colonists endure, they must win," he repeated. "Anybody who lives in Bristol has made the acquaintance of a thousand colonists—they flit about the place like bats in the last light. The death of Empire, Dick! It is the first rattle in our English throats. I have come to know the colonists, and I say they will win."

A strange and ominous sound began to percolate in from outside, a sound of many angry voices; the distorted shapes of passersby flickering unhurriedly across the windows suddenly became blurs moving at a run.

"Rioters!" Richard was getting to his feet even as he handed the child to his wife. "Peg, straight upstairs with William Henry! Mum, go with them." He looked at Mr. Thistlethwaite. "Jem, do you intend to fire with one in either hand, or will you give me the second pistol?"

"Leave be, leave be!" Dick emerged from behind his counter to reveal himself a close physical counterpart to Richard, taller than most, muscular in build. "This end of Broad Street does not see rioters, even when the colliers came in from Kingswood and snatched old man Brickdale. Nor does it when the sailors go on the rampage. Whatever is going on, it is not a riot." He crossed to the door. "However, I am of a mind to see what is afoot," he said, and disappeared into the running throng. The occupants of the Cooper's Arms followed him, including Richard and Jem Thistlethwaite, his horse pistols still snug in his greatcoat pockets.

People were boiling everywhere at street level, people leaned from every penthouse with necks craning; not a stone of the flagged road could be seen, nor a single slab of the new pedestrian pavement down either side of Broad Street. The three men pushed into the crush and moved with it toward the junction of Wine and Corn Streets—no, these were not rioters. These were affluent, extremely angry gentlemen who carried no women or children with them.

On the opposite side of Broad Street and somewhat closer to the hub of commerce around the Council House and the Exchange stood the White Lion Inn, headquarters of the Steadfast Society. This was the Tory club, source of much encouragement to His Britannic Majesty King George III, whose men they were to the death. The center of the disturbance was the American Coffee House next door, its sign the red-and-white flag of many stripes most American colonists used as a general banner when the flag of Connecticut or Virginia or some other colony was not appropriate.

"I believe," said Dick Morgan, on fruitless tiptoe, "that we would do better to go back to the Cooper's Arms and watch from the penthouse."

So back they went, up the shaky crumbling stairs at the inner end of the counter and thus eventually to the casement windows which leaned perilously far out over Broad Street below. In the back room little William Henry was crying, his mother and grandmother bent over his cot cooing and clucking; the hubbub outside held no interest for Peg or Mag while William Henry displayed such terrible grief. Nor did the hubbub tempt Richard, joining the women.

"Richard, he will not perish in the next few minutes!" snapped Dick from the front room. "Come here and see, damn ye!"

Richard came, but reluctantly, to lean out the gaping window and gasp in amazement. "Yankeys, Father! Christ, what are they doing to the things?"

"Things" they certainly were: two rag effigies stuffed quite professionally with straw, tarred all over with pitch still smoking, and encrusted with feathers. Except for their heads, upon which sat the insignia of colonists—their abysmally unfashionable but very sensible hats, brim turned down all the way around so that the low round crown sat like the yolk blister in the middle of a fried egg.

"Holloa!" bellowed Jem Thistlethwaite, spying a well-known face belonging to a well-known, expensively suited body, the whole perched upon a geehoe sledge loaded with tall barrels. "Master Harford, what goes?"

"The Steadfast Society saith it hangeth John Hancock and John Adams!" the Quaker plutocrat called back.

"What, because General Gage refused to extend his pardon to them after Concord?"

"I know not, Master Thistlethwaite." Clearly terrified that he too would be lampooned in some highly uncomplimentary way, Joseph Harford descended from his vantage point and melted into the crowd.

"Hypocrite!" said Mr. Thistlethwaite under his breath.

"Samuel Adams, not John Adams," said Richard, his interest now fairly caught. "Surely it would be Samuel Adams?"

"If the richest merchants in Boston are whom the Steadfast Society mean to hang, then yes, it ought to be Samuel. But John writes and speaks more," said Mr. Thistlethwaite.

In a nautically oriented city, the production of two ropes efficiently tied into hangman's knots did not present a difficulty; two such magically appeared, and the stark, bristly, man-sized dolls were hoisted by their necks to the signpost of the American Coffee House, there to turn lazily and smolder sluggishly. Rage spent, the throng of Steadfast Society men vanished through the welcoming, Tory-blue doors of the White Lion Inn.

"Tory pricks!" said Mr. Thistlethwaite, descending the stairs with a nice mug of rum uppermost in his mind.

"Out, Jem!" said Mine Host, bolting the door until he could be sure the disturbance was definitely over.

* * *

Richard had not followed his father downstairs, though duty said he ought; his name was now joined to Dick's in the official Corporation books. Richard Morgan, victualler, had paid the fine and become an accredited Free Man, a vote-empowered citizen of a city which was in itself a county distinct from Gloucestershire and Somersetshire surrounding it, a citizen of a city which was the second-largest in all of England, Wales, Scotland and Ireland. Of the 50,000 souls jammed within its bounds, only some 7,000 were vote-empowered Free Men.

"Is it taking?" Richard asked his wife, and leaning over the cot; William Henry had quietened, seemed to doze uneasily.

"Yes, my love." Peg's soft brown eyes suddenly filled with tears, her lips trembling. "Now is the time to pray, Richard, that he does not suffer the full pox. Though he does not burn the way Mary did." She gave her husband a gentle push. "Go for a good long walk. You may pray *and* walk. Go on! Please, Richard. If you stay, Father will growl."

A peculiar lethargy had descended upon Broad Street as a result of the panic which seemed to wing citywide in minutes whenever riots threatened. Passing the American Coffee House, Richard stopped for a moment to contemplate the dangling effigies of John Hancock and John/Samuel Adams, his ears assailed by the fitful roars of laughter and spleen originating among the dining ranks of the Steadfast Society inside the White Lion. His lips curled in faint contempt; the Morgans were staunch Whigs whose votes had contributed to the success of Edmund Burke and Henry Cruger at the elections last year—what a circus they had been! And how miffed Lord Clare had been when he polled hardly a vote!

Walking swiftly now, Richard strode along Corn Street past John Weeks's fabulous Bush Inn, headquarters of the Whig Union Club. From there he cut north up Small Street and emerged onto the Key at the Stone Bridge. The vista spread southward was extraordinary. It looked as if a very wide street had been filled with ships in skeletal rigging, just masts and yards and stays and shrouds above their beamy oaken bellies. Of the river Froom wherein they actually sat, nothing could be seen because of those ships in their multitudes, patiently waiting out the days of their twenty weeks' turnaround.

The tide had reached its ebb and was beginning to flood in again at a startling rate: the level of the water in both the Froom and the Avon rose thirty feet in around six and a half hours, then fell thirty. At the ebb the ships lay upon the foetid mud, which sloped steeply and tipped them sideways on their beams; at the flood, the ships rode afloat, as ships were built to do. Many a keel had hogged and buckled at the strain of lying sideways on Bristol mud.

Richard's mind, once over its instinctive reaction to that wide avenue of ships, returned to its rut.

***Lord God**, hear my prayer! Keep my son safe. Do not take my son from me and from his mother. . . .*

He was not his father's only son, though he was the elder; his brother, William, was a sawyer with his own business down along the St. Philip's bank of the Avon near Cuckold's Pill and the glasshouses, and he had three sisters all satisfactorily married to Free Men. There were nests of Morgans in several parts of the city, but the Morgans of Richard's clan—perhaps emigrants from Wales in long ago times—had been resident for enough generations to have gained some standing; indeed, clan luminaries like Cousin James-the-druggist headed significant enterprises, belonged to the Merchant Venturers and the Corporation, gave hefty donations to the poorhouses, and hoped one day to be Mayor.

Richard's father was not a clan luminary. Nor was he a clan disgrace. After some elementary schooling he had served his time as an apprentice victualler, then, certificated and a Free Man who had paid his fine, he struggled toward the goal of keeping his own tavern. A socially acceptable marriage had been arranged for him; Margaret Biggs came from good farming stock near Bedminster and enjoyed the cachet of being able to read, though she could not write. The children, commencing with a girl, came along at intervals too frequent to render the grief of losing an occasional child truly unbearable. When Dick learned sufficient control to withdraw before ejaculating, the children ceased at two living sons, three living daughters. A good brood, small enough to make providing for them feasible. Dick wanted at least one fully literate son, and centered his hopes on Richard when it became apparent that William, two years younger, was no scholar.

So when Richard turned seven he was enrolled at Colston's School for Boys and donned the famous blue coat which informed Bristolians that his father was poor but respectable, staunchly Church of England. And over the course of the next five years literacy and numeracy were drummed into him. He learned to write a fair hand, do sums in his head, plod through Caesar's *Gallic War,* Cicero's speeches, and Ovid's *Metamorphoses,* stimulated by the acid sting of the cane and the caustic bite of the master's comments. Since he was a good though not shining scholar and owned into the bargain a quiet attractiveness, he survived the late Mr. Colston's philanthropic institution better than most, and got more out of it.

At twelve, it was time to leave and espouse a trade or craft in keeping with his education. Much to the surprise of his relations, he went in a different direction than any Morgan thus far. Among his chief assets was a talent for things mechanical, for putting together the pieces of a puzzle; and allied to that was a patience truly remarkable in one so young. Of his own choice, he was apprenticed to Senhor Tomas Habitas the gunsmith.

This decision secretly pleased his father, who liked the idea of the Morgans' producing an artisan rather than a tradesman. Besides which, war was a part of life, and guns a part of war. A man who could make and mend them was unlikely to become cannon fodder on a battlefield.

For Richard, the seven years of his apprenticeship were a joy when it came to the work and the learning, even if a trifle on the cheerless side when it came to physical comfort. Like all apprentices, he was not paid, lived in his master's house, waited on him at his table, dined off the scraps, and slept on the floor. Luckily Senhor Tomas Habitas was a kind master and a superb gunsmith. Though he could make gorgeous dueling pistols and sporting guns, he was shrewd enough to realize that in order to prosper in those areas he must needs be a Manton, and a Manton he could not be outside of London. So he had settled for making the military musket known affectionately to every soldier and marine as "Brown Bess," all 46 inches of her—be they wood of stock or steel of barrel—brown as a nut.

At nineteen Richard was certificated and moved out of the Habitas household, though not out of the Habitas workshop. There he continued, a master craftsman now, to make Brown Bess. And he married, something he was not allowed to do while an apprentice. His wife was the child of his mother's brother and therefore his own first cousin, but as the Church of England had no objection to that, he wed his bride in St. James's church under the auspices of Cousin James-of-the-clergy. Though arranged, it had been a love match, and the couple had only fallen more deeply in love as the years rolled on. Not without some difficulties of nomenclature, for Richard Morgan, son of Richard Morgan and Margaret Biggs, had taken another Margaret Biggs to wife.

While the Habitas gunsmithy had thrived that had not been so awkward, for the young pair lived in a two-roomed rented apartment on Temple Street across the Avon, just around the corner from the Habitas workshop and the Jewish synagogue.

The marriage had taken place in 1767, three years after the Seven Years'

War against France had been concluded by an unpopular peace; heavily in debt despite victory, England had to increase her revenues by additional taxes and decrease the cost of her army and navy by massive retrenchments. Guns were no longer necessary. So one by one the Habitas artisans and apprentices disappeared until the establishment consisted of Richard and Senhor Tomas Habitas himself. Then finally, just after the birth of little Mary in 1770, Habitas was reluctantly obliged to let Richard go.

"Come and work for me," Dick Morgan had said cordially. "Guns may come and go, but rum is absolutely eternal."

It had answered very well, despite the problem with names. Richard's mother had always been known as Mag and Richard's wife as Peg, two diminutives for Margaret. The real trouble was that save for quirky Protestant Dissenters who christened their male progeny "Cranfield" or "Onesiphorus," almost every male in England was John, William, Henry, Richard, James or Thomas, and almost every female was Ann, Catherine, Margaret, Elizabeth or Mary. One of the few customs which embraced every class from highest to lowest.

Peg, deliciously cuddly and willing Peg, turned out not to conceive easily. Mary was her first pregnancy, nearly three years after she had married, and it was not for want of trying. Naturally both parents had hoped for a son, so it was a disappointment when they had to find a girl's name. Richard's fancy lighted upon Mary, not common in the clan and (as his father said frankly) a name with a papist taint to it. No matter. From the moment in which he took his newborn daughter into his arms and gazed down on her in awe, Richard Morgan discovered in himself an ocean of love as yet unexplored. Perhaps because of his patience, he had always liked and gotten on famously with children, but this had not prepared him for what he felt when he beheld little Mary. Blood of his blood, bone of his bone, flesh of his flesh.

Thus his new trade of victualler suited Richard far more than gunsmithing now that he had a child; a tavern was a family business, a place wherein he could constantly be with his daughter, see her with her mother, watch the miracle of Peg's beautiful breast serve as a cushion for the babe's head while the tiny mouth worked at getting milk. Nor did Peg stint her milk, terrified of the day when Mary would have to be weaned from the breast on to small beer. No water for a Bristol child, any more than for a London one! There was not much intoxicant in small beer, but it did have some. Those babes put to it too young, said Peg the farmer's daughter (echoed by Mag), always grew up to be drunkards. Though not prone to espouse women's ideas, Dick Morgan, veteran of forty years in the tavern business, heartily concurred. Little Mary was over two years old before Peg commenced to wean her.

They had run the Bell then, Dick's first tavern of his own. It was in Bell Lane and part of the tortuous complex of tenements, warehouses and underground chambers in control of Cousin James-the-druggist, who shared the south side of the narrow alley with the equally rambling premises of the American woolbrokering firm of Lewsley & Co. It must be added that Cousin James-the-druggist had a splendid shop for local retail on Corn Street; he made most of his money, however, in manufacturing and exporting drugs and chemical compounds from corrosive sublimate of mercury (used to treat syphilitic chancres) to laudanum and other opiates.

When the license of the Cooper's Arms around the corner on Broad Street had come up last year, Dick Morgan had leaped at it. A tavern on Broad Street! Why, even after paying the Corporation £21 a year in rent, the proprietor of a tavern on Broad Street could not help but see a profit of £100 a year!* It had answered well, as the Morgan family was not afraid of hard work, Dick Morgan never watered down his rum and gin, and the food available at dinner time (around noon) and supper time (around six) was excellent. Mag was a splendid cook of plain food, and all the petty regulations dating from the time of Good Queen Bess which hedged a Bristol tavern-keeper around—no bread to be baked on the premises, no animals killed to avoid buying from a butcher—were, thought Dick Morgan, actually benefits. If a man paid his bills on time, he could always get special terms from his wholesalers. Even when things were hard.

I wish, *God, said Richard to that invisible Being, that Thou wert not so cruel. For Thy wrath so often seems to fall upon those who have not offended Thee. Preserve my son, I pray. . . .*

Around him on its heights and marshes the city of Bristol swam in a sea of gritty smoke, the spires of its many churches wellnigh hidden. The summer

* English money was divided into pounds, shillings and pence, with the guinea as an oddment. There were 21 shillings in a guinea, 20 shillings in a pound, and 12 pence in a shilling. A ha'penny was one half a penny, a farthing one quarter of a penny.

had been an unusually hot and dry one, and this August ending had seen no relief. The leaves of the elms and limes on College Green to the west and Queen Square to the south looked tired and faded, stripped of gloss and glitter. Chimneys gouted black plumes everywhere—the foundries in the Friers and Castle Green, the sugar houses around Lewin's Mead, Fry's chocolate works, the tall cones of the glasshouses and the squatter lime kilns. If the wind were not in the west, this atmospheric inferno received additional fugs from Kingswood, a place no Bristolian voluntarily went. The coal-fields and the massive metalworks upon them bred a half-savage people quick to anger and possessed of an abiding hatred for Bristol. No wonder, given the hideous fumes and wretched damps of Kingswood.

He was moving now into real ship's territory: Tombs's dry dock, another dry dock, the reek of hot pitch, the unwaled ships abuilding looking like the rib cages of gargantuan animals. In Canon's Marsh he took the rope walk through the marsh rather than the soggy footpath which meandered along the Avon's bank, nodding to the ropemakers as they walked their third-of-a-mile inexorably twisting the hempen or linen strands, already twisted at least once, into whatever was the order of the day—cables, hawsers, lines. Their arms and shoulders were as corded as the rope they wound, their hands so hardened that all feeling had left them—how could they find pleasure in a woman's skin?

Past the single glasshouse at the foot of Back Lane, past a cluster of lime kilns, and so to the beginnings of Clifton. The stark bulk of Brandon Hill rose in the background, and before him in a steep tumble of wooded hills going down to the Avon was the place of which he dreamed. Clifton, where the air was clear and the dells and downs rippled shivers as the wind ruffled maidenhair and eyebright, heath in purple flower, marjoram and wild geraniums. The trees sparkled, ungrimed, and there were glimpses of the huge mansions which stood in their little parks high up—Manilla House, Goldney House, Cornwallis House, Clifton Hill House. . . .

He wanted desperately to live in Clifton. Clifton folk were not consumptive, did not sicken of the flux or the malignant quinsy, the fever or the smallpox. That was as true of the humble folk in the cottages and rude shelters along the Hotwells road at the bottom of the hills as it was of the haughty folk who strolled outside the pillared majesty of their palaces aloft. Be he a sailor, a ropemaker, a shipwright's journeyman or a lord of the manor, Clifton folk did not sicken and die untimely. Here one might *keep* one's children.

Mary, who used to be the light of his life. She had, they said, his grey-blue eyes and waving blackish hair, her mother's nicely shaped nose, and the flawless tan skin both her parents owned. The best of both worlds, Richard used to say, laughing, the little creature cuddled to his chest with her eyes—*his* eyes—upturned to his face in adoration. Mary was her dadda's girl, no doubt of it; she could not get enough of him, nor he of her. Two people glued together, was how the faintly disapproving Dick Morgan had put it. Though busy Peg had simply smiled and let it happen, never voicing to her beloved Richard her knowledge that he had usurped a part of the child's affections due to her, the mother. After all, did it matter from whom the love came, provided there was love? Not every man was a good father, and most were too quick to administer a beating. Richard never lifted a hand.

The news of a second pregnancy had thrilled both parents: a three-year gap was a worry. Now they would have that boy!

"It is a boy," said Peg positively as her belly swelled. "I am carrying this one differently."

The smallpox broke out. Time out of mind, every generation had lived with it; like the plague, its mortality rate had slowly waned, so that only the most severe epidemics killed many. The faces one saw in the streets often bore the disfiguring craters of pock marks—a shame, but at least the life had been spared. Dick Morgan's face was slightly pock marked, but Mag and Peg had had the cowpox as girls, and never succumbed. Country superstition said that the cowpox meant no smallpox. So as soon as Richard had turned five, Mag took him to her father's farm near Bedminster during a spate of the disease and made the little fellow try to milk cows until he came down with this benign, protective sort of pox.

Richard and Peg had fully intended to do the same with Mary, but no cowpox appeared in Bedminster. Not yet four, the child had suddenly burned with terrible fever, moaned and twisted her pain-racked body, cried in a constant frenzy for her dadda. When Cousin James-the-druggist came (the Morgans knew he was a better doctor than any in Bristol who called themselves doctors) he looked grave.

"If the fever comes down when the spots appear, she will live," he said. "There are no medicaments can alter God's will. Keep her warm and do not let the air get at her."

Richard tried to help nurse her, sitting hour after hour beside the cot he had made and artfully fitted up with gimbals so that it swayed gently without the grind of cradle rockers. On the fourth day after the fever began the spots appeared, livid areolae with what looked like lead shot in their centers. Face, lower arms and hands, lower legs and feet. Vile, horrific. He talked to her and crooned to her, held her plucking hands while Peg and Mag changed her linens, washed her shrunken little buttocks as wrinkled and juiceless as an old woman's. But the fever did not diminish, and eventually, as the pustules burst and cratered, she flickered out as softly and subtly as a candle.

Cousin James-of-the-clergy was overwhelmed with burials. But the Morgans had kinship rights, so despite the calls on his time he interred Mary Morgan, aged three, with all the solemnities the Church of England could provide. Heavy with exhaustion and near her time, Peg leaned on her aunt and mother-in-law while Richard stood, weeping desolately, quite alone; he would not permit anyone to go near him. His father, who had lost children—indeed, who had not?—was humiliated by this torrent of grief, this unseemly unmanning. Not that Richard cared how his father felt. He did not even know. His bubba Mary was dead and he, who would gladly have died in her place, was alive and in the world without her. God was not good. God was not kind or merciful. God was a monster more evil than the Devil, who at least made no pretense of virtue.

An excellent thing, Dick and Mag Morgan agreed, that Peg was about to birth another child. The only anodyne for Richard's grief was a new baby to love.

"He might turn against it," said Mag anxiously.

"Not Richard!" said Dick scornfully. "He is too soft."

Dick was right, Mag wrong. For the second time Richard Morgan was enveloped in that ocean of love, though now he had some idea of its profundity. Knew the immensity of its depths, the power of its storms, the eternity of its reaches. With this child, he had vowed, he would learn to float, he would not expend his strength in fighting. A resolution which lasted no longer than the frozen moment in which he took in the sight of his son's face, the placid minute hands, the pulse inside a brand-new being on this sad old earth. Blood of his blood, bone of his bone, flesh of his flesh.

It was not in the province of a woman to name her babies. That task fell to Richard.

"Call him Richard," said Dick. "It is tradition."

"I will not. We have a Dick and a Richard already, do we now need a Dickon or a Rich?"

"I rather like Louis," said Peg casually.

"Another papist name!" roared Dick. "And it's *Frog!*"

"I will call him William Henry," said Richard.

"Bill, like his uncle," said Dick, pleased.

"No, Father, not Bill. Not Will. Not Willy, not Billy, not even William. His name is William Henry, and so he will be known by everybody," said Richard so firmly that the debate ended.

Truth to tell, this decision gratified the whole clan. Someone known to everybody as William Henry was bound to be a great man.

Richard gave voice to this verdict when he displayed his new son to Mr. James Thistlethwaite, who snorted.

"Aye, like Lord Clare," he said. "Started out a schoolmaster, married three fat and ugly old widows of enormous fortune, was—er—*lucky* enough to be shriven of them in quick succession, became a Member of Parliament for Bristol, and so met the Prince of Wales. Plain Robert Nugent. *Rrrrrrrr*olling in the soft, which he proceeded to lend liberally to Georgy-Porgy Pudden 'n' Pie, our bloated Heir. No interest and no repayment of the principal until even the King could not ignore the debt. So plain Robert Nugent was apotheosized into Viscount Clare, and now has a Bristol street named after him. He will end an earl, as my London informants tell me that his soft is still going princeward at a great rate. You have to admit, my dear Richard, that the schoolmaster did well for himself."

"Indeed he did," said Richard, not at all offended. "Though I would rather," he said after a pause, "that William Henry earned his peerage by becoming First Lord of the Admiralty. Generals are always noblemen because army officers have to buy their promotions, but admirals can scramble up with prize-money and the like."

"Spoken like a true Bristolian! Ships are never far from any Bristolian's thoughts. Though, Richard, ye have no experience of them beyond looking." Mr. Thistlethwaite sipped his rum and waited with keen anticipation for the warm glow to commence inside him.

"Looking," said Richard, his cheek against William Henry's, "is quite close enough to ships for me."

"D'ye never yearn for foreign parts? Not even London?"

"Nay. I was born in Bristol and I will die in Bristol. Bath and Bedminster are quite as far as I ever wish to go." He held William Henry out and looked his son in the eye; for such a young babe, the gaze was astonishingly steady. "Eh, William Henry? Perhaps you will end in being the family's traveler."

Idle speculation. As far as Richard was concerned, simply having William Henry was enough.

The anxiety, however, was omnipresent, in Peg as well as Richard. Both of them fussed over the slightest deviation from William Henry's habitual path—were his stools a little too runny?—was his brow too warm?—ought he not to be more forward for his age? None of this mattered a great deal during the first six months of William Henry's life, but his grandparents fretted over what was going to happen as he grew into noticing, crawling, talking—and thinking! That doting pair were going to ruin the child! They listened avidly to anything Cousin James-the-druggist had to say on subjects few Bristolians—or other sorts of English people—worried their heads about. Like the state of the drains, the putridity of the Froom and Avon, the noxious vapors which hung over the city as ominously in winter as in summer. A remark about the Broad Street privy vault had Peg on her knees inside the closet beneath the stairs with rags and bucket, brush and oil of tar, scrubbing at the ancient stone seat and the floor, whitewashing ruthlessly. While Richard went down to the Council House and made such a nuisancc of himself to various Corporation slugs that the honey-sledges actually arrived en masse to empty the privy vault, rinse it several times, and then tip the result of all this activity into the Froom at the Key Head right next door to the fish markets.

When William Henry passed the six-months mark and began to change into a person, his grandparents discovered that he was the kind of child who cannot be ruined. Such was the sweetness of his nature and the humility of his tiny soul that he accepted all the attention gratefully, yet never complained if it were not given. He cried because he had a pain or some tavern fool had frightened him, though of Mr. Thistlethwaite (by far the most terrifying denizen of the Cooper's Arms) he was not in the least afraid no matter how loudly he roared. His character inclined to thoughtful silences; though he would smile readily, he would not laugh, and never looked either sad or ill-tempered.

"I declare that he has the temperament of a monastery friar," said Mr. Thistlethwaite. "Ye may have bred up a Carthlick yet."

Five days ago a whisper had surfaced at the Cooper's Arms: a few cases of the smallpox had appeared, but too widely dispersed to think of containment by quarantine, every city's first—and last—desperate hope.

Peg's eyes started from her head. "Oh, Richard, not again!"

"We will have William Henry inoculated" was Richard's answer. After which he sent a message to Cousin James-the-druggist.

Who looked aghast when told what was required of him. "Jesus, Richard, no! Inoculation is for older folk! I have never heard of it for a babe barely out of his clouts! It would kill him! Far better to do one of two things—send him away to the farm, or keep him here in as much isolation as ye can. And pray, whichever course ye choose."

"Inoculation, Cousin James. It must be inoculation."

"Richard, I will not do it!" Cousin James-the-druggist turned to Dick, listening grimly. "Dick, say something! Do something! I *beseech* you!"

For once Richard's father stood by him. "Jim, neither course would work. To get William Henry out of Bristol—no, hear me out!—to get William Henry out of Bristol would mean hiring a hackney, and who can tell what manner of person last sat in it? Or who might be on the ferry at Rownham Meads? And how can we isolate anybody in a tavern? This ain't St. James's on a Sunday, lively though that can be. All manner of folk come through my door. No, Jim, it must be inoculation."

"Be it on your own heads, then!" cried Cousin James-the-druggist as he stumbled off, wringing his hands, to enquire of a doctor friend whereabouts he might find a victim of the smallpox who had reached rupture-of-the-pustules stage. Not so difficult a task; people were coming down with the disease everywhere. Mostly under the age of fifteen.

"Pray for me," Cousin James-the-druggist said to his doctor friend as he laid his ordinary darning needle down across a running sore on the twelve-year-old girl's face and turned it over and over to coat it with pus. Oh, poor soul! It had been such a pretty face, but it never would be again. "Pray for me," he said as he rose to his feet and put the sopping needle on a bed of lint in a small tin case. "Pray that I am not about to do murder."

He hastened immediately to the Cooper's Arms, not a very long walk. And there, the partly naked William Henry on his knee, he took the darning needle from its case, placed its point against—against—oh, where ought he to do this murder? And such a *public* one, between the regulars sitting in their usual places, Mr. Thistlethwaite making a show of casually sucking his teeth, and the Morgans looming in a ring around him as if to prevent his fleeing should he take a notion to do so. Suddenly it was done; he pinched the flesh of William Henry's arm just below the left shoulder, pushed the big needle in, then drew it out an inch away by its point.

William Henry did not flinch, did not cry. He turned his large and extraordinary eyes upon Cousin James's sweating face and looked a question—why did you do that to me? It hurt!

Oh why, why did I? I have never seen such eyes in a head! Not animal's eyes, but not human either. This is a strange child.

So he kissed William Henry all over his face, wiped away his own tears, put the needle back in its tin to burn the whole thing later in his hottest furnace, and handed William Henry to Richard.

"There, it is done. Now I am going to pray. Not for William Henry's soul—what babe needs fear for stains on that? To pray for my own soul, that I have not done murder. Have you some vinegar and oil of tar? I would wash my hands."

Mag produced a small jug of vinegar, a bottle of oil of tar, a pewter dish and a clean clout.

"Nothing will happen for three or four days," he said as he rubbed away, "but then, if it takes, he will develop a fever. If it has taken to the proper degree, the fever will not be malign. And at some time the inoculation itself will fester, produce a pustule, and burst. All going well, 'twill be the only one. But I cannot say for sure, and I do not thank ye for this business."

"You are the best man in Bristol, Cousin James!" cried Mr. Thistlethwaite jovially.

Cousin James-the-druggist paused in the doorway. "I am not your cousin, Jem Thistlethwaite—ye have no relations! Not even a mother," he said in freezing tones, pushed his wig back onto his head properly, and vanished.

Mine Host shook with laughter. "That is telling ye, Jem!"

"Aye," grinned Jem, unabashed. "Do not worry," he said to Richard, "God would not dare offend Cousin James."

Having walked for much longer than he had prayed, Richard arrived back at the Cooper's Arms just in time to give a hand with supper. Barley broth made on beef shins tonight, with plump, bacony dumplings simmering in it, as well as the usual fare of bread, butter, cheese, cake and liquid refreshments.

The panic had died down and Broad Street was back to normal except that John/Samuel Adams and John Hancock still swung from the signpost of the American Coffee House. They would probably, Richard reflected, remain there until time and weather blew their stuffing all over the place and naught was left save limp rags.

Nodding to his father as he passed, Richard scrambled upstairs to the back half of the room at their top, which Dick had partitioned off in the customary way—a few planks from floor to near the ceiling, not snugly tenoned and joined like the wales of ships, but rather held together by an occasional strut and therefore full of cracks, some wide enough to put an eye to.

Richard and Peg's back room held an excellent double bed with thick linen curtains drawn about it from rails connecting its four tall posts, several chests for clothing, a cupboard for shoes and boots, a mirror on one wall for Peg to prink in front of, a dozen hooks on the same wall, and William Henry's gimbaled cot. There were no fifteen-shillings-a-yard wallpapers, no damask hangings, no carpets on the oak floor so old it had gone black two centuries ago, but it was quite as good a room as any one would see in any house of similar standing, namely of the middling classes.

Peg was by the cot, swinging it gently back and forth.

"How is he, my love?"

She looked up, smiling contentedly. "It has taken. He has a fever, but it is not burning him up. Cousin James-the-druggist came while you were walking, and seemed very relieved. He thinks William Henry will recover without developing the full pox."

Because his left upper arm was sore, Richard assumed, William Henry lay sleeping on his right side with the offending limb drawn comfortably across his chest. Where the needle had passed through the flesh a great red welt was growing; his palm almost touching it, Richard could feel the heat in the thing.

"It is early!" he exclaimed.

"Cousin James says it often is after inoculation."

Knees shaking from the sheer relief of learning that his son had survived his ordeal, Richard went to a hook on the wall and plucked his stout canvas apron from it. "I must help father. Thank God, thank God!" He was still thanking God as he bounded down the stairs, it having slipped his mind that until he saw William Henry's pustule developing, he had quite given up on God.

For places like the Cooper's Arms the relaxed atmosphere of long summer evenings brought benefits in its wake; the tavern's regular clientele were respectable people who earned a better than subsistence living—tradesmen and artisans in the main, and accompanied by their wives and children. Between threepence and fourpence a head bought them plenty of palatable food and a big pitcher of small beer, and for those who preferred full beer, rum or gin or Bristol milk (a sherry much favored by the women), another sixpence would see them merry enough to tumble into bed and sleep the moment they got home, safe from footpads and the press gangs because that extended gloaming kept darkness at bay.

So Richard descended into a social club still golden-lit as much from the westering sun outside as from the oil lamps fixed to the exposed beams of walls and ceiling, black against the brilliant pallor of whitewashed plaster. The only portable lamp burned at Mine Host's place behind his counter, at the far end of it from Ginger, the tavern's most famous attraction.

Ginger was a large wooden cat Richard had carved after reading of the renowned Old Tom in London—a distinct improvement on the original, he prided himself. It stood diagonally across the boards with its nether regions closest to the drinkers, an orange-striped cat with jaws open in a wide smile and tail at a jaunty angle. When a customer wanted a measure of rum, he put a threepenny coin into its mouth and rested it upon the flexible tongue, which flopped down with an audible click. Then he held his mug beneath the two realistic testicles at its rear and pulled the tail; the cat promptly pissed exactly half a pint of rum.

Naturally the older children present were its greatest users; many a dad and mum were wheedled into drinking more than they ought for the sheer pleasure of putting a coin into Ginger's mouth, pulling his tail, and watching him piss a stream of rum. If Richard had done no more for the Cooper's Arms than that, he had vindicated his father's generosity in taking him into the business.

As Richard crossed the sawdust-strewn floor with wooden bowls full of steaming broth distributed precariously up both arms, he exchanged conversation with everybody, his face lighting up as he told them of William Henry's optimistic prognosis.

Mr. Thistlethwaite was not there. He came at eleven in the morning and stayed until five, sitting at "his" table under the window, which bore an inkwell and several quills (but he could buy his own paper, said Dick Morgan tersely), composing his lampoons. These were printed up by Sendall's bookshop in Wine Street and sold there, though Mr. Thistlethwaite also had outlets on a few stalls in Pie Powder Court and Horse Fair, far enough from Sendall's not to affect its market. They sold extremely well, for Mr. Thistlethwaite owned a rare ripeness of epithet and was apt into the bargain. His targets were usually Corporation officials from the Mayor through the Commander of Customs to the Sheriff, or religious entities addicted to pluralism, or those who presided over the courts. Though quite why he had it in for Henry Burgum the pewterer was a mystery—oh, Burgum was a dyed-in-the-wool villain, but what precisely had he done to Mr. James Thistlethwaite?

And so the supper hour wore down amid a general feeling of repletion and well-being, until promptly at eight o'clock by the old timepiece on the wall next to the slate, Dick Morgan rapped: "Settle up accounts, gentlemen!" After which, his tin cash box satisfyingly heavy, he shepherded the last toddler out the door and bolted it securely. The cash box went upstairs with him and was deposited beneath his own bed with a string tied from its handle to his big toe. Bristol had more than its share of thieves, some of them most artful. In the morning he transferred the mass of coins to a canvas bag and took it to the Bristol Bank in Small Street, a concern headed by, among others, a Harford, an Ames and a Deane. Though no matter which one of Bristol's three banks a man patronized, it would be Quakers looking after his money.

William Henry was sleeping soundly on his right side; Richard lifted the cot closer to the bed, took off his apron, his voluminous white cotton shirt, his linen breeches, his shoes and thick white cotton stockings, and his flannel underdrawers. Then he donned the linen nightshirt Peg had draped across his pillow, untied the ribbon confining his long locks and fitted a nightcap securely over them. All this done, he slipped into bed with a sigh.

Two very different snores emanated through the gaps in the partition between this room and the front one where Dick and Mag slept, but not like the dead. Snores were the epitome of life. Dick produced a resonant rumble, whereas Mag wheezed and whistled. Smiling to himself, Richard rolled onto his side and found Peg, who snuggled up to him despite the warmth of the night and began to kiss his cheek. Very carefully Richard pleated up his nightshirt and hers, then fitted himself against her and cupped a hand around one high, firm breast.

"Oh, Peg, I do love you!" he whispered. "No man was ever gifted with a better wife."

"Nor woman with a better husband, Richard."

In complete agreement, they kissed down to the velvet of their tongues while she nudged her mound against his growing member and purred her pleasure.

"Perhaps," he mumbled afterward, his eyes unwilling to stay open, "we have made a brother or sister for William Henry." He had barely uttered the words before he was asleep.

Though as tired as he, Peg yanked at his nightshirt until it shielded his body from the bottom sheet, then adjusted her own with a dab of its tail to blot the moisture from her crotch. Oh, she thought, I wish Dad and Mum did not snore! Richard does not, and nor, he tells me, do I. Still, snores mean that they sleep and do not hear us. And thank you, dearest Lord, for being kind to my little boy. I know that he is so good You must want him to adorn Heaven, but he adorns this earth too, and he should have his chance. Yet why, dearest Lord, do I feel that I will have no other children?

For she did feel this, and it was a torment. Three years she had waited to fall the first time, then another three years before she fell the second time. Not that she had carried either child poorly, or been unduly sick, or suffered cramps and spasms. Just that somewhere inside her soul she sensed a womb leached of its fertility. The fault did not lie with Richard. Did she so much as look sideways at him with an invitation, he would have her, and never failed (save when a child was ill) to have her when they went to bed. Such a kind and considerate lover! Such a kind and considerate man. His own appetites and pleasures were less important to him than those of the folk who mattered to him. Especially hers and William Henry's. And Mary's. A tear fell into the down pillow and more followed, faster and faster. Why do our children have to go before us? It is not fair, it is not just. I am twoscore and five, Richard is twoscore and seven. Yet we have lost our firstborn, and I miss her so! Oh, how much I miss her!

Tomorrow, she thought drowsily, her spate of weeping ended, I will go to St. James's burying ground and put flowers on her grave. Soon it will be winter, and of flowers there will be none.

Winter came, the ordinary Bristol gloom of fog, drizzle, a damp coldness which seeped into the bones; untroubled by the ice which often pocked the Thames and other rivers of eastern England, the tide in the Avon rose its thirty feet and fell its thirty feet as rhythmically and predictably as in summer.

News from the war in the thirteen colonies trickled in, far behind the events it chronicled. General Thomas Gage was no longer His Britannic Majesty's Commander-in-Chief, Sir William Howe was, and it was being said that the rebellious Continental Congress was courting the French, the Spanish and the Dutch in search of allies and money. The King's retaliation had been much as expected: at Christmastide the Parliament prohibited all trade with the thirteen colonies and declared them beyond the protection of the Crown. For Bristol, hideous news.

There were those among influential Bristolians who wanted peace at any price, including granting the American rebels whatever they demanded; there were those who deemed the rebels sorely wronged, yet who wanted the perpetuation of English imperium because they feared that if England abandoned a thousand miles of naked coast, the French would return with the Spanish hard behind them; and there were those whose outrage was colossal, who cursed the rebels for traitors fit only to be drawn and quartered after they were hanged, and who would not hear of the smallest concession's being made. Naturally this last group of Bristol's mighty had the most power at the Court of St. James, but all three groups cried woe in the drawing rooms of the best houses and huddled grimly over their port and turtle at the White Lion, the Bush Inn and the Plume of Feathers.

Beneath the thin crust of influential Bristolians lay the vast majority of citizens, who knew only that work was getting hard to find, that more and more ships sat permanently along the quays and the backs, and that now was not the time to strike for a raise of a penny a day. Since Parliament knew how to spend money but did not dole it out to the needy, care of the swelling numbers of jobless devolved upon the parishes—provided, that is, that they were genuine parishioners entered in the register. Each parish received £7 per annum per dwelling of the Corporation's rents, and out of this came relief for the poor.

In one respect Bristol differed from all other English cities, for no reason easily explained; its upper crust tended toward an impressive degree of philanthropy, during life as well as in testamentary bequests. Perhaps one reason might have been that to have almshouses or poorhouses or hospitals or schools named after their endower lent their endower a second kind of immortality, for his name was never aristocratic. When it came to birth and lineage, Bristol's upper crust was utterly mediocre. Lord Clare, who had been Robert Nugent the schoolmaster, was about as much of a nobleman as Bristol high society could produce. Bristol might was soundly vested in Mammon.

Thus 1776 arrived like the kind of brooding shadow seen only out of the corners of the eyes. By now, everybody had assumed, the King's Navy and the King's Army would have stamped out the last ember of revolution between New Hampshire and Georgia. But no news of this glorious event came, though those who could read—a large number in education- and charity-conscious Bristol—had taken to frequenting the staging inns to wait for the coach from London and the London flimsies and magazines.

The Cooper's Arms was doing its share of drawing in the belt; and sad it was, too, to find with every passing week a new gap in the ranks of the regular patrons. Expenses kept time with shrinking custom, however; Mag cooked less, Peg carried home fewer loaves from Jenkins the baker, and Dick bought more vile cheap gin than rich aromatic Cave's rum.

"I do not like to sound disloyal," said Peg on a January day when the threat of snow found the Cooper's Arms empty, "but surely some of our folk would find it easier to eat if they drank less."

The look Dick gave Richard was wry, but he said nothing.

"My love," said Richard, taking William Henry from his mother, "it is the way of the world, and we have managed to put a little aside because it is the way of the world. So hush, and do not think of disloyalty. Men and women are free to choose what they want to put in their stomachs. Some can bear the pain of doing without a daily half-pint of rum or gin, but some find the pain of doing without too hard to bear." He shrugged, ruffled William Henry's dark ringlets and smiled down into those amazing eyes, amber flecked with deep brown dots. "Pain is different for everybody, Peg."

As January crept onward, the tally of ships failed to reach expectations. From sympathy with the rebel cause, the feeling within the city was turning to increasingly bitter resentment. The Union Club at the Bush Inn, once engaged in inundating the King with petitions to cease taxing and trying to govern the colonies from afar, was stumbling into mortified silence; at the White Lion the Tories were roaring ever louder, inundating the King with formal avowals of allegiance and support, contributing to the cost of raising local regiments, and starting to ask questions about the two Whig Members of Parliament for Bristol, the Irishman Edmund Burke and the American Henry Cruger.

There, said the Steadfast Society, was Bristol, bleeding from almost a year of war already, with a Whig parliamentary team composed of a golden-tongued Irishman and a leaden-tongued American. Sentiments were changing, feelings were souring. Let all this business three thousand miles away get itself over and done with, let the chief business of the day be *proper* business! And damn the rebels!

On the night of the 16th of January, while the tide was at its ebb, someone set fire to the Savannah La Mar, loading for Jamaica on the Broad Quay not far from Old Nick's Entrance. She had been daubed with pitch, oil and turpentine, and luck alone had saved her; by the time the city's two firemen had arrived with their forty-gallon water cart, several hundred shaken sailors and dock denizens had dealt with the blaze before serious damage had been done.

In the morning the port officials and bailiffs discovered that the Fame and the Hibernia, one to north and one to south of the Savannah La Mar, had also been soaked with incendiaries and set alight. For reasons no one could fathom, neither ship had so much as smoldered.

"Barratry in Bristol! The whole of the Quay could have gone up, and the backs, and then the city," said Dick to Richard the moment he returned from the scene of this shipboard arson. "*Low tide!* Nothing to stop a good blaze leaping from ship to ship—Christ, Richard, it might have been as bad as London's great fire!" And he shivered.

Nothing terrified people quite so effectively as fire. Not the worst the colliers of Kingswood could do could compare, for the angriest mob was a nothing alongside fire. Mobs were made of men and women with children tagging behind, whereas fire was the monstrous hand of God, the opening of the portals to Hell.

On the 18th of January, Cousin James-the-druggist, ashen-faced, ushered his weeping wife and those of his children still at home through Dick Morgan's door.

"Will you look after Ann and the girls?" he asked, trembling. "I cannot persuade them that our house is safe."

"Good God, Jim, what is it?"

"Fire." He grasped at the counter to steady himself.

"Here," said Richard, giving him a mug of best rum while Mag and Peg fluttered around the moaning Ann.

"Give her one too," said Dick as Mr. James Thistlethwaite abandoned his manic quill to join them. "Now tell us, Jim."

It took a full quarter-pint to calm Cousin James-the-druggist enough to speak. "In the middle of the night someone forced the door of my main warehouse—you know how strong it is, Dick, and how many chains and padlocks it has! He got at my turpentine, soaked a big box in a vat of it, and filled the box with tow soaked in more turpentine. Then he put the box against some casks of linseed oil, and lit it. The place was deserted, of course. No one saw him come, no one saw him go."

"I do not understand!" cried Dick, quite as white as his first cousin. "We are right on the corner of Bell Lane, and I swear we have heard nothing, seen nothing—*smelled* nothing!"

"It would not burn," said Cousin James-the-druggist in an odd voice. "I tell you, Dick, it would not burn! It should have burned! I found the box when I came to work. At first I thought the broken door meant someone after opiates or badly needed medicines, but the moment I got inside, I could smell the turpentine." His grey-blue Morgan eyes shone with the light of the visionary. "It is a miracle!" he cried. "It is a miracle! God has been good, and I will give St. James's a thousand pounds for its poorbox."

Even Mr. Thistlethwaite was impressed. "That is enough to make me wish I wrote panegyrics, Cousin James, and could hymn ye in print." He frowned. "But I smell something fishy in the city of Bristol, so I do. The Savannah La Mar, the Hibernia and the Fame all belong to Lewsley, which is an American firm. Lewsley is right next door to you in Bell Lane. Perhaps the arsonist broke down the wrong door. I would tell Lewsley if I were you—this is a plot by the Tories to drive American money out of Bristol."

"Ye see Tories in everything, Jem," said Richard, smiling.

"Tories are in everything dastardly, at any rate." Mr. Thistlethwaite sat down at his table again, rolling his eyes at the clutch of hysterical women. "I do wish ye'd shoo them home, Dick. Leave Richard there with one of my horse pistols—here, take it, Richard! I can defend myself with one. But what I insist upon is *silence.* The muse has beckoned, and I have a new subject to write about."

No one took any notice of this, but as the regular patrons started to drift in for a noon dinner and the flow of enquirers into what had happened at the Morgan drug warehouse steadily increased, Richard decided to do as Mr. Thistlethwaite had suggested. One of the horse pistols in his greatcoat pocket and a dozen paper shot cartridges in the other pocket, he escorted Ann Morgan and her two dismally plain daughters back to their very nice house in St. James's Barton. There he sat himself in a chair in the hallway to repel invading arsonists.

Within the space of two days, Thursday to Saturday, all Bristol had spun into a helpless panic. The wardens and specially appointed constables actually put some effort into their exertions, the lamps were lit at five in the afternoon in those few places lucky enough to have street lighting, and the lampmen got busy with their ladders to refill the oil reservoirs, something they rarely did. People hurried home early and wished that the season were not winter and therefore redolent with the smell of wood smoke. Hardly anyone slept during that Saturday night.

On the 19th, a Sunday, all Bristol save for the Jews were in church to beg that God be merciful and bring this Hellhound to justice. Cousin

James-of-the-clergy, an excellent preacher even when not on form, gave of his best in a manner some slightly startled members of the St. James's congregation described as positively Jesuitical and others as alarmingly Methodical.

"For myself," said Dick, to whom one such remark was addressed, "I care not whether the Reverend sounded Jesuitical or Methodical. If we are to sleep soundly in our beds, the arsonist must be kicking his heels at the end of a rope. Besides, the Reverend's papa was a regular fire-and-brimstone preacher, do you not remember? He gave sermons in the open air to the colliers at Crew's Hole."

"The Steadfast Society blames it on the American colonists."

"Hardly likely! The American colonists look more the victims," said Dick, ending the subject.

In the small hours of Sunday going into Monday, Richard woke with a start from a restless sleep.

"Dadda, Dadda!" William Henry was saying loudly from his cot.

Out of bed in a trice, Richard lit a candle from the tinder box and bent over him, heart pounding, as the child sat bolt upright. "What is wrong, William Henry?" he whispered.

"Fire," said William Henry clearly.

Only his obsession with his son's health could have stoppered his nose—the room was full of smoke.

In an emergency he was neat and quick, preserved his presence of mind; Richard woke his father with a shout even as his hands worked at his clothes and pulled on his shoes. Ready, he did not wait for Dick, but ran down the stairs with his candle, grabbed two buckets, unbolted the tavern door and slid across the pavement, slippery in a little rain. Others were stirring as he ran around the corner into Bell Lane and there came to a halt, aghast. The warehouse complex of Lewsley & Co. was ablaze, flames licking through gaps in the slate roofs, the narrow and dirty confines of Bell Lane pulsing red. A noise of roar and huff filled his ears; the Spanish wool, the grain and casks of olive oil inside were soaking up the fire and the fire was feeding upon them as it had not fed upon tow and turpentine.

Men armed with buckets were coming from all directions and multiple lines of them strung themselves from the Froom at the Key Head to Lewsley & Co.'s warehouse. Though the tide was not all the way in, nor was it out; a fairly easy matter therefore to dip the buckets into the water and send them on their way. This frenzy of activity confined the fire to Lewsley & Co. and half a dozen ancient tenements; Cousin James-the-druggist's complex right next door escaped without a mark. No one died—apparently the arsonist was more interested in destroying property than taking lives. So the occupants of the lost tenements had fled in time, their scant belongings clutched in their arms and their children wailing.

Filthy with soot, Richard went back to the Cooper's Arms as soon as the Sheriff and his minions pronounced Bell Lane out of danger. Both his buckets had gone, only God knew where or to whom. His father and Cousin James-the-druggist were seated together at a table, both showing signs of wear and tear; they were a generation older, had tried to keep up, then gratefully turned their buckets over to younger men as they flocked in from more outlying districts to do their bit.

"There will be a great demand for buckets tomorrow, Richard," said Dick, drawing his son a tankard of beer, "so I intend to be at the cooper's as soon as dawn breaks to buy a dozen more. What a world we live in!"

"Dick," said Cousin James-the-druggist with that same look of exaltation on his face, "for the second time within a day, God has spared me and mine! I feel—I feel as Paul must have done on the road to Damascus."

"I do not see the comparison," said Richard, drinking thirstily. "You have never persecuted the faithful, Cousin James."

"No, Richard, but I have undergone a revelation. I will give every prisoner in the Bristol Newgate and the Bristol Bridewell a shilling as thanks to God."

"Huh!" grunted Dick. "Do so, by all means, Jim, but be aware that they will spend it on booze in the prison taproom."

Their speech had permeated to the upper floor; Mag and Peg came down the stairs well wrapped, Peg with William Henry in her arms, her eyes glowing.

"Oh, it is over and you are safe!"

Richard put his tankard down and crossed to take the child, who clung to him. "Father, it was William Henry who woke me. He said 'fire' as if he knew what it meant."

Cousin James-the-druggist stared at William Henry thoughtfully. "He is pixilated. The fairies have claimed him."

Peg gasped. "Cousin James, do not say such things! If the fairies own him, one day they will take him away!"

Strip that of its fanciful rustic superstition, Cousin James-the-druggist reflected, rising slowly and painfully to his feet, and it means that William Henry's mother recognizes his strangeness. For the truth is that he ought never to have survived inoculation.

* * *

The arsonist did not stop with the destruction of Lewsley & Co. During the Monday after the fire, other torches similar to those which had set the American firm alight were found in a dozen other American-owned or American-affiliated warehouses and factories. On the Tuesday, Alderman Barnes's sugar refining house went up in flames; its owner had strong American ties. But by now the whole of Bristol was hopping up and down in expectation of fire, so the conflagration was snuffed out before too much damage was done. Three days later, Alderman Barnes's sugar house was torched again, and again saved.

Politically, both sides were striving to make capital out of the business; the Tories accused the Whigs and the Whigs accused the Tories. Edmund Burke put up £50 for information, the Merchant Venturers contributed £500, the King a further £1,000. As £1,550 represented more than most could earn in a lifetime, Bristol turned detective and soon winkled out a likely suspect—though, of course, nobody got the reward. A Scotchman known as Jack the Painter, he had lodged at various houses in the Pithay, a tumbledown street which crossed the Froom along St. James's Backs; after the second attempt to burn down Alderman Barnes's sugar house, he suddenly disappeared. Though no real evidence existed to link him physically to the fires, all of Bristol was convinced he was the arsonist. A hue and cry went up, fueled by London and provincial news gazettes clear across the country. From the Tyne to the Channel, no one wanted a fire maniac on the loose. The fugitive was apprehended in the act of robbing a nabob's house in Liverpool, and upon the payment of £128 in expenses by the Corporation and the Merchant Venturers, he was extradited in chains to Bristol for interrogation. Where an unexpected obstacle reared its head: nobody could understand a word the Scotchman said apart from his name, James Aiten. So he was shipped to London on the theory that in such a vast metropolis there would be some who could understand the Scotch dialect. As indeed proved to be the case. James Aiten, alias Jack the Painter, confessed to all the Bristol fires—and to one in Portsmouth which had burned the Royal Navy rope house to the ground. This last crime was heinous in the extreme; ships could not function without miles upon miles of rope.

"What I fail to see," said Dick Morgan to Jem Thistlethwaite, "is how Jack the Painter could have done both Bristol and Portsmouth. The rope house was set afire in December, when he was definitely living in the Pithay for all to see."

Mr. Thistlethwaite shrugged. "He is a scapegoat, Dick, no more. It is necessary that England rest easy, and what better way to ensure that than to have a culprit? A Scotchman is ideal. I do not know about the Portsmouth fire, but the Bristol ones were set by the Tories, I would stake my life on it."

"So you think there will be more fires?"

"Nay! The ruse has succeeded. American money has fled, Bristol is washed clean of it. The Tories can recline comfortably upon their laurels and let poor Jack the Painter bear the blame."

Bear the blame he did. James Aiten, alias Jack the Painter, was tried at the Hampshire Assizes for the Royal Navy rope house fire, and convicted. After which he was conveyed to Portsmouth, where a special gallows had been built for the well-attended occasion. The drop was a full 67 feet, which meant that when Jack the Painter was kicked off a stool and launched into eternity, coming to the end of his tether chopped off his head neater than an axe could have. The head was then displayed on the Portsmouth battlements for all to see, and England rested easy.

Jack the Painter had assured his interrogators that he alone was responsible for all the fires.

"Not," said Cousin James-the-druggist, "that *I* am satisfied by such an assurance. However, Easter has come and gone and there have been no more fires, so—who knoweth, as a Quaker might ask? All *I* know is that God spared me."

Two days later Senhor Tomas Habitas the gunsmith walked into the Cooper's Arms.

"Sir!" cried Richard, greeting him with a smile and a very warm handshake. "Sit down, sit down! A glass of Bristol milk?"

"Thank you, Richard."

The tavern was empty apart from Mr. Thistlethwaite; prosperity was declining rapidly. So this unexpected visitor found himself the center of attention, a fact which seemed to please him.

A Portuguese Jew who had emigrated thirty years ago, Senhor Tomas Habitas was small, slender, olive-skinned and dark-eyed, with a long face, big nose and full mouth. About him hung a faint aura of aloofness, something he shared in common with the Quakers; a knowledge, perhaps, that he was too different ever to fit into the ordinary Bristol mold. The city had been good to him, as indeed it was to all Jews, who, unlike the papists, were permitted to worship God in their own fashion, had their burying ground in Jacob Street and two synagogues across the Avon in Temple parish; Jewishness was less of an impediment to social and economic success by far than Roman Catholicism. Mostly due to the fact that there were no Jewish (or Quaker) pretenders to His Britannic yet Germanic Majesty's throne. Bonnie Prince Charlie and 1745 were still fresh in every mind, and Ireland not very distant.

"What brings you so far from home, sir?" asked Dick Morgan, presenting the guest with a large glass (made by the Jewish firm of Jacobs) of deep amber, very sweet sherry.

The narrow black eyes darted about the empty room, returning to Richard rather than to Dick. "Business is bad," he said in a surprisingly deep voice, only lightly accented.

"Aye, sir," said Richard, sitting down opposite the visitor.

"I am very sorry to see it." Senhor Habitas paused. "I may be able to help." He put his long, sensitive hands upon the table, and folded them. "We have this war with the American colonies to thank, I know. However, the war has brought increased business to some. And to me, very much so. Richard, I need you. Will you come back to work?"

While Richard was still opening his mouth to answer, Dick butted in. "On what terms, Senhor Habitas?" he asked, a little truculently. He knew his Richard—too soft to insist upon terms before he said yes.

The enigmatic eyes in the smooth face did not change. "On good terms, Mister Morgan," he said. "Four shillings a musket."

"Done!" said Dick instantly.

Only Mr. Thistlethwaite was looking at Richard, and in some pity. Did he never have a chance to decide his own destiny? The blue-grey eyes in Richard Morgan's handsome face held neither anger nor dissatisfaction. Christ, he was patient! Patient with his father, with his wife, his mother, the patrons, Cousin James-the-druggist—the list really had no end. It seemed the only person for whom Richard would go to war was William Henry, and then it was a quiet business, steadfast rather than choleric. What *does* lie within you, Richard Morgan? Do you know yourself? If Dick were my father, I'd give him a bunch of fives that knocked him to the floor. Whereas you bear with his megrims and his fits and starts, his criticisms, even his too thinly veiled contempt for you. What is your philosophy? Where do you find your strength? Strength you have, I know it. But it is allied to—resignation? No, not quite that. You are a mystery to me, yet I like you better than any other man I know. And I fear for you. Why? Because I have a feeling that so much patience and forebearance will tempt God to try you.

* * *

Oblivious to Mr. Thistlethwaite's concern for him, Richard returned to the Habitas workshop and settled to make Brown Bess for the soldiers fighting in the American war.

A gunsmith made a gun, but not its component parts. These came from various places: the steel barrel, forged into a tube by a hammer, from Birmingham, as did the steel parts of the flintlock; the walnut stock from any one of a dozen localities throughout England; and the brass or copper fittings from around Bristol.

"You will be pleased to know," said Habitas when Richard reported on his first day, "that we have been commissioned to make the Short Land musket—a little lighter and easier to handle."

At 42 inches, it was 4 inches shorter than the old Long Land still employed at the time of the Seven Years' War, and a distinct improvement as far as an infantryman was concerned. Though its fire was quite as accurate, it weighed a half-pound lighter and was less unwieldy.

When Richard sat down at his bench on a high stool, everything he needed was distributed about him. The polished stocks with their long, half-moon barrel supports were turned in one piece, and stood in a frame to his left. To his right were the tanged barrels, each with pierced tenons on its under side. In receptacles on the bench were the various parts of the flintlock itself—springs, cocks, sears, frizzens, triggers, tumblers, screws, flints—and the brass bands, tubes, flanges and supports which bound the gun together. Between all these receptacles he spread out his tools, which were his own property and carried to and fro each day inside a hefty mahogany box bearing his name on a brass plate. There were dozens of files and screwdrivers; pincers, metal snips, tweezers, small hammers, a drill brace and assorted bits; and a collection of woodworking tools. Having been properly taught, he made his own emery papers out of canvas, sprinkling the abrasive black particles onto a base of very strong fish-glue, and used the same technique to fashion different sizes of emery sticks, some pointed, some rounded, some blunt and stubby. Filing parts down was at least fifty per cent of gunsmithing art, and so expert was Richard that his sawyer brother, William, would let no one else sharpen the teeth of his saws when it came time to set them anew.

What Richard had not realized until he picked up the first barrel to polish off the rust and then brown it with butter of antimony was how much he had missed practicing his craft. Six years! A long time. Yet his hands were sure, his mind enchanted at the prospect of assembling the pieces of a puzzle designed to kill men. A gunsmith's reasoning processes, however, did not progress far enough to come to this ultimate conclusion; a gunsmith simply loved what he did and thought not at all about its destructive outcome.

The largest part of the work concerned the flintlock itself. The stock had to be carved delicately to fit it, then each spring and moving component had to be filed, adjusted, filed, adjusted, filed, adjusted, until finally mechanical harmony was achieved and it came time to put the flint in. Those in Norfolk and Suffolk who knapped the flints were craftsmen too, chipping away until the blocky chunk was faceted at its business end to precise specifications. Richard's job was to line up the angle at which the flint struck the frizzen, a leafy-looking, inch-wide, L-shaped piece of steel whose base covered the powder pan. As the cock snapped forward and the flint struck, they forced the frizzen up and off the powder pan, at the same moment producing a shower of sparks. When the flint was properly positioned in the jaws of the cock, this shower of sparks was great enough to set off the powder in the pan; it flashed through a small touch hole into the breech of the barrel, and here in turn ignited the powder packed beneath the missile. In the case of Brown Bess, the missile was a lead ball .753 inches in diameter.

There was nothing Richard did not know about Brown Bess. He knew that she was useless at any range exceeding 100 yards, and of best use when the range was 40 yards or less. Which meant that opposing sides were very close before Brown Bess was fired, and that a good soldier would get in two shots at most before either engaging with bayonets or retreating. He knew that it was a very rare battle in which a man fired his Brown Bess more than ten times. He knew that her powder charge was a mere 70 grains—less than a fifth of an ounce—and he understood every aspect of gunpowder manufacture, for as a part of his apprenticeship he had spent time in the gunpowder works at Tower Harratz on the Avon in Temple Meads. He knew that there was a strong likelihood that only one in four of the Brown Besses he made would ever be fired in combat. He knew that her caliber was close enough (the ball was two sizes smaller than the smooth interior of the barrel) to French, Portuguese and Spanish caliber to enable cartridges from those three countries to be fired from her. And he knew that if one of her balls did strike a human target, the chances of survival were slim. If a man were chest- or gut-shot, his insides were a butchered shambles; if he were limb-shot, his bones were so fragmented that amputation was the only treatment.

It took him two hours to craft his first Brown Bess, but after that the rhythm came back, and by the end of the day he was making one musket an hour. For him, fabulous money at four shillings a gun, but for Senhor Habitas, far more. After deducting the costs of parts and Richard's labor, Senhor Habitas made a profit of ten shillings a gun. There were cheaper gunsmithies, but a Habitas product *fired.* In the hands of a trained fusilier, no hang fires and no flashes in the pan. Senhor Habitas also made sure that he was present to watch his gunsmiths test fire the guns they made.

"I am not," he said to Richard as they strolled through to the proving butt while there was still light enough to see, "putting on any apprentices. Just qualified gunsmiths, and preferably those I have schooled myself." He looked suddenly very serious. "It will end, my beloved Richard, do not think otherwise. I give this war another three or four years, and I cannot see the French emerging from it in any state to fight us yet again. So we have work aplenty now, but it will cease, and I will have to let you go a second time. One reason why I am willing to pay you four shillings a gun. For I have never seen work as good as yours, and you are quick."

Richard did not reply, which was so much his habit that Tomas Habitas had not expected a reply. Richard was a listener. He took in what was said to him with illuminating intelligence, yet would make no comment for the sake of talking. Information went aboard and straight into the cargo holds of his mind, there to stay until events required that he unload it. Perhaps, thought Habitas, that is why, even apart from his work, I am so fond of him. He is a truly peaceful man who minds his own business.

The ten Brown Besses that Richard had made were standing in a rack, fetched there by the ten-year-old lad whom Habitas employed as a menial. Richard picked up the first one, removed the ramrod from its pipes beneath the part of the stock supporting the barrel, and reached into a bin for a cartridge. The ball and powder lay inside a little bag of paper; Richard produced a mouthful of spit, sank his teeth hard into the base of the paper to rupture and moisten it, tipped the powder into the barrel, screwed up the paper and jammed it after the powder, then pushed the ball in. A deft thrust with the ramrod and the lot was snug in the breech at the bottom of the barrel. As he swung the musket up to his shoulder he rapped it smartly over the firing pan to clear powder out of the touch hole, and pulled the trigger. The cock, chunk of flint in its jaws, came down and struck the frizzen. Sparks, explosion and a huge puff of smoke seemed to happen all at once; a bottle forty yards away on a shelf in the range wall disintegrated.

"You have not lost your touch," purred Senhor Habitas while the lad, barefoot, swept up the glass with a broom and put another dull brown, Bristol-made bottle up.

"Say that after I have fired all ten," said Richard, grinning.

Nine behaved perfectly. The tenth needed a little more filing of the frizzen spring—not a major task, as it lay on the outside of the lock mechanism.

When Richard walked into the Cooper's Arms he snatched William Henry from his high chair and held him tight, curbing his impulse to squeeze and hug until the child could scarcely breathe. William Henry, William Henry, how much I love you! Like life, like air, like the sun, like God in His Heaven! Then, leaning his cheek against his son's curls, his eyes closed, he felt a fine convulsive trembling right through the little body. It was as invisible as a cat's purr; he found it only by way of his fingertips. A vibrating anguish. *Anguish?* Why that word? His eyes snapped open, he held William Henry out at arm's length and looked into his face. Secret, shut away.

"He did not seem to miss ye at all," said Dick comfortably.

"He ate every scrap on his plate," said Mag proudly.

"He was as happy as a lark in my company," said Peg with a sly flash of triumph.

His knees began to buckle; Richard sank into a chair near the counter and cuddled his son close again. The fine tremor had gone. Oh, William Henry, what are you thinking? Did you decide that Dadda was never coming back? Until today Dadda has never been away from you for more than an hour or two, and did anybody remember to tell you that Dadda would be home at twilight? No, nobody did. Including me. And you did not cry, or refuse to eat, or display concern. But you thought I was never coming back. That I would not be here for you. "I will always be here for you," he whispered against William Henry's ear. "Always and always."

"How did it go?" asked Peg, who could still, after eighteen months of watching Richard with William Henry, find herself amazed at her husband's—weakness?—softness? It is not healthy, she thought. He needs our child to feed something in himself, something I have no idea of. Well, I love William Henry every bit as much as he does! And now is my chance to have my son for *me.*

"It went well," said Richard, answering her question, then looked at Dick, his gaze a little remote. "I have earned two pounds today, Father. A pound for you and a pound for me."

"No," said Dick gruffly. "Ten shillings for me, thirty for you. That much will see me through even when the day brings no custom at all. Pay me two shillings more for your family's board, and bank the other twenty-eight shillings for yourself. He means to pay ye every Saturday, I hope? None of this by-the-month business, or when he is paid for the goods?"

"Every Saturday, Father."

That night when Richard turned to find Peg and carefully roll up her nightgown, she slapped his hands away nastily.

"No, Richard!" she whispered fiercely. "William Henry is not asleep yet, and he is old enough to understand!"

He lay in the darkness listening to the rumbles and wheezes from the front room, weary to the bone from an unaccustomed kind of labor, yet wide awake. Today had been the beginning of many new things. A job at work he loved, separation from a child he loved, separation from a wife he loved, the realization that he could hurt people he loved all unknowing. It should be so simple. Nothing drove him save love—he had to work to support his family, to make sure they did not want. Yet Peg had slapped his hands away for the first time since they had married, and William Henry had trembled a cat's purr.

What can I do? How can I find a solution? Today I have unwittingly opened up a chasm, though for the best of reasons. I have never asked for much nor expected much. Just the presence of my family. In that is happiness. I belong to them, and they belong to me. Or so I thought. Does a chasm always open up when things change? How deep is it? How wide?

"Senhor Habitas," he said as dawn broke on his second day of work, "how many muskets do ye expect me to make in a day?"

Not a blink; Tomas Habitas rarely blinked. "Why, Richard?"

"I do not want to stay from dawn to dusk, sir. It is not as it was in the old days. My family have need of me too."

"That I understand," said Senhor Habitas gently. "The dilemma is insoluble. One works to make money to ensure the comfort and well-being of one's family, yet one's family needs more than money, and a man cannot be in two places at the same instant of time. I am paying you per musket, Richard. That means as many or as few as ye care to make." He shrugged, an alien gesture. "Yes, I would like fifteen or twenty in a day, but I am prepared to take one. It is your choice."

"Ten in a day, sir?"

"Ten is perfectly satisfactory."

So Richard walked home to the Cooper's Arms in mid afternoon, his ten muskets completed and successfully tested. Senhor Habitas was pleased; he would see enough of William Henry and Peg as well as bank enough to make that house on Clifton Hill a reality. His son was walking; soon the allurements of Broad Street would beckon through the open tavern door and William Henry would go adventuring. Better by far that his footsteps led him along paths perfumed with flowers than paths redolent with the stench of the Froom at low tide.

But it was neither Peg nor William Henry who reached him first when he walked in; Mr. James Thistlethwaite leaped up from "his" table to envelop Richard in a massive hug.

"Let me go, Jem! Those pistols will go off!"

"Richard, Richard! I thought I'd not see ye again!"

"Not see me again? Why? Had I worked from dawn to dusk—and as you see, I am not—you would still have seen me in winter," said Richard, detaching himself and holding out his arms to William Henry, who toddled into them. Then Peg came, smiling an apology with her eyes, to kiss him full upon the lips. Thus when Richard sat down at Jem Thistlethwaite's table he felt as if his world had glued itself back together again; the chasm was not there.

When Dick handed him a tankard of beer he sipped at it, liking the slightly bitter taste but not desperate for it. The son of a temperate victualler, he too was temperate, drank only beer and then never enough to feel it. Which, had he realized, was why—apart from natural affection—Senhor Tomas Habitas prized him so. The work called for steady, skillful hands properly connected to a fresh, sharp mind, and it was rare to light upon a man who did not drink too much. Almost everybody drank too much. Mostly rum or gin. Threepence bought a half-pint of rum or, depending upon its quality, as much as a full pint of gin. Nor were there any laws on the books to punish excessive drinking, though there were laws to punish almost everything else. The Government made too much money from excise taxes to want to discourage drinking.

In Bristol more rum was made and consumed than gin; gin was what the poorest folk drank. Chief importer of sugar to the whole British Isles, Bristol quite naturally made itself the capital of Rum. As to strength, there was little difference between the two spirits, though rum was richer, lasted longer in the system and was more bearable the morning after.

Mr. Thistlethwaite drank rum of the best kind, and had settled upon the

Cooper's Arms as his home-away-from-home because Dick Morgan bought from the rum house of Mr. Thomas Cave in Redcliff; Cave's rum was peerless.

So by the time that Richard walked in, Mr. Thistlethwaite was well away, more so than usual by three o'clock. He had missed Richard, as simple as that, and had assumed that from now on Richard would never be there before five and it came time for him to leave. That five was his inflexible rule represented a last instinct for self-preservation; he knew that were he to stay for one minute more, he would end lying permanently in the gutter which ran down the middle of Broad Street.

Delighted that Richard was still going to be a part of each tavern day, he righted himself unsteadily and prepared to take his leave. "Early, I know, but the sight of you, Richard, has quite overcome me," he announced, weaving his way to the door. "Though I do not know why," came the sound of his voice from Broad Street. "I really do not know why, for who are ye, save the son of my tavern-keeper? It is a mystery, a mystery." His head, battered tricorn at a rakish angle, appeared around the jamb. "Is it possible that the eyes of a drunken man can plumb the future? Do I believe in premonitions? Hur hur hur! Call me Cassandra, for I swear I am a silly old woman. Ho ho ho, and off into the Beotian air go my Attic lungs!"

"Mad," said Dick. "Mad as a March hare."

The war against the thirteen American colonies went on with, it seemed to the puzzled citizens of Bristol, so many English victories that news must come any day of American surrender. Yet that news never came. Admittedly the colonists had successfully invaded Boston and taken it off Sir William Howe, but Sir William had promptly removed himself to New York, apparently intending to divide and conquer by driving George Washington into New Jersey and placing himself squarely between the northern and southern colonies. His brother, Admiral Howe, had rolled up the fledgling American navy at Nassau and Narragansett Bay, so Britannia ruled the waves.

Until this time Pennsylvania's colonial government had tried to steer a middle path and reconcile the two warring factions of loyalist and rebel; now, just as—to Bristol eyes, anyway—American defeat seemed inevitable, Pennsylvania repudiated its allegiance to the Crown and joined the rebels wholeheartedly! It made no sense, especially to Bristol's Quakers, blood relatives.

In August of 1776 the news gazettes reported that the Continental Congress had accepted Thomas Jefferson's draft of the mooted Declaration of Independence, and signed it into being without the consent of New York. President of the Congress, John Hancock was the first to sign, and with a flourish that his effigy, its emptied skin still dangling from the signpost of the American Coffee House, might well have envied. After General Washington's ragged troops acclaimed the Declaration, New York ratified it. Independence was now unanimous, though New York around Manhattan remained loyalist. And the flag of the Continental Congress now consisted of thirteen stripes, red alternating with white.

Peace negotiations on Staten Island broke down after the colonists refused to rescind the Declaration of Independence, so Sir William Howe invaded New Jersey with his own English soldiers and 10,000 Hessian mercenaries the King had hired to stiffen his army. All fell before the English advance; Washington crossed the Delaware into Pennsylvania, then recrossed it in the teeth of a terrible winter to inflict a crushing defeat on the Hessians, wassailing at Trenton. After a second, smaller victory at Princeton, the rebel army retired into the Morristown hills and the reeling General Howe returned to Manhattan with his equally stunned second-in-command, Lord Cornwallis. Whose family owned Cornwallis House on Clifton Hill, and therefore was dear to every Bristol heart.

For Richard, 1776 had been a year of muskets and money; he had £400 in the Bristol Bank, and the twelve shillings per diem he donated to his father had enabled the Cooper's Arms to keep its door open when many other taverns had closed theirs for good. Hardship gripped high, middling and low alike. Awful times.

The crime rate had soared beyond belief, and carried with it one peculiar symptom of this bitter, frustrating American war: convicts and the poor-without-a-parish were no longer being shipped to the thirteen colonies and sold there as indentured labor. Time honored and convenient, the practice had enabled the Government to implement the harshest punitive measures in Europe while simultaneously keeping its prison population down. For every Frenchman hanged, ten Englishmen were; for every German hanged, fifteen Englishmen were. An occasional woman was hanged. But the vast majority of those convicted of crimes of lesser degree than highway robbery, blatant murder or arson, were sold in job lots to contractors who hustled them aboard ships—many out of Bristol—transported them to some of the thirteen colonies, and there profitably resold them as white slaves. One difference between them and the black slaves lay in the fact that, theoretically at least, their bondage eventually came to an end. Often, however, it did not, particularly if the slaves were female. Moll Flanders had it good.

Transportation of white indentured labor was largely confined to some of the thirteen colonies because the plantation owners in the West Indies preferred negro labor. They believed that black people were used to the heat, worked better in it—and did not, when looked over, closely resemble the Master and Mistress. Now the transportation system had ground to a halt, but the English courts of quarter session and assizes did not in consequence cease to crack down hard on those accused of even the pettiest crime. English penal law was not designed to protect the rights of a few aristocrats; it was aimed at protecting the rights of all persons who had managed to acquire a modicum of wealth, no matter how small. Thus the prison populations swelled at an alarming rate, castles and old buildings were pressed into service as auxiliary places of detention, and the stream of convicted felons continued to pass in chains through gates both old and new.

At which point one Duncan Campbell, a London contractor and speculator of Scotch origins, conceived the idea of using old naval men o' war put into ordinary—that is, retired from service—as prisons. He bought one such ship, Censor, moored her in the Thames at the Royal Arsenal, and filled her with 200 male convicts. A new law permitted convicted felons to be put to work on governmental business, and Censor's felons were required to dredge the river's reaches along this critical sea road as well as construct new docks—work no free man could be prevailed upon to do unless very well paid. Convict labor cost no more than food and lodging, both of which Mr. Duncan Campbell provided on Censor hulk. There were a few early mistakes; hammocks, Campbell discovered, were not beds suitable for felons, whose chains became badly tangled in their supports. So he switched to shelving for beds, and was able to increase Censor's complement to 300 prisoners. His Britannic Majesty's Government was mightily pleased, and happy to pay Campbell for his pains. Surplus felons could be stored on naval hulks until the war was over and wholesale transportation could begin again. What a relief!

To a tavern-keeper the explanation for petty crime was obvious; most of it occurred while its perpetrators were drunk. With the scarcity of jobs, rum or gin became increasingly precious to those who could perceive no ray of hope illuminating their lot. Silk garments, handkerchiefs and fripperies were the hallmark of more affluent folk. Men and women—even children—reduced to begging from the parish took out their rage and frustration in drinking as soon as a coin came their way, and then, drunk, pilfered silk garments, handkerchiefs, fripperies. Things they did not own, could not own. Things the better off prized. Things that—in London and Bristol, at least—might be sold to those who dealt in stolen goods for the price of another drink, another few hours of inebriated well-being. And when they were caught, off to the courts they shuffled to be sentenced to death—or to fourteen years—or, most frequently, to seven years. With the word "transportation" tacked on. Transportation to where? An unanswerable, therefore never asked, question.

As far as Richard was concerned, 1777 ought simply to have been another year of muskets and money, but early in the New Year, while Washington and what troops he had left endured the ordeal of a frightful winter outside Morristown, the Morgans of the Cooper's Arms received a shock. Mr. James Thistlethwaite abruptly announced his departure from Bristol.

Dick flopped onto a chair, something he did so rarely that his elbows were horny from leaning on the counter. "Leaving?" he asked feebly. "*Leaving?*"

"Aye," said Mr. Thistlethwaite aggressively, "leaving, damn ye!"

Peg and Mag began to cry; Richard shooed them upstairs with the bewildered William Henry to have their weep in private, then faced the apparently angry Mr. Thistlethwaite. "Jem, ye're a fixture! Ye cannot leave!"

"I am not a fixture, and I am leaving!"

"Oh, sit down, man, sit down! And stop this prize-fighting posturing! We are not your adversaries," said Richard. He looked stern. "Sit, Jem, and tell us why."

"Ahah!" said Mr. Thistlethwaite, doing as bidden. "So you can come out of that timid shell. Does my going mean so much?"

"It is hideous," said Richard. "Father, give me a beer and Jem some of Cave's best."

Dick got up and did as he was told.

"Now what's amiss?" asked Richard.

"I am fed up, Richard, that is all. I have done my dash in Bristol. Who is there left to lampoon? Old Bishop Newton? I'd not do that to someone with wit enough to call Methodism a bastardized form of popery. And what else can I do to the Corporation? What more stinging quip is there than to say that Sir Abraham Isaac Elton is all jaw and no law, John Vernon is all law and no jaw, and Rowles Scudamore neither law nor jaw? I have exposed Daniel Harson for the Dissenting minister he once was, and John Powell for the medical man on a slaver he once was. No, I have shot my Bristol bolt, and I have a mind to seek greener pastures. So I am off to London."

How to say tactfully that a shining light in Bristol might find itself obscured by the fog of a place twenty times larger than Bristol? "It is such a vast place," Richard ventured.

"I have friends there," Mr. Thistlethwaite countered.

"Ye'll not change your mind?"

"I will not."

"Then," said Dick, reviving a little, "I drink to your good luck and good health, Jem." He lifted his lip. "At least I will save the expense of quills and ink."

"You will write to tell us how you are?" asked Richard somewhat later, by which time Mr. Thistlethwaite's truculence had changed to maudlin self-pity.

"If you write to me." The Bard of Bristol sniffled, wiped a tear away. "Oh, Richard, the world is a cruel place! And I have a mind to be cruel to it on a larger canvas than Bristol offers."

Later that evening Richard sat William Henry on his lap and turned the child to face him. At two and a half, he was strongly knit and tall, and had, his father fancied, the face of a stern angel. It was those eyes, of course, so large and unique—truly unique, for no one could remember ever seeing their ale-and-pepper mix—but also the planes of his bones and the perfection of his skin. No matter where he went, people turned to look and marvel at his beauty, and this was not the judgment of a doting parent. By anybody's standard, William Henry was a ravishing child.

"Mr. Thistlethwaite is going away," Richard said to his son.

"Away?"

"Aye, to London. We will not see him again very often if at all, William Henry."

The eyes did not fill with tears, but they changed in a way Richard had learned meant inward grief, secret and sensitive. "He does not like us anymore, Dadda?"

"He likes us very well. But he needs more room than he can find in Bristol, and that has nothing to do with us."

Listening to them, Peg plucked at the bars of her own cage, a structure as hidden as whatever went on inside William Henry's mind. After that one vindictive reaction against Richard's right to touch her, she had disciplined herself into conjugal obedience, and if Richard noticed that her response to his lovemaking was more mechanical than of yore, he had not commented. It was not that she loved him any less; her emotional withdrawal was founded in her guilt. Her barrenness. Her womb was shriveled and empty, incapable of carrying more than her menses, and here she was married to a man who loved his children almost too much. Who needed a tribe of children so that he could not heap all his eggs into a basket named William Henry.

"My love," she said to Richard as they lay in bed reassured by the snores from the front room and by the deep sound of William Henry's sleeping respiration, "I fear that I will never conceive again." There. It was out at last.

"Have you talked to Cousin James-the-druggist?"

"I do not need to, nor is it something he would know the answer to. It is the way God made me, I just know it."

He blinked, swallowed. "Well, we have William Henry."

"I know. And he is healthy, remarkably so. But, Richard"—she lifted herself up to sit—"it is on that head I wish to speak."

Richard sat up too, linked his arms around his knees. "Then speak, Peg."

"I do not want to move to Clifton."

He leaned sideways, struck the tinder and lit their candle so that he could see her face. Round, softly pretty and strained with anxiety, its big brown eyes looking hunted. "But for the sake of our only child, Peg, we must move to Clifton!"

Her hands clenched, she suddenly resembled her son—whatever she felt, she would not find the right words to express. "It is for William Henry's sake that I speak. I know that you have the money to buy a very nice cottage a little way up the hills, but I would be alone in it with William Henry and there would be no one to call on in an emergency."

"We can afford a servant, Peg, I have told you that."

"Yes, but a servant is not *family.* Here I have your parents to turn to—there are three of us to make sure that William Henry is all right, Richard." She ground her good, hard-water-nourished teeth. "I am having nightmares. I see William Henry going down to the Avon and falling in because I was busy making bread and the servant busy fetching water from Jacob's Well. I see it over and over again—over and over again!"

The flame glittered off a sudden rush of tears; Richard put the candle on the clothes chest beside the bed and pulled his wife into his arms. "Peg, Peg. . . . These are dreams. I have them too, my love. But my nightmare is of

William Henry crushed beneath the runners of a geehoe, or William Henry taken with the bloody flux, or William Henry falling down an open manhole. All things that cannot happen in Clifton. If it worries you so much, then we will have a nursemaid for him too."

"Your nightmares are all different," she wept, "but mine is ever the same. Just William Henry leaping into the Avon at the gorge, William Henry terrified of something I cannot see."

He gentled her until she quietened and finally fell asleep in his arms. Then lay, the candle guttering, fighting his own grief. This was a family conspiracy, he knew it. His mother and father were getting at Peg, Mag because she adored William Henry and loved her niece like a daughter, Dick because—well, perhaps in his heart of hearts he had decided that once Richard was living in Clifton, those twelve shillings a day would cease; a man who is master of his own house has many additional expenses. All his instincts urged that he ignore these pressures and remove his wife and child to the clean air and verdant hills of Clifton, but what Dick Morgan deemed softness in Richard was in fact an ability to understand and commiserate with the actions of others, especially his family. If he insisted upon that cottage in Clifton—and he had found the right one, roomy, beautifully thatched, not too old, with a separate kitchen in its backyard to guard against fire and a garret for the servants—if he insisted upon that cottage in Clifton he knew now that Peg had made up her mind not to thrive in it. She had made up her mind to hate it. How odd, in a farmer's daughter! Not for one moment had he dreamed that she would not espouse a more rural style of living as eagerly as he, a city man born and bred. His lips quivered, but in the privacy of the night marches Richard Morgan did not weep. He simply steeled himself to accept the fact that he would not be moving to Clifton.

Dear God on high, my wife thinks that William Henry will drown in the Avon were he to live in Clifton. Whereas I have a dread foreboding that it is Bristol will kill him. I pray Thee, I *beg* Thee to protect my son! Grant me this one child! His mother says that there will be no more, and I believe her.

"We will remain at the Cooper's Arms," he said to Peg as they rose just before dawn.

Her face lit up, she hugged him in an agony of relief. "Oh, thank you, Richard, thank you!"

The war in America continued to go well for England for some time, despite the fact that a few Tory elements in the Parliament felt strongly enough to secede from the Government as a protest against the King's policies. Gentleman Johnny Burgoyne was told to clear out every rebel in northern New York and demonstrated his tactical prowess by taking Fort Ticonderoga on Lake Champlain, a stronghold the rebels had deemed invulnerable. But between the lake and the headwaters of the Hudson River lay a wilderness that Burgoyne traveled at the rate of a mile a day. He lost his luck; so did his diversionary contingent, defeated at Bennington. Horatio Gates had taken over as rebel commander, and had the brilliant Benedict Arnold with him. Twice brought to battle at Bemis Heights, Burgoyne plummeted to final defeat and surrender at Saratoga.

The news of Saratoga rocked all of England to its foundations. *Surrender!* Somehow Saratoga outweighed all of the victories so far, a mysterious and subtle consequence neither Lord North nor the King had considered. To ordinary Englishmen and Englishwomen, Saratoga said that England was losing the war, that the American rebels owned something the French, Spanish and Dutch did not.

Had Sir William Howe advanced up the Hudson to meet Burgoyne, things might have gone very differently, but Howe had decided to invade Pennsylvania instead. He beat George Washington at Brandywine, then succeeded in capturing Philadelphia and Germantown. The American Congress fled to Pennsylvanian York, which baffled the English in the field—and at home. A people simply did not abandon their capital to the enemy, they defended it to the death! What matter taking Philadelphia when it no longer held the rebel government? Something new was on the face of the earth.

Though Howe's conquests in Pennsylvania occupied more or less the same time frame as Burgoyne's campaigns in upper New York, in England they could not compete with defeat at Saratoga. From Saratoga onward, the Parliament started to wonder if England could win this war. The government of Lord North grew defensive, worried too about events in Ireland, blocked from direct trading across the seas and talking about enlisting volunteers to fight the French, allied to the Americans. Well, everybody in London saw through *that!* If the Irish intended to fight, they would be going to fight the English. Therefore the Irish would have to be conciliated, as the army was 3,000 miles away. Not an easy task with the Tories ruling the House.

In Bristol the economic depression kept on worsening. French and American privateers were sailing the seas and doing better than the English privateers; the Royal Navy was also on the far side of the Western Ocean.

Always eager to mount privateers, many Bristol plutocrats contributed money toward transforming merchant vessels into heavily armed floating fortresses. English privateers had done extremely well during the Seven Years' War against France, so nobody envisioned that this war would see different results.

> "But," said Richard to Mr. James Thistlethwaite in a letter he wrote during the last half of 1778, "our investors have lost disastrously. Bristol launched 21 privateers, but only the two slavers Tartar and Alexander have captured a prize—a French East Indiaman said to be worth £100,000. The shipping trade has declined so much that the Council says the port dues will not cover the Mayor's salary.
>
> "Highwaymen are everywhere. Even the White Ladies Inn on the Aust turnpike is now deemed too dangerous a journey for a Sunday outing, and Mr. and Mrs. Maurice Trevillian of that eminent Cornish family were held up and robbed in their carriage right outside their residence on *Park Street!* They lost a gold watch, some very expensive jewelry and a sum of money.
>
> "In short, Jem, things are in a parlous state."

Mr. Thistlethwaite answered Richard's letter with remarkable promptitude. Some inimical little Bristol birds were whistling a merry tune, to the effect that Jem Thistlethwaite was not prospering in London. He had turned, they trilled, to hacking for certain publishers and even touting for stationers.

> "Richard, how splendid to hear from you! I miss the sight of your comely face, but a letter conjures it up.
>
> "The only difference between a pirate and a privateer is the Letter of Marque from H.M.'s Government, which takes a big share of the profits. What started as a local conflagration has become a world war. English outposts are under attack in nearly all corners of the globe—how can a globe have corners?—even some mighty remote ones.
>
> "I am not surprised that it was two slavers captured the only prize. Especially Alexander and Tartar. Just the right size and weight. 120 men to man 16 guns. Perfect. Besides, slavers sail so

well. Fast and maneuverable. And they may as well be doing something, with slaving wellnigh impossible for the duration.

"If Bristol is in dire straits, Liverpool is poised on the brink of a maelstrom. It is a town almost as large as Bristol, yet it has less than a quarter of Bristol's charitable institutions. *Thousands* have been thrown on its parishes, which, lacking donations from philanthropists, cannot feed them. They are literally starving, and Lord Penrhyn and his Liverpudlian kind have never heard of the word 'philanthropy.' That is what happens in a town whose nabobs are all in the slaving business.

"Though it looks east, London's million souls are suffering too, Richard. The East India Company is feeling a little pinch, and is very afraid of the French, who are doing quite well by their Yankey allies. The United States of America! A grand title for a loose confederacy of little colonies thrown together by urgent need—need which will pass. Then, I predict, each little colony will go its own way, and the United States of America will dissolve into an unattainable philosophical idea in the minds of a handful of brilliant, enlightened, extremely gifted men. The American colonists will win their war, I have never doubted it, but they will emerge as thirteen different states linked by nothing more solid than a treaty of mutual aid.

"A little whisper you will enjoy, I know. Mr. Henry Cruger, Member of Parliament for Bristol and an American, is rumored to be receiving a pension of at least £1,000 a year from the King for information about Yankey doings. Ironic, is it not? There is Bristol screaming that Cruger is a Yankey spy, when all the time he is spying for England.

"And I will conclude, my very dear Richard, by saying that London air is Beotian air too, not fit for my Attic lungs to respire. However, I am well, quite often too drunk—though the rum is not the equal of Thomas Cave's."

A concluding paragraph, thought Richard, putting the letter down, that said the Bristol birds were singing a true song. Poor Jem! Bristol had finite bounds; he had thought to find none in gargantuan London, a city amply provided with its own satirists and in no need of Bristolians.

So the letters with which he continued to inundate Richard contained news Richard had already heard, though he could not bring himself to say so in his replies.

"Oh, Jem!" he exclaimed at the end of 1780 as he read yet another Thistlethwaite missive. "Ye've lost your edge!"

"It is a topsy-turvy world, Richard. Sir Henry Clinton, our latest Commander-in-Chief, has abandoned Philadelphia in order to keep a firm hold on Manhattan and adjacent parts of New York. Which seems to me a little like a fox going to earth before the hounds have started baying. The French have formally recognized the United States of America and are making utter buffoons of themselves over Ambassador Benjamin Franklin's moth-eaten fur hat. All of Europe is now so apprehensive that Catherine, Empress of All The Russias, has negotiated a league of armed neutrality between herself and Denmark, Sweden, Prussia, Austria and Sicily. The only thing these countries have in common is fear of the English and French.

"I wrote a brilliant—and very well received!—article upon the 5,500 Sons of Liberty taken prisoner when Sir Henry Clinton captured Charles Town. They have been impressed into our own navy! A nice touch, eh? My article revolved around a peculiar fact: that American officers do not dare to flog their soldiers or sailors! Imagine then what the Sons of Liberty think when the dear old English cat-with-nine-tails flays the hide from their backs and bottoms!

"I also wrote a defense of General Benedict Arnold's defection, which I regard as a simple consequence of this plaguey slow war. I believe that he and his other turncoat colleagues have grown tired of enduring. The comforts of English commands and pensions must loom large for many American senior officers. Not to mention the attractions of English *professionalism.* It must surely be galling for a spanking-smart commander to see his ragged troops shoeless, hatless, mutinous from lack of pay *and* independent enough to tell him to fuck himself if they do not like his orders. No cat!

"I have laid down £100 at odds of ten-to-one that the rebels will win. Which means that eventually I will be £1,000 richer. Eventually. Ye gods, Richard, how this wretched war drags on! Parliament and the King are ruining England."

But Richard's mind was filled with a pain much closer to home than a war 3,000 miles away. Peg was turning in on herself.

She had her reasons: she would have no more children, William Henry was her sole hope, and Richard was not there all day to gentle her out of her moods and depressions.

Is it because as we grow older we are incapable of sustaining the vividness of our youthful dreams? Does life itself snuff them out? Is that what is happening to Peg? Is that what is happening to me? I used to have such wondrous dreams—the cottage in Clifton amid a garden full of flowers, a handsome pony to ride into Bristol and a trap to take my family up to Durdham Down for picnics, very pleasant congress with my neighbors of like estate, a dozen children and all the thrills and perils of watching them mature. As if I were naught save a witness to the magical purposes of God, warm in His hand, good to mine own, offending no one. Yet here am I turned two-and-thirty, and none of it has come to pass. I have a small fortune in the Bristol Bank, one chick in my nest, and I am doomed to live in my father's house forever. I will never be my own man, for my wife, whom I love too dearly to hurt, is terrified of change. Terrified that she will lose her one chick. How to tell her that her terror is a temptation to God? Long ago I learned that trouble comes when one makes too much of a song and dance, that the best way to avoid trouble is to be quiet, draw no attention to oneself.

His love for William Henry had subtly changed as a result of Peg's obsession with the child. What had been fear that their son would sicken or go wandering had turned to pity at their son's plight. If he ran rather than walked, even inside the tavern, Peg would swoop upon him, ask him why he was running. When Dick took William Henry for his daily walk, Peg insisted on accompanying them, so the boy was doomed to walk hand-in-hand, never to run free. If he tried to stand on the very edge of the Key Head and count (he could count to 100) the number of ships in that amazing avenue, Peg snatched him away with a hard word for Dick's carelessness. The greatest pity of it was that the child was not defiant, didn't have that drive to assert his independence that most boys of six owned almost to excess.

"I have been talking to Senhor Habitas," Richard said one long summer evening after the Cooper's Arms had closed. "There is no fear that Tower Arms will cease to place orders with us for a good time to come, yet things have settled down into such regularity that we can spare attention for someone unskilled." He drew a big breath and looked at Peg across the supper table. "From now on, I am going to take William Henry to work with me."

He had intended to go on and explain that it was only for a little while, that the boy desperately needed the stimulus of new experiences and fresh faces, that he too owned that patience, that mechanical aptitude, that love for fitting together the pieces of a puzzle. But none of it was said.

Peg began to scream. "No, no, no!" came her thin shrieks, so terrifying that William Henry flinched, shivered, scrambled down from his chair and ran to hide his head in his father's lap.

Dick clenched his fists and looked down at them, mouth set; Mag got up, plucked a pitcher of water off the counter and threw its contents in Peg's face. She stopped screaming, began to howl.

"It was just an idea," Richard said to his father.

"Not one of your better ones, Richard."

"I thought—here, William Henry!" He put his arms around the boy and lifted him to sit on his lap, with a glare at Dick that forbade any comment; Dick thought his grandson too old to be cuddled by his father.

"It is all right, William Henry, it is all right."

"Mama?" the child asked, skin bleached white, eyes enormous.

"Mama came over unwell, but she will be better soon. See? Grandmama knows what to do. I said something I ought not, that is all," Richard ended, rubbing his son's back and gazing at Dick with an awful desire to laugh. Not from amusement. From madness. "I cannot do anything right, Father," he said. "I meant no harm."

"I know," said Dick, got up and went to pull the cat's tail. "Here, have a real drop," he said, handing Richard a mug. "I know ye don't like rum, but sometimes strong medicine is the best."

To his surprise, Richard discovered that the rum did him good, steadied his nerves and deadened his pain. "Father, what am I going to do?" he asked then.

"Not take William Henry to Habitas's with ye, at any rate."

"She is something worse than merely unwell, ain't she?"

"I fear so, Richard. The worst of it is that it is not good for him to be so cosseted."

"Who is 'him'?" asked William Henry.

Both men looked at him, then at each other.

" 'Him,' " said Richard with decision, "is you, William Henry. Ye're old enough to be told that your mama worries and fusses about you too much."

"I know that, Dadda," said William Henry. He climbed off Richard's knee and went to stand beside his mother, pat her heaving shoulders. "Mama, you must not worry so. I am a big boy now."

"But he is a little boy!" Peg wailed after Richard had taken her upstairs and put her on their bed. "Richard, how could you be so stupid? A babe in a gunsmithy!"

"Peg, we make guns, we do not use them," said Richard patiently.

"William Henry is old enough to be"—he searched frantically for a telling word—"*broadened.*"

She rolled away from him. "That is ridiculous! How can anyone who calls a tavern 'home' be in need of broadening?"

"A tavern exposes a child to naught save folly," said Richard, keeping the exasperation out of his voice. "Since his eyes could see, he has witnessed inebriation, self-pity, incautious comments, fisticuffs, profanity, lewd behavior and disgusting messes. You think that your presence makes it acceptable, that he cannot be harmed, but I too was a tavern-keeper's child, and well do I remember what tavern life did to me. Frankly, I was glad to go to board at Colston's, and gladder still not to serve my apprenticeship as a victualler. It would do William Henry the world of good to meet and have congress with sober men."

"You will *not* take him to Habitas's!" she spat.

"I can see that for myself, Peg, ye've no need to tell me. But this episode has shown me," he said, sinking onto the bed and putting a hand on her shoulder, "that it is time to speak. You cannot keep William Henry wrapped in swaddling clothes for the rest of his childhood for no better reason than that he is our only child. Today has made me understand that it is high time our son was allowed a little more freedom. You must learn to let William Henry go now, for next year he will be at Colston's School, and that I insist upon no matter what."

"I cannot let him go!" she cried.

"You must. If you do not, Peg, then it is not your child who occupies your thoughts. It is you yourself."

"I know, I know, I know!" she wept through her fingers, rocking. "But how can I stop? He is all I have—all I will ever have!"

"You have me."

For a moment she did not answer. "Yes," she said eventually, "I have you. But it is not the same, Richard, it is not the same. If anything were to happen to William Henry, I would die."

Most of the light had gone; a grey little ray seeped through one of the cracks in the partition and rested like a cobweb on Richard Morgan's face as he sat looking down on his wife. No, it is not the same, he thought. It is not the same.

Colston's School for Boys had enabled many of the sons of the better class of Bristol's poor to become lettered. It was by no means the only such;

every religious denomination except the Roman Catholics had charity schools, particularly the Church of England. Only two of them had distinctive uniforms for their charity pupils, however. Colston's boys wore blue coats, the Red Maids wore red dresses. Both Church of England, though the Red Maids were not so lucky; they were taught to read but not to write, and most of their time was taken up with embroidering silk waistcoats and coats for the gentry, work for which their mistresses were paid but they were not. Literacy and numeracy were better spread among Bristol's males than in any other English city, including London. Elsewhere they tended to be the mark of the wealthy.

Colston's 100 charity boys were boarders, of course, a fate which had befallen Richard; due to school and apprenticeship, he had seen his parents only on Sundays and during vacations between the ages of seven and nineteen. Imagine Peg coping with *that!* Luckily Colston's provided another mode of education; for a fat fee, the child of a prosperous man could attend between seven in the morning and two in the afternoon from Mondays to Saturdays as a day pupil. With generous holidays, of course; no schoolmaster wished more punishment upon himself than the Church of England and the late Mr. Colston's will prescribed.

To William Henry, trotting along beside his grandfather (Mag had thrown a temper tantrum which had effectively prevented Peg's coming too) on that first morning, more than a gate to school and learning was being thrown open; this was the first day of a whole new life, and he was dying of curiosity. Perhaps had he been let go with Richard to see what gunsmithing was like it might not have gripped him so urgently, but the prison walls his mother had erected around him remained unbreached, and he was very tired of them. A more passionate and impulsive child would have railed at them with evident frustration, but William Henry was as patient and as self-controlled as his father. His watchword was "wait." And now, at last, the waiting was over.

Colston's School for Boys looked no different from two dozen other piles which rejoiced in titles like school or poorhouse or hospital or workhouse; grimy and not very well kept up, the glass in its windows never cleaned, its plaster shabby and its timbers crooked. Damp pervaded it from foundations to Tudor chimneys, the interior had never been designed for instruction, and the smell of the Froom mere yards away was nauseating for any save a native Bristolian nose.

It had a gate and a yard and what seemed like a thousand boys, perhaps half of them wearing the famous blue coat. Like the other paying day pupils, William Henry was not required to wear it; some of the day pupils were the sons of aldermen or Merchant Venturers who had no wish to besmirch their offspring with the taint of charity.

A tall, spindling man in the black suit and starched white stock of a clergyman approached Dick and William Henry, smiling to reveal discolored, rotting teeth: a rum drinker.

"Reverend Prichard," said Dick, bowing.

"Mister Morgan." The dark eyes turned to William Henry and widened. "This is Richard's son?"

"Yes, this is William Henry."

"Then come, William Henry." And the Reverend Prichard set off across the yard without a backward glance.

William Henry followed, also without a backward glance; he was too busy digesting the chaos a boys' schoolyard was before discipline cracked down.

"It is fortunate for you," said the day pupil master, "that your birthday should coincide with the commencement of your schooling, Master William Henry Morgan. You will start learning with A for apple and the two-times table. I see ye have your slate, good."

"Yes, sir," said William Henry, whose manners were excellent.

That was the last collected thing he was to say unbidden until dinner time in the refectory, nor were his thought processes in much better order. It was so confusing! There were so many rules, none of which seemed to make any sense. Standing. Sitting. Kneeling. Praying. Parroting words. How to answer a query, how not to answer a query. Who did what to whom. Whereabouts this was, versus that.

His lessons took place in a vast room inhabited by the junior 100 of Colston's pupils; several masters drifted from one group to another, or hectored one group without regard for the welfare of other groups. It was therefore of great advantage to William Henry Morgan that his grandfather, not busy enough in these hard times, had taught him to count, to know his ABC, and even to do a few simple sums. Otherwise he might have been overwhelmed.

Though the Reverend Prichard hovered, he did not take lessons. That duty for William Henry's group rested with a Mr. Simpson, and it soon became apparent that Mr. Simpson had pronounced likes and dislikes when it came to his charges. Since he was willowy, sallow-skinned and looked to be in constant danger of vomiting, it was not surprising that he disliked the boys who snuffled with sickening gusto, or picked their noses, or displayed the sticky brown fingers which betrayed that they used them to wipe their dirty bottoms.

It was no torment for William Henry to do as he was told and—sit still!—don't fidget!—don't kick the bench!—don't pick your nose!—don't snuffle!—and *don't* talk! Therefore Mr. Simpson appeared not to notice him beyond asking him his name and informing him that since there were already two Morgans at Colston's, he would be known as "Morgan Tertius." Another boy, asked the same question and giving a similar kind of reply, was foolish enough to protest that he did not want to be known as "Carter Minor." Which earned him four vicious lashes with the cane, one for not saying "sir," one for being presumptuous, and two for good luck.

The cane was a frightful instrument, one William Henry had no experience of whatsoever. In fact, he had lived for seven years without so much as being smacked. Therefore, he vowed, he would give no master at Colston's any excuse for caning him. For by the time that eleven o'clock came and the entire school sat upon benches down either side of long tables in the refectory, William Henry had worked out who got the cane. The talkers, the nose pickers, the fidgeters, the snufflers, the dullards, the cheeky, and a small number of boys who could not seem to help getting up to mischief.

He did not care much for either of his closest companions in both classroom and refectory, but did like the look of the boy who sat next-but-one from him; cheerful, yet not quite perky enough to have gotten the cane. William Henry glanced at him and essayed a smile which caused one of the masters at the Head's table to draw in a breath and stiffen.

The moment he received the smile, the boy somehow ejected the obstacle between them, who fell on the floor with a clatter and was hauled away by one ear to the Head's table on a dais at the front of the enormous, echoing room.

"Monkton Minor," said the newcomer, grinning to reveal a missing tooth. "Been here since February."

"Morgan Tertius, started today," whispered William Henry.

"It is allowed to talk quietly once Grace has been said. You must have a rich father, Morgan Tertius."

William Henry eyed Monkton Minor's blue coat and looked wistful. "I do not think so, Monkton Minor. Not terribly rich, anyway. He went here, and he wore the blue coat."

"Oh." Monkton Minor thought about that, then nodded. "Is your father still alive?"

"Yes. Is yours?"

"No. Nor is my mother. I am an orphan." Monkton Minor leaned his head closer, his bright blue eyes sparkling. "What is your Christian name, Morgan Tertius?"

"I have two. William Henry. What is yours?"

"Johnny." The look became conspiratorial. "I will call you William Henry and you will call me Johnny—but only if no one can hear us."

"Is it a sin?" asked William Henry, who still catalogued wrongs in that light.

"No, just not good form. But I *hate* being a Minor!"

"And I a Tertius." William Henry removed his gaze from his new friend and glanced guiltily toward the Head's table on high, where the ejected benchmate was receiving what William Henry had already learned was a jawing—far worse than a few licks of the cane because it took so much longer and one had to stand absolutely still until it was over or else teeter on a stool for the rest of the day. Encountering the stare of a master beside Mr. Simpson, he blinked and looked away immediately, quite why he did not know. "Who is that, Johnny?"

"Next to the Head? Old Doom and Froom." Mr. Prichard.

"No, one down. Next to the Simp."

"Mr. Parfrey. He teaches Latin."

"Does he have a nickname too?"

Monkton Minor managed to touch the tip of his snub nose with his pursed lips. "If he does, us juniors don't know it. Latin is for the seniors."

While the two boys discussed them, Mr. Parfrey and Mr. Simpson were busy discussing William Henry.

"I see, Ned, that ye have a Ganymede amongst your swine."

Mr. Edward Simpson understood this without further elucidation. "Morgan Tertius? You should see his eyes!"

"I must make sure I do. But even viewed from afar, Ned, he is ravishing. Truly a Ganymede—ah, to be a Zeus!"

"As well then, George, that by the time he starts amo-ing and amas-ing, he will be two years older and probably as snotty as all the rest," said Mr. Simpson, picking diffidently at his food, though a great deal more palatable than that served to the boys; disease ran in his family, notoriously short-lived.

Their casual exchange was not evidence of prurient intentions; it was merely a symptom of their unenviable lot. George Parfrey had longed to be a Zeus, but he might as easily and as fruitlessly have longed to be a Robert Nugent, now Earl Nugent. Schoolmasters were inevitably genteely impoverished. For Mr. Simpson and Mr. Parfrey, Colston's represented a kind of zenith; they were paid £1 per week—but only when school was up—and had their board and lodging all year round as part of the job. As Colston's ran to very good food (the Head was a famous Epicure) and its masters each had a roomlet to himself, there was very little reason to leave unless one were tapped for Eton, Harrow or Bristol Grammar School. Marriage made things more difficult, of course, and was out of the question until one either took Orders or received a hefty promotion; not that marriage was forbidden, rather that housing a wife and offspring in a roomlet was a daunting prospect. Besides which, Mr. Simpson and Mr. Parfrey were not tempted by the Other Sex. They preferred to make do with their own, and in particular with each other. The love, however, was purely on poor Ned Simpson's side. George Parfrey owned himself completely.

"Perhaps we could go to the Hotwells after Church on Sunday?" Mr. Simpson asked hopefully. "The waters seem to do me good."

"Provided you allow me the indulgence of my watercolors," said Mr. Parfrey, still gazing at William Henry Morgan, who was growing more animated—and more beautiful—with every passing moment. He pulled a face. "I fail to understand how anyone can feel better after drinking the Avon's leavings, but if you are happy to grant me a peaceful interlude by St. Vincent's Rocks, then I will come." A sigh emerged. "Oh, how much I would love to paint that divine child!"

Richard arrived to collect William Henry dry mouthed. What if he were greeted by a distraught little boy begging not to have to return to school tomorrow?

Needless fears. His eyes located his son careering headlong around the yard, laughing as he dodged the sallies of a blue-coated little fellow his own age, tow-headed and painfully thin.

"Dadda!" Up he scampered, his playmate close behind. "Dadda, this is Monkton Minor, but I call him Johnny when no one can hear us. He is a norphan."

"How d'ye do, Monkton Minor?" asked Richard, his own days at Colston's rushing back. He had been Morgan Minor, had graduated to Morgan Major after he turned eleven. And only his best friend had called him Richard. "I shall ask the Reverend Prichard if ye may come to dinner with us after Church next Sunday."

He felt as if he shepherded a stranger, he reflected as he bore William

Henry off; a William Henry who did not walk sedately at his side but skipped and hopped, hummed under his breath.

"I take it that you like school," he said, smiling.

"It is splendid, Dadda! I can run and shout."

The tears came; Richard blinked them away. "But not in the classroom, I trust."

William Henry gave him a withering look. "Dadda, I am an angel in the classroom! I did not get the cane once. A lot of the boys got it a lot, and one boy fainted when he got thirty. Thirty is a walloping lot. But I worked out how not to get caned."

"Did you? How?"

"I keep quiet and do my writing and my sums tidily."

"Yes, William Henry, I know that technique well. Did the big boys make you cry when you were let out to play?"

"You mean when they lined all of us up in the privies?"

"They still do that, do they?"

"Well, they did to us. But I just wrote on the privy wall with the big piece of pooh Jones Major did on my hand—most of it missed—and then they left me alone. Johnny says it is the best way. They pick on the boys who howl and carry on." He gave a particularly high skip. "I wiped my fingers on my coat. See?"

Mouth rigid, Richard eyed the brown smear across the skirt of William Henry's brand-new, mushroom-colored coat and swallowed convulsively several times. Do not laugh, Richard, for Christ's *sake* do not laugh! "If I were you," he said when he was able, "I would not mention the pooh incident to Mama. Or show her where you wiped it off. I will ask Grandmama to clean the mark."

So Richard ushered his son into the Cooper's Arms with an air of triumph only his father noticed. Peg squealed and scooped the hitherto tractable William Henry into her arms to cover his face with kisses, and was pushed away.

"Mama, do not do that! I am a big boy now! Grandpapa, I had such a good time today! I ran ten times around the yard, I fell over and hurt my knee, I made a whole row of a's on my slate, and Mr. Simpson says I am so advanced for my age that he is going to put me up into the next class. Except that that don't make sense. He teaches the next class too, and in the same place. Mama, my knee is a *badge!* Do not fuss so!"

Richard filled in the rest of his afternoon by nailing up some planks to make William Henry his own cubicle at the far side of the bedroom; he slept in a bed these days anyway. The activity was as soothing as it was removed from the turmoil downstairs, from whence he could hear William Henry regaling every newcomer with a censored version of his day at school. Talk! He had not shut up—William Henry, who never said more than two words together!

For Peg, Richard felt an enormous pity tempered by the icy wind of his own common sense. William Henry had flown from the nest, and could never be confined again. But how much of what he had displayed in the stunning space of one small day had he harbored through the years? One day could not possibly have produced so many new thoughts, for all that it had endowed him with a new code of behavior. William Henry is not the saint I deemed him after all. William Henry, God bless him, is an ordinary little boy.

And so he tried to tell Peg, but without success. No matter how he attacked her, Peg refused to accept the fact that her son was alive and well and hugely enjoying a brand-new world. She sought refuge in tears and suffered such black depressions that Richard despaired, tired of her waterworks and having no idea of the depth of her guilt, her consciousness that she had failed in the only task a woman truly had: to give birth to children. His patience with her never diminished, but on the day that he caught her drinking a mug of rum it was sorely tried.

"This is no place for you," he said kindly. "Let me buy that house in Clifton, Peg, please."

"No, no, no!" she screamed.

"My love, we have been married for fourteen years and ye've been my friend as well as my wife, but this is too much. I do not know what ails your heart, but rum is no cure for it."

"Leave me alone!"

"I cannot, Peg. Father is growing annoyed, but that is not the worst of it. William Henry is old enough to notice that his mama is behaving strangely. Please, try to be good for his sake."

"William Henry does not care about me, why should I try for his sake?" she demanded.

"Oh, Peg, that is not true!"

Round and round in circles, that was how it seemed to be; not sweet reason nor Richard's patience nor Dick's irritation served to help placate whatever monsters chewed at her mind, though she did abandon the rum when William Henry asked her outright why she was falling-down drunk. The directness of his question appalled her.

"Though why I do not know," said Dick to Richard later that day. "William Henry is a tavern-keeper's child."

Late in February of 1782, Mr. James Thistlethwaite sent Richard a letter by special courier.

> "I write this on the night of the 27th, my dear friend, and I am the richer by £1,000. Paid by a draft on my hapless victim's bank. It is official! Today the Parliament voted to discontinue offensive warfare against the thirteen colonies, and soon we will begin to withdraw our troops.
>
> "I blame all of it on Franklin's fur hat. The Frogs have proven themselves staunch allies, between Admiral de Grasse and General de Rochambeau—which goes to show that if a man captivates the French sense of fashion, anything is possible. George Washington and the Frogs ran rings around us at Yorktown, though I think what decided the Parliament was the fact that Lord Cornwallis *surrendered.* Yes, I realize that Clinton was having too good a time of it in New York to sail down and relieve Cornwallis, and I realize that it was the French navy enabled Washington and his land Frogs to force Yorktown, but that does not diminish the magnitude of *surrender.* Burgoyne all over again. London is shamed into heartbreak over it.
>
> "Spread the news, Richard, for my courier will reach Bristol first, and do not neglect to say that your source is James Thistlethwaite, late of Cornwallis's Bristol.
>
> "Do I hear you ask what I am going to do with £1,000? Buy a pipe of rum from Mr. Thomas Cave's distillery—and I do know that a pipe contains 105 gallons! I will also stroll down to the Green Canister in Half Moon Street, there to buy a gross of her finest cundums from Mrs. Phillips. These London whores are runny with the pox and the clap, but Mrs. Phillips has come up with the world's most important invention since rum. I shall be able to poke my properly encundumed sugar stick with impunity."

It was another year—March of 1783—before Senhor Tomas Habitas was obliged to let Richard go. The Bristol Bank held over £3,000 by then, scarcely a penny of it touched. Why should he spend it? Peg would not move to Clifton and his father (whom he had tried to talk into taking the Black Horse Inn on Clifton Hill) professed himself happy at the Cooper's Arms. Not all those twelve shillings a day which Richard had paid him for over seven years had been used up, Dick explained ingenuously. He could afford to wait the hard times out right where he was, on Broad Street, in the thick of things.

Yes, the American war was over and in time a treaty would confirm that fact, but prosperity had not returned. Part of that was due to chaos in the Parliament, wherein Charles James Fox and Lord North screamed the roof down about the unwarranted concessions Lord Shelburne was making to the Americans. No one was worrying about mundanities like *government.* Short-lived administrations distinguished by wrangling and power plays wreaked havoc in Westminster; the truth was that no one, including the half-crazed King, knew what to do with a war debt of £232 million and falling revenues.

Food riots broke out among Bristol's sailors, who were paid thirty shillings per month—provided that they were at sea. On shore, not a penny. The situation was so desperate that the Mayor managed to persuade ship owners to give their sailors fifteen shillings per month while on shore. In 1775 the number of ships paying the Mayor's Dues had been 529: by 1783, that number had shrunk to 102. As most of these ships were Bristol based and lying idle along the quays and backs as well as downriver around Pill, several thousand sailors were a force to be reckoned with.

In Liverpool, 10,000 of the 40,000 inhabitants were depending upon the slender charitable resources of that city, and in Bristol the Poor Rates had soared 150 per cent. The Corporation and the Merchant Venturers had no choice other than to start selling off property. New and stringent ordinances were brought in to deal with the ever-increasing flow of rural poor into Bristol, there to throw themselves upon the parishes and eat at least. Some of those caught defrauding the parishes were publicly pilloried and whipped before being banished; yet the flood continued to pour in faster than an Avon tide.

"Did you see this, Dick?" asked Cousin James-the-druggist, calling in on his way home from his Corn Street shop. He waved a sheet of flimsy. "An advertisement from our felons in the Newgate, if you please! Announcing that they cannot afford to eat on their twopence a day—it is a disgrace, with bread at sixteen pence the quartern loaf."

"A penny a day if they are still awaiting trial," said Dick.

"I shall see Jenkins the baker and send them however much bread they need. And cheese and ox cheeks."

Dick grinned slyly. "What, Jim, no shillingses tipped into their outstretched hands?"

Cousin James-the-druggist blushed. "Yes, ye were right, Dick. They did indeed drink it up."

"They always will drink it up. To send them bread is sensible. Just make sure that your philanthropic cronies do likewise."

"How is Richard now that he is not working? I never see him."

"Well enough," said Richard's father curtly. "The reason he is invisible is up there on his bed."

"Drunk?"

"Oh, no. She stopped *that* after William Henry asked her outright why she guzzled rum." He shrugged. "When William Henry is not here, she lies on the bed and stares at nothing."

"And when William Henry is here?"

"She behaves herself." Mine Host hawked and spat copiously into his sawdust. "Women! They are very queer fish, Jim."

A mental picture of his vaporish wife and their two bracket-faced spinster daughters swam before Cousin James-the-druggist's eyes; he smiled wryly and nodded. "I have often wondered," he said, "why the world should choose to liken a face to a bracket?"

Dick roared with laughter. "Thinking of your girls, Jim?"

"Girls no longer, alas. They are past their last prayers." He got to his feet. "I am sorry to have missed Richard. I had thought to see him back here, as in the old days before Habitas."

"The old days are gone, do I need to tell ye that? Look around you! The place is empty, and the quays boil with those poor sailor bastards. How virtuous are our genuine registered parish poor, and how indignant! They cast rocks at their wretched brethren in the pillory rather than pity them." Dick pounded his fist on the table. "*Why* did we ever go to war three thousand miles away? Why did we not simply hand the colonists their precious liberty? Wish them well of something so ridiculous, then go back to sleep, or go fight France? The country is ruined, and all for the sake of an idea. Not our idea at that."

"You have not answered me. If Richard has no job, where is he? And where is William Henry?"

"They walk together, Jim. Always to Clifton. They go—up Pipe Lane—down Frog Lane—across the Brandon Hill footpath to Clifton

Hill—chase the cows and sheep in the Clifton Pound—then come back along the Avon, where they throw stones into the water and laugh a lot."

"That is William Henry's version, not Richard's."

"Richard tells me nothing," said Dick sourly.

"You and he are different natured," said Cousin James-the-druggist, going to the door. "That happens. What ye ought to be thanking God for, Dick, is that Richard and William Henry are like as two peas. It is"—he drew a breath—"quite beautiful."

On the following Sunday after Church and a bracing sermon from Cousin James-of-the-clergy, Richard and William Henry walked to the Hotwells end of Clifton.

A decade or two ago Bristol's own watering place had come near to rivaling Bath as a spa for high society; the guest houses of Dowry Place, Dowry Square and the Hotwells Road teemed with elegant visitors in expensive array, fabulously bewigged gentlemen in embroidered coats mincing along in high heels with bedizened ladies on their arms. There were balls and soirées, parties and routs, concerts and entertainments, even theater in the old Clifton playhouse on Wood Wells Lane. For a while an imitation Vauxhall Gardens had seen its share of masquerades, intrigues and scandals; novelists had situated their heroines at the Hotwells, and society doctors had extolled the medicinal properties of the waters.

And then the fabric of its fascination fell apart, too slowly to call disintegration, yet too quickly to call a rot from within. Fashion had made it: fashion unmade it. The elegant visitors moved back to Bath, or on to Cheltenham, and the Bristol Hotwells became mostly an export industry of bottled spa water.

Which suited Richard and William Henry very well, for it meant that a Sunday outing saw no more than a handful of other visitors on the horizon. Mag had packed them a cold dinner of broiled fowl, bread, butter, cheese and a few early apples her brother had sent from the farm at Bedminster; Richard carried it in a soldier's pack athwart his shoulders, where it rested next to a flagon of small beer. They found a good spot beyond the square bulk of the Hotwells House, which stood on a rock shelf just above the high tide mark where the Avon Gorge terminated.

It truly was a beautiful place, for St. Vincent's Rocks and the crags of the gorge were richly colored in reds, plums, pinks, rusts, greys and off-whites, the river was the hue of blued steel, and a wealth of trees conspired to hide even the chimneys of Mr. Codrington's brass foundry.

"Can you swim, Dadda?" asked William Henry.

"No. Which is why we are sitting here, not right on the edge of the river," said Richard.

William Henry eyed the spate thoughtfully; the tide was still flooding in, and the current curled and swirled visibly. "The water moves as if it were alive."

"You might say it is. And it is hungry, never forget that. It would suck you down and eat you whole here, ye'd never see the surface again. So no high jinks anywhere near it, is that understood?"

"Yes, Dadda."

Dinner eaten, the pair of them stretched out on the sward with their coats rolled up to serve as pillows; Richard closed his eyes.

"The Simp is gone," said William Henry suddenly.

His father opened one eye and grinned. "Can you never be still and quiet?" he asked.

"Not often, and not now. The Simp is gone."

The message sank in. "You mean that he does not teach you? Well, ye've just begun your third year at Colston's, so that was to be expected."

"No, Dadda, I mean that he is gone! Over the summer, while we were on holidays. Johnny says he was too sick to stay any longer. The Head asked the Bishop if he could go to one of the almshouses, but the Bishop said they were not for the sick, they were for the in—in—I do not know the word."

"Indigent?"

"That is it, indigent! So they carried him in a sedan chair to St. Peter's Hospital. Johnny says he cried dreadfully."

"So would I, were I to be carried to St. Peter's," Richard said with feeling. "Poor fellow. Why wait until now to tell me?"

"I forgot," said William Henry vaguely, rolled over twice, kicked his heels bruisingly against the grass, sighed deeply, flapped his hands, rolled over again, and began to pluck the detritus from around a promising stone.

"Time to go, my son. I recognize the signs," said Richard, getting to his feet, stuffing their coats into the soldier's pack and shouldering it. "Shall we hike up Granby Hill and look at Mr. Goldney's grotto?"

"Oh yes please!" cried William Henry, scampering off.

They looked, reflected Mr. George Parfrey from his perch on a shrub-shrouded ledge above them, as if they had not a care in the world. And they probably did not have a care in the world. The boy was a paying pupil;

though they were not ostentatiously dressed, Mr. Parfrey had taken due note of good fine cloth, the absence of frayed or darned hems, the shine on their silver-buckled shoes and a certain air of independence.

He knew everything about Morgan Tertius's father, of course; Colston's was a small place, its paying pupils dissected in the masters' common-room all the more minutely because in a starved existence there was so little else to talk about. A gunsmith in partnership with a *Jew,* and who had earned a small fortune out of the American war. Not often a boy as beautiful as the son appeared. Nor, when such a boy did appear, was he usually as unaffected and unspoiled as Morgan Tertius. However, the boy was not yet old enough to realize what capital he could make out of his beauty.

That had to be the father with him. They were too alike not to be closely related and the odds favored paternity. A sketchbook lay upon Parfrey's knee, on its top page a drawing he had taken of the pair of them resting beside the Avon. A good drawing. George Parfrey himself was a handsome man, and when younger, his looks had effectively scotched any hope of a career as a drawing master in some rich man's house, seeing to the limited education of the rich man's daughters. For no rich man in his right mind would hire a handsome young man to peer over an heiress's shoulder and catch her fancy.

Though his heart had not been touched, he was missing poor Ned Simpson more than he had counted upon; the others of their persuasion at Colston's were paired too neatly to think of switching their affections. With Ned's departure—he had died soon after going into St. Peter's—no one needed him. Neither the Head, the Bishop nor the Reverend Mr. Prichard approved of Greek love, each of them having a suitable wife and other fish to fry. So the discreet liaisons which were conducted within the walls of Colston's were fraught with a thousand tensions. Schoolmasters were a ha'penny a dozen, for who in choosing them cared a straw about whether they could teach or not? They were selected upon the recommendation of a board, a Church committee, an eminent cleric, an alderman, a Member of Parliament. None of whom would approve of homosexuality, no matter how discreet. Supply and demand. Sailors might drink themselves sodden, curse and brawl, ram every arse between Bristol and Wampoa, and still keep their reputations as good workmen intact; no ship owner bothered his head about booze, brawls or bums. The same could probably be said of lawyers or bookkeepers. Whereas schoolmasters were a ha'penny a dozen. No booze, no brawls, and—God forbid!—no bums. Especially in a charity school.

Mr. Parfrey had been thinking about moving on, but understood that his hopes were faint. His world was too small, too enclosed. Colston's would see the end of his career, after which the Bishop might graciously consent to accommodating him in an almshouse. He was turned five-and-forty, and Colston's was *it.*

So he put the sketchbook into his case and left the ledge above the Avon to its own devices, still thinking about Morgan Tertius and his father. Odd, that the father shared the son's amazing good looks, yet did not have the power to turn heads.

Now that William Henry was back in school, Richard had the leisure to pursue both a friendship and an intriguing proposition. Cousin James-the-druggist had been at him to do something better by his £3,000 than leave it in a bank for Quakers to make more from than he did—invest it in the three-per-cents, or at least invest it! urged the businesslike member of the Morgan clan.

He had met Mr. Thomas Latimer when he and William Henry had called into the Habitas workshop. The seven years during which Senhor Habitas had made Brown Besses for Tower Arms had earned him enough to retire in style, but no one who loved his craft as much as Tomas Habitas did would voluntarily retire. Rather, he had advertised in *Felix Farley's Bristol Journal* that he was now available to make sporting guns, and sufficient custom had arrived to keep him just pleasantly occupied.

As Habitas explained after the introductions were performed, Mr. Latimer was a craftsman of a different kind: he made pumps.

"Mostly hand pumps, but ships are converting to chain pumps, and I have an Admiralty contract for making the chains themselves," he said cheerfully. "The hand pump or the pole pump were lucky to lift a ton of bilge water in a week, whereas the chain pump can lift a ton of bilge water in a literal minute. Not to mention that its basis is a simple wooden structure a ship's carpenter can build. All he needs to complete it is the brass chain."

This was news to Richard, who found himself liking Mr. Thomas Latimer enormously. Not anybody's picture of an engineer, he was short, plump, and always smiling—no gloomy Vulcan's brow or blacksmith's sinews about Mr. Latimer!

"I have bought Wasborough's brass foundry in Narrow Wine Street," he explained, "I confess purely because it contains one of Wasborough's three fire engines."

Of course Richard knew what a fire engine was, but once his son was back in school and the hours between seven and two were entirely his to fritter away, he had the time to discover a great deal more about this fascinating device.

The fire engine had been invented by Newcomen early in the century; this was the model that pumped water out of the Kingswood mines and drove the water wheels in William Champion's copper and brass works on the Avon adjacent to the coal. Then James Watt had invented the separate steam condenser, which improved the efficiency of Newcomen's engine so much that Watt had been able to interest the Birmingham iron and steel magnate Matthew Bolton in his idea. Watt had gone into partnership with Bolton and the pair of them maintained a complete monopoly on the manufacture of fire engines through a series of court cases which effectively prevented anyone else's trying to compete; no other inventor could manage to get around incorporating Watt's heavily patented separate steam condenser into his design.

Then Matthew Wasborough, a man in his middle twenties, had met another Bristolian youth named Pickard. Wasborough had come up with a system of pulleys and a fly wheel, Pickard had invented the crank, and together these three new concepts converted the reciprocal motion of a fire engine into circular motion. Instead of the driving force moving up and down, it now turned round and round.

"Water-wheels rotate and can make machinery rotate," said Mr. Latimer as he conducted the sweating Richard through a place filled with furnaces, hearths, lathes, presses, fumes and noise. "But that," said Latimer, pointing, "can make machinery rotate all by itself." Richard gazed at a puffing, chugging monstrosity which occupied pride of place amid a series of spinning lathes, all turning brass into useful objects for ships; iron and ships did not mix, thanks to the corrosive effects of salt water on iron.

"May we go outside?" Richard shouted, ears ringing.

"When Wasborough combined his pulleys and fly wheel with the Pickard crank, they virtually eliminated the water-wheel," Latimer continued as soon as they emerged onto the bank of the Froom just downriver of the Weare where the washerwomen gathered to launder. "It is brilliant, for it means that a manufactory does not need to be sited on a river. If coal is cheap, as it is in Bristol, steam is better than water—provided the engine has circular motion."

"Then why have I never heard of Wasborough and Pickard?"

"Because of James Watt, who sued them because their fire engine contained his patented separate steam condenser. Watt also accused Pickard of stealing his idea for a crank, which is utter nonsense. Watt's solution to the problem of circular motion is rack-and-pinion—he calls it 'sun and planet motion'—but it is devilish slow and complicated. The moment he saw the patent for Pickard's crank, he knew it was the right answer, and could not bear being beaten."

"I had no idea engineering was so cutthroat. What happened?"

"Oh, after a lot of heartaches like losing the contract for a Government flour mill in Deptford, Wasborough died of sheer despair—he was all of eight-and-twenty—and Pickard fled to Connecticut. But I have worked out how to get around Watt's patented separate steam condenser, so I intend to produce the Wasborough-Pickard model before their patents run out and Watt can nip in to collar them."

"It is hard to believe that the most brilliant man in the world is a villain," said Richard.

"James Watt," said Thomas Latimer, not smiling, "is a twisted, stringy little Scotch bastard of no mean ability but a great deal more conceit! If it exists, then Watt has to have invented it—to hear him, God is his apprentice and Heaven is a haggis. Pah!"

Richard eyed the sluggish Froom and noted its cargo of flotsam. Ideal for snarling the buckets of a water-wheel, he thought. "I do see the advantage of steam over water," he said. "We simply cannot continue to conduct industries requiring water power in the midst of cities. Fire engines with circular motion are the way of the future, Mr. Latimer."

"Call me Tom. Consider this, Richard! Wasborough dreamed of incorporating one of his fire engines into a ship, thus enabling it to steer a course as straight as an arrow without regard for seas, currents or tacking and standing to find a favorable wind. His steam device would rotate the blades of a modified water-wheel on either side of the ship, propelling it along. Wonderful!"

"Wonderful indeed, Tom."

When he got home he repeated this sentiment to an audience consisting of his father and Cousin James-the-druggist.

"Latimer is looking for investors," he said then, "and I am thinking of contributing my three thousand pounds to the venture."

"Ye'll lose your money," said Dick grimly.

Cousin James-the-druggist did not agree. "News of Latimer's intentions has created much interest, Richard, and the man's credentials are excellent, even though he is a newcomer to Bristol. I am thinking of investing a thousand in it myself."

"Then ye're both fools," said Dick, a stand from which he refused to budge.

Head bent over his books, William Henry was sitting at Mr. James Thistlethwaite's old table doing his homework; he had gone from a slate to quill and paper, and had enough of Richard's painstaking patience to enjoy producing copperplate script minus the smears and blots which were the bane of most boys' lives.

I am going to make enough money, thought Richard, to educate William Henry right up to Oxford level. He will *not* go at twelve to some lawyer or druggist—or gunsmith!—to serve for seven years as an unpaid slave. I was lucky with Habitas, but how many young apprentices can say they have a good master? No, I do not want that fate for my only child. From Colston's he must go to the Bristol Grammar School, and then to Oxford. Or Cambridge. He likes his schoolwork greatly, and I notice that, just as for me, it is no chore to him to have to read a book. He loves to learn.

Peg was there alongside Mag, both women busy putting the final touches to supper while Richard moved among the occupied tables collecting empties and delivering fulls. The atmosphere was much happier than of yore; Peg seemed to be on the mend at last. She could marshal an occasional smile, did not fuss over William Henry, and in bed she sometimes turned of her own volition to Richard to offer him a little love. Not the old sort of love, no. That was the stuff of dreams, and Richard's dreams were busy dying. Only the young can conquer the mountains of the mind, thought Richard. At five-and-thirty years of age, I am no longer young. My son is nine, and I pass the dreams to him.

Along with a dozen other men, Richard signed his money over to Mr. Thomas Latimer for the express purpose of developing a new kind of fire engine; none of the investors, who included Cousin James-the-druggist, were given any interest in the brass foundry itself, devoted to manufacturing the flat, hook-linked chains for the Admiralty's new bilge pumps.

"I am closing down for Christmas," said Mr. Thomas Latimer to Richard (who was so fascinated that he visited Wasborough's almost every day) on the eve of that foggy, mournfully grey season.

"Unusual" was Richard's comment.

"Oh, the workmen will not be paid! It is just that I have noticed that nothing is done properly during Christmas. Too much rum. Though what the poor wretches have to celebrate I do not know," sighed Latimer. "Times are no better, in spite of young William Pitt as Chancellor for the Exchequer."

"How can times be better, Tom? The only way Pitt can pay for the American war is to raise existing taxes and think of new ones." Richard grinned slyly. "Of course, ye could make a happier Yuletide for your workmen by paying them for the holidays."

Mr. Latimer's cheerfulness did not abate. "Could not do that! Did I, every employer in Bristol would blackball me."

It was pleasant for Richard, however, to be able to spend more time at the Cooper's Arms over Christmas, for William Henry had no school and the tavern was full of wassailers. Mag and Peg had made delicious puddings and pots of brandy sauce to go over them, a haunch of venison roasted on the spit, and Dick made his festive drink of hot, sweet, spiced wine. Richard produced presents: a second cat for Dick, tabby grey, to dispense gin; a green silk umbrella each for Mag and Peg; and for William Henry, a parcel of books, a ream of best writing papers, a splendid leather-covered cork ball, and no less than six pencles made of Cumberland graphite.

Dick was mighty pleased with his gin cat, but Mag and Peg were overwhelmed.

"Such an extravagance!" cried Mag, opening her umbrella to study the effect of lamplight through its thin, jade-colored fabric. "Oh, Peg, how fashionable we will be! Even Cousin Ann will be cast in the shade!" She pirouetted, then shut the umbrella in a hurry. "William Henry, do not *dare* to throw that ball in here!"

Of course the ball was the best present as far as William Henry was concerned, but the pencles were pretty good too. "Dadda, you will have to show me how to sharpen them, I want them to last as long as possible," he said, beaming. "Oh, Mr. Parfrey will admire them! *He* does not have a pencle."

Mr. Parfrey was top of the trees in William Henry's estimation, everybody knew that by now; William Henry had been dinning his excellence in their ears ever since Latin classes had begun early in October. Clearly this was one schoolmaster who knew how to teach, for he had captured William Henry's interest on his first day, and William Henry had not been the only one. Even Johnny Monkton voted Mr. Parfrey first rate.

"He may admire your pencles, but not take," said Richard as he folded William Henry's hand around a small parcel. "Here, this is a present for Johnny. A pity the Head insisted all boarders remain in school for Christmas Day, it would have been nice to have him here with us. Still, he shall have a present."

"It is pencles," said William Henry instantly.

"Aye, pencles."

Peg seized the moment to enfold William Henry in a hug and press her lips to his wide, ivory brow. As if understanding that this was one gift he could give his mother, William Henry suffered her embrace, even kissed her back.

"Ain't Dadda the best father?" he asked his mother.

"Yes," said Peg, waiting in vain to be told that she was the best mother. A year ago her son's indifference coupled with a remark like this would have generated a surge of hatred for Richard, but Peg had learned that hating Richard could not change a thing. Better then to get on with him, please him. Her son adored him so. What else could a woman expect? They were men together.

When the new year of 1784 dawned, Richard walked up to Narrow Wine Street to visit Mr. Latimer at Wasborough's foundry.

What one saw from Narrow Wine Street was a barnlike structure built of limestone blocks so grimed from the smoke of its chimneys that they were black; along its façade were a number of very large, battered wooden doors, always thrown open to reveal the activity within as well as let out some of the heat and noise.

How odd! All the doors were closed. A long holiday indeed for Latimer's poor workmen, not paid since before Christmas. As he walked down the length of the building Richard tried each door in turn: locked. The back way, then. He took advantage of a tiny alley to attain the Froom side of the building, and there found one open door. Silence greeted him as he entered; the furnaces were unlit, the hearths empty, and the quenched fire engine sat brooding among its idle lathes.

Emerging, he walked to the Froom, running full, and as grey and gelid as the sky.

"Richard, oh, Richard!"

He turned to see Cousin James-the-druggist come out of the alley, wringing his hands.

"Dick said you were here—Oh, Richard, it is terrible!"

Something in him already knew, but he asked anyway. "What is terrible, Cousin James?"

"Latimer! He is gone! Absconded with all our money!"

An oak mooring post probably as old as the English Romans stood at the edge of the river; Richard leaned against it and closed his eyes. "Then the man is an idiot. He will be caught."

For answer, Cousin James-the-druggist began to weep.

"Cousin James, Cousin James, it is not the end of the world," said Richard, putting an arm about his shoulders and leading him to a slab of foundry junk upon which they could sit. "Come now, do not cry so!"

"I must! It is my fault! If I had not encouraged you, your money would still be safe. I can afford to pay for my own stupidity, but—oh, Richard, it is not fair that you should lose your all!"

Not conscious of any pain beyond concern for this beloved man, Richard stared at the Froom without seeing it. This was not like losing little Mary, nor was it a millionth as important. The money was an external thing.

"I have a mind of my own, Cousin James, and you should know me better than to believe I can be led where I do not want to go. It is no one's fault, least of all yours and least of all mine. Come, dry your eyes and tell me," said Richard, proffering his nose rag.

Cousin James-the-druggist produced a proper handkerchief and mopped away, gradually calming.

"We will not see our money, Richard," he said. "Latimer has taken it and fled to Connecticut, where he and Pickard intend to manufacture fire engines. Since the American war, Watt's patents are worthless there."

"Clever Mr. Latimer!" said Richard appreciatively. "Can we not take a lien on Wasborough's foundry and get our money back by making chains for the Admiralty?"

"I am afraid not. Latimer does not own Wasborough's. His father-in-law is a wealthy Gloucester cheesemaker, and bought it as a dowry for Latimer's wife. Her papa also owns the house in Dove Street."

"Then let us go home," said Richard, "to the Cooper's Arms. Ye can do with a mug of Cave's rum, Cousin James."

To give him credit, Dick said not one word, let alone "I told you so." His eyes had gone from Richard's calm face to Cousin James-the-druggist's devastated one, and whatever he thought he kept to himself.

"There is really only one significant consequence," Richard said to him later, "and that is that I no longer have the money to educate William Henry."

"Are ye not angry?" Dick asked, frowning.

"No, Father. If losing my money is my share of trouble, then I am glad.

What if it had been losing Peg?" His breath caught. "Or losing William Henry?"

"Yes, I see. I do see." Dick reached across the table and gripped his son's arm strongly. "As for William Henry's education, we will just have to pray that something comes along. He will be able to finish Colston's, I have enough put by for that. So we have three years before we need fret."

"And in the meantime, I must find a job. The Cooper's Arms is not prosperous enough to support my family as well as yours." Richard took Dick's hand from his arm and lifted it to his cheek. "I thank you, Father, so very much."

"Oh!" The exclamation served to cover Dick's embarrassment at this unmanly display of affection. "I have just remembered! Old Tom Cave is in need of a man at his distillery. Someone who can solder, braze and weld. Go and see him, Richard. It may not be the answer to your prayers, but it will pay a pound a week and serve until something better comes along."

Ownership of a rum distillery in Bristol was tantamount to having a license to coin money; no matter how hard the times were and how many souls were out of work, the consumption of rum never fell any more than did the price. Not only was rum Bristol's favorite drink, it was also the drink loaded aboard every ship to make sure unhappy sailors did not mutiny. Provided they got their ration of rum, sailors would eat rotten sea biscuit and salt meat so old it shrank to nothing when boiled—and endure the rope's end.

Mr. Cave's premises were built like a fortress. They occupied most of one short block of Redcliff Street near the Redcliff Backs, from whence he collected his shipments of sugar from the West Indies and loaded his different sizes of casks into lighters the moment an order was paid for. His cellars were vast and impregnable, and like most Bristol cellars ran below the public land constituting a street. Bristol, in fact, was a hollow city mined so extensively that no heavy wheeled vehicle was allowed anywhere within it; all transport of goods was done by the sledges known as geehoes because their runners distributed the load more evenly over a much larger area than wheels did.

The stills were contained in a vast, virtually shapeless room on the ground floor, lit mostly from the reflected glare of the furnaces. The whole effect was of a copper forest of roundly buttressed tree trunks planted in a soil of fire bricks, the foliage strongly cooped oak casks shaped like apex-amputated cones. It reeked of coal smoke, fermenting mash, molasses and head-spinning rum vapors, and Richard loathed it; inhaling the stench of rum day after day did not tempt him to change from a tankard of beer to a mug of Cave's best.

Cave himself hardly ever appeared; the overseer, William Thorne, reigned supreme. As obsequious to Cave as he was cruel to his underlings, Thorne was of that kind who belonged, thought Richard, on a slaver like Alexander, back in the business. Thorne loved to flog an apprentice with a rope's end, and took malicious delight in making life as miserable as possible for as many of Mr. Cave's employees as he could. Though after a measuring look he left Richard severely alone, contenting himself with a series of curt instructions.

"And stay out of the back of the room," Thorne ended. "There is naught there to concern ye, and I do not like prowlers. This is *my* ken, and I will thank ye to do as ye're told."

So Richard stayed out of the back part of the room, more for the sake of peace than because Thorne intimidated him. The stills themselves were copper, as were the pipes which twisted, kinked, looped and ran in many directions; the numerous valves, taps and braces were brass. It was therefore mandatory to have someone on hand who could detect weaknesses before they turned into leaks, and who could deal with those weaknesses while the stills continued to operate. They were paired and one pair was always shut down to permit major repairs to the metal; this was also Richard's job. A job boring to the point of mindlessness, yet constant enough to require that he mind it and himself.

His first day acquainted him with the worst word in Thorne's vocabulary: excise.

His Britannic Majesty's Government had always taxed liquors imported from abroad; those were customs duties, and smuggling (very popular on the Cornish, Devon and Dorset coasts) was punishable by death and gibbetting. Then the Government had realized that there was even more money to be made by taxing spiritous liquors made inside England; those were excise duties. Gin and rum had to be made in licensed premises rigorously inspected by an Excise Man, for excise had to be paid on every drop of spirits a distillery squeezed out of its vats of fermented mash.

"All this," said Richard at the end of his first week, "in order that ships can sail the seas free of mutiny, and folk on land forget their troubles. What a miracle is the mind of Man, that so much cleverness has been spent upon producing stupidity."

"Richard," said Dick, exasperated, "ye're a Quaker at heart, I swear it. We make our *living* out of booze!"

"I know, Father, but I am free to think what I want, and I think that governments want us to drink so they can make money."

"I wish Jem Thistlethwaite could hear ye!" Dick snapped.

"I know, I know, he would demolish my argument in a trice," grinned Richard. "Calm yourself, Father! I am joking."

"Peg, discipline this man of yours!" Dick said.

She turned with such a brilliant smile on her face that Richard drew a breath—oh, she was so much better! Was that all it took, permanent removal of the threat that she would be moved to Clifton? Now that continued residence at the Cooper's Arms was assured because Richard had lost all his money, she was genuinely and happily secure.

She dropped the empty mug she was holding and, grunting, bent quickly to pick it up. A scream of such agony rent the air that the hair on every head in the tavern rose; Peg straightened, both hands to her head, then collapsed to the floor in a huddled heap. So many people crowded around that Dick had to shove most of them forcibly out of the way before he could kneel beside Richard, who had Peg's head in his lap. Mag knelt on the other side with William Henry, who reached for his mother's hand.

"It is no good, Richard. She is dead."

"No! No, she cannot be!" Richard took her other hand and chafed it. "Peg! Peg, my love! Wake up! Peg, wake up!"

"Mama, Mama, wake up!" William Henry echoed, eyes too full of shock to produce tears. "Mama, wake up and I will hug and kiss you! Please, please wake up!"

But Peg lay so inanimate that no pinch or prick could rouse her.

"It was a stroke," said Cousin James-the-druggist, summoned.

"Impossible!" cried Richard. "She ain't old enough!"

"Young folk can have strokes, and they are always of this kind—a sudden scream of pain, then unconsciousness and death."

"She cannot be dead," said Richard stubbornly. How could Peg be dead? She was a part of him. "No, she cannot be dead."

"Believe me, Richard, she is dead. All signs of life are gone. I have held a mirror to her mouth, and it has not clouded. I have put my wooden cone on her chest, and heard no heartbeat. She has lost her irises," said Cousin James-the-druggist. "Accept God's will, Richard. Let us take her upstairs and I will lay her out."

That he did with Mag in attendance, washing her, dressing her in her

Sunday gown of eyelet-embroidered pink cambric, rouging her lips and cheeks, curling her hair and piling it up in the latest fashion, fitting her Sunday-best high-heeled shoes on stockinged feet. Her hands were folded on her breast and her eyes had been closed from the very beginning; she looked peacefully asleep and barely twenty years old.

Richard sat beside her, William Henry alongside him so that he could not see his son's face. Could he, it would break him, and that would not benefit either of them. The room was bright with lamps and candles which would not be allowed to go out until she was put into her coffin and carried in the funeral sledge to St. James's for the burial service in two days' time. This was, for want of a better description, a natural death. All the family from far and near would come to pay their respects, kiss the still kissable mouth, commiserate with the widower, then descend to the tavern and partake of refreshments. Nothing as eerie and outlandish as a wake would be held; in Protestant Bristol, death was coped with soberly and somberly.

Richard sat the long hours of day and night away, joined by various Morgans; for once no snores emanated through the flimsy partition. Just muffled sobs, murmurs of comfort, sighs. No one slept save William Henry, who cried himself into a restless slumber. The shock had been so sudden that Richard felt numbed, but beneath the layers of pain and grief slowly bubbling up he was horrified to find a core of bitter resentment: if you were going to die, Peg, why did you not do so *before* I invested my money? Then I could have taken William Henry to live in Clifton and been rid of the reek of rum. Been my own man.

On the second night and in the coldest marches of the small hours William Henry appeared barefoot in his nightshirt and came to sit with Richard. They had kept the room as cold as so many candles and lamps allowed, so the still figure on the bed looked as serene and beautiful as she had at the moment the laying out was finished. Richard rose and went to fetch a thick blanket and two pairs of stockings, draped the one about his son's body and put the others on his feet.

"She looks so happy," said William Henry, wiping at his tears.

"She was very happy at the instant she died," Richard said, throat controlled, eyes dry. "She smiled, William Henry."

"Then I must try to be happy for her, Dadda, must I not?"

"Yes, my son. There is nothing to fear in such an unexpected, happy death. Mama has gone to Heaven."

"I miss her, Dadda!"

"So do I. That is natural. She has always been here. Now we have to get used to living without her, and that will be hard. But never forget that she looks happy. As if nothing nasty has touched her. Because nothing nasty has, William Henry."

"And I still have you, Dadda." The blanket-shrouded form edged close; William Henry put his curly head on his father's arm and hiccoughed. "I still have you. I am not a norphan."

In the morning Cousin James-of-the-clergy interred Margaret Morgan, born in 1750, dearly beloved wife of Richard Morgan and mother of William Henry, next to her daughter, Mary. As it was the end of January, there were no flowers, only evergreens. Richard did not weep, and William Henry seemed to have cried himself into acceptance. Only Mag sobbed, as much for her niece as for her daughter-in-law. The Lord giveth, and the Lord taketh away. That is life.

The death of his mother drew William Henry more tightly to his father, but his father was strapped with a job he worked at six days a week from dawn to dusk, which left only Sunday and a few snatched bedtime minutes for William Henry. The distillery was no gunsmithy, and Thomas Cave no Tomas Habitas. Special terms of employment were for William Thorne alone, who would disappear with impunity for sometimes hours on end, then return looking smug. Richard noticed that whenever Thorne did absent himself, Thomas Cave would be there waiting anxiously for his return—yet not in anger. Rather, in an eager apprehension. Puzzling. Had Richard been less preoccupied with his private worries and sadnesses, he would undoubtedly have seen more and come to some conclusions, but work was a solace only if he applied himself to it wholly.

The distillery saw an occasional visitor, the chief of whom was the Excise Man. William Thorne always showed the inspector around personally, and disapproved of observers.

The other frequent caller apparently had no business being in the distillery beyond friendship with Thorne; an odd relationship between two men who could surely have little in common. John Trevillian Ceely Trevillian was rich, foppish, and monumentally silly. His wigs were white as snow with starch powder and he tied them with naught save black velvet; his vacuous countenance was painted and patched; he wore embroidered velvet coats and lavish waistcoats; his heels were so high that he tittuped along with the aid of a clouded amber cane; and he exuded a perfume so strong it overpowered even the smell of rum.

Naturally Thorne performed no introductions on the occasion of Mr. Trevillian's first visit after Richard started at Cave's, but Ceely, as Thorne called him, paused in front of the new worker and eyed him in some appreciation. Apparently he enjoyed bare and sinewy forearms, thought Richard sourly when Mr. Trevillian, having looked his fill, tripped off in Thorne's wake. He knew well enough who John Trevillian Ceely Trevillian was: the elder son of Mr. and Mrs. Maurice Trevillian of Park Street, the same wealthy couple who had been robbed by a highwayman outside their own front door. A Cornish family with large interests in Bristol commerce, and related by blood to a very ancient clan of London merchants named Ceely who had been prominent since the twelfth century. This Ceely, all of Bristol knew, was a bachelor of questionable sexual tastes, an idle and brainless fribble completely eclipsed by his younger brother.

Several further visits by Mr. Trevillian caused Richard to doubt Bristol's judgment; that silly, whinnying, vapid manner of his concealed a brain both shrewd and intelligent. He knew a great deal about distilling, and a great deal about business. The ruse of idiocy was extremely effective: as Mr. Trevillian stood around the Exchange looking a simpleton, those in his vicinity did not bother to lower their voices when they talked of business deals in the making. And perhaps in consequence lost out to Mr. Trevillian.

To round the matter of Mr. Ceely Trevillian off, in April he appeared arm-in-arm with Mr. Thomas Cave. Ah! thought Richard. Ceely has a financial interest in this place—must have, to see old Tom Cave smarm and grovel so. Yet Ceely was not on the books, else Dick would have mentioned the fact; he was a sleeping partner who provided nothing beyond capital when it was needed, and thereby paid no taxes.

In himself, Richard was managing, though he chafed at the tiny amount of time he had to spend with William Henry. Sundays were infinitely precious. Occasionally Richard varied the route of their walk so that William Henry would get to know every part of Bristol, but their favorite destination remained Clifton, where the cottage Richard had almost bought mocked him. Of his own choice he might have gone elsewhere than Clifton, but William Henry adored the place.

"Mr. Parfrey told us a new one yesterday," said William Henry, skipping along.

Stifling a sigh, Richard resigned himself to another paean about this paragon of a teacher who managed to turn boring old Latin into a game of puns and mnemonics; William Henry's Latin was far more advanced than Richard's had been at the same age.

"What?" he asked dutifully of his son.

"Caesar adsum iam forte—Caesar had some jam for tea."

"And can you translate it?"

" 'As it so happened, and quite by chance, Caesar was at hand.' "

"Very good! He is a wit, your Mr. Parfrey."

"Yes, he is very funny, Dadda. He makes us laugh so much that the Head and Mr. Prichard disapprove. I do not think they really like it that Mr. Parfrey never uses the cane either."

"I am surprised Mr. Parfrey has survived at Colston's," said Richard dryly.

"We are all so good at our Latin," William Henry explained. "We *have* to be! Otherwise we would get Mr. Parfrey into trouble with the Head. Oh, Dadda, I do like him! He smiles a lot."

"In which case, William Henry, ye're very lucky."

At the end of May all the pieces of the puzzle at Cave's distillery fell into place.

William Thorne had done one of his disappearing tricks and the acolytes who danced attendance on the stills had also disappeared, the latter rather in the manner of mice after cheese, twitching with apprehension but determined to consume the prize. In the case of Mr. Cave's employees the prize was rum. Not the good rum which went into holding casks and would be blended by none save Mr. Cave himself, but the feint-ridden second distillate; no one would notice if a little were siphoned off the second receiver tub.

In no need of rum or company, Richard continued with his work. The huge room had so many corners, nooks and crannies that it was difficult to assign it a shape, and this was particularly true of its back regions, into which Richard was expressly forbidden entry. Nor would he have entered, had he not heard the unmistakable hiss of liquid escaping under pressure. A careful check of the rows of paired stills and their confusing network of pipes revealed nothing, but as he approached the last pair in the back row he became convinced that the noise was coming from somewhere behind. So he hauled himself up onto the uncomfortably warm bricks of the furnace and squeezed between the left and right still, ducking his head to avoid the receiver tubs.

It was then that he noticed some pipes which ought not to have been there, and stiffened. For a full minute he stood without moving and let his eyes accustom themselves to the gloom, then he looked upward and found a number of pipes hidden among festoons of spider-web and what might have passed at a casual glance for hempen lagging come adrift. Each of these pipes came off a receiver tub which held the final distillate, not at its bottom but well up its side—at a point, in fact, which would allow a runoff only if the tub were full to its tapping level. No valve was attached to each of these unwarranted pipes; once the contents of a tub reached the level of the pipe, the liquid ran off down it into the darkness at the back of the chamber.

There, hidden behind a false section of wall, were two rows of 50-gallon hogsheads. Lips pursed in a silent whistle, Richard calculated how much excise-free spirit was flowing off each and every day—no wonder that William Thorne always drained the final distillate from its receiver tub! Only a skilled distiller with experience elsewhere would have wondered at the slowness of Mr. Cave's apparatus, and there were no such men at 137 Redcliff Street. Except for William Thorne. And Thomas Cave. Was he in it too?

As he jumped back onto the top of the furnace Richard found the source of the hiss—the right-hand still was spraying a thin jet of fluid backward from a pinhole in its worn copper skin. As he crouched to plug it, Thorne walked in.

"Here! What are ye doing up there?" he demanded, face ugly.

"My job of work," said Richard tranquilly. "A temporary one, I fear. I think ye'll have to stand this pair down very soon."

"Fucken shit! I keep telling old Tom to invest some of his profits in new stills, but he always has a reason not to." Thorne stalked away, mollified, roaring for his acolytes, who had not been quick enough; the cat had come back sooner than anticipated.

When he returned to the Cooper's Arms that evening Richard did not mention his discovery to Dick. Time enough when he knew more—knew, for instance, how many were involved in this huge excise fraud. Thorne, of course. Cave, possibly. And what about John Trevillian Ceely Trevillian? Why should a well-born idler like Ceely haunt a location far from the pastures where such ornamental ponies usually grazed?

When do they clear out the illicit liquor? Richard wondered. During the night, certainly, and probably on a Sunday night. The streets are deserted even of sailors and press gangs.

Getting out of the Cooper's Arms on the next Sunday night was easy; he slept alone, Dick and Mag were snoring, and William Henry never roused, even in a thunderstorm. The moon was full and the sky cloudless—what good luck! As he reached the vicinity of 137 Redcliff Street, a lone bell was tolling midnight. He sought the dark shelter of a crane belonging to the pipe maker across the court and settled patiently to wait.

Two hours. They certainly cut it fine, he thought; two more hours would see the commencement of a leisurely dawn. And there were three of them: Thorne, Cave and Ceely Trevillian. Though it was difficult to recognize the last man; the mincing Bartholomew Baby had been replaced by a slim, decisively energetic man clad in black, with raggedly cropped short hair and boots on his feet.

Cave arrived on his elderly gelding, Thorne and Ceely drove up in a sledge drawn by a pair of massive horses, and the three of them proceeded to unload four dozen obviously empty hogshead casks from the geehoe. Cave unlocked a disused door into the back part of his distilling chamber and the barrels disappeared inside. A minute later Thorne was back, grunting as he rolled a full barrel; Cave bustled to the sledge and let down a ramp at its rear. It took Thorne and Trevillian combined to push each hogshead up the ramp, where they flipped it from its side onto one end with a deftness born of much practice.

Sixty minutes by Richard's watch saw the job done; no doubt inside the building the empty hogsheads were in place beneath the illicit pipes—how often did they do this? Not every Sunday night or someone would notice, but, if Richard's calculations were right, at least once in every three weeks.

Thomas Cave mounted his horse and rode off up Redcliff Street while the other two boarded the sledge, which headed on very smooth and silent runners eastward to the Temple Backs; Richard followed the sledge. At the river the casks were tipped onto their sides again and rolled down into a flat-bottomed barge tended by a man who was a stranger to Richard, though not to Thorne and Ceely. Finished, the three unharnessed one of the horses and tethered it to the barge; the stranger scrambled up onto its huge back and kicked it hard until it began to plod down the deplorable towpath in the direction of Bath, the floating cargo, with Ceely aboard, following behind. Once sure everything was going to plan, William Thorne drove off in the geehoe.

I know it all, said Richard to himself. The rum goes to some place nearer Bath, where Ceely and the stranger either sell it or trans-ship it to Salisbury or Exeter, and a fat, excise-free profit is divided by four. I would be willing to bet, however, that it is Ceely Trevillian gets the biggest share.

What was he actually going to do? After turning it over in his mind all the way home, Richard decided that the time had come to tell his father.

Dick and Mag were up and about, William Henry still slumbering when Richard walked into the Cooper's Arms. His parents cast each other a conspiratorial glance, having noticed on their way downstairs that Richard's bed was empty. How to let a recent widower know that they did understand an occasional absence?

"Mum, go away," said Richard without ceremony. "I have to speak to Father in private."

Looking worldly, Dick prepared to listen to a tale of basic urges and some pretty female face seen in St. James's yesterday morning, only to hear a tale of staggering villainy.

"What should I do, Father?"

A shrug, a wry look. "There is only one thing a decent man can do. Go at once—and in secret!—to the Collector of Excise at Excise House. His name is Benjamin Fisher."

"Father! Your business—your friendship with Tom Cave—it would ruin everything for you!"

"Nonsense," said Dick strongly. "There are other makers of good rum in Bristol, and I know 'em all. Stand on best terms with 'em too. Tom Cave is more a very old acquaintance than a friend, Richard. Ye've not seen him sup at my table, nor do I sup at his. Besides," he grinned, "I always knew he was a sly boots. It is in his eyes, ain't you noticed? Never gives ye a good frank stare."

"Yes," said Richard soberly, "I have noticed. Still, I feel sorrier for him than I do for Thorne. As for Ceely"—he made a gesture as if to push something horrible away—"the man is a turd. What an actor! The apparent nincompoop is a very clever man."

"No work for you today," said Dick, pushing Richard stairward. "Go and put on your best Sunday clothes, my new hat, and off to Excise House—and do not breathe a word to anyone, hear? There is no need to look so down in the mouth, either. If those beauties have tapped off half as much rum as ye think they have, then ye'll get a hefty reward for your pains. Enough to see William Henry is educated to your heart's content."

It was that thought drove Richard, clad in his dark-hued Sunday clothes, Dick's best hat on his head, to walk toward Queen Square. Excise House occupied the end of a block between the square and Princes Street (upon which desirable avenue Mr. Thomas Cave's house was situated), and Richard soon discovered that the Excise Men of Excise House were slugs who used their desks to sleep off their hangovers, especially on a Monday. They were unorganized, uninterested, and preferred to be unoccupied. Thus it took Richard several hours to ascend the hierarchical ladder. Looking at each of the bored faces, Richard declined to say anything more than that he had discovered an excise fraud, and wanted to see the Collector himself. As distinct from the Commander, higher up still.

An interview he finally achieved at three o'clock in the afternoon, dinnerless and with his famous patience distinctly frayed.

"Ye have five minutes, Mr. Morgan," said Mr. Benjamin Fisher from behind his desk.

No need to wonder if the Collector of Excise had ever been in the field himself; he peered at Richard through the small round lenses of a pair of spectacles which he did not need to peruse the neatly stacked documents on his desk. Short-sighted. His home had always been a desk. Which meant that he would not understand in the way any of his field officers would. On the other hand, Richard's mind went on, that might mean that he does not accept bribes. For surely the men in the field do, else I would not be here.

Richard told his story in a few succinct words.

"How much rum d'ye estimate these persons draw off in a week?" Mr. Benjamin Fisher asked when Richard ended.

"If they pick up their hogsheads every three weeks, sir, about eight hundred gallons per week."

That put a different complexion on it! Mr. Fisher straightened, put his quill down and pushed the piece of paper on which he had been taking notes to one side. On went the spectacles again; his eyes, two pale blue marbles swimming beneath layers of glass, goggled.

"Mr. Morgan, this is a huge fraud! Could ye be mistaken in your calculations?"

"Aye, sir, of course I could. But if they change the hogsheads every three weeks, then 'tis eight hundred gallons weekly. Yesterday was the first of June, and I can testify that the casks the three men brought into the distillery were completely empty, for one man could kick one cask around like a ball. Whereas the casks they took out were so full that it took two of them to roll one up an easy ramp. The Sunday I imagine they will use next is the twenty-second of June. If your men are hiding nearby from midnight on, ye'll apprehend all three of them in the very act," Richard said, betting that he was right.

"Thank you, Mr. Morgan. I suggest that ye return to work and conduct yourself as usually until further notified by this office. On behalf of His

Majesty, I must convey the Excise Office's sincere thanks for your diligence."

Richard was going to the door when the Collector of Excise spoke again. "If the fraud is as large as you say, Mr. Morgan, there will be an eight-hundred-pound reward, five hundred pounds of which will go to you. After testifying at their trial, of course."

He could not resist asking. "Who gets the other three hundred?"

"The men who arrest the culprits, Mr. Morgan."

And that was that. Richard went home.

"You were right, Father," he said to Dick. "If all turns out as I expect it will, then I will receive five-eighths of an eight-hundred-pound reward."

Dick looked skeptical. "Three hundred pounds seem excessive for a dozen Excise Men to share for nothing more than the act of arrest."

Which made Richard laugh. "Father! I had not thought ye so green! I imagine that the Excise Men who do the actual arresting will share fifty pounds of it. The other two hundred and fifty will undoubtedly find their way into Mr. Benjamin Fisher's pockets."

On Sunday the 22nd of June a dozen Excise Men chopped down the back door of the Cave distillery, charged into the deserted premises with staves at the ready, and there located four dozen full 50-gallon hogsheads of illicit rum connected to the stills by illicit pipes.

When Mr. Thomas Cave rode up on his horse at two on Monday morning and Mr. William Thorne and Mr. John Trevillian Ceely Trevillian drove up in their geehoe shortly thereafter, the gaping tatters of the door and the Excise seals on everything inside told an unmistakable tale.

"We were rumbled," said Mr. Thorne, showing his teeth.

Cave shivered in terror. "Ceely, what do we do?"

"As the rum is gone, I suggest we go home," said Ceely coolly.

"Why are they not here to arrest us?" Cave asked.

"Because they wanted no trouble, Tom. The amount of rum will have told them that there are some ruthless characters involved—it is a hanging offense. An Excise Man is not paid enough to risk a pistol ball in his guts."

"Our sources should have informed us ahead of time!"

"That they should," said Ceely grimly, "which leads me to think that this came from the very top and that foreign men were used."

"Richard Morgan!" snarled Thorne, pounding one fist into the palm of his other hand. "The fucken bugger rumbled us!"

"Richard Morgan?" Trevillian frowned. "You mean that damned good-looking fellow fixes the leaks?"

Thorne's eyes dwelled on him in wonder; he lifted his lantern to inspect Ceely's face closely. "Ye're a mystery to me, Ceely," he said slowly. "Is it women ye fancy, or men?"

"Who I fancy is not important, Bill. Go home and start putting a story together for the Collector of Excise. 'Tis you who'll bear the blame."

"What d'ye mean, me? We will all bear it!"

"Afraid not," said Ceely Trevillian lightly, jumping up into the geehoe. "Did you not tell him, Tom?"

"Tell me what, Tom?"

But Mr. Cave could only shiver and shake his head.

"Tom made you the licensee," said Ceely. "Some time ago, as a matter of fact. I thought it might be a good idea, and he saw my point at once. As for me—I have no connection whatsoever with Cave's distillery." He shook the reins to gee up the horses.

William Thorne stood leaden-footed, unable to move. "Where are you going?" he asked feebly.

Ceely's teeth, very white, flashed in a laugh. "To the Temple Backs, of course, to alert our confederate."

"Wait for me!"

"You," said Mr. Ceely Trevillian, "can walk home, Bill."

The sledge glided off, leaving Thorne to confront Cave.

"How could ye do this to me, Tom?"

Cave's tongue came out to lick at his lips. "Ceely insisted," he bleated. "I cannot stand against the man, Bill!"

"And you thought it an excellent idea. You would, you lily-livered old turd!" said Thorne bitterly.

"It is Ceely," Thomas Cave insisted. "I'll not leave ye unsupported, that is a promise. Whatever it takes to get you off will be done." Panting with the effort, he managed to haul himself onto his horse; Thorne made no move to help him.

"I will hold you to that promise, Tom. But more important by far is the murder of Richard Morgan."

"No!" Cave cried. "Whatever else you do, not that! Excise knows, you fool! Kill their informant and we will all hang!"

"If this comes to trial, I am certainly going to hang, so what matters it to me, eh?" He was shouting now. "Best make sure it never does come to trial,

Tom! And that goes for Ceely too! If I go down, Richard Morgan will not be the only snitch! I will bring you and Ceely down with me—we will all go to the gallows! Hear me? All of us!"

Mr. Benjamin Fisher summoned Richard to Excise House early in the morning of the next day, the 23rd of June.

"I advise you not to return to work, Mr. Morgan," said the Collector of Excise, two spots of color burning in his cheeks. "My fools of men raided Cave's distillery during the day, so no one was apprehended. All they did was seize the liquor."

Richard gaped. "Christ!"

"Well but fruitlessly said, sir. I echo your sentiment, but the damage is done. The only one Excise can prosecute is the licensee for having illicit rum on his premises."

"Old Tom Cave? But he is *not* the principal villain!"

"Thomas Cave is not the licensee. That is William Thorne."

Richard gaped again. "And what of Ceely Trevillian?"

Looking absolutely disgusted, Mr. Fisher squeezed his hands together and leaned forward. "Mr. Morgan, we have no case against anyone save William Thorne." He put on his spectacles, grimacing. "Mr. Trevillian is extremely well connected, and general opinion around town is that he is an amiable, harmless simpleton. I will interview him for myself, but I must warn you that were it to come to court, it would be your word against his. I am very sorry, but unless new evidence comes to light Mr. Trevillian is unimpeachable. I am not even sure," he ended, sighing, "that we have enough to hang William Thorne, though he will certainly go down for seven years' transportation."

"*Why* did your men not wait to catch them in the act?"

"Cowardice, sir. It is ever the way." Mr. Fisher took his spectacles off and polished them vigorously, blinking away tears. "Though it is early, Mr. Thomas Cave is already waiting downstairs, I imagine to negotiate a settlement by offering to pay a very large fine. That is where the money lies, Mr. Morgan—I am not so blind that I cannot see that William Thorne is a red herring. Excise will get no recompense out of the licensee, whereas it may from the owner. That includes you. Your reward, I mean."

As Richard left he encountered Thomas Cave in the foyer, but was wise enough to say nothing as he passed. No point in going to the distillery; he went back to the Cooper's Arms.

"So I have no job and at least two of the three culprits are to escape justice," he told Dick. "Oh, if only I had known!"

"It sounds as if Tom Cave will buy Thorne off," said Dick, and cheered up. "Be thankful for one thing, Richard. No matter which way it goes, ye'll get that five hundred pounds."

That was true, but less of a comfort than Dick suspected. At least a part of Richard wanted to see Mr. John Trevillian Ceely Trevillian in the dock. Quite why he did not know, except that it lay in Ceely's insultingly blatant look of appreciation on that first meeting. I am less than the dust to that conceited, whinnying fop, and I hate him. Yes, hate. For the first time in my life, I am filled with an emotion that held no personal significance for me until now; what used to be a word has become a fact.

He missed Peg in these trying times. The grief at her going had been great, but diminished by those last years of opposition, tears, drinking, wandering in the mind. Yet as the days went by and he searched Bristol for a job, that Peg was fading, to be replaced by the Peg he had married seventeen years ago. He needed to cuddle against her, to converse softly with her in the night, to seek the only kind of sexual solace he deemed truly satisfactory—one wherein love and friendship contributed at least as much as passion. There was no one left to talk to, for though his father was firmly on his side, Dick would always look down on him as too soft, a trifle spineless. And Mum was Mum—cook and scullery maid in one. In a few years William Henry would be his equal; then all he would lack was sexual solace. And that, Richard had resolved, would have to be put away until after William Henry was grown to full maturity. For he would not inflict a stepmother on this beloved only child, and whores were a kind of woman he could not stomach no matter how he ached for the simplest, most basic relief.

On Monday, which was the last day of June, Richard left at the crack of dawn—very early at this time of summer solstice—to walk the eight miles of hilly road between the Cooper's Arms and Keynsham, a hamlet along the Avon made larger and much dirtier by folk like William Champion, brass maker. Champion had patented a secret process for refining zinc from calamine and old tailings, and it had come to Richard's ears that he was looking for a good man to deal with zinc. Why not try? The worst that could happen was a refusal.

William Henry left for school at a quarter to seven as usual, grumbling because the Head had insisted that school be held on the last day of June when it fell on a Monday. His grandmother's response was a good-natured cuff over the ear; William Henry took the hint and departed. Tomorrow was the commencement of two months of holiday, for the wearers of the blue coat as well as the paying pupils. Those who had homes and parents to go to would doff their blue coats and quit Colston's until the beginning of September, while those like Johnny Monkton who had neither parents nor home would spend the summer at Colston's under a somewhat relaxed code of discipline.

Dadda had explained why he could not keep William Henry company over the next two months, and William Henry understood completely. He was well aware that all of Dadda's efforts were on his behalf, and that put a burden on his young shoulders that he did not even know was there. If he worked very hard over his books—and he did—it was to please Dadda, who valued an education more highly than any nine-year-old boy possibly could.

At the gates of Colston's School he stopped, amazed; they were festooned with black ribbons! Mr. Hobson, a junior master, was waiting just inside them to put a hand on William Henry's arm.

"Home again, lad," he said, turning William Henry around.

"Home again, Mr. Hobson?"

"Aye. The Head passed away in his sleep during the night, so there is no school today. Your father will be notified about the funeral, Morgan Tertius. Now off you go."

"May I see Monkton Minor, sir?"

"Not today. Goodbye," said Mr. Hobson firmly, giving William Henry a little push between his shoulder blades.

At the Stone Bridge the child paused, frowning. What a bother! Dadda off to Keynsham, Grandpapa and Grandmama busy with the Monday chores—what was he going to do all day without Johnny?

This was the first time that life had presented William Henry with the opportunity to do exactly what he wanted without anybody's knowing. The Cooper's Arms thought him at Colston's, yet Colston's had sent him home. There to kick his heels to no purpose. Mind made up, William Henry galloped off the Stone Bridge, but not in the direction of home. In the direction of Clifton.

The steep, bluffy cone of Brandon Hill was his first stop; he scrambled all the way up to its top fancying himself a Roundhead soldier in Cromwell's army besieging Bristol, and there stood to gaze across the lime kiln chimneys and marshlands, then to the ruins of the Royalist fort on St. Michael's Hill. Game over, he leaped down from ledge to ledge until he reached the footpath and hopped, skipped and jumped to Jacob's Well, which had once been the only convenient source of water for Clifton. There were houses around it now, none of them attractive to a small boy. So he gamboled on past St. Andrew's church, turned somersaults on the springy turf of Clifton Green, and decided to walk to Manilla House, last in the row of mansions atop the hill.

"Holloa there, young spindle-shanks!" said a friendly voice outside the stable yard attached to Boyce's Buildings.

"Holloa yourself, sir."

"No school today?"

"The Head died," William Henry explained briefly, and perched himself on the gate-post. "Who are you?"

"Name's Richard the groom."

"Richard is my dadda's name too. I am William Henry."

Out came a horny hand. "Pleased to meet you."

For two hours he followed Richard the groom around, patting the few horses, peering into mostly empty stalls, helping draw buckets of water from the well and fetch hay, talking merrily. At the end of it Richard the groom gave him a tankard of small beer, a hunk of bread and some cheese; greatly refreshed, William Henry waved him a cheerful goodbye and continued on up the road.

Manilla House was as deserted as Freemantle House, Duncan House and Mortimer House—where to now?

He was still debating his alternatives when he heard the sound of horse's hooves behind him, and turned to discover that the rider bore a very familiar and much-loved face. "Mr. Parfrey!" he called.

"Good lord!" said George Parfrey. "What are you doing here, Morgan Tertius?"

William Henry had the grace to blush. "Please, sir, I am on a walk," he said lamely. "There is no school today, and Dadda has gone to Keynsham."

"Ought you to be here, Morgan Tertius?"

"Please, sir, my name is William Henry."

Mr. Parfrey frowned, then shrugged and held out his hand. "I see more than perhaps you know, William Henry. So be it. Hop up and come for a ride, then I will see you home."

Ecstasy! In all his life he had never been upon a horse! Now here he was, sitting astride the saddle in front of Mr. Parfrey, so high off the ground that looking down made him feel quite dizzy. A whole new world, like being in the top of a tree that ran! How smooth and regular the motion! How wondrous to be on a new adventure with a friend almost as best as Dadda! William Henry succumbed to absolute bliss.

They cantered off up Durdham Down, scattering several flocks of sheep, laughing at anything and everything they chanced upon. And when William Henry let him get a word in edgeways, Mr. Parfrey revealed that he knew about lots of things besides Latin. They rode to the parapet of the Avon Gorge, where Mr. Parfrey pointed out the colors in the rock and told the eager little boy how iron tinted the grey and white of the limestone those richly ruddy pinks and plums; he pointed with his crop at the flowering plants in the summer grass and recited their names, then minutes later jokingly quizzed William Henry as to the identity of this one or that one.

Finally the bridle path atop the gorge led them down to the Hotwells House on its ledge jutting into the Avon.

"We may find some dinner here," said Mr. Parfrey, letting the boy slide to the ground before dismounting. "Hungry?"

"Yes, sir!"

"If I am to call you William Henry away from the portals of Colston's, I think you must call me Uncle George."

There were very few people taking the waters in the pump room—a few consumptive, diabetic or gouty men, a very old lady and two crippled younger women. It had seen better days; the gilding had tarnished, the wallpaper was peeling, the drapes had frayed and accumulated visible layers of dirt, the spindling chairs needed new upholstery. But the sour lessee—who was still in the midst of a battle with Bristol over the rates he charged to drink the waters—provided dinner of a kind. To William Henry, accustomed to much better food at the Cooper's Arms, it tasted of nectar and ambrosia simply because it was different—and because he shared it with such a magical companion. Who, when they were done, suggested a walk outside before they rode back to the city. The old lady and the crippled women cooed over William Henry as they left; he suffered their exclamations and pats with the same patience he used to give his dead mother, a side of him that fascinated George Parfrey.

For George Parfrey had found a magical companion too. It had been, in fact, a magical day, starting off with the news that the Head had expired during the night. The Reverend Prichard, his long dark face betraying none of the elation he felt inside (he hoped to be the new Head), was too preoccupied to take any notice of the masters once he had acquainted them with the situation. Apart from giving Harry Hobson the duty of turning the day pupils away as they arrived, he issued no orders whatsoever.

Very well, said Mr. Parfrey to himself, I hereby declare that today is a holiday. If I remain here, Prichard or one of the others will think of something for me to do. Whereas if no one sees my face, no one will remember my existence.

His one extravagance was a horse. Not to own—that was far beyond his slender means—but to hire on some Sundays from a stable near the gallows on St. Michael's Hill. Mondays, he discovered when he arrived at the stable carrying his tray of watercolors and his sketchbook, offered him a wider choice of mount. The handsome black gelding he had hankered for was munching placidly on hay and no doubt expecting a day of rest after hectic Sunday excursions. Not to be. Ten minutes later Mr. Parfrey was in its saddle and trotting off across Kingsdown in the direction of the Aust road. A fine horseman, he gentled the black gelding out of its resentment and settled to enjoying his favorite pastime.

For a moment the old depression threatened to engulf him, but the day was too glorious not to be relished to its fullest, so he tucked his loneliness and apprehensions of a bitter old age into the back of his thoughts and concentrated upon the beauty around him. At which moment, hacking up Clifton Hill to Durdham Down, he saw Morgan Tertius ahead of him. Company! The little devil, he had decided to have a holiday from responsibilities too. Then why not be devils together? A question which carried the reassurance that he would be doing the boy a service by keeping him safe.

William Henry. The double name suited him, a nice conceit which age might perhaps confirm as a wise choice. All the masters had seen the potential in Morgan Tertius, though his beauty warped the judgment of some. As indeed it had Parfrey's judgment, until exposure to Morgan Tertius in Latin class had shown him that the face merely reflected the beauty of the soul as a clouded mirror did the sun. What he had not seen until today was the naughty little boy, for in class William Henry was an angel. Because, the child had explained gravely as they cantered across Durdham Down, he did not want to get the cane and he did not want to be *noticed.*

How to tell him that he would always be noticed? Interesting that the father, so like him in the face, lacked the son's vital spark. Richard Morgan would never turn heads, never stop the world spinning. Whereas William Henry Morgan did the first every day of his life, and might possibly manage to do the second one day. His conversation was typical of his age, though it did indicate a careful upbringing—until, that is, he got onto tavern doings and betrayed that there were few of the baser human passions he had not witnessed, from flashing knives to lust to manic furores. Yet none of it had tainted him; not the faintest whiff of corruption emanated from him.

So when they walked together out of the Hotwells House it seemed perfectly natural to turn their footsteps in the direction of the place where William Henry had picnicked with his father, and George Parfrey had watched them from above. Not a large spot, nor contiguous with the long stretch of the Avon bank on the Bristol side of the Hotwells House. A mere twenty feet of grassy verge between St. Vincent's Rocks and another, lower outcrop. Inside a forest, it would have been a dell.

Though nine months had gone by since the day the two Morgans had picnicked there, the scene was curiously static; the Avon was at exactly the same level, flooding in toward its full, the grass was exactly the same shade of green, the cliffs reflected exactly the same intensity of light. Time out of mind. A chance to put one foot into the future and keep the other in the past. As if today were plucked from existence, time out of mind.

William Henry sat while George Parfrey produced his sketchbook and a piece of charcoal.

"May I watch you, Uncle George?"

"No, because I am taking your likeness. That means you must keep still and forget that I am looking at you. Count the daisies. When I am done, you may see yourself."

So William Henry sat and George Parfrey looked.

At first the charcoal moved swiftly and surely, but as the minutes passed the strokes on the paper grew fewer, and finally ceased to be made. All Parfrey could do was look. Not only at so much beauty, but at the shape of his fate.

The timing is wrong—utterly wrong. I am fathoms deep in love with a complete innocent who is over thirty-five years my junior. By the time that I could awaken him to love, he would find nothing in me to love. Now that, Bill Shakespeare, is a tragedy worth the writing. When he is Hamlet, I will be Lear.

The hair ribbon had long fluttered away, so the dark mass of curls fell around the face with the same drama as dense coal smoke taken in a high wind. The skin was satin—peach—ivory—the thin blade of aquiline nose as patrician as the bones of the cheeks, and the mouth, full and sensuous, creased in its corners as if on the verge of a secret smile. But all that was as nothing compared to the eyes!

As if sensing Parfrey's change in mood, William Henry looked up and directly at him, the enigmatic smile suddenly seeming to the dazzled Parfrey an invitation offered from some part of himself that William Henry did not know existed. The eyes filled with light and the dark flecks danced amid the gold because the sun, glancing off a water-slicked rock, was caught up in them too.

He could not help himself. It was done before a thought could flicker into his mind. George Parfrey crossed the distance between himself and his nemesis and kissed William Henry on the mouth. After that he had to hold the boy—could not *bear* to let him go—had to sample the skin of brow and cheek and neck with his lips—caress the small body which vibrated as a cat purred.

"Beautiful! Beautiful!" he was whispering. "Beautiful!"

The boy tore himself away frantically, leaped to his feet and hovered, eyes rolling in shock, uncertain which way to run. Terror was not yet a part of it; all of him was concentrated upon flight.

As his madness lifted Parfrey rose to stand with one hand outstretched, not understanding that he was blocking the route William Henry saw as his only avenue of escape.

"William Henry, I am so sorry! I did not mean to harm you, I would never harm you! I am so sorry!" Parfrey gasped, spreading his arms wide in an appeal for forgiveness.

Terror came. William Henry saw hands reaching for him, not the appeal, and turned to flee another way. There at his feet lay the Avon, the color of blued steel, coiling and twisting as it poured out of the gorge in a sinuous torrent. Mr. Parfrey was edging closer, his arms wanting to grab and imprison, a smile on his mouth that was no smile. The Cooper's Arms had taught him what such smiles meant, for while Father and Grandfather were not looking other men had smiled so, whispered invitations. William Henry knew the smile was false, yet he mistook the reason for its falseness.

His head came up, he gazed into the sun blindly.

"Daddaaaaa!" he wailed, and jumped into the river.

The Avon in this place was not swimmable, nor could Parfrey swim. Even so, as he ran madly up and down the short piece of bank between the rocks looking for anything in that tide, he would have leaped into the water at the glimpse of a hand, an arm—*anything!* But nothing appeared. Not leaf, not twig, not branch, let alone William Henry. He had sunk like a stone, unresisting.

What had the child thought? What had he seen as he stood on the brink of the river? Why *so much* horror? Had he actually preferred the river? Did he know what he was doing when he jumped? Or was he incapable of reason? He had cried out for his dadda, that was all. And jumped. Not stumbled. Not fallen. Jumped.

At the end of half an hour Parfrey turned away. William Henry Morgan was not going to bob gasping to the surface. He was dead.

Dead, and I have killed him. I thought of self and self alone, I wanted an invitation and I deluded myself into believing he was giving me an invitation. But he was nine years old. *Nine.* I am cast out. I am anathema. I have murdered a child.

He found his horse, mounted it slackly and rode toward Bristol, oblivious to the interested regard of one old lady and two crippled women. How extraordinary! There went the man, but where was the dear little boy?

The horse he abandoned outside Colston's gates and passed into the mourning institution without seeing a soul, though some saw him, and looked startled. In his cubicle he put the sketchbook on his table where he could see William Henry's face from every corner, then took a small key from his fob and unlocked the wooden box which held those objects he did not want the likes of snooping Reverend Prichard to see. Inside among an untidy collection of memorabilia—a lock or two of hair, a polished agate stone, a tattered book, a painted miniature—lay another box. Inside it reposed a tiny gun and all the paraphernalia necessary to keep the gun in working order. A lady's muff pistol.

Ready, he went to the table, sat upon the narrow chair, dipped his quill in the inkwell, automatically wiped its tip free of excess ink, and wrote across the bottom of the sketch.

"I have caused the death of William Henry Morgan."

He signed his name and shot himself in the temple.

Consternation began at the Cooper's Arms well before William Henry was due home from school at a quarter past two; news of the Head's death had twinkled around the city at the speed of sunlight on water. The school was closed for the day, but William Henry had not come home. When Richard, tired and discouraged, walked through the door at three o'clock, he was greeted by two agitated grandparents and the news that his son was missing.

A crawling march of numbness paralyzed his mouth and jaw, but his physical exhaustion fled immediately. He tried to speak, open—close—open—close, and finally managed to mumble that he would start looking for William Henry.

"You go in the direction of Colston's," said Dick, untying his apron. "I will go toward Redcliff. Mag, shut up shop."

Words were a little easier. "He will have gone to Clifton, Father. I will go across Brandon Hill, you go along the rope walk. We will meet at the Hotwells House."

His heart was pounding at twice its normal speed, his mouth was so dry that he could find no spit to swallow, but Richard hurried as much as pausing to question everybody he saw allowed; by the time he reached the Brandon Hill footpath there were few to inquire of, but he stopped to knock on the doors of the apartment houses around Jacob's Well—no, no one had seen an errant little boy.

At Boyce's Buildings he had his first success; Richard the groom was still pottering around the stable yard.

"Aye, sir, I saw him early this morning—devilish fine young chap! Helped me hay and water the horses, and I gave him a bit to eat and drink. Then he went on up Clifton Hill, free as a bird."

There was nothing in face or eyes to lead Richard to suspect that the man lied; Richard the groom was exactly what he purported to be, a friendly fellow who enjoyed the company of errant little boys without stopping to think that his first duty ought to have been a box on the ears and a boot up William Henry's backside to push him in the direction of home.

With a muttered thank you, Richard toiled at an accelerated pace up Clifton Hill until he was high enough to see for miles. But the downs were deserted save for grazing sheep, and though he probed the eaves of every grove of trees, no William Henry emerged from their shelter.

At six o'clock he walked into the Hotwells House to find Dick already waiting there, and big with news.

"Richard, he was here for dinner! Came on horseback with a man in his forties—good-looking fellow, according to Mrs. Harris—an old lady who was here at the time. And they stood on very good terms. Laughed and joked as if they knew each other real well. They walked off toward St. Vincent's Rocks. About an hour later, Mrs. Harris and two other women saw the man ride off alone, looking sick. William Henry was not with him."

The lessee was hovering, very alarmed at developments. All he needed at this moment was a scandal, so he thrust a big glass of the Hotwells water into Richard's hand free of charge and slunk off a little way to watch.

Without tasting its bitterness or smelling its odor of rotten eggs, Richard drained it at a gulp. His whole body was trembling, his clothes soaked with sweat; the eyes he turned to his father were horrified. "Come," he said curtly, and walked out.

There was evidence that William Henry and his companion had been in the spot Richard knew from that previous visit; the grass was trampled and daisies had been picked, lay in a wilting heap. They called and called, but no one answered, then they climbed the rocks to inspect every crevice, ledge, hollow. No one was anywhere. The Avon, ebbing now, was shrinking backward into its gorge.

Dick made no attempt to persuade Richard to cease searching until twilight came, then he put a hand on his son's arm and shook it gently. "Time to go back to the Cooper's Arms," he said. "In the morning we will mount a full party and look again."

"Father, he is here, he did not leave here!" said Richard on a sobbing breath.

Do not mention the river! Do not put that thought into his poor head! "If he is here, we will find him in the morning. Now come home, Richard. Come home."

They plodded toward Bristol, neither man vouchsafing a word—Richard in a fever of anguish, Dick cold to his marrow.

Though the door to the Cooper's Arms bore a sign that it was closed, three men sat around the table near the counter, looking at their hands until the door opened. Cousin James-of-the-clergy, Cousin James-the-druggist, and the Reverend Mr. Prichard. Between them on the table was a sketchbook, face down.

"William Henry!" Richard cried. "Where is William Henry?"

"Sit down, Richard," said Cousin James-the-druggist, who, as senior member of the clan, was always the one delegated to break bad news. Cousin James-of-the-clergy served as his assistant, ready to take over once the bad news had been given.

"*Tell me!*" said Richard through his teeth.

"William Henry's Latin master is a man named George Parfrey," said Cousin James-the-druggist in even tones, and managing to meet those half-crazed eyes. "This afternoon Parfrey shot himself. He left this." He turned the sketchbook over.

The identity of the subject was unmistakable, even through the spatters of blood. "I have caused the death of William Henry Morgan."

His knees gave. Richard fell upon them, his face whiter than the paper. "It cannot be," he said. "It cannot be."

"It must be, Richard. The man shot himself dead." Cousin James-the-druggist crouched down beside Richard and smoothed his matted hair.

"He imagined it! Perhaps William Henry ran away."

"I doubt that very much. Parfrey's words indicate that he—he killed William Henry. If ye have not found the child, then he must have thrown William Henry into the Avon."

"No, no, no!" Hands over his face, Richard rocked back and forth.

"What have *you* to say?" Dick asked Mr. Prichard aggressively.

Prichard wet his lips, turned grey. "We heard the shot and found Parfrey with his brains blown out. The drawing was near him. I went straight to the Reverend Morgan"—he indicated Cousin James-of-the-clergy—"and then we came here. I am—I do not know—words cannot say—oh, Mr. Morgan, if you knew my sorrow and regret! But Parfrey had been at Colston's for ten years, he seemed a decent man, and his pupils thought him wonderful. What lies at the base of this is a mystery I cannot even begin to solve."

Still on his knees, Richard heard as if in the far, far distance the voices rising and falling; Dick was recounting today's expedition to Clifton, the events at the Hotwells House, the trodden grass and the plucked daisies in the little cove along the Avon.

"William Henry must have fallen into the river and drowned," said Mr. Prichard. "We wondered at the way Parfrey phrased it—as if he witnessed the death, rather than committed murder."

"Though he *caused* the death," said Cousin James-of-the-clergy, in tones harder than a minister's had any right to be. "May he rot!"

The voices continued to come and go, accompanied by the sobs of Mag in a corner, her apron thrown over her head, Hecuba mourning.

"He is not dead," said Richard what seemed like hours later. "I know William Henry is not dead."

"Tomorrow we will have half of Bristol looking, Richard, that I promise you," said Cousin James-the-druggist. What he did not say was that most of the looking would be done along the banks of the Avon and the Froom, especially at low tide. Bodies did wash up—cats, dogs, horses, sheep and cows in the main, but occasionally some drowned man or woman or child would be found lying on the mud, one more piece of wreckage vomited up by the rivers.

They got Richard upstairs, put him on his bed and undressed him; he had worn holes in the bottom of his shoes, for he had walked almost thirty miles between dawn and dusk. But when Cousin James-the-druggist tried to make him swallow a dose of laudanum, he pushed the glass away.

No, William Henry was not dead. Would never have gone close enough to the river to drown. He had lectured his son on the subject, said that the Avon was hungry, and William Henry had listened, had understood the danger. Richard knew as well as Dick, the Cousins James and Mr. Prichard what must have transpired between boy and man: Parfrey had made amorous advances and William Henry had fled. But not in the direction of the river. An agile, clever little boy like William Henry? No, he would have scrambled up into the rocks and made his escape across country; even now he might be curled up asleep beneath some sheltering bank on Durdham Down, prepared to make the long walk home tomorrow. Terrified, but alive.

And so Richard comforted himself, talked himself away from the truth everybody else saw clearly, glad of one thing: that Peg had not lived to witness this. Truly God was good. He had taken Peg as if with a bolt of lightning, and closed her eyes before they could know despair.

Some thousands flocked with the Mayor's consent to help search for William Henry. Every sailor on watch scanned the mud in his vicinity, sometimes leaped overboard to examine a huddled, greasy grey heap amid the four-legged carcasses and the refuse of 50,000 people. To no avail. Those who could afford horses rode as far afield as the Pill, Blaize Castle, Kingswood, and every village within miles of Clifton and Durdham Down; others prowled the river-banks turning over barrels, sloppy floats of turf, anything that might catch and conceal a body. But no one found William Henry.

"'Tis a week," said Dick gruffly, "and there is no sign. The Mayor says we must give it up."

"Yes, I understand, Father," said Richard, "but I will never give it up. Never."

"Accept it, please! Think what it is doing to your mother."

"I cannot and will not accept it."

Was this blind refusal to accept better than those oceans of tears he had shed when little Mary died? At least they had been an outlet. This was awful. More awful by far than Peg or little Mary.

"Did Richard lose all hope of finding William Henry," said Cousin

James-the-druggist over a mug of rum, "he would have nothing whatsoever to live for. His whole family is gone, Dick! At least this way he can hope. I have prayed and the Reverend James has prayed that there never is a body. Then Richard will survive."

"This ain't survival," said Dick. "It is a living Hell."

"For you and Mag, yes. For Richard, it is the prolongation of hope—and life. Do not badger him."

Richard had not found a job either, but that did not carry the same urgency it would have were his father not in the tavern business. Ten years had gone by since Dick took up the license of the Cooper's Arms, which had outlived most of the other less pretentious taverns in Bristol's center. Though it could never expect the likes of the Steadfast Society or the Union Club to darken its door, and despite those dreadful years of depression, the Cooper's Arms still had its customers. The moment an old regular got his job back or found a new one, he returned with his family to his old watering place. So the summer of 1784 saw the Cooper's Arms in fairly good condition—not as full as it had been in 1774, but sufficiently so to keep Dick, Mag and Richard busy. Nor was it necessary to find school fees for William Henry.

Two months went by. In September, Colston's opened its gates to paying pupils again—though not with Mr. Prichard as the new Head. The disappearance of William Henry Morgan and the suicide of George Parfrey, Latin master, had effectively ruined his chances to succeed to that august position. As the old Head was not there to bear the blame for this nightmare, the Reverend Mr. Prichard inherited its mantle—and its odium. Questions were being asked in the Bishop's Palace by some very important Bristolians.

At about the same moment as Colston's reopened, Richard had a letter from Mr. Benjamin Fisher, Collector of Excise, asking to see him at once.

"Ye may wonder," said Mr. Fisher when Richard reported in, "why we have not yet arrested William Thorne. That we will do only as a last resort—so far we have concentrated our energies upon Mr. Thomas Cave in the hope that he will produce the sixteen hundred pounds' fine necessary to settle the matter without prosecution. However," he went on, beginning to smile in quiet satisfaction, "evidence has come to light which puts a different complexion on the case. Do sit down, Mr. Morgan." He cleared his throat. "I heard about your little boy, and I am very sorry."

"Thank you," said Richard woodenly, seating himself.

"Do the names William Insell and Robert Jones mean anything to you, Mr. Morgan?"

"No, sir," said Richard.

"A pity. Both of them worked at Cave's distillery during your time there."

"As still men?"

"Yes."

Frowning, Richard tried to remember the eight or nine faces he had seen around the gloomy cavern, regretting now that he had held himself aloof from those workmen's parties while Thorne was away. No, he had no idea which one was Insell, or Jones. "I am sorry, I simply do not remember them."

"No matter. Insell came to me yesterday and confessed that he had been withholding information, it seems from fear of what Thorne might do to him. At about the time that you discovered the pipes and casks, Insell overheard a conversation between Thorne, Cave and Mr. Ceely Trevillian. They were talking about the illicit rum in plain terms. Though Insell had not suspected the swindle as he went about his work, this conversation made it clear that there was collusion among the three to defraud the Excise. So I intend to prosecute Cave and Trevillian as well as Thorne, and Excise will be able to get its money by garnishing Cave's property."

A small shaft of feeling penetrated Richard's numbness; he sat back and looked contented. "That is excellent news, sir."

"Do nothing, Mr. Morgan, until the case comes to trial. We will have to investigate matters some more before we move to arrest the three, but rest assured that it is going to happen."

Two months ago the news would have sent him whooping back to the Cooper's Arms; today it was merely of passing interest.

"I cannot remember Insell or Jones," he said to his father, "but my evidence is corroborated."

"That," said Dick, pointing into a corner, "is William Insell. He came while ye were away and asked to see you."

One look at Insell's face jogged Richard's memory. A fresh young fellow, good-natured and hardworking. Unfortunately he had been Thorne's chief butt; twice he had felt Thorne's rope's end, and twice he had suffered the flogging without fighting back. Not unusual. To fight back meant losing one's job, and in hard times jobs were too precious to lose. Richard would never have suffered so much as the threat of a flogging, but Richard had never been in a situation where the rope's end was an alternative. Like William Henry, he had the knack of avoiding corporal punishment without needing to be obsequious; he was also a qualified craftsman, not a simple workman. Insell was a perfect victim, poor fellow. Not his own fault. Just the way he was made.

Richard carried two half-pints of rum to the corner table and sat down. This was indicative of a change in his behavior that no one had thought it wise to comment upon; Richard was drinking rum these days, and increasingly so.

"How d'ye do, Willy?" he asked, pushing one rum toward the pallid Mr. Insell.

"I had to come!" Insell gasped.

"What is it?" asked Richard, waiting for the burning fluid to start deadening his pain.

"Thorne! He has found out I went to the Excise."

"I am not surprised, if ye blurt it out to everyone. Now calm yourself. Have some rum."

Insell drank thirstily, gulped and half-retched on the power of Dick's unwatered best stuff, and ceased to tremble. Finished with his own half-pint, Richard went to draw two more mugs.

"I have lost my job," said Insell then.

"In which case, why d'ye need to fear Thorne?"

"The man is a murderer! He will find me and murder me!"

Privately Richard considered that Ceely Trevillian was more likely to do any murders necessary, but did not attempt to argue. "Where d'ye live, Willy?"

"In Clifton. At Jacob's Well."

"And what has Robert Jones to do with it?"

"I told him what I had overheard. Mr. Fisher of the Excise was interested in that, but he thinks I am far more important."

"Rightly so. Does Thorne know you live at Jacob's Well?"

"I do not think so."

"Does Jones know?" Richard suddenly remembered Robert Jones, who was a crawler, smarmed up to Thorne. He was how Thorne knew, definitely.

"I never told him."

"Then rest easy, Willy. If ye've nothing better to do, spend your days here. The Cooper's Arms is one place Thorne will not look for you. But if you drink rum, ye'll have to pay for it."

Horrified, Insell pushed the second mug away. "Do I have to pay for this?" he asked.

"These are on my slate. Cheer up, Willy. In my experience, rogues are not very clever. Ye'll be safe enough."

The days were beginning to draw in a little, which limited the amount of time Richard had to search for William Henry. His first call was always the dell by the Avon, from which place he would clamber up the frowning cliffs, calling William Henry's name; from the top of the gorge he would strike across Durdham Down, and so come eventually to Clifton Green. The walk home led him past William Insell's lodging place, but he usually met Insell on the footpath across Brandon Hill, hurrying to beat the darkness, yet too afraid to leave the Cooper's Arms until after sunset.

He had worn out two more pairs of shoes, but no one in the extended Morgan family attempted to remonstrate with him; the more Richard walked, the less time he had to drink rum. Brother William suddenly needed to have his saws set and sharpened more often (he pleaded a new West Indian timber), and that gave Richard some other place to walk than Clifton. Who knew? Perhaps the little fellow had gotten himself all the way to Cuckold's Pill, so the journeys to William's sawpits were not entirely wasted time. And he could not drink rum when he needed his eye to set a saw properly.

He had not wept, could not weep. The rum was a way to dull his pain, which was the pain of hope, hope that one day William Henry would walk through the door.

"I never thought to say this," Richard said to Cousin James-the-druggist halfway through September, "but I am beginning to wish that I had found William Henry's body. Then I could have no hope. As it is, I must assume William Henry is alive somewhere, and that in itself is torture—what sort of life must he be leading, not to come home?"

His cousin once removed eyed him sadly. Richard was thinner yet physically fitter—all that walking and climbing had honed down a body always in good trim until now it was probably capable of lifting anvils or withstanding the ravages of any disease. How old was he now that he had just had another birthday? Six-and-thirty. The Morgans tended to make old bones, and if Richard did not ruin his liver with rum, he looked as if he would live to be ninety. Yet what for? Oh, *pray* he put this awful business behind him, took another wife and begot another family!

"Two and one-half months, Cousin James! Not a sign of him! Perhaps"—he shuddered—"that abominable creature hid his body."

"Dear fellow, put it behind you, please."

"I cannot."

William Insell did not arrive at the Cooper's Arms the next day; glad of an excuse to walk out to Clifton earlier than usual, Richard put his hat on and went to the door.

"Off already?" asked Dick, surprised.

"Insell has not come, Father."

Dick grunted. "That is no loss. I am very tired of him in his corner looking so woebegone that he puts the customers off."

"I agree," said Richard, managing a grin, "but his absence is a worry. I will see for myself why he ain't here."

The path across Brandon Hill was so familiar by now that he could have negotiated it blindfold; Richard was outside William Insell's house within fifteen minutes of leaving home.

A girl sat hunched on the stoop. Hardly aware of her, Richard went to step around her. Her foot came out.

"Bon jour," she said.

Startled, he looked down into the most bewitching female face he had ever seen. Big, saucily demure black eyes, long-lashed—a dimple in either rosy cheek—a pair of lush, unpainted red lips—a glowing skin—an uncoiffured mop of glossy black curls. Oh, she was pretty! And so *clean*-looking!

"How d'ye do?" he asked, removing his hat to bow.

"Very well, monsieur," she said in French-accented English, "but I cannot say as much for poor Willy."

"Insell, mistress?"

"Oui." She got to her feet to reveal that her figure was as graciously endowed as her face, and fetchingly dressed in pink silk. Expensive. "Yes, Willy," she added, pronouncing the name so adorably that Richard smiled.

She gasped. "Oh, monsieur! You are very 'andsome."

Ordinarily shy with strangers, Richard found himself not shy with her at all, despite her forwardness. Conscious that he had reddened, he wanted to look away but found that he could not. She really was amazingly pretty, and the upper halves of two smooth, creamy breasts were even more beguiling than her expression.

"I am Richard Morgan," he said.

"And I am Annemarie Latour, serving maid to Mrs. Barton. I live 'ere." She chuckled. "Not with Willy, you understand!"

"He is sick, ye say?"

"Come and see for yourself." She walked ahead of him up the narrow stairs, her dress kilted high enough to see two beautifully turned ankles below a foam of ruffled petticoats. "Willy! Willy! You 'ave a visitor!" she called as she reached the landing.

Richard entered Insell's room to find him lying on his bed looking very bilious. "What is it, Willy?"

"Ate some bad oysters," Insell groaned.

Annemarie had followed him in and was surveying Willy with interest but no pity. " 'E *would* eat the oysters Mrs. Barton gave me. I told 'im that old thing would not give me fresh oysters. But Willy sniffed them and said they were good, so 'e ate them. Et voilà!" She pointed dramatically.

"Then serves ye right, William. Have ye seen a doctor? D'ye need anything?"

"Just rest," moaned the sufferer. "I have cast up my accounts so many times that the doctor says there cannot be any more oysters left down there. I feel awful."

"But ye'll live, which is a good thing. Without you to confirm my testimony, Mr. Fisher of the Excise Office has no case. I will drop in tomorrow to see how you are."

Richard descended the stairs conscious that Annemarie Latour was close enough behind him to smell the fresh scent of best Bristol soap. Not perfume. Soap. Lavender-scented soap. What was a girl like this doing living alone in a Clifton lodging house? Maids usually lived in. And no maid Richard had ever met wore silk. Mrs. Barton's cast-offs, perhaps? If so, then Mrs. Barton, apostrophized by Annemarie as an "old thing," must have an excellent figure.

"Bon jour, Monsieur Richard," said Mistress Latour on the step. "I will see you tomorrow, non?"

"Yes," said Richard, clapped his hat on his head and walked away up the hill toward Clifton Green.

His mind was battling to do two things at one and the same moment: William Henry had to be searched for, yet Annemarie Latour was there too, eating away like a worm. For so he saw her, instincts not awry just because his traitorous body was twitching and stirring. A lifetime around taverns had shown him on countless occasions that a man's reason and good sense could fly out the window at the merest flick of a feminine skirt.

But why now, and why with this woman? Peg had been dead for nine months and by tradition he was still in mourning for her, ought not even to be thinking of his body's needs. Nor was he a man who had ever dwelled upon his body's needs. His wife had been his only lover, he had never seriously coveted any other woman.

It is neither the time nor the situation, he thought as he continued to wear out his fourth pair of shoes. It is simply *her.* Annemarie Latour. Whenever he had met her, in whatever situation he had met her, were Peg alive or dead, Richard divined that Annemarie Latour would have provoked this same bodily reaction in him. Thank God then that Peg was dead. The girl exuded some invisible lure, she was a siren whose chief pleasure was the act of seduction. And I am not Ulysses bound to the mast, nor are my ears stoppered with wax. I am an ordinary man of humblest origins. I do not love her, but Christ, I want her!

Then the guilt began. Peg was dead, he was still in mourning. William Henry had not been gone three months—these feelings were impious, disgusting, unnatural. He began to run, shrieking his son's name to the indifferent winds of Clifton Hill. William Henry, William Henry, save me!

But he was back at Willy Insell's door at eight the next morning, turning his hat around in his hands, looking in vain for Annemarie Latour. No one on the stoop, no one inside. Knocking gently, he pushed at the door to Insell's room and discovered him asleep in the bed, his chest rising and falling regularly. He tiptoed out.

"Bon jour, Monsieur Richard."

There she was! On the stairs leading to the garret.

"He is asleep," said Richard lamely.

"I know. I gave him laudanum."

She was wearing much less than yesterday, but perhaps she had just risen from her own bed: a pink lace robe, some kind of thin pink shift beneath it. Her hair, unpinned, cascaded in masses over her shoulders.

"I am sorry. Did I wake you?"

"No." She put her finger to her lips. "Sssssh! Come up."

Well, he was up already, just at the sight of her, but he followed her to the tiny eyrie where she lived and stood with his hat across his groin, gazing about like a bumpkin. Cousin Ann had much finer furniture, but Mistress Annemarie had much finer taste; the room was tidy, smelled of lavender rather than sweaty clothes, and was delicately fitted out in purest white.

"Richard? I may call you Richard?" she asked, plucking his hat away and staring round-eyed. "Oooooh, la la!" she exclaimed, and helped him out of his coat.

He was used to the decencies of nightclothes and darkness, but Annemarie believed in neither. When he tried to keep his shirt on she would not let him, pulled it over his head and left him standing defenseless, not a stitch on.

"You are very beautiful," she said in a surprised tone, going all the way around him while the lace robe fell, then the pink silk shift. "I am very beautiful too, am I not?"

He could only nod, wordless. No need to worry what to do next; she was in complete control, and clearly preferred it that way. A less humble man might have balked at her mastery, but Richard knew himself a novice at this sort of activity, and had all a humble man's pride. Let her take the initiative, then he could not be mortified by making a move she did not approve of, or might find laughable.

There were many beautiful ladies paraded around the better bits of Bristol, but voluminous skirts might hide spindled shanks or legs of mutton, and the breasts forced up by stays might sag to a suddenly spreading waist, a wobbling pudding of belly. Not so, Mistress Annemarie! She was, as she had complacently announced, very beautiful. Her breasts were as high and full as Peg's had been, her waist smaller, her hips and thighs rounded, her legs slender yet well shaped, her belly flat, her black mound triumphantly, juicily plump.

She strolled around him again, then fitted her front to his back and rubbed herself against him with purrs and murmurs; he could feel the soft hair of her mound against his legs, jumped when she suddenly sank her manicured nails into his shoulders and pulled herself up until the hair was sliding voluptuously across his buttocks. Teeth clenched—for he feared that he would come right then and there—he forced himself to stand perfectly still while she inched around him, rubbing and cooing. Then she sank to her knees in front of him, threw her shoulders back so that her breasts reared up like red-capped, rounded pyramids, tossed her hair out of her face and grinned gleefully.

"I think," she said in the back of her throat, "that I will play the silent flute."

"Do that, madam," he gasped, "and the tune will be drowned in a second!"

She cupped his balls in her hands and smirked. "No matter, cher Richard. There is many a tune in this 'andsome flute."

The sensation was—sensational. Eyes closed, every fiber of him concentrated upon drawing this astonishing pleasure out for as long as his flesh could bear, Richard tried to store up as many different nuances of the experience as he could. Then, defeated, let himself come in dazzling colors, jerks and black velvet, his hands clutching her hair as she gulped and swallowed him down.

But she had been right; no sooner was the convulsion over than the tyrant at the base of his belly was up and wanting more.

"Now it is my turn," she said, stalked as if she still wore high heels to the bed, and sprawled upon it, swollen crimson lips sparkling in the depths of her mound. "First the tongue in a la-la-la, then the flute in a march, and then—the tarantelle! Bang, bang, bang with the stick upon the drum!"

That was what she wanted, and that was what she got. All pretense at thought had long since gone; if madam demanded a full performance, then let it be a symphony.

"Ye're a musical wench," he said several hours later, utterly spent. "Nay, do not bother trying. The flute is tweetled out."

"You are full of surprises, my dear," she said, still purring.

"And you. Though I doubt ye learned such a varied repertoire on the likes of my poor single drumstick. It must have taken—flutes—clarinets—oboes—bassoons even."

"Somewhere, cher Richard, you 'ave picked up an education."

"Five years at Colston's is a sort of an education, I suppose. But most of it I learned in making guns."

"Guns?"

"Aye, from a Portuguese gentleman of Jewish persuasion. My master gunsmith," said Richard, so exhausted that speaking was an effort, but realizing that she liked to chat after concerts. "He played the violin, his wife the harpsichord, and his three daughters harp, cello and—flute. I lived in their house for seven years, and used to sing because they liked my voice. My blood is probably Welsh, and the Welsh are much addicted to singing."

"You also 'ave a sense of humor," she said, hair brushing his face. "Very refreshing in a Bristolian. Is the humor Welsh too?"

He got off the bed and into his underdrawers, then sat on its edge to pull on his stockings. "What I cannot understand is why ye're a lady's maid, Annemarie. Ye should be some nabob's mistress."

She twinkled her fingers in the air. "It amuses me."

"And the silk gowns? This—this *virtuous* room?"

"Mrs. Barton," she said, tone oozing contempt, "is a stupid old cow of a bitch!"

"Do not use that word!" he snapped.

"Bitch! Bitch—bitch—bitch! There! I 'ave shocked you greatly, cher Richard." She sat up and crossed her legs under her like a tailor. "I cheat Mrs. Barton, Richard. I cheat 'er blind. But she thinks she is the clever one, lodging me 'ere to keep 'er silly old 'usband away from me." She lifted her lip. "As for 'er, she can parade around Clifton to all the big 'ouses and boast that she 'as a genuine Frrrrrench maid. Bah!"

Dressed, Richard eyed her ironically. "D'ye want to see more of me?" he asked.

"Oh yes, my Richard, very definitely."

"When?"

"Tomorrow at the same hour. Mrs. Barton is not early out of 'er bed."

"You cannot keep Willy on laudanum forever."

"There is no need. I 'ave you now—why should Willy mind?"

"Quite. Until tomorrow, then."

That day William Henry was, if not forgotten, buried under many layers of his father's mind. Richard walked straight back to the Cooper's Arms, up the stairs without saying a word to anyone, fell fully clothed on his bed and slept until dawn. Rumless.

"Your fish," said Annemarie Latour to John Trevillian Ceely Trevillian, "is 'ooked."

"I do wish you would abandon those Frenchified affectations," Mr. Trevillian sighed. "Was it very awful, my poor darling?"

"Quite the opposite, cher Ceely. His clothes were clean. So was his person. No nits, no lice, no crabs." She was emphasizing her aitches. "He washes." A smile of pure cruelty curved her mouth. "His body is very beautiful. And he is very, very much a *man.*"

The barb struck home to fester and spread its poison, but he was too clever to betray that. Instead he patted her on the bottom, gave her twenty golden guineas and dismissed her; Mr. Cave and Mr. Thorne were coming to call, and he had not seen them in some time. For one who lived with his doting mama on Park Street it was not advisable to be seen too often receiving low visitors.

"The best thing we can do," said William Thorne when he and Cave arrived, "is to grab Insell and put him on a slaver as crew."

"And have the suspicion of murder hanging about us like smoke around a foundry chimney?" asked Ceely. "Oh, no."

"I will make sure he is listed as pressed and on the roster."

"I want Richard Morgan done for too," said Trevillian.

"It is not necessary!" wailed Thomas Cave. "Richard Morgan is well connected—the other is a nobody. Let Bill have Insell taken on a slaver, then let me go back to the Excise, please. I am not asking you to pay the fine, Ceely, but until it is paid the threat of trial hangs over all of us. We are being watched."

"Look," said Ceely Trevillian slowly and carefully, "I am too well-born to earn a living, and my late father, Devil take him, disinherited me. Knowing that I must live on my wits has sharpened them something brilliant. M'mother does what she can, including housing me and donating gold when m'brother is not looking, but I needed that excise money, and I am not pleased to be deprived of it. Nor will I be pleased to be deprived of either my freedom or my breathing and swallowing apparatus. Morgan and Insell have put a stop to my income, and I want to put a stop to them." His face twisted. "Insell is a nothing, I agree. It is Morgan who will send us down. Besides, I *need* to ruin Richard Morgan."

When Richard woke, the first thing he did was go to look in William Henry's cubicle. The bed was empty. Tears stung at his eyes, the first since William Henry had disappeared, but they did not fall. His sleep had been long enough to banish bodily aches, though his penis felt raw and he could feel her bites and scratches. A shocking word, bitch, but Annemarie Latour was a first-rate bitch.

The habits of the household at dawn went back past his very earliest memories. Dick descended to the kitchen and carried a kettle of hot water and a bucket of cold water up to Mag for her small tin bath. When Peg had been alive the two women had shared it, and after them the servant girl got it. While they washed upstairs, Dick and Richard washed downstairs.

Dick passed through to his bedroom with Mag's kettle and bucket, cast a glance in Richard's direction on his way out and ascertained that his son had finally come to. Leaving his slept-in clothes for the servant girl to deal with, Richard found more in his chest and ran down the stairs, naked, to join his father, who had already shaved and was standing in the small bath trickling water over himself with a tin dipper and slicking his wet skin with soap.

Dick gaped. "Christ! Where have you been?"

"With a woman," said Richard, preparing to shave.

"About time too." The soap was sloshed away with the dipper. "A whore, Richard?"

Richard grinned. "If she is, Father, then she is a very rare sort of a one. By that I mean that I have never seen her like."

"A strong statement from a tavern man." Dick stepped out of the oversized dish and rubbed himself vigorously with an old linen sheet while Richard stepped into his father's used water.

"Finished?" came Mag's voice from upstairs.

"Not yet!" Dick yelled, and dragged Richard, still drying himself, to the bullioned window and a shade more wan light. There he looked his son over grimly. "I hope ye're not clapped or poxed."

"I would bet I am not. The lady is particular."

"What happened?"

"I met her at Insell's place."

"She's *Insell's* leavings?"

"Nay! She'd as soon cut her throat. Very high and mighty." He frowned, shook his head. "Truth to tell, I know not why she fancied me. There is little enough between Insell and me."

"Ye're no more like Insell than a silk purse is a sow's ear."

"I am to see her again at eight o'clock this morning."

Dick whistled. " 'Tis hot, then?"

"Like a fire." Richard finished tying his stock and combing his damp hair. "The thing is, Father, that I dislike her hugely, yet I cannot get enough of her. Ought I go? Or stay away forever?"

"Go, Richard, go! When it is a fire, the only way out is to walk through it to the other side."

"And if it consumes me?"

"I will pray that it does not."

At least, thought Richard at a quarter to eight, shutting the Cooper's Arms door behind him, I have my father's approval. I never dreamed he would understand. I wonder who was *his* fire?

He still had very little idea why he was going, whether it was as complex as sexual enslavement or as simple as sexual starvation. In Bristol "sex" and "sexual" were not words employed in the context of the act—too brutally explicit for a godfearing small city, not mealy-mouthed about many things. "Sex" stripped the act of love or morality. "Sex" made the act an animal event. In which case, sex and sex alone was why he walked to Jacob's Well for more Annemarie.

But it was William Henry he thought about. Alive out there in someone else's world, unable to get home. Which meant that he had been taken as a ship's boy. It happened, especially to beautiful boys. Oh, dear God! Not my lad in that life! Please, dear God, let him be dead first! While I go to copulate with a French bitch who transfixes me the way I once saw a hooded snake transfix a rat at the Bristol Fair. . . .

The fire burned more fiercely each time Richard met her, which was every day for the next week. But the pain of it and the pain of deserting William Henry, of imagining William Henry as a ship's boy, forced him back to the rum; his days became a muddled blur of Annemarie, of his father's worried face, of William Henry crying out from a great distance amid a vast sea, of sex and music and hooded snakes and rum, rum to find oblivion at the end of each hideous bout. He hated her, the French bitch, yet he could not get enough of her. Worse than that, he hated himself.

Then out of the blue she sent a note with Willy Insell that she could not see him for some time—but she gave no reason. Dazed at the affair, Insell could provide no reason either, save that the knocker was off her garret door and he fancied she was staying with Mrs. Barton. I cannot deal with losing both of them, Richard thought as he wandered in search of either of them. What I feel for her is base metal, heavy and dull and dark as lead, so how can I mourn at losing her? The fire still consumes me.

Giving up the search, he spent his days inside the Cooper's Arms drinking rum, talking to nobody, the quill and paper he had taken to write to Mr. James Thistlethwaite lying dry and blank.

"Jim, please tell me what to do," Dick begged of Cousin James-the-druggist.

"I am an apothecary, not a doctor of the soul, and it is poor Richard's soul is sick. No, I do not blame it on the woman. She is merely a symptom of his disease, which has been coming on ever since William Henry drowned."

"D'ye really think he drowned?"

Cousin James-the-druggist nodded emphatically. "I have not the slightest doubt." He sighed. "At first I thought it was better for Richard to cherish hope, but when he took to rum I changed my mind. His soul needs a doctor, and rum is no cure."

"Except," Dick objected, "that the Reverend James is such a—a *fizzing* sort of minister. 'Tis you has good sense and can see all sides, not the other

James. Imagine trying to tell him about this French whore—he would be off with his prayer book in one hand and a Roman crucifix in the other to do battle with one of Satan's imps! For so he would regard her. Whereas I think she is just a meddler, and very attracted to Richard. Why can he never see that women fancy him? They do, Jim! You must have seen it for yourself."

As both his bracket-faced spinster daughters had been in love with their cousin Richard for years, Cousin James-the-druggist had no hesitation in nodding emphatically a second time.

By the 27th of September Richard was soaked to the core in rum; when he received a note from Annemarie Latour saying that she was back in residence and dying to see him, he floundered from his chair and was off at a run.

"Richard! Oh, how marvelous to see you! Mon cher, mon cher!" She drew him inside, covering his face with kisses, took his hat and coat from him, purred and murmured and cooed.

"Why?" he asked, hanging back, determined this once to be his own man. "Why have I not seen you for a week?"

"Because Mrs. Barton has been ill and I have been with her—Willy should have told you. I asked him to tell you."

"So far you have not dropped a single aitch," he said.

"Because I have been with Mrs. Barton, 'oo—*who*—hates it when I speak the bad English. I have had to nurse 'er—*her,*" said Annemarie, looking injured.

Richard slumped onto the bed, feeling the rum. "Oh, what the hell does it matter, girl? I have missed ye and I am glad to be back. Kiss me."

So they played at sex with lips, tongues, hands, wetness and fire, the sodden ecstasies of utter shamelessness. Hour upon hour, he upon her, she upon him, upside down, right way up, she fertile of imagination, he consumed to go in whichever direction she pointed.

"You are astonishing," she said at the end of it.

His eyes were closing, but he summoned up a huge effort and kept them open. "In what way?"

"You stink of rum, yet you can still fuck—that is a *good* word—like a boy of nineteen."

"You would know, my dear." He grinned and did close his eyes. "It takes more than a few pints of rum to knock the stuffing out of me," he said. "I have lasted a great deal longer than John Adams and John Hancock."

"What?"

He vouchsafed no answer; Annemarie lay back against the soft pile of pillows and gazed at the ceiling, wondering how she was going to feel when this was over. When Ceely had persuaded her—assisted by several rouleaux of golden guineas—to seduce Richard Morgan, she had stifled a sigh, taken the money and reconciled herself to however many weeks of boredom. The trouble was that she had not been bored. For one thing, Richard was a gentleman. Which was more than she could say for that two-faced, double-gaited monster Ceely, who by profession called himself a gentleman yet would not have recognized one on the street.

What she had not counted upon was the victim's attractiveness (to herself, however, she called it beauty). On the surface, a drab and genteel ordinary man of Bristol with no pretensions to fashion and no ability to turn heads. Then when first he smiled at her he seemed to whip a veil from his face, was suddenly strikingly handsome. And beneath the clothes of the time, designed to make all men look paunchy, round shouldered and sway backed, lay the physique of an ancient Greek statue. He hides, she thought, groping after the English adage, his light under a bushel. It is there only for those with the eyes to see. What a pity that he has never valued himself enough to stand forth. A superb lover. Oh yes, superb!

How then might she feel when all this was over? Not long now, depending upon how malleable Richard was—Ceely wanted it done soon, and the rum would be a great help. Her own part, she suspected, was a minor one, and she would never know the outcome. But playing that part meant goodbye to Ceely and to England. Her looks were still at their peak, she could pass for twenty even though she was thirty; between what Ceely would pay her shortly and what he had already paid her over the course of four years, she would be able to quit this country of dirty pigs and go home to her beloved Gironde, there to live like a lady.

For an hour she dozed; then she leaned over and shook Richard awake. "Richard! Richard! I 'ave an idea!"

His head felt swollen and his mouth was parched; Richard got off the bed and went to the white pitcher in which Annemarie kept small beer. A good beaker of that and he felt a little better, though he knew it would be several days before he cleared the rum from his system. If he stopped drinking it. But did he want to?

"What?" he asked, sitting on the bed, head in his hands.

"Why do we not set up house together? Mrs. Hale downstairs is moving out and the rent for two floors is only half a crown a week—we could move our bedroom down so there are not as many steps, and put Willy up here or in the cellar. His rent would be a help—he pays a shilling. Oh, it would be so nice to 'ave a proper establishment—do say yes, Richard, please!"

"I have not got a job, my dear," he said through his hands.

"But I 'ave—*have*—with Mrs. Barton, and you will soon get one too," she said comfortably. "Please, Richard! What if some horrible man moves in? How would I protect myself?"

He took his hands away from his face and looked at her.

"I could say we were married, that would make it respectable."

"Married?"

"Just to satisfy the neighbors, cher Richard. Please!"

It was difficult to think, and the small beer was making him feel a little sick; Richard grasped the proposition and turned it over in his befuddled mind, wondering if this might not be the best way. He was outwearing his welcome at the Cooper's Arms—or else the Cooper's Arms was outwearing him. "Very well," he said.

She jigged up and down on the bed, beaming. "Tomorrow! Willy is helping Mrs. Hale move today, then he can help me. Tomorrow!"

The news that Richard was leaving stunned his parents, who looked at each other and resolved to say nothing against it. His consumption of rum between coming home and going to bed was greater than ever—if he transferred himself to Clifton he would have to pay for at least a part of what he drank.

"For I cannot deny my own son what he has here," said Dick.

"You are right, it is too readily available," Mag agreed.

So Dick lent him the handcart in which they fetched sawdust and provisions, watched a grim-faced Richard load two chests upon it. "What about your tools?"

"Keep them," said Richard tersely. "I doubt I will need those kind of tools in Clifton."

The house in which Mistress Latour and Willy Insell lodged was the middle one of three conjoined premises on Clifton Green Lane not far from Jacob's Well. That the edifice had once been a single dwelling was patent in the narrowness of the stairs and the rough partitions which divided it into three separate sections, thereby increasing the rents. The boards did reach the ceilings, but were typically slipshod—full of gaping cracks and thin enough to hear a woman's voice shrilling next door. Annemarie's garret rose alone like a single eyebrow and had afforded a great deal more privacy, Richard now discovered as he surveyed her fine bed in its new location one floor down.

"Our lovemaking will be rather more public," he said dryly.

A Gallic shrug. "All the world makes love, cher Richard." Suddenly she gasped and reached into her reticule. "I forgot! I 'ave a letter for you."

He took the folded sheet and stared at the seal curiously; not anyone's he knew. But the front was clearly addressed—by the copperplate hand of a scrivener—to Mr. Richard Morgan.

> "Sir," said the letter, "your name has been drawn to my attention through the kind services of Mrs. Herbert Barton. I believe that you are a gunsmith. If this be true, and you are able to furnish good references and perhaps demonstrate your skills in my own presence, then I may have employment for you. Kindly present yourself at nine of the clock to my establishment at 10, Westgate Buildings, Bath, on the 30th of September."

It was signed, in a shaky, unschooled hand, "Horatio Midder." Who on earth was Horatio Midder? He had thought he knew the name of every gunsmith between Reading and Weymouth, but Mr. Midder was new to him.

"What is it? Who is it from?" Annemarie was asking, trying to peer over his shoulder.

"From a gunsmith in Bath named Horatio Midder. Offering me a job," said Richard, blinking. "He wants to see me on the thirtieth at nine in the morning, which means I will have to leave tomorrow."

"Oh, it is the friend of Mrs. Barton's!" caroled Annemarie, clapping her hands in joy. She hung her head until her long black lashes cast shadows on her cheeks. "I mentioned you to her, cher Richard. You do not mind?"

"If it means a job," said Richard, picking her up and tossing her into the air, "I would not care did ye mention my name to Old Nick himself!"

"It is too bad," she pouted, "that you will have to go away tomorrow. I have told everybody in these 'ouses—*houses*—that we are married and you have moved in, and we have many invitations to visit." The pout grew poutier. "Perhaps you will have to stay in Bath on Friday night too—I will not see you until Saturday."

"Never mind, if it means a job of work," said Richard, taking one of his chests to a spot where he thought Annemarie would not want to put anything of her own. "I am still sorry that ye moved the bed downstairs," he hinted. "Since Willy has elected to live in the cellar, there was no need."

"What does it matter, Richard, if you get a job in Bath?" she asked with inarguable logic. "We will be moving again anyway."

"True."

"Is it not nice to have a room for my desk?" she asked. "I love to write letters, and it was so cramped upstairs."

He walked to the room behind the bedroom and looked at the desk, very solitary. "We will have to buy furniture to keep it company. How odd! In all my life I have not needed to furnish a place, even when Peg and I lived on Temple Street."

"Peg?"

"My wife. She is dead," said Richard curtly, suddenly needing a drink. "I shall go for a walk while you write letters."

But she followed him downstairs, where the living room and the kitchen lay, the one containing four wooden chairs, a table and a sideboard, the other a counter and crude fireplace. Could Annemarie cook? Would Annemarie have the time to cook, if she spent her afternoons and evenings with the late-rising Mrs. Barton?

On the doorstep she stood on tiptoe and kissed him.

"Egad!" cried an affected voice. "Mr. Morgan, is it not?"

Richard broke the kiss with a jerk and slewed around to see Mr. John Trevillian Ceely Trevillian posing not three feet away in all the glory of cyclamen velvet embroidered in black and white. The hair on the back of his head rose, but, aware of Annemarie, he could not do what he longed to do—turn his rump on Ceely Trevillian and stride away down the lane.

"Mr. Trevillian, as I live and breathe," he said.

"Is this the wife I have been hearing about?" the fop fluted, pursing his painted lips in admiration. "Do introduce me!"

For a long moment Richard stood silent, striving to keep his face expressionless as his rum-clouded mind raced through all the possible consequences of this unhappy, inopportune encounter. To one side of and behind Mr. Trevillian stood a small group of men and women he had not so far met, but assumed from their indoor dress that they lived in one or the other of the boarded-off sections on either side of Annemarie's apartment. What should he do? How should he answer? "Do introduce me!" Ceely had said.

Like almost every other Englishman, Richard knew very little about the law, but he did know that once he spoke of a woman as his wife, in effect she became his wife at Common Law. When Annemarie had proposed that she tell her friends and neighbors of a marriage between herself and Richard, he had retained, even in his hungover state, sufficient sense to resolve that she could prattle on about marrying him as much as she wanted, but he would make sure he never confirmed her talk.

Now here he stood, confronted by his inimicus Ceely Trevillian in the midst of Annemarie's neighbors, neatly impaled on the horns of a dilemma: if his introduction implied that she was his wife, then as long as he cohabited with her, she was his Common Law wife; if he publicly disavowed her, she acquired the status of a whore in the eyes of her neighbors and the persecution would start.

He gave a mental shrug. So be it. His wife she would have to be until—or if—he ceased to cohabit with her. Though he loathed her tasteless musical analogies quite as much as he loathed himself for being caught in her sexual toils, he could not turn her from a respectable maidservant into a trollop. Of their two lives, hers was the one that revolved around Jacob's Well and its denizens.

"Annemarie," he said curtly. Then: "What are you doing here?"

"My dear fellow, visiting my hairdresser—Mr. Joice, y'know." Ceely indicated a simpering man at his elbow. "Lives next door, which is how I learned ye're married and come to live here." Out came a lace handkerchief; he passed it delicately across his brow. " 'Tis a warm day for the end of September, is it not?"

"Oh, sir, please to come in," said Annemarie, curtseying in a flurry of petticoats. "A rest in the cool of our living room will soon make you feel better." She ushered the unwelcome visitor in and sat him on one of the chairs, then fanned his brow with the edge of her apron. "Richard, my dear, do we 'ave anything to offer the gentleman?" she asked dulcetly, obviously impressed with so much style.

"Until I fetch beer and rum from the Black Horse, naught," said Richard ungraciously.

"Then I will find you a pitcher for beer and one for small beer," she said, and bustled with many twitchings of her skirts into the kitchen, making sure that Ceely got an eyeful of ankle.

"I owe you no thanks, Morgan," said Ceely as soon as they were alone.

"That tale you fabricated about me has led to several very unpleasant interviews with the Commander of Excise. I do not know what I did to offend you while you tinkered with Mr. Cave's apparatus, but it was certainly not sufficient to deserve the tissue of lies you told the Collector."

"No lies," said Richard levelly. "I saw ye at work by the light of a full moon on a cloudless night, and heard your name." He smiled. "And because ye were injudicious enough to converse frankly with Mr. Cave and Mr. Thorne while another listened, you will be exposed as the villain you are, Mr. Ceely Trevillian."

Annemarie came in, an empty white pitcher in each hand. "Is beer acceptable, sir?" she asked the visitor.

"At this hour of day, quite," said Mr. Trevillian.

A pitcher in either hand, Richard went off to the Black Horse under Brandon Hill while Annemarie settled in another chair to talk to the awesomely grand gentleman.

When he returned he discovered that his trip had been for nothing; Mr. Trevillian was standing on the stoop, busy kissing Annemarie's hand.

"I 'ope we see you again, m'sieur," she said, dimpling demurely.

"Oh, I can promise you that!" he cried in his falsetto voice. "Do not forget that my hairdresser lives right next door."

Annemarie gasped. "Mrs. Barton! I will be late!"

Mr. Trevillian offered his arm. "As I know the lady well, Madame Morgan, pray permit me to escort you to her house."

And off they went, heads together, he mouthing pretty nothings, she giggling. Richard watched them turn at the corner of a nearby lane of half-finished houses, emitted an angry growl and went to get his father's handcart. It had to be returned. The silly French bitch! Simpering and groveling to the likes of Ceely Trevillian just because he wore cyclamen velvet some poor workhouse child had been forced to embroider without seeing a farthing's recompense.

The daily coach to Bath left the Lamb Inn at noon and made the trip in four hours for a price of four shillings an inside seat or two shillings on the box. Though he had saved scrupulously during the six months he had worked for Mr. Thomas Cave, there was very little money left; the trip to Bath would cost him a minimum of ten shillings he could ill afford. He had come to no arrangement with Annemarie over domestic expenses, and yesterday's two meals had been taken at the Black Horse, a more costly business than the Cooper's Arms; she had not offered to pay the shot, nor apparently disapproved of the amount of rum he drank. Her tipple was port.

Thus Richard set off to walk clear to the other side of Bristol in time to secure a two-shilling seat on the box; this necessitated sitting on top of the coach exposed to the elements, but the day did not promise rain.

Posting inns were busy places, endowed with large interior courtyards in which grooms and horses trailing harness walked to and fro restlessly, ostlers ran in all directions, and servants bearing trays of refreshments tendered them to the prospective passengers. Finding the team of six horses not hitched to his vehicle yet, Richard paid two shillings for a seat on the box and went to lounge against a wall until Bath was announced ready for boarding.

He was still lounging there when William Insell ran through the gates and paused to look about, chest heaving.

"Willy!"

Insell came hurrying over. "Oh, thank God, thank God!" he gasped. "I feared ye might have left."

"What is it? Annemarie? Is she ill?"

"Not ill, no," said Insell, pale eyes goggling. "Worse!"

"*Worse?*" Richard grasped his arm. "Is she dead?"

"No, no! She has made an assignation with Ceely Trevillian!"

Why did that not surprise him? "Go on."

"He came to see the hairdresser fellow next door—or so he said, but the next moment he was aknocking on our door, and I had not got up the stairs from the cellar when Annemarie opened it." He wiped the sweat from his brow and looked at Richard pleadingly. "I am so thirsty! I ran all the way."

Richard disbursed a penny for a tankard of small beer for Insell, who drained it at a gulp. "There! Better!"

"Tell me, Willy. My coach will be called at any moment."

"They made no secret of it—it was just as if they had clear forgotten I was in the house. She asked him if he wanted to do business with her, and he said yes. But then she did one of her flouncing acts—said the time were not right, you might come back. Six o'clock this evening, she said, and he could stay the night. So he went next door to Joice the hairdresser—I could hear him neighing through the wall. Then I waited until Annemarie went upstairs, and ran to find you." His anxious face fixed its hang-dog eyes on Richard, begging for approval.

"Bath! Bath!" someone was shouting.

What to do? Damn it, he needed this job! And yet the man in him was outraged that Annemarie could prefer Ceely Trevillian to himself—Ceely Trevillian, of all men! The slur was insupportable. He straightened. "No job in Bath," he said ruefully. "Come, we will go to my father's and wait there. At six o'clock, Mistress Latour and Mr. Ceely Trevillian are in for a nasty surprise. It may be that he will never see the inside of a court for excise fraud, but he will remember what happens this evening, and so I swear it."

How, wondered Dick, sensing terrible trouble brewing but not able to find out what kind of trouble, can I demand the truth from a thirty-six-year-old man, son though he is? What is going on, and why will he not tell me? That cringing creature Insell sits fawning at his feet—oh, there is no harm in him, but a good friend for Richard he is definitely not. Richard, Richard, steady on the rum!

At a little before six, just as Mag was about to serve supper to a pleasantly full tavern, Richard and Insell got up. Amazing how well he stood the rum, thought Dick as Richard walked an arrow-straight line to the door with Insell weaving behind him. My son is horribly drunk, trouble's in the wind, and he has shut me out.

Twilight still infused the sky with a subtle afterglow because the weather was fine; Richard walked so swiftly that Willy Insell was hard put to keep up with him, the rage in him growing with every step he took.

The front door was unlocked; Richard slipped inside. "Stay down here until I call you," he whispered to Willy, then ground his teeth. "With Ceely! *Ceely!* The bitch!" He started up the stairs, fists clenched.

To find the scene inside the bedroom one straight out of a classical farce. His lusty inamorata lay on the bed with legs akimbo, Ceely on top of her clad in his lace-trimmed shirt. They were heaving up and down in the traditional motion, Annemarie giving vent to small moans of pleasure, Ceely emitting grunts.

Richard had thought himself prepared for it, but the anger which invaded him drove reason from his brain. In one wall was a fireplace, beside it a scuttle of coal and a hammer for breaking down the larger chunks. Before the pair on the bed could blink, he had crossed the room, picked up the hammer and faced them.

"Willy, come up!" Richard roared. "No, do not move! I want my witness to see ye exactly as ye are."

Insell walked in and stood gaping at Annemarie's breasts.

"Are you prepared to testify, Mr. Insell, that ye've seen my wife in bed doing business with Mr. Ceely Trevillian?"

"Aye!" gulped Mr. Insell, trembling.

Annemarie had told Trevillian that Richard was drinking very heavily, but he had not imagined in any of his rehearsals for this moment what the sight of a very big man in a black rage would do to him; the cool and collected excise defrauder felt the blood drain from his face. Christ! Morgan meant murder!

"Damned bitch!" Richard shouted, turning his head to glare at Annemarie, quite as frightened as Trevillian. Shivering, she eeled up the bed and tried to retreat into the wall. "You bitch! You whore! And to think that I acknowledged ye as my wife to save your reputation! I did not deem ye a whore, madam, but I was mistaken!" His furious gaze went from her to the window-sill, whereon sat Trevillian's watch, purse and fob. "Where is your candle, madam?" he asked, snarling. "Whores advertise for custom by putting a candle in the window, but I see no candle!" He reeled, staggered, sat heavily on the side of the bed and put the hammer to Trevillian's forehead. "As for you, Ceely, 'twas you forced me to call this slut my wife, so you can take the consequences! I'll have you up in court on charges of wife-stealing!"

Trevillian tried to slither away; Richard took his shoulder in an agonizing grip and tapped the hammer very gently against his sweating brow. "No, Ceely, do not move. Otherwise your blood will be all over this pretty white counterpane."

"What are you going to do?" whispered Annemarie, sounding very afraid. "Richard, you are drunk! I beg you, not murder!" Her voice rose shrilly. "Put the hammer down, Richard! Put the hammer down! Not murder! Put it down!"

Richard obeyed with a spitting sound of contempt, though the hammer remained much closer to his hand than to Trevillian's.

Think, Ceely Trevillian, think! He is murderous but not by nature a murderer—work on him, calm him, get this thing going in the direction it was intended to go!

Richard lifted the hammer amid Annemarie's shrieks of terror and used its head to flick Trevillian's shirt up around his belly. Then he looked at Annemarie in feigned amazement. "Is *that* what ye wanted? My, ye must be desperate for gold!" He didn't know which one of the guilty pair he hated more—Annemarie for selling her favors or Ceely Trevillian for putting him in this cuckold's situation by forcing him to indicate that she was a wife; so he hurtled, rum-impelled, down the only path he could see would make both of them pay. At least on this memorable evening and for however long after it that his rage endured. Not as far as a court, no. Not as far as a profit, no. But if he died for it, he would make them fear him and fear the consequences.

His hand shot out too quickly to see, took Trevillian by the throat and lifted him bodily to kneel in the middle of the bed. "I have here a witness that ye stole my wife, sir. I intend to prosecute ye for"—he hesitated, plucked a figure out of nowhere—"a thousand pounds in damages. I am a respectable artisan and I do not relish the role of a cuckold, especially when my cuckolder is a turd like you, Ceely Trevillian. Ye were willing to pay for my wife's services—well, the fee has just gone up."

Think, Ceely, think! It is going where I thought *I* would have to lead it without his aid. He is talking more, acting with less violence. The rum is slowing him down at last.

Trevillian wet his lips and found the words he had rehearsed. "Morgan, I acknowledge that ye have the right to take measures at law, and I admit that ye'd get *some* damages. But let us not air this matter in a court, please! My mama and brother—! And think of your wife, of her public reputation! Were her name to be bandied about in a court, she would be jobless and cast out."

Yes, the rage was dying; Morgan looked suddenly confused, ill, at a loss. Trevillian babbled on. "I admit my guilt freely, but let me settle this out of court—here and now, Morgan, here and now! Ye would not get a thousand pounds, but ye might get five hundred. Let me give you my note of hand for five hundred pounds, Morgan, please! Then we can call the matter settled."

Thrown off balance by this cow-hearted surrender, Richard sat on the edge of the bed wondering what to do now. He had envisioned Trevillian fighting back, resisting, daring him to do his worst—why had he envisioned that? Because of memories of the slim, crisp excise defrauder stripped in the moonlight of his fancy clothes and fancy manners? But that, he realized now, was a Trevillian in complete control of a situation. The man had no genuine sinew, he was a fraud in every way.

" 'Tis a fair offer, Richard," said Willy Insell timidly.

"Very well," Richard said, and got off the bed. "Dress yourself, Ceely, ye look ridiculous."

Having scrambled any old how into his plush jade green outfit embroidered in peacock blue, Trevillian followed Richard into the back room and sat down at Annemarie's desk. Hopeful that he would see a share in Richard's windfall, Willy Insell followed; what Willy did not realize was that Richard had no intention of cashing any note of hand. All Richard wanted was to make the fellow sweat over the next few days at the prospect of losing £500.

The note of hand for £500 was made payable to Richard Morgan of Clifton, and signed "Jno. Trevillian."

Richard studied it, tore it up. "Again, Ceely," he said. "Sign it with all your wretched names, not half of them."

At the top of the stairs the temptation was too much; Richard applied the toe of his shoe to Trevillian's meager buttocks and sent him pitching down with a roll and a somersault, the noise of his body when it struck the flimsy board partition echoing like thunder. By the time he reached the tiny square of hall, Trevillian was yelling at the top of his lungs. No cool excise defrauder now! He tugged at the door and fell into the lane, weeping and howling, there to be succored by all the neighbors.

Richard shot the bolt and went up the stairs to Annemarie, but without Willy Insell, who scuttled down into his cellar.

She had not moved. Her eyes followed Richard as he crossed to the bed and picked up the hammer again.

"I ought to kill you," he said tiredly.

She shrugged. "But you will not, Richard. It is not in you, even with the rum." A smile tugged at her mouth. "Ah, but Ceely believed for a moment that you would. A surprise for that one, so confident, so full of himself, so fond of complicated schemes."

He might have fastened upon this remark as betraying a more intimate knowledge of Ceely Trevillian than a chance encounter in a bed, but someone was pounding on the front door. "Now what?" he asked, and went downstairs. "Yes?" he called.

"Mr. Trevillian wants his watch back," said a man's voice.

"Tell Mr. Trevillian that he can have his watch back after I have had satisfaction!" Richard roared through the bolted door. "He wants his watch back," he said as he re-entered the bedroom.

The watch was still lying on the window-sill, though the fob and purse had gone.

"Give it back," said Annemarie suddenly. "Throw it out the window to him, please."

"I'm damned if I will! He can have it back, but when I am good and ready." He picked it up and examined it. "What a conceit! Steel. All the go, top of the trees, very dapper." The watch went into his greatcoat pocket alongside the note of hand.

"I am out of here," he said, feeling very sick.

She was off the bed in an instant, throwing on a dress, shoving her bare feet into shoes. "Richard, wait! Willy, Willy, come and help me!" she called.

Willy appeared as they reached the bottom of the stairs, face dismayed. "Here, Richard, what are ye going to do? Leave be!"

"If it is Ceely ye're worried about, there is no need," said Richard, stepping into the lane and inhaling fresh air deeply. "He ain't here now. The performance stopped two minutes ago."

He set off toward Brandon Hill, Annemarie on one side of him and Willy on the other, three vague outlines in the pitch darkness of a place not lit by any lamps.

"Richard, what will happen to me if you go?" Annemarie asked.

"I care not, madam. I did ye the honor of allowing Ceely to think ye were my wife, but I'd not have the likes of you to wife, and that is the truth. What will change for ye? Ye're still in employment, and Ceely and I between us have seen to it that your reputation is pure." He grinned mirthlessly. "Pure? Madam, ye're a black-hearted whore."

"What about me?" Willy asked, thinking of £500.

"I will be at the Cooper's Arms. With the Excise case still coming up, we have to stick to each other."

"Let us see ye over the hill," Willy offered.

"No. Take madam back to her house. It is not safe."

Thus they parted in the night, one man and the woman returning to Clifton Green Lane, the other man striding off along the Brandon Hill footpath, heedless of its dangers. Mrs. Mary Meredith stopped outside her front door, glad she had arrived, but wondering at the fearlessness of the walker, whose companions had left him. They had been talking in low voices and had seemed on excellent terms, but who they were she had no idea. Their faces were invisible on this late September evening.

Too empty to be sick, Richard stumbled home feeling the rum far more than he had in the heat of that confrontation. What a business! And what was he going to say to his father?

> "But at least I can say that the fire is out," he ended a letter to Mr. James Thistlethwaite the next day, which was the last day of September, 1784. "I do not know what came over me, Jem, save that the fellow I met inside myself I do not like—bitter, vengeful and cruel. Not only that, but I find myself in possession of the two articles I want least in the world—a steel watch and a note of hand for £500. The first I will return as soon as I can bear to set eyes

upon Ceely Trevillian's face and the second I will never present to his bank for payment. When I return the watch I will tear it up under his nose. And I curse the rum.

"Father sent a man over to Clifton for my stuff, so I have not set eyes on Annemarie, nor will I ever again. False from hair of head to hair of—I will not say it. What a fool I have been! And at six-and-thirty years of age. My father says I should have gone through an experience like Annemarie at one-and-twenty. The older the fool, the bigger the fool, is how he put it with his usual grace. Still, he is an excellent man.

"The business has made me understand much about myself I had no inkling of. What shames me is that I have betrayed my little son—thought not a scrap about him or his fate from the time I met Annemarie until today, when I woke to find her spell no longer upon me. Maybe a man has to have one fling of a sexual sort. But how have I offended God, that He should choose this time of loss and grief to try me in such a horrible way?

"Please write, Jem. I can understand that it might be very difficult to write in the aftermath of our news about William Henry, but we would all like to hear from you, and worry at your silence. Besides, I need your words of wisdom. In fact, I am in *dire* need of them."

But if Mr. James Thistlethwaite intended to reply, his letter had not reached the Cooper's Arms by the 8th of October, when two sober-looking men in drab brown suits walked into the tavern.

"Richard Morgan?" asked the one in the lead.

"Aye," said Richard, emerging from behind the counter.

The man came close enough to him to put his right hand on Richard's left shoulder. "Richard Morgan, I hereby arrest ye in the name of His Majesty George Rex on charges laid by Mr. John Trevillian Ceely Trevillian."

"William Insell?" he asked then.

"Oh! Oh!" squeaked Willy, cowering in his corner.

Again the hand on the shoulder. "William Insell, I hereby arrest ye in the name of His Majesty George Rex on charges laid by Mr. John Trevillian Ceely Trevillian. Come with us, please, and do not try to make trouble. There are six more of us outside the door."

Richard held out his hand to his father, standing thunderstruck, and opened his mouth to speak before he realized that he had no idea what to say.

The bailiff dug him sharply between the shoulder blades with the same hand he had lain upon Richard's shoulder. "Not a word, Morgan, not a word." He stared around the silent tavern. "If ye want Morgan and Insell, ye'll find them in the Bristol Newgate."

PART TWO

From
October of 1784
until
January of 1786

The Briſtol Newgate was two buildings down from Waſ-borough's brass foundry on Narrow Wine Street. Richard and Willy Insell in their midst, the eight bailiffs made short work of the walk and entered the prison through a massively barred door not unlike a portcullis. A narrow passageway with an opening on either side was Richard's first sight of Newgate's interior; hardly pausing, the head bailiff hustled them through the left-hand portal with a shove from behind by his henchmen, who remained outside.

"Prisoners Morgan and Insell!" he barked. "Sign, please."

A man lounging on a chair behind a table reached for the two pieces of paper the bailiff presented. "And where d'ye expect me to put them?" he asked, signing each paper with a large X.

"Your business, Walter, not mine," said the bailiff smugly. "They are on a writ of habeas corpus," he added, walking out.

Willy was weeping copiously; Richard stood dry-eyed and composed. The shock was wearing off, he was able to feel and think again, and knew himself unsurprised. What was he charged with? When would he find out? Yes, he had Ceely's watch and note of hand, but he had told the person in the lane that Ceely would get his watch back, and he had not taken the note of hand to Ceely's bank. Why hadn't he *thought?*

Overcrowding would help him be acquitted. The practical men of Bristol's Bench were prone these days to come to an agreement with any accused who could marshal the funds to make restitution, pay something extra by way of damages. Though he would be loaded down for the rest of his life with a debt only another war and more guns could pay off, he knew that his family would not desert him.

"A penny a day for bread," the gaoler named Walter was saying, "until ye're tried. If ye're convicted, it goes up to tuppence."

"Starvation," said Richard spontaneously.

The gaoler came around his desk and struck Richard across the mouth so hard that his lip split. "No smart remarks, Morgan! In here ye live and die according to my rules and at my convenience." He lifted his head and bellowed, "Shift yerselves, ye bastards!"

Two men carrying bludgeons rushed into the room.

"Chain 'em," said Walter, rubbing his hand.

Staunching the blood with his shirt cuff, Richard walked with the blubbering Willy Insell across the passageway and into the room on the right-hand side. It looked a little like a saddler's shop, except that the multitude of straps hanging all over its walls were made of iron links, not leather.

Leg irons were considered sufficient in the Bristol Newgate; Richard stood while the sorry-looking individual responsible for this storehouse of misery kitted him out with his fetters. The two-inch-wide band which confined his left ankle was locked, not riveted, and it was joined to the similar band on his right ankle by a two-foot length of chain. This permitted him to walk at a shuffle, but not to step out or run. When Willy panicked and tried to fight, he was beaten to the ground with bludgeons. His split lip still bleeding, Richard said and did nothing. The remark to Walter the gaoler was the last time, he vowed, that he would court abuse. It was back to his days at Colston's—sit quietly, stand quietly, do whatever was bidden quietly, attract nobody's attention.

The passageway terminated in another barred gate; a keeper unlocked it with a massive key and the two new prisoners, Morgan and Insell, were thrust through it into Hell. Which was a very big room, its stone walls oozing moisture so consistently yet insidiously that in many places the surface had sprouted long limestone icicles gone black and furred with the soot of the factoried Froom. Not a stick of furniture. A flagged floor filthy with the slicks of age and ammoniac human emissions. A crowded mass of leg-ironed prisoners, all male. They mostly sat on the floor with their legs stretched out in front of them; some moved aimlessly about, too leached of life to lift their burdened feet over the legs of some other wretch, who continued to sit as if he had not felt the blow of the walker's chain. To someone accustomed to Bristol mud, the stench was familiar—rot, muck, excrement. Just stronger from poor ventilation.

The only purposeful activity was going on around an arched opening in the far end of the room; though he had never been inside the Bristol Newgate, Richard deduced that through the aperture lay the prison taproom. In there, those who could scrape up the coins necessary would be served with rum, gin, beer. Hearing Dick and Cousin James-the-druggist talk had given Richard an idea of what the Newgate might be like, and he had visualized it as boiling with fights over money and booze, bread and property. But, he understood now, the gaolers were too shrewd to let that happen. None of these men had the strength to fight. They were starving, and a good proportion of them were also drunk on empty bellies, drooling and humming tunelessly, sitting with their legs stretched out, far away from care.

Willy would not leave him. Willy stuck to him like a burr. No matter which direction Richard took, there was Willy shuffling in his wake, weeping. I shall go mad. I cannot bear it. And yet I will not go back to rum. Or take to gin as cheaper. After all, this hideous ordeal will be over in some months—however long it takes for the courts to get around to our turn, mine and Willy's. Why must he howl so? What good does that do him?

At the end of an hour he was weary; the iron bands around his ankles were beginning to hurt. Finding a vacant piece of wall big enough to accommodate him and his shadow, he lowered himself to the ground and stretched his legs out in front of him with a sigh of relief, understanding immediately why the prisoners adopted this posture. It took the weight off the fetters, let their backs rest on the floor. An examination of his thick knitted stockings revealed that after a mere hour of walking, the fabric was already showing signs of wear and tear. Another reason why these people did not move around.

He was thirsty. A pipe poked through the Froom wall and sent a steady trickle of water into a horse trough; a tin dipper on a chain served as a drinking vessel. Even as he stared at it, one of the ambulating wretches paused to piss into the trough. Which, he noted, was situated right next to four naked privies optimistically deemed sufficient for the needs of over 200 men. If Cousin James-the-druggist is right, he thought, drinking that water will kill me. This room is stuffed with sick men.

As if the very name had the power to work a miracle, Cousin James-the-druggist appeared in the barred doorway from the passage; Dick was with him, hanging back.

"Father! Cousin James!" he called.

Eyes distended in horror, they picked their way over to him.

For the first time in anyone's memory, Dick fell to his knees and broke down. Richard sat patting his heaving shoulders and looked across them at the apothecary.

"We have brought you a flagon of small beer," said Cousin James-the-druggist, producing it out of a sack. "There is food too."

Willy had cried himself into an exhausted doze, but woke when Richard shook him. Never had anything tasted as good as that beer! Passing the unstoppered jug to Willy, Richard reached into the sack and found bread, cheese and a dozen fresh apples. In a corner of his mind he had wondered if perhaps the sight of these goodies would bring that apathetic throng to a fever of clawing hands and bared teeth, but it did not. They were truly lost.

Regaining his composure, Dick wiped his eyes and nose on his shirt. "This is awful! Awful!"

"It will not last forever, Father," said Richard, unsmiling; he did not want to split the lip again and alarm Dick even more. "In time my trial will come up and I will be freed." He hesitated. "Am I able to go bail?"

"I do not yet know," said Cousin James-the-druggist briskly, "but I am going to see Cousin Henry-the-lawyer first thing in the morning, and then we will beard the lion in the Prosecutions Office at the courthouse. Be of good cheer, Richard. The Morgans are well known in Bristol and ye're a Free Man in good standing. I know the popinjay who is pressing the charges—usually to be found ee-awing in the vicinity of the Tolzey like the donkey he is."

"I do not know how the news spread so far so fast," said Dick, "but before we left to find you here Senhor Habitas turned up. His eldest daughter is married to an Elton, and Sir Abraham Isaac Elton is a very good friend. He said you may be certain that Sir Abraham Isaac will be the presiding judge at your trial, and while he may serve ye a hideous homily on the temptations of a Lilith, the charges will not stick. Everything depends upon the advice a judge gives to his jury. This Ceely Trevillian is despised—every man on the jury will recognize him instantly and laugh himself sick."

The two Morgans did not stay long, and shortly after their departure Richard became profoundly glad of it. The ordeal and the small beer were working cruelly on his bowels. He had to sit on a filthy privy seat with his breeches and underdrawers around his knees, on full view. Not that anyone cared save he. Nor was there a breech-clout to wipe himself with, drop into the soapy water of the laundering bucket; he had to get to his feet and pull up his underdrawers over the last of a runny mess, his eyes closed against the most appalling shame he had ever experienced. From that moment on, he was more conscious of his own smell than of the ghastly fug around him.

Nightfall saw them shifted from this common-room up a flight of steps to the men's dormitory, another enormous room, and endowed with too few pallets to accommodate those in residence. Figures lay on some, apparently had so lain all day in the throes of fever; one or two would never move again. But as he and Willy were new and therefore quick, they found a pair of vacant stretchers and took possession. No mattresses, no sheets, no pillows, no blankets. And stiff with the dried remnants of dysentery and vomit.

Sleep seemed unlikely to come. The place was freezingly damp and his only covering was his greatcoat. For Willy, who had wept so, the terrors of the Bristol Newgate had not the power to keep him awake; Richard profoundly thanked a merciless God for the small mercy of Willy's silence. He lay listening to the moans and snores, the occasional hacking cough, someone retching, and the terrible sound of a little boy's weeping. For not all the prisoners were grown men. Among the crowd he had counted about twenty boys who might have been any age from seven to thirteen, none of them depraved or riddled with vices, though at least half of them were drunk. Caught pinching a mug of gin or a handkerchief and prosecuted for it by the irate victim. Not things which happened at the Cooper's Arms, simply because Dick did not permit them to happen. If some ragamuffin did sneak in and whip a mug of rum from under a dreaming nose, Dick always managed to calm feelings down, would boot the urchin out the door and give the violated customer a free drink. It did not happen more than once or twice a year. Broad Street saw few crimes other than filched wallets or reputations.

The news that Dick and Cousin James-the-druggist had brought was cheering, no denying that. Senhor Habitas was an unexpected ally—still writhing over the fact that it had been he who introduced Richard to Mr. Thomas Latimer, clearly. Poor man! What blame could be laid at his door? These things happen, thought Richard drowsily, closed his eyes and fell immediately into dreamless darkness.

Late in the afternoon on the morrow Dick appeared alone with a sack of food and small beer over his shoulder.

"Jim is still at Cousin Henry's chambers," he explained as he squatted on his hunkers close enough to keep what he said private from all ears but those of the avidly eavesdropping Willy.

"It has not gone as we expected," said Richard flatly.

"Yes." Dick clenched his hands and gritted his teeth. "You are not to be tried in Bristol, Richard. Ceely Trevillian lodged his suit with the authorities in Gloucester on the ground that the crime occurred in Clifton, and therefore outside Bristol's borders. Your detention in our Newgate is temporary—only until the papers are officially approved and the witnesses' testimony processed, whatever that means." He waved his hands about wildly. "My head is ringing with legal talk! I do not understand it—I never have understood it—and I never will understand it!"

Richard leaned his head against the blackened wall and gazed beyond his father's hunched form to the pissy horse trough and the four disgusting privies. "Well," he said at last through a tight throat, "be all that as it may, Father, I have some more urgent needs." He gestured toward his feet. "First of all, I must have rags to pad these irons. One day, and my stockings have worn through. Tomorrow it will be my skin, and the day after that, my flesh. If I am to come out of this—and I swear I will!—I must keep my good health. As long as I can drink small beer and eat bread, cheese, meat and fruit or green vegetables, I will not suffer."

"They will send ye to Gloucester Castle," said Dick, lips quivering. "I do not know a soul in Gloucester."

"Nor does any other Morgan, I suspect. What a clever fellow is this Ceely Trevillian! And how much he wants me down. Is it for the excise fraud and his neck, or because I derided him as a man?" He shook his head, smiled. "Both, probably."

"I heard a rumor," said Dick doubtfully.

"Tell me, Father. My weeping days are over, you need not be afraid that I will shame ye," said Richardly gently.

His father's face reddened. "Well, it came to me through Davy Evans, my new rum distiller—*beautiful* drop, Richard! He told me that the trade is saying that Cave and Thorne went to Trevillian the moment they heard about your rumpus in Clifton, and asked him to prosecute you and Willy. You and I know that Trevillian is actively involved in the excise fraud, but the trade is ignorant of that, and has made the connection a different way. Davy Evans says Cave and Thorne want you and Willy convicted felons before the excise case can come to court. Then there is no case, for felons cannot testify. Furthermore, Cave has been to see the *Commander* of Excise—your Benjamin Fisher's brother, John—it is all in the family, as usual—and offered to make a sixteen-hundred-pound restitution. The Brothers Fisher are of course aware that you and Willy have been arrested and know perfectly well why Trevillian is doing this, but there is absolutely no proof."

"So we are to be convicted felons disbarred from testifying."

Willy began to howl like a dismal dog; Richard swung around with one of those lightning moves that defied sight and grasped his arm so hard that he squealed shrilly.

"Shut up, Willy! *Shut up!* Cry one more tear and irons or no, I will kick you to the other end of this establishment—*and* leave ye to die of fever!"

Dick gaped. Willy shut up.

Just as well, thought the stunned Dick, that Cousin James-the-druggist chose that moment to appear, lugging a wooden box the size of a small trunk. Otherwise, what was there to say to a stranger?

"A few things for you, Richard, but later," the newcomer said, putting the box on the floor with a grunt. His eyes shone liquid with tears. "It looks worse and worse for you."

"That comes as no surprise, Cousin James."

"The Law is so peculiar, Richard! I confess I had no idea what it says or does beyond my own small part in the scheme of things, and I suppose that is true for everybody, especially the poor." He held out his hand to Richard, who took it and found its grip convulsive. "You have almost no rights, especially outside the bounds of Bristol. Cousin Henry has tried and both the Reverend James and I have seen every important man we know, but the Law says that we cannot get a glimpse of Ceely's sworn statement, nor even know the names of his witnesses. It is shocking, shocking! I had hoped to post bail, but bail is not granted for crimes ranked as felonies, and ye're charged with"—he gulped, swallowed—"grand larceny *and* extortion! Both are capital crimes—Richard, ye could hang!"

"Well," said Richard tiredly, "I brought it all upon myself, though 'twould be interesting to know what Ceely has sworn about extortion. He *offered* a wronged husband a note of hand as an out-of-court settlement. Or is he now saying I am not a husband and so extorted under false pretenses? If I call her my wife, then she is my wife under the Common Law unless I already have a wife, which I do not. That much I do know about the Law."

"We have no idea what he has sworn," said Dick hollowly.

"The first thing we must do is lay hands on Annemarie Latour. She can verify my story when I tell it in court."

"Ye're not allowed to testify on your own behalf, Richard," said Cousin James-the-druggist quietly. "The accused is bound to silence, he is not allowed to tell his side of the story. All he may do in his defense is produce character witnesses and—if he can afford it—retain counsel to cross-examine the prosecution's witnesses. His counsel cannot examine him, nor introduce any new evidence. As for the woman—she has disappeared. By rights she ought to be in the women's section of the Newgate equally charged, but she is not. Her rooms in Clifton have been vacated, and no one seems to know whereabouts she went."

"What a place is England, and how little we know of how it works until it touches us," said Richard. "Am I not even allowed to have my counsel read out a sworn statement to the jury?"

"No. You may speak only in reply to a direct question from the judge, and then you must confine your answer entirely to it."

"What about finding Annemarie through Mrs. Herbert Barton?"

"There is no Mrs. Herbert Barton."

Willy Insell emitted a loud sob.

"Do not, Willy," said Richard softly. "Just—do—not."

"It is diabolical!" Dick cried, borrowing a Dissenter word.

"To sum up, then, we have no idea how Ceely is going to go about prosecuting me, nor who his witnesses are, nor what they will say," said Richard levelly. "And all of it is going to take place in Gloucester, forty miles away."

"That is the sum of it," said Cousin James-the-druggist.

For as much as a minute Richard sat silent, chewing his lower lip, in thought rather than in anxiety. Then he shrugged. "That is for the future," he said. "In the meantime I have urgent needs. Rags to pad my fetters. Rags for washing. And rags for wiping my arse." His face contorted. "I will launder the last under the water pipe and use them damp if I have to. These poor creatures are too far gone to have much energy for stealing, but I doubt my rags would survive being hung up to dry. I will have to pay one of the gaolers to cut off my hair. I want soap. Changes of some clothing every few days—shirts, stockings, underdrawers. And clean rags, always clean rags. Plus money enough to drink small beer. That water over there comes out of the Pugsley's Well pipe, I would bet, and will not be fit for drinking. So many in here are sick." He drew a breath. "I know this means I will cost ye money, but I swear that the moment I am free, I will begin to pay it back."

In answer, Cousin James-the-druggist opened up the wooden chest with the flair of a fairground conjurer. "I did think of rags already," he said, burrowing. "If it is possible to keep custody of this box, do so. Sit on it, or be like Dick and tie it to your big toe. The gaoler inspected it minutely when I came in, of course." He tittered. "No files or hacksaws, which is all he was worried about. Though it seems odd to me, ye're allowed a razor and a pair of scissors. Perhaps the gaolers do not care if ye cut each other's throats. A strop and a whetstone." He lifted the scissors and handed them to Dick. "Start cutting, Cousin."

"Cut Richard's hair? I could not!" cried Dick, appalled.

"You must. Places like this are riddled with every kind of vermin. Short hair will not keep them entirely at bay, but at least it means far fewer. I have put in a fine-toothed comb as well, Richard. Trim your body hair too, or pluck it."

"I have very little, so cutting it will suffice."

Cousin James-the-druggist was still ferreting, trying to get his hands around something heavy and awkward. Finally he succeeded in dragging it out, and set it triumphantly on the flagging. "Is it not wondrous?" he demanded.

Richard, Dick and Willy stared at the object blankly.

"I am sure it is, Cousin James, but *what* is it?" asked Richard.

"A dripstone," said Cousin James-the-druggist proudly. "The stone part, as you can see, is a slightly conical-bottomed dish which holds about three pints of water. The water soaks through the stone and drips from its bottom into the brass dish below it. Whatever magic happens within the stone I do not know, but the water in the collecting dish is as sweet and fresh as the best spring water. Which," he explained, launched into one of his scientific enthusiasms, "is pure and sparkling because it too makes a journey through porous rocks! I had heard that the Italians—clever people!—have these dripstones, but I could not lay my hands on one. Then about a year ago my friend Captain John Staines came home from Brazilian parts with a cargo of cocoa beans for Joseph Fry and cochineal for me. He called into Teneriffe for water, which that isle has in abundance. Someone showed him this, thinking to interest him for an English market—it is at present exported to those parts of Spain where the water is terrible. Thus he gave it to me rather than to Fry, who cannot think beyond chocolate. I tested it on the water from the Pugsley's Well pipe—as ye rightly said, Richard, undrinkable. Since the pipe is wooden and passes through four burying grounds, little wonder."

"How did ye test it, Jim?" asked Dick with a long-suffering look, wincing as he snipped off Richard's thick and curling hair.

"I drank the water the dripstone produced myself, naturally."

"I knew ye'd say that."

"I have begun to import dripstones from Teneriffe, and thought of you immediately," said Cousin James-the-druggist, tucking the dripstone back into the box. "It will come in handy, Richard, though I warn ye that it does not last forever. My trial one became smelly and the water cloudy after nine months, but it is easy to see when the corruption begins because the inside of the stone bowl grows a sticky brown substance. However," he went on, "the paper which came with my first shipment says that a dirty dripstone can be purified by soaking it for a week or two in clean sea-water and then drying it in the sun for another week or two." He sighed. "Not possible in England, alas."

"Cousin James," said Richard, smiling with enormous affection, "I kiss your hands and feet."

"No need to go that far, Richard." He rose and dusted his hands together, then suffered a change of mood. "I brought the box today," he said carefully, "because no one will tell me when ye're likely to be moved to Gloucester. Since the next assizes are not due until Lent, it may not be soon. But it may be tomorrow. And James-of-the-clergy said to tell ye he will be visiting."

"It will be a joy to see him," said Richard, feeling light-headed. He rose while Dick, still squatting, scooped up his shorn hair. "Father, wash your hands in vinegar and oil of tar when you get home, and do not touch your face until you do. Bring me clean underdrawers and soap, I beg you!"

The move did not happen on the morrow. Richard and Willy remained in the Bristol Newgate until into the new year of 1785. A blessing in some ways—his family could see to his needs; a curse in others—his family witnessed the misery of his situation.

Determined to see Richard for herself, Mag came once. But after the horrors of finding him amid that horde of wraiths, one look at his face and bristling scalp saw her faint dead away.

That was not to be the worst. Cousin James-the-druggist came alone just after Christmas. "It is your father, Richard. He has had a stroke."

The eyes Richard turned upon him had changed out of all recognition. Even through William Henry the tranquillity and flashes of humor had not completely vanished, but now they had. Life was not gone from them, but they observed rather than reacted. "Will he die, Cousin James?"

"No, not of this stroke. I have put him on a strict diet and hope to ensure that no second and third follow. His left arm and left leg are affected, but he can speak and his thought processes are not disordered. He sends all his love, but we feel that it is not wise for him to visit the Newgate."

"Oh, the Cooper's Arms! It will kill him to have to leave it."

"There is no need for him to leave it. Your brother has sent his oldest boy to train as a victualler there—a good lad too, not so money-hungry as William. And pleased to be out of that household, I suspect. William's wife is as hard as she is watchful—well, I do not need to tell ye *that.*"

"I daresay 'tis she has put her foot down and forbidden Will to visit me in gaol. He must be mourning the loss of his gratis saw-setter," said Richard without rancor. "And Mum?"

"Mag is Mag. Her answer for everything is to work."

Richard did not reply, just sat on the flags with his legs stretched out in front of him, Willy the shadow on his far side. Fighting tears, Cousin James-the-druggist tried to study him as if he were a stranger—not so difficult these days. How could he be so much handsomer than he used to be? Or was it that his handsomeness had gone unnoticed? The raggedly cropped trying-to-curl hair, no more than half an inch long, revealed the fine shape of the skull, and the sharp cheekbones and aquiline blade of nose stood forth in the smooth, unlined face. If that face had altered, then the change lay in his mouth; the sensuous lower lip remained, yet the whole had firmed and straightened, lost its dreamily peaceful contours. His thin, peaked black brows had always lain close to the eyes beneath, though now they looked—oh, more as if they belonged, as if they had been etched in as emphasis.

He is six-and-thirty, and God is trying him as He tried Job, but somehow Richard is turning the table on God without cheating or insulting Him. Over the course of the last year he has lost wife and only child—lost his fortune—lost his reputation—lost family like his selfish brother. Yet he has not lost himself. How little we know of those we think we know, in spite of a whole lifetime.

Richard suddenly smiled brilliantly, his eyes lighting. "Do not worry about me, Cousin James. Prison has not the power to ruin me. Prison is just something I have to live through."

Possibly because few felons were transferred from Bristol to Gloucester, Richard and Willy received two days' notice of their going, a bare week into January.

"You can take whatever ye can carry," said Walter the chief gaoler when they were brought into his presence, "not a fleabite more. Ye're not allowed a cart or barrow."

He did not say whereabouts they were to start their journey, nor what kind of conveyance they would inhabit, and Richard did not ask. Willy—dying to ask—was too busy wincing at the pain of Richard's foot on top of his.

The truth was that Walter was very sorry to see the end of Richard Morgan, who had brought him a very nice profit over the three months of his incarceration. His relatives fed both him and Insell, which meant that Walter had an extra tuppence a day; his father sent a gallon jug of good rum to his office once a week; and his cousin the fancy druggist regularly dropped a crown into Walter's cupped hand. Had it not been for these gratuities, he would have deemed Richard Morgan a potentially violent madman and sent him to be locked up in St. Peter's Hospital out of harm's way until Gloucester demanded him. He really was mad!

Every day he washed his entire body with soap and freezing water from the pipe—he wiped his bum on a rag and then washed it—he hovered over the privy rather than sat on it—he kept his hair shorn—he never visited the taproom—he spent most of his time reading the books his cousin the rector of St. James's brought him—and, maddest act of all, every day he filled a great thick stone basin with water from the pipe and drank what dripped out of it into a brass dish underneath. When Walter had demanded to know what he thought he was doing, he answered that he was turning water into wine as at the wedding feast. Mad! A March hare weren't in it!

What the two days' grace meant to Richard was a chance to make his stay in Gloucester Gaol more comfortable.

Cousin James-of-the-clergy brought him a new greatcoat. "As you see, your cousin Elizabeth"—who was his wife—"has sewn a thick lining of wool into your coat, Richard, and given ye two sorts of gloves. The leather ones have no fingertips, the knitted ones do. And I have packed the pockets of the greatcoat."

No wonder it was so heavy. Both pockets contained books.

"I ordered them from London through Sendall's," Cousin James-of-the-clergy explained, "on the thinnest paper, and I tried not to visit you with too much religion. Just a Bible and the Book of Common Prayer." He paused. "Bunyan is a Baptist, if that can be called a religion, but I think that *Pilgrim's Progress* is a great book, so I put it in. And Milton."

There were also a volume of Shakespeare's tragedies, one of his comedies, and John Donne's translation of Plutarch's *Lives.*

Richard took the Reverend James's hand and held it to his cheek, eyes closed. Seven books, none very big, so thin was the paper, so flexible the cloth binding. "Between the coat, the gloves, the Bible, Bunyan, Shakespeare and Plutarch, ye've managed to care for my body, my soul and my mind. I cannot thank you enough."

Cousin James-the-druggist concentrated on Richard's health. "A new stone for your drip apparatus, though do not change it until ye have to—it is just as well the stone is not much heavier than pumice, eh? Oil of tar and some new, very hard-wearing soap—ye go through soap too fast, Richard, too fast! Some of my special asphalt ointment—'twill heal anything from an ulcer to psoriasis. Ink and paper—I have wired the cork down so the bottle cannot leak. And do look at these, Richard!" he burbled, as always delighted out of a slough of despond by some new device. "They are called 'nibs' because they perform the same function as the tip of a trimmed quill, and they slide into the steel end of this wooden handle. I imported them from Italy, though they were made in Araby—geese are few and far between in Araby, it seems. Another razor, just in case. A big tin of malt for when ye do not get fruit or green vegetables—it prevents the scurvy. And rags, rags, rags. Between my wife and your mother, the drapers are out of sheets. A roll of lint and some styptic. And a bottle of my patented tonic, to which I have added a drachm of gold so that ye do not break out in boils. If ye get boils or carbuncles after ye've no tonic left, chew some lead shot for a few days. What is not padded with rags is padded with clothes." Busy packing the chest, he frowned. "I fear ye'll have to stuff some of it into your greatcoat pockets, Richard."

"They are already full," said Richard firmly. "The Reverend James brought me books, and I cannot leave *them* behind. If my mind fails, Cousin James, physical well-being is irrelevant. All that has kept me sane these past three months has been the chance to read. The worst horror of a prison is the idleness. The utter lack of anything to do. In Bunyan's day—yes, I have *Pilgrim's Progress*—a man could perform useful work and even sell what he made to support his wife and children, as Bunyan did for twelve long years. In here, the gaolers do not even like us to walk. Without books I would truly have gone mad. So I must keep them."

"I understand."

After much packing, unpacking and rearranging, the entire treasure trove was squeezed into the box. Only after Willy sat on its lid could its two stout locks be snapped shut; the key, on a thong, went around Richard's neck. When he lifted the chest, he estimated that it weighed at least fifty pounds.

There was a box for Willy too, smaller and much lighter.

"The words have not been invented to tell ye of my gratitude," Richard said, his eyes alive with the purest love.

"And I thank you," said Willy, moved to tears despite Richard.

They parted then, to meet in Gloucester at the Lent assizes.

* * *

At dawn on the 6th of January, Richard and Willy picked up their boxes and shuffled through the barred gate into the passageway, where Walter waited with another individual, a stranger armed with a cudgel. They were thrust into the ironing room; for a fleeting moment Richard thought that they were to be divested of their irons for the journey, and breathed a sigh of relief. The box was heavy enough without the weight of fetters. But no. The sorry-looking fellow who ran this chamber of horrors took a two-inch-wide band of iron and locked it around Richard's waist. His wrists were fitted with manacles, their two-foot chains attached to the lock at the front of his belly. After which the chain between his ankles was removed and replaced with two chains, one going from his left ankle to the lock on the belt, the other from his right ankle to the lock on the belt. He could walk with a normal stride, but never with sufficient agility to escape. Four lengths of chain met at the lock above his navel.

Somehow he managed to pick up his chest, and found with an odd surge of pleasure that the wrist chains formed a cradle for it, distributing the load between his arms and his trunk.

"Hold your box so, Willy," he said to his shadow, "and it will bear better."

"Hold your *tongue!*" barked Walter.

The piercing air outside felt and smelled like a distillation of Heaven. Nostrils and eyes dilated, Richard set out in front of their escort, who so far had not spoken a word. A Bristol bailiff?

How wondrous to be rid of that stinking dungeon! Gloucester, he knew, was a small town, therefore its gaol was bound to be more tolerable than the Bristol Newgate. Crime in rural areas was not unknown, but all the gazettes said that it was far greater in big cities. He could also comfort himself with the knowledge that he had more time in prison behind him than before him: the Gloucester Lent assizes were to be held in the latter part of March.

Oh, the air! Threatening snow, said the lowering black sky, but the only cold parts of him were his ears, unprotected now by hair. His hat shielded his scalp, but its upturned three-cornered brim could do nothing for his ears. Who cared? Eyes shining, he strode out down Narrow Wine Street, his chains jingling.

Though the hour was very early, Bristol was an early-rising sort of place; people were expected to be at work shortly after dawn, there to spend eight hours in winter, ten hours in spring and autumn, and twelve hours in summer. So as the three men walked, the two felons in front, there were plenty of people to see them. Faces would contort in terror, figures would plunge precipitously to the far side of the street—no one wanted to brush by a felon.

Wasborough's brass foundry doors were wide open, its interior an inferno of flame and roar. The Royal Navy was getting the flat, hook-linked brass chains for its new bilge pumps, obviously; he had never walked up to see since losing his money.

"Dolphin Street," said the bailiff curtly as they reached its corner. Not in the direction of the Cooper's Arms, then, but north across the Froom. Well, that made sense. The Gloucester Turnpike ran north.

Which led to a new thought: who was paying for all this? He and Willy were being extradited from one county to another, and the importing county was the one had to pay. Were he and Willy so significant to Gloucestershire, then, that it was willing to disburse several pounds on forty miles of travel and the cost of their bailiff escort? Or was it Ceely paying? Yes, of course it was Ceely paying. With pleasure, Richard imagined.

From Dolphin Street it was left into Broadmead and the wagon yard of Michael Henshaw, who operated freight wagons to Gloucester, Monmouth and Wales, Oxford, Birmingham, and even Liverpool. There they were shoved into an alcove full of horse dung and allowed to put their boxes down, Willy gasping in distress.

At least, thought Richard, three months of inertia have not stripped me of all my strength. Poor Willy is not strong, is all. But three months more will see me reduced to Willy's plight unless Gloucester Gaol offers me the opportunity to work and feeds me enough to work on. But if I do work, who will guard my box, keep thieving hands out of it? I will not lose things like my oil of tar and dripstone, but my rags and clothes will vanish in a second and someone might find the hollow compartment holding my golden guineas. *My books might go!* For certainly I am not the only prisoner in England who reads books.

The huge wagon Willy and Richard climbed into was provided with a canvas cover stretched taut across iron half-hoops; they would be protected from the worst of the elements, including what looked like a coming snowstorm bound to be more severe away from the heat of Bristol's chimneys. A team of eight big horses were harnessed to the wagon, and looked fit to struggle through the mud and mire of the Gloucester Turnpike. The interior was jammed with so many barrels and crates that there was nowhere to put their feet, and the wagoneer began to insist that their boxes stay behind.

"They has their property, man, that is the Law," said the bailiff in a tone brooking no argument. He climbed into the wagon to unlock the chains between their ankles and waists, fastening them instead to the half-hoops supporting the canvas shroud. The best they could do was dispose themselves among the cargo with legs stretched out. The bailiff jumped down, and for a moment Richard wondered if he was leaving them here. The wagon jerked into motion; the bailiff's back was ranged alongside the wagoneer's on the driver's seat, over which an adequate shelter was rigged.

"Willy, stir yourself," said Richard to his doleful companion, clearly dying to burst into tears. "Help me shift my box to rest against this sack, then I will do the same for you. We will have something to lean against. And do not cry! Cry, and ye're dead."

The pace was tormentingly slow on that completely plastic, unpaved road, and from time to time the wagon bogged to its axles in mud. Richard and Willy would be unchained and unloaded and set to digging and pushing—as was, Richard noted with amusement, the indignant bailiff. The snow was coming down hard, but the temperature was not low enough to freeze the surface. By the end of the first day, unfed and unwatered save by mouthfuls of snow, they had covered eight of the forty miles.

Which pleased the wagoneer, disembarking in front of the Stars and Plough in Almondsbury.

"I owe ye a bed and blankets," he said to the prisoners with a great deal more good humor than he had displayed in Bristol. " 'Twere your efforts got us out of the muck half a dozen times. And as for you, Tom, ye deserve a quart of ale—'tis good here, the landlord makes his own brew."

He and Tom the bailiff disappeared, leaving Richard and Willy inside the wagon wondering what happened now. Then Tom the bailiff came to unlock the chains binding them to the hoops, cudgel at the ready, and conducted them to a stone barn wherein lay straw. He found a beam with several iron staples in it close to the floor, and locked them to that. After which he vanished.

"I am so hungry!" whimpered Willy.

"Ye may pray, Willy, but do not cry."

The barn smelled clean and the straw was dry, a better nest than any which had come Richard's way for three months, he thought, burrowing around. In the midst of this, the landlord and a hefty yokel walked in, the landlord bearing a tray upon which reposed two tankards, bread, butter, and two big bowls of steaming soup. The yokel went to an empty stall and reappeared with horse blankets.

"John says ye helped the wagon considerable," said Mine Host, putting down his tray where they could reach it and then stepping backward quickly. "Have ye money to pay more than the penny each the bailiff will for ye? Otherwise I am out of pocket and must charge John's firm, since he says ye've earned laborer's wages."

"How much?" Richard asked.

"Threepence each, including the quarts of ale."

Richard produced a sixpence from his waistcoat pocket.

Three pence got them bread and small beer at dawn, then it was back into the wagon for a second day of eight miles, broken by much digging, pushing and heaving. A blissful night's rest amid straw and blankets combined with the nourishing hot food had worked wonders for Richard's frame, ache though it did from his exertions. Even Willy was more cheerful, put more heart into the work. It had ceased to snow and snapped colder, though never cold enough to freeze the ground; eight miles in one day were as many as they could go, a progress which perfectly satisfied John the wagoneer—and probably enabled him to put up each night at his regular stop.

Thus Richard expected to be deposited at Gloucester Gaol on the evening of the fifth day. The wagon, however, ceased to roll when it reached the Harvest Moon on Gloucester's outskirts.

"I am not of a mind to put ye into that foul place in the dark," John the wagoneer explained. "Ye have paid your way like gentlemen, and I feel sorry for ye, very. This will be your last night of decent rest and decent food for only God can say how long. 'Tis hard to think of ye as felons, so good luck, both of ye."

At dawn the next day the wagon crossed the Severn River on the drawbridge and entered the town of Gloucester through its west gate. In many ways it was still medieval, had retained most of its walls, ditches, drawbridges and cloisters, half-timbered houses. His view of the town was limited to what he could see through the uncovered back of the wagon, but that was sufficient to tell him that Gloucester was a minnow to Bristol's whale.

The wagon drew up to a gate in a heavy, ancient wall; Richard and Willy were unloaded and conducted, together with Tom the bailiff, into a large open space which seemed given over to the cultivation of plants only spring would name. In front of them was Gloucester Castle, which was also Gloucester Gaol. A place of frowning stone turrets, towers and barred windows, yet more of a ruin than a fortress last defended in the time of Oliver Cromwell. They did not enter it, but went instead to a fairly large stone house set against the outer wall and ditch surrounding the castle. Here lived the head gaoler.

The real reason they had been escorted from Bristol, Richard decided here, lay more in the fact that the Bristol Newgate wanted its irons back than cared about escaping prisoners. They were divested of every piece of iron they wore, Tom the bailiff gathering them to himself like a woman her new baby. As soon as all were accounted and signed for, he strolled off with his cargo in a sack to catch the cheap coach home. Leaving Richard and Willy to be put into fresh sets of the familiar locked fetters with a two-foot length of chain between. This deed done, a gaoler—they never saw the head gaoler himself—hustled them, carrying their precious boxes, to the castle.

What little of it was still habitable was such a crush of prisoners that sitting down with the legs stretched out was quite impossible. If these wretches sat, it was with knees drawn up beneath their chins. The chamber was exactly twelve feet square and contained around thirty men and ten women. The gaoler who had escorted them bawled an incomprehensible order and everybody who had managed to find enough space to sit got to their feet. They then filed outside, Richard and a weeping Willy in their midst, still carrying their boxes, and came to a halt in a freezing yard where twenty more men and women already stood.

It was Sunday, and the complement of Gloucester Gaol were to receive God's message from the Reverend Mr. Evans, a gentleman so old that his reedy voice drifted into the winds eddying around the roughly rectangular space and rendered his words of repentance, hope and piety—if such they were—unintelligible. Luckily he considered that a ten-minute service and another twenty minutes spent sermonizing constituted adequate labor for the £40 per annum he was paid as prison chaplain, especially because he also had to do this on Wednesdays and Fridays.

After, they were herded back to the felons' common-room, far smaller than that for debtors, of whom there were only half as many.

"It ain't as bad as this Monday to Saturday," said a voice as Richard put his box down by shoving someone else out of the way, and sat on it. "What a lovely man ye are!"

She squatted at his feet, elbowing those on either side of her roughly, a thin and stringy creature of about thirty years, clad in much-mended but reasonably clean clothes—black skirt, red petticoat, red blouse, black jerkin and an oddly cheeky black hat which sat with its wide brim to one side and bore a goose feather dyed scarlet.

"Is there no chapel where the parson can make his sermon heard?"

Richard asked with a slight smile; there was something very likable about her, and talking to her meant he did not have to listen to Weeping Willy.

"Oh, aye, but it ain't big enough for all of us. We are real full at the moment—need a decent dose of gaol fever to cut the numbers back. Name is Lizzie Lock." And she thrust out a hand.

He shook it. "Richard Morgan. This is Willy Insell, who is the bane of my life as well as my shadow."

"How de do, Willy?"

Willy's answer was a fresh spate of tears.

"He is a water fountain," said Richard tiredly, "and one day I am going to strangle him." He gazed about. "Why are there women in with the men?"

"No separate gaol, Richard my love. No separate gaol for the debtors either, which is why we got a mention in John Howard's report on England's Bridewells about five year ago. And that is why we are abuilding of a new gaol. And that is why we ain't so crowded Monday to Saturday, when the men are abuilding," she said, rattling it off.

He picked one fact out of this. "Who is John Howard?"

"Fellow wrote this report on the Bridewells, I already told ye that," said Lizzie Lock. "Do not ask me more for I do not know no more. Would not know that except it set Gloucester by the ears—the Bishop and his grand College and the beadles. So they got a Act of Parliament to build a new gaol. Supposed to be finished in another three years, but I will not be here to see it."

"Expecting to be released?" asked Richard, whose smile was growing. He liked her, though he was not attracted to her in the slightest; just that her beady black eyes had not given up on life.

"Lord bless ye, no!" she said with great good cheer. "I went down for the sus. per coll. two year ago."

"The what?"

"Hangman's rope, Richard my love. Sus. per coll., which is what the gent who swings ye writes in his official book as soon as ye've stopped kicking. In London, 'tis called the nubbing cheat."

"But you are still alive, I see."

"Got reprieved Christmas before last. Transportation for seven years. So far, ain't been transported nowhere, but 'tis bound to happen."

"From what I hear, Lizzie, there is nowhere to transport you. Though there was talk about Africa in Bristol."

"Ye're a Bristol man! Thought so. Ye've a twang, not a burr."

"Willy and I are both Bristol men. We came in today by wagon."

"And ye're a gentleman," she said, tone wondering.

"Of sorts only, Lizzie."

She poked a finger at the wooden box. "What is in there?"

"My belongings, though for how long is difficult to say. I note that some of these folk look sick, but most look a lot spryer than anyone in the Bristol Newgate."

"Because of the new goal abuilding, and Old Mother Hubbard's vegetable patches. Those who work get fed proper. 'Tis cheaper to use the prisoners than hire Gloucester laborers—something to do with a Act of Parliament letting prisoners labor. Us women got jobs too, mostly gardening."

"Old Mother Hubbard?"

"Hubbard the head gaoler. Important thing is not to sicken—quarter rations if ye do. Gaol fever runs riot here. Lost eight to the smallpox over Christmas of eighty-three." She patted the wooden box. "Do not fret about it, Richard my love. I will look after it—for a consideration."

"What consideration?" he asked warily.

"Protection. I earn full rations by darning and mending, and a few pence too. Ye might say I rent my services in a mode the parson do not disapprove of. But the men are always after me, especially that Isaac Rogers." She pointed to a big, burly fellow who looked a genuine villain. "A bad lot, that one!"

"What did he do?"

"Highway robbery. Brandy and chests of tea."

"And what did you do?"

She giggled and flicked her hat. "I pinched the most wondrous silk hat! I cannot help myself, Richard—I *love* hats!"

"Do you mean they sentenced you to death for stealing a *hat?*"

The black eyes twinkled; she hung her head. " 'Twas not my first offense," she said. "I told ye, I love hats."

"Enough to swing for, Lizzie?"

"Well, I did not think of that when I pinched 'em, did I?"

He held out his hand to Lizzie for the second time. "Ye've a bargain, my girl. Consider yourself under my protection, in return for which I expect you to guard my box with your life. And do not try to pick its locks, Lizzie Lock! There are no hats inside, I swear." He got to his feet by shoving people aside. "If I can move through the crowd, I intend to explore the full extent of my new domain. Mind my box."

Fifteen minutes were enough to complete the tour. A number of small cells led off the common-room, unlit, unventilated and unpopulated, though two of them held privies. A set of crumbling stairs led to regions aloft, barred by a gate. The debtors' common-room, also barred from the felons by a gate, was ten by twenty feet, but, like the cells, it contained no kind of window or vent and would have lain in stygian darkness were it not that its inmates had broken down a section of wall at its top to admit light and air. The yard lay beyond that. Though they had more space, the debtors' lot was more invidious than that of the felons'; they did not work, and so subsisted on quarter rations. Like the inmates of the Bristol Newgate, they were emaciated, partially clothed in rags, and apathetic.

He returned to the felons' common-room to find Lizzie Lock vigorously defending his box from Isaac Rogers the highwayman.

"Leave her and my belongings alone," said Richard curtly.

"Make me!" said Rogers with a snarl, shaping up.

"Oh, piss off, do! Ye're a tub of lard I would eat at one sitting," said Richard, his tone as weary as it was unintimidated. "Just go away! I am a peaceful man by name of Richard Morgan, and this lady is under my protection." He put his arm about Lizzie's waist while she shrank against him gleefully. "There are other women here. Bother one of them."

Rogers weighed him carefully and decided discretion was the better part of valor. Had Morgan betrayed a trace of fear it would have gone differently, but the bugger had no fear in him. Too calm, too contained. Fellows like that fought like cats, teeth and nails and boots, and they were agile. So he slouched away with a shrug, leaving Richard to sit on his box and perch Lizzie on his knee.

"When do they feed us?" he asked. What a clever female she was! No fear that she would misinterpret his gallantry. It suited Lizzie Lock to have a protector who did not desire her.

"Soon for dinner," she answered. "It being Sunday, we get new bread, meat, a hunk of cheese, turnips and cabbage. No butter or jam, but there is plenty to eat. Felons got their own kitchen, through there"—she pointed to the far end of the room—"and Cook will issue ye with a wooden trencher and a tin mug. Supper is more bread, small beer and cabbage soup."

"Is there a taproom?"

"What, in *here*? Fond of the booze, are ye, Richard my love?"

"No. I drink naught but small beer or water. I wondered."

"Simmons—his nickname is Happy and he is an under-gaoler—will bring booze in for ye for a penny profit. That is when ye'll have to watch yon Isaac. He is savage in his cups, is Ike."

"Drunk men are clumsy, I have dealt with them all my life."

By the end of February there was nothing that Richard did not know about Gloucester Gaol, including all its felon inmates, whom proximity rendered intimates rather than acquaintances. Fourteen of them were up for trial at the Lent assizes; the rest were already judged and sentenced, mostly to transportation. And of those fourteen, three were women—Mary (known as Maisie) Harding, charged with receiving stolen goods—Betty Mason, charged with stealing a purse containing fifteen guineas from a house in Henbury—and Bess Parker, charged with housebreaking in North Nibley and the theft of two linen garments. Bess Parker had formed a firm relationship with a 1783 felon, Ned Pugh; Betty Mason had bewitched an under-gaoler named Johnny. Both were due to have babies at any moment.

What a fine little world is ours! Richard reflected wryly. A common-room one can hardly stand up in, and, when a gaoler opens the gate, a disgusting men's dormitory up the steps. He had become quite case-hardened; stripped and bathed at the pump in an airless black cell without regard for the women, washed his bum rags under it with calm unimpaired, and filtered his drinking water through his dripstone under the gaze of more than three dozen pairs of incredulous eyes. A degree of selfishness had crept into him, for he made no attempt to share his purified water with either Lizzie or Willy; the dripstone was slow, taking an hour to produce two pints of filtered water. Nor did he share his soap or rags. What few pence he disbursed from his hoard went to Maisie, the laundress, for washing his underdrawers, shirts and stockings; as for breeches and other outer wear—well, they simply stank of sweat.

Maisie was the only one of the women without a protector and dispensed her favors gratis, whereas two or three of the others could be had for a mug of gin. When the urge visited a couple, they lay down on whatever vacant piece of floor they could find, or, failing that, stood against the wall. Not an erotic business, as clothes stayed on and the most a curious individual could see was a glimpse of a fleshy pole or hairy mound, though usually not even that. What fascinated Richard most was that none of the copulating happened in one of the adjacent cells; everybody seemed terrified of the dark.

Bess Parker and Betty Mason broke their waters on the felons' common-room floor early in March and were carried off to the female dormitory to finish the birthing process in that foul place. Two other women were nursing babies born in Gloucester Gaol, and Maisie had a toddler she had brought into gaol with her. Most of the babes died at or soon after birth. Toddlers were a miracle.

But there was plenty of work to do, a blessing. Richard was put to carrying limestone blocks from the castle dock to the new prison, which gave him both fresh air and a chance to look around. Gloucester's tiny port was just north of the castle precinct on the same bank of the Severn, which was navigable to this point for small snows and large barges. One of the town's two foundries made church bells, whereas the other contented itself with small iron items readily sold in the neighborhood. They gave out smoke, but not nearly enough to foul the air, which Richard found sweet and crisp. Nor did the Severn look fouled, though the endemic gaol fever indicated that the gaol's water source was contaminated. Or else it was spread by the fleas and lice, which Richard dealt with by scrubbing his filthy pallet with oil of tar and keeping himself and his clothes picked over constantly. Oh, God, to be clean! To live clean! To have a meed of privacy!

The gaol fever broke out scant days after Richard and Willy were admitted, which brought the population of the common-room down from forty to twenty; only a small influx of new faces kept the number due to be tried at fourteen.

Time and shared work had introduced him to all the men, some of whom he found himself able to like well enough to call them friends: William Whiting, James Price and Joseph Long. They were all on the Lent assizes list with him.

Whiting stood accused of stealing a wether sheep at the same place had harbored Richard and Willy amid the straw of the Stars and Plough, Almondsbury.

"Absolute rubbish!" said Whiting, who was a regular wag. No one was quite sure if what he said could be taken seriously. "Why on earth would *I* steal a sheep? All I wanted to do was fuck it. Would've had it back in its pen the next morning and no one the wiser. Except that the shepherd was not asleep."

"Desperate, Bill?" asked Richard without cracking a smile.

"Not so much desperate as—well, I plain like fucking, and a sheep's arse feels much the same as a woman's quim," said Whiting chirpily. "Smells the same, at any rate, and 'tis a bit tighter. Besides, sheep don't answer back. See, ye stick its back legs in the tops of your boots and away ye go."

"Whether it is bestiality or sheep stealing, Bill, ye're up for the rope. But why *Almondsbury?* Another eight miles and ye could have found a thousand whores of either sex in Bristol—they do not answer back either."

"Could not wait, just could not wait. Had the loveliest face—reminded me of a parson I once knew."

Richard gave up.

Jimmy Price was a Somerset yokel with a poor head for rum. He and a companion had robbed three houses in Westbury-upon-Trim and stolen a large quantity of beef, pork and mutton, three hats, two coats, an embroidered waistcoat, riding boots, a musket and two green silk umbrellas. His confederate, whom he called Peter, had since perished of the gaol fever. He was unrepentant because he considered his conduct blameless. "Didn't mean to do it—don't remember doing it," he explained. "What would I need with two green silk umbrellas? Ain't nowhere to sell them in Westbury. Wasn't hungry neither, and none of the clothes fit me or Peter. And never took no powder or shot for the musket."

The third of the trio, whom Richard pitied deeply, was far sadder. Weak-willed, weak-witted, Joey Long had stolen a silver watch in Slimbridge. "I were drunk," he said simply, "and it were so pretty."

Of course Richard had answered the same sort of questions; the felons' common-room was a kind of Grand Larceny Club. His explanation was always brief: "Extortion and grand larceny. A note of hand for five hundred pounds and a steel watch." A reply which earned him much respect, even from Isaac Rogers.

"A useful term, grand larceny," he said to Bill Whiting as they lugged limestone blocks; Whiting was literate and intelligent. "For me, a steel watch. For poor Bess Parker, a couple of workaday linen shifts worth sixpence, if that. For Rogers, four gallons of brandy and forty-five hundredweight of best hyson tea at a pound a pound retail. Over five thousand in plunder. Yet we are all charged with grand larceny. It is senseless."

"Rogers will dance," was Whiting's comment.

"Lizzie got the sus. per coll. for stealing three hats."

"Repeated offenses, Richard," said Whiting with a laugh. "She was supposed to reform her ways and never do it again. The trouble is that we are most of us drunk at the time. Blame the booze."

* * *

The two Cousins James arrived in Gloucester by hired post chaise on Monday, the 21st of March. As they could find no decent accommodation in the town itself, they ended in putting up at the Harvest Moon, in the barn of which Richard and Willy had spent their last night before entering Gloucester Gaol.

Like Richard, they had confidently expected to find the new prison more bearable by far than the old. Besides, they had not imagined that any prison could be worse than the Bristol Newgate.

"It is pretty fair at the moment, Cousin James, Cousin James," said Richard, surprised at their horror when conducted into the felons' common-room. "The gaol fever has cleared it out greatly." He had pecked each of them on the mouth, but would not let them enfold him in hugs. "I stink," he said.

A table and benches had suddenly appeared after the Sunday service; warned that the Parliament was paying severe attention to John Howard's report on debtors' prisons and that in consequence the Baron Eyre might ask to inspect his premises, the head gaoler had responded by doing what he could.

"How is Father?" was Richard's first question.

"Not well enough to make the journey, but better all the same. He sends his love," said Cousin James-the-druggist. "And prayers."

"Mum?"

"Herself. She sends her love and prayers too."

The Cousins James were amazed at how well Richard looked. His coat, waistcoat and breeches were very smelly and shabby, but his shirt and stockings were clean, as were the rags padding his ankle irons. The hair was cropped as short as it had been in the Newgate and showed no sprinkling of grey; his nails were clean and well trimmed, his face freshly shaven; and his skin showed not a single line. The eyes were remote and stern, a little terrifying.

"Is there any news of William Henry?"

"No, Richard, not a peep."

"Then all this does not matter."

"Of course it does!" said Cousin James-of-the-clergy strongly. "We have engaged counsel for you—not a Bristol man, alas. These county assize courts do not welcome foreigners. Cousin Henry-the-lawyer instructed us to seek out a proper Gloucester assizes man. There are two judges, one a Baron of the superior court of the Royal Exchequer—that is Sir James Eyre—and the other a Baron of the superior court of Common Law—that is Sir George Nares."

"Have you seen Ceely Trevillian?"

"No," said Cousin James-the-druggist, "but I am told he is lodging at the best inn in town. This is a big event for Gloucester—conducted with great ceremony, I hear, at least on the morrow, when everybody parades through the town to the city hall, which is also the court house. The two judges stay in special lodgings nearby, but most of their serjeants, barristers and clerks put up at inns. Tomorrow the Grand Jury sits, but it is merely custom. Ye'll all go to trial, so your attorney says."

"Who is he?"

"Mr. James Hyde, of Chancery Lane, London. He is a barrister who travels the Oxford circuit with Barons Eyre and Nares."

"When is he coming to see me?"

"He will not do that, Richard. His duties are in the court. Do not forget that he cannot present your side of the story. He listens to the witnesses and tries to find a chink in their testimony for cross-examination. As he does not know who the witnesses are nor what they will say, it is useless his seeing you. We have briefed him very adequately. He is very down-to-earth and able."

"What is his fee for so much work?"

"Twenty guineas."

"And ye've paid him already?"

"Aye."

It is a travesty, thought Richard, producing a warm smile and squeezing the arm to either side of him. "You are so very good to me. I cannot tell you how much I appreciate your kindness."

"You are family, Richard," said Cousin James-of-the-clergy, sounding surprised.

"I have brought you a new suit and a new pair of shoes," the apothecary James announced. "And a wig. Ye cannot go into court crop-skulled. The women—your mother, Ann and Elizabeth—have sent ye a whole box of underdrawers, shirts, stockings and rags."

To which Richard made no reply; his family had prepared for the worst, not the best. For if the day after tomorrow were to see him set free, why did he need a whole box of new clothes?

The sounds of Gloucester celebrating the beginning of its assizes came clearly to Richard's ears the next day as he lumped his blocks—the blare of trumpets and horns, the roll of drums, cheers and oohs of admiration, music from a band of drums and fifes, the sonorous singsong of voices orating in fluent Latin. The mood of Gloucester was festive.

The mood within the prison was dour. No one, Richard realized when he looked at his sixteen fellow accused (the tally had risen again), truly expected any verdict other than "guilty." Two others could afford counsel: Bill Whiting and Isaac Rogers. Mr. James Hyde was their man too, which led Richard to assume that Mr. Hyde was the only candidate.

"Do none of us hope to get off?" Richard asked Lizzie.

Veteran of three trials in these same assizes, Lizzie looked blank. "We do not get off, Richard," she said simply. "How can we? The evidence is given by the prosecutor and witnesses, and the jury believes what it hears. Almost all of us are guilty, though I have known several who were the victims of lies. It is no excuse to be drunk, and if we had friends in high places, we would not be in Gloucester Gaol."

"Is anyone ever acquitted?"

"Perhaps one, if the assizes are big enough." She sat on his knee and smoothed his hair much as she would have a child's. "Do not get your hopes up, Richard my love. Being in the dock is all the damnation the jury needs. Just wear your wig, please."

When Richard shuffled off at dawn on the 23rd of March, hands in manacles and everything chained to his waist, he wore his new suit, a very plain affair of black coat, black waistcoat and black breeches, with his new black shoes on his feet and clean padding on his wrists and ankles. But he was not wearing the wig; the feel of the thing was too horrible. Seven others went with him: Willy Insell, Betty Mason, Bess Parker, Jimmy Price, Joey Long, Bill Whiting and Sam Day, a seventeen-year-old from Dursley charged with stealing two pounds of yarn from a weaver.

They were ushered into the city hall through a back door and hustled down some stairs to the cellars without gaining a glimpse of the arena in which combat was verbal but death possible just the same.

"How long does it take?" Bess Parker whispered to Richard, eyes big with apprehension; she had lost her child of the gaol fever two days after he was born, and it was a grief to her.

"Not long, is my guess. The court will not sit for more than six hours in a day, if that, yet there are eight of us waiting to be tried. It must happen like a butcher turning out sausages."

"Oh, I am so frightened!" cried Betty Mason, whose girl-child had been born dead. A grief to her.

Jimmy Price was taken away first, but had not returned when Bess Parker's turn came; only after Betty Mason had gone did those remaining in the cell realize that once a prisoner's hearing had concluded, the prisoner apparently went straight back to the gaol.

Sam Day was marched off, leaving Richard and Willy in the cell with Joey Long and Bill Whiting. Several hours went by.

"Dinner time for their lordships," said the irrepressible Whiting. He licked his lips. "Roast goose, roast beef, roast mutton, flummeries and flans and flawns, pastries and puddens and pies—it looks well for us, Richard! Their lordships' bellies will be full and their wits fuddled with claret and port."

"I think that bodes ill," said Richard, in no mood for jollity. "Their gout will play up, so will their guts."

"What a Job's comforter ye are!"

He and Willy were last of all, taken upstairs at half past three by the timepiece on the wall of the court room. The well from the bowels of the hall opened directly into the dock, where he and Willy stood (it had no seats) blinking at the brightness. A javelin man kept them company, his regalia medieval and his pose lethargic. Though the room was not enormous, it did have audience galleries on high; those on its floor all apparently had a role to play in the drama. The two justices sat on a tall dais clad in all the majesty of fur-trimmed crimson robes and full-bottomed wigs. Other court officials sat around and below them, while yet others moved about—which one was his counsel, Mr. James Hyde? Richard had no idea. The jury of twelve men stood in what looked a little like a sheepfold, easing their sore feet by surreptitiously stepping. Richard was aware of their plight, which figured large in every Free Man's resentment of jury duty from the Tweed to the Channel: no sitting down on the job and no compensation for the loss of a day's wages. Which encouraged the jury to get its business over and done with as quickly as the judge could say "Gallows!"

Mr. John Trevillian Ceely Trevillian was sitting in the company of a formidable-looking man clothed in the garb of a participant in the drama—robe, tie-back wig, buckles, badges. A different Ceely than any Richard had so far seen; this Ceely was soberly clad in the finest black cloth from head to foot, wore a conservative wig, black kid gloves and the mien of an amiable idiot. Of the mincing laughingstock or the brisk excise defrauder, no sign whatsoever. The Ceely who sat in Gloucester's city hall was the quintessential dupe. Upon Richard's entry into the dock he had emitted a shrill little squeak of terror and shrunk against his companion, after which he looked anywhere but in the direction of the dock. At law, Ceely himself was the prosecutor, but his counsel did the work, addressing the jury to tell it of the heinous crime the two felons in the dock had committed; Richard put his manacled hands on the railing, set his feet firmly on the ancient board floor, and listened as the prosecutor extolled the virtues—and idiocies—of this poor harmless person, Mr. Trevillian. There would be, he understood, no miracles in Gloucester today.

Ceely told his story amid sobs, gulps and long pauses to find words, rolling his eyes in his head, sometimes covering his face with his ungloved hands, agitated, trembling, twitching. At the end of it, the jury, impressed by his mental impoverishment and his material prosperity, clearly deemed him the victim of a lewd woman and her irate husband. Which in itself did not necessarily indicate that a deliberate felony had occurred, nor that the note of hand for £500, though extricated by force, was true extortion.

The job of establishing that fell to two witnesses, Joice the hairdresser's wife, who listened through her wall, and Mr. Dangerfield in the other house, who saw through his wall. Mrs. Joice's hearing was superlative, and Mr. Dangerfield was able to see a 360° world through a quarter-inch crack. One heard phrases like "Damned bitch! Where is your candle?" and "I will blow your brains out, you damned rascal!", while the other saw Morgan and Insell threatening Ceely with a hammer and forcing him to write at a desk.

Mr. James Hyde, acting for Richard, turned out to be a tall, thin man who looked much like a raven. He cross-examined well, it seemed with the object of establishing that the three houses near Jacob's Well contained a nest of gossips who had actually heard and seen extremely little and constructed their stories upon what Ceely had said to them in the lane afterward—followed by the Dangerfields' sheltering him in their house with Mrs. Joice in attendance.

On one point Ceely could make little headway: the witnesses both testified that Richard had shouted through the door that Mr. Trevillian could have his watch back after Richard had obtained satisfaction. That sounded very much like a wronged husband, even to the jury.

It is ridiculous! thought Richard as the testimony went on and that trip to the Black Horse to fetch liquid refreshments was shifted to the following day. If Willy and I could speak for ourselves, we could establish easily that at the time we were both in the Lamb Inn courtyard. There is only one coach to Bath and it goes at noon and I was supposed to be in Bath, even Ceely says that. Yet they all say I was in Clifton!

During Mrs. Joice's testimony it came out that she had overheard Richard and Annemarie plotting Annemarie's assignation with Ceely in their hall—as if, thought Richard, anyone with criminal intent would choose to have such a conversation right next to a thin partition! But the very mention of the word "plot" caused both judge and jury to stiffen.

Mrs. Mary Meredith testified that she had seen the two men in the dock and a woman near Jacob's Well as she was returning home about eight o'clock in the evening, and recounted hearing talk between them about a watch and Ceely's having to go to law to get it back. Amazing! At eight o'clock at the end of September no one could have seen facial features farther away than a yard, as Mr. Hyde reminded Mrs. Meredith, much to her confusion.

A faint ray of hope began to suffuse Richard's gloom; no matter how hard the prosecution tried, the jury still had not made up its mind whether what had happened was deliberate or the result of anger at being cuckolded.

Cousin James-the-druggist and Cousin James-of-the-clergy were called as character witnesses on Richard's behalf; though the prosecutor made much of their close relationship to the accused, there could be no doubt that two such pillars of probity made a profound impression on the jury. The trouble was that this case, thanks to a defending counsel, was dragging out toward an hour in length, and the jurymen were dying to get off their feet. No one wanted a long case at the end of the day, including the judges.

Mr. James Hyde called Robert Jones as a character witness.

Richard jumped. Robert Jones testifying on his behalf? The smarmer who sucked up to William Thorne and had told Thorne of Willy's visit to the Excise?

"Do you know the accused, Mr. Jones?" Mr. Hyde asked.

"Oh, aye, both of them."

"Are they decent, law-abiding men, Mr. Jones?"

"Oh, aye, very."

"Have they, to your knowledge, ever run foul of the Law?"

"Oh, nay, never."

"Are ye privy to any information—apart from the general gossip which seems rife there—about the events at Jacob's Well on the thirtieth of September last?"

"Oh, aye, that I am, sir."

"To what effect?"

"Eh?"

"What do you know, Mr. Jones?"

"Well, to start with, Mrs. Joice ain't no missus. She is just a whore who moved in with Mr. Joice."

"Mrs. Joice is not on trial, Mr. Jones. Confine yourself to the events."

"I talked to her and to Mr. Dangerfield. Mr. Dangerfield took me to the place upstairs in his house where he saw through, but he said he could not hear nothing, and what he saw was mighty little. Mrs. Joice said she did not hear nor see a thing."

The prosecuting attorney was frowning; Mr. Trevillian, the real prosecutor, sat looking as if this were all far too much for his sadly limited understanding.

The prosecutor's attorney elected to cross-examine.

"When did this conversation with Mrs. Joice and Mr. Dangerfield occur, Mr. Jones? Please be explicit."

"Eh?"

"Absolutely clear."

"Oh, aye. Happened the next day when I went to see Willy—Mr. Insell the accused, that is—at Jacob's Well. Heard the story from him and asked the neighbors what they had seen and heard. Mrs. Joice—who *ain't* a missus!—said she did not hear or see nothing. Mr. Dangerfield showed me the place he saw from, but when I looked, I could not see nothing."

Mrs. Joice was recalled, and explained that naturally she had denied seeing or hearing anything next door—she was not the sort of woman to encourage snoopers!

Mr. Dangerfield was recalled, and repeated that he had never said he could hear, only see.

"Call Mr. James Hyde!" said the prosecuting attorney loudly. Richard's counsel jumped, looked startled. "Not you, my learned colleague. Mr. James Hyde, servant to Mr. Trevillian's mother."

This James Hyde was a small, sandy man in his fifties with the unobtrusive and faintly obsequious air of a senior house servant. He stated that Mr. Dangerfield had come to see him on the first of October and informed him that a Robert Jones had told him that for the sum of five guineas, he could prove that Morgan had plotted with his wife to rob Mr. Trevillian.

The jury stirred and muttered, Sir James Eyre the judge sat up straighter.

"A plot, Mr. Hyde?"

"Yes, sir, a plot."

"Did it involve Mr. Insell too?"

"Mr. Dangerfield did not say it did. Morgan and Mrs. Morgan."

Recalled, Mr. Dangerfield admitted that he had gone to Mrs. Maurice Trevillian's house to see his friend Mr. James Hyde and told Hyde of Robert Jones's offer.

On re-examination, Mr. Robert Jones said that all of this was true. He knew Mr. Dangerfield was friendly with the Trevillian household, and he was a bit short of money, so. . . .

"What of this plot between Morgan and his wife to rob Mr. Trevillian? Did it exist?" asked the prosecuting attorney.

"Oh, aye," said Robert Jones cheerfully. "But Willy were not in on it, on my oath."

"Ye're on your oath, Mr. Jones."

"Oh, aye, so I am!"

"How did ye know of this plot?"

"Mrs. Morgan told me."

More stirs from the jury and judge.

"When?"

"At—oh, a bit after noon on the day it happened, when I came to see Willy the first time. Did not see him, ran into Mrs. Morgan instead. She said she were expecting Mr. Trevillian, but that he would have to come back later, after Morgan had gone to Bath. She were real pleased, said when Mr. Trevillian did come, Morgan would pounce on him for having a bit of slap-and-tickle with her—you know, the sort of thing husbands do when they find out they are wearing horns. She said her husband thought they would get five hundred pounds out of the silly clunch, he were so simple."

Sir James Eyre looked in the direction of the dock. "Morgan, what have you to say about this plot with your wife?"

"There was no plot, your lordship. I am innocent," Richard said strongly. "There was no plot."

His lordship pulled the corners of his mouth down. "Where is Mrs. Morgan?" he demanded of, it seemed, anyone in the court room. "She ought to be in the dock with her husband, so much is clear." He shot a fierce look at Richard. "Where is your wife, Morgan?"

"I do not know, your lordship. I have never seen her from that day to this," Richard answered steadily.

The prosecuting attorney made much of the plot and little of the absence of the co-conspirator, Mrs. Morgan. And when Sir James Eyre directed the jury, he too made much of the plot.

The twelve good men and true looked at each other in enormous relief. In less than a minute they could go home. It had been a very long, hard day; Gloucester's Free Men were nowhere near enough to staff separate juries for each accused. There was no deliberation. Richard Morgan was found not guilty of stealing a watch, but guilty of grand larceny in the matter of extortion. William Insell was found not guilty on all counts.

Sir James Eyre turned his gaze to the dock, wherein Willy had sunk to his knees, weeping, and the shorn Richard Morgan—what a villain!—stood staring at something a great deal farther off than Gloucester's city hall.

"Richard Morgan, I hereby sentence ye to seven years' transportation to Africa. William Insell, ye may go free." He banged his gavel to wake Sir George Nares up. "The court will come together again at ten of the clock tomorrow morning. God save the King."

"God save the King," everybody echoed dutifully.

The javelin man prodded the prisoners; Richard turned to descend into the dock well without bothering to look in Mr. John Trevillian Ceely Trevillian's direction. Ceely had passed from his life as all things passed. The Ceelys did not matter.

And by the time he had plodded halfway back to Gloucester Gaol Richard found himself truly happy; he had just realized that very shortly he would be rid of Weeping Willy.

The sun was nudging the western horizon when Richard and Willy—still weeping, presumably from joy—passed through the castle gate under escort by two gaolers. Here Richard was detained, Willy sent onward. Is this the beginning of the difference between a man awaiting trial and a convicted felon? His gaoler indicated the head gaoler's house; Richard moved off as passively as he did everything under an official eye. After three months he knew all the gaolers, good, bad and indifferent, though he avoided striking up any sort of acquaintance with them and never called any by his name.

He was ushered into a comfortable-looking room furnished as a place for social congress. It contained three people: Mr. James Hyde the attorney and the Cousins James. Both the Cousins James were in tears and Mr. Hyde looked mournful. In fact, thought Richard as the door was closed behind him with his escort on its far side, they look worse than I feel. This has come as no surprise, I knew it would happen thus in my bones. Justice is blind, but not in the romantic sense they taught us at Colston's. It is blind to individuals and human motives; its dispensers believe the obvious and are incapable of subtleties. All of that witness testimony from the Jacob's Well people had its roots in gossip; Ceely merely entered the gossip chain and contributed the right mite. Robert Jones he paid—well, he paid all of them, but save for Jones he was able to disguise his payments as thoughtful gifts to folk who know him and his family and its servants. Oh, they understood! But on oath they could deny had anybody asked. Jones he bought outright.

Or else Annemarie fed Jones the story of the plot. In which case she belonged to Ceely body and soul, was involved in the conspiracy from its beginning. If that is so, then she lay in wait for me and all of it was a fabulous lie. I have been convicted on the testimony of a witness who did not appear: Annemarie Latour. And the judge, having asked me where she was, did not follow through.

His silence after he entered the room enabled the Cousins James to mop their eyes and compose themselves. Mr. James Hyde took the time to examine Richard Morgan at closer quarters than the court room had allowed. A striking fellow, big and tall—a pity he had not worn a wig, it would have transformed him. The case had hinged upon whether the accused was a decent man insulted beyond bearing at finding his wife in bed with another man, or whether the accused had, so to speak, cashed in on the opportunity his wife's infidelity had offered. Of course he knew from the Cousins James that the woman was not his client's wife, but had not made capital of it because, were she known as a mere whore, the case would have been blacker. It was the unveiling of a plot had done for Richard Morgan; judges were notoriously prejudiced against accused felons who committed their crimes with cold-blooded forethought. And juries found as the judge instructed them to find.

Cousin James-the-druggist broke the long silence, handkerchief tucked away. "We have bought this room and all the time we want with you," he said. "Richard, I am so sorry! It was a complete fabrication—every one of those people, however menial, was a part of Ceely's circle."

"What I want to know," said Richard, sitting down, "is why Mr. Benjamin Fisher of the Excise did not appear for me as a character witness? Had he, things might have gone very differently."

The Reverend James's mouth compressed to a thin line. "He was too busy, he said, to make a journey of eighty miles. The truth is that he is busy concluding a deal with Thomas Cave, and cares not about the fate of his chief witness."

"However," said Mr. Hyde, who looked far less imposing out of his attorney's gear, "ye may be sure, Mr. Morgan, that when I write your letter of appeal to Lord Sydney, the Secretary of State for Home Affairs, I will have a letter from Mr. Fisher attached. But not Benjamin. His brother John, the Commander."

"Can I not appeal in a court?" Richard asked.

"No. Your appeal takes the form of a letter begging the King's mercy. I will draft it as soon as I return to London."

"Have some port, Richard," said Cousin James-the-druggist.

"I have had naught to eat today, so I dare not."

The door opened and a woman brought in a tray bearing bread, butter, grilled sausages, parsnips, cabbage and a tankard. She put it down without any expression on her face, bobbed a curtsey to the gentlemen, and departed.

"Eat, Richard. The head gaoler told me that supper has been served already in the gaol, so I asked for food."

"Thank you, Cousin James, truly thank you," said Richard with feeling, and dug in. But the first piece of sausage on his knife's point was subjected to a long sniff before being gingerly tasted; satisfied, Richard chewed with gusto and carved off another slice. "Sausages," he said, his mouth full, "are usually made from rotten meat when they are served to felons."

His meal finished, Richard did sip at the glass of port, then grimaced. "It is so long since I have had sweet things that I seem to have lost my appetite for them. We get no butter with our bread, let alone jam."

"Oh, Richard!" chorused the Cousins James.

"Do not feel sorry for me. My life is not over because I must spend the next seven years of it under some form or other of imprisonment," said Richard, rising to his feet. "I am six-and-thirty and I will be six months short of four-and-forty when my sentence is done. The men of our family are long-lived, and I intend to keep my health and my strength. Those five hundred pounds from the Excise Office are mine no matter what happens, and I will write to the lackadaisical Mr. Benjamin Fisher directing that he pay them to you, Cousin James-the-druggist. Take what I have cost ye out of them, and use the rest to keep me supplied with dripstones, rags, clothes and shoes. With some to the Reverend James for books, including those he has already given me. I am not idle here, and my labor means that I am fed. But on Sundays I read. A blessing."

"Remember, Richard, that we love you dearly," said Cousin James-the-druggist, hugging and kissing him.

"And we pray for you," said Cousin James-of-the-clergy.

Willy Insell was the only prisoner acquitted at the assizes held in Gloucester during that March of 1785. Six were sentenced to be hanged: Maisie Harding for receiving stolen goods, Betty Mason for stealing fifteen guineas, Sam Day for stealing two pounds of weaving yarn, Bill Whiting for stealing a sheep, Isaac Rogers for highway robbery, and Joey Long for stealing a silver watch. The rest, some ten in all, were sentenced to seven years' transportation to Africa, wherein His Britannic Majesty possessed no formal colony. Richard was well aware that had the Cousins James not testified as to his character, he too would have gotten the rope; though Bristol was far away, two of its leading citizens could not be quite ignored.

More importantly, how were they all going to fit into this tiny place? Within a week the answer was manifest: nine of the prisoners died of a malignant quinsy in the throat, as did the remaining children and ten debtors on the Bridewell side.

The situation in England's prisons was absolutely desperate, which had not prevented the Gloucester judges from handing down their drastic sentences.

Between 1782 and 1784 three attempts had been made to deliver felons to America. The Swift was turned away on her first voyage, though some of her transportees escaped, assisted to do so by the Americans. On her second voyage in August of 1783 she took 143 prisoners on board and sailed from the Thames for Nova Scotia. But she got no farther than Sussex, where her human cargo mutinied and beached the ship near Rye. After which they scattered to the four winds. Only 39 were recaptured; of those, six were hanged and the rest sentenced to transportation to America for life. Just as if transportation to America were still an option, so slowly did the mills of government grind, not to mention the judicial mills.

In March of 1784 a third attempt to unload transportees in America was tried. This time the ship was the Mercury and the destination was Georgia (which, along with the other twelve newly united states, had already served stern notice to England that it would not, repeat, *would not* accept any transported felons). The Mercury took 179 men, women and children felons aboard and sailed from London. The mutiny occurred off the coast of Devon and the Mercury fetched up near Torbay. Some were still on board when recaptured, most had fled; 108 all told were apprehended, a few having ranged as far afield as Bristol. Though many of them were sentenced to hang, only two actually were. The political climate was shifting.

The Recovery in January of 1785 represented the last attempt of a disorganized nature to relieve gaol overcrowding; she took a cargo of felons to the equatorial wetlands of Africa and dumped them ashore without guards, supervision or much by way of necessities to survive. They died hideously, and the African experiment was never repeated. Clearly future transportees would have to be cared for in ways less provocative of public scandal. Between the prison reformers John Howard and Jeremy Bentham, the Quaker agitators against slavery and African expansion in general, and the two new names of Thomas Clarkson and William Wilberforce looming on the horizon, Mr. William Pitt the Younger's fledgling government deemed it wise to provide no ammunition for social crusaders of any kind. Especially since Bentham and Wilberforce were important men in Whig Westminster. The extra taxes economic necessity had made unavoidable were odious enough. Mr. William Pitt the Younger owned one quality in common with a convicted felon named Richard Morgan: he intended to survive for many years to come. And in the meantime, Jeremy Bentham was allowed to tinker with the plans for the new Gloucester Gaol, while Lord Sydney of the Home Department was instructed to find somewhere—anywhere!—to dump England's huge surplus of convicts.

In the as yet unmodified Gloucester Gaol disease and proximity worked their wills.

Weeping Willy Insell, still weeping, was discharged, a free man, on the 5th of April. On the same day Mr. James Hyde the attorney forwarded the Humble Petition of Richard Morgan to Lord Sydney, together with a letter from Mr. John Fisher, Commander of the Bristol Excise Office. Lord Sydney's indefatigable and highly efficient secretary, Mr. Evan Nepean, forwarded it on the 15th of April to the chambers of Sir James Eyre in Bedford Row; it would be up to him, the presiding judge in Morgan's case, to review that case and advise Lord Sydney as to whether the King's Mercy might or might not be extended to Richard Morgan. All very prompt, given that the trial had taken place on the 23rd of March. But there in Bedford Row the Humble Petition of Richard Morgan moldered; Mr. Baron Sir James Eyre was so busy that he had not the time to deal with any petitions, humble or otherwise.

In late July a letter came from Mr. Jem Thistlethwaite, who had disappeared from his lodgings and the London scene at much the same date as William Henry had vanished. Richard took it from Old Mother Hubbard with a sinking sensation in his chest; he would now have to open up that wound and air it. From the time that he had entered the Bristol Newgate it had been buried beneath conscious thought. Though what he had not realized was that his blotting out of William Henry had generated his determination to survive, even spurred him to perform the rituals he had established for himself, the rituals of purification which set him apart from all his fellows and caused them to regard him as somewhere between untouchable and mad. Why survive? To get through these seven years in a fit state to resume his search for William Henry, buried deep in his mind.

"Richard, I have just received a letter from your father, and I am utterly overset by his awful news. Getting through the last few gallons of my pipe of rum apparently caused me to *think* I had written to inform you of my intended flight, but that letter was either not written or went astray. I have been absent abroad since June of last year—Italy beckoned, I went running into her glorious embrace. It is our combined luck that upon my return a bare week ago, I was able to engage my old lodgings again, and so your father's pages reached me.

"I have always known that your life would not go as you thought it would—do you remember? You said, 'I was born in Bristol and I will die in Bristol.' Even as you said it, William Henry on your knee, I understood that it would not turn out so. I feared for you. And I, who am quite incapable of love, loved you then as I love you now. I just do not know the how or why, save that I see something in you that you do not realize is there.

"Of William Henry I will say no more than that you will never find him. He was not meant for this earth, but wherever he is, Richard, he is happy and at peace. The truly good have no business here, for they have nothing to learn. And even atheists like me can believe that sometimes these things happen because, did they not, the future would hold worse. Be glad for William Henry."

Richard put the letter down blindly, unable to see for the tears he had never been able to shed for William Henry. The other prisoners in the felons' common-room, including Lizzie Lock, made no attempt to approach him as he sat on his box and wept. How strange that it should be Jem Thistlethwaite who broke down the dam and let the torrent of grief flow free at last. But he was not right. William Henry would come back one day, he was not gone from this world forever.

He took up the letter again at dinner time the following day, having spoken to no one, and no one having spoken to him.

"I have carved a little niche for myself among the new breed of Whigs the presence of a young leader like Pitt has permitted.

Oligarchy, though it must ever rule in the Lords, has quit the Commons. Men of ideas abound, and Pitt, could he only find the money, would indulge them all.

"Getting to you yourself, the prospect of transportation is nonexistent. The African experiment was such a disaster that no one at Westminster has the courage—or the stupidity, miraculously enough—to revive it in any form. India has been suggested, and discarded the way a man would divest himself of a shirt made of snakes. Our outposts there are perilous and circumscribed. Though these are not the reasons behind the decision. *They* are firmly based in the opposition of the East India Company, which wants no felons jeopardizing its activities in Bengal and Cathay. The West Indies want none but negroes for indenture or slavery, and the English grip on places like Nova Scotia and Newfoundland does not allow transportation. The French hover. As do the Spanish in the south.

"So it would seem that you will serve out your time in Gloucester. Rest assured, however, that as soon as I hear anything, I will pass it on to you. Dick says that you have organized yourself with what Cousin James-the-druggist calls a 'cool kind of passion.' "

His answer had to wait until Sunday, when he took possession of the end of the table Old Mother Hubbard had installed in the felons' common-room just before the assizes and not removed after them, on the theory that it gave some felons an extra storey to perch upon when the place was over-crowded. As if it knew times of undercrowding.

A rash of visitors had broken out, envoys of a friend of Mr. Pitt's named Jeremy Bentham, at present touring Russia with the intention of writing a legal code for the Empress Catherine, but also the author of a treatise on the virtues and vices of setting felons to hard labor on public works, and exponent of a new kind of prison-in-the-round. His envoys popped in and out of the gaol inspecting it minutely and shaking their heads gloomily, gazing at the extensions its inmates were erecting and muttering about its all having to be pulled down again. Square! Why did the minds of men think square when round had no corners?

"I would rather be in Italy than in Gloucester Gaol, Jem, of that I can assure you.

"Of Ceely Trevillian and the affair at the distillery I can say no more than that I had the misfortune to run up against a man of birth and brain with no better outlet for his talents than intrigue, conspiracy and manipulation. He belongs on the stage, where he would have out-acted Kemp, Mrs. Siddons and Garrick combined. My only consolation is that when Cave and Thorne have arrived at a settlement with the Excise Office, I will be able to pay my debts and ensure that the Cousins James are not out of pocket when they buy me more things. I am never without a new book, though reading some of them is painful, as Clifton and the Hotwells keep cropping up. Two places I would rather not be reminded of, even by an Evelina or a Humphry Clinker. Not so much because of William Henry or Ceely as because of Annemarie Latour, with whom I sinned grievously. I can see the exasperation at my prudishness on your ugly face from here, but you were not there, nor could you have loved the man I became with her. Pleasure meant too much. Can you understand that? And if you cannot, how can I make you? I was a bull, a stallion. I *rutted,* I did not make love. And I loathed the object of my animality, who was an animal too.

"In Gloucester Gaol we are all in together, men and women—and children. Though it is a place of more fucking than suckling. The babies usually die, poor little creatures. And their poor mothers, who constantly carry and bear for nothing. At first the presence of the women appalled me, but as time has gone on I have come to realize that they make Gloucester Gaol endurable. Without them, we would be a collection of men brutalized beyond recognition.

"My own woman is Lizzie Lock, who has been here since the beginning of 1783 for stealing hats. When she sees one she fancies, she pinches it. Ours is a platonic friendship, we neither make love nor rut. I protect her from other men and she protects my box of belongings whilst I am laboring. Jem, if solvency permits it, would you find a grand hat for Lizzie? Red, or red and black, preferably with feathers. It would cast her into ecstasies.

"I must go. Even my elevated status in here does not guarantee tenure of so much table for a whole Sunday afternoon. That is the oddest part about it, Jem. For some reason (possibly that I am deemed mad) I notice that I am, for want of a better word, respected. Write to me sometimes, please."

* * *

Cousin James-the-druggist came to see Richard in August, loaded with a new dripstone, more rags and clothes, medicines, books.

"But keep your present dripstone going, Richard, for I see no evidence that it is tainting. The more spare stones ye have, the better, and I have brought ye a good stout sack for surplus items. The Gloucester water is purer by far than any Bristol can produce, even from the Bishop's feather off Jacob's Well." He was very ill at ease, talking for the sake of talking, and finding it very hard to meet Richard's eyes.

"There was no real reason to make this journey in such hot weather, Cousin James," said Richard gently. "Tell me the bad news."

"We have finally heard from Mr. Hyde in Chancery Lane. Sir James Eyre got around to your petition for the King's Mercy on the ninth of last month, or at least that is the date on his letter to Lord Sydney. He denied ye mercy, Richard, and most emphatically. There is no doubt in his mind that ye conspired with that woman to rob Ceely Trevillian. Even though she was never found."

"The damning witness who was not there," said Richard under his breath. "Not there, but believed."

"So that is it, my poor dear fellow. We have exhausted all our avenues. Your reward is safe, however. It cannot be garnished because it is not related to the crime for which ye were convicted. I know ye've a few guineas, but when next I come I will bring ye a new box with a hollow long *side* to it—tops and bottoms are more likely to be examined than sides, I am told. It will contain gold coins packed in lint so that, no matter how hard the box is shaken or rapped, they will make no noise. The lint also sounds solid."

Richard took both his hands and held them strongly. "I know I keep saying it, but I cannot thank you enough, Cousin James. What would I have become without you?"

"A bloody sight dirtier, Richard my love," said Lizzie Lock after Cousin James-the-druggist had gone. " 'Tis the apothecary gives ye your drips, soaps, oil of tar and all the rest of your popish ceremonials. Ye remind me of a priest saying Mass."

"Aye, he is a fussy bugger," said Bill Whiting, smiling. "It ain't necessary, Richard my love—look at the rest of us."

"Talking of buggery, Bill, I saw you sneaking around my sheep the other day," said Betty Mason, who kept a flock for Old Mother Hubbard. "Leave them alone."

"What chance do I have to bugger anybody except Jimmy and Richard my love? And they will not be in it. I hear, by the by, that all our lugging of rocks is to go for naught—Old Mother Hubbard says there is talk of a new style for the new prison."

"I hear that too," said Richard, sopping up the last of his soup with a piece of stale bread.

Jimmy Price sighed. "We are like whosit thingummabob who kept on having to roll the boulder up the hill but it always came down again. Christ, it would be nice to work for some purpose." He glanced across to where Ike Rogers was hunched at the far end of the table the old brigade defended against all presumptuous comers. "Ike, ye have to eat. Otherwise Richard my love will have your soup too, the hungry bugger. I ain't noticed the other five gallows birds off their food, nor worried much either. Eat, Ike, eat! Ye will not hang, I swear it."

Ike vouchsafed no reply; the blustering bully was no more. Highwaymen were considered the aristocrats of criminals, but Ike could not seem to come to terms with his fate or adopt the die-hard attitude of the other five in similar case.

Richard went to sit on the bench beside him and put an arm about his shoulders. "Eat, Ike," he said cheerfully.

"I am not hungry."

"Jimmy is right. Ye will not go to the gallows. It is over two years since anybody hanged at Gloucester, though many have been sentenced to it. Old Mother Hubbard needs us to work to get his thirty pence a week for each of us. If we do not work, he gets but fourteen pence."

"I do not want to die, I do not want to die!"

"Nor will you, Ike. Now drink your soup."

"What a gloomy bugger Ike is, always mincing along in his riding boots as if he wore high heels. Jesus, his feet must stink! He even wears the things to bed, Richard my love," said Bill Whiting the next day as they lugged their stones. "If he swings, so do I. It does not seem fair, does it? His loot was worth five thousand, my sheep ten shillings." His demeanor was resolutely brave, but now he suddenly shivered. "Goose walked over my grave," he laughed.

"Our geese would do more than walk over it, Bill. They would be digging after your worms."

There were eight of them staunch friends: the four women, Bill, Richard, Jimmy and the pitiable Joey Long, who was their child. Richard shivered in his turn. Four of his seven friends might not live to see 1786 arrive.

Then three days after Christmas, all six condemned to death were reprieved, their sentences commuted to fourteen years' transportation to—Africa. Where else? Jubilation reigned, though Ike Rogers never did recover his bombast.

The year 1785 had seen Richard a prisoner from beginning to end; its last day brought a couriered letter from Mr. James Thistlethwaite.

> "There is movement at Westminster, Richard. All sorts of rumors are flying. The most pertinent one as far as you are concerned goes as follows: transportees to Africa held in all gaols outside London are to be put on the Thames hulks in readiness for shipment to foreign parts, but not across the King's herring pond, which is the Western Ocean—on the maps, Oceanus Atlanticus. Since it is no longer his own private fishery, the rumors I hear (more strongly every day) talk of the Eastern Ocean—on damned few maps, Oceanus Pacificus.
>
> "Not much more than a decade ago, the Royal Society and its powerful Royal Navy connections sent one Captain James Cook to Otaheite to observe the transit of Venus across the sun. This Cook fellow kept discovering lands of milk and honey during what were, I gather, nosy wanderings. Little wonder that in the end his curiosity got him killed by the Indians of Lord Sandwich's isles. The land of milk and honey which concerns us now reminded Captain Cook of the coast of south Wales, so he dubbed it, imaginatively, New South Wales. On the maps it can be found as 'Terra Incognita' or 'Terra Australis.' How far it goes from east to west is anybody's guess, but it is certainly 2,000 miles from north to south.
>
> "At about the same latitude south as the new American state of Georgia is north, Cook found a place he christened 'Botany Bay.' Why this name? Because that obnoxious, interfering man of letters and President of the Royal Society, Sir Joseph Banks, snuffled around ashore there with Linnaeus's pupil Dr. Solander to gather botanical specimens.
>
> "Enter a gentleman of Corsican extraction, Mr. James Maria Matra. He was the first to put the idea into official heads, who huddled in countless consultations with Sir Joseph Banks,

authority on everything from the birth of Christ to the music of the spheres. The result is that Mr. Pitt and Lord Sydney are convinced they have found the answer to a hideous dilemma: what to do with the likes of you. Namely, to send you to Botany Bay. Not precisely to be abandoned ashore there, as happened in Africa, but rather to put a few Englishmen and Englishwomen in a land of milk and honey neither the French, the Dutch nor the Spanish have gotten to yet. No place that I have ever heard of was *settled* by convicts, but such seems to be the intention of His Majesty's Government in regard to Botany Bay. However, I am not sure that the verb 'to settle' is the proper one to use in this context. It is more likely that Mr. Pitt's verb is 'to dump.' Though should the experiment actually work, Botany Bay will end in taking our leavings for generations upon generations and two goals will have been achieved. The first—and by far the more important—is to send England's felons so far away that they cease to be either an embarrassment or a nuisance. The second—a ploy to lull the suspicions of our ever-multiplying Do Gooders, I am sure—is that His Majesty will own a new, if exploitably worthless, colony for the Union flag to float over. A colony populated by felons and gaolers. Undoubtedly its name in time will be 'Felonia.'

"Enough punning. Be prepared, Richard, for removal from Gloucester. I have already written to Cousin James-the-druggist, who should descend upon you armed with tools of survival not far into 1786. And gird your loins for a shock. Once you board the hulks moored around the Royal Arsenal, you encounter *London.* There are three of these penal palaces. The Censor and the Justitia have been there for a decade and have earned much attention and many visits from Mr. John Howard. The third, the Ceres, is only now coming into commission. The hulks are operated under contract to the Government by a London speculator named Duncan Campbell. A canny Scotchman, of course.

"I am very sorry to have to tell you that the Thames hulks are for male prisoners only. You will enjoy no tender female ministrations nor calming influences. The hulks are floating hells, and I mean every word of that. I know I am comforting Job, but Job you are, Richard. And better a Job who knows what he is in for. Guard yourself well."

* * *

"I have news," said Richard, putting the letter down.

"Oh?" asked Lizzie, darning complacently. It couldn't be bad news because his face was placid.

The needle stopped moving; her eyes rested fondly upon Richard my love (which had become his nickname). She knew absolutely nothing about him, for he had volunteered no information about himself beyond the terminology of his crime. Of course she loved him, for all that she would never bed him. In bedding lay a pain she knew she could not bear—a child with death snapping at its heels.

Her new hat, a dizzying confection of black silk and scarlet ostrich feathers, was perched incongruously on her head. He had given it to her for Christmas, carefully explaining that it was not a gift from him, but from someone he knew in London named Mr. James Thistlethwaite. A lampoonist, which he had informed her was someone who made obnoxious politicians, prelates and officials look very small and ridiculous through the power of the written word. She had no trouble believing that; as she could neither read nor write, persons who could earn a living from being literate were next door to God Himself.

So now, complacent needle going in and out and around a hole in one of Old Mother Hubbard's stockings, she could ask in mild interest, "Oh?"

"My lampoonist friend in London says that everybody sentenced to transportation to Africa will be moved from the county gaols to the hulks in the Thames. Men convicts, that is. He says naught about what is to happen to the women."

They were going through an underpopulated phase, so much so that the Michaelmas assizes had not been held that year. Scarlet fever had claimed too many lives to warrant Michaelmas assizes; instead there would be Epiphany assizes in January of 1786—if the numbers made it worthwhile.

Therefore some twenty people heard Richard's news, and stilled to immobility. Those awaiting trial stirred first. The old brigade revived very slowly, eyes widening, heads turning, all attention riveted upon Richard my love.

"Why?" Bill Whiting asked.

"Somewhere in the world—I am not sure exactly where—is a place called Botany Bay. We are to be transported there, and I suppose we sail from London, as they are sending us to the Thames hulks, not to

Portsmouth or Plymouth. The men only. Though it seems that women felons will also be going to Botany Bay."

Bess Parker huddled against a white-faced Ned Pugh and wept. "Ned! They are going to separate us! What will we do?"

No one had words of comfort; best ignore her question. "Is Botany Bay in Africa?" asked Jimmy Price to break the silence.

"It seems not," Richard said. "Farther away than Africa or America. Somewhere in the Eastern Ocean."

"The East Indies," said Ike Rogers, grimacing. "Heathens."

"No, not the East Indies, though they cannot be too far away. It is south, very south, and but newly discovered by a Captain Cook. Jem says it is a land of milk and honey, so I daresay it will not be too bad." He groped for a geographical anything. "It must be on the way to or from Otaheite. Cook was going there."

"Where is Otaheite?" asked Betty Mason, as devastated as Bess; Johnny the gaoler would not be going to Botany Bay.

"I do not know," Richard confessed.

The next day—New Year's Day of 1786—the convicted felons of both sexes were marched to the gaol chapel, where they found Old Mother Hubbard, Parsnip Evans and three men they recognized only because they occasionally accompanied the mystery men from London who examined the construction work. John Nibbet was the Gloucester sheriff; the other two rejoiced in the appellation of Gentlemen Sheriffs—John Jefferies and Charles Cole.

Nibbet had been appointed spokesman. "The city of Gloucester in the county of Gloucestershire has been notified by the Home Department and its Secretary of State, Lord Sydney, that certain of the prisoners held in the gaol under sentence of transportation to Africa are to be transported elsewhere than Africa!" he bellowed.

"He did not draw a breath," muttered Whiting.

"Do not court a thrashing, Bill," Jimmy whispered.

Nibbet continued, apparently not needing to draw breath. "And further to this, the city of Gloucester in the county of Gloucestershire has been notified by said Home Department that it is to act as collecting agent for male transportees from Bristol, Monmouth and Wiltshire. When all have been assembled here, they will be joined by the following prisoners already in the Gloucester gaol: Joseph Long, Richard Morgan, James Price, Edward

Pugh, Isaac Rogers and William Whiting. The entire group will then proceed to London and Woolwich, there to wait on the King's pleasure."

A long wail terminated the Sheriff's proclamation. Bess Parker ran forward, stumbling in her fetters, to throw herself at Nibbet's feet, wringing her hands together and weeping wildly. "Sir, sir, honored sir, please, sir, I beg you! Ned Pugh is my man! See my belly? I am to have his child, sir, and any day! Please, sir, do not take him away from me!"

"Cease this caterwauling, woman!" Nibbet turned to Old Mother Hubbard with a direful frown. "Does the prisoner Pugh have a permanent connection with yon yowling female?" he demanded.

"Aye, Mr. Nibbet, for some years. There was an earlier child, but it died."

"My instructions from Under Secretary Nepean specifically state that only male felons without wives or wives at common law imprisoned with them are to be sent to Woolwich. Therefore Edward Pugh will remain in Gloucester Gaol with the female transportees," he announced.

"Damned considerate," said Gentleman Sheriff Charles Cole, "but I do not see the need for it."

Old Mother Hubbard murmured into Nibbet's ear.

"Prisoner Morgan, d'ye have a permanent connection with one Elizabeth Lock?" barked the Sheriff.

Every part of Richard's being longed to say that he had, but his papers would be examined and they would inform these men that he had a wife. The fate Annemarie had given him lived on. "I do have a permanent connection with Elizabeth Lock, sir, but she is not my wife even in common law. I am already married," he said.

Lizzie Lock mewed.

"Then ye'll proceed to Woolwich, Morgan."

The Reverend Mr. Evans said a prayer for their souls, and the meeting was over. The prisoners were escorted by a very glad Johnny the gaoler back to the felons' common-room. Where Lizzie lost no time in hauling Richard into a fairly private corner.

"Why did you not tell me you are married?" she demanded, her plumes nodding and bouncing.

"Because I am not married."

"Then why did ye tell the Sheriff ye were?"

"Because my papers say I am."

"How can that be?"

"Because it is."

She took him by the shoulders and shook him vigorously. "Oh, damn you, Richard, damn you! Why do you never tell me anything? What point is there in being so close?"

"I am not intentionally close, Lizzie."

"Yes, you are! You never tell me a thing!"

"But you never ask," he said, looking surprised.

She shook him again. "Then I am asking now! Tell me all about yourself, Richard Morgan. Tell me everything. I want to know how ye can be married yet not married, damn you!"

"Then I may as well tell the lot of you."

They gathered around the table and heard a very edited story relating only to Annemarie Latour, Ceely Trevillian and a distillery. Of Peg, little Mary, William Henry and his other family he told them nothing because he could not bear to.

"Weeping Willy said more than that," Lizzie stated sourly.

"It is all I am prepared to say." Richard assumed a worried look and neatly changed the subject. "It sounds as if we are to be moved very soon. I pray that my cousin James gets here in time."

By the 4th of January the number of men in the felons' section of Gloucester Gaol had swollen. Four men came in from Bristol and two from Wiltshire. Two of the Bristol men were very young, but two were in their early thirties and had been close friends since childhood.

"Neddy and I got drunk one night in the Swan on Temple Street," said William Connelly, slapping Edward Perrott companionably on the shoulder. "Not sure what happened, but the next thing we were in the Bristol Newgate and got seven years' transportation to Africa at last February's quarter sessions. Seems we stole clothes."

"Ye look well for spending a year in that place. I was there for three months just before," said Richard.

"Ye're a Bristol man?"

"Aye, but tried here. My crime was committed in Clifton."

William Connelly was obviously of Irish extraction; thick auburn hair, short nose and cheeky blue eyes. The more silent Edward Perrott had the bumpy big nose, prominent chin and mousy fairness of a true Englishman.

The two Wiltshire men, William Earl and John Cross, were at most twenty years old, and had already struck up a friendship with the two Bristol youngsters, Job Hollister and William Wilton. Joey Long was so simple that he gravitated naturally to this young group from the moment they clanked into the felons' common-room, and—which Richard found strange at first—Isaac Rogers elected to join these five. A few hours saw Richard change his mind—no, not at all strange. Oozing glamour and seniority, the highwayman could retrieve some of the clout he had lost among his Gloucester fellows when he had funked at the prospect of hanging.

Then the Monmouth man arrived to make the twelfth for Woolwich and informed them that he was William Edmunds.

"Christ!" cried Bill Whiting. "There are twelve of us for Woolwich and five of us are fucken Williams! I lay claim to Bill, and that is that. Wilton from Bristol, ye remind me of Weeping Willy Insell, so ye're Willy. Connelly from Bristol, ye're Will. Earl from Wiltshire, ye're Billy. But what the devil are we to do with the fifth? What did you do to get here, Edmunds?"

"Stole a heifer at Peterstone," said Edmunds with a Welsh lilt.

Whiting roared with laughter and kissed the outraged Welshman full on his lips. "Another bugger, by God! I borrowed a sheep for the night—only wanted to fuck it. Never *thought* of a heifer!"

"Do not do that!" Edmunds scrubbed at his mouth vigorously. "You can fuck whatever ye like, but ye'll not fuck me!"

"He is a Welshman and a thief," said Richard, grinning. "We call him Taffy, of course."

"Did ye get the gallows?" Bill Whiting asked Taffy.

"Twice over, Da."

"For *one* heifer?"

"Nay. I got the second for escaping. But the Welsh ain't too happy at the moment, would not have liked to see a Welshman hanged even in Monmouth, so they reprieved me again and got rid of me," Taffy explained.

Richard found himself drawn to Taffy as much as he was to Bill Whiting and Will Connelly. He had Welsh moods like clouds chasing the sun in and out on a heath-purple hillside. But then, Richard's own roots were Welsh.

Cousin James-the-druggist made it to Gloucester just in time on the 5th of January, loaded down with sacks and wooden boxes.

"The Excise Office paid over your five hundred pounds at the end of December," he said, burrowing. "I have six new dripstones, five of them with their brass frames and catching dishes because I felt that you must keep the five friends around ye safe and well."

"Why five friends, Cousin James?" Richard asked, intrigued.

"Jem Thistlethwaite said in his letter to me that the men on the Thames hulks are separated into groups of six who live and work together." He did not go on to tell Richard any of the other things Jem had explained about the hulks; he could not bring himself to. "That is why there are five new boxes, all containing what yours does, save not in the same quantity. I brought your tool box too."

Richard sat back on his heels and thought about that, then shook his head. "Nay, Cousin James, not my tools. I will need them for this Botany Bay, but there are enough rays of enlightenment dancing inside my head to feel very strongly that did I take them with me now, they would not survive to see Botany Bay. Keep them until ye know what ship I will be on, then send them to me."

"Here are more books from the Reverend James. He has concentrated this time on books about the world, geography, voyages. Heavier, because most are on ordinary paper and leather bound. But he thinks they may help, and hopes that ye'll be able to carry them and all your others to Botany Bay."

After which Cousin James-the-druggist could find nothing to say about practical matters. He got to his feet. "Botany Bay is at the other end of the world, Richard. Ten thousand miles if ye could fly, more like sixteen thousand as a ship must sail. I fear that none of us will ever see you again, and that is a terrible grief. All for something you never meant. Oh dear, oh dear! Remember that you will be in my prayers every day for the rest of my life, and your father's, and your mother's, and the Reverend James's. Surely so many good intentions cannot be lost upon God. Surely He will preserve ye. Oh dear, oh dear!"

Richard reached for him, held him close, kissed his cheeks. Then he pattered away, head bent, and did not look back.

But Richard's eyes followed him down the path between the vegetable patches, through the castle gate. He turned a corner, and was gone. *And I will pray for you, Cousin James, for I love you more than I love my father.*

Lizzie Lock draped around his shoulders, he gathered his troops at the table in the felons' common-room.

"It is not that I wish to lead," he said to his five chosen companions—Bill Whiting, Will Connelly, Neddy Perrott, Jimmy Price and Taffy Edmunds. "I am seven-and-thirty, which makes me the oldest amongst us, but I am not the stuff makes leaders, and ye should all know that now. Each of us must look for strength and guidance within himself, as is fit and proper. Yet I do have some learning, and a source of information in political London as well as a very clever druggist cousin in Bristol."

"I know him," said Will Connelly, nodding. "James Morgan of Corn

Street. Recognized him the moment he came in. Thought, phew! Yon Richard Morgan is well connected."

"Aye, enough. First I have to tell ye that the men on the hulks are divided into groups of six who live and work together. An it pleases you, I would have the six of us form one such group before some hulk gaoler does it for us. Is that agreeable?"

They nodded soberly.

" 'Tis our good fortune to be twelve to London from here. The other six are young save for Ike, and he seems to prefer their company to ours. So I am going to advise Ike to do the same thing with his five. That way, there will be twelve of us on the hulk to form up as mutual protection."

"You expect trouble, Richard?" asked Connelly, frowning.

"I do not honestly know, Will. If I do, it is more because of what my informants have not said, than said. We are all from the West Country. That will not be so on the hulks."

"I understand," said Bill Whiting, serious for once. "Best to decide what to do now. Later might be too late."

"How many of us can read and write?" asked Richard.

Connelly, Perrott and Whiting held up their hands.

"Four of us. Good." He pointed to the five boxes standing on the floor alongside him. "On a different note, these contain the things that will enable us to stay healthy, like dripstones."

"Oh, Richard!" Jimmy Price exclaimed, exasperated. "Ye make a fucken religion out of your wretched dripstone! Lizzie is right, ye're like a priest saying Mass."

"It is true that I have made a religion out of staying well." Richard looked at his group sternly. "Will and Neddy, how did ye manage to stay well through a year in the Bristol Newgate?"

"Drank beer or small beer," said Connelly. "Our families gave us the money to eat well and drink healthy."

"When I was there, I drank the water," said Richard.

"Impossible!" gasped Neddy Perrott.

"Not impossible. I filtered my water through my dripstone. Its function is to purify bad water, which is why my cousin James imports them from Teneriffe. If ye think for one moment that Thames water will be more drinkable than Avon water, ye'll be dead in a week." Richard shrugged. "The choice is yours entirely. If ye can afford to drink small beer, well and good. But in London we will not have families on hand to help us. What gold we have ought to be saved for bribing, not spent on small beer."

"Ye're right," said Will Connelly, touching the dripstone on the table reverently. "I for one will filter my water if I cannot afford to drink small beer. It is good common sense."

In the end they all agreed to filter their water, including Jimmy Price.

"That settles that," said Richard, and went to talk to Ike Rogers. He was sorry that he did not have twelve dripstones, but not sorry enough to share six of them among twelve. Ike's group would have to manage as best it could, and at least Ike always seemed to have plenty of money.

If the twelve of us stick together as two groups, we stand a chance to survive.

PART THREE

From
January of 1786
until
January of 1787

The wagon to London and Woolwich arrived at dawn the next day, the 6th of January; exactly a year since his last wagon trip had commenced, Richard realized. But this was a gaol parting of higher magnitude and much sorrow, the women weeping desolately.

"What will I do without you?" Lizzie Lock asked Richard as she followed him to Old Mother Hubbard's house.

"Find someone else," said Richard, but sympathetically. "In your circumstances, a protector is essential. Though 'twill be hard to find another like me, willing to forgo sex."

"I know, I know! Oh, Richard, I shall miss you!"

"And I you, skinny Lizzie. Who will mend my stockings?"

She grinned through her tears, gave him a shove. "Get away with you! I have shown you how to use a needle and ye sew well."

Then two gaolers came and took the women back to the prison, waving, howling, protesting.

And back to the iron belt around the waist, the four sets of chains joined together at its front.

In appearance this wagon looked the same as the one from Bristol to Gloucester—drawn by eight big horses, covered with a canvas semicircle. Inside it was quite different, having a bench down either side long enough for six men to sit with plenty of space between each. Their belongings had to be piled on the floor between their legs and would pitch and slide every time the vehicle jarred, thought the experienced Richard. What road was smooth, especially at this time of year? Dead of winter, and a rainy one.

Two gaolers traveled with them, but not inside with them; they sat with the driver up front, which had a fine shelter built over it. No one in the back was going to slip out and escape; once seated, a length of chain was run through an additional loop on each man's left fetter and bolted to the floor at either end. If one man moved, his five companions had to move.

The pecking order was now established. Muffled in his warmly lined greatcoat, Richard sat at the open end of the wagon on one side, with Ike Rogers, leader of the youngsters, facing him.

"How long will it take?" asked Ike Rogers.

"If we cover six miles in a day we will be lucky," answered Richard, grinning. "Ye've not been on the road before—in a wagon, I mean, Ike. I do not know how long. It depends which way."

"Through Cheltenham and Oxford," said the highwayman, taking the joke in good part. "Whereabouts Woolwich is, however, I do not know. I have been to Oxford, but never to London."

Richard had conned his first geography book, a text on London. "It is well east of London but on the south bank of the Thames. I do not know if they mean to make us cross over—we are going to hulks moored in the river, after all. If we go through Cheltenham and Oxford, then we have about a hundred and twenty miles to travel to Woolwich." He did some calculations in his head. "At six miles a day, it will take almost three weeks to get there."

"We sit here for three weeks?" asked Bill Whiting, dismayed.

Those who had already been on the road in a wagon laughed.

"No need to worry about sitting idle, Bill," said Taffy. "We will be out and digging half a dozen times in a day."

As indeed proved to be the case. Wayside hospitality, however, fell far short of that extended to Richard and Willy by John the wagoneer. No barns, no warm horse blankets, nothing to eat save bread, nothing to drink save small beer. Each night saw them bed down in the wagon by transferring their belongings to the seats and occupying the floor to stretch out, greatcoats for covers, hats for pillows. The canvas roof leaked in the perpetual rain, though the temperature stayed well above freezing, a small mercy for damp and shivering prisoners. Only Ike had boots; the rest wore shoes and were soon caked to above their fettered ankles in mud.

They did not see Cheltenham or Oxford, the driver preferring to skirt both towns with this cargo of felons, and High Wycombe was no more than a short row of houses down a hill so slippery that the team of horses became entangled in the traces and nearly turned the wagon over. Bruised by flying wooden boxes, the prisoners were set to work righting the perilously leaning vehicle; Ike Rogers, who had a great affinity with horses, engaged himself in calming the animals down and sorting out their harness.

Of London they saw absolutely nothing, for one of the gaolers fixed a shield over the open back and blinded them to what was going on outside. Soon came a trundling motion rather than a lurching one; they had reached some paved main road, which meant that their services would not be needed to dig the wagon out. Noises percolated inside: cries, whinnies, brays, snatches of song, sudden babbles which perhaps meant they passed by an open tavern door, the thump of machinery, an occasional crash.

When night fell the gaolers pushed bread and small beer in through the shielding flap and left them to their own devices; he who needed to urinate or defecate was now provided with a bucket. More bread and small beer in the morning, then onward through that confusing racket, joined now by the cries of vendors and some very interesting stenches—rotten fish, rotten meat, rotten vegetables. The Bristolians stared at each other and smirked, while the rest looked a little sick.

For two nights they lay somewhere within the reaches of the great city, and on the afternoon of the third day—their twentieth since leaving Gloucester—someone yanked the shield away and let in the London daylight. In front of them lay a mighty river, grey and slick and bobbing with refuse; judging from the position of the sun, a pale and watery brilliance in the midst of a whitish sky, they had crossed the stream somewhere, and were now on its south bank. Woolwich, Richard decided. The wagon stood alongside a dock, to which was moored a dilapidated semblance of a ship which bore a barely discernible name on a bronze plate: Reception. Most appropriate.

The gaolers removed the chain which had linked them together and told Richard and Ike to get out. Legs a little shaky, they jumped down, their companions following.

"Remember, in two groups of six," said Richard to Ike softly.

They were marched up a wooden gangplank and onto the vessel before anyone had a good opportunity to take in much of the river or what lay upon it. Once inside a room they were divested of their chains, manacles, belts and fetters, which were handed back to the Gloucester gaolers.

Boxes, sacks and bundles around them, they stood for some time aware of the guards at the door of this ruined wardroom or whatever it might have been; escape was impossible unless all twelve of them made a combined rush—but after that, what?

A man walked in. "Dowse yer nabs n toges!" he shouted.

They looked at him blankly.

"Nabs n toges orf!"

When nobody moved he cast his eyes at the ceiling, stormed up to Richard, who was closest, knocked his hat off and yanked at his greatcoat and the suit coat he wore beneath it.

"I think he wants us to take off our hats and coats."

Everybody obeyed.

"Nah kicks araon stampers n keep yer mishes orn!"

They looked at him blankly.

He ground his teeth, shut his eyes and said, with a very odd accent, "Britches round your feet but keep your shirts on."

Everybody obeyed.

"Ready, sir!" he called.

Another man strolled in. "Where are you lot from?" he asked.

"Gloucester Gaol," said Ike.

"Oh, West Country. Ye'll have to speak something akin to the King's English, Matty," he said to the first man, and then to the prisoners, "I am the doctor. Is anybody sick?"

Apparently assuming that the general murmur was a negative, he nodded and sighed. "Lift your shirts, let us see if there are any blue boars." He inspected their penises for syphilitic ulcers, and having found none, sighed again. "Bene," he said to Matty, and to them, "Ye're a healthy lot, but all things change." About to leave the room, he said, "Put your clothes on, wait here, and keep quiet."

They put their clothes on and waited.

It was a full five minutes before Bill Whiting, the chirpiest of the twelve, recovered enough of his cheek to find speech. "Did anybody understand anything yon Matty said?" he asked.

"Not a word," said young Job Hollister.

"Perhaps he was from Scotland," said Connelly, remembering that no one in Bristol had understood Jack the Painter.

"Perhaps he was from Woolwich," said Neddy Perrott.

Which silenced all of them.

An hour went by. They had subsided to the floor and leaned their backs against the walls, feeling the slight shifting under their legs as the ship moved sluggishly against its moorings. Rudderless, thought Richard. We are as rudderless as this thing that was once a ship, farther away from home than any of us has ever been, and with no idea of what awaits. The youngsters are dumbstruck, even Ike Rogers is unsure. And I am filled with dread.

Came the sound of several pairs of feet thumping on wooden planking, the familiar dull clinking of chains; the twelve men stirred, looked at each other uneasily, got up wearily.

"Darbies f y dimber coves!" said the first man through the door. "Fetters, ye pretty hicks! Sit down and nobody move."

Six inches longer than the Bristol or Gloucester versions, the chains were already welded to the cuffs, which were much lighter, flexible enough for the heavily muscled smith to bend apart around a man's ankle, then close until the holes in either end overlapped. Then he pushed a flat-headed bolt through the holes from the ankle side, grabbed the prisoner's leg and slipped the long tongue of an anvil between it and the fetter. Two heavy blows with his hammer and the rivet ends were smashed flat against the iron band forever.

I will wear these for the next six and more years, thought Richard, easing his aching bones by rubbing them. They do not do that for a mere six and more months. Which means that even after I reach Botany Bay, I will wear these until I finish my sentence.

Another smith had fettered the second six from Gloucester, and just as competently. Within half an hour the two of them had the job done, prodded their assistants into gathering the tools up, and left. Two guards remained; Matty must have belonged to the doctor. However, Matty had passed the message on, for when one of the guards spoke, it was in that peculiarly accented English, not in what time would inform the prisoners was "flash lingo"—the speech of the London Newgate and all those who had dealings with that place.

"Ye'll mess and sleep here tonight," he said curtly, tapping the knobbed end of his short bludgeon against the palm of his other hand. "Ye can talk and move about. Here, have a bucket." Then he and his companion moved out, locking the door.

The two Wiltshire lads were wiping away tears; everyone else was dry-eyed. Not in a mood for talking until Will Connelly got up and prowled about.

"These feel better on the legs," he said, lifting one foot. "Chain must be thirty inches long too. Easier to walk."

Richard ran his fingers over the cuffs and found that they had rounded edges. "Aye, and they will not rub so much. We will go through fewer rags."

"Proper working irons," said Bill Whiting. "I wonder what sort of work it will be?"

Just before nightfall they were given small beer, stale and very dark brown bread, and a mess of boiled cabbage with leeks.

"Not for me," said Ike, pushing the pot of cabbage away.

"Eat it, Ike," Richard ordered. "My cousin James says we must eat every vegetable we can get, otherwise we will get scurvy."

Ike was unimpressed. "That muck could not cure a runny nose."

"I agree," said Richard, having tasted it. "However, it is a change from bread, so I will eat it."

After which, windowless, womanless and cheerless, they lay down on the floor, wrapped their greatcoats about them, used their hats as pillows, and let the gently moving river rock them to sleep.

The next morning, amid a drizzling grey rain, they were taken off Reception and loaded into an open lighter. So far nothing hideously cruel had happened to them; the guards were surly brutes, but as long as the prisoners did as they were told at the pace demanded, they kept their bludgeons to themselves. The wooden boxes were a source of curiosity, obviously, yet why had no one inspected them? On the dock they learned why. A short, rotund gentleman in an old-fashioned wig and a fusty suit came hurrying down from the ship's remnant of a poop, hands outstretched, beaming.

"Ah, the dozen from Gloucester!" he said brightly, with an accent they would discover later was Scotch. "Doctor Meadows said ye were fine specimens, and I see he was right. My name is Mr. Campbell, and this is my idea." His hand swept the soft rain aside in a grand gesture. "Floating prisons! So much healthier than the Newgate—than any gaol, for that matter. Ye've your property, yes? Good, good. 'Tis a black mark for anybody does not respect a convict's right to his property. Neil! Neil, where are ye?"

A person who appeared enough like him to be his twin rushed from the bows of Reception down onto the dock and came to a halt with a puff. "Here, Duncan."

"Oh good! I did not want ye to miss setting eyes on these splendid fellows. My brother is my assistant," he explained, just as if the prisoners were real people. "However, he is responsible for Justitia and Censor at the moment—I am too busy with my dear Ceres—she is superb! Brand new! Of course ye're going to dear Ceres—so convenient that ye're the round dozen and in such good condition. Two teams for the two new dredges." He actually began to prance. "Splendid, splendid!" And off he galloped, his brother bleating in his wake like a lost lamb.

"Christ! What a quiz!" said Bill Whiting.

"Tace!" barked the overseeing guard, and brought his bludgeon down with a sickening thump on Whiting's arm. "Nah *hike!*"

That they understood; with Ike Rogers unobtrusively supporting the half-conscious Whiting, the twelve men edged, hanging on to their goods, down a flight of slimy steps to the waiting lighter.

Stretches of a low, swampy shore and misty profiles of a few ships came and went through the ghostly grey rain; collars turned up, hats oriented to cascade water onto their shoulders rather than down their necks, they sat amid their boxes, sacks and bundles. A silent crew of twelve oarsmen, six to a side, pushed the lighter off, turned it, and stroked toward the middle of the great wide river with a long, easy motion that hardly disturbed the sliding water.

There were four ships sitting one behind the other like a line of cows about three hundred yards off this south or Kentish shore. Each was moored more thoroughly than Richard had ever seen a vessel moored, even in the Kingroad of the Severn Estuary. To fix them, he thought, too firmly to allow them to swing at anchor, of which each had many on chains rather than the normal rope cables. The smallest ship was farthest upriver in London's direction and the largest brought up the rear, with perhaps a hundred yards separating each from its neighbors in the line.

"Hospital ship Guardian—then Censor, Justitia and Ceres," said a guard, pointing.

The lighter struck for Censor, opposite the dock, then turned to run downriver with an ebbing tide to make life easier for the oarsmen. Thus they had the chance to look at each of the three prison hulks. Travesties of ships only, mizzens long gone, mainmasts broken off forty feet aloft in cracks and splinters, foremasts more or less intact but stripped of shrouds, clothing hanging limp and wet from lines strung between each fore and main, as well as on the stays connecting the fore with a stub of bowsprit. The decks sported a shambles of wooden huts and jutting penthouses with a forest of iron chimneys kinked at all angles; more of these stood atop quarterdecks, forecastles and roundhouses. Censor and Justitia looked old enough to have gone to sea with Good Queen Bess's fleet against the Spanish Armada—no scrap of paint left, no copper nail ungreened, no strake unchipped.

By comparison Ceres looked a mere century old; its naval black-and-yellow paint still showed in places and it had the remnant of a figurehead beneath its bowsprit, some sort of wheaty bare-breasted female a wag had finished off with bright red nipples. The gun ports of Censor and Justitia were closed fast, but those of Ceres had been removed entirely and replaced by grilles of thick iron bars which led the Bristolians, experienced in such matters, to conclude that it had two decks below the upper or surface deck—a lower deck and an orlop deck. Once a second-rate ship of the line with 90 guns, then. No cargo vessel or slaver ever owned so many ports along her sides.

How, Richard wondered, are we going to manage to get ourselves and our belongings up a rope ladder? Our chains will be our undoing. However, the ebullient Mr. Duncan Campbell had fitted his pride and joy with a flight of wooden steps attached to a bobbing landing. Box in his arms, two sacks of additionals slung over his shoulders, Richard found himself first over the side of the lighter behind a bludgeon-bearing guard, and mounted the steps to an opening in the rail sixteen feet above. Ceres had been a big second-rater.

"Gigger dubber!" roared the overseeing guard.

An important-looking but slovenly fellow emerged from between two wooden shacks picking his teeth; in the background Richard saw an occasional flick of a skirt, heard women's voices, and realized that most of the guards must live in these ramshackle quarters.

"Ah?" asked the important-looking individual.

"Twelve convicts from Gloucester Gaol, Mr. 'Anks. Ain't flash so don't know the lingo. Mr. Campbell says they are the two new teams for the new dredges. No hum durdgeons among 'em, Doc says."

"More 'icks!" said Mr. Hanks in disgust. "Nigh 'alf aboard are 'icks now, Mr. Sykes." He turned to the prisoners. "Me name is 'Erbert 'Anks an I am the gigger dubber—gaol keeper to youse. Into the orlop wiv 'em, Mr. Sykes. An 'ere ye ain't prisoners, ye're convicts. Got it?"

They nodded wordlessly, trying to sort out an English wherein the th's were pronounced as v's and the f's as th's. Sort of.

"Prisoners," Mr. Hanks went on conversationally, " 'ave a chance to get theirselves unsnabbled. Convicts is convicts, in for the 'ole duration. 'Ere are the rules, so put yer lugs to listening 'cos they will not be said again. Visitors allowed on Sundees after the autem bawler's service—autem is compulsory—that's church to youse—an ain't no autem quavers nor dippers nor cacklers of any Dissenting sort allowed. Just the King's autem 'ere. All visitors will be searched, 'ave to lodge their blunt wiv me, an any grub they got will be confiscated. Why? 'Cos flash coves smuggle files aboard in their cakes an puddens."

He paused to eye his auditors with a curious mixture of glee and severity; he was enjoying this. "When ye're aboard, the orlop is 'ome. I am the only one can dub the gigger—open the door—an that don't 'appen hoften. Up to work, down to sleep, Mondees to Sattidees. Weather permitting, youse work, an I mean youse *work.* Today, frinstance, is not a day for work 'cos the rain is too fucken 'ard. Youse eat what ye're fed an drink what I decide. Blue tape—gin—comes very dear, an I am the only purveyor of such delights. 'Alf a borde—sixpence—a 'alf-pint."

Another pause ensued, this time to allow Mr. Hanks to hawk and spit at their feet. "Youse mess in sixes an get yer grub from the purser. Sundees, Mondees, Wensdees, Thursdees an Sattidees the following rations are issued to each six men—one ox cheek or ox shin, three pints of pease, three pounds of vegubbles, six pounds of bread an six quarts of small beer. On Tuesdees an Fridees it is burgoo—as much aqua Thames as ye want, three pints of oatmeal wiv simples, three pounds of cheese an six pounds of bread. That is *all* ye get. If ye eat it all up at supper, ye go 'ungry an thirsty of a morning, got it? Mr. Campbell says youse 'ave to wash every day an shave every Sundee before the autem bawler comes aboard. When youse come up for work or autem, ye'll bring yer night buckets wiv youse an empty 'em over the side. One bucket each mess. Ye are locked in, me dimber cullies, so what youse do inside I do not care hany more than Mr. Campbell do."

His pleasure increased. "But first," he said, squatting down while Mr. Sykes and his minions remained standing behind him, "I 'ave to cast me ogles over them boxes an bags, so dub 'em—*now!*"

This lecture having informed them that to dub was to open, the convicts unlocked their boxes, spread open their additionals.

Mr. Herbert Hanks was very thorough. By chance he commenced with the belongings of Ike Rogers and his team, whose boxes were smaller, not uniform, and in the case of the two Wiltshire lads, nonexistent. Rags he discarded, clothing he discarded, but each and every rag and item of clothing was nonetheless passed up to Mr. Sykes, who ran them between his hands and squeezed at every tiny swelling. This yielded nothing. Nor did any of the other articles appeal, evidently.

"Where's yer money?" he demanded.

Ike looked respectfully surprised. "Sir, we have none. We have been in Gloucester Gaol for a year. The blunt got spent."

"Huh." Mr. Hanks turned to Richard's team, eyes glistening. "Rum coves, eh? A lot of loot." Out of Richard's box and sacks came the clothing, the bottles and jars, the framed dripstone and several spares, the rags used as packing, the books, the ream of paper, the pens—very curious objects!—

and two spare pairs of shoes. He held the shoes up and studied them in disappointment, shrugged at the equally disappointed Mr. Sykes. "Ain't for nothing ye're called clodhoppers. No one here got feet that size, cully, even Long Joyce. What is this, then?" he asked, displaying a bottle.

"Oil of tar, Mr. Hanks."

"An what is this contraption?"

"A dripstone, sir. I use it to filter my drinking water."

"Water is already filtered in 'ere. Got a big strainer under every pump. What's yer name, big feet?"

"Richard Morgan."

He snatched a list from one of Mr. Sykes's offsiders and cast his ogles over it; read he could, but painfully. "Not any more it ain't. From now on, Morgan, ye're convict number two 'unnerd an three."

"Yes, sir."

"A booky cove, I note." Mr. Hanks riffled through the pages of a few in search of salacious etchings or erotic prose, then laid each one down with a frustrated slap. "An what's this?"

"A tonic, sir, to cure boils."

"An this?"

"A salve, sir, for cuts and ulcers."

"Shite, ye're an apothecary's shop! Why'd ye bring all this clutter?" He removed the cork from the bottle of tonic and sniffed suspiciously. "Aaaaaagh!" He slammed it down on the deck and let its cork roll away. "Smells bad enough to come from the river."

Expression unconcerned, Richard stood while the head gaoler picked up the empty box, shook it to hear if it rattled, rapped all four sides, top and bottom. After which he felt every seam of the sacks. Nothing. He appropriated Richard's better razor, the strop and whetstone, and Richard's best pair of stockings. Then he moved on to Will Connelly's box and bag. Very quietly and unobtrusively Richard knelt to retrieve his tonic, cork it and put it to one side. A glance at Mr. Sykes told him that he was probably expected to repack his things at this juncture, so he nodded to the immobile Rogers and began his task. Rogers and the youngsters followed suit.

Finished with the twelve of them, Mr. Hanks exuded pleasure. "Right, now where's yer coach wheels? Where's yer blunt, cullies?"

"Sir, we have none," said Neddy Perrott. "We have been in gaol for a year and there were women. . . ." He trailed off apologetically.

"Pockets inside out!"

Every coat pocket was empty save Richard's, Bill's, Neddy's and Will's, stuffed full of books.

"Dowse yer toges—take 'em off!" snapped Mr. Hanks.

Off came greatcoats and suit coats; Mr. Sykes felt over every inch of every one. "Nowt," he said, grinning.

"Frisk 'em, Mr. Sykes."

This they interpreted as an order to search their persons; Mr. Sykes proceeded to feel their bodies, with obvious enjoyment when he groped around genitals and buttocks. "Nowt," he said, exchanging a look of keen anticipation with Mr. Hanks.

"Dowse yer kicks an bend over," said Mr. Hanks in a resigned but quivering voice. "Though I am warning youse! If Mr. Sykes 'ere finds any coach wheels up yer arses, ye'll wash 'em in yer blood."

Mr. Sykes was brutally, lingeringly efficient. The four young men and Joey Long wept in pain and humiliation, the others endured it without exclamation or evident discomfort. "Nowt," said Mr. Sykes. "Fucken nowt—not nuffink, Mr. 'Anks."

"We are from Gloucestershire," said Richard as he pulled up his underdrawers and breeches. "It is a poor part of England."

And I have got your measure. Shame and money. God rot you.

"Take 'em below, Mr. Sykes," said the gigger dubber, and went off into the warren of shacks a disappointed man.

As of this January 28, 1786, Ceres held 213 convicts; the twelve from Gloucester were admitted as numbers 201 to 213, Richard at 203. The only gaoler, however, who used their numbers was Mr. Herbert Hanks of Plumstead Road, near the Warren, Woolwich.

Someone in his wisdom—probably to placate the felons of the London Newgate, who loathed associating with hicks—had separated the London Newgaters from the hicks by putting them on different decks. The London Newgaters occupied the lower deck and the hicks occupied the orlop deck. Or perhaps this wisdom stemmed from the perpetual war which went on between the London felons and all the non-Londoners on Censor and Justitia, wherein everybody was so hopelessly intermingled that not even Mr. Duncan Campbell could unravel the tangle. With Dunkirk in Plymouth he was to go further than with Ceres, segmenting the ship to create seven convict compartments according to a system of classification he had concocted himself.

The divisions between Englishmen were very deep. Those who used the London Newgate flash lingo spoke what sounded like an alien tongue, though many could—if pushed to it, and in a bizarre accent—speak a more general kind of English. The problem was that by far the greater number of them refused to as a matter of principle, preferring their flash exclusivity. Those from the lands of the north as far south as Yorkshire and Lancashire could more or less comprehend each other's speech, but, no matter how literate, could not make head or tail of anyone who hailed from farther south. Complicated by the fact that Liverpudlians spoke something known as Scouse, another foreign language. The Midlanders could communicate fairly well with those from the West Country and both these groups could understand convicts from Sussex, the Channel parts of Kent, Surrey and Hampshire. But those from the Thames part of Kent spoke something akin to flash lingo, and the same had to be said of those from the parts of Essex closest to London. As for those from north Essex, Cambridgeshire, Suffolk, Norfolk and Lincoln—quite different again. So polyglot was this assemblage of Englishmen, indeed, that Censor owned two convicts from Birmingham who could not understand each other; one had lived in the village of Smethwick, the other in the village of Four Oaks, and neither had been a mile from home until caught in the judicial net.

The result was that people clumped. If one group of six could understand another group of six, they mingled to some degree. When dialects or accents became insuperable, the twain never met. The Gloucester men therefore entered a divided camp, united only in a universal hatred of the London Newgaters one deck up, who were said to get the lion's share of everything from grub to cheaper gin because they and the gaolers could understand each other and were allied in depriving the non-Londoners of their rightful share.

This last assumption might well have been true of the gin, as the London Newgaters were in their own bailiwick and likely to have more sources of money, but it certainly was not true of the grub.

That jolly little prancing person Mr. Duncan Campbell became exceedingly thrifty about things he had to pay for out of the £26 per convict per year he obtained from His Majesty's Government, and grub was an item he had to pay for. Ten shillings per week per man: on the Thames hulks that January his gross income was £360 per week, and there were things a canny contractor could do to keep the gross and the net figures closer together. Such as growing his own vegetables and brewing his own small beer. The more obvious ploys of falsifying his convict numbers or letting scurvy run riot were, alas, out of the question. Too many nosy officials. He bought his bread and his beef from the garrison at the Tower of London—ox heads and shins only, hard bread only—and at first he had not been fussy about their condition. Then along came Mr. John Howard; bread and beef had to improve somewhat. Notwithstanding these irksome constrictions and a staff of 100 assorted persons, Mr. Campbell managed to make a profit of £150 a week from his Thames hulks. He also had a hulk in Plymouth—Dunkirk—and two in Portsmouth—Fortunee and The Firm. His total profit from all his enterprises was around £300 a week; he was also engaged in some delicate dickering for the tender to supply the bruited expedition to Botany Bay.

The 'tween decks on the Ceres orlop were six feet, which meant that Richard cleared the ceiling of moldering planks by half an inch and Ike Rogers could not fully straighten. The beams which ran from side to side were a foot lower than this, however, and were spaced six feet apart. Thus turning the act of walking into a parody of a monkish parade, heads bent in a reverence every double pace.

For a Bristol man the smell was bearable, as the wind moaned around the iron grilles and swept through the chilly, red-painted chamber extending from a bulkhead athwart the foremast to the entrance bulkhead in the stern. All told, it was about 40 feet wide and 100 feet in length. Along either outer wall—the hull—were wooden platforms at about the height of a table, and such they seemed to be, for men were sitting at them on benches. The conundrum was that they also seemed to function as beds, for in some places men were lying on them, apparently resting or else gripped by fever. The platform width of six feet also suggested that they were beds. Another table-like platform six feet wide ran down the middle. Perhaps 80 men inhabited this garish crimson chamber, and upon the entry of twelve new inmates all conversation stilled and most heads turned to look.

"Where from?" asked a man sitting at the middle table near the entrance.

"Gloucester Gaol, all twelve of us," said Will Connelly.

The man rose to his feet, revealing himself as short enough to pass beneath the beams, though he had more the physique of a jockey than a midget, and had the face of a man who had spent most of his life around horses—creased, leathery, faintly equine. He might have been any age between forty and sixty.

"How de do," he said more than asked, advancing to meet them and holding out a diminutive paw. "William Stanley from Seend. That is near Devizes in Somerset, but I was convicted in Wiltshire."

"We most of us know of Seend," said Connelly with a grin, then performed introductions. He put his box down with a sigh. "And what happens now, William Stanley from Seend?"

"Ye move in. That would be Sykes did the bum fuck. A real Miss Molly. 'Tis his way of getting to know the convicts from the inside, ye might say. No money, eh? Or did he find it?"

"We have no money," said Connelly, sitting on the bench. He winced. "After Mr. Sykes, this is hard. What does happen now?"

"This end is Midlands, West Country, Channel, Wolds and Wealds," said Stanley, producing an unlit pipe and sucking on it when he was not using it to point in some direction. "Center is the boys from Derby, Cheshire, Stafford, Lincoln and Salop. Far end—bows—is Durham, Yorkshire, Northumbria and Lancashire. Liverpudlians have that end of this middle table. They have a few Irish, all but one Liverpudlian. Got four blackamoors, but they are upstairs with the Londoners. Sorry, Taffy, no Welsh." He eyed their boxes and bags. "If ye've valuables, ye'll lose 'em. Unless," he added, tone loaded with meaning, "we can plain deal."

"Oh, I think that will be possible," said Connelly affably. "I take it we eat off what we sleep on?"

"Aye. Put your tackle right here at this middle table, it has plenty of room for twelve this end. Mats ye sleep on are rolled up under it, and that is where ye'll stow your tackle too. One mangy blanket each two men." He giggled. "We are in the Yankey business of bundling here, not too private if ye're of a mind to toss off. But we all got to toss off—bum fucking ain't popular with the troops after a taste of Mr. Sykes. Upstairs they get women in on Sundays—call 'em their aunties, sisters or cousins. Don't happen here because we are all too far from home and them as has got money prefer to spend it on Hanks's sixpenny gins. Robber!"

"How can ye help us hang on to our things, William?" asked Bill Whiting, suffering two kinds of pain: one from the escort's bludgeon, the other from Mr. Sykes's hand and fingers.

"I do not work, ye see. They tried me in the vegetable patch, but I got eight brown fingers and two brown thumbs—even the turnips curled up their toes. So they gave me up as too old, too stunted and too hard to keep the darbies on." He lifted one tiny foot and surreptitiously wriggled it in his fetter until the iron band sat across his instep. "Ye might say I am the caretaker of this establishment. I run a mop around it, swill out the night buckets, roll up the mats, fold up the blankets and keep the mad Irish at bay. Though our Irish, being Liverpudlians, are not too bad. But there are two on Justitia can only speak Erse—got snabbled the day they hopped off the boat from Dublin. No wonder they run mad. 'Tis hard this side of the Irish sea, and they are soft folk. Gulled in a twinkle, drunk on a dram." He chuckled, sighed. "Ah, 'tis good to see some new West Country blood! Mikey! Here, Mikey!"

A young man slouched up, dark-haired and dark-eyed, with the faintly furtive air West Country men recognized as belonging to a Cornish smuggler. "Nay, not Cornwall," he said, reading their minds. "Dorset. Poole. Seaman in the customs division. Name, Dennison."

"Mikey helps me look after the place—cannot do it on my own. He-me are surplus, never manage to hook up in a six. Mikey has fits—real corkers! Goes black in the face, bites his tongue. Frightens the shit out of Miss Molly Sykes." Stanley eyed the newcomers shrewdly. "Ye're already two lots of six, ain't ye?"

"Aye, and that fellow who says not a word is our leader," said Connelly, pointing to Richard. "Just will not own up to it. Bill Whiting and I have to do all the talking while he sits back, listens, and then makes the decisions. Very peaceful, very clever. I ain't known him all that long, but if Sykes had done that before I met Richard, I would have gone at him—and for what? A sore head as well as a sore arse. And a flogging, eh?"

"A bludgeoning, Will. Mr. Campbell do not hold with the cat, says it keeps too many men off work." William Stanley from Seend half-shut his eyes. " 'Tis you I come to terms with, Richard—what was the surname?"

"Morgan."

"Welsh."

"Bristol born and bred for generations. Connelly has an Irish name, but he is a Bristolian too. Surnames do not mean much."

"Why," asked Ike Rogers suddenly, having spent most of this exchange gazing about, "is this place painted red?"

" 'Twas the orlop on a second-rater," said Mikey Dennison, the smuggler from Poole. "The thirty-two pounders lived in here and so did the surgeon's hospital. Paint the place red and the blood ain't visible. Sight of blood puts the gunners off terrible."

William Stanley from Seend pulled a huge turnip watch from his waistcoat pocket and consulted it. "Grub up in an hour," he said. "Harry the fucken purser will dole out your trenchers and mugs. Today being Friday, 'tis burgoo. No meat, apart from what's in the bread and cheese. Hear the racket overhead?" He poked his pipe at the ceiling. "They are grubbing in London now. We get whatever is left. There be more of them than us."

"What would happen if Mr. Hanks decided to put some Londoners in here?" asked Richard, curiosity stirred.

Little William Stanley chuckled. "He'd not dare do that! If the Irish did not cut their throats in the darkmans—that is their flash lingo for night—the North Country would. Who loves London and Londoners? Tax the whole of England drier than a bog trotter at a Methodist meeting, then spend all of it in London and Portsmouth, London being where the Parliament, the Army and the East India Company are, and Portsmouth where the Navy is."

"Burgoo. If I remember my Mr. Sykes correctly, that means we drink aqua Thames," said Richard, getting up with a dazzling smile. "My friends with dripstones, I think we should conduct a little ceremony. Since ye accused me of being the leader, Will, follow my lead." He put his box on the table, unlocked it with the key he kept around his neck, and pulled a large rag out of it. Once it was draped across his cropped head he began to hum musically; Mr. Handel would have recognized the tune, but nobody on the Ceres orlop did. Bill Whiting forgot his injuries to don a rag, then Will, Neddy, Taffy, and Jimmy followed suit, though they left the music to Richard. Out came Richard's dripstone; the hum became a long, rising and falling aaaah. He passed his hands across it, bent to touch his brow to it, then scooped it up and stalked to the pump, his five acolytes behind him in emulation. Taffy had picked up the melody and sang a high counter to Richard's baritone, notes rather than words. By now only those in the throes of fever were not watching, transfixed; William Stanley's eyes goggled.

Luckily the pump produced a series of trickles rather than gushes; they fell into a copper kettle somone had punched a few holes in. Mr. Campbell's filtration system did serve to confine an occasional horrible lump or tiddler fish, but was incapable of anything else. From there the water dribbled into the scuttles, and so escaped bilgeward.

With a grand gesture Richard indicated to Jimmy Price that he was to work the pump handle, and held his dripstone to catch his three pints. The others followed, Bill Whiting bowing lavishly to Jimmy before filling his dripstone as well, while Richard's fine voice swelled into a loud string of hallelujahs. Then off back to the table, where the six objects were set in its exact center amid many gesticulations. Richard banished his acolytes to two paces behind and spread his hands, wiggling his fingers.

"King of Kings! Lord of Lords! Hallelujah! Hallelujah!" he sang. "Hosannah! O Hippocrates, receive our supplications!" After a final reverential bow, he doffed his rag, folded it with a kiss and sat down. "Hippocrates!" he yelled, so suddenly that everyone jumped.

"Christ! What was that all about?" asked Stanley.

"The rites of purification," said Richard solemnly.

The horsey little man looked suddenly wary. "Is it a joke? Are ye gammoning me?"

"Believe me, William Stanley from Seend, what all six of us are doing is no joke. We are placating Father Thames by invoking the great god Hippocrates."

"Is this going to happen every time ye drink water?"

"Oh, no!" cried Bill Whiting, perfectly understanding the method in Richard's madness. He was setting them apart, endowing them with special qualities, helping to preserve them and their property. How quick he was! All this out of Jimmy's and Lizzie's remarks about his turning filtration into a religion. Miss Molly Sykes would get to hear of it—William Stanley from Seend was a gossip, and had all day inside Ceres. "No," he went on earnestly, "we conduct the rites of purification only on special occasions, like entering a new place of abode. It—it alerts Hippocrates."

"Mind you," said Will Connelly, contributing his mite, "we use the stones every time we drink water, just not with the whole ceremony. That is for the first day of each month—and when we enter a new place of abode, of course."

"Is it witchcraft?" asked Mikey Dennison suspiciously.

"Did ye smell brimstone and sulphur? Did the water turn to blood or soot?" Richard demanded aggressively. "Witchcraft is nonsense. *We* are serious."

"Oh, oh!" Stanley exclaimed, brow clearing. "I forgot! Ye are mostly from Bristol, home to every Dissenter there is."

"Ike," said Richard, getting up, "a word in your ear." They moved a few paces away, every eye still on them. "Confirm our story, and next time we perform join in the chorus. If ye back us we will all keep our things—and our money. Where d'ye hide yours?"

Rogers grinned. "In the heels of my riding boots. They look low on the outside, but inside—I am up on stilts. And yours?"

"One side of every box has a thin inside lining. Those of us with coins can keep them there. They cannot rattle because of lint wadding. Will, Neddy and Bill have a few, I have more than a few, but the other boxes are empty, so if any of us acquire more money there is space for it. Yon William Stanley from Seend can be bought, but the question is, will he tell Sykes?"

The highwayman considered this carefully, then shook his head. "I doubt it, Richard. If he sings, Miss Molly will get the lot. What we have to do is convince the jockey that we only have so much—Christ, I wish we had a regular visitor from London! If we did, we could explain our wealth that way. Ye're right about the water—it is foul. My lads and I will have to drink small beer on burgoo days and I warrant yon William Stanley from Seend can get it for us."

Richard clapped his hand to his head. "Jem Thistlethwaite!" he exclaimed. "I think I can arrange for that visitor, Ike. Are ye of the opinion that Stanley runs an efficient postal service?"

"I am of the opinion that he runs most things efficiently."

When Richard and his team were led on deck the next morning they understood why evacuation from the orlop had been a gradual business; Ceres had the use of a certain number of lighters, but not nearly enough, even with men jammed in, to ferry the convicts en masse to their places of work. Luckily no place of work was farther from Ceres than 500 yards, but they were water yards. The oarsmen plied their open boats with a will simply because this was better work by far than other kinds. Convicts from Censor, they were chained to the under side of the gunwales. Why do they not simply make a run for the shore and escape? Richard wondered, learning later that in days gone by they had escaped, only to be recaptured and sometimes hung.

The chief advantage of "Campbell's academies" (as the hulks were known to their inmates) lay in the fact that they floated; very few Englishmen could swim. That fact also kept a pressed crew on board a vessel once it sailed. Richard could not swim, nor could any of his eleven friends. Which endowed them with a horror of deep water.

His belly was empty, though he had saved half his bread and cheese to eat when dawn came; the half-pint of oatmeal gruel flavored with the bitter herbs called simples he drank as soon as it had been issued to him, gone cold by then, but surely worse twelve hours later. At least Old Mother Hubbard had realized that men performing hard labor had to be fed sufficient to keep their strength up, but less than a day on Ceres had shown him that Mr. Duncan Campbell, more isolated from his superiors than Old Mother Hubbard was, cared not a rush about quality work.

The convicts destined for shore duty had already gone when Richard's lighter ferried its complement of four dredging teams slightly downriver of the ship and somewhat closer to the shore. His dredge was the first of the four, moored by chains on both sides of both ends. It was a true barge, absolutely flat-bottomed and rectangular in shape, its hull (it had neither bow nor stern) curving out of the water at each end to make it easy to run aground and climb on and off when unloading. Being new, its interior was empty, its paintwork unsullied.

They stepped over the gunwale of the lighter onto a five-foot-wide plank platform which ran down one side of the barge only; no sooner was Jimmy Price, the last man, out of it than the lighter shoved off and headed for the next dredge some 50 yards away. After a wave for Ike and his youngsters, they turned to inspect the premises. One end of the barge was a simple shell, whereas the other had a broad deck on which stood a small wooden shack complete with iron chimney stack. Feeling the impact of men coming aboard, their keeper strolled out of his domain puffing away at a pipe of tobacco, a bludgeon in his other hand.

"We do not," said Richard instantly and courteously, "speak the flash lingo, sir. We are from the West Country."

"S'all right, cullies, that don't worry me." He inspected them. "Ye're new to Ceres." As no one volunteered to comment on this observation, he continued to converse with himself. "Ye're not that young, but ye're real strong-looking. Might get a few tons of ballast out o' ye before ye weaken. Any of ye dredgemen?"

"No, sir," said Richard.

"Thought not. Any of ye swim?"

"No, sir."

"Best not lie to me, cullies."

"No lies, sir. We do not come from swimming parts."

"What about I throw one of ye in to find out, eh?" He made a sudden move at Jimmy, who squealed in terror, then on each of the others in the row, watching their eyes. "I believe ye," he said then, returned to his shack, disappeared inside and emerged with a chair, upon which he sat himself, one shin resting on the other leg's knee, pipe blowing a delectable cloud their way. "Me name is Zachariah Partridge and ye call me *Mister* Partridge. I am a Methodist, hence the name, and I have been a dredger since me youth in Skegness on the Wash, which is why I do not care for flash lingo. In fact, I asked Mr. Campbell to make sure I did not get no Londoners. Wanted some Lincoln men, but West Country ain't bad. Any of ye from Bristol or Plymouth?"

"Three from Bristol, Mr. Partridge. I am Richard Morgan, the other two Bristolians are Will Connelly and Neddy Perrott." He pointed each man out. "Taffy Edmunds is from coastal Wales, Bill Whiting and Jimmy Price are from Gloucester."

"Then ye know a bit about the sea." He leaned back in his chair. "This here establishment aims at deepening the channel by dredging out the mud on the bottom with that"—he waved his hand at what looked like a giant, gape-mouthed purse—"bucket. It runs around a chain—there at your feet now, but waist level when bucket is in—which can be shortened or lengthened according to the depth of the water. Adjusted just right for this here spot, did it meself."

Clearly enjoying giving this oration (though there seemed to be no malice in him), Mr. Zachariah Partridge spoke on. "Ye might well wonder why this spot? Because, cullies—that be a word I have picked up local-like—the Royal Arsenal over there supplies the entire army with ordnance, yet there ain't a tenth enough wharfage for the ordnance tenders. Your colleagues in crime on shore are building the new wharves by filling in the marshes around the Warren. And we dredgemen give them their ballast, which of course they have to mix with rock, gravel and lime, else it would all wind up back in river."

"Thank you, Mr. Partridge, for explaining," said Richard.

"Most folk never do, do they?" He waved at the huge purse again. "That there bucket goes in water at my end and comes up where the davit is down far end. If ye do the job right, it will hold fifty pounds of mud and muck—terrible, some of the things what come up! This here barge holds twenty-seven tons of ballast, as we dredgemen refer to it. That means ye will have to dredge up one thousand, one hundred buckets of ballast to fill it. This being winter, ye'll work six hours—they waste two hours getting ye here and back again. A good day's work will give me twenty buckets, which is half a ton. Subtracting"—he is literate and numerate, thought Richard—"Sundays and allowing for another day a week for foul weather, especially this time of year, ye should fill this here establishment with ballast in about ten weeks. When it is full it is towed to the Warren, where ye'll shovel it out before it is towed to a new spot and ye start again."

He loves facts and figures; he is a disciple of John Wesley; he is not from London; and he enjoys what he does—particularly because he does not have to lift a finger. How then do we burrow our way into his affections, or, failing that, gain his approval? Is the degree of labor he expects from us feasible? If it is not, then we will suffer in some subtle Wesleyan way. No brute, he.

"Are we allowed to speak to you, Mr. Partridge? For instance, may we ask questions?"

"Give me what I want, Morgan, and ye'll have no trouble from me. By that I do not mean that I will pamper ye, and if I want, I can break your arm with this here club. But I do not want to, for one good reason. I aim to stand real high in Mr. Campbell's estimation, and to do that I need to produce ballast. I have been put in charge of this here brand-new establishment because my dredge has always produced the most ballast. You help me, and I might be willing to help you," said Mr. Partridge, getting up. "I will now proceed, cullies, to tell ye what to do and how to do it."

The bucket was a thick leather bag about three feet long, with a round maw of iron a little over two feet in diameter. Fused to the iron on its underside was a steel extension shaped like an oval spoon, shallow and sharp-edged. A chain was attached to either side of the iron ring and joined in a Y to the single chain which ran, uninterrupted, in a circuit from one end of the barge to the other with sufficient slack to put the bucket on the river bottom. The chain went around a winch which dropped the bag into the water at Mr. Partridge's end; it sank under its own weight, its leather butt tethered to a rope manipulated from the barge. A geared and pulleyed davit at the other end dragged the iron maw and its steel spoon along the bottom gathering in mud. When the bucket reached the end of the run the davit exerted a vertical pull; up it came, dripping, was swung inboard by turning the davit and hung over the ballast compartment. Then, working the rope on its butt, the bag was upended and vomited its contents. It came down, empty, ran along its chain to the winch, and went over the side again for its next meal of Thames mud.

Getting used to the job took a full week, during which Mr. Partridge did not see anything like his expected half-ton a day. He was calculating upon one bucket every twenty minutes, whereas the new team took an hour. But Mr. Partridge said and did nothing, simply sat on his chair and sucked at his pipe, a mug of rum at his feet and all the activity of the great river to occupy his attention when he was not staring contemplatively at his toiling team. A dinghy was attached to the barge by a painter, which may have meant that he rowed himself ashore at the end of the day, though he seemed to spend at least some nights on board, for he bought wood for his stove and food for his larder from two of the hordes of bum boats which plied their wares around the river; his rum and his ale came from a third.

There were knacks and tricks, his team discovered from sheer experience. The bucket was prone to lift off the bottom and had to be kept down with a pole put in exactly the right place, which was the top of the iron ring, only three inches wide. A matter of sense and feel in water owning no visibility thanks to churning mud. Four men worked the davit and rope, one man the winch, and one man the pole keeping the bucket down. The brute force was almost all on the davit, though the pole man had to be as strong as he was skillful. Mr. Partridge having done and said nothing, Richard was left to sort out the team. Jimmy Price on the winch, which required the least brawn. Bill, Will and Neddy on the davit, Taffy on the rope, and himself on the pole.

Slowly, slowly, slowly their speed increased, as did the amount of ballast in the bucket. When they achieved their twenty buckets in a six-hour day a week after they had started, a genial Mr. Partridge broke out six big tankards of small beer, a pat of butter and six one-pound loaves of fresh, yeasty bread.

"I knew ye were good when I set eyes on ye. Leave men to find their own way, I always says. I get a bonus of five pounds for every load of ballast I deliver to the Warren—ye rub my back and I will rub yours. Give me more than twenty buckets a day and I will give ye lunch—a quart of small beer and a pound of good bread each. Ye're all thinner than ye were a week ago, cannot have that. I have a reputation to look after." He stroked the side of his nose reflectively. "Mind, could not buy ye lunch *every* day."

"We might be able to contribute funds," said Richard. "As a Bristol man, I know the smell of that tobacco—Ricketts. Must be very expensive in Woolwich—even in London, I daresay. It may be possible for me to have some of Ricketts's best sent to you, Mr. Partridge, if ye can give me an address. I fear that were it to go to Ceres, Mr. Sykes would have it."

"Well, well!" Mr. Partridge looked tickled. "Find me just one shilling every day, and I will provide lunch. And send the tobacco to me at the Ducks and Drakes tavern in Plumstead."

At first Ike Rogers and his team did not fare happily, but after a few conferences with Richard and his men they quickened their dredging and came to the same kind of arrangement with their dredgeman, a Kentishman from Gravesend.

The worst feature of the work was its filthiness. From hair of head to soles of feet, they were plastered in blackish, stinking mud; it coated the chain as it ran waist-high along the platform, it dripped from the bucket, it splashed everywhere as the bucket was emptied. By the end of that first week the brand-new barge looked the twin of any of the older rigs.

When Richard realized that once a day two of them would have to descend into the ballast compartment to shovel the gluey mud and its grisly inclusions away from the mound under the bucket, he made a decision.

"Has anybody a sore foot? A cut, a scratch, a blister?"

"Aye, me," said Taffy. "Corn looking nasty, Da."

"Then tonight after we wash I will give ye some of my salve, but it means that ye cannot dig until the foot is better. I am not going into that slime in my shoes. In fact, as soon as it gets a little warmer, I will ask Mr. Partridge"—avidly listening—"if we may put our shoes on his deck and work in bare feet. In the meantime, we do our turns on the shovels in bare feet."

At least they could wash, and did so every evening the moment they were let into the Ceres orlop; for the non-Bristolians the sight of what the Thames dredge brought up was horrifying enough for them to be eager to emulate Richard—strip off, soap and wash at the pump, muddy chains, fetters and all. And they had a nice arrangement with William Stanley from Seend, who had Mikey wash their clothes during the day. Wash them *all,* thanks to Mr. Duncan Campbell the canny Scotch contractor.

For that worthy had issued new clothing—he did this about once a year—to the denizens of his academics four days after the men from Gloucester had arrived: two pairs of coarse, heavy linen trowsers, two checkered linen shirts of the same weight, and one unlined linen jacket. The trowsers, the Gloucester men discovered to their delight, might feel like hacksaws along their seams, but they came down past their ankles, though on Richard and Ike they were shorter. Ike's height had shrunk several inches, but due to their newness in Ceres, no one save his Gloucester companions had noticed, and mum was the word when he switched to shoes.

Wearing trowsers, the men of ordinary height did not have to pad their fetter cuffs, and did not need to wear stockings to keep out the cold Thames winds. Richard, a dab hand with a sewing needle thanks to Lizzie Lock, obtained enough cloth off the ends of Jimmy's trowsers to add to his own, while Ike paid Stanley a mug of gin for his offcuts and had Richard sew them on. What a wonderful invention trowsers were! Theirs were rust-colored, hard-wearing, eminently washable and differently constructed from breeches, which came only to the knees. Whereas breeches opened at the waist on a broad flap held by buttons along the waistband, trowsers opened up the front seam with buttons in a vertical row from a man's genitals to his waist. A great deal easier to take a piss in too.

* * *

Mr. James Thistlethwaite arrived on the second Sunday after they were admitted to Ceres. He appeared in the doorway warmly shaking Mr. Sykes's hand, stepped across the threshold and stared at the crimson prison in disbelief.

"Jem! Jem!"

They embraced unashamedly, then held each other off to look. Close enough to ten years had gone by since last they met, and those ten years had wrought many changes in both men.

To Richard, Mr. Thistlethwaite looked mighty prosperous. His wine red suit was of the finest cloth, his buttons mohair, his head bewigged, his hat trimmed with gold braid, his fob gold, his watch gold, his black top boots absolutely gleaming. The paunch was noble, the face fuller and therefore less lined than it used to be, though the grog blossoms on his bulbous nose had flowered to an empurpled perfection. Beneath the shock, the look in his watery, bloodshot blue eyes was full of love.

To Mr. Thistlethwaite, Richard was like two men moving within each other, one surfacing briefly, the other taking his place for an equally short span of moments. The old Richard and the new, inextricably intertwined. Christ, he was handsome! How had he managed that? The stubble of hair seemed actually to have turned blacker than its old very dark brown, and his skin, weathered though it was, had the same flawless look ivory did. He was shaven and very clean, and the Sunday shirt open on his chest showed the ridges and columns of fatless muscle. Did he not feel the cold? This blood-red chamber was freezing, yet he wore no coat and seemed comfortable. His shoes and stockings were clean—oh, the fetters! Chains on patient, peaceful Richard Morgan. That did not bear thinking of. In his grey-blue Morgan eyes lay most of the change; they had used to be a little dreamy, a little smiling in a serious way, and always very gentle of expression. Now they were more directly focused on whatever he looked at, did not dream, did not smile, and were definitely not gentle of expression.

"Richard, how much you have *grown!* I had expected all kinds of changes, but not that." Mr. Thistlethwaite pinched the bridge of his nose and blinked.

"William Stanley from Seend, this is Mr. James Thistlethwaite," Richard said to a wizened, tiny little man who hovered. "Now give us some elbow room. Everybody leave us in peace, hear? I will do the introductions later. Privacy," he said to Jem, "is the scarcest commodity aboard Ceres, but it can be obtained. Sit down, do!"

"Ye're the head man!" Jem said in wonder.

"No, I am not. I refuse to be. It is just that occasionally I have to be a trifle forceful—but we all do that when provoked. The head man is a notion full of sound and fury, and I am no more a talker now than I was in Bristol. Nor do I want to lead any man other than myself. Needs must, Jem, is all. They are sometimes like sheep, and I would not have them go to the slaughter. Save for Will Connelly, another Bristolian from Colston's under a good Head, they have little skill in using their wits. And the true difference between Will Connelly and me can best be summed up as Cousin James-the-druggist. Had I not known him and had he not been so good to me, the Richard Morgan ye see now would not exist. I would be like those poor Liverpudlian Irish down there, a fish out of water." He smiled brilliantly, leaned forward to take Mr. Thistlethwaite's hand. "Now tell me all about yourself. Ye look exceeding grand."

"I can afford to look exceeding grand, Richard."

"Did ye marry money like any true Bristolian?"

"Nay. Though I do make my money from women. Ye're looking at a man who—under a nom de plume, naturally—writes novels for the delectation of ladies. To read novels is the latest female passion—comes of all this teaching them to read but not letting them *do* anything, y'see. Between bookshops, episodes published serially in magazines and the lending libraries, I do amazing better than ever I did out of lampooning. The counties are stuffed with genteel reading females in every vicarage, parsonage, manor and hotel, so my audience is as big as Britain, for ladies in Scotland and Ireland read also. Not only that, but I am read in America too." He grimaced. "I do not, however, drink Cave's rum anymore. In fact, I have eschewed rum entirely. I now drink only the best French brandy."

"And are ye married these days?"

"Nay again. I have two mistresses, both of whom are married to other, lesser men. And that is enough about me. I want to hear about you, Richard."

Richard shrugged. "There is little to tell, Jem. I spent three months in the Bristol Newgate, exactly a year in Gloucester Gaol, and am now two weeks into however long I shall be aboard Ceres. In Bristol I sat and read books. In Gloucester I lumped stones. On Ceres I dredge the Thames bottom, which is a nothing to one weaned on Bristol mud at low tide. Though all of us find it hard when we bring up the corpse of a baby."

They passed then to the important consideration of money and how to safeguard hoards of gold coins.

"Sykes will be no trouble," said Jem. "I slipped him a guinea and he rolled over to present me with his belly like any other cur. Be of good cheer. I will come to an arrangement with Mr. Sykes to buy ye whatever ye need by way of food or drink. That goes for your friends too. Ye look as trim as a sloop, but ye're thin."

Richard shook his head. "No to the food, Jem, and small beer only. There are almost a hundred men in here, give or take the few who die regularly. Each man watches hawkish to see how much the pursers dish out to every other man. All we need to do is preserve our existing money and perhaps beg more from you if it becomes necessary. We have been lucky enough to encounter an ambitious dredgeman and the Thames is full of bum boats. So we eat well at midday on our dredge for tuppence a man, everything from salt fish to fresh vegetables and fruit. Ike Rogers and his youngsters are succeeding in taming their dredgeman too."

"It is hard to credit," said Jem slowly, "but ye're full of purpose and almost enjoying this. 'Tis the responsibility."

" 'Tis belief in God sustains me. I still have faith, Jem. For a convict, I have had remarkable good luck. A woman called Lizzie Lock in Gloucester, who kept my belongings safe and taught me how to ply a needle. She turned cartwheels over the hat, by the way, and I cannot thank ye enough. We miss the women, for reasons I explained to ye in one of my letters, as I remember. I have kept my health and sharpened my wits. And here in this assemblage of womanless brutes, we have managed to carve a niche for ourselves, thanks to an avaricious jockey and an ambitious dredgeman who combines Methodism with rum, tobacco and laziness. Queer bedfellows, but I have known queerer."

His dripstone was standing on the table near him, and, it seemed absently, he put his hand out to stroke it. A curious hush and murmur arose among those in the crimson chamber, intrigued enough at the advent of a visitor to watch in hang-dog envy. But the reaction of all those men to Richard's idle gesture was a mystery Mr. Thistlethwaite's sensitive nose itched to explore.

"Provided he has a little money, avarice is a convict's best friend," Richard went on, putting his hand back on top of its fellow. "Here, men come far cheaper than thirty pieces of silver. 'Tis folk like the Northumbrians and Liverpudlians I feel sorriest for. They have not a penny between them. So they mostly die of disease or pure hopelessness. Some of them it seems God has a purpose for—they survive. And the Londoners upstairs are astonishing hardy, with all the cunning of starving rats. They live by different rules, I think—perhaps gigantic cities are entire countries in themselves, with their own way of looking at life. Not our way, but I discount a lot of what I hear on the Ceres orlop about the Londoners. The Ceres orlop contains the rest of England. Our gaolers are venal and deviant into the bargain. And then ye must stir the likes of William Stanley from Seend into the mixing bowl. He milks the way this place functions better than a dairymaid her pet cow. And we all of us from Hanks and Sykes through the rum coves, snitches, hicks, cullies and boozers to the dying wretches on that platform over there walk a rope across a pit of fire. One inch too far either way, and we fall." He drew a breath, surprised at his own eloquence. "Though no one in his right mind could call what we play a game, it does share some things in common with a game. There is plenty of wit involved, but also some luck, and it seems God has given me luck."

It was during this speech that Mr. Thistlethwaite suddenly understood much about Richard Morgan that had always teased and tormented him. Richard had spent his life in Bristol as a raft, pushed and pulled at the direction, sometimes the whim, of others. Despite his griefs and disasters, he had remained that passive raft. Even William Henry's disappearance had not provided him with a rudder. What Ceely Trevillian had done for him was to pitch him into an ocean wherein a raft would founder. An ocean wherein Richard perceived his brethren as incapable of floating, and therefore took them upon his own shoulders. Prison had given him a star to steer by, and his own will had swelled sails he did not even know he possessed. Because he was a man who had to have someone to love more than he loved himself, he had undertaken the task of saving his own people, those he had brought with him from Gloucester Gaol into alien and storm-tossed seas.

After the introductions had been performed, the fourteen convicts (William Stanley from Seend and Mikey Dennison had to be included) settled to hear what Mr. James Thistlethwaite could tell them about what might happen to them.

"Originally," said the purveyor of reading delights for most of Britain's literate women, "those on board Ceres were destined for a place called Lemaine, which, as I understand, is an island in the midst of a great African river about the size of the island of Manhattan in New York. Where undoubtedly all of ye would have died of some pestilence within a year. 'Tis

Edmund Burke ye have to thank for striking Lemaine and all Africa from the list of places thought possible transportation destinations.

"Aided and abetted by Lord Beauchamp, last March and April Burke launched an attack on Mr. Pitt's schemes to rid England of its felons. Better, cried Burke, to hang the lot of ye than ship ye off to some place where death would be a great deal slower and a sight more painful. After the inevitable parliamentary committee of enquiry, Mr. Pitt was forced to abandon Africa, probably forever. Hence attention turned to the suggestion of Mr. James Matra—that Botany Bay in New South Wales might be a good place. Lord Beauchamp had made a huge fuss over the fact that Lemaine Island was outside the limits of English territory in an area the French, the Spanish and the Portuguese all frequent for slaving. This Botany Bay, on the other hand, though it certainly lies outside the limits of English territory, is also not anybody else's territory. So why not kill two birds with the same stone? The raven—a far bigger, nastier feathered specimen—is the likes of you, costing England vast sums with little or no return. The quail—a demure and most toothsome little sweeting—is the possibility that, after a few years of outlay, Botany Bay will turn a fat profit for England."

Richard got out a book and tried to show the group whereabouts Botany Bay was on one of Captain Cook's maps, but the only faces to display any kind of comprehension belonged to the literate men.

Mr. Thistlethwaite tried. "How far is it from London to, say, Oxford?" he asked.

"A long way," offered Willy Wilton.

"Fifty miles or thereabouts," said Ike Rogers.

"Then Botany Bay is two hundred times farther from London than Oxford is. If it takes a week for a wagon to journey from London to Oxford, then it would take two hundred weeks for the same wagon to make the journey from Oxford to Botany Bay."

"But wagons cannot travel on water," Billy Earl objected.

"No," said Mr. Thistlethwaite patiently, "but ships can, and much faster than wagons. Four times as fast at least. That means a ship will take a year to go from London to Botany Bay."

"That is excessive," said Richard, frowning. "Ye should know that from Bristol days, Jem. In a good wind a ship can sail near two hundred miles in a single day. Allowing for time spent in ports of call as well as periods of standing and tacking, the time might be as few as six months."

"Ye're splitting hairs, Richard. Be it a mere sixmonth or a whole twelvemonth, Botany Bay is not only on the far side of the globe, but on its underside as well. And I have had enough. I am off." Suddenly sapped, Mr. Thistlethwaite rose to his feet.

As well that they are the infinitely patient Richard's burden! Were they mine, he thought, banging loudly on the door to be let out, I would side with Edmund Burke and hang the lot of them. I can see neither rhyme nor reason in this Botany Bay experiment. It smacks of utter desperation.

"Adieu, adieu!" he cried as the gigger dubber on duty dubbed the gigger for his benefit. "We shall meet anon!"

"Mr. Thistlethwaite is a great swell," said Bill Whiting as he usurped the departed visitor's place alongside Richard. "Is he your London informant, Richard my love?"

The old nickname jarred. "Do not call me that, Bill," he said a little sadly. "It reminds me of Gloucester Gaol's women."

"Aye, it does. I am sorry." He was not the old, cheeky Bill these days; Ceres tended to reject jokers. He thought of something else. "At first I thought that Stanley from Seend would become one of us, but he is only with us for what he can get."

"What could ye expect, Bill? You and Taffy made off with live animals. Stanley from Seend was caught skinning a dead one. He will always fleece what cannot fight back."

"Oh, I do not know," said Bill with a dreamy look at variance with his perky round countenance. "If you and Mr. Thistlethwaite are only half right, 'tis a long sail from here to Botany Bay. A spar might fall on Stanley's pate. And would it not be a sight for sore eyes if Mr. Sykes met with an accident before we go?"

Richard took him by the shoulders and shook him. "Do not even think such things, Bill, let alone say them! There is only one way any of us can ever hope to see an end to misery, and that is to endure it without ever attracting attention to ourselves from those who have the power to increase our misery. Hate them, *but bear them.* All things end. Ceres will. And so, sooner or later, will Botany Bay. We are not young, but we are not old either. Do ye not understand? In surviving, we win! That alone must concern us."

And so time wore on, marked by the little circuits of the dredge bucket's chain—in, out, around. Piles of stinking mud. The stinking orlop of Ceres. The stinking bodies hustled out once a week for burial in a piece of waste ground near Woolwich that Mr. Duncan Campbell had acquired for the purpose. New faces kept arriving; some of them went to the waste ground. Old faces went to it too, but none belonging to Richard or to Ike Rogers.

A certain camaraderie existed between everyone on the orlop, born out of tribulations in common, remotest between groups who could hardly communicate. By the end of the first seven months every face which lasted was known, nodded to, gossip and news exchanged, sometimes simple pleasantries. There were fights, some very serious; there were feuds, some very bitter; there were a certain number of snitches and toadies like William Stanley from Seend; and, rarely, someone died violently.

As in any other enforced congress of very different kinds of men, the grains of single individuals and the various layers of similar weight shook until they settled into stability. Though a monthly repetition of Handelian and Hippocratic invocations served to keep other groups too wary to encroach on their domain, both Richard's and Ike's groups achieved confraternity as well as an exclusivity. They were not bully boys or pranksters or predators, but nor were they the prey of those who were. Live and let live: it was a good rule to go by.

Mr. Zachariah Partridge found no reason to alter his opinion of his dredging crew; as the days lengthened and the hours of labor increased, he was paid his £5 bonus for a full load more frequently than he had dreamed possible. These fellows made a ritual out of keeping fit by working and eating well.

Like everybody else on that populous river from the bum boat denizens to the hulk gaolers, he was well aware that Botany Bay loomed. This disposed him to be generous with his crew because he knew that were they chosen to sail, his chances of getting another crew half as good were slender. The Ricketts tobacco had arrived, together with a small keg of wonderful rum. So when Richard and his men wanted the services of a bum boat vending sometimes peculiar wares, he indulged them provided that the dredge scooped in its stipulated amount of ballast. Fascinated, he watched them accumulate duck clothing, sea soap, shoes, scissors, good razors, strops, whetstones, fine-toothed combs, oil of tar, extract of malt, underdrawers, thick stockings, liniment, string, stout sacks, screws, tools.

"Ye're touched in the noddle," he observed. "D'ye expect to be Noahses?"

"Aye," said Richard solemnly. "That is a fitting comparison. I doubt there are any bum boats at Botany Bay."

News came from Jem Thistlethwaite whenever he had more of it. In late

August he was able to tell them that Lord Sydney had written formally to the Lords Commissioners of the Treasury and notified them that 750 convicts were to be ferried to a new colony in New South Wales likely to be situated at Botany Bay. They would be in the custody of His Majesty's Royal Navy and under the direct control of three companies of marines, who were to sign on for three years' duty dating from arrival in New South Wales.

"They will not simply throw ye ashore," he said, "so much seems certain. The Home Office is awash in lists, from convicts to rum, and tenders for the contracts. Though," he grinned, "it is to be an expedition of male convicts only. They plan to provide women from islands in the vicinity, no doubt in the same manner as Rome obtained women from the Sabines on the Quirinal. Which reminds me that I must give ye the existing volumes of Gibbon's *Decline and Fall.*"

"Christ!" Bill Whiting exclaimed. "Indian wives! But what *sort* of Indians? They come in all varieties from black through red to yellow, and fair as Venus or ugly as Medusa."

But in October Mr. Thistlethwaite informed them that there were to be no Indian wives. "The Parliament was not amused at a reference to the rape of the Sabine women, for all could see that the Indian men would not offer their women as a gift, or maybe even sell them. The Do Gooders shrieked a treat. So women convicts will sail too—how many, I do not know. As forty of the marines are taking their wives and families, it has been agreed that husbands and wives in prison together will both go. There are some such, apparently."

"We knew a pair in Gloucester," said Richard. "Bess Parker and Ned Pugh. I have no idea what has become of them, but who can tell? Perhaps they have been chosen if both live. . . . Yet what a shame to send men like Ned Pugh and women like Lizzie Lock when by next year they will have served five of their seven years."

"Do not hope for Lizzie Lock, Richard. I hear that the women to go will be drawn from the London Newgate."

"Ugh!" was the general reaction to that.

A week later their fount of knowledge was back.

"A governor and a lieutenant-governor have been appointed for New South Wales. A Captain Arthur Phillip of the Royal Navy is to be the governor, and a Major Robert Ross of the Marine Corps is his lieutenant-governor. Ye'll be in the hands of the Royal Navy, and that means ye'll be introduced to the cat. No naval man, even a marine sort, can live without the cat, and I do not mean a four-legged creature which says meow." He shuddered, decided to change the awful subject. "Other appointments have been made. The colony is to exist under naval law—no elected government whatsoever. The judge-advocate is a marine, I believe. There will be a chief surgeon and several assistant surgeons, and of course—how could ye live without a good, stoutly English God?—a chaplain. For the moment, however, it is all hush-hush. No public announcement has been made."

"What is this Governor Phillip like?" asked Richard.

Mr. Thistlethwaite guffawed. "He is a nobody, Richard! A true naval nobody. Admiral Lord Howe was very disparaging when he heard, but I imagine he had some young nephew in mind for a thousand-pound-a-year commission. My source is a very old friend—Sir George Rose, Treasurer of the Royal Navy. He informs me that Lord Sydney chose this Phillip personally after a long conversation with Mr. Pitt, who is determined this experiment will work. An it don't, his government will face defeat on something as piddling as the prison issue. All those felons with nowhere to go, and ever more of them into the bargain. The problem is that transportation is linked to slavery in zealous, reforming Do Gooder minds. So when a Do Gooder espouses the one, all too often he espouses the other."

"There are similarities," said Richard dryly. "Tell me more about this Governor Phillip, who will be the arbiter of our fates."

Mr. Thistlethwaite licked his lips, wishing he had a glass of brandy. "A nobody, as I have already said. His father was a German and taught languages in London. His mother had been the widow of a naval captain, and was a remote connection of Lord Pembroke's. The boy went to a naval version of Colston's, so they were poor. After the Seven Years' War he was put on half-pay and chose to serve in the Portuguese navy, which he did with distinction for several years. His biggest Royal Navy command was a fourth-rater, in which he saw no action. He has come out of a second retirement to take this present commission. Not a young man, nor yet a very old one."

Will Connelly frowned. "It sounds distinctly odd to me, Jem." He sighed. "In fact, it sounds very much as if we are to be dumped at Botany Bay. Otherwise the governor would be—oh, I do not know, a lord or an admiral at the very least."

"Give me the name of one lord or admiral who would consent to go to the far ends of the earth for a mere thousand pounds a year, Will, and I shall offer ye England's Crown and Scepter." Mr. James Thistlethwaite grinned evilly, the lampoonist in him stirred. "A refreshing trip to the West Indies, perhaps. But this? It is very likely a death trap. No one really knows what lies at Botany Bay, though all are assuming it is milk and honey for no better reason than that to think thus is convenient. To be its governor is the sort of job only a nobody would accept."

"You still have not told us why *this* nobody," said Ike.

"Sir George Rose suggested him originally because he is both efficient and compassionate. His words. However, Phillip is also a rarity in the Royal Navy—speaks a number of foreign tongues very fluently. As his German father was a language teacher, he probably absorbed foreign tongues together with his mother's milk. He speaks French, German, Dutch, Spanish, Portuguese, and Italian."

"Of what use will they be at Botany Bay, where the Indians will speak none of them?" asked Neddy Perrott.

"Of no use at all, but of great use in getting there," said Mr. Thistlethwaite, striving manfully to be patient—how did Richard put up with them? "There are to be several ports of call, and none of them are English. Teneriffe—Spanish. Cape Verde—Portuguese. Rio de Janeiro—Portuguese. The Cape of Good Hope—Dutch. It is a very delicate business, Neddy. Imagine it! In sails a fleet of ten armed English ships, unannounced, to anchor in a harbor owned by a country we have warred against, or gone a-poaching in its slaving grounds. Mr. Pitt regards it as imperative that the fleet be able to establish excellent relations with the various governors of these ports of call. English? No one will understand a word of it, not a word."

"Why not use interpreters?" asked Richard.

"And have the dealings go on through an intermediary of low rank? *With the Portuguese and the Spanish?* The most punctilious, protocolic people in existence? And with the Dutch, who would do Satan down if they thought there was a chance to make a profit? No, Mr. Pitt insists that the governor himself be able to communicate directly with every touchy provincial governor between England and Botany Bay. Captain Arthur Phillip's was the only name came up." He rumbled a wicked laugh. "Hur-hur-hur! It is upon such trivialities, Richard, that events turn. For they are *not* trivialities. Yet who thinks of them when the reckoning is totted up? We envision the likes of Sir Walter Raleigh—ruffler, freebooter, intimate of Good Queen Bess. A flourish of lace handkerchief, a sniff at his pomander, and all fall at his feet, overcome. But quite honestly we do not live in those times. Our modern world is very different, and who knows? Perhaps this nobody, Captain Arthur Phillip, has exactly the qualities this particular task demands. Sir George Rose seems to believe so. And Mr. Pitt and Lord Sydney agree with him. That Admiral Lord Howe does not is immaterial. He may be First Lord of the Admiralty, but the Royal Navy does not rule England yet."

The rumors flew as the days drew in again and the intervals between Mr. Zachariah Partridge's £5 bonuses stretched out, not helped by two weeks of solid rain at the end of November which saw the convicts completely confined to the orlop. Tempers shortened, and those who had come to some sort of arrangement with their shore supervisors or dredgemen whereby they ate extra food on the job found it very hard to go back to Ceres rations, which had not improved in quality or quantity. Mr. Sykes trebled his escort when obliged to be in the same area as a large group of convicts, and the racket upstairs on the Londoners' deck was audible on the orlop.

They had ways of passing the time; in the absence of gin and rum, chiefly by gambling. Each group owned at least one deck of playing cards and a pair of dice, but not everyone who lost (the stakes varied from food to chores) was gallant about it. Those who could read formed a substratum; perhaps ten per cent of the total number of men exchanged books if they had them or begged books if they did not, though ownership was jealously guarded. And perhaps twenty per cent washed their linen handouts from Mr. Duncan Campbell, stringing them on lines which crisscrossed the beams and made walking for exercise even harder. Though the orlop was not overcrowded, the available space for walking limited the shuffling, head-bowing parade to about fifty men at any one time. The rest had either to sit on the benches or lie on the platforms. In the six months between July and the end of December, Ceres lost 80 men of disease—over a quarter of the entire convict complement, and evenly distributed between the two decks.

Late in December Mr. Thistlethwaite was able to tell them more. By now his audience had greatly enlarged and consisted of all who could understand him—and that number had grown too, thanks to propinquity. Only the slowest rustics among the orlop inmates by now could not follow the speech of those who spoke an English somewhat akin to that written in books, as well as grasp a great deal of flash lingo provided the users of it spoke slowly enough.

"The tenders have been let," he announced to his listeners, "and some tears have been shed. Mr. Duncan Campbell decided that he had sufficient on his plate with his academies, so ended in not tendering at all. The cheapest tender, from Messrs. Turnbull Macaulay and T. Gregory—seven-and-a-third pence per day per man or woman—did not succeed. Nor did that of the slavers, Messrs. Camden, Calvert & King—Lord Sydney did not think it wise to use a slaving firm for this first expedition, though again the price was cheap. The successful tender is a friend of Campbell's named William Richards Junior. He describes himself as a ship's broker, but his interests go well beyond that. He has partners, naturally. And I take it that he is co-operating closely with Campbell. I should tell ye that the lot of the marines to go with ye is not enviable, for they are included in the tender price on much the same rations save that they get rum and flour daily."

"How many of us are to go?" asked a Lancastrian.

"There are to be five transports to carry about five hundred and eighty male convicts and almost two hundred female, as well as about two hundred marines plus forty wives and assorted children. Three storeships have been commissioned, and the Royal Navy is represented by a tender and an armed vessel which will function as the fleet's flagship."

"What are they calling 'transports'?" asked a Yorkshireman named William Dring. "I am a seaman from Hull, yet it is a sort of ship I do not know."

"Transports convey men," said Richard levelly, meeting Dring's eyes. "In the main, troops to an overseas destination. I believe there are some such, though they would be old by now—the ones used to send troops to the American War had already been used during the Seven Years' War. And there are coastal transports for ferrying marines and soldiers around England, Scotland and Ireland. They would be far too small. Jem, were there any specifications in the tender for transports?"

"Only that they be shipshape and capable of a long voyage through uncharted seas. They have, I understand, been inspected by the Navy, but how thoroughly I could not say." Mr. Thistlethwaite drew a breath and decided to be honest. What was the point in giving these poor wretches false hopes? "The truth, of course, is that there was not a rush to offer vessels. What Lord Sydney had counted on, it seems, was an offer from the East India Company, whose ships are the best. He even dangled the bait of the ships' proceeding directly from Botany Bay to Wampoa in Cathay to pick up cargoes of tea, but the East India Company was not interested. It prefers that its ships call in to Bengal before proceeding to Wampoa, why I do not know. Therefore no source of vessels proven sound for long voyages was at Lord Sydney's disposal. It may well be that naval inspection consisted in culling the best out of a poor lot." He looked around at the dismayed faces and regretted his candor. "Do not think, my friends, that ye'll be embarked upon tubs likely to sink. No ship's owner can afford to risk his property unduly, even if his underwriters allowed him the opportunity. No, that is not what I am trying to tell ye."

Richard spoke. "I know what ye're trying to say, Jem. That our transports are slavers. Why should they not be? Slaving has fallen off since we have been denied access to Georgia and Carolina, not to mention Virginia. There must be any amount of slavers looking for work. And they are already constructed to carry men. Bristol and Liverpool have them tied up along their docks by the score, and some of them are big enough to hold several hundred slaves."

"Aye, that is it," sighed Mr. Thistlethwaite. "You are to go in slavers, those of you who will be picked to go."

"Is there any word of when?" asked Joe Robinson from Hull.

"None." Mr. Thistlethwaite looked around the circle of faces and grinned. "Still, 'tis Christmastide, and I have arranged for the Ceres orlop to be issued with a half-pint of rum for all hands. Ye will not have the chance for any on the voyage, so do not guzzle it, let it sit a while on your tongues."

He drew Richard to one side. "I have brought ye another lot of dripstones from Cousin James-the-druggist—Sykes will hand them over, have no fear." He threw his arms about Richard and hugged him so tightly that none saw the bag of guineas slip from his coat pocket into Richard's jacket pocket. " 'Tis all I can do for ye, friend of my heart. Write, I beg, whenever that may be."

"My thumbs are pricking," said Joey Long over supper on the 5th of January, 1787, and shivered.

The others turned to look at him seriously; this simple soul sometimes had premonitions, and they were never wrong.

"Any idea why, Joey?" asked Ike Rogers.

Joey shook his head. "No. They are just pricking."

But Richard knew. Tomorrow was the 6th, and on each 6th of January for the past two years he had begun the move to a new place of pain. "Joey feels a change coming," he said. "Tonight we get our things together. We wash, we cut our hair back to the scalp, we comb each other for lice, we make sure no item of clothing or sack or bag or box is unmarked. In the morning they will move us."

Job Hollister's lip quivered. "We might not be chosen."

"We might not. But I think Joey's thumbs say we will."

And thank you, Jem Thistlethwaite, for that half-pint of rum. While the Ceres orlop snored, I was able to secret your guineas in our boxes, though no one knows save me.

PART FOUR

From
January of 1787
until
January of 1788

At dawn the tranfportees were culled, a total of 60 men in their habitual groups of six, leaving another 73 convicts looking vastly relieved at being passed over. Who, how or why the ten groups chosen to go from the Ceres orlop had been selected no one knew, save that Mr. Hanks and Mr. Sykes had a list and worked from it. The ages of those going varied from fifteen to sixty; most of them (as all the old hands knew) were unskilled, and some of them were sick. Mr. Hanks and Mr. Sykes ignored such considerations; they had their list and that, it seemed, was that.

William Stanley from Seend and the epileptic Mikey Dennison were hopping from foot to foot in glee because they were not on the list. Life on the Ceres orlop was comfortable, there would soon be fresh fleeces.

"Bastards!" Bill Whiting hissed. "Look at them gloat!"

The door opened; four new convicts were thrust inside. Will Connelly and Neddy Perrott squawked simultaneously.

"Crowder, Davis, Martin and Morris from Bristol," explained Connelly. "They must have been sent from Bristol just for this."

Bill Whiting gave Richard a broad wink. "Mr. Hanks! Oh, Mr. Hanks!" he called.

"What?" asked Mr. Herbert Hanks, who had been liberally greased in the palm by Mr. James Thistlethwaite and had promised to do his utmost to favor Richard's and Ike's groups if they were among those to go. That he was inclined to honor his promise lay in the fact that Mr. Thistlethwaite had whispered of additional largesse after they had gone if his spies informed him that what could be done had indeed been done. "Speak up, cully!"

"Sir, those four men are from Bristol. Are they going?"

"They are," said Mr. Hanks warily.

The old, merry Whiting looked sideways at Richard, then the round face assumed an expression of diffident humility for Mr. Hanks. "Sir, they are but four. The thing is, we do so hate being parted from Stanley and Dennison, Mr. Hanks, sir. I wondered. . . ?"

Mr. Hanks consulted his list. "I see that the two who were to go with them died yesterday. They is four too many or two too few, whichever way youse looks at it. Stanley and Dennison will round it off real nice."

"Got you!" said Whiting beneath his breath.

"Thankee, you bugger!" said Ike through his teeth. "I was looking forward to life without that pair."

Neddy Perrott giggled. "Believe me, Ike, two craftier shits than Crowder and Davis do not exist. William Stanley from Seend will meet his match and more."

"Besides, Ike," said Whiting, smiling angelically, "we will need a couple of workers to mop the deck and do the washing."

The convicts to go were fitted with locked waist bands and locked manacles, but no extensions to their ankles; instead, a long chain was passed from one waist to the next and fused each six men together. Weeping and wailing because they had not sufficient time to gather all the things they needed, Stanley and Dennison were hitched to the four newcomers from Bristol.

"That makes sixty-six of us in eleven groups," said Richard.

Ike grimaced. "And at least that many from London."

But that, as they found out later, was not the case. Only six groups of six were chosen from upstairs, and by no means confined to the true flash coves of an Old Bailey conviction and the London Newgate; most were from around London and many of those from Kent of the Thames, particularly Deptford. Why, no one knew, even Mr. Hanks, who simply followed his list. The whole expedition was a mystery to all who had dealings with it, whether a part of it or whether remaining behind.

His box and two canvas sacks by his side, Richard told the orlop transportees off: one gang from Yorkshire and Durham, one from Yorkshire and Lincolnshire, one from Hampshire, three from Berkshire, Wiltshire, Sussex and Oxfordshire, and three from the West Country. With an occasional oddment. But Richard's puzzle-loving mind had long ago made certain deductions: some parts of England produced convicts galore, while others like Cumberland and a large tract of counties around Leicestershire produced none at all. Why was that? Too bucolic? Too sparsely populated? No, Richard did not think so. It depended upon the judges.

* * *

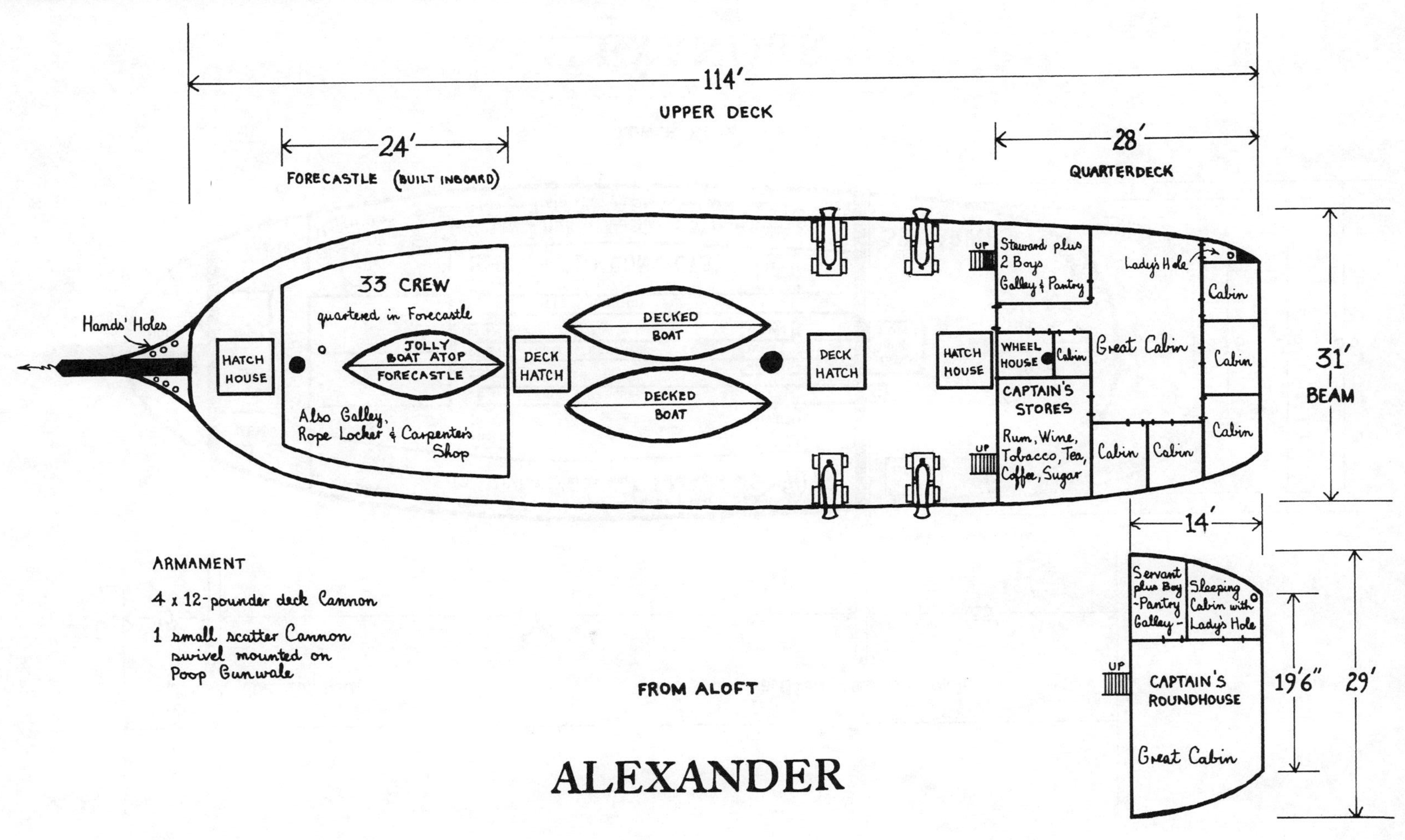
114′
UPPER DECK
24′
FORECASTLE (BUILT INBOARD)
28′
QUARTERDECK
Hands' Holes
HATCH HOUSE
33 CREW
quartered in Forecastle
JOLLY BOAT ATOP FORECASTLE
Also Galley, Rope Locker & Carpenter's Shop
DECK HATCH
DECKED BOAT
DECKED BOAT
DECK HATCH
HATCH HOUSE
UP
Steward plus 2 Boys Galley & Pantry
WHEEL HOUSE
Cabin
CAPTAIN'S STORES
Rum, Wine, Tobacco, Tea, Coffee, Sugar
Lady's Hole
Great Cabin
Cabin
Cabin
Cabin
Cabin
Cabin
31′
BEAM
14′
Servant plus Boy -Pantry Galley-
Sleeping Cabin with Lady's Hole
CAPTAIN'S ROUNDHOUSE
Great Cabin
19′6″
29′
ARMAMENT
4 x 12-pounder deck Cannon
1 small scatter Cannon swivel mounted on Poop Gunwale
FROM ALOFT
ALEXANDER

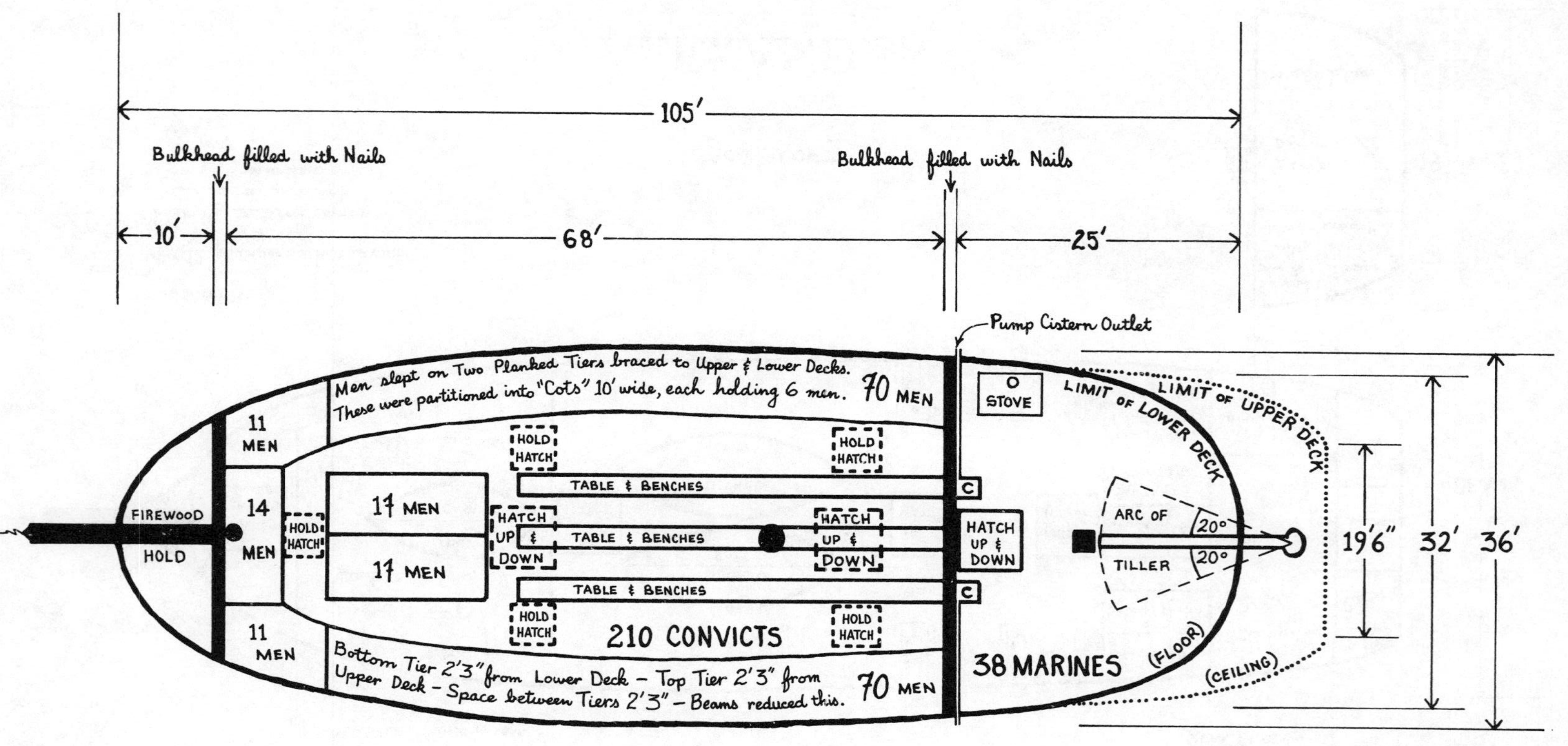

LOWER DECK

ALEXANDER

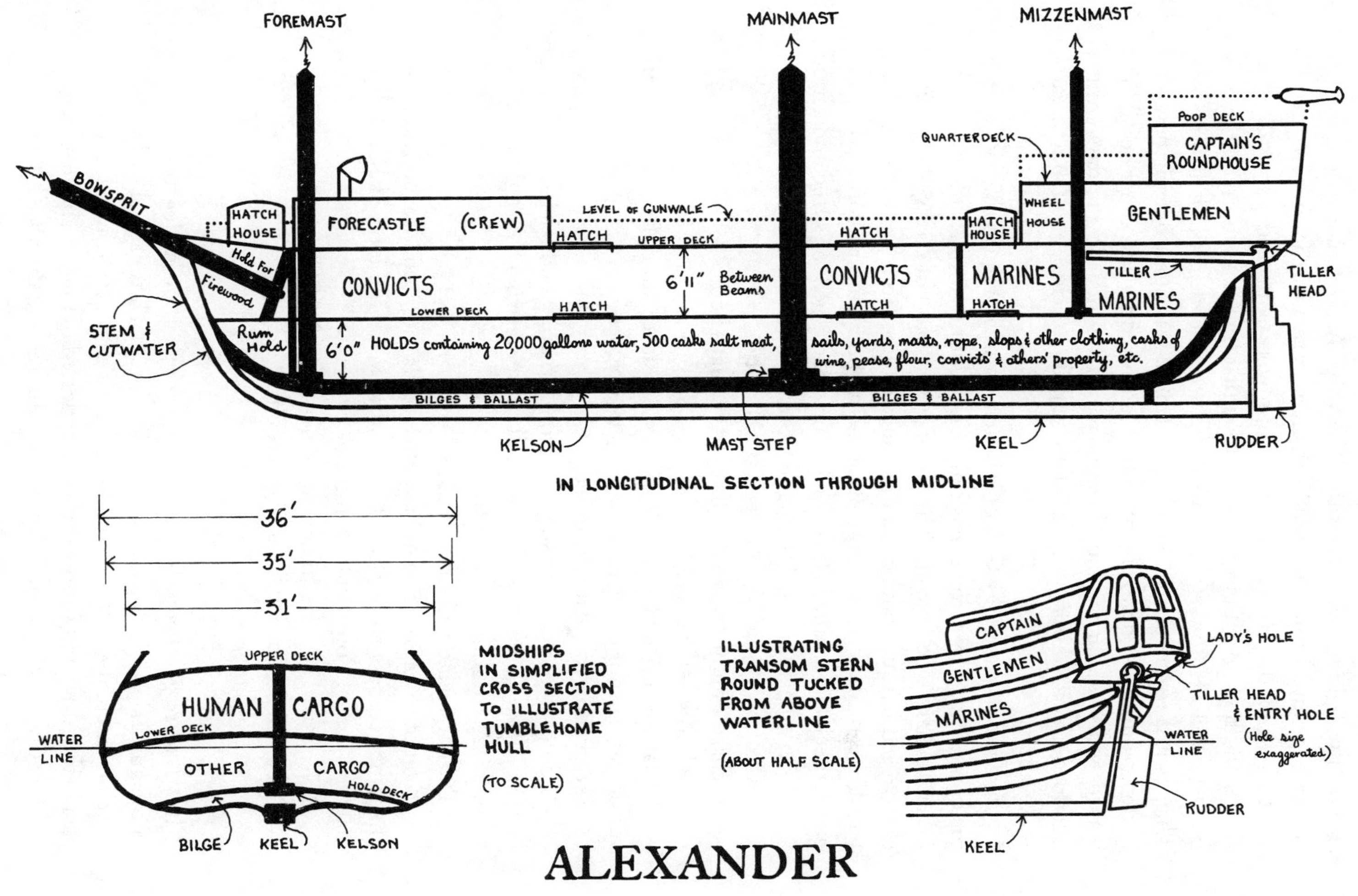
FOREMAST
MAINMAST
MIZZENMAST
POOP DECK
QUARTERDECK
CAPTAIN'S ROUNDHOUSE
BOWSPRIT
HATCH HOUSE
FORECASTLE (CREW)
LEVEL OF GUNWALE
HATCH
UPPER DECK
HATCH
HATCH HOUSE
WHEEL HOUSE
GENTLEMEN
Hold For Firewood
CONVICTS
6'11" Between Beams
CONVICTS
MARINES
TILLER
MARINES
TILLER HEAD
LOWER DECK
HATCH
HATCH
HATCH
STEM & CUTWATER
Rum Hold
6'0" HOLDS containing 20,000 gallons water, 500 casks salt meat,
sails, yards, masts, rope, slops & other clothing, casks of wine, pease, flour, convicts' & others' property, etc.
BILGES & BALLAST
BILGES & BALLAST
KELSON
MAST STEP
KEEL
RUDDER
IN LONGITUDINAL SECTION THROUGH MIDLINE
36'
35'
31'
UPPER DECK
HUMAN CARGO
LOWER DECK
WATER LINE
OTHER CARGO
HOLD DECK
BILGE
KEEL
KELSON
MIDSHIPS IN SIMPLIFIED CROSS SECTION TO ILLUSTRATE TUMBLEHOME HULL
(TO SCALE)
ILLUSTRATING TRANSOM STERN ROUND TUCKED FROM ABOVE WATERLINE
(ABOUT HALF SCALE)
CAPTAIN
GENTLEMEN
MARINES
LADY'S HOLE
TILLER HEAD & ENTRY HOLE
(Hole size exaggerated)
WATER LINE
RUDDER
KEEL
ALEXANDER

Two big lighters lay alongside. The three West Country groups and the two groups from around Yorkshire were loaded into the first—a tight fit—and the six remaining groups were squeezed perilously into the second boat. At about ten o'clock on that fine, cold morning the oarsmen stroked off downriver toward the great bend in the half-mile-wide Thames just to the east of Woolwich. Traffic was light, but the news had gotten around; the denizens of bum boats, dredges and other small craft waved, whistled shrilly and cheered, while the men on the dangerously overloaded second boat prayed no one sailed past close enough to create a wake ripple.

Around the curve lay Gallion's Reach, an anchorage for big ships occupied on that day by two vessels only, one about two-thirds the size of the other. Richard's heart sank. The larger vessel had not changed a scrap—a ship-rigged barque standing about fourteen feet from gunwales to water, which meant she had no cargo aboard—no poop and no forecastle, just a quarterdeck and a galley aft of the foremast. Stripped for speed and action.

His eyes met those belonging to Connelly and Perrott.

"Alexander," said Neddy Perrott hollowly.

Richard's mouth was a thin line. "Aye, that's her."

"Ye know her?" asked Ike.

"That we do," said Connelly grimly. "A slaver out of Bristol, late a privateer. Famous for dying crews and dying cargoes."

Ike swallowed. "And the other?"

"I do not know her, so she ain't from Bristol," said Richard. "She will have a bronze plate screwed to her hull at the stern, so we ought to be able to see it. We are going to Alexander."

The nameplate said she was Lady Penrhyn.

"Out of Liverpool and built special for slaving," said Aaron Davis, one of the newcomers from Bristol. "Brand new, by the look of her. What a maiden voyage! Lord Penrhyn must be desperate."

"No sign of anyone going aboard her," said Bill Whiting.

"She will fill up, never fear," said Richard.

They had to get themselves and their gear up a rope ladder to an opening in the gunwale amidships, a twelve-foot climb. Those ahead of his group were not encumbered by boxes, but even when their chains became entangled in the rungs and supports no one appeared in the gap above to help.

Luckily the chain connecting them ran free and distance between each of them could be expanded or contracted. "Bunch up and give me all the chain," said Richard when their turn came. He tossed both his sacks up, used his manacles to cradle his box, and scaled those few feet in a hurry to make sure no one already up had the presence of mind to pinch one of his sacks. Once aboard, he gathered in his stuff and took the boxes his fellows handed up to him.

Alexander's two longboats and her jollyboat had been taken off the deck and put in the water, so there was room for Richard to move his three West Country groups out of the way. Confusion was his initial impression; knots of scarlet-coated marines stood about looking like thunder, two sashed marine officers and two corporals manned a small scatter cannon swiveled on the quarterdeck rail, and a motley collection of sailors hung from the shrouds or perched on various kennels like spectators at a boxing match in a meadow.

What happens now? As there was no one to ask, he watched the confusion grow ever worse. Long before all eleven lots of convicts were on the deck the place resembled a menagerie—an impression added to by dozens of goats, sheep, pigs, geese and ducks running all over the place pursued by a dozen excited dogs. Feeling someone watching him fixedly from above, he lifted his head to see a large marmalade cat balanced comfortably on a low spar surveying the chaos with an expression of bored cynicism. Of gaolers there were none; they had stayed behind on Ceres, responsibility for the transportees ended.

"Soldiers," whispered Billy Earl from rural Wiltshire.

"Marines," corrected Neddy Perrott. "White facings on their coats. Soldiers have colored facings."

Finally a first lieutenant of marines descended in a snappy fashion from the quarterdeck and surveyed the scene with a nasty look in his pale blue eyes. "My name," he bellowed with a burr in his voice, "is First Lieutenant James Shairp of the 55th Company, Portsmouth! Ye convicts are under my command and will answer to no one except His Majesty's Marines. It is our duty to feed ye and keep ye from annoying anybody, including us. Ye will do as ye are told and not speak unless ye are spoken to." He pointed to a yawning hatch aft of the mainmast. "Get yourselves and your rubbish below, one lot at a time. Sergeant Knight and Corporal Flannery will precede ye and show ye where ye are to be stowed, but before ye move I will inform ye what the business is. Ye will go to the berths the sergeant assigns ye and ye will not change from those berths because ye will be counted and told off by number and by name every day. Each man is allowed twenty inches, no more and no less—we have to fit two hundred and ten of ye into a very small space. If ye fight among yourselves, ye will be flogged. If ye steal rations, ye will be flogged. If ye answer back, ye will be flogged. If ye want what ye are not allowed, ye will be flogged. Corporal Sampson is the company flogger and he takes pride in his work. If ye like to lie down—and lie down is all ye will be able to do—then do not court a bloody back. Now get going." He turned on his heel and marched back to the quarterdeck and the scatter cannon.

Though Scotch convicts were nonexistent, Richard recognized the speech pattern by now, particularly Shairp's constant use of "ye." The old form of "you" was slowly disappearing; he used it himself, but not when "you" needed special emphasis. So this marine officer was a Scotchman; he had heard that most marine officers were.

Sergeant Knight and Corporal Flannery disappeared down the hatch. Nothing ventured, nothing gained, thought Richard as everyone hung back. He jerked his head and led his three groups to the six-foot-square opening in the deck. God help us and God save us! he prayed, handed his box to Bill Whiting behind him, dropped his two sacks down the hatch, and leaned over it. About four feet below him was a narrow plank table; he sat on the edge of the opening and dropped neatly onto it, reached up for his box, and waited until Bill had enough slack on the chain to follow. All six got down, each stepping off the table onto a bench and thus to the deck, where they found themselves penned in by another table and set of benches. Everything seemed bolted to the floor, for nothing moved a fraction of an inch when shoved.

"Get over!" barked the sergeant.

They got over and stood in an aisle of deck less than six feet wide. Looking forward into the darkness, they were on the left, or larboard, side. Fixed to the larboard hull were two tiers of platforms very similar to those on Ceres, save that these were double. Each was firmly braced by stanchions and had a curved outer edge which followed the line of the hull, and they were actually quite beautifully made. No one would be able to dismember them in a fit of lunacy. At ten-foot intervals the platforms were partitioned off; the top tier was a little over two feet below the upper deck, the bottom tier was a little over two feet above the lower deck, and the distance between the two tiers was a little over two feet. As even Ike Rogers could comfortably stand upright in the aisle between the beams, Richard calculated that the 'tween decks height was close to seven feet; his head cleared the beams themselves with half an inch to spare.

"These are yer cots," said the sergeant, a villainous individual who grinned to display the rotten teeth of a heavy rum drinker as he pointed at the tiers. "You lot, up on top, first cot agin the bulkhead, and gimme yer names and numbers. Corporal Flannery here is an Irishman and writes a treat. Look sharp, now!"

"Richard Morgan, number two hundred and three," said Richard, put a foot on the lower platform and hauled himself and his goods onto the top platform, the other five following; they were still chained together. Ike's six were directed into the adjoining top "cot," partitioned off from theirs by thin boards down the middle of a beam that ran from larboard to starboard hull. Stanley, Mikey Dennison and the four late arrivals from Bristol were put into the cot below theirs; underneath Ike were six Northmen including the two sailors from Hull, William Dring and Joe Robinson.

"Cozy," said Bill Whiting with a rather hollow chuckle. "I always wanted to sleep with you, Richard my love."

"Shut up, Bill! There are plenty of sheep on deck."

Six of them were crammed into a space ten feet long, six feet wide and twenty-seven inches high. All they could do unless they lay down was to sit hunched over like gnomes, and, sitting like gnomes, each of them tried to cope with leaden despair. Their boxes and sacks occupied room too—room they did not have. Jimmy Price began to weep, Joey Long and Willy Wilton in the next cot were howling—oh, dear God, what to do?

Across the three tables and six benches in the middle was another double tier of platforms on the starboard side; even craning into the darkness did not reveal how far the chamber extended or what it really looked like. A steady trickle of chained men were dropping onto the middle table, then were herded into the aisle and inserted into a cot. When six of their eleven groups had been put on the larboard side, Sergeant Knight started directing men to starboard and again filled up the cots from the stern bulkhead forward—up, up, down, down.

Over the worst of his shock, Richard summoned the will to act. Did he not, all of them would be in tears, and that he could not have. "All right, first we deal with our boxes," he said crisply. "For the moment we stack them upright against the hull—there will be just enough room between them to put our feet. 'Tis lucky we put the solids in the boxes and filled at least one sack with clothes and rags, because a soft sack will be a pillow." He felt the coarse matting under him and shuddered. "No blankets as yet, but we can bundle for warmth. Jimmy, stop crying, please. Tears do nothing to help." He eyed the beam where the partition was between them and Ike's cot. "That beam will take extra things once I manage to get out a screwdriver and hooks—cheer up, we will manage."

"I want my head against the wall," said Jimmy, snuffling.

"Definitely not," said Will Connelly firmly. "We put our heads where we can hang them over the edge to puke. Do not forget, we are going to sea and we will be doing a lot of puking for a while."

Bill Whiting achieved a laugh. "Just think how lucky we are! We puke on those below us but they cannot puke on us."

"Good point," said Neddy Perrott, and leaned his head over. "Hey, Tommy Crowder!"

Crowder's head appeared. "What?"

"We get to puke on you."

"Do, and I will personally fuck ye!"

"In fact," said Richard cheerfully, interrupting this exchange, "there is a lot of beam vacant—all the way to the starboard cots. We may be able to build some sort of shelf off it on either side to hold spare stuff—even our boxes, certainly our sacks of books and spare dripstones. Yon Sergeant Knight looks as if he would not say no to an extra pint of rum, so he might be willing to gift us with planks, brackets and rope for trussing. We will manage, boys."

"Ye're right, Richard," said Ike, poking his head around the partition. "We will manage. Better this than the nubbing cheat."

"The hangman's rope is the end, I agree. This will not last forever," said Richard, glad that Ike and his boys were listening.

The prison was almost pitch-black; its only light came from the open hatch to the deck above. And the stench was frightful, a stale foulness that was a mixture of rotting flesh, rotting fish and rotting excrement. Time passed, how much of it was impossible to tell. Eventually the hatch was closed with an iron grille that permitted some light and a hatch in the forward end of the chamber was opened. From where they huddled this extra illumination still did not tell them what their prison was like. Another stream of convicts dribbled in, voices muffled, attenuated; many wept, a few started to scream and were suddenly silenced—with what and by whom, the six in Richard's cot had no idea. Except that what they felt, everybody obviously felt.

"Oh, God!" came Will Connelly's voice, loud in despair. "I will not be able to read! I will go mad, I will go mad!"

"No, you will not," said Richard strongly. "Once we settle in and stow our things properly, we will think of things to do with the only instruments we have left—our voices. Taffy and I can sing, so I am sure can others. We will have a choir. We can play at riddles and conundrums, tell stories, jests." He had made his men change places so that he now sat against Ike's partition. "Listen to me, all of you who can hear! We will learn to pass the time in ways we have not yet dreamed of, and we will not go mad. Our noses will get used to the smell and our eyes will become sharper. If we go mad they win, and I refuse to allow that. *We* will win."

No one spoke for a long while, but no one wept either. They will do, thought Richard. They will do.

Two strange marines came aft from the forward hatch to take off their waist bands and the chain connecting them together, though the manacles remained on. Free to move now, Richard came down off the platform to see if he could locate the night buckets. How many were there? How long would they have to last between emptyings?

"Under our platform," said Thomas Crowder. "I think there is one for each six men—at least there are two beneath this cot. *Cot!* What a divine description of something Procrustes would have been proud to invent!"

"Ye're educated," said Richard, perching his rump on the edge of the lower tier and stretching his legs out with a sigh.

"Aye. So is Aaron. He is a Bristolian, I am not. I was—er—apprehended in Bristol after I escaped from the Mercury, is all. Got snabbled doing some dirty work there. Our accomplice—Aaron was in it too—was a snitch. We tried a bit of hush money—would have done the trick in London, but not in Bristol. Too many Quakers and other autem cacklers."

"Ye're a Londoner."

"And ye're a Bristolian, judging by the accent. Connelly, Perrott, Wilton and Hollister I know, but I never saw you in the Bristol Newgate, cully."

"I am Richard Morgan and I am from Bristol, but I was tried and convicted at Gloucester."

"I was listening to what ye said about passing the time. We will do it too if there is not enough light for cards." Crowder sighed. "And I thought Mercury was Satan's ferry! Alexander will be hard going, Richard."

"Why did ye think it would be otherwise? These things were built to house slaves, and I doubt they could have jammed many more slaves in than they have us. Save that we do have those three long tables there, so I presume they feed us seated."

Crowder sniffed. "Marine cooks!"

"Surely ye did not expect the cook at the Bush Inn?" Richard went up to impart the news of the night buckets and got his dripstone out. "Now more than ever we have to filter our water, though we need not fear anyone will encroach on our space or steal our things." His white teeth flashed in a smile. "Ye were right about Crowder and Davis, Neddy. True villains."

They were fed by lamplight and two surly private marines who seemed extremely disgruntled. Though each table was 40 feet long and a total of six narrow benches was provided, the three tables were men from end to end; counting heads, Richard thought that Alexander had taken about 180 men aboard that sixth day of January, 1787. That was 30 short of the total Lieutenant Shairp had mentioned. Not all were from Ceres; there were a few from Censor and rather more from Justitia, though not all the Justitia men managed to drag themselves to the tables. Some kind of sickness was among them, marked by a low fever and aching bones. Not the gaol fever, then. It was there too, however, because it always was.

Each man was issued with a wooden bowl, a tin spoon and a tin dipper which held two quarts* comfortably; two quarts were the day's ration of water per man. The food consisted of very hard, dark bread and a small chunk of boiled salt beef. Those with poor teeth fared badly, were reduced to trying to break up their bread with their spoons, which bent and twisted.

But there were advantages to being near the after hatch of the prison. I will now, Richard decided, risk a flogging by standing up and offering to help these young marines do a task they have no skill at whatsoever.

"May I give ye a hand?" he asked, smiling deferentially. "I used to be a tavern-keeper."

The sullen face nearest him looked startled, was suddenly quite attractive. "Aye, it would be appreciated. Two of us to feed near two hundred men ain't enough, that is certain."

Richard passed bowls and dippers down for some time in silence, having deftly established a routine between himself, the youth he had addressed and his equally young confrere. "Why are you marines so unhappy?" he asked then, voice low.

" 'Tis our quarters—they are lower down than yours are and nigh as

* The modern imperial liquid measures of pint, quart and gallon are larger than the American, but in the eighteenth century are likely to have been the same as the modern American; leaving the British fold in 1776 meant that the United States of America kept many of the old British ways, probably including measures. Thus Richard's quarts were likely to have contained 32 fluid ounces, not the modern imperial 40 fluid ounces.

crowded. We do not eat no better either. Hard bread and salt beef. Except," he added fairly, "that we get flour and a half-pint of drinkable rum."

"But ye're not convicts! Surely—"

"On this ship," said the other marine, snarling, "there is little difference between convicts and marines. The *sailors* are quartered where we should be. The only light and air we get comes through a hatch in the floor of their place—they are abaft of this bulkhead in steerage, while we are down in the hold. Alexander is supposed to be a two-decker, but no one mentioned that the second deck is being used as a hold because Alexander carries a lot of cargo and has no proper hold."

"She is a slaver," said Richard, "so she does not need a true hold. Her captain is accustomed to putting the hard cargo on his orlop, the negroes in here where we are, and the crew in the stern compartment. Hence no forecastle for the crew. The quarterdeck is the captain's." He looked sympathetically curious. "I take it that he is accommodating your officers on the quarterdeck?"

"Aye, in a cupboard, and with no access to his galley, so our officers have to mess with us," said the disher-up of salt beef and bread. "They are not even allowed to use the great cabin—he keeps that for himself and the first mate, a very grand fellow. This ain't like any ship I have ever been in. But then, 'tis the first ship I have been in what did not belong to the Navy."

"Ye'll be below the water line when the cargo is aboard," said Richard thoughtfully. "She will be carrying a mighty big cargo if she is contracted to cargo as well as convicts. I would reckon she will have near twenty thousand gallons of water alone if the legs are two months long."

"Ye know a lot about ships for a tavern-keeper," said the lad scooping out water.

"I am from Bristol, where ships matter. My name is Richard. May I know yours?"

"I am Davy Evans, he is Tommy Green," said the water-scooper. "We cannot do much about our situation here, but when we get to Portsmouth next week 'twill be different. Major Ross will soon tidy Captain Duncan Sinclair up."

"Ah yes, the Commandant of Marines *and* Lieutenant-Governor."

"How d'ye know that?"

"From a friend."

So a great many questions have been answered, Richard reflected as he filtered his water. The owners grabbed at the tender, falsified a few little details about Alexander's history, and chose to ignore the fact that she would have to accommodate marines as well as convicts. Yon lads are right—the contractors see little difference between marines and convicts. So we are for Portsmouth next week, and a captain named Duncan Sinclair is as sure to be Scotch as a man named Robert Ross, Commandant of Marines. The confrontation between them will be horrible. If I remember my Newton, the irresistible force will collide with the immovable object.

Alexander did not sail for Portsmouth that week, the next week or the week after that; she still sat at anchor in the Thames. On the 10th of January she did get under way to an accompaniment of moans and whimpers from those who expected to be seasick, but she sailed only as far as Tilbury, and that by courtesy of a towline from a tender. Still well inside the sheltered waters of the Thames, hardly even rocking.

By now there were 190 convicts on board, though a couple had died and Lieutenant Shairp had delegated the top tier of a midline set of platforms forward of the tables as a receiving place for the sick in an attempt to contain whatever was threatening to rage. This total of 190 would fall by one, be added to by two as the days went by, so that even precise men like Richard finally gave up trying to count at around 200.

The presence of manacles was bitterly resented, but Sergeant Knight (very co-operative about planks, brackets and whatever else was needed in return for rum money—nor were Richard's men the only ones to make use of the sergeant's little weakness) refused to remove these exasperating restraints. Until convict discontent boiled into a very vocal and terrifying demonstration of anger on the release of one man, pardoned. A maddening, relentless banging, shouting and thumping began. When the marines came down to issue food and water they descended in force, perched the scatter cannon on the hatch border and circled it with muskets. Only then did they realize how few of them there were to control 200 furious men.

As it was his ship, Captain Duncan Sinclair ordered that the convicts be taken permanently out of their manacles and paraded on deck twelve at a time for a few minutes during each day. However, an escaped convict would have cost him £40 out of his own pocket, so Sinclair had the marines and some of his crew man the ship's boats, then had them row in constant circles around Alexander.

Those few minutes on deck were among the best Richard had ever experienced. His fetters felt like feathers, the freezing air smelled sweeter than wallflowers and violets, the turgid river was a ribbon of liquid silver, and the sight of the animals frisking cheekily a greater pleasure than bedding Annemarie Latour. It seemed as if half the marines owned at least one dog, as did some of the crew; there were liver-colored hounds, dewlapped bulldogs, silly spaniels, terriers and a great many mongrels. The big marmalade cat had a tortoiseshell wife and a family of six, and most of the ewes and sows were gravid. Ducks and geese roamed loose, but the chickens were penned in a coop near the crew's galley.

After that first walk the foetid prison was more bearable, a sentiment Richard was not alone in feeling. The demonstration had died down the moment hands were freed of manacles, and the deck privilege was not withdrawn.

On his third outing Richard finally saw Captain Duncan Sinclair, and stared in amazement. *Hugely* fat! So fat that all his pleasures were certainly of the table—how did he piss accurately when his arms couldn't possibly reach his penis? Looking very humble and as if the word "escape" were not a part of his vocabulary, Richard clinked across the deck to take a turn from larboard to starboard below the quarterdeck upon which Captain Sinclair stood. For a moment his eyes met a pair of extremely shrewd grey ones; he bowed his head respectfully and moved away. Not a mere tub of lard, for all his size. . . . Lazy to the point of inertia he may be, but when the Devil takes the reins and drives, I will warrant he can rise to the challenge. What a to-do there will be in Portsmouth when he and the Commandant of Marines clash over whereabouts the marine contingent will sling their hammocks! A pity that I will never know what passes between them, albeit I am bound to learn the outcome. Davy Evans and Tommy Green will be dying to tell me.

Toward the end of January two more ships hove to off Tilbury Fort, an oversized sixth-rater and a neat-looking sloop. When it came time for Richard's turn on deck he went straight to the rail near the bows and stared at them intently; rumors of their advent had already spread around the prison. By mutual agreement Richard and his five companions separated the moment they emerged on deck, hugging a tiny span of freedom from proximity to each other. Since no one had yet tried to escape, the marines were more relaxed about their guard duty; provided that the convicts were quiet and orderly in their progress, no one bothered them. Thus Richard stood alone, his hands on the rail, gazing. And had no inkling that he was one of the human cargo the sharp eyes of the crew had singled out as interesting.

"They are our escort to Botany Bay," said a voice in his ear. A pleasant voice containing a great deal of charm.

Richard turned his head to see the man who had been pointed out to him as Alexander's fourth mate. She carried a very big crew for this mammoth voyage, hence four mates and four watches. Tall, willowy, with a handsomeness some would have called slightly pretty, and like Richard in coloring—very dark hair, light eyes with jet lashes. His eyes were the blue of cornflowers, however, and merry.

"Stephen Donovan from Belfast," he said.

"Richard Morgan from Bristol." Edging a little away from Mr. Donovan to make it appear as if they were not teamed up for a chat, Richard smiled. "What can ye tell me about them, Mr. Donovan?"

"The big one is an old Navy storeship, the Berwick. She has just undergone a refit to turn her into a sort of a ship of the line and she has been renamed Sirius, since that is a southern star of first magnitude. They have given her six carronades and four six-pounders as armament, though I hear that Governor Phillip is refusing to sail with less than fourteen six-pounders. I do not blame him, when ye think that Alexander has four *twelve*-pounders as well as the scatter cannon."

"Alexander," said Richard deliberately, "is not only a slaver out of Bristol, but was once a privateer with sixteen twelve-pounders. Even with four she will outgun most of those who try to take her—if they can catch her, that is. She's capable of near two hundred nautical miles a day in the right wind."

"Ah, I do like a Bristol man!" said Mr. Donovan. "A seaman?"

"Nay, a tavern-keeper."

The vivid blue eyes rested on Richard's face with a caress in them. "Ye look like no tavern-keeper I have ever seen."

Quite aware of the overture, Richard feigned bland ignorance. "It runs in the family," he said easily. "My father is one too."

"I know Bristol. Which tavern?"

"The Cooper's Arms on Broad Street. My father still has it."

"While his son is being transported to Botany Bay. For what, I wonder? There is no look of the booze bibber about ye and ye're an educated man. Are ye *sure* ye're a simple tavern-keeper?"

"Absolutely. Tell me more about yon two ships."

"Sirius is about six hundred tons, a wee bit under, and she is carrying mostly people—wives of marines and the like. She has her own captain, one John Hunter, who is commanding her alone at the moment. Phillip is in

London battling the Home Department and the Court of St. James. I hear her surgeon is the son of a doctor of music and takes his pianoforte with him. Yes, she is a good old girl, Sirius, but on the slow side."

"And the sloop?"

"The tender Supply, a very old girl indeed—one might say, at near thirty, past her last prayers. Commander's name is Lieutenant Harry Ball. This will be a cruel voyage for her—she has never been farther from the Thames than Plymouth."

"Thank you for the information, Mr. Donovan." Richard stood straight and saluted him in naval fashion before shuffling away.

And that is a kind of man loves being at sea, but never in the same vessel for more than two voyages. Loves come and go for Stephen Donovan, who is married to the sea.

Once back in the gloom of the prison Richard related his news about their naval escorts. "So I imagine we will be off any day now, at least to Portsmouth."

Ike Rogers had his own item to impart. "We will have women at Botany Bay," he said with great satisfaction. "Lady Penrhyn is carrying naught but women—a hundred of them, 'tis said."

"Half a one for each Alexander man," said Bill Whiting. "It would be my luck to get the half that talks, so I think I will stick to sheep."

"There are more women going from Dunkirk in Plymouth."

"Together with more sheep and maybe a heifer, eh, Taffy?"

On the first day of February the four ships finally sailed, having been delayed twenty-four hours by a merchant seaman pay dispute—very common.

It took four days of placid sailing to cover the 60 miles to Margate Sands; they had not yet rounded the North Foreland into the Straits of Dover, but a few men were seasick. In Richard's cot all was well, but Ike Rogers became ill the moment Alexander felt a slight sea and continued very poorly until some hours after the anchor went down off Margate.

"Peculiar," said Richard, giving him a little filtered water to drink. "I fancied that a horseman would not turn a hair at the sea—riding is perpetual motion."

"Up and down, not side to side," whispered Ike, grateful for the water, all he could keep down. "Christ, Richard, I will die!"

"Nonsense! Seasickness passes, it lasts only until ye get your sea legs."

"I doubt I ever will. Not a Bristolian, I suppose."

"There are many Bristolians like me who have never been aboard a ship afloat. I have no idea how I will fare when we get into real seas. Now try to eat this pap. I soaked some of the bread in water. It will stay down, I promise," Richard coaxed.

But Ike turned his head away.

Neddy Perrott had come to an arrangement with Crowder and Davis in the cot below; in return for a loud warning whenever someone above was going to puke, William Stanley from Seend and Mikey Dennison would be delegated to clean the messes off the deck and empty the night buckets. Against the stern bulkhead on either aisle was a 200-gallon barrel full of seawater which the convicts could use to wash themselves, their clothes and the premises. It had been a shock to discover that the night buckets had to be emptied into the lead-lined scuttles which ran below the bottom platform against larboard and starboard hulls; these drained into the bilges, which were supposed to be evacuated daily by means of two bilge pumps. But those with experience of ships like Mikey Dennison vowed that Alexander's bilges were the foulest they had ever, ever encountered.

During January they had had to use the emptied night buckets to flush the excrement away down the scuttle drains, which meant they had nothing bigger than a two-quart dipper for all other sorts of washing. Inspecting at Margate and revolted by conditions in the prison, Lieutenant Shairp issued an extra bucket to each cot and also provided mops and scrubbing brushes. That meant a bucket for bodily waste and deck scrubbing and a second for washing clothes and persons.

"But that ain't going to help the bilges," said Mikey Dennison. "Bad!" Dring and Robinson from Hull agreed fervently.

While ever there was daylight outside, a few faint rays percolated through the iron grilles which closed off the hatches; at sea, said Lieutenant Shairp, no one would be allowed on deck for any reason. Which meant that in this winter season the 200 men in Alexander's prison were far longer in utter blackness than in that comforting grey gloom, though sailing helped the monotony. Heeling into a bigger swell as Dover and Folkestone passed, they rounded Dungeness into the English Channel. Richard felt queasy for a day, dry-retched twice, then recovered feeling remarkably well for a man who had eaten naught except hard bread and salt beef for over a month. Bill and Jimmy were the sickest, Will and Neddy only a trifle greener than Richard, while Taffy existed in some kind of Welsh ecstasy because there was still nothing to do, but at least they were *moving.*

Ike Rogers grew steadily worse. His lads nursed him devotedly, Joey

Long most devotedly of all, but nothing seemed to help the prostrated highwayman find his sea legs.

"Eastbourne just went aft, Brighton is next," said Davy Evans the marine to Richard as the days wore into their third week at sea.

Convicts started to die on the 12th of February. Not of any familiar disease, but of something bizarre.

It started with a fever, a runny nose and a soreness beneath one ear, then one chop began to swell just as it did when a child caught the mumps; swallowing and breathing were not impaired, but the pain of that aching, tender mass was intense. As the side affected deflated, a worse swelling came up on the other side. By the end of two weeks it too shrank back to normal and the sufferer began to feel better. At which moment his testicles commenced to puff up to four and five times their usual size, with such pain that none of the victims screamed or thrashed about; they lay as still as possible and whimpered as their fevers rose again, higher this time than in the beginning. About a week later some recovered and others died in agony.

Portsmouth at last! The four ships anchored at the Mother Bank on the 22nd of February, a boat trip away from shore. By this time the appalling swelling disease had spread to the marines and one of the sailors was sickening. Whatever it might be, it was not gaol fever, the malignant quinsy, typhoid, scarlet fever or the smallpox; a whisper began that it was the Black Death—hadn't that produced hideous buboes?

Three of the crew deserted as soon as they could beg a boat ride ashore, and the marines were so terrified that Lieutenant Shairp departed immediately to find his superiors, Major Robert Ross and First Lieutenant John Johnstone of the 39th Company of Marines, based at Plymouth. Three marines were sent to hospital, and more were ailing.

The next day Lieutenant John Johnstone—another Scotchman—boarded in the company of a Portsmouth doctor, who took one look at the victims, withdrew in a hurry with his handkerchief plastered over his nose, sent more marines to hospital, and declared that in his opinion the disease was as malignant as it was incurable. He did not employ the word "plague," but this omission only served to highlight his private diagnosis. All he could suggest was that fresh meat and fresh vegetables be served to everybody on board at once.

It is like Gloucester Gaol, thought Richard. As soon as that place held more people than it could bear, it produced a disease to cull the flock. So too with Alexander.

"We will stay well if we remain where we are, confine our exercise to deck we have washed, wipe our bowls and dippers out with oil of tar, filter our water and keep taking a spoonful of malt extract. This disease came aboard from Justitia, I am sure of it, which means it is forward."

That evening they ate hard bread and boiled beef as usual, but the beef was fresh rather than salted, and a pot of cabbage and leeks came with it. They tasted like ambrosia.

After that they were forgotten, as was the order to supply fresh food. No one came near them save for two terrified young marines (Davy Evans and Tommy Green were gone) deputed to feed them salt beef and the inevitable hard bread. The days passed in a dull, brooding silence broken only by the moans of the sick and an occasional terse conversation. February turned into March, and March dragged away while the sick continued to die and were simply left where they lay.

When finally someone opened the forward hatch it was not to remove the bodies; 25 new convicts were thrust into the freezing, filthy air of the prison.

"Fucken Christ!" came the voice of John Power. "What do the fucken buggers think they're doing? There is sickness down here and they fill us up to overflowing again! Christ, Christ, *Christ!*"

An interesting man, John Power, thought Richard. He rules up forward, the flash boy from the Old Bailey and the London Newgate who usually speaks in plain English. Now he possesses not only the hospital platforms, but a new detachment of inmates. Poor bastard. Alexander had trimmed from 200 down to 185, now there are 210 of us.

By the 13th of March four more men were dead; six corpses lay on the hospital platforms, several of them there for over a week. No one could be persuaded to come down and touch them; by now it was commonly known that the disease was plague.

Not long after dawn on the 13th of March the forward hatch was opened and a party of marines wearing gloves and with scarves muffling their faces took the six bodies away.

"Why?" asked Will Connelly. "Not that I am sorry to see them go, mind. Just—why?"

"I would say that one of the big wigs is coming to visit," said Richard. "Tidy up, lads, and look bursting with health."

Major Robert Ross arrived shortly after the bodies had gone, accompanied by Lieutenant John Johnstone, Lieutenant James Shairp and a man who appeared to be a doctor, judging from his manner. A slender, handsome fellow with a long nose, enormous blue eyes and a pretty little curl of fair hair on his broad white brow. They brought lamps and an escort of ten marine privates, who preceded them down the after hatch and filed along larboard and starboard aisles like men being sent to their doom, young enough to be intimidated, old enough to know what sort of specter squatted here.

The chamber filled with a soft golden glow; Richard finally saw the shape of his fate in all its terrible detail. The sick now occupied all 34 berths which sat isolated in the middle section forward of the tables; beyond them, where the foremast went through near the bows, was a bulkhead much narrower than the one astern behind Richard's cot. The double tier of platforms was continuous all the way around, it contained no break whatsoever. That is how they do it! That is how they have managed to squeeze 210 poor wretches into a space 35 feet at its widest and less than 70 feet from end to end. They have packed us in like bottles on shelving. No wonder we die. Compared to this, Gloucester Gaol was a paradise—at least we got out into the fresh air and could work. Here is only darkness and stench, immobility and madness. I keep prating to my people of survival, but how can we survive this place? Dear God, I despair. I despair.

All three of the marine officers were Scotch, Ross having the broadest burr and Johnstone the least. A dour and sandy man, Ross, slight of build, nondescript of face save for a thin, determined mouth and a pair of cold, pale grey eyes.

First he toured the establishment in a leisurely fashion, commencing on the starboard side. He walked as if participating in a funeral, head going from side to side with clockwork timing, steps slow and deliberate. At the isolation cots he paused, it seemed quite without fear, to examine the sick in company with his medical man, murmuring inaudibly to this attractive fellow, who kept shaking his head emphatically. Major Ross continued around the curve between the isolated platforms and those at the foremast, then began to walk down the larboard aisle toward the stern.

At Dring below and Isaac Rogers above he stopped, looked down at the deck beneath his feet, gestured to one of the privates and directed that the boy should pull out the night buckets, which had been emptied and rinsed out. His eyes rested on Ike, trembling as he lay with his head on Joey Long's lap.

"This man is sick," he said to Johnstone rather than to the doctor. "Put him with the others."

"No, sir," said Richard instantly, too shocked to think of prudence. "It is not what you think, we have none of that down here. He nearly died from seasickness, that is all."

An extraordinary look came over the Major's face, of horror and comprehension combined; he reached up and took Ike's hand, squeezed it. "I know what ye go through, then," he said. "Water and dry biscuit, nothing else helps."

A marine major who got dreadfully seasick!

The eyes traveled then to Richard's face, to all the faces in those two last upper cots, assimilating the cropped hair, the damp clothing and rags strung on lines between the beams, recently shaven chins, a certain air of pride having nothing to do with defiance. "Ye have kept very clean," he said, and plucked at the matting. "Aye, very clean."

No one replied.

Major Ross turned and stepped onto a bench just where the open hatch provided him with a little fresh air. He had not betrayed a sign of disgust at the vapors which swirled through the prison, but he did seem more comfortable on this perch.

"My name," he announced in a parade-ground voice, "is Major Robert Ross. Commandant of Marines on this expedition, and also Lieutenant-Governor of New South Wales. I am the sole commander of your persons and your lives. Governor Phillip has other concerns. Mine are all ye. This ship is not at all satisfactory—men are dying in her and I intend to find out why. Mr. William Balmain here is surgeon on Alexander and will commence his duties tomorrow. Lieutenant Johnstone is senior marine officer aboard and Lieutenant Shairp is his second-in-command. It seems ye have had few fresh provisions in over two months. That will be rectified while this ship is in port. This deck will be fumigated, which will necessitate the removal of most of ye to other accommodation. Only those seventy-two men in the cots adjacent to the stern bulkhead will remain on board and will be expected to help."

He gestured to his two lieutenants, who sat down together at the table alongside his booted feet and produced paper, ink and quills out of a writing case Lieutenant Shairp carried. "I will now proceed to take a census," the Major said. "When I point at a man, he will give me his name and the name of the hulk from which he boarded. You can start." He pointed at Jimmy Price.

It took a very long time. Major Ross was thorough, but his two scribes were as awkward as they were slow; writing was clearly not a pleasure. Some twenty names into the procedure and Major Ross stepped down to con what his scribes were producing.

"Ye illiterate boobies! What did ye do, buy your commissions? Numskulls! Idiots! Ye could not find a fuck in a bawdy house!"

Phew! thought Richard. He has a shocking temper, and he cares not at all that he has just humiliated his junior officers in front of a parcel of convicts.

Oh, but when the marines departed the darkness was hard to bear! A veil had been lifted to reveal the prison in all its monstrous, festering hideousness, but the golden light had been kind and the sight of so many men hunched in their cots round-eyed as owls had somehow reduced danger to human proportions. With the going of the last lamp, what was left could not be imagined, let alone seen or palpated. The night had come, and despite Major Ross's promise of fresh food, no one had thought to feed them anything.

In the morning the move began through the forward hatch; the sick were handled through gloves and scarf masks, those who did the handling insensitive to the screams of agony which shifting them provoked. By noon the only men left in the prison were located in the three double cots on starboard and larboard at the stern bulkhead. A great deal of lamplight had been provided; minus most of the convicts it was easy to see what kind of cesspool two-and-a-half months on board had created. Vomit, feces, overflowing night buckets, filthy decks and platforms.

Then it was their turn to move, but through the after hatch. I do not care, thought Richard, who steals what below; they are welcome to it, for I will not leave one of mine on guard down there alone. Though as long as the rumor of plague is about, our things are probably safe.

Fumigation consisted of exploding gunpowder in every part of Alexander below her upper deck and sealing the hatches fast.

They lay in a calm stretch of water well offshore, which was a fascinating sight: great bastions and fortresses bristling with gigantic guns ringed the place around, for this was England's naval headquarters and stood looking south past the Isle of Wight to the French coast at Cherbourg, where the ancient, traditional enemy lay watchful. Where or what kind of town was Portsmouth was a mystery beyond the mighty fortifications, some of them older than the time of Henry VIII, some of them still under construction. Was it here that Admiral Kempenfeldt and 1,000 men went down on the Royal George only five years ago? Careened for a leak, the biggest first-rater England had ever built filled up through her thirty-two-pounder portholes and sank in a swirling vortex.

Johnstone and Shairp had a difference of opinion as to whether the convicts left on board should be manacled; Johnstone prevailed and hands stayed free. Having lost the argument, Shairp took the jollyboat and went to visit a congenial colleague aboard another vessel bound for Botany Bay. There were several such now, one of them almost as large as Alexander.

"Scarborough," said fourth mate Stephen Donovan, cradling the big marmalade cat in his arms. "Yonder is Lady Penrhyn—ye know her—and the addition, Prince of Wales. They could not manage to get all aboard five transports, so she is the sixth. Charlotte and Friendship have sailed to Plymouth to pick up those on Dunkirk."

"And the three loading from lighters closer in shore?" Richard asked, turning his head to glare a fierce warning at Bill Whiting, who looked as if relative liberation might loosen his tongue in a Miss Molly jest Miss Molly Donovan might not appreciate.

"The storeships—Borrowdale, Fishburn and Golden Grove. We are to carry sufficient supplies to last for three years from the time we reach Botany Bay," said Mr. Donovan, eyes caressing.

"And how long does the Admiralty think it will take to get to Botany Bay?" asked Thomas Crowder, smarming sweetly.

As Crowder was not to Mr. Donovan's taste—too simian—the fourth mate chose to direct his answer to Richard Morgan, whom he found very fascinating. Not so much because of his looks, though they were wonderful—more because of his aloofness, his air of keeping most of what he thought to himself. A head man, but of far different kind from Johnny Power, whom all the crew knew well. A Thames seaman with the sense not to talk flash, Power and sailors had a natural affinity.

"The Admiralty estimates that the voyage will take between four and six months," Mr. Donovan said, pointedly ignoring Crowder.

"It will take longer than that," said Richard.

"I agree. When the Admiralty does its calculations it always thinks that winds blow forever in the right quarter—that masts never snap—that spars never come adrift—and that sails never split, fall in the slings or work loose from the reefing pendants." He tickled the loudly purring cat beneath its chin.

"No dog?" asked Richard.

"Bastards of things! Rodney here is Alexander's cat and the equal of any dog aboard, which is why they don't mess with him. He is named after Admiral Rodney, with whom I served in the West Indies when we thrashed the Frogs off Jamaica." He lifted his lip at a hovering bulldog; so did Rodney, whereupon the bulldog decided it had urgent business elsewhere. "There are twenty-seven dogs aboard, all of them belonging to the marines. They will soon diminish. The spaniels and terriers ain't too bad, they rat, but a hound is simply shark bait. Dogs fall overboard. Cats never do." He kissed Rodney on top of his head and put him on the rail to illustrate his contention. Indifferent to the lapping water below, the cat settled with paws tucked under and continued to purr.

"Where have they sent the rest of the convicts?" asked Will Connelly, rescuing Richard, who moved unobtrusively away.

"Some to The Firm, some to Fortunee, the sick to a hospital ship and the rest to that lighter there." Mr. Donovan pointed.

"For how long?"

"I suspect for one or two weeks at least."

"But the men in the lighter will freeze to death!"

"Nay. They put them ashore each night in a camp, manacled and chained together. Better to be on a lighter than on a hulk."

The following day Alexander's surgeon, Mr. William Balmain, brought two other doctors aboard, apparently to look at the ship, since the sick convicts were gone. One, whispered Stephen Donovan, was John White, chief surgeon to the expedition. The other, they could see for themselves, was the Portsmouth medical man Lieutenant Shairp had called in when Alexander first arrived.

Having received no work orders yet, the convicts stood about in close proximity to the doctors and listened to what was said; the equally curious crew were genuinely too busy to eavesdrop—cargo was arriving in lighters.

The Portsmouth doctor was convinced the illness was a rare form of bubonic plague; surgeons White and Balmain disagreed.

"Malignant!" cried the doctor. "It is bubonic!"

"Benign," said the surgeons. "It is not bubonic."

But all three concurred about preventative measures: the 'tween decks would have to be fumigated again, scrubbed thoroughly with oil of tar, then thickly coated with whitewash—a solution of quicklime, powdered chalk, size and water.

Left on board to supervise the loading of cargo, Stephen Donovan was not amused; the decks were piling up with casks, kegs, sacks, crates, barrels and parcels.

"I have to get them below!" he snapped to White and Balmain. "How can I do that when ye've got them hatches battened all day for your wretched fumigations? There is only one thing will rid Alexander of what ails her, and that is better bilge pumps!"

"The smell," said Balmain loftily, "is due to dead bodies. A week or two at sea after extensive fumigation will remove it."

White had wandered away to discover how the crew could load cargo through an intervening prison; a look below showed him that the tables and benches in the prison had been removed to reveal six-foot-square hatches beneath them exactly in line with those on the upper deck. Winched inboard on davits, even the gigantic water tuns were dropped straight into the orlop hold. He came back with his air of brisk superiority very much to the fore, brushed Balmain and Donovan aside, and issued orders.

The 36 starboard prisoners were despatched into the prison to mop, scrub and sponge the place with vinegar before fumigation with gunpowder; the 36 larboard convicts were sent down into the marines' quarters below steerage, there to do the same.

"Christ!" squeaked Taffy Edmunds. "Poor little Davy Evans was right—we convicts are in heaven compared to this, though 'twould be nice to sleep in hammocks."

The hold floor was awash in bilge overflow which stank worse than the prison compartment and released gases which had turned the pewter buttons on those brave scarlet coats as black as coal. The 'tween decks was scarcely six feet, which meant bending to pass under the beams, as on Ceres.

Thus it was that Richard and the larboard convicts were made privy to what took place between the irresistible force and the immovable object; Major Ross and Captain Sinclair came to grips in the marines' hold under the fascinated eyes of 36 men. This stupendous battle was heralded by the arrival of the Major at the bottom of the wooden ladder from the crew's quarters above.

"Get your bloated blubber down here, ye torpid bag of shit!" Ross bellowed. "Come and look, damn ye!"

And down the ladder on dainty booted feet came Captain Duncan Sinclair, for all the world like a glob of syrup trickling down one side of a smooth string. "No one," he puffed, reaching the deck below, "speaks to *me* like that, Major! I am not only captain of this ship, but also one of her owners."

"Which only makes ye all the more guilty, balloon-arse! Go on, look around ye! Look at where ye expect His Majesty's Marines to live for God knows how many months! Almost three months already! They are sick and very afraid, for which I do not blame them one wee bit! Their dogs are better off—so are the sheep and pigs ye have aboard to pile on your own overloaded table! Sitting up there like King Muck of Dunghill Palace with a night cabin, a day cabin and the great cabin all to yourself, and my two officers in an airless cupboard! Eating with the privates! It will change, Sinclair, or I will personally spill your swollen guts into this liquid *shit!*" He put his hand on his sword hilt and looked perfectly capable of following the threat with the deed.

"Your men stay here because I have no other place to stow them," said Sinclair. "As a matter of fact, they are occupying valuable space my firm contracted to fill up with more useful cargo than a lot of thieving, rum-swilling twiddle-poops not clever enough to get into the Navy nor rich enough to get into the Army! Ye're the entire world's leavings, Ross, you and your marines! 'Tain't for nothing they call an empty bottle a marine! Cluttering up my crew's galley, letting two dozen dogs shit from bowsprit to taffrail—look at my boot! Dog turd, Ross, fucken dog turd! Two of my hens dead, four of my ducks, and one goose! Not to mention the ewe I had to shoot because one of the fucken bulldogs got its teeth in and would not let go! Well, I shot the fucken dog first, ye Lowlands bastard without a mother!"

"Who's the Lowlands bastard, ye Glasgow bitch's by-blow?"

A pause ensued as both the combatants searched wildly for a new and mortally wounding thing to say and the convicts stood as still as statues for fear they might be noticed and sent on deck.

"The Lords of the Admiralty accepted Walton's tender, which was specific about Alexander's appointments," said Sinclair, eyes two blazing slits. "Blame your superiors, Ross, do not blame me! When I heard I was to have forty marines as well as two hundred and ten convicts, I was not a happy man! The marines stay right here, and ye can like or ye can lump it."

"I do not like it and I will not lump it, ye elephant's arse! Ye will shift my lads up into steerage and accommodate my officers properly or I will have words to say from Governor Phillip all the way to Admiral Lord Howe and Sir John Middleton—not to mention Lord Sydney and Mr. Pitt! Ye have two choices, Sinclair. Either put your crew down here and my marines where they are, or move the stern bulkhead of the prison twenty-five feet forward. Now that the fleet has Prince of Wales, the displaced convicts can go to her. And that," said Ross, brushing his white-gloved hands together, "is that, suet-face!"

"It is not!" Sinclair snapped through his teeth; the sight of so much adiposity in such a ferment was Homeric. "Alexander was contracted to transport two hundred and ten convicts, not one hundred and forty convicts and forty marines in a space belonging to seventy more convicts! The purpose of this expedition is not to cosset a parcel of scabby marines, but to get as many of England's felons to the far end of the earth as possible. I will keep my entire contracted complement of convicts and—if ye like—I will take full responsibility for their confinement through the agency of my crew. It is very clear and simple, Major Ross. Move your precious marines off Alexander. I will lock the convicts in the prison permanently and feed them through the hatch bars for the duration, which does away with the need for marine guards."

"Lord Sydney and Mr. Pitt would not approve," said Ross, on safe and sure ground. "They are both modern men who insist that the convicts be delivered at Botany Bay in better condition than ye used to deliver your slaves to Barbados! If ye lock these men in for as much as a year, they will half of them be dead on arrival and the other half fit only for a Bedlam. Therefore," he continued, looking as malleable as a cast-iron thirty-two-pounder, "it might behove ye to build yourself a poop roundhouse and a forecastle within the next month. Ye may then move yourself one deck up to live in solitary splendor and turn your quarterdeck over to my officers. Do not forget, Sinclair, that ye have also to accommodate the ship's surgeon, the naval agent and the contractor's agent, all of whom have quarterdeck rank. They will fill it without your presence, ye cheeseparing bile bag! As for your crew—put them where a crew belongs, in a forecastle. My enlisted men can then move up into steerage and I will undertake to provide them with a galley stove on which they can cook for themselves and the convicts. Thus your crew can keep their galley, you can build yourself a new one in your roundhouse, the officers can use the quarterdeck one, and Alexander will turn into something like a ship rather than a slaver, ye fat flawn!"

The grey slits of eyes had changed during this masterly speech, from furious rage to a more natural cunning. "That," Sinclair said, "would cost Walton's at least a thousand pounds."

Major Ross turned on his heel and mounted the ladder. "Send the bill to the Admiralty," he said, and disappeared.

Captain Duncan Sinclair looked at the ladder, then suddenly seemed to see the silent ring of men around him for the first time. "Ye need a bucket chain to get rid of this overflow," he said to Ike Rogers curtly, "and while ye're about it, lift that hatch over there and start baling out the starboard bilge. Some more of ye can bale out larboard. Tip fresh sea-water in and bale until the bilge water is clear. I can smell it on the quarterdeck." He stared at the ladder again. "You, you and you," he said to Taffy, Will and Neddy, all much of a height, "get your shoulders under my arse and push me up this fucken ladder."

Once the sound of his progress upward had faded, the convicts collapsed into shrieks of laughter.

"I thought," gasped Ike, "that for a moment there, Neddy, ye were going to tip him flat on his puss in the bilge water."

"I was tempted," said Neddy, wiping his eyes, "but he is the captain, and 'tis best not to offend the captain. Major Ross don't care who he offends, so much is sure." He giggled. "An elephant's arse! Oh, it fits! Getting him up that ladder near killed us."

"Major Ross won the engagement," said Aaron Davis thoughtfully, "but has bared *his* arse to the Admiralty boots. If Captain Sinclair goes ahead and builds a roundhouse and a forecastle, the Admiralty will refuse to pay the bill and Major Ross will be in a kettle of boiling water."

"Somehow," said Richard, smiling, "I cannot see Major Ross's arse bare for anybody's boot. His spotless white breeches will stay up, mark my words. He was right. Alexander cannot hold so many people without a roundhouse and a forecastle." He huffed. "Who wants to be on the bucket chain? If, that is, we can persuade Lieutenant Johnstone to let us have more buckets, for I will not use the prison ones on this disgusting foulness. Bristolians, we head the chain at the bilges themselves. Jimmy, go and smile at the pretty Lieutenant for more buckets."

Captain Sinclair made his renovations, but for a great deal less than £1,000. While the convicts kept on board toiled with oil of tar and whitewash, the loading of cargo went on around them, which gave them a good idea of what was stowed where. The spare masts were lashed on deck below the boats, whereas spars, sails and rope went below; the 160-gallon water tuns, by far the heaviest objects, were put in clusters among other, lighter cargo. Cask after cask of salt beef and salt pork came aboard, sack after sack of hard bread, dried peas and the chickpeas called calavances, kegs of flour, bags of rice, and a great many parcels sewn in coarse cloth and inked with the name of the owner. There were also bales of clothing the sailors called "slops," apparently destined for the convicts when their present clothing wore out.

Everybody knew that there were pipes of rum aboard; neither crew nor marines would stand for a dry voyage. Rum was what made the miseries of cramped quarters and poor food bearable, so rum there had to be. But it did not go into the general holds, either beneath the prison or steerage.

"He is clever, our big fat captain," said William Dring from Hull with a grin. "Right up forward there is another hold in two decks. Top one is for firewood—they pack it everywhere around bowsprit and partnerson. Bottom deck has an iron cover and that is where rum is. Cannot be got at from prison because bow bulkhead is a foot thick and stuffed with nails, just like stern bulkhead. And cannot be got at from firewood hold without shocking racket. Rum on issue is in big cupboard on quarterdeck and captain doles it out himself. No one can steal it because of Trimmings."

"Trimmings?" asked Richard. "Sinclair's steward?"

"Aye, and completely Sinclair's creature. Spies and pries."

"He is using his own chips to do the alterations," said Dring's friend Joe Robinson; seamen, they had scraped acquaintance with the crew. "He took five convicts as well, all fit to hammer in nails. Got 'em off lighter and Fortunee. Forecastle is just a forecastle, but some real pretty mahogany panels have gone up roundhouse way. Captain pinched all the great cabin furniture, so Major Ross has to obtain more for quarterdeck and ain't happy about it."

Major Ross was never happy. His displeasure extended a great deal further than Captain Duncan Sinclair and Alexander, however. The new battle, as several marines informed the convicts (gossip was everybody's main recreation), was to have the expedition's rice exchanged for wheat flour. Unfortunately the contract with Mr. William Richards Junior had been drafted in the same format as for the transportation of Army personnel, which had enabled the frugal purveyor of food to convicts and marines alike to substitute rice for some of the flour. Rice was cheap, he had a warehouse full of it, and it stowed smaller because it expanded in cooking. The issue was that rice did not prevent scurvy, whereas flour did.

"I do not understand," said Stephen Martin, one of the two quiet Bristolians sent down with Crowder and Davis. "If flour can prevent scurvy, why cannot bread? 'Tis made on flour."

Richard tried to remember what Cousin James-the-druggist had said about such matters. "I think it is the baking," he said. "Our bread is hard—sea biscuit. There is as much barley and rye in it as wheat, if not more. Flour is ground wheat. So the—the *antiscorbutic* must be in wheat. Or it might be that the flour is made into dumplings in stew or soup and does not cook long enough to ruin whatever it is prevents scurvy. Vegetables and fruit are best, but no one gets those at sea. There is a pickled cabbage called 'sour crout' my cousin James imports from Bremen for some of the Bristol sea captains because it is cheaper than extract of malt, which is a very good antiscorbutic. But the trouble with sour crout is that sailors loathe it and have to be flogged to eat it."

"Is there anything ye do not know, Richard?" asked Joey Long, who deemed Richard a walking encyclopedia.

"I know hardly anything, Joey. It is my cousin James is the fount of knowledge. All I had to do was listen."

"And ye're very good at that," said Bill Whiting. He stood back to survey their work, which was almost done. "There is one grand thing about all this whitewash. Even when the bars are down on the hatches, there will be a lot more light inside." He threw an arm about Will Connelly's shoulders. "If we sit at the table right under the after hatch, Will, we will have enough light to read."

The entire complement of convicts were back on board shortly into April, while the erection of forecastle and roundhouse went on apace. Had the convicts only known it, Major Ross was still to write to the authorities about conditions on Alexander, preferring that the alterations be too far along to stop before he roared. Captain Sinclair had chosen to build his crew's new quarters inboard, allowing a three-foot-wide gangway along either side for easy access to the bows, where the crew's holes were situated. For those convicts left aboard Alexander during the hygienic measures it had been bliss; the hatches were open and they too could use the crew's holes rather than their night buckets. The hatch forward of the foremast was now sheltered with a house (a structure a little like a dog kennel with a curved roof) to afford the cooks weatherproof access to the firewood hold; the hatch just in front of the quarterdeck which led down into the steerage compartment was also housed, whereas the two hatches above the prison were simple deck hatches, equipped with iron grilles over which a solid cover could be battened.

They will be battened down, thought Richard, whenever the seas break over the deck, and we will be absolutely blinded for however long the tempest lasts. No light, no air.

Despite fresh meat and fresh vegetables every day and despite being permitted onto the deck in small groups for air and exercise, the sickness aboard Alexander continued. Willy Wilton died, the first casualty among the West Country people, though not of the mumpish disease. He had caught cold in the perishing weather and it settled on his chest. Surgeon Balmain applied hot poultices to draw out and loosen the phlegm, but Willy died during much the same treatment a free Bristolian would have received from his doctor. Poultices were the only remedy for pneumonia. Ike Rogers grieved terribly. He was not the same man Richard had met in Gloucester Gaol; that blustering pugnaciousness was all bluff. Underneath was a man who worshiped horses and the freedom of the road.

Others died too; by the end of April the month's toll among the convicts stood at twelve. And sickness was spreading through the marines as well—fevers, lung inflammations, deliriums, paralyses. Three terrified privates absconded, a fourth on the last day of the month. A sergeant, a drummer and fourteen privates had been shipped off to hospital and replacements were hard to find. Alexander was getting a reputation as the death ship of the fleet—a reputation she was to keep. Every so often all but the original convicts (now 71 men, with Willy Wilton dead) were sent elsewhere and the vinegar, fumigation, scrubbing with oil of tar and whitewashing began all over again. Each time Richard's larboard group found the bilges fouled.

"She may as well not have bilge pumps," said Mikey Dennison in disgust. "They do not work."

Three more men died. The toll now stood at fifteen dead since the 1st of April, and the number of convicts had shrunk from 210 to 195.

On the 11th of May, more than four months after boarding the death ship, news came that Governor Phillip had at last arrived on his flagship, Sirius, and that on the morrow the fleet of eleven ships would sail. But it did not. The crew of the storeship Fishburn had not been paid and refused to leave until they were. The occupants of the Alexander prison lay in their cots to sleep, finally provided with blankets—one per two men. Perhaps that was some kind of reward for having been stripped and searched—what for, nobody knew. Only that with Major Ross there to supervise, no one was rectally examined. Nor was anything confiscated.

About an hour after dawn on the 13th of May—summer solstice was coming, so dawn was early—Richard woke to find Alexander moving, her timbers creaking, a faint sighing of water nudging her sides, the slightest roll. Enough for Ike, already puking, but they had dealt with that by giving him poor dead Willy's wooden eating bowl, which Joey Long had undertaken to empty into the night bucket whenever necessary.

Robert Jefferies from Devizes died that day of pneumonia; the blankets had come far too late for many men.

Once through the Needles at the western end of the Isle of Wight, which happened on that same day, Alexander grew more frisky than at any time on the slow sail from Tilbury to Portsmouth. She rolled a lot and pitched a little, which sent most of the convicts to their cots in the throes of sickness. Richard became conscious of nausea, but not to a degree beyond controlling, and it passed within three hours after a single dry heave. Maybe sea legs grew automatically on Bristolians? The other Bristolians—Connelly, Perrott, Davis, Crowder, Martin and Morris—were in similar case to himself. It was the country boys seemed the worst, though none was as bad as Ike Rogers.

The next day Lieutenant Shairp and Surgeon Balmain came down the after hatch more awkwardly than in still water, but with sufficient dignity to look impressive. The two privates with them collected the body of Robert Jefferies while Shairp and Balmain negotiated the heaving aisle by hanging on to platform edges, Shairp very careful not to put his hand on anyone's vomit. The order was the same: get out and clean your deck, get out and empty your night bucket, get out and clean your cot, I do not care how sick you think you are. If you have puked on your blanket, wash it. If you have puked on your matting, wash it. If you have puked on yourself, wash yourself.

"If they do that every day the place will stay clean," said Connelly. "Oh, I do hope!"

"Do not hope," said Richard. "This is Balmain's doing, not Shairp's, but Balmain is not a methodical man. Luckily the food has already been puked up, so the worst we will have to cope with is shit. They will just lie there and shit themselves, and half of them at least have never had a wash in their lives. If we are clean and our cleanliness is spreading, it is because of my cousin James and the fact that I badger all within hailing distance so much that they fear me more than they do a wash." He grinned. "Once they get used to washing, they start to like being clean."

"You," said Will Connelly, "are a very strange man, Richard. Deny it as much as ye like, but ye're definitely the head man on the larboard side." He closed his eyes and concentrated upon his internal mechanisms. "I feel well, so I am going to try to read." He sat on the bench along the central table right under the open hatch with the three volumes of *Robinson Crusoe,* found his place in the first and was soon absorbed in it, apparently quite oblivious to the ship's motion.

Richard joined him with his gazetteer of the world; the coats of whitewash had made all the difference.

By the time Alexander passed well to the south of Plymouth most of the men had found their sea legs, though Ike Rogers and a handful of others had not. It was even possible to walk the aisles once a man got used to the way the deck rose to meet his feet, then fell away from beneath them. And thus it was that Richard, exercising, made the acquaintance of John Power, the forward head man.

Power was a fine-looking young fellow, lithe and supple as a cat, with a fierce look in his dark eyes and a curious habit of making highly expressive gestures with his hands as he talked. Very Frog, very Italian, not at all English, Dutch or German. He had an air of someone under pressure, not with anxiety or ill temper but rather with colossal energies and enthusiasms. And his eyes said that he liked to take risks.

"Richard Morgan!" he said as Richard passed by his cot, the top corner one where the forward bulkhead met the starboard hull. "I bid ye welcome to enemy territory."

"I am not your enemy, John Power. I am a quiet man who minds his own business."

"Which is the larboard side. Very neat and clean and tidy, I am told. Bristol fashion, real shipshape."

"I am indeed a Bristol man, but visit us and see for yourself. 'Tis true we keep ourselves to ourselves—but then, we none of us speak the flash lingo."

"My men like to talk flash, though I do not much care for it myself—sailors hate it." Power slipped off his cot and joined Richard. "Ye're an old man, Morgan, now I see ye close up."

"Eight-and-thirty last September, though so far I have not felt my years overmuch, Power. My strength is a little diminished after nigh five months of Alexander, but we did get some work to do in Portsmouth, which was a help. They always put Bristolians on bilge duty—our noses are immune to the foulest airs. Did ye go to the lighter, The Firm or Fortunee?"

"The lighter. I get on well with Alexander's crew, so my men never experienced Portsmouth's hulks." He heaved a great sigh, hands signaling exultation. "As soon as maybe I intend to work on Alexander as a seaman. Mr. Bones—he is third mate—promised. Then I will get my strength back."

"I had thought we would be below deck for the whole voyage."

"Not if Mr. Bones is right. Governor Phillip says we are not to be allowed to waste away, he needs us fit enough to work when we reach Botany Bay."

They reached the starboard bulkhead barrel of sea-water and turned to walk forward. Power glanced sideways at Will Connelly hunched over Mr. Daniel Defoe. "Do all of ye read?" he asked with a tinge of envy.

"Six of us do, and five of us are Bristolians—Crowder, Davis, Connelly there, Perrott and me. The odd man out is Bill Whiting," said Richard. "Bristol is full of charity schools."

"London has almost no charity schools. Though I always thought it a waste of time to read books when the signs above any sort of shop tell a man what is inside." The hands waggled wryly. "Now I think it would be good to read books. It passes the time."

"When ye're aloft 'twill not seem so dreadful. Are ye married?"

"Not I!" Power turned his thumbs down. "Women are poison."

"Nay, they are just like us—some good, some bad, and some indifferent."

"How many of each kind have ye known?" asked Power, smiling to reveal strong white teeth—not a boozer, then.

"More good than bad, and none indifferent."

"And wives?"

"Two, according to my records."

"And of records, Lieutenant Johnstone tells me, there are none!" Power clenched his fists in glee. "Can ye imagine that? The Home Office never got around to sending Phillip a list of us, so no one knows what our crimes are, nor how long we have to serve. I intend to take advantage of that, Morgan, the moment I reach Botany Bay."

"The Home Office sounds as efficient as the Bristol Excise Office," said Richard as they reached Power's cot and he climbed into it without seeming to move at all. As graceful as Stephen Donovan, whose company Richard was missing now that they were below. A Miss Molly he might be, but he was well read and not a convict, so could talk of something other than prison.

Richard walked back to his own cot in a thoughtful mood. An interesting snippet, that no one in authority had any idea of the nature of convict offenses, the time each still had to serve. . . . It might work as Power confidently expected it would, but there was also the possibility that the Governor might make an arbitrary decision to the effect that all convicts were to serve fourteen years. No one would want hordes of convicts claiming to have served their time within six months or a year of arriving. Which thought told Richard why they had been searched in Portsmouth. It cost money to buy passage home on a ship; they all knew that a return fare was not a part of the Parliament's plan. Someone in Phillip's retinue was shrewd enough to guess that there might be quite a lot of men and women concealing a nest egg aimed at buying passage home. Ye should have done a Mr. Sykes, Major Ross! But that brutish ye're not, for all ye must have known. I have read ye aright: a man with a code of honor, a fierce partisan and protector of your men, a Scotch pessimist, violent-tempered, salty-tongued, not hugely ambitious, and prone to seasickness.

On the 20th of May, while Alexander frisked into a strong swell and driving rain, the convicts were brought up on deck a few at a time to have their leg irons removed. The sick went up first, even including Ike Rogers, so bad that Surgeon Balmain had put him on a glass of potent Madeira wine twice a day.

When Richard's turn came he emerged into a minor gale; it was impossible to see anything beyond the ship and a few yards of white-capped ocean, but the skies wept fresh, wholesome, genuine, honest-to-goodness *water.* Someone thrust him down onto the deck with his legs extended in front of him. Two marines sat on stools side by side; one slid a broad smith's chisel under the fetter to pin the cuff to a sheet of iron and the other smashed his hammer down on its butt. The pain was excruciating because the force of the blow was transmitted to his leg, but Richard didn't care. He lifted his face to the rain and let it cascade over his skin, his liberated spirit soaring into the grey tatters of cloud. One more excruciating pain as his other leg came free and there he was light-footed, light-headed, soaking wet, and utterly, blissfully, perfectly happy.

Someone, he had no idea who, gave him a hand to help him up. Dizzily he wavered on feathers to get himself out of the way and come to terms with the fact that he, who had been ironed for thirty-three months, was suddenly stripped of them.

Once back in the prison he began to shiver, took his clothes off, wrung the sweet clean water out of them into his dripstone, draped them across a line between the sea-water barrel and a beam, dried his body with a rag and donned a brand-new outfit. It was that kind of day, a milestone.

In the morning he looked at his friends and tried to see each of them as he saw himself. How did they feel? What did they think about the enormity of this great experiment in human lives? Had any of them realized that home was probably gone forever? Did they dream? Did they hope? And if they did, what did they dream about, hope for? But he couldn't know because none of them knew. If he had voiced those questions, asked them outright, they would have answered in the way men always did: money, property, comfort, sex, a wife and family, a long life, no more troubles. Well, he hoped and dreamed of all those things himself, yet they were not what he yearned to know.

All of them looked at him with trust and affection, and that was somewhere to start, though nowhere to finish. Somehow each of them had to be made to see that his own fate was in his own hand, not in Richard Morgan's. The head man on the larboard side was perhaps a father, but he could not be a mother.

They were now allowed on deck provided that the whole prison did not appear there at one time, and provided that they kept out of the crew's way. Though John Power, fizzing with joy, was let work as a seaman, as were Willy Dring and Joe Robinson. However peculiar Richard found it, by no means every convict wanted to go above. Those still seasick he could understand—the Bay of Biscay had felled some unaffected until then—but now that they were free of their irons others were content to lie about in their cots or congregate in groups around a table to play cards. Of course it was still squalling and blustering, but Alexander was not a hefty slaver for nothing. It would take bigger seas than she was ploughing through at the moment to swamp her decks and elicit the order to batten down the hatches.

By the time that the command came from Lieutenant Johnstone that men might proceed on deck, the weather was clearing rapidly; they had been fed and watered with the inevitable hard bread, salt beef and horrible Portsmouth water. Six marine privates were delegated to tip buckets of salt water into the prison barrels, and stiff, proper Lieutenant Shairp stalked up and down the aisles commanding slack cots to clean their decks and platforms. Secure in the knowledge that Shairp would have no complaints about their area, nine of Richard's eleven hauled themselves through the hatch with a wave for Ike and Joey Long.

A rush to the rail, there to look at the ocean for the first time. Its grey was suffusing with a steely blue and still bore many white-caps, but the horizon was visible and so were other ships, some to larboard, some to starboard, and two so far astern that they were hull down, only their masts showing. Close by was the other big slaver, Scarborough, a magical sight with her sails filled, pennants flying in some unknown sea code, her blunt bows biting at the swell, which ran on her starboard stern beam in communion with the wind. She had a larger superstructure than Alexander, which perhaps was why Zachariah Clark, the contractor's agent, had elected to sail in her instead. The naval agent, Lieutenant John Shortland, was another had defected; he was in Fishburn the storeship, though one of his two sons was second mate in Alexander. The other was aboard Sirius. Nepotism reigned.

As at Tilbury, Richard's six parted company the moment they smelled fresh air and a chance to be relatively alone. Richard hauled himself atop one of the two longboats tied upside down athwart the spare masts and counted ships. A brig about half the size of Alexander was at the head of the field, then came Scarborough and Alexander, after them the two-masted sloop Supply clinging to Sirius like a cub to its mother. Behind them was a ship he thought Lady Penrhyn, then the three storeships, and those two sets of masts on the horizon. Eleven vessels if none were out of sight.

"Good day to you, Richard Morgan from Bristol," said Stephen Donovan. "How do your legs feel?"

Half of Richard wanted to be alone, but the other half was very glad to see Miss Molly Donovan, whom he read correctly enough to think was too intelligent not to know that his sexual inclinations were not shared. So he smiled and nodded with the correct degree of courtesy. "In regard to the sea or the irons?" he asked, liking the sensation of lifting and dropping.

"The sea is no grief, that is evident. Irons."

"Ye would have to have worn them for three-and-thirty months to understand how I feel without them, Mr. Donovan."

"Three-and-thirty months! What did you do, Richard?"

"I was found guilty of extorting five hundred pounds."

"How long did ye get?"

"Seven years."

Donovan frowned. "That makes little sense to me. By rights ye should have hanged. Were you reprieved?"

"No. My original sentence was seven years' transportation."

"It sounds as if the jury was not very sure."

"The judge was. He refused to recommend mercy."

"Ye do not look resentful."

Richard shrugged. "Why should I be resentful? The fault was my own, nobody else's."

"How did ye spend the five hundred pounds?"

"I did not try to cash the note of hand, so I spent naught."

"I *knew* ye were an interesting man!"

Disliking the memories this conversation provoked, Richard changed the subject. "Tell me which ship is which, Mr. Donovan."

"Scarborough keeping pace with us, Friendship in the lead—a snappy little sailer, that one! She will show the rest a clean pair of heels all the way."

"Why exactly? I am not a seafaring Bristolian."

"Because she is—shipshape. Her steering sails provide just the right proportionate area for holding in a zephyr or a gale." He stretched out a long arm to point at Supply. "Yon sloop is rigged brig-fashion, which don't suit her one wee bit. Since she has a second mast, Harry Ball would have done better to rig her as a snow. She's a slug as soon as the seas turn heavy because she's so low in the water and she cannot crowd on enough sail. Supply is a light-wind sailer, at home in the Channel, where she has had her career. Harry Ball must be praying for good weather."

"Is that Lady Penrhyn behind the Royal Navy pair?"

"No. Prince of Wales, the additional transport. Then Golden Grove, Fishburn and Borrowdale. The two snails in the rear are Lady Penrhyn and Charlotte. Were it not for them we would be farther along, but the Commodore's orders are specific. No ship is to be out of sight of the rest. So Friendship cannot set her topgallants and we cannot set our royals. Ah, 'tis good to be at sea again!" The brilliant blue eyes spotted Lieutenant John Johnstone emerging from the gentleman's domain of the quarterdeck; Stephen Donovan leaped down with a laugh. "There is naught more certain, Richard, than that I will see ye some day soon." And off he went to join the marine commanding officer, with whom he seemed on excellent terms.

Two of a kind? Richard wondered, not moving from his perch. His belly rumbled; in all this wondrous air he needed more food, but more food he was not going to get. An underweight pound of hard bread and more like half than three-quarters of a pound of salt beef a day, plus two quarts of Portsmouth water. Not nearly enough. Oh, for the days of the Thames bum boats and a good lunch!

All the convicts save the seasick or ill were conscious of perpetual, gripping hunger. While he and the others from the larboard cots toward the stern were on deck, some of the starboard lazybones opposite them had manufactured a jimmy out of an iron bolt on the mainmast and levered up the hold hatches dotted at intervals along the aisles. They found no rum; they found a cache of bread sacks. But there was always a snitch somewhere. The next moment a dozen marines were piling down the after hatch to snabble the thieves as they feasted and threw the rock-hard little loaves blithely to any imploring hands or voices.

Six men were hauled onto the deck, there to face Lieutenants Johnstone and Shairp.

"Twenty lashes and back into irons," said Johnstone tersely. He nodded to Corporal Sampson, who had appeared out of the after hatch house with his cat. Not, as Mr. Thistlethwaite had once put it, a four-legged creature that said meow. An instrument with a thick handle of rope coiled around a central core and nine thin hempen strings knotted at intervals and ending in a bead of something lead-colored.

Richard's first impulse was to bolt back into the prison, only to find that everybody was being driven on deck to witness the floggings.

The six men were stripped to the waist—twenty lashes were not considered sufficient to bare buttocks as well—and the first victim was tied over the curving roof of the after hatch house. The thing whistled, and it did not require much effort in the plying. A whip, a cane or a cudgel raised welts and a bludgeon one massive bruise; this vile implement broke the skin with its first stroke, and where the very small bulb of lead at the end of each of its nine tails struck the body, a great scarlet lump arose in the same instant. Corporal Sampson knew his job; the marines were flogged too, usually to the tune of twelve lashes but sometimes many more. Each stroke landed in a slightly different place, so that by the twentieth the man's back was a grid of bloodied stripes and lumps the size of a baby's fist. The victim got a bucket of salt water on the mess which set him to screaming thinly, then his place was taken by the next. While Corporal Sampson ploughed indifferently—he did not appear either to love or hate what he did—through the six, those he had finished with were fitted with locked fetters and a Ceres length of chain. No one sent them below; Lieutenant Johnstone simply nodded dismissal to his flogger and the dozen green-hued privates.

Richard's gorge rose. He jumped off the longboat and walked quickly to the rail, leaned over it and retched. But as he was too hungry to have anything to bring up, he contented himself with staring down into the water a scant ten feet below him. Water, he noticed as his eyes focused, so pure that the translucent jellyfish everywhere in it were like delicate ghosts, umbrellaed in sheerest silk, with long trails of lustrous frilly tentacles abandoned to the tug of ship and current.

Something went "Whoof!" so suddenly that he jumped; a long, sleek, iridescent body shot past and rose clear of the sea's surface in an arc of absolute freedom, total joy. A dolphin? A porpoise? There were others frolicking, a great band of them playing chasings with dirty, decrepit Alexander.

The tears poured down his face, but he made no attempt to wipe them away. All of this was a part of this. The beauty of God and the ugliness of Man. What place could Man have in such a gorgeous universe?

The floggings sobered everyone as Alexander continued on her way south toward the Canaries, which was just as well; John Power had learned from his friend Mr. Bones that a convict he knew slightly, Nicholas Greenwell, had been pardoned the day before the fleet left Portsmouth and was smuggled off in secret. Lieutenant Shairp had remembered the discontent following the pardon of James Bartlett while Alexander had lain off Tilbury.

"I never noticed the fucken bastard was missing at first, then I assumed he'd died," Power said to Richard and Mr. Donovan up on deck where the wind blew their words away. "Bastard! Oh, *bitch!* I should have been pardoned, not Greenwell!"

Power constantly maintained that he was innocent, that it had not been he who was with Charles Young (of whose present whereabouts he knew nothing) when a quarter-ton of rare wood belonging to the East India Company was spirited off a London wharf in a boat. The watchman had recognized Young, but would not swear that Power was the second man. As usual, the jury hedged its bets by returning a verdict of guilty; best be on the safe side in case the second man *had* been Power, even if the watchman was not sure. The judge, concurring, handed down seven years' transportation.

"It should have been me!" Power cried, his dark face twisted in pain. "Greenwell was a robber, pure and simple! But I ain't got his connections, just a sick dad I am not there to look after! Bitch, bugger, fuck 'em all!"

"There, there," soothed Donovan, suddenly very Irish, for all that he said he was a good Protestant Ulsterman. "Johnny, 'tis too late to cry. Remember the cat and get yourself home the minute your sentence is over."

"My dad will be dead by then."

"Ye cannot say that for sure. Now do what Mr. Shortland told ye to do, else ye'll be back to idleness."

The rage simmered down, the pain did not. John Power surveyed the tall fourth mate with eyes full of tears, then marched away.

"It is a wonder," said Richard thoughtfully, deciding it was high time things were brought into the open, "that ye do not fancy him. Why a stringy old man like me?"

The too-handsome face aped astonishment but the eyes danced. "If I do fancy ye, Richard, 'tis an unrequited passion. Even a cat can look at a king."

"Bog trotter."

"Mud skipper."

"What is a mud skipper?" asked Richard, intrigued.

"A miraculous fish-out-of-water I read of. Maybe 'twas Sir Joseph Banks described it, I do not remember. It skips on mud."

More deaths had occurred; there were now 188 convicts left on board Alexander.

At about the moment that Thomas Gearing from Oxford was in extremis, Teneriffe loomed out of fog and drizzle so quietly that the inmates of the prison, ordered below, scarcely knew when their ship made harbor.

Having had little to do for three weeks save feed the convicts and dwell upon their own injuries, the marines now went seriously on duty. Their most onerous task at sea was to boil up kettles of the salt beef chunks which Sergeant Knight was supposed to weigh up on the scales Lieutenant Shortland, the naval agent, had himself checked. As the naval agent was not present to witness this ritual, however, Sergeant Knight simply chopped the beef or pork into half-pound bits for the convicts and pound-and-a-half pieces for the marines. The convicts were supposed to get pease or oatmeal as well, but Sergeant Knight confined such treats to Sundays after prayers had been said. He was fed up with playing nursery maid to a lot of felons before Alexander put to sea—*scales,* for pity's sake! Even if Lieutenant Shairp came down to watch, Knight made no attempt to weigh or be fair about the rations, and Shairp said not a word. Better fucken not say a word!

Above and beyond the differences natural in a group of almost forty men unable to escape from each other's company, the marines were very unhappy. Moving up into steerage should have mollified them, but it did not. Oh, it was a great deal more comfortable to occupy that peculiarly shaped space wherein the ceiling was far larger than the floor, admittedly. But the tiller came inboard along the ceiling—and groaned—and screeched—and clattered hollowly—and occasionally walloped a body swinging aloft in his canvas nest when the helmsman swung the wheel hard over just as the sea was running the wrong way. They had air and light from several ports, the stink was not unbearable, and the crew had been decent enough to leave steerage relatively clean.

Yet what they did not have far outclassed all of these improvements: they were not getting their full half-pint of rum every day. Captain Duncan Sinclair, in whose purlieu the liquor lay, had taken it upon himself to water the rum down to what was known as "grog." There had been a furious outcry about it before Alexander left Portsmouth and for a few days thereafter the rum was served the way it was supposed to be served—neat. Now they were back on watery grog, had been since the Scillies. No dreamless sleeps despite the tiller, and definitely no kindly thoughts. On board ship rum was the beginning and end of all earthly pleasures to a sailor or a marine, and now both kinds of seafaring man were on grog. The hatred for Sinclair among crew and marines was as immense as it was intense. Not that Sinclair cared, dwelling on high in a roundhouse he had turned into a fortress. A little further into the voyage he intended to start selling the rum he was currently hoarding. If the bastards wanted a full half-pint of neat rum, then they could pay for it. *He* had to pay for his roundhouse, as he knew perfectly well that the Admiralty would not.

Now, with port in Santa Cruz attained, was the prospect of going ashore to find as much rum as a marine could drink—and Major Ross issued orders that no marine was to have much shore leave! Lieutenant Johnstone had informed them in his languid voice that a full guard would have to be mounted during daylight hours, as Governor Phillip did not want the convicts confined below decks interminably. Further to that, Johnstone announced, Governor Phillip and his aide-de-camp Lieutenant King were expected to come aboard at some unpredicted time while at Teneriffe. So woe betide the marine whose choking black leather stock was not properly fastened around his neck or whose knee-length black leather spatterdashes were not properly buttoned. The ship was stuffed with the most desperate criminals, said Lieutenant Johnstone with a weary wave of his hand, and Teneriffe was not far enough away from England to relax. Sergeant Knight, facing court martial over his grog protests, was not a happy man. Nor were his underlings.

To make matters worse on Alexander, the ship had not inherited one of the senior officers. Now that they were deliciously tucked into cabins on the quarterdeck, Lieutenants Johnstone and Shairp were not in any way dependent upon their subordinates for any of their creature comforts. They had servants (officers' servants were always crawlers) and a galley of their own, the chance to keep their own livestock on board to supplement their table, and the use of a ship's boat if they felt like visiting friends on one of the other transports while Alexander was at sea. What the privates, drummers, corporals and lone sergeant had not taken into account was the remorseless nature of their task, to feed and guard nearly 200 felons. Port, they had been sure, would see the felons locked up. Now they discovered that this lunatic governor insisted the felons have freedom of the deck even in port!

Of course the rum came on board the moment the crew was set at liberty, the marines having contributed to a pool which ensured that, shipbound or no, they would still be able to moisten their parched throats with something stronger than Sinclair's fucken grog. Luck served them another good turn when, late in the afternoon of the 4th of June, Alexander was the first ship Governor Phillip and his party boarded to inspect. Captain Sinclair actually waddled out of his roundhouse to converse politely with the Governor while the convicts were lined up on deck under the eyes of the marines on duty, eyes bloodshot and breath reeking, but leather stocks and spatterdashes perfect.

"It is a tragedy," said Phillip, walking around the prison, "that we cannot afford better accommodation for these fellows. I see fourteen too sick to parade and I doubt there is room for more than forty men at a time to get a little exercise in these aisles. Which is why they must be given as much freedom of the deck as is possible. If ye have trouble," he said to Major Robert Ross and the two Alexander lieutenants, "double-iron the offenders for a few days, then see how they go."

Lined up with the other convicts on deck wherever there was space to stand, Richard found himself looking at a man who could have been Senhor Tomas Habitas's brother. Governor Phillip had a long, curved, beaky nose, two vertical worry lines hedging in the bridge of that nose, a full and sensuous mouth, and a balding dome of head; he wore his own hair, curled into rolls above his ears and confined in a queue on the back of his neck. Richard remembered that Jem Thistlethwaite had said that the Governor's father, Jacob Phillip the language teacher from Frankfurt, had fled Lutheran-inspired persecution of German Jews. His mother was respectably English, but her relative Lord Pembroke had not seen fit to assist the promising young man educationally or financially, nor had he given Arthur Phillip a push up the naval ladder. All done the hard way, including a long stint in the Portuguese navy—yet another link with Senhor Habitas. As he stood there understanding that this was as close as he would ever get to His Excellency the Governor of New South Wales, Richard felt oddly comforted.

Phillip's aide-de-camp and protégé, Lieutenant Philip Gidley King, was still in his twenties. An Englishman who probably had quite a lot of Celt in him, judging by the way he talked constantly and enthusiastically. The English showed in his meticulous recounting of facts, figures, statistics as the party toured the deck. Major Ross clearly despised him as full of waffle.

Thus it was Tuesday before the convicts had the leisure to look at Santa Cruz and what parts of Teneriffe their moorings in the harbor revealed. They had been fed that midday with fresh goat's meat, boiled pumpkin, peculiar but edible bread and big, raw, juicy onions. Neither vegetable found favor with many, but Richard ate his onion as if it were an apple, crunching into it and letting the juice run down his chin to join the tears its vapors produced in abundance.

The town was small, treeless and very tired and the land around it was precipitous, dry, inhospitable. Of the mountain Richard had so hoped to see after reading about it, nothing was visible above a layer of grey cloud which seemed to hang over the island only; the sky out to sea was blue. Teneriffe had a lid jammed upon it like the hat on a donkey he saw near the stone jetty, the first truly novel impression he had of a non-English world. Bum boats either did not exist or were turned back by the longboats patrolling the area where the transports were all moored together. Alexander lay between two anchor cables suspended taut from the sea bed by floating kegs; because, one of the more sober sailors explained to him, the harbor bottom was littered with sharp chunks of iron the Spanish (who brought it out as ballast) simply dumped into the water as they took on cargo. If the cables were not kept taut, the iron tended to fray them.

They had chosen a good time of year to arrive, he learned from another sailor who had been here several times; the air was warm but neither hot nor humid. October was the most unendurable month, but from July to November hideous winds blew as hot as a furnace from Africa, and carried on them a wealth of stinging sand. But Africa was several hundred miles away! A place, he had always believed, of steaming jungles. Obviously not at this latitude, which was fairly close to the place where Atlas held the world up on his broad shoulders. Yes, he remembered, the deserts of Libya went all the way to Africa's west coast.

On Wednesday, Stephen Donovan came down to the prison to find him shortly after dawn.

"I need you and your men, Morgan," he said curtly, mouth tight in displeasure. "Ten of ye will do—and make it lively."

Ike Rogers was a little better with every day that passed at anchor; yesterday he had eaten his onion with such relish that he found himself the recipient of several more. The pumpkin had also been devoured, though he seemed to have no appetite for meat or bread. His loss of weight was increasingly worrisome: the full, brash face had fallen away to bones and his wrists were so thin that they were knobbed. When Joey Long refused to leave him, Richard decided to take Peter Morris from Tommy Crowder's cot.

"Why not me?" demanded Crowder peevishly.

"Because, Tommy, the fourth mate does not come down into the prison looking for men to clerk for him. He is wanting labor."

"Then take Petey with my blessing," said Crowder, relaxing; he was in the midst of delicate negotiations with Sergeant Knight which might lead to a little rum, even if at an inflated price.

On deck the ten convicts found Mr. Donovan pacing up and down looking like thunder. "Over the side and into the longboat," he rapped. "I have barely enough sober men to bring the empty water tuns up, but none to take the tuns to the jetty and fill them. That is going to be your job. Ye'll be under orders from the cargo hand, Dicky Floan, and ye're going because there are not enough sober marines to put a guard on you. How many of ye can row?"

All the Bristol men could, which made four; Mr. Donovan, an abstemious man, looked blacker. "Then ye'll have to be towed in and out—though where I am to find a lighter to do it, I have no idea." He spotted the naval agent's second-mate son and grabbed him. "Mr. Shortland, I need a towing lighter for the water tun longboat. Any suggestions?"

After a moment of frowning thought Mr. Shortland decided upon nepotism and flagged Fishburn, where his father was ensconced. Fishburn answered so promptly that not more than half an hour went by before Alexander's longboat, loaded with empty tuns all standing upright, was towed away jettyward.

For such an arid and desolate place Teneriffe had excellent water; it came down from a spring somewhere in the interior near a town called Laguna, was conduited through the customary elm pipes (imported, Richard imagined, from Spain) and ran out of a series of mouths dispersed along a short stone jetty. Unless some ship were filling its tuns, the water dissipated in the salty harbor. Since leaving Portsmouth Alexander had used 4,000 gallons, so there were 26 of these 160-gallon receptacles to fill, and each one took two and a half hours. The system was quite ingenious, however, and permitted the filling of six tuns at once; had the Spanish put in a wooden jetty on piers, a boat containing tuns could actually have maneuvered itself underneath and filled all its tuns without man-handling either boat or tuns. As it was, the longboat had been stacked with six tuns on either side and had to be turned constantly to part-fill the tuns on one side, then turn the boat around and part-fill the tuns on the other side. Otherwise the weight—a full tun weighed over half a ton—would have capsized them. Hence the need for ten men to labor, pushing, pulling and oaring the longboat around, mindful of the fact that Donovan had said they had to finish filling the tuns that day. Tomorrow was booked for Scarborough.

The second Alexander longboat was brought in by another towing crew and contained fourteen tuns. Hoping for a little shore time, the towing crew was ordered to haul Alexander's first boat back. Not an order the men would have taken from everybody, but were obliged to; it came from Mr. Samuel Rotton, one of the master's mates off Sirius, and supervisor of watering. A sickly fellow, he did his job beneath the shelter of a green silk umbrella borrowed from delightful Mrs. Deborah Brooks, wife of Sirius's boatswain and a *very* good friend of the Governor's.

"Is she?" Richard asked Dicky Floan, who knew all the gossip.

"Oh, aye. A bit of naughty there, Morgan. All of Sirius is in the know, including Brooks. He's an old shipmate of Phillip's."

Darkness had long fallen before the last tun was filled, and the ten convicts were trembling with fatigue. They had not been fed and for once Richard's scruples had had to be set aside; it was impossible to labor in the sun, veiled though it was most of the time, without drinking, and the only water to drink came from the pipe originating at Laguna's spring. They drank it.

Returning to Alexander well after eight, draped over the tuns in exhaustion, the convicts found that the harbor had come alive with a horde of tiny boats, each dewed with twinkling lights, and fishing for something that apparently was not catchable during the day. A fairyland of bobbing lamps, the occasional golden gleam of nets glittering with whatever milled inside them.

"Ye've done remarkable well," said the fourth mate when the last of them, Richard, had clambered clumsily up the ladder. "Come with me." He walked off toward the crew's mess in the forecastle. "Go in, go in!" he cried. "No one has fed ye, I know, and there is not a marine sober enough to boil anything on their wretched stove without setting fire to the ship. Crew's not in any better condition, but Mr. Kelly the cook kindly left ye food before retiring to his hammock cuddling a bottle."

They had not had a feast like that one since leaving Ceres and their bum boat lunches six months ago—cold mutton that had been roasted, not boiled—a mess of pumpkin and onion stewed with herbs—*fresh* bread rolls slathered in butter—and the whole washed down by small beer.

"I do not believe the butter," said Jimmy Price, chin shining.

"Nor did we," said Donovan dryly. "It seems the butter loaded for the officers was put in the wrong sort of firkins—perishables are supposed to go into double-lined containers, but the contractors cut corners as usual and used ordinary ones. So the butter is on the turn and the whole fleet has been issued with it to get rid of it before it spoils. Then the coopers will get to work to make proper butter firkins—which cannot be filled until we get to the Cape of Good Hope. There are no milch cows this side of it."

Bellies full, they stumbled back to their cots and slept until the church bells woke them at midday Angelus. Shortly after that they ate again, goat's meat, fresh corn bread and raw onions.

Richard gave Ike the fresh, buttered bread roll he had purloined the evening before and hidden in his shirt. "Do try to eat it, Ike. The butter on it will help ye."

And Ike did eat it; after three days and four nights at anchor he was beginning to look better.

"Come look!" cried Job Hollister, excited, sticking his head inside the hatch.

"Ain't she *grand?*" he asked when Richard appeared on deck. "I never saw a ship half her size in Bristol, even at Kingsroad."

She was a Dutch East Indiaman of 800 tons and dwarfed Sirius, though she sat a little lower in the water—on her way home, Richard decided, laden with the spices, peppercorns and teak the Dutch East Indies produced in such abundance—and probably with a chest of sapphires, rubies and pearls in her captain's strong-box.

"Going home to Holland," said John Power, pausing. "I would bet she's lost a fair number of her crew. Our East Indiamen do, at any rate." Mr. Bones beckoned, Power scampered off.

Secure in the knowledge that the official inspection was not going to be repeated, the marines had settled down to drinking now that Sergeant Knight's rather impromptu court martial had concluded with no more than a disciplinary rap over the knuckles; privates like Elias Bishop and Joseph McCaldren had had a hand in Alexander's "grog rebellion" as well, had expected 100 licks of the cat, and were profoundly glad that marine officer sympathy was more with them than with Captain Duncan Sinclair. The two lieutenants had hardly been aboard, busy dining with their fellows on better ships or dickering for goats and chickens in the Santa Cruz marketplace, not to mention journeying inland to see the beauties of a fertile tableland on the mountain's flank.

Some of the convicts had managed to obtain rum as well, and Scarborough was selling Dutch gin she had picked up floating at sea off the Scilly

Isles. To English palates, very harsh and bitter; English gin was as sweet as rum, the main reason why so many men (and women) had rotten teeth. Tommy Crowder, Aaron Davis and the rest in the cot below were snoring on rum they had bought from Sergeant Knight; in fact, the snores which emanated from the Alexander prison were louder than they had been since embarkation. On Friday only those like Richard who preferred to keep their money for more important things were on deck at all, and on Friday night the ship's timbers reverberated.

They were five hours into Saturday morning's daylight when the very haughty and superior first mate, William Aston Long, came looking for John Power.

The faces turned to him blankly were patently innocent; Mr. Long departed looking grim.

Several marine privates, stupid from drink, began yelling that they had better get their fucken arses on deck, and look lively! Startled, the convicts tumbled out of their cots or from around the tables; they were expecting to be fed at any moment.

Captain Duncan Sinclair emerged from his roundhouse, his face pouting in extreme displeasure.

"My dad had a sow looked just like Captain Sinclair," said Bill Whiting audibly enough for the thirty-odd men around him to hear. "Don't know why all the huntsmen talk about wild boars—I never knew a wild boar or a bull could hold a candle to that awful old bitch. She ruled the yard, the barn, the coops, the pond, the animals and us. Evil! Satan would have given her a wide berth and God did not want her either. She would charge at the drop of a hat and she ate her piglets just to spite us. The boar near died of fright when he had to service her. Name was Esmeralda."

From that day on Captain Duncan Sinclair was known to the entire complement of Alexander as "Esmeralda."

Heads aching, tempers ruined, those marines not ashore were put to turning the prison inside out, and when it yielded nothing, to turning every other place inside out. Even rolled sails on spars were searched for John Power, who had disappeared. So, when someone thought to look, had Alexander's jollyboat.

Major Ross came aboard during the afternoon, by which time the hapless marines had managed to look as if they were halfway sober. Lieutenants Johnstone and Shairp had been summarily ordered back from Lady Penrhyn, where they were in the habit of dining with marine captain James Campbell and his two lieutenants. Because of the "grog rebellion" Ross was in no mood to suffer more trouble from this most troublesome of the fleet's eleven ships. The convicts kept dying, the marines were the worst assortment of malcontents the Major had ever encountered, and Duncan Sinclair was the bastard son of a Glasgow bitch.

"Find the man, Sinclair," he said to that worthy, "else your purse will be the lighter of forty pounds. I have reported this matter to the Governor, who is not pleased. *Find him!*"

They did, but not until after dawn on Sunday morning, with the fleet ready to sail. Enquiries aboard the Dutch East Indiaman had revealed that Power had arrived alone in the Alexander jollyboat and begged for work as a seaman on the voyage to Holland. As he was wearing the same kind of clothes as the many English convicts the Dutch captain had seen on the English ships, he was courteously refused and told to be on his way. Not before someone, moved at the sight of his terrible grief, had given him a mug of gin.

It was the jollyboat the search parties from Alexander and Supply found first, tied by its painter to a rock in a deserted cove; Power, sound asleep thanks to sorrow and Dutch gin, was curled up behind a pile of stones, and came quietly. Sinclair and Long wanted him given 200 lashes, but the Governor sent word that he was to be put into double irons and stapled to the deck. The stapling was to last for twenty-four hours, the irons were to remain on at the Governor's pleasure.

Alexander put out to sea. Chips, the ship's carpenter, stapled John Power to the deck by screwing down his manacles and fetters, thus pinning him prone and face down. The orders were that nobody was to go near him on pain of the cat, but as soon as night enfolded the ship Mr. Bones crept to give him water, which he lapped like a dog.

The weather was fine, sunny and gently windy the moment the fleet extricated itself from Teneriffe's morning overcast. This time sight of the island stayed with them for a full three days, a vision that late afternoon rendered unforgettable. Pico de Teide reared up 12,000 feet clear from the ocean, its jagged tip shining starkly white with snow, its waist encircled by a band of grey-hued cloud. Then in the setting sun the snow glowed rose-pink, the cloud crimsoned, and what looked in the ruddiness like molten lava poured down one flank all the way to the sea, some flow of ancient rock whose uniqueness had never been obliterated by sun, wind or blasts of sand from the far off African deserts. So beautiful!

On the morrow it was still there, just farther away, and on the third day out, with the wind freshening and the sea getting up, it looked as if the straight and steady hand which had drawn the horizon had been suddenly jarred to produce a tiny fang. Teneriffe was 100 miles away when the horizon became perfect again.

On the 15th of June they crossed the Tropic of Cancer, an event marked by much ceremony. Every soul on board who had not been south of this imaginary line was obliged to stand trial before none other than Father Neptune himself. The scene on deck was set with shells, nets, seaweed and a huge copper tub filled with sea-water. Two sailors blew on conches while a fearsome individual was carried from the forecastle on a throne made from a barrel; it took a hard look to recognize Stephen Donovan. His head was crowned with seaweed and a jagged brass ring, his beard was seaweed, his face, bare chest and arms were blue, and from the waist down he was clad in the tail of a swordfish caught the previous day, flesh and guts scooped out to accommodate his legs. In one hand he bore his trident, which was actually Alexander's grains—a three-pronged, barbed instrument the sailors successfully used to spear big fish. Each man was brought forward by two blue-painted, seaweed-draped sailors, asked if he had crossed the line, and if he said no, was thrust into the copper of sea-water. After which Father Neptune slapped a bit of blue paint on him and let him go. The best fun for the audience was watching Lieutenants Johnstone and Shairp get dunked, though both knew enough about the ceremony to wear slops.

Rum was issued—and continued to be issued—to all hands, including the convicts; someone produced a penny whistle and the sailors fell to dancing in their strange way, bobbing up and down with arms folded, jigging in circles, teetering from one foot to the other. From that they passed to chanties, after which the convicts—the crew heard them singing often—were begged for a song or two. Richard and Taffy sang a lay by Thomas Tallis, passed into "Greensleeves," and brought the rest into it to sing tavern ballads and popular ditties. Everybody was served a brimming bowl of Mr. Kelly's swordfish chowder, which soaked up the hard bread and actually made it seem tasty. On nightfall lamps were lit and the singing continued until after ten o'clock, when Captain Sinclair sent a message through Trimmings, his steward, that all hands except the Watch were to go to fucken bed.

They picked up the northeast trades, which carried them on south and west at a goodly rate. No square-rigged ship could sit with the wind directly behind her sails; it had to blow on the leading edge of the sail, which meant more to the side or beam. An ideal wind blew from abaft the beam, somewhere between the stern and the midships. As the natural tendency of winds and currents pushed ships toward Brazil and away from Africa as they went down the Atlantic, everyone was aware that sooner or later the fleet must arrive at Rio de Janeiro. The vexed question was, *when?* Though every water tun was full when they left Teneriffe, Governor Phillip thought it prudent to top up the casks again in the Cape Verde Islands, owned by Portugal and positioned almost directly west of Dakar.

On the 18th of June in blowy, hazy weather, the Cape Verde Islands began to pass—Sal, Bonavista, Mayo. Alexander was scudding along at the rate of 165 nautical miles a day, which were 190 land miles. Though mileage was not counted as the actual miles sailed; only those miles which proceeded in the right direction were. On some days a ship might achieve a minus mileage, having spent her time going backward when latitude and longitude were determined at noon. Sea days were noon to noon, when the sun could possibly be shot with a sextant for latitude; accurate longitude was calculated from the chronometers, of which the fleet possessed only one set aboard Sirius, the flagship. As soon as longitude was known on Sirius it was signaled to the other ten ships by flying the appropriate flags.

Big and mountainous St. Jago loomed on the morning of the 19th of June. All went well until the fleet, close together, rounded the southeastern cape to make harbor in Praya. Suddenly they were becalmed, stripped of all wind save what seamen called "catspaws"—little puffs from all points of the compass. To make matters worse, a strong swell was running inshore and breaking upon the reefs; after a few tentative essays the Governor, seeing Scarborough and Alexander within half a mile of the surf, ordered the fleet back to sea. There would be no additional water.

Then Alexander got into trouble again. Lieutenants Johnstone and Shairp had a good thing going with Lady Penrhyn, always one of the two laggards. Both groups of marine officers owned sheep, pigs, chickens and ducks; they not only cooked for themselves, they killed for themselves. Captain, mates and crew had their own stock on board, and so jealously was fresh food regarded that fish caught by the crew were not shared with the marines, and vice versa. There were always several expert fishermen among the crew, but the marines had come equipped with hand-lines, hooks, floats and sinkers for fishing as well. If a convict was discovered to be a handy fisherman, he too would be pressed into service in return for fish-chowder on the convict menu that day or the following one.

The fowls were comfortably consumed by the marine officers of one ship, but in these tropical latitudes a whole carcass of mutton or pork would spoil before it could be eaten. It might have seemed the sensible thing to a hungry convict like Richard Morgan that the marine officers should negotiate with the captain and crew of their vessel to share meat. But no. What belonged to the marine officers would be eaten by none except marine officers. So when Johnstone and Shairp killed a pig or sheep (the goats were kept for milk), they hung a tablecloth over the stern of Alexander; on seeing it, Captain Campbell and his two lieutenants would send a boat to pick up their half of the kill. Similarly, whenever Lady Penrhyn hung a tablecloth over her bows, Alexander's lieutenants took a boat to Lady Penrhyn to pick up half the kill.

To the great joy of Johnstone and Shairp, on the 21st of June Lady Penrhyn hung out a tablecloth. The two marines promptly commandeered a longboat and went to collect their share of the feast. Governor Phillip, Captain Hunter, Major Ross, Judge Advocate David Collins and various other senior persons aboard Sirius watched with amazement as Alexander's marine officers set off gaily into the teeth of a huge swell running from the northwest. Skillfully rowed by twelve marine privates, the longboat made the round trip and arrived safely back to Alexander. While it was being stowed in its usual resting place on deck, Johnstone and Shairp drooled at the prospect of succulent pork loins and Teneriffe onions braised in goat's milk.

Captain Sinclair sent for them.

"Sirius," he said in a monotone, "is awash in flags. I suggest ye go up to the poop and read what they are saying."

The two first lieutenants mounted the steps to the poop, where Sinclair kept his chicken coop, a pen of sheep and goats, and six plump porkers in a mudless sty well shielded from the sun and having a salt water pool so that the pigs could submerge their knees and keep their body temperature down.

"No boat is to leave Alexander without specific permission from the Governor," said the flags.

Such brevity could not convey any emotion whatsoever, but Major Ross rectified this omission a little later in the day when he and a Sirius longboat visited Alexander.

"Ye pair of fucken cretins, I'll flay ye until your ribs show!" he roared, as usual in front of anybody who cared to listen; his conveyance was heaving up and down larboard and he was not about to waste his valuable time by hauling the miscreants into the privacy of the quarterdeck to tell them what he thought of them. "I do not give a fucken shit what Campbell and his ninnies on Lady Penrhyn have to do with ye, or ye with them—this fucken traffic will cease forthwith!"

Back he marched to the rope ladder, down it and into the Sirius longboat without picking up so much as a single drop of sea foam; then it was off to Lady Penrhyn to repeat his sentiments.

Since the marine underlings were laughing quite as hard as the crew and convicts, Lieutenants Johnstone and Shairp shut themselves into the quarterdeck and contemplated suicide.

While the northeast trades held the fleet made good time, but toward the end of June the steady wind failed and progress depended upon whatever breeze could be found. This involved a great deal of tacking and standing; the helmsman would bring the ship onto a different tack and then everybody would wait to see if it brought a wind with it which would send the ship in the right direction. If no such wind appeared, the ship was again turned a little, and the waiting began once more. Tack, stand, tack, stand. . . .

Richard had been put on fishing detail, not so much because he demonstrated any degree of luck as because he was so patient; when people like Bill Whiting decided to fish, they expected a bite within a minute of sending the line down, and refused simply to stand, leaning on the rail with line in the water, for hours if necessary. With the sun directly overhead, deck was not such a comfortable place anymore, particularly for fine white English skins. In that respect Richard's luck held; he had pinkened on the voyage to Teneriffe but then darkened slowly to a good brown, as did Taffy the dark Welshman and others who tended to dark hair. For the fair and freckled Bill Whiting and Jimmy Price came a long period during which they had to retire below, there to nurse pain and blisters, suffering sparing applications of Richard's salve and the calamine lotion Surgeon Balmain slapped on heartlessly.

So when Richard saw the sailors rigging canvas awnings from the stays to the shrouds or any handy projection which would not inconvenience men climbing aloft, he was very pleased.

"I did not know Esmeralda was so considerate of sunburn," he said to Stephen Donovan.

Donovan hooted with laughter. "Richard! Esmeralda don't give a fuck about shelter! No, we are getting close to the line Line—the Equator—

which is why we spend so much of our lives becalmed. Esmeralda knows the storms are about to start, is all. The awnings are to catch rain-water—see? They put a tun at the lowest corner to take the runoff. 'Tis an art to string the canvas—old pieces of sail—so that it forms a saucer with just one edge sagging to form a funnel. We have lost the trade, I think, and so does dear Esmeralda."

"Why are ye fourth mate, Mr. Donovan? It seems to me as I go about the deck that ye carry almost as much weight as Mr. Long, and certainly more than Mr. Shortland or Mr. Bones."

The blue eyes crinkled up at their corners and the mouth wore a smile, but to Richard it looked a little bitter.

"Well, Richard, I am an Irishman of sorts, and despite time with Admiral Rodney in the West Indies, I belong to the merchant sail. Esmeralda put me on as second mate, but the naval agent wanted a berth for his son. Esmeralda got very piggy when he was informed that Mr. Shortland would be coming aboard as second mate—he and the father, Lieutenant Shortland, had a rare old barney. The result was that Lieutenant Shortland thought it better to shift himself to Fishburn. But the son stayed. Mr. Bones was not about to give up his third mate's ticket, so I became fourth mate. There is one of us for each Watch, ye might say."

Richard frowned. "I thought the captain was master of his own ship and had the final say."

"Not when ye're in partnership with the Royal Navy. Walton's want to do more of this transportation work—that is why Captain Francis Walton, one of the family, is master of Friendship. Esmeralda Sinclair is a partner in Walton & Company. Ye'd find, if ye looked hard enough, that almost all the masters of the transports and storeships are shareholders in their companies." Donovan gave a shrug. "If the Botany Bay experiment is a success, there will be a brisk trade in shipping convicts."

"It is nice to know," Richard grinned, "that we miserable wretches bring prosperity to some people."

"Especially to people named William Richards Junior. He is the contractor—and the one ye have to thank for the food ye get, God rot the bastard to Hell forever. And, God, send us a fish or two!"

The line in Richard's hand jerked. So did the one Donovan was holding. A whoop went up from a sailor farther astern; they had come into a huge school of albacore, and hauled the big fish in at such a rate that those standing watching were put to baiting hooks so the lines could go down again before the fish were gone. By the end of this exhilarating spurt of activity there were over fifty large albacore flipping and flapping around the deck, and sailors and marines were sharpening their knives to clean and scale and fillet. A task not allowed to convicts, devoid of knives.

"Chowder aplenty tonight," said Richard with satisfaction. "I am glad too that we do not eat at midday anymore. A man sleeps better on a full belly. I know our lieutenants complain that these beautiful creatures are dry eating, but the meat is *fresh.*"

The sea was great company; something was always happening in it. Richard had grown used to the sight of huge porpoises and somewhat smaller dolphins chasing, playing and leaping far out of the water, though they never ceased to fascinate. Life for sea dwellers, he fancied, could not simply be a matter of survival. These creatures *enjoyed* themselves. Nothing as carefree as a leaping porpoise could possibly not know pleasure in the act, no matter what dour men like Mr. Long said about the leap being a device to frighten predators away, coming down with such a splash and rumpus.

Birds were always present in sometimes great numbers—pintada birds, various petrels, even gulls. As Alexander was not liberal with scraps save when fish guts were tipped out, Richard learned that the presence of lots of birds meant there were schools of fish about, usually too small to bother catching.

He saw his first shark and his first whale on the same day, one of great calm, just a long swell rolling too placidly to break into ruffs of foam. The water was like crystal and he longed to swim in it, wondered if perhaps somewhere along the way Mr. Donovan or some other sailor would teach him to swim. What puzzled him was why they never went over the side, even on days like this, when a man would have no trouble climbing back on board.

Then along it came, this chilling creature. Just why the mere sight of it should freeze him to his marrow he did not understand, for it was beautiful. He saw its fin first, cutting through the water like a knife. The fin stood two feet into the air, heading for a bloody mess of albacore ruins bobbing along their side and in their wake. The thing swam past like a dark shadow and seemed to go on forever; it was, he estimated, twenty-five feet long, as round as a barrel in its mid section but narrowing to a pointed snout in front and terminating in a slender, tapering tail equipped with a forked double fin as rudder. A dull black eye as large as a plate broke the mass of its head, and just as it came up with the fish guts floating in a tangle it turned over on its side to scoop the mess into a vast maw armed with terrible teeth. Its belly flashed white, then the albacore remains were gone; it gulped down every bit it could find, then cruised off into the gentle wake to see if there were more goodies near the ships in Alexander's rear.

God Jesus! I have heard of whales and I have heard of sharks. I knew that a shark is a big fish, but I never dreamed they came as large as whales. Now that is a thing does not know joy. Its eye said that it has no soul.

The whale erupted into the air perhaps a cable's length from the ship, so suddenly that only those like Richard fishing from the starboard side saw the mighty creature breach the surface in a shimmering explosion of water. A beaky head, a small eye that sparkled cognizance, a pair of speckled flippers—it just kept coming up and up and up, forty feet of it in ridged, blue-grey glory, its hull as barnacled as any ship's. When it fell it crashed in clouds of spray and disappeared; a moment's breathless wait and the magnificent fluked tail towered, poised like a banner, before it smacked with a clap like thunder amid dazzling rainbows of foam. The leviathan of the deep, grander than any ship of the line.

Others appeared, spread all over the sea like an etching he had seen of grazing elephants, spouting fountains of mingled air and water, sailing along majestically or breaching the surface in those gargantuan dances. A mother and child sported around Alexander for a long while; she was terribly scarred as well as barnacled, her calf was flawless. Richard wanted to go down on his knees to thank God for so honoring him, but he couldn't bear not to watch for as long as the whales remained. Where was *their* fleet going? Like the porpoises and dolphins, the whales were joyous voyagers.

The squalls began not long after the wind died, and had to be used. They arrived out of a clear sky, the clouds piling up fast, curling dark blue billows tipped with pure white fans, and growling ominously. Then a huge gale descended, the sea turned into a fury, the rain teemed down, lightning flashed, thunder boomed. An hour later saw the sky blue and the ship becalmed again.

A number of convicts and marines were sleeping on deck, though it surprised Richard that more men did not choose to do this. The convicts at any rate were accustomed to sleeping on hard flat boards, yet most elected the stinking prison as soon as darkness fell, which it did at these latitudes with stunning swiftness. There was comfort in a hammock, no matter how stifling the weather, but his fellows—he could only conclude that men feared the elements.

Not Richard, who would find a piece of uncluttered deck out of the way of seamen's feet and lie watching the fantastic play of lightning in and out of the clouds, waiting to be drenched to the skin, waiting to feel his heart stop with the shock of flash and thunderclap together if the storm drifted overhead. The best of all was the rain. He brought his soap with him and stowed his clothes under the edge of one of the longboats, loving the feel of sudsy lather, knowing the rain would last long enough to rinse it off. He brought anything washable up—the matting, everyone's clothes, even the blankets in spite of bleating protests that they were shrinking rapidly.

"If it is not screwed or nailed down, Richard, ye take it up and wash it!" said Bill Whiting indignantly. "How can ye stay out in the open? When the ship is struck and we sink, I want to be below to start with."

"The blankets have shrunk as far as they are going to, Bill, and I do not understand why ye fret so. Everything is dry again in an hour. Ye do not even know that I have taken the stuff, ye're so busy snoring."

The fact that Bill had regained his cheek was an indication of how often they were eating fish, an aspect of transportation across the King's herring pond which Richard had not thought to take into account. The bread was very poor by now, full of grossly wriggling mites he preferred not to see, a reason why most men now ate it with their eyes closed. It had gone softer, apparently a signal for these noisome things to start multiplying. Nothing could live in salt meat, but the pease and oatmeal had their share of livestock. And Richard's group was running low on malt extract.

"Mr. Donovan," he said to the fourth mate who was by rights second mate, "when we reach Rio de Janeiro would ye do me a good turn? I would not presume to ask, save that I trust ye and can trust no one else going ashore."

That was true. Those hours and hours of fishing together had forged a friendship as strong, Richard felt, as any between himself and his men. Stronger, even. Stephen Donovan had both weight and lightness, sensitivity and keen humor, and an uncanny instinct for divining what was going on in Richard's mind. More a brother than William had ever been, and somehow it had ceased to matter that Donovan did not regard Richard in the light of a brother. At first the convicts, near and far, had had a fine time of it poking fun at Richard because of this odd friendship, and his absences on deck during the night had lent an interesting nuance. To all his tormentors Richard turned a blind eye and a deaf ear, too wise to react defensively, with the result that as time went on everybody settled down to accept the relationship as a simple friendship.

They were fishing on the day that Richard put his request; one of those distracting days when nothing would bite. Donovan was wearing a straw sailor's hat and so was Richard, who had bought his from the carpenter's mate, more addicted to rum than the sun.

Donovan made a small sound of pleasure. "I would be delighted to do ye a good turn," he said.

"We have a little money and there are things we need—soap, malt extract, some sort of old woman's recipe for nips and stings, oil of tar, new rags, a couple of razors and two pairs of scissors."

"Keep your money, Richard, to buy your passage home. I will be glad to get what ye want without payment."

Shoulders hunched into his neck, Richard shook his head. "I cannot accept gifts," he said emphatically. "I must pay."

One eyebrow flew up; Donovan grinned. "D'ye think I am after your body? That is hurtful."

"No, I do not! I cannot accept gifts because I cannot give gifts. It has nothing to do with bodies, damn ye!"

Suddenly Donovan was laughing, a clear sound the sky snatched and hurled away. "Oh, my dialogue is grand! I sound like a young maiden in a lady's magazine! Nothing is more ridiculous than a Miss Molly in the throes of unrequited love! Take the gift, 'tis meant to ease your lot, not load ye down with obligations. Did ye never notice, Richard? We are friends."

Richard blinked quickly, smiled. "Aye, I know it very well. Thank you, Mr. Donovan, I will accept your gift."

"Ye could give me a greater one."

"What?"

"Call me Stephen."

"It is not fitting. When I am a free man I will be glad to call ye Stephen. Until then I must keep my place."

A shark cruised by, as hungry as everyone else on this fishless day. A shovel-nose, not above twelve feet long. In this ocean, a tadpole. It turned, gave them an expressionless stare, went off.

"That thing is evil," said Richard. "A whale has a knowing twinkle in its eye, so does a porpoise. That thing looks from out of the pits of Hell."

"Oh, ye're a true product of Bristol! Did ye never preach?"

"No, but there are preachers in the family. Church of England ones. My father's cousin is rector of St. James's, and his father preached in the open air at Crew's Hole to the Kingswood colliers."

"A brave man. Did he live through it?"

"Aye. Cousin James was born after it."

"Are ye never plagued by the flesh, Richard?"

"I was once, with a woman who could open the gates of paradise to any man. *That* was terrible. Going without is a nothing."

Something tugged at Donovan's line, and he whooped. "A bite! There is a fish down there!"

There was. The shark had come back and taken the bait. Also the hook, float and sinker. Donovan plucked his hat off, stamped on it and cursed.

Perhaps it was the weather, sultry, hot, airless; or perhaps Alexander had simply given death a short holiday before the old troubles began afresh. On the 29th of June the convicts began to die again. Surgeon Balmain, who loathed going into the prison because of the smell, was suddenly obliged to spend a great deal of time there. His physics did little, nor did his emetics, nor did his purgatives.

How easily superstitions took hold! Just as the sickness started Alexander ploughed into a solid sea of brilliant cobalt blue, and the unaffected convicts, crowding on deck to see, were immediately convinced that this was the manifestation of a curse. The sea had turned to blue pebbles and everyone was going to die.

"They are nautiluses!" cried Surgeon Balmain, exasperated. "We have encountered a great shoal of nautiluses—Portuguese men o' war! Bright blue jellyfishy creatures! They are natural, they are not evidence of divine displeasure! *Christ!*" Waving his arms about, he disappeared to despair in the privacy of his cluttered cabin on the quarterdeck.

"Why do they call them Portuguese men o' war?" asked Joey Long, yielding his place to Richard, whose turn it was to nurse Ike.

"Because Portuguese ships of the line are painted that same shade of blue," said Richard.

"Not black with yellow trim like ours?"

"If they were painted the same as ours, Joey, how would anybody tell friend from foe? The moment there is powder smoke all about, 'tis very hard to distinguish flags and badges. Now take a turn on deck, there's a good fellow. Ye spend too much time below." Richard sat beside Ike, stripped off the shirt and trowsers and began to sponge him down.

"Balmain is an idiot," Ike croaked.

"Nay, he is simply at his wits' end. He don't know what to do for the best."

"Does anybody? I mean anybody at all, anywhere at all?" Ike had leached away to skin stretched over bones, a collection of sticks wrapped in parchment; his hair had fallen out, his nails had turned white, his tongue was furred, his lips cracked and swollen. Though Richard found the most horrifying talismans of his illness in his nude, shrunken genitals; they looked as if they had been tacked on like an afterthought. Oh, Ike!

"Here, open your mouth. I have to clean your teeth and tongue." Touch gentle, Richard used a screwed-up corner of rag moistened in filtered water to do what he could to make the highwayman's day more bearable. Sometimes, he thought as he worked, it is worse to be a big man. If Ike were the size of Jimmy Price, it would all have been over long since. But there was a sizable mountain of flesh there once, and life is tenacious. A very few give up without a protest, but most cling to whatever is left like limpets to a rock.

The smell was worsening and its source was the bilge water. Though he had been a naval surgeon for seven years and had staffed a surveying expedition to the west African coast at the time when the Parliament had still thought of using Africa as a convict dumping ground, Balmain found Alexander a task beyond his abilities. At his insistence wind sails had been installed in the suffocating corners of the prison—useless canvas funnels supposed to deliver a good draft of air through a hole bored in the deck. Captain Sinclair had protested vigorously for such a torpid man, but the surgeon would not back down. Perturbed because Alexander was now nicknamed the Death Ship, Sinclair gave way and ordered Chips to deface his deck. But very little if any fresh air came prisonward, and men continued to come down with fever.

Thin though he was, Richard was well. So too were his cot mates and the four others in Ike's cot. Willy Dring and Joe Robinson had abandoned below deck entirely, which left three others (they had lost a man outside Portsmouth) to spread out in a space designed for six at twenty inches apiece. The cot belonging to Tommy Crowder and Aaron Davis had such a good thing going with Sergeant Knight that they lived very comfortably. Despite these good indications, Richard's instincts told him that the new outbreak of disease was going to be a bad one.

"Save for whoever is nursing Ike, we move onto the deck and we catch as much rain-water for ourselves as we can," he ordered.

Jimmy Price and Job Hollister began to whimper, Joey Long to howl; the rest looked mutinous.

"We would rather stay below," said Bill Whiting.

"If ye do, ye'll catch the fever."

"You said it yourself, Richard," Neddy Perrott snapped. "As long as we filter our water and keep everything clean, we will live. So no deck. 'Tis fine for you with your skin, but I burn."

"I will come up," said Taffy Edmunds, gathering a few things. "You and I have to practice for the concert. We cannot let our ship be the only one unable to get a concert together. Look at Scarborough. She has a concert every week. Corporal Flannery says that some of the acts are so polished they have to be seen to be believed."

"Scarborough," said Will Connelly, "might have more convicts than we do these days, but the reason they are well is because they are spread between the lower deck and the orlop. We're jammed in half the space Scarborough has because we're carrying cargo too."

"Well, I for one am very glad that Alexander has cargo in her orlop," said Richard, giving up the fight, which he could see was pointless. "Look what happened to the marines when they were one deck farther down. Scarborough's bilge pumps work. It all goes back to the master. They have Captain Marshall, we have Esmeralda, who don't care if his bilge pumps work as long as his table groans. Alexander's bilges are absolutely fouled."

By the 4th of July another man had died and there were thirty men on the hospital platforms. It was, thought Surgeon Balmain, as if the whole of Alexander's hull was packed solid with corpses in the worst stage of decomposition. How could these unfortunate wretches *live* amid the putrescence?

The next day two orders came from Sirius. The first said that John Power was to come out of his irons; the moment he was unlocked he was back to report to Mr. Bones, nothing having been said to forbid his working. The second order displeased Lieutenants Johnstone and Shairp hugely. The water ration for every man in the fleet (women and children got less) was to go from four pints to three pints, be he sailor, marine or convict. One pint was to be issued at dawn to all convicts, two pints in mid afternoon. A detail to be under the supervision of a marine officer, with two marine subordinates and two convicts as witnesses; the marines and convicts were to be changed each and every time to prevent cheating or collusion. The holds were to be locked, the water tun in use locked and kept under strict guard. Custody of the keys went to the officers. Additional water for the coppers and kettles was to be issued in the morning, together with water for the animals. Animals drank copiously; cattle and horses got through ten gallons per day per head.

Three days later the calms and storms vanished and the southeast trades began to blow. This despite the fact that the ships had not yet crossed the

Equator. Spirits picked up immediately, though the fleet was hard-pressed to maintain its course in terms of real miles, which were less than 100 a day. Alexander ploughed into a huge head swell, her rigging creaking, parallel as usual with Scarborough the concert ship, Sirius and Supply not far behind, Friendship out in front, the swell over her bows in masses of spray she shook off as a dog does water.

When the silver buttons on Johnstone's and Shairp's scarlet coats began to blacken and the smell was pervading the quarterdeck almost as badly as below deck, the two lieutenants and Surgeon Balmain went as a deputation to see the captain, who received them and dismissed their complaints as nonsense. What concerned him was that the convicts were stealing his bread and ought to be flogged within an inch of their lives.

"You ought," said Johnstone tartly, "to thank your stars that they are not stealing your rum!"

The dirty teeth showed in a smile of pure pleasure. "Other ships may have trouble with their rum, sirs, but my ship does not. Now go away and leave me alone. I have given the starboard bilge pump to Chips to fix, it is not working properly. That, no doubt, accounts for the state of the bilges."

"How," said Balmain through his teeth, "can a carpenter fix an object whose capacity to work depends upon metal and leather?"

"Ye had better pray he can. Now go away."

Balmain had had enough. He flagged Sirius and received permission to take a boat to Charlotte and the Surgeon-General, John White. With Lieutenant Shairp in command, the longboat headed away into the swell; Charlotte, a heavy sailer, was lagging far behind. The trip back to Alexander was frightful, even for Shairp, who never turned a hair in the worst seas. So when Surgeon White clambered up Alexander's ladder he was not in a good mood.

"You Bristol men, ye're wanted," said Stephen Donovan. "In steerage with Mr. White and Mr. Balmain."

Strictly speaking, thought Richard, who had learned a lot about pumps during the time he had spent with the absconding Mr. Thomas Latimer, Alexander's pumps should have been down a deck to reduce the height of the column of bilge water they had to lift, but she was a slaver and her owners did not like low holes in the hull; the truth was that no one had ever worried much about the bilges between dry-dockings for careening.

There were two cisterns in the marines' steerage compartment, one larboard and one starboard, each equipped with an ordinary suction pump owning an up-and-down handle. A pipe led from each cistern and emptied through a valve into the sea. The starboard pump had been dismantled; the larboard one refused to budge.

"Down we go," said Surgeon White, face ashen. "How does a man exist in this place? Your men, Lieutenant Johnstone, are to be commended for their forbearance."

Richard and Will Connelly took up the hatch and reeled. The hold below was in utter darkness, but the sound of liquid slopping around the water tuns was audible to the rest, hanging back.

"I need some lamps," said White, tying a handkerchief over his face. "One of us is going to have to go down there."

"Sir," said Richard courteously, "I would not put a flame in there. The air itself would burn."

"But I must see!"

"There is no need, sir, truly. We can all hear what is going on. The bilges have overflowed into the hold. That means they are completely fouled. Neither pump is working and may never have worked—the last time we were in here we cleared the bilges by bucket. We have had this problem since Gallion's Reach."

"What is your name?" asked White through his mask.

"Richard Morgan, sir, late of Bristol." He grinned. "We men of Bristol are used to fugs, so they always put us on bilge duty. Though cleaning them by bucket will not remedy anything. They have to be pumped, and pumped every day. But not with suction pumps like these. They take a week to evacuate a ton of water, even when they are working properly."

"Is the carpenter capable of fixing them, Mr. Johnstone?"

Johnstone shrugged. "Ask Morgan, sir. He seems to know. I confess I know nothing about pumps."

"Is the carpenter capable of fixing them, Morgan?"

"Nay, sir. There are so many solids in the bilge that pipes and cylinders of this size will block at every lift. What this ship needs are chain pumps."

"What does a chain pump do that these cannot?" White asked.

"Cope with what is down there, sir. It is a simple wooden box of much larger internal size than these cylinders. The lifting is done by means of a flat brass chain strung over wooden sprockets at the top and a wooden drum at the bottom. Wooden shelves are linked to the chain so that on the way down they flop flat, then unfold on the way up and exert suction. A good chips can build everything except the chain—it is so simple a device that two men turning its sprocketed drum can lift a ton of water in a minute."

"Then Alexander must be fitted with chain pumps. Is there any of the chain aboard?"

"I doubt that, sir, but Sirius has just undergone a refitting, so she is bound to have chain pumps. I imagine she will have chain to spare. If she does not, some of the other ships might."

White turned to Balmain, Johnstone and Shairp. "Very well, I am off to Sirius to report this to the Governor. In the meantime the hold and bilges will have to be baled out. Every marine and convict who is not sick will take his turn, I will not have these Bristol men forced to do it all," he said to Johnstone. He turned then to glare at Balmain. "Why, Mr. Balmain, did ye not report the situation a great deal earlier, if it has been going on for over seven months? The captain of this vessel is a slug, he could not move out of his own way if the mizzen fell on his roundhouse. As surgeon, it is your clear duty to preserve the health of every man on board, including convicts. Ye have not done that, and so I will tell the Governor, rest assured."

William Balmain stood flying a scarlet flag in each cheek, his handsome countenance rigid with shock and anger. A Scotchman, he was six years younger than the Irishman White and they had not taken to each other upon meeting. To be dressed down in front of two marines and four convicts was disgraceful—that was the kind of thing Major Ross did to feckless subordinates. Now was not the time to have it out with White, but Balmain promised himself that after the fleet reached Botany Bay he would have satisfaction. His large eyes passed from one convict face to another in search of mirth or derision, but found none. He knew this lot for the oddest of reasons: they were never sick.

At which moment Major Robert Ross arrived at the bottom of the steps, curiosity stirred because Shairp had been gallivanting all over the ocean again. One sniff was sufficient to acquaint him with the problem; Balmain withdrew stiffly to his cabin to sulk and plot revenge while White explained what was going on.

"Ah yes," said Ross, staring at Richard intently. "Ye're the clean head man, I remember ye well. So ye're an expert on pumps and the like, are ye, Morgan?"

"I know enough to be sure Alexander is in sore need of chain pumps, sir."

"I agree. Mr. White, I will convey ye to Sirius and then on to Charlotte. Mr. Johnstone and Mr. Shairp, get everybody onto baling out the bilges.

And cut two holes in the hull lower than the ports so the men can tip the stuff straight into the sea."

Lieutenant Philip Gidley King, arriving with Major Ross and Surgeon-General White the next day, took one look at the larboard pump Richard had removed and dismantled, and gave vent to a noise of derisive disgust. "That thing could not suck semen out of a satyr's prick! This ship is to be fitted out with chain pumps. Where is the carpenter?"

English meticulousness combined with Celtic enthusiasm worked wonders. Royal Navy and therefore senior in rank to a marine lieutenant, King remained on board long enough to be sure that Chips understood exactly what he was to do—and was capable of doing it—then left to report to the Commodore that in future Alexander ought to be a far healthier ship.

But the poison was in her timbers, so Alexander never was a truly healthy ship. The gaseous effluvia which had lain everywhere below gradually dissipated, however. Living inside her became more bearable. And was Esmeralda Sinclair pleased that his bilge problem had been solved at no cost to Walton & Co.? Definitely not. Who the hell, he demanded from his poop perch (Trimmings had inspected and reported), had cut two fucken holes in his ship?

The fleet crossed the Equator during the night between the 15th and 16th of July. On the following day the ships ran into their first roaring gale since leaving Portsmouth; the hatches were battened down and the convicts plunged into utter darkness. To those like Richard who spent all their time on deck it was a nightmare alleviated only by the fact that the worst of the stench had gone. The sea was running off the larboard bow, so Alexander was pitching more than rolling, an extraordinary sensation alternating between crushing pressure and weightlessness as she reared into the air and slammed with a noise like a huge explosion back into the sea. At right angles to the motion, they rolled from the bulkhead to the partition. Seasickness, deemed a thing of the past, erupted again; Ike suffered terribly.

Too terribly. As the fleet emerged from the storm with its rain butts filled sufficiently to permit ordinary water rations again, it became clear to everyone, even the desolate Joey Long, that Isaac Rogers was not going to live.

He asked to see Richard, who crouched opposite Joey, cradling Ike's head and shoulders on his lap.

"The end of the road for this highwayman," he said. "Oh, I am so glad,

Richard! Be glad for me too. Try to look after Joey. He will feel it."

"Rest easy, Ike, we will all look after Joey."

Ike lifted one skeletal arm to indicate the shelf along the beam. "My boots, Richard. Ye're the only one big enough to wear them and I want ye to have them. *As they are, whole and complete.* Ye know?"

"I know. They will be used wisely."

"Good," he said, and closed his eyes.

About an hour later he died, not having opened them.

So many men had died aboard Alexander that her sailmakers had had to beg old canvas from other ships; clad in clean clothes, Isaac Rogers was sewn into his envelope and carried on deck. As he owned a Book of Common Prayer, Richard read the service, committing Ike's soul to God and his body to the deep. It slid off the board and sank immediately, weighted down with basalt stones collected off the same beach in Teneriffe where John Power had slept. The Death Ship had run out of metal scraps.

Surgeon Balmain ordered another fumigation, a scrub with oil of tar, a new coat of whitewash. His was rather a lonely life, stuck on the quarterdeck with only two marine lieutenants for company. They messed separately from him and shared absolutely nothing with him. Like Arthur Bowes Smyth, the surgeon on Lady Penrhyn, Balmain sustained himself with an interest in the many sea creatures they chanced upon, and if they were small enough, preserved them in spirits. Admittedly it was a great deal easier to descend into the prison these days of chain pumps, but he was still smarting from Surgeon White's jawing and determined that it would not be *his* fault if the wretched convicts kept dying.

When a convict using the crew's holes in the bow was washed overboard by a freak wave, the complement went down to 183.

At the beginning of August the fleet made landfall at Cape Frio, a day's sail to the north of Brazil's chief city. But the high, jagged mountains of that coast behaved as had St. Jago's peaks; once around the cape the wind failed into catspaws and calms. They groped down to Rio de Janeiro, not reaching it until the night between the 4th and 5th. The season was winter now: Rio de Janeiro was so far south of the Equator that it lay just to the north of the Tropic of Capricorn. Out of the realms of both crab and sea goat. The passage from Teneriffe had taken 56 days and they were 84 days out of Portsmouth, figures which rounded neatly into 8 weeks and 12 weeks. And 6,600 land miles.

Permission to enter the colonial domains of Portugal had to be secured, a time-consuming business. At three in the afternoon the fleet crossed the mile-wide bar between the Sugarloafs to the thunder of a thirteen-gun salute from Sirius answered by the guns of Fort Santa Cruz.

From dawn on, everyone on Alexander had crowded to the rails, fascinated by this alien, fabulously beautiful place. The south Sugarloaf was a thousand-foot-tall egg of pinkish-grey rock crowned with a wig of trees, the north Sugarloaf less spectacularly bare. Other crags reared, their tops sheared and jarred, flanks thick with lushly green forests, flashes of brilliant grassland, jutting grey, cream, pink faces of rock. The beaches were long, curved and yellow-sanded, creamy with surf where the ocean beat in, still and placid once across the bar. They dropped anchor not far inside, opposite one of the many fortresses erected to guard Rio de Janeiro from maritime predators. It was not until the next day that the eleven ships were towed to their permanent moorings off the city of São Sebastião, which was the proper name for urban Rio. It occupied a squarish peninsula on the western shore and sent tentacles of itself into the valleys between the peaks all around.

The harbor was alive with bum boats, most of them paddled by near-naked negroes, each craft sporting an awning painted in bright colors. Richard could see the spires of churches crowned with golden crosses, but of other tall buildings Rio had few. No one had forbidden the convicts access to the deck, nor had they been ironed, even John Power. A patrol of longboats rowed constantly around the six transports, however, and turned the bum boats away.

The weather was fine and very hot, the air still. Oh, to be allowed ashore! Not possible, all the convicts understood that. When midday came they were served with huge pieces of fresh beef, pots of yams and beans, messes of rice and loaves of strange-tasting bread made, Richard was told later, from a root called "cassada." But all that was as nothing when the boats arrived and laughing negroes threw hundreds upon hundreds of oranges up onto the deck, making a game of catchings out of it, white teeth flashing in ebony faces. Richard knew of oranges, as did a few others; he had read that some great houses contained "orangeries" and had once seen an orange displayed by Cousin James-the-druggist, who imported lemons to obtain their oil. Lemons were less perishable.

Some of these oranges were six and seven inches in diameter, deep and rich in color; others were almost blood-red and had blood-red flesh inside. Having discovered that the unpalatable skin peeled off easily, the convicts and marines gorged on oranges, ravished by their sweetness and juiciness. Sometimes they ate fat, bright yellow lemons to cut the saccharine taste of so many oranges or sucked at less juicy limes, which lay somewhere between the astringency of a lemon and the syrup of an orange. They never got tired of the citrus, could not get enough. Finding that the palest fruit had been picked before it was fully ripe, Neddy Perrott began at the end of their third week in Rio to stockpile any succulent globes he thought might last a few days; once made aware of it, more convicts followed suit. And a number of men, including Richard, saved orange and lemon seeds.

Every single day they got fresh beef, fresh vegetables of some kind, and fresh cassada bread. Once the marines found out that Rio rum might be poor in quality but was almost as cheap as water, discipline and supervision of the convicts was close to nonexistent. The two lieutenants were hardly ever on board, nor was Surgeon Balmain, who took himself off on country expeditions to look at enormous, brilliant butterflies and flowers of waxen glory called orchids. Hungry for pets, the crew and marines often came back bearing quite tame parrots of gorgeous colors; only two of the dogs were left, the rest, as Donovan had predicted, bait for sharks. Rodney the cat, his wife and rapidly growing family were thriving. Alexander might be more sanitary now, but she was full of rats and mice.

There was a less attractive side to Rio; it was a cockroach paradise. England did own a very small and meek creature in the roach, but these things were giants that flew, clattered, and oozed the same kind of evil intent that sharks did. Aggressive and clever, they would charge a man rather than run away. From Sirius's top echelons all the way down to Alexander's most picked-on convict, men were driven to the verge of dementia by cockroaches.

Most shipbound people slept almost nude on deck, though not as peacefully as at sea. Rio never went to bed. Nor did it ever grow dark; the churches and other buildings were illuminated all night. As if the few Portuguese and their innumerable black slaves feared what lurked amid the nocturnal shadows. After hearing some creature emit a bloodcurdling sound halfway between a shriek and a roar in the small hours of one night, Richard began to understand why they kept darkness at bay.

At least two or three times a week there were fireworks, always in honor of some saint, or the Virgin, or an event in the life of Jesus Christ—there was nothing sober or toned down about Rio's religious life. This offended Knoxian individuals like Balmain and Shairp, who regarded Catholicism as immoral, degenerate and satanic.

"I am surprised," said Richard to John Power as they watched colored sparks and tendrils float down from a skyrocket, "that ye've not tried to escape, Johnny."

Power looked wry. "Here? Not speaking Portuguese? I would be snabbled in a day. Apart from Portuguese slavers and cargo snows, the only ship in port is an English whaler having her bottom scraped. And she is to take a party of naval invalids from Sirius and Supply home with her." He changed the subject, obviously too painful. "I see that Esmeralda is neglecting his ship as usual. He never makes any attempt to scrape her."

"Didn't Mr. Bones tell ye? Alexander is copper sheathed." Richard flicked his chest, sticky with orange juice. "I am going over the side to wash."

"I did not know ye could swim."

"I cannot. But I dunk myself in the water and hang on to the ladder. In the hope that sooner or later I will be able to do without the ladder. Yesterday I let go and actually kept afloat for two seconds. Then I panicked. Today I might not panic."

"I can swim, but dare not," said Power ruefully. Slack discipline or no, Power had his own guard.

Richard was in the water one day when Stephen Donovan returned in a hired boat. He had not succeeded in swimming; as soon as he let go of the ladder he began to sink. With a boat coming in he had to get out, and was ready to when he saw who stood in its bow.

"Richard, ye idiot, there are sharks in this harbor!" said Donovan, gaining the deck. "I would not continue were I you."

"I very much doubt that any shark would fancy my stringy frame in the midst of the bounty Rio harbor offers," grinned Richard. "I am trying to learn to swim, but so far I am a dismal failure."

Donovan's eyes twinkled. "So that if Alexander goes down in an ocean gale ye can swim for Africa? Fear not, Alexander has a good tumblehome hull and she's shipshape in spite of her age. Ye could lay her right over on her beam until her spars went under or poop her in a following sea, and she'd not sink."

"No, so that when we get to Botany Bay and perhaps buckets are in short supply, I can at least bathe in sea-water without needing to worry about being over my head in a hole. There may be lakes and rivers there, but Sir Joseph Banks does not mention them. In fact, he indicates that fresh water is exceeding scant—just a very few small brooks."

"I understand. Look at yon dog Wallace." He pointed to where Lieutenant Shairp's Scotch terrier was striking out for the ship alongside a hired boat, encouraged by a laughing Shairp.

"What about Wallace?"

"Watch him swim. Next time ye go down the ladder to brave the sharks, pretend that ye've got four legs, not two. Tip yourself onto your belly, stick your head up out of the water and move all four of your limbs like a duck's paddles. Then," said Donovan, bestowing a silver sixpence upon a beaming black man after he put a heap of parcels on the deck, "ye'll swim, Richard. From Wallace and four legs ye'll go easily to treading water, floating, all the tricks and treats of swimming."

"Johnny Power swims, yet he is still with us."

"I wonder would he have come so tamely in Teneriffe if he had known what I found out today?"

Alerted, Richard put his head to one side. "Tell me."

"This fleet sailed from Portsmouth with what cartridges the marines had in their pouches and not a grain of powder or a single shot more."

"Ye're joking!"

"Nay, I am not." Donovan began to chuckle, shaking his head. "That is how well organized this expedition is! They forgot to supply any ammunition."

"Christ!"

"I only found out because His Excellency Governor Phillip has managed to purchase ten thousand cartridges here in Rio."

"So they could not have contained a serious mutiny on any one of these ships—I have seen how our Alexander marines care for their pieces and ammunition—there would not be one cartridge worth a man's spit."

Mr. Donovan glanced at Richard sharply, opened his mouth to say something, changed his mind and squatted down near the parcels. "Here are some of your things. I will pick up more tomorrow. I also heard talk of sailing." He piled the bundles into Richard's arms. "Oil of tar, some ointment from a crone so hagged and ugly that she cannot help but know her craft, plus some powdered bark she swears cures fevers. And a bottle of laudanum in case aqua Rio spreads the dysentery—the surgeons are suspicious of it, Lieutenant King sanguine. Lots of good rags and a couple of fine cotton shirts I could not resist—got a few for myself and thought of you. For coolness and comfort in hot weather, cotton has no equal. Malt is proving elusive—the surgeons got to the warehouses first, damn their eyes and cods. But dry some of your orange and lemon peels in the sun and chew them. 'Tis common sailor talk that citrus prevents the scurvy."

Richard's eyes dwelled upon Donovan's face with affection and gratitude, but Donovan was too wise to interpret what they held as more than it actually was. Friendship. Which was to die for with this man, who must surely have loved, but was not willing to do so again. Whom had he lost? How had he lost? Not the woman who had opened the gates of sexual heaven. That, from the expression on his face, had revolted him. Not any woman. Nor yet any man. One day, Richard Morgan, he vowed, I will hear all of your story.

As he went to leave the ship the next morning, he found Richard waiting for him by the ladder.

"Another favor?" he asked, looking eager to do it.

"No, this I must pay for." Richard pointed to the deck and bent down as if something of interest lay there. Donovan hunkered down too; nobody saw the seven gold coins change hands.

"What is it ye want? Ye could buy a topaz the size of a lime for this, or an amethyst not much smaller."

"I need as much emery powder and very strong fish-glue as it will buy," said Richard.

Mouth slightly open, Donovan looked at him. "Emery powder? Fish-glue? What on earth for?"

"It would probably be possible to buy them at the Cape of Good Hope, but I believe the prices there are shocking. Rio de Janeiro seems a much less expensive place," Richard hedged.

"That does not answer my question. Ye're a man of mystery, my friend. Tell me, else I'll not buy for ye."

"You will, you know," said Richard with a broad smile, "but I do not mind telling you." He looked out across the bay toward the northern hills, smothered in jungle. "I have spent a great deal of time during this interminable voyage wondering what I should do when finally we reach Botany Bay. There are hardly any skilled men among the convicts—we all hear the marine officers talking, especially since arriving in Rio, what with all the visiting goes on. Little Lieutenant Ralph Clark never shuts up. But sometimes our ears glean a useful item between his whines about the drunken antics on Friendship's quarterdeck and his fond moans about his wife and son." Richard drew a breath. "But do not let me start on marine second lieutenants! Back to what I began to say, that there are hardly any skilled men among us convicts. I do have some skills, one of which I will certainly be able to use, as I imagine there will be much tree felling and sawing of timber. I can sharpen saws. More importantly, I can set the teeth on saws, a rarer art by far. It may be that my cousin James managed to get my box of tools somewhere aboard these ships, but he may not have. In which case, I cannot do without emery powder and glue. Files I imagine the fleet must have, but if it has been as sketchily provided with tools as it has been poorly victualled, no one will have thought of emery powder or fish-glue. Hearing the news about musket cartridges has not exactly cheered me either. What did they expect us to do if the Indians of New South Wales are as fierce as Mohawks and besiege us?"

"A good question," said Stephen Donovan solemnly. "What d'ye do with emery powder and fish-glue, Richard?"

"I make my own emery paper and emery files."

"Will ye need ordinary files if the fleet has none?"

"Yes, but that is all the money I can spare, and I will not encroach further on your generosity. I am hoping for my tools."

"Getting information out of you is like squeezing blood out of a stone," said Mr. Donovan, smiling, "but I am a little ahead. One day I will know all."

"It is not worth hearing. But thank you."

"Oh, I am your servant, Richard! Were it not for having to search high and low for your medicaments, I would never have found half the fascinating sights I have seen in Rio. Like Johnstone and Shairp, it would have been coffee houses, sticky buns, rum, port and smarming up to Portuguese officials in the hope of being dowered with precious little keepsakes." And off he went down the ladder with the careless ease of someone who has done something ten thousand times, whistling merrily.

On the last Sunday in Rio the Reverend Mr. Richard Johnson, chaplain to the expedition and noted for his mildly Methodical view of the Church of England (*very* Low!), preached and gave service aboard Alexander to the accompaniment of blatantly Catholic church bells clanging and cascading all over town. The decks were being cleared, a sure sign that sailing time was imminent.

They began the business of getting eleven ships out of Rio de Janeiro's island-littered harbor on the 4th of September and completed it on the 5th, having remained at anchor for a month of oranges and fireworks. Fort Santa Cruz and Sirius outdid themselves with a twenty-one-gun salute. Water rationing to three pints a day had already been instituted, perhaps an indication that the Governor concurred with the surgeons about the quality of Rio's water.

By nightfall land was out of sight; the fleet headed out to find its eastings in the hope that the 3,300 land miles to the Cape of Good Hope would be a swift passage. From now on it would be eastward and southward into seas charted as far as the Cape, but not populous. Thus far they had encountered a Portuguese merchantman occasionally, but from now on they would see no ships until they neared the Cape and the route of the big East Indiamen.

Richard had his replenished stocks plus emery powder, glue and several good files; his chief worry was the dripstones, of which he still had two spares but his five friends had none. If Cousin James-the-druggist was right, they had to be nearing the end of their usefulness. So with Mr. Donovan's help he rigged up a rope cradle and trailed one dripstone in the sea, praying that a shark did not fancy it. One shark had fancied a pair of marine officer's trowsers being towed behind for a good bleaching, snapped the line in half, swallowed the trowsers and spat them out in disgust. As it would a dripstone. But once the line was gone, so was the item attached to it. After one week he pulled it out and screwed it to the deck to get plenty of sun and rain. A second one went in for a long bath. He hoped to get through all of them before any started showing signs of deterioration.

As they drew farther south, still waiting on the great current which would assist them to cross from Brazil to Africa, they began to see groups of spermaceti whales, also heading south. Massive creatures, they had snouts which in profile looked like small cliffs, beneath which sat ludicrously slender lower jaws armed with fearsome teeth. Their tails were blunter, their flukes smaller, and they were less acrobatic than other whales they had seen. The usual marine life of porpoises, dolphins and sharks were there aplenty, but edible fish were harder to catch because they were sailing faster and into heavy swells. Sometimes a school came along to provide fish-chowder, but the fare was mostly salt meat and hard bread seething with weevils and worms. No one had much of an appetite. The convicts did have a large sack of dried citrus peelings, however, and shared it out to chew on, a small piece every day.

Gigantic sea birds called albatrosses grew more and more numerous as they inched southward, but when an ambitious marine got out his musket because he fancied roast albatross for dinner, the crew restrained him in horror; it was bad luck to the ship to kill one of these kings of the air.

The new sickness broke out among the marines first, but soon spread into the prison. So it was back to fumigating, scrubbing and whitewashing. The central isolation platforms were full once more and one convict died in the midst of a roaring gale. Surgeon Balmain—happier to visit in these days of sweeter smells—spent a lot of time between the prison and steerage. Whenever the weather permitted it he ordered yet another fumigation, scrub, and whitewash, though clearly the ritual did nothing save steal a little more light for Richard, Bill, Will, Neddy and others to read by if the deck was a shambles of sail and sailors. It turned out during this series of blows that Captain Sinclair was no mean sailor himself; he would make sail the moment the wind was right, then shorten sail not many minutes later if the wind went sour. Make, shorten, make, shorten, make. . . . Little wonder that John Power, Willy Dring and Joe Robinson never made an appearance in the prison. The mates could use all the hands they could get. Nothing was worse than having too few hands to get a decent rest between watches.

By the end of September the equinoctial gales died a little, the seas became easier, deck accessible. In fair weather or foul she sailed well, did Alexander, so at no time did the seas break over her hard enough to batten the hatches. That fate had happened only the once since leaving Portsmouth.

Looking as exalted as he did exhausted, John Power returned to the prison from time to time once his services were not so much in demand, as did Willy Dring and Joe Robinson, who seemed edgy and restless; they made no attempt to go forward and join Power's clique around the bow bulkhead, which puzzled Richard, who had expected that shared work would see them grow increasingly friendly with their fellow sailor. Instead, they looked uneasy whenever they saw him.

Things went along much as they had for weeks on end—an excursion on deck to fish or pat animals, a read, a singsong, talk between groups, games of dice or cards, some sort of struggle to eat; they were all growing thin again, the little bit of padding acquired in Rio dwindling on that terrible diet. No one near the stern bulkhead on the larboard side noticed anything different—no change in the atmosphere, no furtive whispering, no descending into the hold to steal bread—well, who would want to? Willy Dring and Joe Robinson had gone to earth in their cot and seemed to sleep or doze constantly; that last was the only symptom Richard noticed, and he dismissed it as odd but not really remarkable. They had worked hard for two solid weeks.

Then on the 6th of October and not very far from the African continent, a party of ten marines descended into the prison and took John Power away. He went fighting, was knocked senseless and lifted out through the after hatch while the convicts stared in amazement. A few minutes later the marines were back to remove two men from Nottingham, William Pane and John Meynell, whose cot was next to Power's. Then—nothing. Except that Power, Pane and Meynell never came back.

Richard got most of the story from Stephen Donovan and a little from Willy Dring and Joe Robinson.

Power and some of the crew had planned a mutiny which hinged on the fact that two-thirds of the marines were not fit for duty.

"A wilder, more harebrained scheme I have never heard of," said Donovan, confounded. "They simply intended to take over the ship! Without any method to their madness at all, at all. I was not in on it, I would stake my life young Shortland was not, and his eminence William Aston Long would not so demean himself—he is up for a master's ticket when he gets home, besides. Old Bones? He says not, though I do not believe him and nor does Esmeralda. Once the quarterdeck and the scatter cannon were secured, the idea was to batten the marines and the convicts in below deck, take the helm and steer for Africa. Presumably Esmeralda, Long, Shortland, self and the dissenting crew were to be locked up with you lot in the prison. I doubt any murder was planned."

"Do not go away," said Richard, and went back to the prison to beard Willy Dring and Joe Robinson.

"What did you know about it?" he demanded.

They looked as if an enormous weight had been lifted from them.

"We heard about it from Power, who asked us to be in on it," said Dring. "I told him he was mad, and to give it up. After that he made sure he spoke to no one while we were about, though he knew we'd not do the whiddle on him. Then Mr. Bones dismissed us."

Richard returned to the deck. "Dring and Robinson knew, but would not be in on it. Bones I think was. What *happened?*"

"Two convicts informed on him to Esmeralda."

"There are always snitches," said Richard, half to himself. "Meynell and Pane from Nottingham. Bad bastards."

"Well, Dring and Robinson adhered to the code of honor among thieves, whereas this other couple are in the business of earning official commendations and better food. Ye called them bad. Why?"

"Because there have been other snitchings. I have had my suspicions about them for some time. Once the names are known, it all falls into place. Where are they now?"

"Aboard Scarborough, to the best of my knowledge. Esmeralda took a longboat to see His Excellency the moment the pair informed. I went along to heave him up ladders. Sirius sent two dozen marines and the sailors whom the snitches named were arrested. About Mr. Bones and some others—we have no proof. But they will not try it again, no matter how much they hate Esmeralda for watering the rum and then selling it to them."

"What of Power?" Richard asked, throat tight.

"Gone to Sirius, there to stay stapled to the deck. He will not come back to Alexander, that is certain." Donovan stared at Richard curiously. "Ye truly do like the lad, don't ye?"

"Aye, very much, though I could see he'd end in trouble. Some men attract trouble the way a magnet does iron nails. He is one. But I do not believe that he was guilty of the crime he was convicted for." Richard brushed his eyes, shook his head angrily. "He was desperate to get home to his sick dad."

"I know. But if it is any consolation, Richard, I think that once we get beyond Cape Town and there is no chance for Johnny to return home, he will settle to being a model convict."

It was not much consolation, perhaps because Richard felt that he himself had not fulfilled his filial obligations; most of his thoughts lay with Cousin James-the-druggist, not with his father.

There was one thing he could do to help John Power, and he did it without a qualm: he let the names of the snitches be known from one bulkhead to the other. Snitches were snitches, they would snitch again. When Scarborough came into Cape Town the word would travel to her. Pane and Meynell would be known for what they were to every convict at Botany Bay. Life for them would not be easy.

Surgeon Balmain had the answer for the general mood of gloom and depression in the prison; he made them fumigate, scrub and whitewash again.

"I want," said Bill Whiting passionately, "to do two things, Richard. One is to grab fucken Balmain, explode gunpowder in his face, scrub him with oil of tar and a wire brush, and paint him solid white. The other is to change my fucken name. *Whiting!*"

Cape Town was beautiful, yes, but could not hold a candle to Rio de Janeiro in the judgment of the convicts, doomed always to look, never to sample. Not only had Rio been visually stunning, but it had also been filled with happy and natural people, with color and vitality. Cape Town had a more windswept and bleakly dusty kind of appeal, and its harbor lacked those hordes of gay bum boats; what black faces they saw did not smile. This might have been a simple reflection of its sternly Calvinistic, extremely Dutch character. Many buildings were painted white (not the favorite color of Alexander's convicts) and there were few trees inside the town itself. A grand mountain, flat and bushy on top, reared behind the tiny coastal plain, and what the books said about it was quite true: a layer of dense white cloud did come down and spread a cloth over Table Mountain.

They had been 39 days at sea from Rio and arrived at the height of the southern spring on the 14th of October. It was now 154 days—22 weeks—since the fleet left Portsmouth and it had sailed 9,900 land miles, though it still had a long way to go. At no time had the eleven ships become separated; Governor/Commodore Arthur Phillip had kept his tiny flock together.

For the convicts, making port consisted in decks which didn't move and food which didn't move. The day after they arrived fresh meat came aboard, accompanied by fresh, soft, *marvelous* Dutch bread and a few *green* vegetables—cabbage and some sort of strong-tasting, dark green leaf. Appetites revived at once; the convicts settled to the critical business of trying to put on enough condition to survive the next and final leg, said to be 1,000 miles longer than the trip from Portsmouth clear to Rio.

"There have been but two voyages gone where we are going," said Stephen Donovan seriously, wishing Richard would let him donate some butter for their bread. "The Dutchman Abel Tasman left charts of his expedition more than a century ago, and of course we have the charts of Captain Cook and his subordinate Captain Furneaux, who went down to the bottom of the world and a land of ice on Cook's second voyage. But no one really *knows.* Here we are with a great host aboard eleven ships, attempting to reach New South Wales from the Cape of Good Hope. Is New South Wales a part of what the Dutch call New Holland, two thousand miles west of it? Cook was not sure because he never laid eyes on any southern coast joining the two. The best he and Furneaux could do was to prove that Van Diemen's Land was not a part of New Zealand, as Tasman had thought, but rather the southernmost tip of New South Wales, which is a strip of coast going over two thousand miles north from Van Diemen's Land. If the Great South Land exists, it has never been circumnavigated. But if it does exist, then it must contain three million square miles, which are more than in the whole of Europe."

Richard's heart was not behaving placidly. "You are saying, I think, that we have no pilot."

"More or less. Just Tasman and Cook."

"Is that because the explorers all entered the Pacific Ocean by sailing around Cape Horn?"

"Aye. Even Captain Cook chose Cape Horn most of the time. The Cape of Good Hope is regarded as the way to the East Indies, Bengal and Cathay, not to the Pacific. Look at this harbor, filled with outgoing ships." Donovan indicated more than a dozen vessels. "Yes, they will sail east, but also north, taking advantage of an Indian Ocean current to get them as far as Batavia. They will reach those latitudes at the beginning of the summer's monsoon winds and will be blown farther north. The winter trades send them home, laden, with three great currents to help them. One runs south through a strait between Africa and Madagascar. The second sweeps them around the Cape of Good Hope into the south Atlantic. The third carries them north along the west coast of Africa. Winds are important, but currents are sometimes even more important."

Donovan's seriousness had increased, which worried Richard. "Mr. Donovan, what is it ye're not saying?"

"Aye, ye're a clever man. Very well, I will be frank. That second current—the one which flows around the Cape of Good Hope—flows from east to west. Wonderful going home, Hell outbound. There is no avoiding it because it is over a hundred miles wide. Going northeast to the East Indies it can be overcome. But *we* have to seek the great westerly winds well *south* of the Cape, and that for a mariner is a far harder task. The length of our last leg will be much increased because we will not find our eastings in a hurry. I have sailed to Bengal and Cathay, so I know the southern tip of Africa well."

Curiosity suddenly piqued, Richard stared at the fourth mate in some wonder. "Mr. Donovan, why did ye sign on for this vague voyage to somewhere only Captain Cook has been and seen?"

The fine blue eyes burned brightly. "Because, Richard, I want to be a part of history, no matter how insignificant a part. This is an epic adventure we have embarked upon, not a trudge to the same old places, even if those places have alluring names like Cathay. I had not the connections to midshipman into the Royal Navy, nor to get myself on some Royal Society expedition. When Esmeralda Sinclair asked me to come aboard as second mate, I leaped at the chance. And have suffered my demotion without protest. Why? Only because we are doing something no one has ever done before! We are taking over fifteen hundred hapless people to live in a virgin land without having done any sort of preparation. As if we were shipping ye from Hull to Plymouth. It is quite insane, ye know. The height of madness! What if, after we get to Botany Bay, we find it is not possible to scratch a living? 'Tis too far to go on to Cathay with so many people. Mr. Pitt and the Admiralty have thrown us onto the lap of the gods, Richard, with no forethought, no planning, no compunction. An expedition of skilled craftsmen should have gone two years earlier to tame the place a little. But that did not happen because it would have cost too much money and not ridded England of a single convict. What d'ye truly matter? The answer to that is—ye don't matter beyond a parliamentary enquiry or two. Even if we perish, this expedition is great history and I am a part of it. And happy to die for the chance." He drew a breath and smiled brilliantly. "It also offers me an opportunity to join the Royal Navy as something like a skilled man of officer material. Who knows? I may end up commanding a frigate."

"I hope ye do," said Richard sincerely.

"I would give it all up for you," Donovan said mischievously.

Richard took the statement literally. "Mr. Donovan! By now I know ye well enough to understand that your deepest passions are not of the flesh. That is a typical Irish exaggeration."

"Oh, flesh, flesh, flesh!" Donovan snapped, tried beyond calm endurance. "Honestly, Richard, you could give lessons to a papist celibate! What do they do to people in Bristol? I never met a man so riddled with guilt about what are natural functions as you are! Don't be such a dolt! The company, man, the *company!* Women are no company. They are hamstrung into smallness. If poor, they drudge. If well off, they embroider, draw and paint a little, speak Italian and issue orders to the housekeeper. Of good conversation they have none. Nor are most men satisfactory company, for that matter," he said more evenly, putting a rein on his temper. He tried to look carefree. "Besides, I am not a true Irishman. There is much Viking blood in Ulstermen. Probably why I love going to sea to visit new and strange places. The Irish in me dreams. The Viking needs to turn dreams into realities."

But the realities of Cape Town were not the stuff of dreams. The Dutch burghers who ran the town (which had a considerable English population, there to look after the interests of the Honourable East India Company) rubbed their hands in glee at the prospect of fat profits and prolonged the negotiations for victualling the fleet into weeks. There had been a famine—the harvest had failed two years in a row—animals were in short supply—and so on, and so forth. Governor Phillip sat through meeting after meeting with calm unimpaired, perfectly aware that these were tactics aimed at securing higher prices. He had never expected it to be otherwise at Cape Town.

Perhaps too he understood better than some of his subordinates that these long stops in port were all that kept the convicts—and the marines—going. It had been he who had arranged for the oranges, the fresh meat and bread, whatever vegetables were to be had. The maritime world was not organized to carry hundreds of passengers for a year. Therefore let them fuel their bodies on decent food in port for long enough to sustain them on the next leg: a thought the convicts and marines had conceived for themselves.

Captain Duncan Sinclair had a furious quarrel with the agent for the contractor, Mr. Zachariah Clark, and rejected the first shipment of newly baked hard bread as rubbishy sawdust. He was busy loading as many animals as his decks could carry, mostly sheep and pigs, half of which were Publick Sheep and Publick Swine, and had to be preserved for Government use at Botany Bay. Chickens, ducks, geese and turkeys went on as well; the poop looked like a farmyard, as did what was left of the quarterdeck; Sinclair's view forward from his roundhouse now consisted of woolly bottoms. Bales of hay and sacks of fodder were stored under the lower platforms in the prison, leaving scant space for night buckets and the additional belongings many of the convicts had evicted from their cots to make extra room for sleeping. The thieves among them were well known by this time; it was an easy matter for a deputation to visit each of the light-fingered ones until property was retrieved. Most thefts were of food caches and rum illicitly purchased through Sergeant Knight, in great trouble for it thanks to a marine private snitch. Even after so many months at sea, there were those who would almost kill to obtain rum.

None of the Brazilian parrots had survived, but Wallace the Scotch terrier and Lieutenant John Johnstone's bulldog bitch, Sophia, remained. She was pregnant, apparently by Wallace (Shairp thought it exquisitely funny), and everybody on board was dying to see what the progeny would be like. Rodney the cat's family had been reduced by gifts of catlings to other ships, but he and it were waxing fat.

When the at-sea provisions started to arrive at the end of the first week in November, Captain Sinclair had the crew scrub that part of Alexander's hull not sheathed in copper. Inspired by this activity, Surgeon Balmain ordered a fumigation, scrub and whitewash below deck, marines' steerage as well as the prison. His head was full of the delightful excursions he had taken out of the town to the foothills, choked with the glory of exotic bushes and shrubs in profligate spring flower—and what strange blossoms! Many of them looked like pastel-colored astrakhan mounds framed by giant petals.

"I knew there was something I meant to ask Mr. Donovan to do in Cape Town," said Richard, savagely slapping a paint brush. "Tell all the vendors of whitewash that our surgeon was not authorized to buy an ounce of the stuff!"

The fleet left that shippy harbor on the 12th of November as a Yankee merchantman from Boston sailed in; its crew crowded to gape, never having witnessed such a mass exodus from any port. Port had occupied thirty days, and every ship was crammed full. The women convicts had been moved off Friendship to make room for sheep and a few cattle; Lady Penrhyn carried a stallion, two mares and a colt for the use of the Governor; other ships held more horses and cattle; there were sheep, pigs and poultry everywhere, and water was looming as a huge problem. A great deal of attention was paid to the accommodation of the horses, which could not be permitted to lie down or move more than a couple of inches in any direction; a horse with sufficient space to be tipped off balance was a dead one. Cattle too were pampered as much as possible.

That last leg commenced exactly as Stephen Donovan had said it would. Every wind as well as the current ran against the fleet. Nor did they do so modestly; minor gales blew and whipped up heavy seas. The susceptible became seasick all over again. Finally the Commodore ordered the fleet into Sirius's wake, and there the eleven ships remained while Captain John Hunter, master of Sirius, strove fruitlessly to find a favorable wind. The gales died a day later and the agony of standing and tacking began, never with much if any good results.

In thirteen long days they had managed to get a mere 249 miles southeast of the Cape. Water was back to three pints a day, which every soul aboard every ship found intolerable; four pints were not enough. Alexander's lieutenants groaned at this order, to be policed as in earlier periods of rationing, which turned it into a proper *business.* Sergeant Knight had been suspended from duty indefinitely, which meant the lieutenants had to rely upon three very mediocre corporals to do water duty with them while Knight, not at all dismayed by his suspension, lay in his hammock and snoozed on the rum he was buying from Esmeralda against his marine pay. Major Ross had thought that suspension without pay would curb Knight's activities, but he had no idea how much money Knight had made on the voyage selling rum to men like Tommy Crowder.

Whales abounded. The fascinated convicts spent hours on deck during those first two weeks, trying to count them. The ocean looked as if it had been strewn with boulders spouting fountains, for they were mostly spermaceti whales. A new kind of porpoise appeared, very large and blunt-snouted; some sailors called them "grampuses," though there was some debate as to what exactly was a grampus. The sharks were so big that they sometimes attacked a small whale, leaping out of the sea to crash with open jaws on the whale's head, leaving gaping, bleeding craters behind. If they were thresher sharks they also used the long blade uppermost on their tails to cut and slash. On one unforgettable moonlit night, as restless as he was sleepless, Richard saw a titanic battle go on in the midst of the silver sea between a whale and what he swore had to be a giant cuttlefish, its tentacles wrapped around the whale's body. Then the whale sounded and bore its foe down into the depths. Who knew what might lurk in a realm where leviathans were eighty feet long and sharks close to thirty?

Rumors began to fly that Governor Phillip intended to split the fleet, take two or three ships and go on ahead as rapidly as he could, leaving the laggards to come on behind. Charlotte and Lady Penrhyn were hopeless, the storeships tended to be slow, and Sirius was a bit of a slug too. The navigators had tried every way they knew to find a favorable wind, including having all vessels stand facing in different directions, with no success.

Two weeks at sea, and they had a little luck at last, found a good fair breeze and surged southeast in company at eight knots an hour. The seas were so enormous, however, that Lady Penrhyn—carrying Phillip's precious horses—first stood over on her side far enough to dunk the gunwale and the ends of the spars under, then was pooped when a massive wave crashed down on her stern and ran right through the ship. She took on so much water that all hands were put to the pumps and baling buckets. But the horses had not suffered at all, nor had the cattle.

Then the wind swung against once more. Bowing to the inevitable, Governor Phillip decided to separate the fleet. He would remove himself to Supply and take Alexander, Scarborough and Friendship with him, while Captain Hunter on Sirius took command of the seven slower ships. Supply would forge on ahead alone; Lieutenant John Shortland, the naval agent, would board Alexander and command Scarborough and Friendship from her, keeping those three vessels together.

This decision of the Governor's was not without its critics. Many of the naval, marine and medical officers felt that Phillip should have split the fleet after Rio de Janeiro if he intended to split it at all. A course that was not in Phillip's nature, thought Richard, overhearing Johnstone and Shairp grizzling because they would now have to share their quarterdeck heaven. Phillip was a mother hen who hated the idea of abandoning any of his chicks. Oh, how he would worry! His segment carried the bulk of the male convicts, who could be put to work at Botany Bay without the chaos of women and children; he estimated that this first segment would make harbor at least two weeks before Hunter's segment arrived.

Convicts who were known to be gardeners, farmers, carpenters and sawyers (appallingly few) were removed to Scarborough and Supply, though Alexander patently had more room. But no one wanted valuable men put into the Death Ship's prison. Alexander's quarterdeck, however, was now overcrowded. Lieutenant Shortland transferred himself and a mountain of gear from Fishburn; Zachariah Clark, the contractor's agent, was dismissed from Scarborough to Alexander when Major Ross usurped his Scarborough cabin; and Lieutenant James Furzer, the marine quartermaster (an *Irishman,* horrors!), was also shifted to Alexander. William Aston Long naturally refused to give up his bit of the quarterdeck, so—so—!

"I almost died of laughing," said Donovan to Richard on deck as they watched the longboats ply back and forth. "The two Scotch marines detest the new Irish one, Clark is a very odd fish at the best of times, and Shortland is not pleased at being on the ship he was supposed to be on in the first place. Young Shortland has moved in with Papa, and Balmain is furious because he has had to throw out a lot of his collection of specimens, which clutter up every corner of the great cabin. Mr. Bones and I are delighted to be where we have always been—in the forecastle."

"Won't they love it when Wallace decides to yowl at the moon around two on a calm night?"

"That is not the worst. Sophia snores like thunder and has made her nest on Zachariah Clark's cot, from which he is too afraid of her to move her."

The parting happened during the morning of the 25th of November in the midst of a calm sea and little wind. Once everybody else had been transferred, Governor Phillip left Sirius in a longboat to the sound of three lusty cheers from every soul left aboard her. He returned the salute and was rowed swiftly to Supply. From what Donovan had said, a grand sailer in light conditions, a wet and wallowing one in foul weather. A brig-rigged sloop which ought to have been a snow.

By half after noon Supply was gone and the three other Racers (as they had been christened), with Alexander in the lead, had also made way. The oddest aspect of the exercise was that the moment Phillip had transferred to Supply, a fine fair wind sprang up and Hunter decided to chase the Racers. So the seven laggards were visible until the morrow, then went hull down over the horizon until the ocean engulfed the tips of their masts. In this sort of weather Supply had no trouble forging ahead; by nightfall she was gone and Alexander, Scarborough and Friendship cruised along abreast of each other just a cable's length apart—exactly two hundred yards.

Two days later they were back to standing and tacking.

"I do not believe that eastings exist," said Will Connelly to Stephen Donovan, who had come off watch and gone to the rail to see if he could find a fish for his dinner.

Donovan laughed softly. "We are about to find them, Will—and with a vengeance. See yon brown birdies?"

"Aye. They look like swifts."

"Mother Carey's chickens, the prophets of gales—*real* gales. And the day is greasy. Very greasy."

"What is 'greasy'?" asked Taffy Edmunds, delegated to look after the quarterdeck sheep in tandem with Bill Whiting—a choice which had provoked considerable mirth in the prison but did not displease the shepherds, both farm boys far too canny to admit that they were farm boys.

"It is a fine day, not so?" Donovan asked, teasing.

"Aye, very fine. The sun is out, there is no wind."

"Yet the sky is not blue, Taffy. Nor is the sea. We seamen call such days 'greasy' because sky and sea look as if smeared with a thin film of grease—dull, no life in them. By afternoon there will be a few frail white clouds scudding like sheets of paper in a wind because there will be a big wind up there pushing them—a wind too high for us to feel. By early tomorrow we will be in the midst of a mighty gale. Secure your stuff and prepare for hatches to be battened down. In a few hours ye'll know what finding the eastings can be like." Donovan yipped joyfully. "A bite!" He hauled in a fish somewhat like a small cod and danced away.

"You heard him," said Richard. "We'd best get below and warn the rest what is to come."

"Greasy," said Taffy thoughtfully. He went off toward the quarterdeck, where Bill was strewing fodder from a bucket. "Bill! Our sheep! Bill, we are in for the mother of all blows!"

They ate that day at the same hour as those thin high clouds were scudding, but no one came to feed them on the following day. The gale kept getting worse, throwing the ship around like a tiny ball; her sides boomed and reverberated like the inside of a drum, though the hatches had not yet been battened down.

At about the moment when the denizens of the prison realized that they would get nothing to eat until the weather died a little, Richard stood on the table and poked his body out of the after hatch, clinging to it for dear life, to witness the ocean hanging over Alexander from four directions at once. The temptation was too much; he levered himself out onto the deck and found a spot out of harm's way against the mainmast, there to watch the sea come at the ship without rhyme or reason. There were head seas, beam seas and following seas, but this was all of them simultaneously. The rigging creaked and groaned in agony, though he could only hear it above the howling wind and roaring sea by pressing his ear to the timber of the mainmast; water cascaded off the sails while sailors spidered from spar to spar shortening some sail and reefing in others completely. The bows and bowsprit would go right under, then rear up amid flurries and vast washes even as a second wave thundered on larboard, a third wave on starboard, and a fourth on the stern. Prudently Richard had used a piece of rope to tie himself securely; these monstrous waves crashed across the deck with massive force no man lower than a spar could resist without a lifeline.

Impossible to spy Scarborough or Friendship until an immense surge carried Alexander with it up onto its crest, there to dangle for just long enough to see poor Friendship rolled right on her side, the seas breaking clean over her. Down slid Alexander into a trough, decks running a foot deep in water, then up, up, up—oh, it was wonderful! And what a seaworthy old girl Alexander was, poison-soaked timbers and all.

They had battened down the hatches just after he had left the prison, though he never noticed, too entranced with the immensity of what was surely one of the mightiest tempests that ever blew. When night fell he loosed himself and crawled, exhausted and blue with cold, under one of the longboats, where he made himself a warm and fairly dry nest amid the hay. Thus he slept through the very worst of it and woke in the morning, still very cold, to find the sky blue but not greasy and that mammoth sea still running, though less chaotically. The hatches were open; he slid down onto the table and twisted to the deck feeling as if he had just midwifed the birth of the end of the world.

The cries of joy which greeted him astonished him; from Rio onward he had fancied that the rest were growing more independent.

"Richard, Richard!" cried Joey Long, hugging him with tears running down his cheeks. "We thought ye drowned!"

"Not I! I was too busy watching the storm to notice them at the hatches, so I was marooned. Joey, calm yourself. I am well, just wet and cold."

While he rubbed himself vigorously with a dry rag he learned from the others that John Bird, a convict up forward, had broken into the hold and passed out bread.

"We all ate it," said Jimmy Price. "No one fed us."

Which did not stop Zachariah Clark from demanding that John Bird be flogged for stealing the contractor's property.

Lieutenant Furzer, who turned out to be a curious mixture of compassion and confused inertia, calculated the amount of bread missing and announced that it was about the same amount as would have been issued had it been issued. Therefore, he said, no punishment would be administered, and today every convict would receive a double portion of salt meat as well as hard bread.

Despite that quarrel with Zachariah Clark in Cape Town, Captain Sinclair had recognized a soul mate in rapacity; no sooner had Clark moved onto Alexander's quarterdeck than Sinclair started inviting the contractor's agent to share his sumptuous dinners—in return for a blind eye about rum. As Sophia was using Clark's cabin as a childing room, Esmeralda graciously consented to let Clark sleep in his day cabin, not really needed. So when Sinclair heard of Furzer's verdict he sent a message to the marine through Clark to the effect that John Bird be flogged for the unauthorized appropriation of the contractor's property.

"Nothing is missing that ought not to be missing," said Furzer frostily, "so why don't ye go off and toss your tossle, arsehead?"

"I shall report your impudence to the captain!" Clark gasped.

"Ye can report it until ye're blue in the cods, arsehead, but that ain't going to change a thing. *I* decide about the convicts, not fucken fat boy Esmeralda."

* * *

Every sailor aboard Alexander was eager to tell anybody prepared to listen that the blow had been the worst he had ever, ever encountered, chiefly due to those awful seas coming from all points of the compass at once—ominous, very ominous. Word was flagged from Scarborough that all was well; poor Friendship was in worse case, having been pooped as well as right over on her beam—nothing on board her was dry from animals to clothing to bedding.

But the eastings had been found and the three ships, keeping abreast of each other with a cable's length in between, ploughed forward to log up a minimum of 184 land miles a day. They were now down at 40° south latitude and inching steadily farther south than that. Early in December came an even worse gale than the famous one, but at least it blew itself out faster. The weather was freezing cold, despite the summer season; the truly impoverished and less farsighted convicts huddled together for warmth in their thin contractor-issue linen slops, though thanks to the number of deaths there were spare blankets. The hay came in handy.

Dysentery broke out among convicts and marines; men started to die again. Then came news from Scarborough and Friendship that they had dysentery too. Richard insisted that every drop of water his men drank be filtered through the cleaned dripstones. In these tossing seas that meant a few spoonfuls at a time. If all the ships were suffering, whatever water they were on was contaminated. Surgeon Balmain did not order fumigation, scrubbing and a new coat of whitewash, probably because he realized that did he, mutiny would break out.

Though Friendship had set more sail than at any time during the voyage so far, she could not keep up with Alexander and Scarborough, flying along at 207 and more land miles a day. Almost a week into December and the weather warmed a little; Shortland ordered the two big slavers to slow down and let Friendship catch up. Then came a morning of dense, pure white fog that glowed from within like a gigantic pearl, eerie, beautiful, dangerous. The three ships loaded their guns with powder only and fired regularly while a sailor rang Alexander's bell in its belfry on the starboard rail, clang-clang—long pause—clang-clang. Muffled booms and faint clang-clangs drifted back from Scarborough and Friendship, which kept as true to course as Alexander, a cable's length apart. Then at ten o'clock the fog lifted in a twinkle to reveal a fine, fair day and a fine, fair breeze.

Great drifts of seaweed appeared—a sign of land, said the sailors, though no land was sighted, just large numbers of grampuses having terrific fun streaking around, under and between the three ships forging along together. The seaweed became mixed with broad trails of fish sperm in meandering ribbons, of what kind no one knew. Somewhere to the south was the Isle of Desolation* where Captain Cook had once spent a very strange Christmas Day.

Two days later the entire sea turned to blood. At first the awed and fascinated occupants of Alexander thought it must be blood from a slain whale, then realized that no leviathan could exsanguinate enough to dye the water scarlet as far as the eye could see. Yet another mystery of the deep they would never solve.

"I understand at last," Richard said to Donovan, "why ye itch to see foreign places. I was never visited by a wish to go any farther from Bristol than Bath because that was my narrow, familiar world. A man cannot help but grow when he is plucked out of his narrow, familiar world. Either that, or like some in the prison below, he will die of the uncertainty. Place is very strong in people. It was in me, perhaps still is."

"To have a sense of place is common, Richard. That I have none may be thanks to poverty and a burning desire to be free of it, get out of Belfast, out of anywhere tied me down."

"Did ye go to a charity school, then?"

"No. A kind gentleman took me under his wing and taught me to read and write. He said—and rightly so—that literacy would be my ticket to better things, whereas booze is a ticket to nowhere."

Donovan was smiling as at a fond memory; reluctant to probe, Richard changed the subject.

"Why is the sea turned to blood? Have ye seen it before?"

"Nay, but I have heard of it. Sailors are a superstitious lot, so ye'll find most of them describe it as a sign of doom, or the wrath of God, or a portent of evil. For myself—I do not know, except that I believe it is as natural as wanting sex." Donovan wriggled his brows expressively and grinned at Richard's discomfort, knowing full well that Richard hated being called a prude chiefly because he knew that at heart he was a prude. "Perhaps some huge convulsion on the sea floor has thrown up a mass of red earth, or perhaps the blood is composed of tiny red sea creatures."

They ran into more gales, always terrible. In the midst of one memorable squall Alexander sustained her only accident of the voyage by carrying away her fore topsail yard in the slings, which meant that the

* Kerguelen Island.

short chains tethering the wooden yard to the mast snapped and the sail, still attached to its yard, flew free. Scarborough and Friendship backed their main and fore topsails to halt onward progress and waited until the sail was caught—a risky business—and the slings were reconnected.

Then right on the summer solstice it rained—after which it snowed heavily—and followed this up with a bombardment of hailstones the size of hen's eggs. Nothing the sheep felt, but for pigs and men, a bruising nuisance. The joys of summer at 41° south! 41° north was the latitude of American New York and Spanish Salamanca, where it did *not* snow heavily at the time of the summer solstice. Perhaps being on the bottom of the world was more than a metaphorical upside-down? The bottom of the world, thought many of the sailors, marines and convicts, must be a lot heavier than the top could possibly be.

By Christmas Day the three ships were at 42° south and maintaining their 184-land-mile-a-day average through dirty weather. The most enormous whale of the entire voyage followed the trio while the light lasted; he was a bluish-grey in color and well over 100 feet long. As well then that apparently he was just wishing them a merry Christmas, for he would have made shivered timbers out of little Friendship.

Christmas well-being reigned in the prison. Served in the mid afternoon, dinner consisted of pease soup flavored with salt pork, the usual chunk of salt beef and the usual small loaf of hard bread. The treat was in receiving a full half-pint of neat Rio rum each. They also got a chance to win one of Sophia's pups. She had produced five healthy offspring in Zachariah Clark's cot, Surgeon Balmain acting as midwife. They were extraordinary. Two looked like pug dogs, two rather like stiff-haired terriers with overslung lower jaws, and one was the image of Wallace. Lieutenant Shairp, the proud surrogate father, gave Balmain the pick of the litter; he chose a puggy one. So did Lieutenant Johnstone, the proud surrogate mother. That left Lieutenant John Shortland and first mate Long to take the salmon-jawed pair.

Things became complicated when Lieutenant Furzer refused to accept the Wallace look-alike because he looked so Scotch (though he did not say that—it was Christmas, after all).

"What shall we do with him?" asked Shairp.

"Esmeralda and his bum boy Clark?" asked Johnstone.

The entire quarterdeck sneered.

"Then I have a mind to give young MacGregor to the prison for Christmas. No convict has a dog," said Shairp.

The entire quarterdeck thought this an excellent idea, worth toasting in a postprandial amalgam of port and rum.

On Christmas Day the two marine parents appeared in the prison as soon as dinner was finished, Shairp carrying little MacGregor. Both officers were falling-down drunk, though that was not an occurrence peculiar to the festive season. No one ever got any sense out of a marine officer after dinner time on any ship save Friendship, where the lemonade-sipping Ralph Clark used his rum ration to trade to carpenters for writing cases and bureaus, and convicts for tailoring everything from shirts to gloves.

The lots for MacGregor were cast using four decks of cards: those who drew an Ace of Diamonds were in the running. To whoops and cheers, three men showed an Ace of Diamonds. Shairp, sitting on the table, then asked for three straws, though he was so drunk that Johnstone had to wrap his hand around them snugly.

"Long straw wins!" cried Shairp.

Joey Long drew it, weeping in delight.

"The long straw to Long!" Shairp was so amused that he fell off the table and had to be helped tenderly to his feet by Richard and Will, while Joey took the wriggling scrap and covered it in kisses.

"We will keep him with his mama until we get to Botany Bay," caroled Johnstone. "Once ashore, MacGregor is yours."

God could not have been kinder, thought Richard as he drifted into a rummy sleep, for once not consumed with a desire to get up on deck. Since Ike died, poor simple Joey has had no purpose. Now he has a dog to love. God has emancipated one of my dependents. I pray the others are as fortunate. Once we leave these confines it will be much harder to keep together.

The pace increased to over 207 land miles a day until the end of December; the weather was as foul as it could be—heavy seas, squalls, howling gales. At south of 43° the winds really roared.

1788 arrived in filthy weather with the wind against; the New Year storms blew on the bow as the latitude crept up to 44°. Then along came a breeze so fair that it shoved the three ships along at 219 miles a day. As the southern capes of Van Diemen's Land were expected at any time, Lieutenant Shortland signaled that cables were to be put to anchors just in case.

The gale increased and Friendship lost her fore topmast studding sail boom and rent the canvas to pieces, but still no land.

Afraid of reefs and uncharted rocks, at seven in the evening of the 4th of January, Shortland ordered the ships to stand to. Next morning came the long awaited cry: "Land ahoy!" There it was! The southernmost tip of New South Wales! A massive cliff.

Once around the southeast cape their course altered radically from east to north by northeast; the last 1,000 miles to Botany Bay were the most frustrating of the whole voyage, so near and yet so far. The winds were against, the currents were against, everything was against. On some days the three ships ended miles south of yesterday's position, on other days they stood and tacked, stood and tacked what seemed eternally. Then there were days when the winds were, as the sailors put it, "horrible hard-hearted." One night Friendship split her fore top main stay sail, followed by her peak halyard in the morning. They would inch up to 39°, fall back to 42°. Friendship's main stay sail split to shreds—her fifth sail disaster since Cape Town. They battled to make any kind of headway.

Though this lack of progress did not dampen the spirits of the convicts the way it did those of the ships' navigators, lack of palatable food had much the same effect. There were brief glimpses of New South Wales, too far away to gauge what sort of land it was. Luckily a new delight arrived; countless seals frisked and frolicked around the ships, absolute clowns as they floated with their flippers on their chests, dived, twisted, huffed and snuffled. Gorgeous, jolly creatures. And where they were, so too were hordes of fish. Chowder appeared on the menu again.

By the 15th of January they had struggled north to 36° and at noon saw Cape Dromedary, which Captain Cook had named for its resemblance to the Ship of the Desert.

"Only a hundred and fifty miles to go," said Donovan, off his watch and ready to fish.

Will Connelly sighed; the weather was so hot, albeit cloudy, that he could not settle to read, had elected to fish instead. "I am beginning to believe, Mr. Donovan," he said, "that we will never get to Botany Bay. Four more men have died since Christmas Eve and all of us below know why. Not fever or dysentery. Just despair, homesickness, hopelessness. Most of us have been in this terrible ship for over a year now—we boarded her on the sixth of January last year. *Last year!* What an odd thing to say. So they died, I believe, because they had passed the point where they could credit that a day would dawn when they were not in this terrible ship. A hundred and fifty miles, ye say. They may as well be ten thousand. If this year has taught us nothing else, it has shown us how far it is to the end of the world. And how far away is home."

Donovan's mouth tightened; he blinked rapidly. "The miles will pass," he said eventually, eyes riveted on his line, floating from a small piece of cork. "Captain Cook warned of this counter current, but we are making headway. What we need is a fair breeze out of the southeast, and we will get it. A sea change is coming. First a storm, then a wind out of the southeast. I am right."

They tacked and stood, tacked and stood. The seals were gone, replaced by thousands of porpoises. Then, after a suffocatingly hot and humid day, the heavens erupted. Red lightning of a ferocity and brilliance beyond English imagination empurpled clouds blacker than Bristol smoke, cracked with deafening thunder; and it began to rain a wall of solid water, so hard that it fell straight down despite a wildly blowing northwest wind. At an hour before midnight, with dramatic suddenness, the show was over. Along came a beautiful fair breeze out of the southeast which lasted long enough to see white cliffs, trees, yellow cliffs, trees, curving golden beaches, and the low, nuggety jaws of Botany Bay.

At nine in the morning of the 19th of January, 1788, Alexander led her two companions between Point Solander and Cape Banks into the reaches of a wide, poorly sheltered bay. Perhaps fifty or sixty naked black men stood gesticulating on either headland, and there at rest on the bosom of choppy steely water was Supply. She had beaten them by a single day.

Alexander had sailed 17,300 land miles* in 251 days, which amounted to 36 weeks. She had spent 68 of those days in port and 183 of them at sea. All told, 225 convicts had sampled her, some for a single day; 177 arrived.

The anchors down and Lieutenant Shortland gone in the jollyboat to Supply to see Governor Phillip, Richard stood alone at the rail and gazed for a long time at the place to which, by an Imperial Order-in-Council, he had been transported until the 23rd of March, 1792. Four years into the fu-

* 15,034 nautical miles. The nautical mile contained 2,025 yards; the land mile 1,760 yards.

ture. He had turned nine-and-thirty in the south Atlantic between Rio de Janeiro and Cape Town.

The land he surveyed was flat along the foreshores, slightly hilly farther away to north and south, and it was a drab, sad vista of blue, brown, fawn, grey and olive. Blighted, juiceless.

"What d'ye see, Richard?" asked Stephen Donovan.

Richard stared at him through eyes misted with tears. "I see neither paradise nor Hell. This is limbo. This is where all the lost souls go," he said.

PART FIVE

From
January
until
October of 1788

Nothing very much happened over the next few days ex-cept that the seven slow ships turned up surprisingly soon after the Racers; they had been blown by the same winds and kept close enough behind to experience the same weather. Heaving in the restless water, all the ships remained at anchor unloaded, people crowding their rails, anyone with a spyglass peering at shoregoing parties of marines, naval officers and a few convicts, and at many Indians. None of this shore activity appeared significant. Rumor now said that the Governor did not consider Botany Bay an adequate site for this all-important experiment and had gone in a longboat to look at nearby Port Jackson, which Captain Cook had noted on his charts, but had not entered.

Richard's feelings about Botany Bay were very much like those in every other breast, free or felon: a shocking place, was the universal verdict. It reminded no one of anywhere, even sailors as traveled as Donovan. Flat, bleak, sandy, swampy, inclement and dreary beyond all imagination. To the inhabitants of Alexander's prison, Botany Bay loomed as a gigantic graveyard.

Orders came that the site of the first settlement was to be Port Jackson, not Botany Bay; they made ready to sail, but the winds were so against and the swell coming across the narrow bar so huge that all thought of leaving had to be abandoned. Then—*a miracle!* Two very big ships were sighted beating in for harbor.

" 'Tis as strange a coincidence as two Irish peasants meeting at the court of the Empress of all the Russias," said Donovan, who had shared a spyglass with Captain Sinclair and Mr. Long.

"They are English, of course," said Jimmy Price.

"No, they are French. We think the expedition of the Comte de la Pérouse. Third-raters, which is why they are such big ships. One therefore must be La Boussole and the other L'Astrolabe. Though I imagine that we are a greater surprise to them than they to us—la Pérouse left France in 1785, long before our voyage was being talked about. Unless they have learned of us somewhere along their way. La Pérouse was given up as lost a year ago. Now—here he is."

Another attempt to get out of Botany Bay was made on the morrow, with equal lack of success. The two French ships were not in sight at all, blown away southward and seaward. Toward sunset Supply managed to wriggle through the swell and headed north the ten or eleven miles to Port Jackson, while Governor Phillip's chicks stayed another night in limbo.

A southeaster in the morning made things better, for the French ships too; La Boussole and L'Astrolabe passed inside Botany Bay as the ten ships of the English fleet hauled anchor and made for that dangerous entrance. Sirius, Alexander, Scarborough, Borrowdale, Fishburn, Golden Grove and Lady Penrhyn all departed gracefully. Then unlucky Friendship could not keep in her stays, drifted perilously close to the rocks, and collided with Prince of Wales. She lost her jib boom and compounded her woes by running into Charlotte's stern. A considerable part of her decorative galleries destroyed, Charlotte almost went aground.

All this havoc caused much mirth on Alexander, shaking her own sails free to take advantage of the southeaster. The day was hot and fine, the view off the larboard side fascinating. Crescent-shaped yellow beaches foaming with surf alternated with reddish-yellow cliffs which grew ever taller as the miles passed by. A wealth of trees, somewhat greener than those in the distance at Botany Bay, spread inland beyond the beaches, and the smoke of many fires smudged the western sky. Then came two awesome 400-foot bastions, between them an opening about a mile wide. Alexander heeled and sailed into a wonderland.

"This is more like!" said Neddy Perrott.

"If Bristol had such a harbor, it would be the greatest port in Europe," said Aaron Davis. "It could take a thousand ships of the line in perfect safety from every wind that blows."

Richard said nothing, albeit his heart felt a little lighter. These trees at least were a kind of green, very tall and numerous, shimmering with a faint blue haze. But very strange trees! They had height and girth of wood, yet were leafed in sparse and ungainly fashion, like shredded flags. Little sandy bays free of surf scalloped the harbor to north and south, though the headlands inside were lower save for one immense bluff exactly opposite the entrance. They sailed to the south of it into what seemed a very long, wide

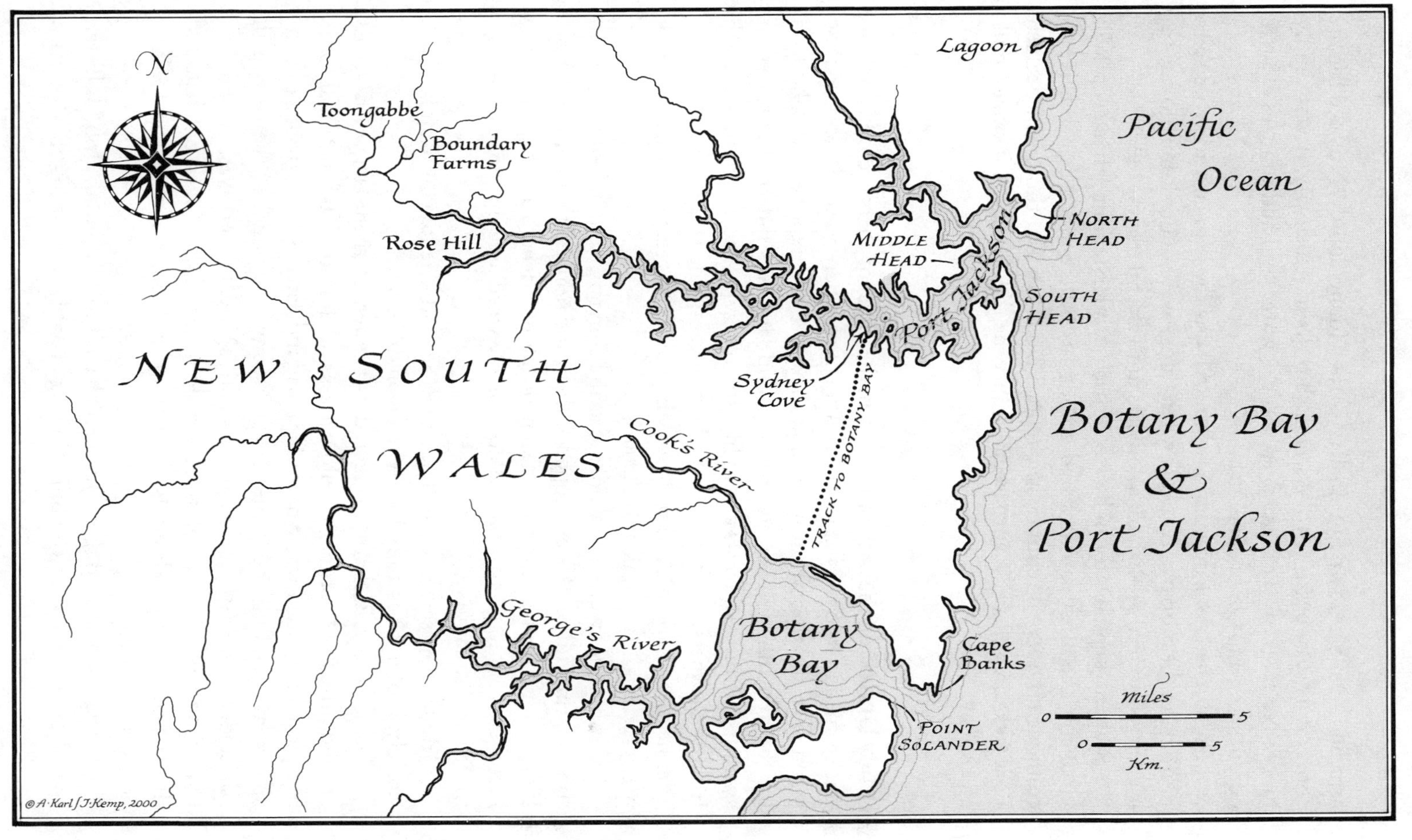

Botany Bay & Port Jackson
Pacific Ocean
N
Lagoon
Toongabbe
Boundary Farms
Rose Hill
NEW SOUTH WALES
MIDDLE HEAD
NORTH HEAD
SOUTH HEAD
Port Jackson
Sydney Cove
TRACK TO BOTANY BAY
Cook's River
George's River
Botany Bay
Cape Banks
POINT SOLANDER
Miles
0
5
0
5
Km.
© A·Karl / J·Kemp, 2000

arm, and six miles down in a small cove they found Supply. No need for anchors, at least to begin with. As each ship floated in slowly, it was simply moored to trees on shore, so deep was the water. Still and calm, as clear as ocean water, and full of small fish.

The sun had gone down in a welter of flame the seamen said promised a fine day on the morrow. As usual when things were out of kilter, no one remembered to feed Alexander's convicts until after darkness fell.

Richard kept his thoughts to himself, understanding that even Will Connelly, the most sophisticated among his little band, was too naive to confide in the way he could with Stephen Donovan. For though he deemed Port Jackson a place of surpassing beauty, he did not think it oozed milk and honey.

They landed on the 28th of January in the midst of chaotic confusion. No one seemed to know what to do with them or where to send them, so they stood with their possessions around their feet and experienced solid land for the first time in over a year. Oh, solid land was hideous! It tossed, it swooped, it refused to stay still; like the rest who had not suffered much from seasickness, Richard was to be constantly nauseated for six weeks after he disembarked. And realized why sailors on terra firma walked with big, wide, slightly drunken footsteps.

The marines were as bewildered as the convicts, who milled about until some marine junior officer yapped at them and pointed them in a direction. Finally, amid the last hundred or so male felons, Richard and his nine satellites were told to go to a fairly flat, sparsely treed area on the eastern side, there to make camp.

"Build yourselves a shelter," said Second Lieutenant Ralph Clark vaguely, looking blissfully happy to be on dry land.

Using what? Richard wondered as the ten of them staggered across ground tufted with crunchy yellow grass and dotted with occasional rocks to a place he decided was where Clark had indicated. Other groups of convicts were standing about the area in a confusion equal to their own; all Alexander men. How can we make shelters? We have no axes, no saws, no knives, no nails. Then a marine came along carrying a dozen hatchets and thrust one at Taffy Edmunds, who stood holding it limply and looking helplessly at Richard.

I have not divorced them yet. I still have Taffy Edmunds, Job Hollister, Joey Long, Jimmy Price, Bill Whiting, Neddy Perrott, Will Connelly,

Johnny Cross and Billy Earl. Most of them rustics, many of them illiterate. Thank God that Tommy Crowder and Aaron Davis have found Bob Jones and Tom Kidner from Bristol—that means they have enough in their circle to fill a hut. If filling a hut is the official intention. Does no one have *any* idea what we are supposed to do? This is the worst planned expedition in the history of the world. The higher-ups have sat on Sirius for the best part of nine months, but all they have done, I suspect, is drink too much. There is no method, no trace of a system. We should have been kept on board until the clearing was done and shelters erected, even if our tables and benches have been dismantled to expose the big hold hatches. At least at night. The marines do not like being shepherds, they clearly want to be nothing but guards in the narrowest sense. Build ourselves a shelter. . . . Well, we have one hatchet.

"Who can use a hatchet?" he asked.

All of them—for chopping up kindling.

"Who can build a shelter?"

No one, save for watching houses being built of brick, stone, plaster and beams. No hedgerow denizens among his flock.

"Perhaps we should start with a ridge pole and a support for either end," said Will Connelly after a long silence; he had read *Robinson Crusoe* on the voyage. "We can make the roof and walls out of palm fronds."

"We need a ridge pole, but also two other poles for the eaves," said Richard. "Then we need six forked young trees, two taller than the other four. That will give us a frame. Will and I can begin on those with the hatchet. Taffy and Jimmy, see if ye can find a marine who can donate us a second hatchet, or an axe, or one of the huge knives we saw in Rio. The rest of you, find some palms and see if the fronds come off by pulling on them."

"We could escape," said Johnny Cross thoughtfully.

Richard stared at him as if he had grown another head. "Escape to where, Johnny?"

"To Botany Bay and the French ships."

"They would not offer us asylum any more than the Dutch did Johnny Power in Teneriffe. And how are we to get to Botany Bay? You saw the Indians on shore there. This is a little kinder, so it must have Indians too. We have no idea what they are like—they might be cannibals like those in New Zealand. Certainly they will not welcome the advent of hundreds of alien people."

"Why?" asked Joey Long, whose mind could not get beyond the fact that Lieutenant Shairp had not yet given him MacGregor.

"Put yourselves in the place of the Indians," said Richard patiently. "What must they think? This is an excellent cove with a stream of good water—it must surely be popular among them. But we have usurped it. We are, besides, under strict orders not to harm any of them. Therefore, why court them by escaping into places where we will have none of our own English kind? We will stay here and mind our own business. Now do what I asked, please."

He and Will found plenty of suitable young trees, none more than four or five inches in diameter. Ugly they might be when compared to an elm or chestnut, but they did have the virtue of growing up without low branches. Richard bent and swung the hatchet, made a nick.

"Christ! The wood is like iron and full of sap," he said. "I need a saw, Will."

But, lacking a saw, all he could do was chip away. The hatchet was neither sharp nor of good quality, would be useless by the time the three poles and six supports were cut. Tonight he would get out his files and sharpen it. The contractor, he thought, has supplied us with the rubbish the foundries in England could not sell. And he was light-headed and panting after cutting and trimming the ridge pole; all those months of poor food and lack of work were no preparation for this. Will Connelly took the hatchet to attack a second young tree and proved even slower. But in the end they had their ridge pole and their two main forked supports for the roof ridge, and chose four smaller ones for the side supports. By then Taffy and Jimmy had returned with a second hatchet, a mattock and a spade. While Richard and Will went in search of trees to connect their side support poles and complete the framework, Jimmy and Taffy were set to digging holes to plant the six supports in. Having no kind of measuring device, they paced it out as accurately as they could. Digging revealed that six inches down was bedrock.

The others had found plenty of palms, but the fronds were too high off the ground to reach. Then Neddy had a bright idea, climbed a neighboring tree, leaned out dangerously, grabbed the end of a frond, and dropped off his perch to pull the frond away by sheer weight. It worked with the older, browner appendages, but not with anything looking lush.

"Find Jimmy," said Neddy to Job Hollister, "and change places with him. You dig. I have a better use for nimble Jimmy."

Jimmy arrived trembling from the unaccustomed effort of digging.

"Have ye a head for heights?" Neddy asked him.

"Aye."

"Then rest a moment before ye climb yon palm. Ye're the most agile and smallest of us. Richard sent us the second hatchet, so tuck it in your waistband. Once ye get up the palm, chop down the fronds one at a time."

The sun was westering, which gave them some means of orienting themselves—south and west of the area where the Governor was going to erect his portable house, a couple of storehouses, and the big round marquee in which Lieutenant Furzer had established himself and the commissariat. They had had the presence of mind to bring their wooden bowls, dippers and spoons, also their blankets, mats and buckets; Richard found the stream and put Bill Whiting to setting up the dripstones, then fetching water. It looked clean and healthy, but he trusted nothing here.

Of all of them, Bill Whiting looked the worst. His face had long since lost its roundness, of course, but now there were black crescents beneath his eyes. The poor fellow trembled as if he had a fever. He had not; his brow was cool. Simple exhaustion.

"It is time to stop," said Richard, collecting his brood. "Lie down on your mats and rest. Bill, ye need a walk—yes, I know ye do not feel like walking, but come with me to find the commissariat. I have an idea."

Lieutenant James Furzer was nothing like organized; that was too much to hope for. Richard and Bill entered chaos.

"Ye need more men, sir," said Richard.

"Volunteering?" asked Furzer, recognizing their faces.

"One of us is," said Richard, putting an arm around Whiting. "Here is a good man ye can trust, never been in any trouble since I met him in Gloucester Gaol in eighty-five."

"That's right, ye were the larboard head man on Alexander, and none of your men gave trouble. Morgan."

"Aye, Lieutenant Furzer, Morgan. Can ye use Whiting here?"

"I can if he has brain enough to read and write."

"He does both."

They walked back to their camp bearing some loaves of hard bread, all the commissariat was able to issue. It had been baked in Cape Town and was very weevily, but it was food.

"We now have a man in the commissariat," Richard announced, doling out the bread. "Furzer is going to use Bill to help deal with the salt meat. Which we cannot have until the kettles and pots are unloaded because from now on we cook for ourselves."

Bill Whiting was looking a little better already; he would be working inside a shaded place, no matter how stifling, and doing something easier than clearing, sawing or gardening, which seemed to be what everybody was going to do eventually. "Once Lieutenant Furzer gets himself settled, we are to be issued with a week's rations at a time," Bill contributed, grateful for Richard's perceptiveness. "There is supposed to be a storeship coming on from Cape Town soon, so we have enough provisions to last."

At nightfall they put bags of clothing down as pillows and used their Alexander mats and blankets as ground cover, their old and tattered greatcoats over them. Though it had been such a hot day, the moment the sun went down it grew cold. Their weariness was so great that they slept despite the unmentionable things which crawled everywhere.

Morning brought a sultry, steamy end to darkness's chill. They went back to building their hut, hampered because they had nothing whatsoever to keep the palm fronds in place except long, strappy palm leaves they tried to turn into twine. The shelter itself seemed strong enough, though it worried Richard and Will, the best engineers, that they had no better foundation than six inches of sandy soil. They piled that soil up around their support posts and began to cut more saplings to lie flat on the ground as anchors, notching their supports and sliding the new poles into the notches.

Others were building around them with varying degrees of success. No one had any real enthusiasm for the task, but it was easy to see by the middle of that second day ashore which groups were either well led or had a mind for construction, and those owning neither. Tommy Crowder's lot had started to wall their hut with a palisade of very thin saplings, an idea Richard resolved to imitate. Education and broader experience definitely showed; the Londoner Crowder had had a very checkered career and was besides a clever man.

There were a few marines around and about now, checking progress and counting heads; some convicts had absconded into the forest, including a woman named Ann Smith. Probably headed for Botany Bay and the French ships, which gossip said were staying a few days.

"Christ, what a place for ants and spiders!" said Jimmy Price, sucking at the edge of his hand. "That bugger of an ant bit me, and it hurts. Look at the size of the things! They are half an inch long and ye can *see* their nippers." He cast a splendid, white-skinned tree a glance of loathing. "And what is it that deafens us with its—its croaking? My ears are ringing."

His complaints about the croaking were as justified as about the ants; it was a good year for cicadas.

Billy Earl came through the trees white-faced and shaking. "I just saw a snake!" he gasped. "Christ, the thing was taller than Ike Rogers in his boots! Thick around as my arm! And there are huge fierce alligators on the other side of the cove, so Tommy Crowder told me. Oh, I *hate* this place!"

"We will get used to the creatures," Richard soothed. "I've not heard that anybody has been bitten or eaten by anything bigger than an ant, even if the ant is the size of a beetle. The alligators are giant lizards, I saw one run up a tree."

The house was finished by mid afternoon of that humid, torrid day full of surprises and terrors. The sun went in and the clouds began to pile up in the skies to the south of them. Black and dark blue, with faint flickers of lightning. They had built the hut in the lee of a large sandstone rock that had a little pocket in its under side, as if scooped out by a spoon.

"I think," said Richard, looking at the approaching storm, "that we ought to put our belongings under our rock just in case. These palm fronds will not keep rain out."

The tempest arrived an hour later with greater ferocity than that one at sea off Cape Dromedary, and more terrifying by far; every one of its colossal, brilliant bolts came straight to earth amid the trees. No wonder so many of them were split and blackened! Lightning. Not thirty feet in front of where they huddled, a huge tree with a satiny vermilion skin exploded in a cataclysm of blinding blue fire, sparks and thunder; it literally disintegrated, then burned fiercely. But not for long. The rain came in a cold, howling wind to put it out and wreck their palm-frond thatching within a single minute. The ground turned to a sea and the thick, hurtful rods pelted down, soaked them to the point of drowning. That night they slept amid the frame of their hut with chattering teeth, their only consolation the fact that their belongings were safe and dry under the rock ledge.

"We have to have better tools and something to hold our house together," said Will Connelly in the morning, close to tears.

Time, thought Richard, to seek a higher authority than Furzer, who could not organize himself to save himself. I do not care if convicts are forbidden to approach those in authority—I am going to do just that.

He walked off in the cool air, pleased to see that the ground was so sandy it was incapable of turning to mud. When he reached the stream at the place where the marines had put three stones across it as a ford, he caught a glimpse of naked black bodies farther up the brook, smelled a strong odor of rotting fish. Not his imagination, then; he had been told that the Indians stank of a fish oil quite the equal of Bristol mud. When they came no closer he skipped across the stepping stones and turned to walk into the bigger settlement on the western side of the cove, where most of the male convicts were already encamped and all the female convicts would be located (the women were still being landed, a few at a time). There also stood the hospital tent, the marines' tents, the marquees of the marine officers, and Major Ross's marquee. On this side of the cove, he noted, the convicts lived in tents. Which simply meant that not enough tents had been put on the ships. Thus he and the rest of the last 100 male convicts had been relegated to the eastern side under whatever kind of shelter they could manufacture, out of sight and out of mind.

"May I see Major Ross?" he asked the marine sentry on duty outside the big round marquee.

The marine, a stranger to Richard, looked him up and down in contempt. "No," he said.

"It is a matter of some urgency," Richard persisted.

"The Lieutenant-Governor is too busy to see the likes of you."

"Then may I wait until he has a free moment?"

"No. Now piss off—what's your name?"

"Richard Morgan, number two-ought-three, Alexander."

"Send him in," said a voice from inside.

Richard entered a space fairly well lighted by open flaps on all sides, and having a wooden plank floor. An interior curtain divided it into an office and what were probably the Major's living quarters. He was there at a folding table which served him as a desk and, typically, alone. Ross despised his subordinate officers quite as much as he did his enlisted men, yet defended the rights, entitlements and dignity of the Marine Corps against all Royal Navy comers. He considered Governor Arthur Phillip an impractical fool and deplored lenience.

"What is it, Morgan?"

"I am on the east side, sir, and would discuss that with ye."

"A complaint, is it?"

"Nay, sir, merely a few requests," said Richard, looking him straight in the eye and conscious that he must be one of the very few persons at Port Jackson who rather liked the picturesque Major.

"What requests?"

"We have nothing to build our shelters with, sir, apart from a few hatchets. Most of us have managed to get up some sort of frame, but we cannot thatch with palm fronds unless we have twine to tie them down. We would happily dispense with nails, but we have no instruments to bore holes, or saw, or hammer. The work would go faster if we had at least some tools."

The Major rose to his feet. "I need a walk. Come with me," he said curtly. "Ye have," he went on as he preceded Richard out of the marquee, "a level head, I noted it in the matter of Alexander's pumps and bilges. Ye're a no-nonsense man and ye don't pity yourself one wee bit. If we had more like ye and less like the scum of every Newgate in England, this settlement might have worked."

From which Richard gathered, walking at the Major's rapid pace, that the Lieutenant-Governor had no faith in this experiment. They passed the bachelor marine encampment and approached the four round marquees in which the marine officers dwelled. Lieutenant Shairp was sitting in the shade of an awning outside Captain James Meredith's dwelling in the company of the Captain, drinking tea out of a fine china cup. On sight of the Major they rose to their feet, but in a manner which suggested that they actively disliked their outspoken, salty commandant. Well, everybody knew that, including the felons; fueled by rum and port, the divisions in the ranks of the officers led to quarrels, courts martial and, always, opposition to Ross. Who had his supporters in some circumstances, however.

"Are the sawpits under construction?" asked the Major frostily.

Meredith waved in a direction behind him. "Yes, sir."

"When did ye last inspect, Captain-Lieutenant?"

"I am about to. *After* I have finished my breakfast."

"Of rum rather than tea, I note. Ye drink too much, Captain-Lieutenant, and ye're quarrelsome. Do not quarrel with me."

Shairp had saluted and disappeared, returning a moment later with MacGregor in one hand. "Here, Morgan, take him. 'Twas one of your men won him, so I am told." He giggled. "Cannot quite seem to remember, myself."

Wanting to sink into the ground, Richard took the joyous scrap from Shairp and followed Major Ross down to the ford.

"D'ye mean to carry that thing to the commissary?"

"Not if I can find one of my men, sir. Our camp is on the way," said Richard with a tranquillity he did not feel; he always seemed to be there when the Major had hard words to say to people.

"Well, 'tis time I visited the surplus. Lead the way, Morgan."

Richard led the way, hanging on to the struggling MacGregor.

"He will survive by ratting," said Major Ross as they arrived at the dozen or so shelters dispersed among the trees. "The place has as many rats as London."

"Give this to Joey Long," said Richard, thrusting MacGregor at a startled Johnny Cross. "As ye see, sir, we managed to get up a fair sort of frame, but I think convict Crowder has the best idea for walls. The trouble is that without tools and materials the work proceeds at a snail's pace."

"I did not know that there was so much ingeniousness among the English" was Ross's comment, touring thoroughly. "Once ye're done here, ye can start building another camp between where ye are and the Governor's farm, which is being cleared and laid out already. If we get no fresh vegetables the scurvy will kill us all. There are too many women all together over on the western side. I will divide them, send some over here. Which does not mean congress, Morgan, understand?"

"I understand, sir."

They proceeded to the commissariat, where confusion still reigned. The horses, cattle and other livestock had come off and were confined inside hastily erected barricades of piled branches, looking as miserable as everybody else.

"Furzer," said the Lieutenant-Governor, erupting into the big marquee, "ye're a typical fucken Irishman. Have ye *never* heard of method? What d'ye think ye're going to do with those animals unless ye get them into grazing? Eat them? There is no corn left and very little hay. Ye're not a quartermaster's arsehole! Since there is nothing for the carpenters to do until they have some timber, get them onto building pens for the animals *right now!* Find someone who knows good grazing when he sees it and build the pens there. The cattle will have to be shepherded and the horses hobbled—and God help ye if they get away! Now where are your lists of what was on what ship, if it has come off, and where it is now?"

Lieutenant Furzer could produce no lists worth mentioning, had little idea of whereabouts anything landed had been stored; the only storehouses up were temporary canvas ones.

"I had thought to list things when they went into permanent storage, sir," he faltered.

"Jesus, Jesus, Jesus, Furzer, ye're a cretin!"

The quartermaster swallowed and stuck his chin out. "I cannot do it all with the men I have, Major Ross, and that is honest!"

"Then I suggest ye conscript more convicts. Morgan, have ye any ideas as to suitable men? Ye're a convict, ye must know some."

"I do, sir. Any amount. Commencing with Thomas Crowder and Aaron Davis. Bristol men and fond of clerking. Villains, but too clever to bite the hand gives them clerical work, so they'll not steal. Threaten to put them to chopping down trees at the rate of a dozen a day and they will behave perfectly."

"What about yourself?"

"I can be of more benefit elsewhere, sir," Richard said.

"Doing what?"

"Sharpening saws, axes, hatchets and anything else in need of a keen edge. I can also set a saw's teeth, which is a craft. I have some tools with me now and if my tool box was put on a ship, I will have everything I need." He cleared his throat. "I do not mean to cast aspersions on those who are in command, sir, but the axes and hatchets are sadly inferior. So too the spades, shovels and mattocks."

"I have noticed that for myself," said Major Ross grimly. "We have been diddled by experts, Morgan, from the penny-pinching Admiralty officials to the contractor and the transport captains, some of whom are busy selling slops and better clothing already—including, I have reason to believe, personal possessions of the convicts." He prepared to leave. "But I will make it my business to see if there is a tool box for one Richard Morgan. In the meantime, get what ye need from Furzer here, be it awls, nails, hammers or wire." He nodded and marched out, clapping his cocked hat on his head. Always neat as a bandbox, Major Ross, no matter what the weather.

"Get me Crowder and Davis and ye can have whatever ye want," said Lieutenant Furzer, beyond mortification.

Richard got him Crowder and Davis, and collected sufficient tools and materials to finish their own shelters and start on more for the women convicts.

Women convicts had suddenly become the focus of all attention as male convicts and single marines attempted to rid themselves of passions and urges largely unfulfilled for a year and more. The comings and goings after dark were so many that not ten times the number of marines on duty could have prevented them, even if the marines on duty had not been equally determined upon sexual relief. Complicated by the fact that there were not nearly enough women to go around, and further complicated by the fact that not all the women were interested in providing sexual relief for starved men. Luckily some women accepted their lot and cheerfully obliged all comers, while others would do so for a mug of rum or a man's shirt. The rarity of rape lay somewhere between some women's willingness to serve multiples of men and most men's scruples about forcing themselves on unwilling women.

From the Governor to the Reverend Richard Johnson, however, those in command were horrified at the comings and goings in the women's camp, viewing them as depraved, licentious, utterly immoral. Naturally this stemmed from their own access to women, be she Mrs. Deborah Brooks or Mrs. Mary Johnson. Something *had* to be done!

Richard's group sneaked off after dark, of course. Except for himself, Taffy Edmunds and Joey Long. For Joey, having MacGregor was apparently enough. Taffy was a different breed, a loner with misogynistic tendencies that the sudden proximity of women actually reinforced. He was odd, that was all. Singing did it for Taffy. Of his own reasons for eschewing the women's camp Richard was not sure, except that there was some Taffy in him, it seemed; the prospect of succeeding in having a woman after two years away from their company and more than three years since Annemarie Latour was not one he could face. Since Annemarie Latour his penis had not stirred, and why that was he did not know. Not extinction of the life force. More perhaps a terrible shame and guilt, coming as it had in the midst of William Henry and on the heels of so many other losses. But he did not know and did not want to know. Only that a part of him had died and another part of him had passed into a dreamless sleep. Whatever had happened inside his mind had banished sex. Whether that was confinement or liberation he did not know. He did not know. More importantly, it was not a grief to him.

On the 7th of February there was to be a big ceremony, the first the convicts were commanded to attend. At eleven in the morning they were marshaled, male separated from female, on the southeastern point of the cove amid ground cleared for the vegetable garden; carrying muskets and properly dressed for parade, every marine marched in to the music of fifes and drums, colors and pendants flying. His Excellency Governor Phillip arrived shortly thereafter, accompanied by the blond giant Captain David Collins, his Judge Advocate; Lieutenant-Governor Major Robert Ross; the Surveyor-General, Augustus Alt; the Surgeon-General, John White; and the chaplain, the Reverend Richard Johnson.

The marines dipped their colors, the Governor doffed his hat and complimented them, and the marines marched past with their band. After which the convicts were bidden sit upon the ground. A camp table was set in front of the Governor and two red leather cases were solemnly laid upon it. They were unsealed and opened in sight of all, after which the Judge Advocate read Phillip's commission aloud, then followed it with the commission for the Court of Judicature.

Richard and his men heard mere snatches: His Excellency the Governor was authorized in the name of His Britannic Majesty George the Third, King of Great Britain, France and Ireland, to have full power and authority in New South Wales, to build castles, fortresses, and towns, erect batteries, as seemed to him necessary. . . . The sun was hot and the Governor's duties apparently endless. By the time the legal commission was read out, some of the listeners were half-asleep and the ship's captains, who had all come ashore to listen, were straggling off because no one had provided them with nice shady seats. Captain Duncan Sinclair was the first to go.

Thankful for his straw sailor's hat, Richard strove to pay attention. Especially when Governor Phillip mounted a little dais and directed an address to the convicts. He had tried! he shouted—yes he had tried! But after these ten days ashore he was rapidly coming to the conclusion that few among them were worthwhile, that most were incorrigible, lazy and not worth feeding, that out of the 600 at work no more than 200 labored at all, and that those who would not work would not be fed.

Most of what he said was audible; out of that spare small frame there issued quite a voice. In future they would be treated with the utmost severity because evidently nothing else was going to have any effect. Theft of a chicken was not punishable by death in England, but here, where every chicken was more precious than a chest of rubies, theft of a chicken would be punishable by death. *Every* animal was reserved for breeding. The most trifling attempt to pilfer any item belonging to the Government would be a hanging matter—and he meant what he said, every word of it! Any man who tried to get into the women's tents at night would be fired upon because they had not been brought all this way to fornicate. The only acceptable congress between men and women was through the agency of marriage, else why had they been provided with a chaplain? Justice would be fair but remorseless. Nor should any convict value his labor as equal to an English husbandman's, for he did not have any wife and family to support on his wages—he was the property of His Britannic Majesty's Government in New South Wales. Nobody would be worked beyond his ability, but everybody had to contribute to the general well-being. Their first duty would be to erect permanent buildings for the officers, then for the marines, and lastly for themselves. Now go away and think about all of that, because he truly did mean every word he said. . . .

"How lovely it is to be wanted!" sighed Bill Whiting, getting to his feet.

"Why did they not simply hang us in England if they intend to hang us here?" He blew a derisive noise. "What piffle! We were not brought all this way to fornicate! What did they think would happen? I joke about sheep, but it is no joke to be shot at for going near my Mary."

"Mary?" Richard asked.

"Mary Williams off Lady Penrhyn. Old as the hills and ugly as sin, but both halves are mine, all mine! Or at least they were until I learned that I am to be shot at for yielding to a natural impulse. In England the only one could shoot me is her husband."

"I am right glad to hear of Mary Williams, Bill. That was not the Governor speaking, that was the Reverend Johnson," said Richard. "The fellow ought to have been a Methodist. I daresay that is why he took this job—he is too radical by far to have appealed to any Church of England bishop."

"Why did they bring any women convicts out here if we are forbidden to go near them?" Neddy Perrott demanded.

"The Governor wants marriages, Neddy, to keep the Reverend Mr. Johnson happy. Also, I suspect," Richard said, thinking out loud, "to make this whole expedition seem sanctified by God. The appearance of fornication in the flock looks like Satan's work."

"Well, I ain't marrying my Mary yet a while," said Bill. "I ain't long enough out of one set of chains to take on another."

Which may have been how Bill felt, but they were not feelings shared by all of his fellows. From the following Sunday on, more and more convict couples were married by a delighted chaplain.

Rations were now issued weekly. How difficult that was! To stay resolute and not wolf down the lot within two days. So very little, especially now they were working. Thanks to Lieutenant Furzer's abject gratitude they now had good kettles and pots, even if there was not much to put in them.

The hut was finished down to a double layer of saplings for its walls, one lot vertical, the other horizontal, with enough slender slats in the roof to support densely interwoven palm fronds. They were fairly dry even in hard rain, though when the wind rose to a gale it penetrated the spaces between the lattice; to keep it out they covered the outside walls with palm fronds. It had no windows and but one door facing the sandstone boulder. Humble it might be, but it was still a great deal better than the Alexander prison. The smell was of a clean, pungent resin rather than a sickening mixture of oil of tar and decomposition, and the floor was a carpet of soft dead leaves. The group was, besides, unfettered and relatively free from supervision. The marines had their work cut out in keeping an eye on the known rogues, so those who never gave trouble were left to their own devices apart from regular checks to make sure they were at their places of work.

Richard's place of work was a small, open bark shelter near the series of sawpits being dug behind the marines' tents, not an easy business with bedrock six inches down. The pits had to be excavated by stone-splitting wedges and picks.

Though the saws had not yet come to light (unloading was a painfully slow business), the axes and hatchets were piling up faster than Richard could put edges on them.

"I could use help, sir," he said to Major Ross within a day of commencing work. "Give me two men now and by the time the saws need attention I will have one man ready to deal with the axes and hatchets."

"I see your reasons, dozens of 'em. But why two men?"

"Because there have already been arguments over ownership and I have not the facilities to keep a list. Better than a list would be a lettered helper to gouge the owner's name on the helve of every axe and hatchet. When the saws come to light, he could do the same to them. 'Twould end in saving marine time, sir."

The cold pale eyes crinkled up at their corners, though the mouth did not smile. "Aye, Morgan, ye do indeed have a head. I suppose ye know whom ye want?"

"Aye, sir. Two of my own men. Connelly for the lettering and Edmunds to learn to sharpen."

"I have not yet located your tool box."

Richard's grief was genuine. "A pity," he sighed. "I had some grand tools."

"Do not despair, I will go on looking."

February wore on with thunderstorms, an occasional cool sea change and a great deal of stifling, humid weather which always ended in a pile of black clouds in southern or northwestern sky. The southern tempests brought those blessed cool snaps in their wake, whereas the northwestern ones produced hail the size of eggs and continued sultriness.

Save for different kinds of rats and millions of ants, beetles, centipedes, spiders and other inimical insects, life forms anchored to the ground seemed rare. In contrast to the sky and trees, both full of thousands upon thousands of birds, most of them spectacularly beautiful. Of parrots there were more sorts than imagination dreamed existed—huge white ones with striking sulphur-yellow crests, grey ones with cyclamen breasts, black ones, rainbow-hued ones, tiny speckled chartreuse ones, red-and-blue ones, green ones, and dozens more besides. A big brown kingfisher bird killed snakes by breaking their backs on a tree branch, and laughed maniacally; one large ground bird had a tail like a Greek lyre and strutted in the manner of a peacock; there were reports from those who walked in the Governor's train on his explorations of *black* swans; eagles had wing spans of up to nine feet, and competed with hawks and falcons for prey. Minute finches and wrens, cheeky and vivid, darted about fearlessly. The whole bird kingdom was gorgeously painted—and vocal to the point of distraction. Some birds sang more exquisitely than any nightingale, some screeched raucously, some chimed like silver bells—and one, a huge black raven, owned the most soul-chilling, desolate cry any Englishman had ever heard. Alas, the saddest fact about these myriads of birds was that none was worth eating.

Though some animal animals had been seen, like a fat, thickly furred waddler which burrowed, the one animal everybody yearned to see was a kangaroo. To no avail, if camp bound. Kangaroos never appeared within the precincts; they were obviously shy and timid. Not so the enormous tree-climbing lizards. They stalked through the camp as if men were beneath contempt, and rivaled the hungriest convict or thirstiest marine when it came to ransacking an officer's marquee. One of the things was fully fourteen feet long and justifiably inspired the same terror an alligator would have.

"I wonder what to call it?" asked Richard of Taffy Edmunds when it strolled past their bark shelter, wicked head snaking.

"I think I would call it 'sir,' " said Taffy.

The axes and hatchets kept coming to have new edges put on them, and by the end of February the saws started coming as well. The western saw-pits had started working and a series of eastern ones was being dug under the same difficulty—bedrock. A new obstacle reared its head; the trees, felled and trimmed and put above the pit, were virtually impossible to saw into even the most mediocre of planks. The wood was not only sappy, it was as hard as iron. The sawyers, all convicts, labored so terribly that the Governor was obliged to give them extra rations and malt, else they collapsed. That irritated the marine privates, who forgot that they received butter, flour and rum in addition to the same rations of bread and salt meat as the convicts; they started to keep a ledger of grievances versus convict "privileges." Only Major Ross and ruthless discipline kept them under control, but ruthless discipline meant more floggings—than the convicts, they whined.

The worst aspect of Richard's life was the saws themselves. Only 175 hand saws and 20 pit saws had been sent, and all 20 of the pit saws were rip saws designed to rip the wood down its grain. No pit saw could cut across the grain of wood like this. Which meant that every tree had to be felled by an axe and segmented by an axe. Both kinds of saw were supposed to be of the best steel, but they were not. Months and months at sea had rusted them and there was no butter of antimony on any list for any ship.

25 hand saws and 5 pit saws had gone with Lieutenant Philip Gidley King to Norfolk Island when Supply sailed for that remote place halfway through February to establish a separate settlement there, turn the native flax into canvas and the huge pine trees Captain Cook had reported into ship's masts.

"Sir, it is almost impossible," said Richard to Major Ross. "I have made my own emery paper and removed the grosser rust, but the saws are not sleek enough. Whale oil is wondrous protective, but we have none. The oils we do have congeal to glue the moment heat builds up inside the cut. I need some substance like whale oil or butter of antimony. The saws are besides of such poor steel that, sawing timber as hard as this, I am terrified of breakages. We have fifteen pit saws, which means no more than fourteen pits—I will always be working on one saw because this timber ruins the teeth. But most importantly, sir, I need a rust remover."

Ross looked grimmer than ever; he had heard the same story from the sawyers. "Then we will have to look for a local substance," he said. "Surgeon Bowes Smyth is an inquisitive sort of fellow, always tapping trees and boiling roots or leaves for curatives, resins and probably the elixir of life. Give me one of the very rusty hand saws and I will ask him to experiment."

Off he stumped. Richard felt very sorry for him; he had great talent for organization and action, yet he had no sympathy for the frailties of others, especially if they were his own marines. Whom, when they transgressed, he was at liberty to flog. When he wanted to flog a convict, he had at least to mention the matter to the Governor. To crown the many woes this conflict within his breast generated, Ross had developed an affinity for lightning; his small stock of sheep had perished sheltering under a tree, then his marque had been struck and most of his papers and records were burned together with much else. What Richard thought as he watched the military figure disappear was that without Major Ross, chaos at Port Jackson would be infinite. The Governor is an idealist; the Lieutenant-Governor is a realist.

Richard's bark shelter had grown much larger and he had added two more men to his team, Neddy Perrott and Job Hollister. Billy Earl, Johnny Cross and Jimmy Price had gone to join Bill Whiting in Government Stores, which left only Joey Long without a delegated job. Richard scrounged a grubbing hoe to add to their spade and mattock and set him to making a garden outside their hut, praying that no one would commandeer him for other work, or question his activities; he was fairly well known to be simple in the head, which made him less desirable. If Joey stayed at the hut, their inedible belongings would be safe. The pillaging of food was so universal that every man and woman carried their rations with them to their place of work—and then had to be vigilant to make sure nothing was stolen. Most food thefts were internecine and therefore of no interest to the Governor or the marines; the strong convicts stole from the weak or sickening convicts with impunity.

Dysentery had broken out within two weeks of landing. Richard's instincts about the stream of water were right, though how it had become polluted at the place where water was drawn was a mystery the surgeons could not solve. Their theory was that the water of New South Wales was too alien for an English gut. Three convicts in the hospital tent died and a second hospital had to be erected out of whatever was to hand. Scurvy was rife too; the sallow skin and painful limping gave it away long before the gums started to swell and bleed. Richard still had malt and could stretch it further because Lieutenant Furzer in Government Stores prized his small band of convict helpers so much that he secretly dosed them with malt. This kind of favoritism, as with the sawyers, was inevitable in the face of growing privation.

"But if it comes to it," said Richard to his group in a tone brooking no argument, "we will eat sour crout. I do not care if I have to sit on your chests and force it down your throats. Remember your mothers—we were all brought up to believe that medicine did no good unless it tasted abominable. Sour crout is medicine."

Port Jackson had no natural remedies for the scurvy in anything like sufficient quantity to feed its new population; very few local plants and berries did not cause symptoms of poisoning. The germinating plants faithfully watered in the Government gardens poked up shoots to look at the sun and the sky, and died of sheer discouragement. Nothing would grow, nothing.

It is late summer here, coming into autumn, thought Richard, considering the citrus seeds he had saved from Rio de Janeiro. So I will not sow my seeds until September or October, when it is spring. Who knows how chill the winter is here? In New York the summer is very hot, yet in winter the sea can freeze. From the look of our Indians, I doubt it ever gets that cold, but I cannot afford to take chances by planting anything now.

Three convicts—Barrett, Lovell and Hall—were caught in the act of stealing bread and salt meat from the Government Stores, and another was caught in the act of stealing wine. The three food thieves were sentenced to death; the wine thief was appointed the Publick Executioner.

On the western shore of the cove between the men's and the women's tents stood a tall, solid, handsome tree with one oddity: a strong, straight, aberrant branch projected from it ten feet off the ground. Thus did it become the Hanging Tree, for there was no timber to spare for erecting a gallows. On the 25th of February the three wretches were escorted to it under the gaze of every convict, ordered to attend on pain of 100 lashes. Governor Phillip was determined that this last-ditch lesson would have the desired effect—they *had* to be made to stop stealing food! His own belly, of course, like the belly belonging to every senior person, was at least full. So, as in the business of fornication, the desperate measures introduced to rectify the trouble could not succeed. The hope that they would arose from empty scrotums and full bellies.

Many among the audience, free or felon, had seen a hanging; in England they were occasions of fete and celebration. But many had not, preferring, like Richard and his men, to leave that kind of macabre pleasure to others.

The first condemned man, Barrett, was placed atop the stool and the Publick Executioner was directed to put the looped rope about his neck, tighten it. This he did white-faced and weeping, but he refused to kick the stool away until several marines put powder and ball in their muskets and aimed at him from point-blank distance. Very pale but composed, Barrett kept himself steady. A die-hard. Because the drop was not sufficient to break his neck, he lunged and writhed at the end of his rope for what seemed an eternity. When he did eventually die, it was from lack of air. A full hour later the body was removed and the stool positioned to receive Lovell.

Lieutenant George Johnston, the Governor's aide-de-camp now that Lieutenant King was gone to Norfolk Island, stepped forward and announced that Lovell and Hall had been granted a twenty-four-hour reprieve. The convicts were then dismissed. Phillip's lesson was wasted; those of a mind to steal would continue to steal, and those of a mind not to steal would not. The most that hanging could do was to reduce the number of thieves by simple subtraction.

While Richard was moving away he chanced to look at the ranks of the women convicts, and there he saw some scarlet ostrich feathers nodding over a glamorous black hat. Stunned, he stopped in his tracks. Lizzie Lock! It had to be Lizzie Lock. She had been transported along with her cherished hat. Which looked remarkably fine in light of its travels. But then, she had probably looked after it better than she had her own person. Now was not the time to try to approach her; a moment would arrive. Knowing she was here was sufficient comfort.

On the morrow everybody was again compelled to assemble—in the midst of pouring rain—only to be informed that His Excellency the Governor had reprieved Lovell and Hall in favor of exile to some place as yet to be determined. However, said Lieutenant George Johnston in minatory tones, His Excellency was *seriously* considering shipping all recalcitrants to New Zealand and dumping them ashore to be eaten by the cannibals. Once Supply could be spared, that was where they were all going, and he meant every single word of it, make no mistake! In the meantime, exiles were to go in irons to a barren rock near the cove which had already earned the name "Pinchgut" and subsist there on quarter-rations of bread plus a little water. Yet Pinchgut, the noose and the threat of cannibal feasts did not stop the desperate from stealing food.

If the convicts concentrated upon edibles, the marines preferred to plunder rum and women; marine floggings went from 50 to 100 to 150 lashes, though the flogger never laid it on as hard as he did were his victim a convict—understandable. That the marines could concentrate upon booze and sex lay in the fact that they doled out the food; no matter how this operation was supervised, the portions for marines were always much larger than the portions for convicts. Again, understandable.

The natives were becoming harder to control into the bargain, took to filching fish, spades, shovels and what few vegetables had managed to survive on a fertile isle to the east of the cove where the big Government Farm was under construction in the hope that the ground would be ready for wheat by September. If this ground could ever grow wheat. Men sent to cut rushes for thatch in a bay farther around than Garden Island were first attacked by some Indians, who wounded one; after that two men were killed in the same place. A search up the stream to its swampy source revealed the carcasses of several big lizards decomposing in it, a signal that the natives were neither stupid nor unaware of how to foul water.

Guard duty for the marines grew more taxing as the settlement expanded on a needs-must basis. A tree Sir Joseph Banks had classified as casuarina was found to yield very good shingle timber, but was located some distance away around the stream swamp, and excellent brick clay was discovered a mile inland. The parties foraged into virgin territory and had to be guarded. To make matters worse, the natives were less gun-shy and bolder in their stealing forays, it seemed aware that the orders were not to harm them at any cost.

Governor Phillip went to explore another harbor in the north called Broken Bay, only to return dejected; it afforded good shelter for ships, but had no arable land whatsoever. His Excellency had the best reasons for his dejection. The Heads of a Plan as prepared at the Home Office had blithely assumed that crops would shoot out of ground needing only to be tickled, that splendid timber would be readily available for all conceivable purposes, that the livestock would multiply by leaps and bounds, and that within a year New South Wales would be virtually self-sufficient. Hence the neglect on the part of the Home Office, the Admiralty and the contractor to make sure that there really were three years' worth of supplies with the fleet. The reality was more like a year, which meant that the first storeship due would not come in time. And how could men—or women—work fruitfully when they were perpetually hungry?

Two months around Sydney Cove, as the original landing place was called, had proven only that this place was hard, indifferently and indiscriminately cruel. It seemed mighty, changeless and alien, the kind of land wherein men might eventually scratch a subsistence living but never truly prosper. The natives, primitive in the extreme to English eyes, were a very accurate indicator of what New South Wales promised: misery allied to squalor.

The last week of March saw a cessation in the thunderstorms and the worst of that humid heat. Those possessed of hats had turned them into Yankey headpieces by snapping tricorn brims down all around, but Richard had kept his tricorn a tricorn because he had his bark shelter to work in and his straw sailor's hat—and because he liked to be properly dressed for Sunday service. The habits of Bristol died hard.

Sunday service was held in any one of a number of places, but on Sunday the 23rd of March—the third anniversary of his conviction and sentence at Gloucester—it happened near the bachelor marines' camp on a stack of rocky shelves which gave the congregation some chance to see and hear the Reverend Mr. Richard Johnson exhort them in the Name of the Lord to rein in their shameful urges and join the ranks of those who were marrying.

Having resolved on a course of action, Richard had wanted to pray and receive enlightenment, but the sermon did not do a thing to help. Instead, God answered him by presenting him with the figure of Stephen Donovan, who ranged himself alongside Richard and walked with him around the cove, across the stepping stones and down to the water's edge near the new farm.

"Terrible, is it not?" asked Donovan, breaking the silence as they sat, arms around their knees, on a rock five feet above the placidly lapping water. "I hear that it takes six men a whole week to grub out one stump from yon wheat field, and that the Governor has decided the ground will have to be hoed by hand to receive the grain, for put a plough in it he dares not."

"And that in turn means that one day I will not eat," said Richard, taking off his best coat and disposing his person in the shade of an overhanging tree. "How thin the shade is here."

"And how hard the life. Still," said Donovan, flicking dead leaves into the water, "it will improve, you know. 'Tis like any brand-new venture, at its worst during the first six months. I am never sure why it then begins to look more bearable, save perhaps that the strangeness goes away. One thing is certain. Whenever it was that God made this corner of the globe, He used a different template." His voice dropped, grew softer. "Only the strong will survive, and you will be one of those who survives."

"Oh, ye can depend on that, Mr. Donovan. If I managed Ceres and Alexander, I can manage this. Nay, I do not despair. But I have missed ye. How goes Alexander and dear fat Esmeralda?"

"I would not know, Richard, for I am not in Alexander. The parting of the ways came after I caught Esmeralda opening all the convicts' belongings and parcels stored in his holds. To see what he could sell for a fortune."

"Bastard."

"Oh, Sinclair is all of that and more." The long, supple body stretched and twisted luxuriously. "I have a far better berth now. You see, I fell in love."

Richard smiled. "With whom, Mr. Donovan?"

"Would you believe, Captain Hunter's valet? Johnny Livingstone. As Sirius is down six or seven seamen, I applied to join her crew, and was accepted. Captain Hunter's nose may be a trifle out of joint over the affair, but he ain't about to turn down a seaman of my experience. So I am on good rations and have a little love into the bargain."

"I am pleased," said Richard sincerely. "Also very glad to see ye on this day above all others. As it is a Sunday, I do not have to work. Which means that I am at your disposal. I need an ear."

"Only say the word and ye can have more than an ear."

"Thank you for the offer, but remember Johnny Livingstone."

"The water," said Mr. Donovan, "looks good enough to sport in. I would, but for the fact that Sirius caught a shark the other day measured six and a half feet around the shoulders. Inside Port Jackson!" He rolled up his coat for a pillow and lay flat. "I never did ask ye, Richard—did ye succeed in swimming?"

"Oh, aye. The moment I imitated Wallace, it was easy. Joey Long got his pup, by the way. Winsome little fellow, rats a treat. Eats better than we do, though I am not tempted to change to his diet."

"Have ye seen a kangaroo?"

"Not even the swish of a tail through the trees. But I do not get out of camp—I sharpen our wretched saws and axes." Richard sat up. "I do not suppose Sirius has any butter of antimony?"

The thick black lashes lifted, the eyes gleamed blue. "Cow's butter we have, but not any other kind. How d'ye know about things like butter of antimony?"

"Any good saw setter and sharpener does."

"Not any I ever met before." The lids fell. "A lovely Sunday, here in the open air with you. I will enquire about the butter. I also hear that the timber is unsawable."

"Not quite, just exceeding slow work. Made slower because the saws are rubbish. Everything, in fact, seems to be rubbish." Richard's face hardened. "That is how I know what England thinks of us. She equipped her rubbish with rubbish. She did not give us a fair chance to succeed. But there are some like me who are more steeled and stubborn knowing that."

Donovan got to his feet. "Make me a promise," he said, putting on his hat.

Conscious of huge disappointment, Richard tried to look as if this abrupt departure did not matter. "Name it," he said.

"I will be gone an hour. Wait here for me."

"I will be here, but will use the time to change. 'Tis too hot for Sunday clothes."

Richard returned before Donovan did, clad as most of the convicts were two months into their sojourn at Sydney Cove; canvas trowsers cut off below the knee, bare feet, a checkered linen shirt so faded that the pattern was as subtle as shade inside shade. When Donovan appeared he too wore simple gear, and staggered under the weight of a Rio orange basket.

"A few things ye may need," he said, dumping it down.

His skin prickled, the color drained from his face. "Mr. Donovan, I cannot take Sirius's property!"

"None of it is—or rather, all of it was gotten legitimately—well, almost all," said Donovan, quite unruffled. "I confess I did pluck some of Captain Hunter's watercress—he grows it on wet beds of lint. So we have a good lunch, and there will be plenty to take back to the others. The marines will not bother ye if I walk home with ye and carry the basket myself. I bought malt from our commissary, another sailor's hat, some good stout fishing line, hooks, a piece of cork to make floats, and some old scuttle lead for sinkers. The main reason why the basket is so heavy," he went on as he dug around, "is due to the books. Would you believe that some of the marines on board from Portsmouth disembarked and left their books behind? Christ! Ah!" He held up a little pot. "We have butter for our bread rolls, baked fresh this morning. And a jug of small beer."

The only other meal of his life which could compare was the one Donovan had provided after they had filled the water tuns in Teneriffe, but even it paled at the taste of watercress—*green!* Richard ate ravenously while Donovan watched, donating him all the cress and butter, most of the rolls.

"Have ye written home yet, Richard?" he asked afterward.

Richard savored the small beer. "There is neither the time nor the—the will," he said. "I dislike New South Wales. All of us do. Before I write any letters, I want to have something truly cheerful to say."

"Well, ye have a little time yet. Scarborough, Lady Penrhyn and Charlotte sail in May, but to Cathay to pick up cargoes of tea. Alexander, Friendship, Prince of Wales and Borrowdale sail direct for England about the middle of July, I hear, so give your letters to one of them. Fishburn and Golden Grove cannot leave until thief-proof buildings have been erected to receive their rum, wine, porter and even the surgeons' proof spirits."

"What of Sirius? I understood that she was to return to naval duties as soon as may be."

Donovan frowned. "The Governor is reluctant to let her go until he is sure that the settlement here will survive. To retain only Supply—thirty years old and so small—brrr! Captain Hunter, however, is not pleased. Like Major Ross, Captain Hunter thinks this whole enterprise is a waste of English time and money."

The last mouthful of small beer went down. "Oh, what a feast! I cannot thank you enough. And I am delighted that ye won't be leaving in a hurry." Richard grimaced, shook his head. "I cannot even take small beer without feeling dizzy."

"Lie down and nap a while. We have the rest of the day."

Richard did just that. The moment he put his head on a nest of leaves, he was asleep.

Curled into a defensive position, Stephen Donovan noted, having no intention of dozing himself. Perhaps because he was a free man and a sailor who genuinely loved the sea, he looked at New South Wales very differently from captive Richard Morgan; there was naught to stop him picking up his traps and moving on. That he owned a desire to stay could in most measure be attributed to Richard, whose fate he cared about—no, whose whole person he cared about. A tragedy that his affections had fixed upon a man unable to return them, but not a tragedy of epic proportions; having voluntarily chosen his sexual preferences before he went to sea, he had lived with them in a spirit of optimism and content, keeping his affairs light-hearted and his sea bags packed to shift ship at a moment's notice. He had felt no premonition when he boarded Alexander that Richard Morgan was about to destroy his complacency. Nor really did he know why his heart had settled upon Richard Morgan. It had just happened. Love was like that. A thing apart, a thing of the soul. He had crossed the deck on winged feet, so sure of his instincts that he had expected a kindred recognition. Failing to find it was irrelevant; at first glance it was already too late to retreat.

This alien land also prompted him to stay. Its fate drew him. The poor natives would perish, and knew it in their bones. That was why they were beginning to fight back. But they were neither as sophisticated nor as organized as the American Indians, whose tribal ties extended into whole nations and who understood the art of war, vide their alliances with the French against the English, or the English against the French. Whereas these indigenes were simply not numerous enough, and appeared to war one small tribe against another; concepts like military alliances were not in their nature, which Donovan suspected was highly spiritual. Unlike

Richard, he was in a position to listen to those who had had some contacts and dealings with the natives of New South Wales. The Governor had the right attitude, but the marines did not share it. Nor was it shared by the convicts, who saw the natives as just one more enemy to be feared and loathed. In a funny way, the convicts were in the middle, like the piece of iron between the anvil and the hammer. A good analogy. Sometimes that piece of iron became a sword.

The countryside fascinated Donovan, though like everybody else he had no idea whether it could be tamed to something like English prosperity. One thing he did know: it would never breed a cozy village life, wherein a man tilled a few small fields and pastured a few more, and could walk to the local tavern in half an hour. If this place was tamed, the distances would be enormous and the sense of isolation all-pervasive, from how far away the tavern was to how far away a kindred civilization was.

He liked the feel of it, maybe because he communed with birds, and this was a land of birds. Soaring, wheeling, free. He flew the ocean, they flew the skies. And the sky was like no sky anywhere else, illimitable, pure. At night the heavens spread a sea of stars so dense they formed gauzy clouds, a web of cold and fiery infinity that rendered a man less significant than a drop of rain fallen into the ocean. He loved his insignificance; it comforted him, for he did not want to matter. Mattering reduced the world to Man's toy, a grief. Richard sought God in a church because he had been brought up to do so, but Donovan's God could not be so confined. Donovan's God was up there amid that splendor, and the stars were the vapor of His breath.

Richard woke after sleeping for two hours, curled up and not moving or sighing once. "Have I been out to it for long?" he asked, sitting up and stretching.

"D'ye have no watch?"

"Aye, I do, but I keep it safe in my box. 'Twill come out when I have my own house and the stealing dies down." His gaze was caught by the sudden appearance of hordes of little fish in the water, striped in black and white with yellow fins. "We have not heard what happened when Lieutenant King got to Norfolk Island—d'ye know?" he asked. A great deal of convict talk revolved around Norfolk Island, which had taken on the allure of an alternative destination kinder and more productive than Port Jackson.

"Only that it took King five days and many trips ashore to find a landing place. Of harbors there are none, just a lagoon within a coral reef beset by surf, and in the end that proved the only possible spot to land. There is one section of the reef is sufficiently submerged to get a jollyboat over. But of flax King could find none, and the pine trees, even if suitable for masts, will never be able to come aboard a ship, as there is nowhere to load them and they do not float. However, the soil is remarkable rich and deep. Supply left before further news was available, but she is to go back soon. Then we will know more. The isle is tiny—not above ten thousand acres in all—and is thickly forested with these giant pines. I am afraid, Richard, that Norfolk Island is no more a paradise than Port Jackson."

"Well, that stands to reason." Richard hesitated, then decided to take the plunge. "Mr. Donovan, there is a matter I need to talk about, and ye're the only one I trust to advise me truthfully. Ye have no personal interest in the way my men do."

"Speak, then."

"One of my chatterboxes in Government Stores said too much—Furzer has discovered that Joey Long can mend shoes. So I am going to be without my house guard. I asked Furzer for a week's grace because we have a few vegetables coming up in our garden thanks to Joey's labors, and Furzer is a man one can talk business with. I got my week's grace in return for a share of whatever survives," Richard said without resentment.

"Vegetables are almost as good a currency as rum" was Donovan's dry comment. "Go on."

"While I was in Gloucester Gaol I had an arrangement with a woman convict named Elizabeth Lock—Lizzie. In return for my protection, she looked after my belongings. I have just found out that she is here. I have a mind to marry her, since no less formal way to obtain her services exists."

Donovan looked startled. "For you, Richard, that sounds sadly cold. I had not thought you so"—he shrugged—"detached."

"I know it sounds cold," said Richard unhappily, "but I can see no other solution to our problems. I had hoped that one of my men might wish to marry—most of them visit the women in spite of the Governor's threat—but so far none of them shows a desire to."

"Ye're talking about inanimate possessions in the same breath as a legal union for life—as if the first is worth the second and no different in nature. Ye're a man, Richard, and a man for women. Why can't ye simply admit that ye'd like to take this Lizzie Lock to wife? That ye're as starved for feminine company as most others are? When ye said that ye gave her your protection in Gloucester Gaol, I presume that meant ye had sex with her. I presume ye intend to have sex with her now. What baffles me is how cold-blooded ye sound—noble for the wrong reasons."

"I did *not* have sex with her!" Richard snapped, angry. "I am not talking about sex! Lizzie was like my sister, and so I still think of her. She is terrified of conceiving, so she did not want sex either."

Hands cupping his face, Donovan leaned his elbows on his knees and stared at Richard in consternation. What *was* the matter with him? All this because of too much pleasure? No! He is a subtle man who gets his own way by being in the right place at the right time and knowing how to approach those who rule him. Not a crawler like most such because he has too much pride to crawl. I am looking at a mystery, but I do have some ideas.

"If I knew the story of your life, Richard, I might be able to help," he said. "Tell it to me, please."

"I cannot."

"Ye're very much afraid, but not of sex. Ye're afraid of love. But what is there to be afraid of in love?"

"Where I have been," said Richard, drawing a breath, "I would not go again because I do not think I could survive it a second time. I can love Lizzie like a sister and you like a brother, but further than that I cannot go. The wholeness of the love I had for my wife and children is sacred."

"And they are dead."

"Yes."

"Ye're young still—this is a new place—why not begin anew?"

"All things are possible. But not with Lizzie Lock."

"Then why marry her?" Donovan asked, eyes shimmering.

"Because I suspect her lot is very hard, and I do love her in a brotherly way. Ye must know, Mr. Donovan, that love is not a thing expedience can conjure up. Were it, then I would perhaps elect to love Lizzie Lock. But I never will. We were a whole year together in Gloucester Gaol, it would have happened."

"So what ye're proposing is not so cold-blooded after all. And ye're right. Love is not a thing expedience can conjure up."

The sun had gone behind the rocks on the western side of the cove and the light was long and golden; Stephen Donovan sat and thought about the vagaries of the human heart. Oh yes, he was right. Love came unasked, and sometimes was an unwelcome visitor. Richard was attempting to insulate himself from it by espousing a sister whom he pitied and would help.

"If ye marry Lizzie Lock," he said finally, "ye'll not be free to marry elsewhere. One day that might matter very much."

"You would advise me not to, then?"

"Aye."

"I will think about it," said Richard, scrambling up.

* * *

On Monday morning Richard secured permission from Major Ross to see the Reverend Mr. Johnson, and asked him for permission to see Elizabeth Lock, convict woman in the women's camp, with the *possible* intention of asking her to marry him.

In his early thirties, Mr. Johnson was a round-faced, full-lipped and slightly feminine-looking man of carefully episcopal dress, from his starched white stock to his black minister's robe; this latter garment tended to conceal his paunch, for naturally he did not want to look *too* well fed in this hungry place. The pale eyes burned with the kind of fervor Cousin James-of-the-clergy called Jesuitically messianic, and at New South Wales he had found his mission: to uplift the moral tone, care for the sick and the orphaned, run his own church his own way, and be deemed a benefactor of humanity. His intentions were genuinely good, but the depth of his understanding was shallow and his compassion entirely reserved for the helpless. The adult convicts he regarded as universally depraved and hardly worth the saving—if they were not depraved, then why were they convicts?

On learning that Richard's first cousin (once removed) was the rector of St. James's, Bristol, and discovering that Morgan was an educated, courteous and apparently sincere fellow, Mr. Johnson gave him his pass and provisionally arranged that Richard should marry Elizabeth Lock during next Sunday's service, when all the convicts could see how successful his policy was.

As soon as the sun went down Richard walked from his bark shelter to the women's camp, presented his pass to the sentry and asked whereabouts lay Elizabeth Lock. The sentry had no idea, but a woman hefting a bucket of water overheard and pointed to a tent. How did one knock on a tent? He compromised by scratching at the flap, which was closed.

"Come in if ye're good-looking!" cried a female voice.

Richard pushed the flap aside and entered a canvas dormitory which would have held ten women comfortably, but instead had been made to house twenty. Ten narrow stretcher beds were jammed cheek by jowl down either long wall, and the space between was littered with impedimenta varying from a hat box to a mother cat nursing six kittens. The inhabitants, having eaten at the communal cooking fire outside, were disposed upon their beds in various stages of undress. Thin, frail and indomitable, all of them. Lizzie was on the bed owned the hat box. Of course.

An absolute silence had fallen; nineteen pairs of round eyes surveyed him with keen appreciation as he threaded his way between the impedimenta to the hat box and the dozing Lizzie Lock.

"Asleep already, Lizzie?" he asked, a smile in his voice.

Her eyes flew open, stared up incredulously at the beloved face. "*Richard!* Oh, Richard my love!" She launched herself off the bed and clung to him in a frenzy of weeping.

"No tears, Lizzie," he said gently when she quietened. "Come and talk to me."

He guided her out, an arm about her waist, all eyes following.

"Half your luck, Lizzie," said one woman, not young anymore.

"A quarter of it would do," said her companion, very pregnant.

They walked down to the water of the cove near the temporary bakehouse, Lizzie hanging on to his hand for dear life, and found a pile of quarried sandstone blocks to sit on.

"How was it after we left?" he asked.

"I stayed on in Gloucester for a long time, then was sent to the London Newgate," she said, shivering. It was beginning to be cool, and she was wearing a skimpy, tattered slops dress.

Richard took off his canvas jacket and draped it around her emaciated shoulders, studying her closely. What was she now, two years past thirty? She looked two years past forty, but the beady black eyes had still not given up on life. When she threw her arms around him he had waited for a surge of love or even of desire, but felt neither. He cared for her, pitied her. No more than those. "Tell me all of it," he said. "I want to know."

"I am very glad I did not stay long in London—the prison is a hell-hole. We were sent on board Lady Penrhyn, which carried no male convicts and no marines worth speaking of. The ship was much as it is in the tent—shoved together. Some women had children. Some were heavy and bore their babes at sea. The babes and children mostly died—their mothers could not give them suck. My friend Ann's boy died. Some fell on the voyage and are heavy now."

She clutched his arm, shook it angrily. "Can you imagine, Richard? They gave us no rags for our bleeding courses, so we had to start tearing up our own clothes—slops like this. Whatever we wore when we came on board went into the hold for here. In Rio de Janeiro the Governor sent us a hundred hempen bread sacks to wear because no women's clothing reached Portsmouth before the fleet sailed. He would have done us a better turn to send us some bolts of the cheapest cloth, needles and thread and scissors," she said bitterly. "The sacks could not be used for rags. When we stole the sailors' shirts to use as rags they flogged us, or cut off our hair and shaved our heads. Those who gave them cheek were gagged. The worst punishment was to be stripped naked and put inside a barrel with our heads, arms and legs poking out. We kept washing the rags as long as we could, but seawater sets the blood. I was able to make a few pence by sewing and mending for the surgeon and the officers, but many of the girls were so poor that they had nothing, so we shared what we had."

She shivered despite the coat. "That was not the worst of it!" she said through shut teeth. "Every man on Lady Penrhyn looked at us and spoke to us as if we were whores—whether we were whores or not, and most of us were not. As if to them, we had no other thing to offer than our cunts."

"That is what many men think," said Richard, throat tight.

"They took away our pride. When we arrived here, we were given a slops dress and our own clothes out of the hold if we had any—my hat box came, is that not wondrous?" she asked, eyes shining. "When came Ann Smith's turn, Miller of the Commissary looked her up and down and said nothing could improve her slovenly appearance—she had naught, being very poor. And she *threw* the slops on the deck, wiped her feet on them and said he could keep his fucken clothes, she would wear what she had with pride."

"Ann Smith," said Richard, in agonies of anger, grief, shame. "She absconded soon after."

"Aye, and has not been seen since. She swore she would go—the fiercest monsters and Indians held no terrors for her after Lady Penrhyn and Englishmen, she said. No matter what they did to her, she would not truckle. There were others who would not truckle and were sad abused. When Captain Sever threatened to flog Mary Gamble—that was just after we boarded—she told him to kiss her cunt because he wanted to fuck her, not flog her." She sighed, snuggled. "So we had our few victories, and they kept us going. Samsons that we are, it was always the women who broke through the bulkhead to get in among the sailors, *lusting* after men! Never the men doing the lusting or the breaking in, saints that they are. Still, never mind, never mind. It is over and I am on dry land and you are here, Richard my love. I have prayed for nothing more."

"Did the men come after you, Lizzie?"

"Nay! I am not pretty enough or young enough, and the first place I lose weight is where I never had any to begin with—in the tits. The men were after the big girls, and there were not a lot of men—just the sailors and six marines. I kept to myself except for Ann."

"Ann Smith?"

"No, Ann Colpitts. She is in the next bed to me. The one who lost her baby boy at sea."

Darkness was falling. Time to go. *Why* did this happen? What under the sun could these poor creatures have done to deserve such contempt? Such humiliation? Such misery, beggared even of their pride? Given sacks to wear, reducing themselves to rags to get rags. How could the contractors have forgotten that women bleed and must have rags? I want to crawl away and die . . .

Poor wretch, not young enough or pretty enough to attract a satiated eye—what a time of it the sailors must have had! And what kind of fate does Lizzie face here, where nothing is different from Lady Penrhyn save that the land does not move? I do not love her and God knows she does not stir me, but it is in my power to give her a little status among old friends. Stephen might say that I am playing God or even condescending, but I do not mean it thus. I mean it for the best, though whether it is for the best I do not know. All I do know is that I owe her a debt. She cared for me.

"Lizzie," he said, "would ye be willing to take up the same sort of arrangement with me that we had in Gloucester? Protection in return for your looking after me and my men."

"Oh, yes!" she cried, face lighting up.

"It means marrying me, for I can get you no other way."

She hesitated. "Do you love me, Richard?" she asked.

He hesitated. "In a way," he said slowly, "in a way. But if you want to be loved as a husband loves the wife of his heart, it would be better to say no."

She had always known she did not move him, and thought well of him for being honest. After she landed she had looked in vain for him among the men who thronged the women's camp, sent out feelers to ascertain if any woman there could boast of bedding Richard Morgan. Nothing. Therefore she had deduced that he was not among the men sent to Botany Bay. Now here he was, asking *her* to marry him. Not because he loved her or desired her. Because he needed her services. Pitied her? No, that she could not bear! Because he needed her services. That she could bear.

"I will marry you," she said, "on conditions."

"Name them."

"That people do not know how things stand between us. This is not Gloucester Gaol, and I would not have your men think that I am—I am—in need of anything."

"My men will not bother you," he said, relaxing. "Ye know them. They are either old friends or the few who came in shortly before we were sent to Ceres."

"Bill Whiting? Jimmy Price? Joey Long?"

"Aye, but not Ike Rogers or Willy Wilton. They died."

Thus it was that on the 30th of March, 1788, Richard Morgan married Elizabeth Lock. Bill Whiting stood in dazed delight as his witness, and Ann Colpitts stood for Lizzie.

When Richard signed the chaplain's register he was horrified to discover that he had almost forgotten how to write.

The Reverend Johnson's face made his feelings about the union quite clear: he thought Richard was marrying beneath him. Lizzie had come in the outfit she had preserved since entering Gloucester Gaol—a voluminous-skirted lustring gown of black-and-scarlet stripes, a red feather boa, high-heeled black velvet shoes buckled with paste diamonds, white stockings clocked in black, a scarlet lace reticule and Mr. James Thistlethwaite's fabulous hat. She looked like a harlot trying to make herself respectable.

A sudden, savage urge to wound invaded Richard's mind; he leaned over and put his lips close to the Reverend's ear. "There is no need to worry," he whispered, winking at Stephen Donovan over Mr. Johnson's shoulder, "I am simply obtaining a servant. It was so clever of ye to think of marriage, honored sir. Once married, they cannot get away."

The chaplain stepped back so quickly that he trod heavily on his wife's foot; she yelped, he apologized profusely, and so managed to get away with dignity more or less intact.

"A perfectly matched couple," said Donovan to their retreating backs. "They labor with equal zeal in the Lord's Name." Then he turned his laughing eyes upon Lizzie, scooped her up and kissed her thoroughly. "I am Stephen Donovan, able seaman off Sirius, Mrs. Morgan," he said, bowing with a flourish of his Sunday tricorn. "I wish ye the whole world." After which he wrung Richard's hand.

"There is no wedding feast," said Richard, "but we would be pleased if ye'd join us, Mr. Donovan."

"Thankee, but no, I have the Watch in an hour. Here, a small present," he said, thrust a package into Richard's hand and walked off blowing lighthearted kisses to a group of ogling women.

The parcel contained butter of antimony and a lavishly fringed scarlet silk shawl.

"How did he know I love red?" asked Lizzie, purring.

How *did* he? Richard laughed and shook his head. "That is a man sees through iron doors, Lizzie, but he is another ye can trust."

In May the Governor located a patch of reasonably good land about fifteen miles inland to the west and decided to shift some convicts to the site, crowned by Rose Hill (after his patron, Sir George Rose), to clear it fully and prepare the ground for wheat and maize. Barley he would continue to try to grow on the farm at Sydney Cove. A very little timber was coming out of the sawpits, but quantities of palm logs were now being freighted from coves nearer to the rearing bastions of the Heads. These round, fairly straight boles were flimsy and rotted quickly, but they could be easily sawed and chinked with mud, so most of the increased spate of building was done with palm logs and a thatch of palm fronds or rushes. The casuarina shingles were being weathered and saved for permanent structures, starting with the Governor's house.

The bricks of the nucleus of this had been landed and the wonderful field of brick clay not so very distant was already being worked—brick making went on as fast as the miserable twelve brick molds put on board could be turned around. There was, however, one problem about building in brick or the stunning local yellow sandstone: no one had found a single trace of limestone anywhere. *Anywhere!* Which was—it was ridiculous! Limestone was like soil—it was always so abundant that no one in London had given it a thought. Yet how, in the absence of limestone, could any mortar be mixed to join bricks or sandstone blocks together?

Needs must. The ships' boats were sent out to collect every empty oyster shell dumped around Port Jackson's beaches and rock shelves, a heavy undertaking. The natives were partial to oysters (very tasty oysters, all the senior officers pronounced) and left the shells piled up like miniature slag heaps. If there was no alternative, then the Government would burn oyster shells to make lime for mortar. Experience proved that it took 30,000 empty shells to produce enough mortar to lay 5,000 bricks, the number contained in a tiny house, so as time went on the forays in search of this only source of lime extended to Botany Bay and Port Hacking to the south and almost 100 miles north of Port Jackson. Millions upon millions of empty oyster shells, burned and ground to dust, went between the bricks and blocks of the first solid, imperishable buildings around Sydney Cove.

Almost everybody began to display the early symptoms of scurvy, including the marines, whose flour rations were being cut back to eke out what flour was left in the stores. The convicts chewed at grass and any sort of tender leaf not redolent with resin. If it stayed down, they ate more of it—if it came up or they collapsed in agony, they avoided it. What else could they do? Having the time and the armaments to venture afield, the senior free men reaped the minute supply of edible greens: samphire (a succulent growing in the salt swamps of Botany Bay), a wild parsley, and a vine leaf which, when infused in boiling water, yielded a sweet, palatable tea.

No matter how many were banished in irons to Pinchgut, flogged, or even hanged, thefts of food continued. Whoever possessed any thriving vegetables was sure to lose them the instant vigilance was relaxed; in that respect Richard's men were lucky, for they had MacGregor, a splendid watchdog during the night hours, and Lizzie Morgan to watch during daylight.

The death toll was mounting alarmingly among the free as well as the felon, and included women and children. A few convicts had absconded, hardly ever to be seen again. Some attrition, but not enough; Sydney Cove still held over 1,000 people on Government rations. Scurvy and semi-starvation meant that the pace of work was appallingly slow, and there were of course a proportion of convicts—and marines—who objected to work on principle. With a governor like Arthur Phillip they were not flogged to work; an excuse was easy to find.

May also saw the first frosts of coming winter, heavy enough to kill almost everything in the gardens. Lizzie looked at her vegetable patch and wept, then went scratching dangerously farther afield in search of anything she thought green and edible. After two convict bodies were carried naked into the camp, killed by the natives, Richard forbade her to leave the cove environs. They had sour crout *and it would be eaten.* If the rest of the world chose scurvy in preference, that was hard luck.

On the 4th of June came the King's birthday and a celebration, perhaps Governor Phillip's way of injecting some heart into his dwindling, apathetic chicks. Guns thundered, marines marched, a bit of extra food was issued, and after dark a huge bonfire was kindled. The convicts were given a whole three days off work, but what mattered far more was the gift of a half-pint of rum broken down into grog by the addition of a half-pint of water. The free people each received a half-pint of neat rum and a pint of porter, which was a thick, black beer. To mark the occasion with some official deed, His Excellency the Governor determined the boundaries of the first county in New South Wales and christened it Cumberland County.

"Tchah!" Surgeon-General White was overheard to exclaim. "It is without a doubt the largest county in the world, but there is absolutely nothing in it. Tchah!"

This statement was not quite accurate; somewhere in Cumberland County were four black Cape cows and one black Cape bull. The precious Government herd of cattle, pastured near the farm under the care of a convict, took advantage of his rummy state, swished their tails and broke out of their compound. The search for them was frenzied and signs of their passing were found in heaps of dung and chewed shrubs, but they had no intention of being recaptured, and were not. A disaster!

Supply had come back from a second trip to Norfolk Island with some cheering news and some depressing news. The pine logs could not be loaded whole thanks to lack of an anchorage, nor could they be towed because they were so heavy they sank, but they could provide plenty of sawn beams, scantlings and boards for Port Jackson. This meant that Port Jackson could erect better wooden buildings than palm log, and concentrate upon a liquor store in stone—Fishburn and Golden Grove were stuck until some secure premises were erected on shore for the liquor.

On the other hand, Supply reported, growing plants in Norfolk Island was proving almost insuperably difficult because the place was infested with literally millions of caterpillars and grubs. Lieutenant King was so desperate that he was sitting his handful of women convicts among the plants to pick the grubs off by hand. But as fast as they picked, two replaced every one grub removed. Such rich, deep, fertile soil! Yet he could not grow in it. What did shine through in Lieutenant King's despatches, rumor had it, was an unquenchable enthusiasm for Norfolk Island. Despite its myriad pests, he truly believed that it had more potential to support people than did the environs of Port Jackson.

Among the ailing were pockets of healthy convicts, the majority of them led by resourceful men with the ability to general their dependents toward good health, a minority led by men of different resource—robbing the weak. There were no regulations to the effect that convicts who encountered patches of wild parsley or the sweet tea vine (samphire was just too far away) must surrender their spoils to those in command. The chief restriction on plant-gathering expeditions was fear of the natives, who were getting bolder and now even came into the camp from time to time. The Governor was hoping to capture and tame a few—introduce them to the English language and English ways—and thus, by returning them, Anglicized, to their tribes, persuade these wretched people to ally themselves with the English effort. Did they, he was convinced, their own standard of living would be immeasurably improved; it never began to occur to him that perhaps they preferred their own way of life—why should they, when it was so draggled and pathetic?

To English eyes the indigenes were ugly, far less prepossessing than African negroes because they stank, daubed themselves with a white clay, mutilated their faces either by knocking out an incisor tooth or perforating the gristle between their nostrils with a small bone. Their unashamed nakedness offended grossly, as did the behavior of their women, who on some occasions would coquette brazenly, on others scream vituperation.

Poles apart, neither group stood a chance of understanding the other, nor did sensitivity rule conduct. Inundated by exhortations from the Governor that the natives were to be handled through kid gloves, the convicts grew to loathe these feckless primitives, especially as they were immune from punishment when they stole fish or vegetables or tools. To make matters worse, the Governor always blamed the convicts for the occasional attacks and murders; even if there were no witnesses, he assumed that the convicts had done something to provoke the natives. Whereas the convicts assumed that this was not so: the Governor would side with Satan if a convict were involved because convicts were an even lower form of life than natives. Those first few months at Sydney Cove cemented attitudes which were to persist far into the future.

The winter was cold, yet not unbearably so; no one would freeze to death. Had the invaders been decently fed, they would probably not have shivered the way they did. Food warmed. A few hut owners piled sandstone into unmortared chimneys and reduced their residences to cinders so frequently that the Governor issued orders—no chimneys were to be put on any save brick or stone houses. The smithy burned down; luckily perishable items like bellows were rescued, as were the rest of the tools, but clearly the smithy would have to go high on the priority list of solid buildings. So too the bakehouses, one communal, the other devoted to baking bread for Sirius and Supply.

Ned Pugh from Gloucester Gaol presented himself to his old comrades. He had been sent to Friendship with his wife, Bess Parker, and their little girl, two years old when they landed in New South Wales. Within three weeks Bess and the child were dead of dysentery. Ned was so inconsolable that Hannah Smith, a convict who had become friendly with Bess between Rio de Janeiro and Cape Town, took him under her wing. She had an eighteen-month-old son, who died at Sydney Cove on the 6th of June. Nine days later she and Ned Pugh married. Aside from lack of food they were prospering; Ned was a carpenter by trade and a good worker. A child was on the way and both prospective parents were determined to keep this one.

Maisie Harding, the cheerful giver of favors in Gloucester Gaol, had not been transported, though she was a fourteen-yearer reprieved from the noose; what had happened to her, no one knew. Whereas Betty Mason had come out on Friendship, pregnant yet again to her Gloucester gaoler. Her baby son died at sea out of Cape Town, and that plus her yearning for Johnny the gaoler had eroded her thought processes; she turned bitter and hard, was one of those who was occasionally lashed for stealing men's shirts. Though Lizzie Morgan stoutly maintained that another convict woman had it in for her and victimized her.

In Richard's hut all was well apart from perpetual hunger. Lizzie was so well known to at least half the men that they accepted her as a sister returned to the fold; the only one she could not charm was Taffy Edmunds, whose misogynistic tendencies worsened. He refused to be fussed or clucked over, did his own washing and mending, and came to life only on Sunday evenings, when the group lit a fire outside next to the fallow vegetable garden and he could sing counter to Richard's baritone.

Richard and Lizzie had their own small room, added onto the basic structure, though they slept apart even through the coldest weather. On some nights when sleep was far away Lizzie would toy with the idea of making overtures, but never did. She was too afraid of rejection, preferred not to test the temperature of his affections and drives. Men were supposed to suffer powerfully from sexual deprivation, but among her ten men there were three who seemed to give the lie to this—Joey Long, Taffy Edmunds and her own Richard. She knew too from congress with the other women at the laundering place and around and about that Joey, Taffy and Richard were not unique; there were certainly some men who liked men, but there were others scattered here and there who elected to be monks, who had shut themselves away from sexual solace of any kind—even, she suspected, tossing off. If Richard tossed off, it was extremely silently and without moving. So she was afraid, too afraid to attempt anything he might dismiss her for.

Not all of life revolved around food and the lack of it, and there were good moments. Despite the two-thirds rations issued to their mothers (convict and marine wife alike) and the half-rations they themselves received, the children who managed to survive played, whooped, got into mischief and rejected the attempts of the Reverend Mr. Johnson to confine them in a school to learn reading, writing and arithmetic. Those he could not capture were the offspring of living parents; orphans had to do as he bade them. Family life did exist among the convicts and enlisted marines, often of a happy nature. Feuds existed too, especially between the women, who could conduct vendettas any Sardinian might have been proud of. As they refused to be bullied and answered back with profane fluency, the women were lashed more frequently than the men. Not for stealing food. They stole men's shirts.

Of Stephen Donovan, Richard saw absolutely nothing. Since the 30th of March he had absented himself, Richard deduced because he hoped that the marriage would work itself into something both parties to it enjoyed. Oh, he missed Stephen! He missed the easy friendship, the sparkling conversation, the discussions they used to have about a book one had read and the other was reading. Mrs. Richard Morgan was no substitute. He admitted her loyalty, her capacity to work, her simplicity, her cheerfulness. Qualities which inspired him to care for her. But love her as a wife he could not.

The first of the transports and storeships had sailed in May, and Alexander, Friendship, Prince of Wales and Borrowdale were due to sail halfway through July.

So when the convict couple Henry Cable and Susannah Holmes from Norfolk prosecuted Captain Duncan Sinclair for loss of most of their belongings early in July, the convicts who had sailed in Alexander exulted, even if Sinclair was bound to win the case. Cable had fallen in love with Susannah in Yarmouth prison, and Susannah had borne a son. But when she was sent alone to Dunkirk hulk in Plymouth, she was not allowed to take her baby with her. This London callousness provoked an outcry around Yarmouth and resulted in a petition's being sent to Lord Sydney. When Cable followed Susannah to Dunkirk hulk, he brought their baby with him. Their plight had touched many Yarmouth hearts; a goodly amount of clothing and some books were wrapped in canvas and sewn into a parcel by their well-wishers in Norfolk and sent aboard Alexander, though the Cables had sailed on Friendship. At Sydney Cove all Sinclair gave them were the books; the clothing could not be found.

As it was a civil case, the panel which sat to hear it was presided over by the Judge Advocate, marine captain David Collins, assisted by the Surgeon-General, John White, and the Reverend Mr. Johnson. Sinclair's contention was that the parcel had broken when being moved from one part of the hold to another and that the books had fallen out, so had been kept separately. As to what happened to the parcel itself, he had no idea. The court found in favor of the Cables, whom the Reverend Johnson had married after they landed. The worth of the books was assessed at £5 of the £20 total value; Captain Duncan Sinclair was ordered to pay the Cables £15 in damages.

"I will not!" he cried, outraged. "Let them pay me fifteen pounds! They owe me for freightage of their wretched parcel!"

"Pay up, sir," said Judge Advocate Collins wearily, "and stop wasting this court's precious time. Your ship was in the service of Government and you were remunerated accordingly for the sole purpose of conveying these people and the little property they possess to this country. Fifteen pounds, sir, and no nonsense!"

A verdict which told Alexander's convicts that the higher-ups were well aware that Esmeralda Sinclair had been selling convicts' belongings at Sydney Cove.

The episode had one curious consequence. Two days after the court case Major Robert Ross sent for Richard to his palm log house; a stone house was being built for him with haste, as his accommodations were not fitting for the Lieutenant-Governor. His nine-year-old son, John, had been disembarked from Sirius and was now living with him; the child's mother and younger brothers and sisters had remained behind in England.

The Major was in a wonderful mood, smiles from ear to ear.

"Ah, Morgan! Ye heard that Captain Sinclair lost the case?"

"Aye, sir," said Richard, returning the grin cautiously.

"Take that—'tis your property," said Ross. "It magically appeared out of nothing in Alexander's hold. But first, ye'd best look to see what's missing."

There on a camp stool stood Richard's big wooden tool chest, bare of any cloth wrappings; had it not still borne the brass plate with his name on it, who would ever have known? The locks had been broken; his heart sank. But when he opened it and removed all its nested trays, he could find nothing missing.

"I'll be buggered!" said the Major, peering at the contents of the trays. "Ye're no saw sharpener, Morgan—ye're a gunsmith."

Everything was perfectly ordered. Senhor Tomas Habitas must have packed the box himself because it contained whole flintlocks, parts of flintlocks, screws, pins, bolts, brass and copper cladding, springs, various liquids—*whale oil!*—special brushes. Far more than he had ever needed to carry to and from work. Nothing had moved or broken; everything was so tightly wadded in lint that a bedbug could not have crawled inside. With what was in here, he could make a gun did he have an unfinished stock and a freshly forged barrel and breech.

"I *am* a master gunsmith," Richard admitted apologetically. "However, sir, I am a genuine saw sharpener too. My brother in Bristol is a sawyer and I always set his saws for him."

"Ye've been very close about the gunsmithing."

"As a convicted felon, Major Ross, I thought it inadvisable to air my skills at handling weapons. My interest might have been misinterpreted."

"Fuck that!" rapped the Major, delighted. "Ye can turn to and overhaul every musket, pistol and fowling piece in this camp. I'll have a proving butt built immediately—there are too many children running loose to pot bottles on tree stumps. How is your apprentice saw sharpener coming on?"

"He is as good as I am at it, sir."

"Then he sharpens saws and you work on guns."

"To work on guns, Major Ross, I will need a proper work-bench of the right height, some sort of stool, and shade allied to plenty of light. 'Tis not work can be done well otherwise."

"Ye shall have whatever ye need—the rust, Morgan, the rust! There is not a gun in this place smaller than a cannon is not full of rust. Half the muskets aimed above the natives' heads or at the kangaroos hang fire, flash in the pan or fizzle. Well, well!" The Major rubbed his hands together gleefully. "I knew that fat fucken flawn Sinclair had your tools, so as soon as the court rose I took him by the collar and told him I had an informer willing to give evidence that he'd stolen a chest of tools belonging to the convict Richard Morgan. Next morning I took delivery of it." He emitted a short bark which Richard decided was his version of a hearty laugh. "He must have taken one look inside it and thought it more profitable to sell the thing intact in London."

"I cannot thank ye enough, sir," said Richard, wishing he might shake the Major's hand.

The Major clapped a hand against his forehead. "Wait a moment! Nearly forgot I have something else for ye." He scrabbled around in a heap of items rescued from his lightning-ruined marquee and held up a large bottle of sluggish fluid. "Assistant Surgeon Balmain distilled this while he was—er—slightly incapacitated last month. 'Twas Mr. Bowes Smyth found the tree before he sailed for Cathay. He thought it not unlike a turpentine, though its sap is a sort of a blue color. It fell to Mr. Balmain to test it on the rusty saw. He said it worked very well."

Richard stood expressionless as the Major gave him this information, well aware (as were all his fellow convicts) of what the officers were convinced they had kept a close secret: that Mr. William Balmain and Mr. John White, who had loathed each other ever since the affair of Alexander's bilge pumps, had had such a fierce and drunken quarrel at the King's birthday feast that they promptly went out with a pair of pistols and fought a duel. Mr. Balmain had received a flesh wound in the thigh, and the Governor had been forced to tell the two combatants very gently that surgeons should concentrate upon letting blood out of patients, not out of each other.

"Then I shall save my butter of antimony and whale oil for the guns and give Edmunds this bottle of whatever-it-is for the saws," said Richard, and departed hardly crediting his good fortune.

Within two days he was ensconced beneath the shelter of a stout canvas tent, its sides retractable, at a work-bench of the right height and with a stool to match. Major Ross had not exaggerated; the settlement's armaments were shockingly rusted.

"What a close-mouthed bastard you are, Richard," said Stephen Donovan, arriving to investigate the latest rumor.

Oh, how *good* to see him! "I did not think it right to speak of things that were behind me, Mr. Donovan," he said, making no attempt to conceal his joy, written all over his face. "Now that I am officially a gunsmith, I am happy to discuss it with you."

Chin tucked in, eyes gleaming derisively, Donovan said no more for perhaps an hour, contenting himself with watching Richard work on his first consignment, a pair of pistols belonging to the Major. What a treat to be privileged to watch a consummate craftsman doing something he loved to do! The strong sure hands moved over the gun delicately, applying a drop of whale oil with the tip of a lint-bound stick, working at the frizzen spring.

"The frizzen is soft," Richard explained, "so 'twill not strike sufficient spark. Aside from that, the Major has kept his pistols very nicely. I have removed the rust and browned them with my butter of antimony again. Thank you for the wedding present, it is more appreciated now than it was then. What have ye been doing with yourself?"

"Captaining a longboat to bring oyster shells, mostly. We are taking the boats out to sea now that Port Jackson is exhausted."

"Then ye'd better go back to your longboat, captain. I can see Major Ross approaching," said Richard, putting the pistol down with a sigh of content.

Donovan took the hint and departed.

"Done?" asked Ross brusquely.

"Aye, sir. All remaining is to test them."

"Then come with me to the proving butt," said the Major, taking the walnut case from Richard. "Once the muskets are something like workable, there will be practice every Saturday at the butt, and ye will supervise. This place should be fortified, but since His Excellency deems battlements and gun emplacements frivolous, the best I can do is have my men prepared for emergencies. What happens if the French arrive? There is not a ship moored in a defensive position nor a cannon could be fired in under three hours."

The proving butt was a log house with no front wall and sand piled inside it; a post bearing a chunk of blackened wood was the target. The Major fired at it while Richard loaded his second gun, fired that, and grunted in satisfaction. "Better than when I first bought them. Ye can start on the muskets tomorrow. And I have found ye an apprentice."

That, thought Richard, is the trouble with dictators. I just hope my Ross-appointed apprentice has the right temperament for this painstaking work. Dealing with pretty pistols—he is an honest man, this one, and offered up his own possessions for sacrifice in case I was ham-fisted—dealing with pretty pistols is all very well, but I have to break down, clean and reassemble about two hundred Brown Besses, if not more. A good helper will be a godsend, an unsuitable one a handicap.

Private Daniel Stanfield was a godsend. A slight, fair young man with no pretensions to good looks, he spoke a grammatical, fairly regionless English and had, he said in answer to Richard's question, been carefully tutored by his mother before going to a charity school. His taste inclined more to reading than to rum, and while he was extremely eager to learn, he had sufficient good sense not to make a nuisance of himself. He listened and remembered, put things back where they belonged, and was deft with his hands.

"This is a peculiar situation," he remarked as he watched Richard break down a musket.

"How so?" asked Richard, driving the pins out along the barrel stock. "I am preparing to separate the piece into its component parts, so do not take your eyes off me. There is always a correct direction to punch out the pins, it is not mere brute strength. They taper, so if you strike them with your punch on the wrong side ye'll ruin the pins—and possibly the gun."

"This is a peculiar situation," Stanfield repeated, "because officially I am your master, yet in this tent ye're my master. I am not comfortable to have you address me as 'mister' while I call ye 'Morgan.' An it pleases ye, I would have ye call me Daniel while I call ye Mister Morgan. Inside this tent."

Blinking in surprise, Richard smiled. " 'Tis up to you, but I would be glad to call ye Daniel. Ye're almost young enough to be my son." An indiscreet thing to say: Richard felt his heart twist. Go back to sleep, William Henry, go back to sleep in the bottom of my mind.

"Ye're well known as one of the quiet convicts," said Daniel some days later, able to break down a musket himself. "I know not what ye did nor why, but we marines all know who is who, if not what and why. Ye're also the head man of a number of quiet groups, which means ye're respected in the marine camp. Less work."

Richard did not look up to grin, he grinned to a Brown Bess between his knees.

When Major Ross had summoned him, Daniel Stanfield had gone secure in the knowledge that he had committed no crimes, even in the matter of women. His attentions were devoted to Mrs. Alice Harmsworth, who had lost her baby son a month after landing and her marine husband two months after that. Now a widow with two surviving children, she existed as best she could. Stanfield's protection, which as yet displayed no amorous side, made the world of difference to her and her children.

"I need to train one of my own men as a gunsmith, Stanfield," said Major Ross, "and my eye has lighted upon ye because ye're the best shot here and ye're also good with your hands. I have found a convict who is a master gunsmith—Morgan, late Alexander. His Excellency the Governor is leaning more and more toward making a larger settlement at Norfolk Island, and that means we will need a saw sharpener and a gunsmith for both settlements. Therefore I am sending ye to Morgan to learn at least the rudiments of gunsmithing. Whichever one of ye goes to Norfolk Island will have to be skilled enough to attend to the muskets there. If 'tis ye who goes to Norfolk Island, I would have to send a saw sharpener as well, which means I lean to sending Morgan there. But only if ye can maintain Port Jackson's pieces. So start learning, Stanfield—and learn fast."

* * *

Winter was proving itself the rainy season; at the beginning of August, well after the men of Richard's hut had waved an ironic farewell to Alexander, it rained without let for fourteen days. The stream flooded and drove the married marines out of their camp conveniently close by, even this sandy soil tried to turn to muck, and every chinked log house was a death trap of whistling chilly winds after the mud plaster melted. The thatched roofs did not merely leak, they let waterfalls through, property stored in the open was irreparably damaged, and the Government Stores was beset with molds, damp, crawlies and deterioration.

As usual, the more enterprising suffered less. Having no garden to tend, Lizzie made use of the astonishing trees of this place, which may not have been lushly beautiful of foliage, but did own some spectacular trunks. Some had brown or grey-brown bark like English trees, but many had skins of different colors—white, grey, yellow, soft pink, deep pink, vermilion, cream, a grey almost blue, an occasional rich pink-brown. And these trunks varied in other ways: the basis might be covered in aimless corneille scribbles—striped with other colors—smooth as silk or stringier than unraveling rope—patched—spotted—scaled—tattered. No tree appeared to lose its leaves over winter, but many seemed to shed their bark.

The ones Lizzie was interested in were the ones the natives used to make their humpies; they yielded sheets of leathery, rust-colored bark. Having pestered Ned Pugh into making her a short ladder, she used the bark to cover the palm thatch on their ever-growing hut, then sewed it down and together with twine and a baling needle cadged from Stores on condition that the needle came back. So when the rains arrived they had no leaks could not be fixed by another bark appliqué; Lizzie kept a stock of bark in a room added on to store their belongings. At the painful rate the brick and stone buildings were going up, it would be years before any convict had a more substantial dwelling than palm log or sapling lattice. And sapling lattice like theirs, curtained as it was with woven palm leaflets, was proving itself more desirable in this cold rain than fruitlessly chinked logs.

In fact, they were quite cozy. All of them were able to keep working through the fortnight's bad weather; Major Ross had given the saw sharpeners a tent the moment one came free. His own stone house became habitable just before the rain, his first stroke of luck in some time. As was true of other senior men, most of his more luxurious possessions had remained in England to come out on a storeship thought to be Guardian, expected in

New South Wales at any time after the dawn of 1789. She would also be bringing more food, more cattle, horses, sheep, goats, pigs, chickens, turkeys, geese and ducks. London had been hopelessly over-optimistic about how long things like flour sent with the fleet would last because London had counted on rapid crops of grain and lots of vegetables, melons and other quick-yielding fruit within the first year. That was not going to happen, everybody from highest to lowest knew it. The hard bread was all used up, they were now baking minute loaves from weevily flour, and the salt meat had been in the casks so long that a pound of it yielded four tiny bits after boiling. Yet on this plus pease and rice the convicts were expected to live; they did not get bread anymore save on Sundays, Tuesdays, Thursdays.

Rations were being doled out daily again; no one could keep a week's rations on hand without their being stolen, even after a desperate Governor Phillip hanged a seventeen-year-old boy for stealing food. Sickly babies and children died; the miracle was that any survived at all, yet some did. Orphans became common, deprived of both convict parents; these the Reverend Mr. Johnson gathered in, cared for, fed, and rejoiced that their depraved parents were dead. Depraved beyond redemption they definitely were—why, otherwise, would God have visited Port Jackson with an earthquake and the reek of sulphur for a day afterward?

The natives were becoming steadily more aggressive and took to stealing goats. Apparently they did not fancy sheep, perhaps not sure what lay beneath all that wool. Goat hide resembled the hide of a kangaroo.

A goat, in fact, was the source of the only trouble Richard's men got into. When one of the Stores workers, Anthony Rope, married Elizabeth Pulley, Johnny Cross stumbled upon a dead goat, which he appropriated with delight and presented to the newlyweds as the basis for a wedding feast. They made a sea-pye out of its meat, nesting it in a crust of bread for want of pastry. The whole group was arrested and tried for killing the goat rather than for eating it. Amazingly, the military court believed the convicts' frantic oaths that the goat was already dead; all of them were acquitted, including Johnny Cross and Jimmy Price.

The ships save for Fishburn and Golden Grove had sailed, but Richard wrote no letters. He had taken to copying excerpts out of books to keep his handwriting steady, but write letters home he would not. As if, did he not, the pain would stay buried.

At the end of August spring arrived with a cessation of the rains and typical equinoctial winds. Flowers bloomed everywhere. Undistinguished small trees and bushes suddenly produced brilliant, fluffy yellow balls, spiky crimson pendants that resembled bottle brushes, spidery-looking pink and fawn and orange tufts. Even the tallest trees nodded with masses of cream-lashed eyes and produced young foliage of an exquisite pink. The mode of flowering was mostly of this brushy, wispy kind than English or American petaled blossoms. For petals they had to look among the grasses, where little shrubs were laden with cyclamen flowers like miniature tulips. The clean, sweetly resinous air was filled with a thousand perfumes, some subtle, some suffocating.

And on the 5th of September came a night sky the like of which few had ever seen, and that never with such structure as this huge display of celestial fireworks. The vault glowed and shimmered with fabulously draped curtains and arches dripping luminous fringes in greenish-yellow, crimson and violet; great steely-indigo beams shot from all horizons to the zenith, moving as fast as lightning or eerily still and radiant. There had been an aurora in England in 1750, but no one remembered it as more than a cloudy, colorful glow. This was, the sailors assured people the next day, more wondrous by far than any Northern Lights.

Spirits picked up, even though there had been no real winter, nor any dramatic increase in warmth. But sheep were lambing, goats kidding, hens hatching eggs. None of which could be touched, yet at least augured well for some vague future. If anybody lived to see it; rations did not improve.

Lizzie applied for and received more seeds, and set to in the garden again with renewed enthusiasm. Oh, for a seed potato! Still, if the carrots and turnips came up they would eat something having substance, real belly-filling nourishment. Greens might be good for the scurvy, but they were not filling.

Governor Phillip had decided to send Sirius to Cape Town for more provisions; storeship Guardian was just too distant a prospect to cherish hopes of survival without something to go on with. She was to sail east for Cape Horn on her way there; the decision as to whether she would return around Van Diemen's Land or Cape Horn was left to Captain Hunter. And Golden Grove would leave Port Jackson with her because the liquor store was almost finished. She would sail first to Norfolk Island bearing the first consignment of convicts under Phillip's scheme to add to the tiny settlement and subtract from the big and overburdened one.

When Major Ross sent for him on the last day of September, Richard knew what he was going to say. He had not long turned forty years old and every birthday since his thirty-sixth had been spent in a different place—Gloucester Gaol, Ceres hulk, Alexander and New South Wales. He would go somewhere else before he turned one-and-forty, though this was sooner than he had expected. In a few weeks he would be at Norfolk Island. Nothing surer.

"Ye've worked wonders with Private Stanfield, Morgan," said the Lieutenant-Governor, "and ye've left us with two trained saw sharpeners as well. I had thought of sending Stanfield to Norfolk Island, but he is concerned for the welfare of Mistress Harmsworth and her children, and I am obliged to consider not only my marines, but also their wives, widows and dependents. Stanfield will stay here and continue with the muskets. Ye'll go to Norfolk Island as a sawyer, saw sharpener and gunsmith. Lieutenant King has informed His Excellency that his only skilled sawyer has drowned. While ye're not a skilled sawyer, Morgan, I have no doubt ye'll soon pick up the art. Ye're that sort of man. I have told Lieutenant King in my own despatches that ye'll be an asset to Norfolk Island." The thin lips stretched in a sour smile. "As well that *some* who go will be assets."

"May I take my wife, sir?" Richard asked.

"I am afraid not. There are no vacant berths for women—His Excellency has given me a list of the women who will be going. I have Blackall from Alexander in mind as another sawyer because I suspect ye'll have a lot of sharpening to do. Our building timber for Port Jackson is coming from Norfolk Island until we can find a proper source of limestone to use stone or brick. The local timber is impossible, whereas the beams and planks Supply has brought back with her are ideal. Supply had a very rough voyage and has to be laid up, which is why Golden Grove has been commissioned to drop ye off at Norfolk Island."

"May I take my tools with me?"

Ross looked offended. "His Majesty's Government of New South Wales is not empowered to deprive ye of a single nail or stocking," he said stiffly. "Take *all* that belongs to ye, that is an order. I am sorry about your wife, but that is not in my command. Private Stanfield will manage on Government issue now that he knows how to make emery paper and files. Go and get your things together. Ye board tomorrow afternoon at four. Be waiting at the east jetty—and do not bring a great company to farewell ye, hear?"

Private Daniel Stanfield was absorbed in a Brown Bess, did not look up when Richard entered the tent.

"Mr. Stanfield," Richard said.

That made him jump. "Ah! Ye're to Norfolk Island."

"Aye, and have been ordered to take every tool and item I own, for which I am sorry. Major Ross assures me that ye'll be able to continue out of Government issue."

"Indeed I will," said Stanfield cheerfully. He got to his feet and held out his hand. "I thank ye, Richard, for your generosity and time. And I am sorry it has to be you who goes. If it were not for poor Mistress Harmsworth, I would welcome the change."

Richard shook the hand warmly. "I hope we meet again, Daniel."

"Oh, I fancy that we will. I am not of a mind to go home in a hurry. Nor is Mistress Harmsworth. Sooner or later there will be plenty of food, we both believe that. As a private of marines I would be lucky to end my career as a sergeant, so life in England upon retirement would be hard. Whereas here I have the opportunity to be a landowner once my three years are expired, and I can farm. Looking twenty years into the future, I believe I will be better off in New South Wales than in England," said Daniel Stanfield. He began to help Richard pack his tool chest. "When does your sentence end?"

"March of 1792."

"Then in all probability ye'll finish your time at Norfolk Island. Where," said Stanfield, making sure a cork was tied down thoroughly, "I am undoubtedly going to be sent at some time or other before I am through. Major Ross does not intend to have any marines permanently stationed on the island, we will all do our turns. Which is why I have to persuade Mistress Harmsworth to marry me before I am posted there."

"She would be foolish to turn ye down, Daniel. However, if history continues as it has with me," Richard said, adjusting the lint wadding, "by the time ye're sent to Norfolk Island the Crown will have developed another settlement elsewhere in this vast place and I will have been sent there."

"Not for some years at least," said the young marine emphatically. "Those here have first to prove that settling Englishmen so far away will succeed. Especially because few of them wanted to come or had any choice. The Governor is determined not to fail, but there are many others not very junior to him who do not feel the same." His fine, light grey eyes looked at Richard very directly. "I take it that this conversation will not go any further?"

"Not from my mouth," said Richard. "There is nothing wrong here that could not have been solved before we set sail. Whatever the official attitudes are here, it is lack of planning and specific orders in London to blame. And the rivalries between naval officers and marine officers."

"In a nutshell." Stanfield smiled.

Richard drew a breath and put the welfare of his back in Daniel Stanfield's hands. "The Major is a curious mixture," he said.

"That he is. He sees his commissioned duties as any marine major would, and disapproves of duties which don't contribute to the well-being of the Corps or marines' pockets. So he will let those of us with a trade work as carpenters or masons or smiths, but he will not countenance his officers serving on criminal courts because they are not paid for the extra duty. The Governor insists that it is every man's duty to do whatever the Crown asks, and in New South Wales he is the Crown. Then there is Captain Hunter, who sides with the Governor for no other reason than that both are Royal Navy." He shrugged. "It makes things very difficult."

"Especially," said Richard thoughtfully, "because ye're more grown up than many of the officers, Daniel. They act like children—quarrel in their cups, fight duels—refuse to get on together."

"How," asked Stanfield, "d'ye know that, Richard?"

"In a place this size? With not many more than a thousand souls? We may be felons, Daniel, but we have eyes and ears the same as free men. And, no matter how low our status at the moment, all of us were born free Englishmen, even if some of us hail from Ireland or Wales. None from Scotland, where they do not use English judges."

"Aye, that is another bone of contention. The majority of our officers are Scotchmen, whereas the sailors can be anything."

"Let us hope," said Richard, locking his chest, "that those who do remain in this place learn to bury the differences this place renders meaningless. Though I doubt that will happen." He held out his hand a second time. "I wish ye luck."

"And I you."

The men were all home to dinner, which Lizzie cooked; had she only a few ingredients it would have been obvious that she was a good cook. As it was, the menu consisted of pease pottage to coat a kettle of rice. And a spoonful of sour crout each.

Richard put his tool box away and joined the circle around the fire; of wood for sawing there might be none, but of wood for burning there was plenty.

How to do it? How to tell them? Ought he to tell Lizzie in private? Yes, of course he had to tell her first, and in private, no matter how he dreaded the tears and protestations. She would assume he had asked not to take her with him.

He ate his food in silence, glad that no one had noticed him deposit the tool box in their belongings room. Of long experience they saved a little of the pease-and-rice for a cold breakfast, even though every one of them could have devoured the lot and still felt hungry.

How would they survive without him? Well enough, he thought; after eight months here, each of them has forged some kind of life for himself independent of the group. Only food and shelter keep them intact. The Government Stores men—and that is most—have excellent relationships with other convicts in Stores and with Lieutenant Furzer, and the others all sharpen together. If I worry about any of them, it is Joey Long, such a simple and easily led soul. I pray the rest watch out for him. As for Lizzie—she would survive the sinking of the Royal George. Mine has never been a push sort of leadership; they will hardly know I am gone, and maybe some of them will be glad to strike out on their own.

"Walk with me, Lizzie," he said when the meal was over.

She looked surprised, but accompanied him without a murmur, aware that something bothered him tonight, yet sure it was nothing she had done.

Dusk was thickening but the official curfew stayed at eight o'clock all year round, still well after dark. Richard led his wife to a quiet place by the water and found a seat for them on a rock. Crickets were making a racket in the grass and the huge huntsman spiders were on the prowl, but there was little else to disturb them.

"Major Ross summoned me today," he said steadily, looking out across the cove to where the myriad lights of the western shore flickered and flamed. "He informed me that tomorrow I am to board Golden Grove. I am being sent to Norfolk Island."

His voice told her that she was not to accompany him, but she had to ask. "Am I to go with you?"

"No. I did ask that ye might, but I was refused. Apparently the Governor has already picked the women."

A tear splashed on the rock, still warm from the last sunlight; her mouth began to tremble, though she fought valiantly to maintain her calm. He would not like a scene, this man of the shadows. Not wanting to stand out from the rest, yet speared on his own abilities and excellences. Nothing will draw him out of his armor, nothing can weaken him, nothing will deflect him from what he sees as his purpose. And I too am a nothing in his eyes, for all that he does genuinely care about my well-being. If he ever had a light inside of him he has snuffed it out. I know nothing about him because he never speaks of himself; when he is angry it only shows as a different sort of silence, after which he proceeds to get his own way by some other means. I am sure that inside his mind he was able to intrude his name into Major Ross's mind. Silly thought! How can one mind influence another without the necessity for speech and glances and nearness? Yet he can do it. Who else in this place has managed to get on the right side of Major Ross? Without smarming or greasing—well, Major Ross cannot be so cozened, as all know who have tried. He wants to go. Richard wants to go. I am sure he did ask for me, but I am quite as sure that he knew the answer would be no. Were he evil, I would say he had sold his soul to the Devil, but there is no evil in him. Has he sold his soul to God? Does God buy souls?

"It is all right, Richard," she said in a voice which did not betray her grief. "We go where we are sent because we are not free to choose. We are not paid for our labors and we cannot insist on having what we want. I will continue to live here and look after our family. If I behave soberly and decently they cannot force me back into the women's camp. I am a married woman separated from her husband at the Governor's whim. And I have a good arrangement with Lieutenant Furzer about vegetables, so he will not want me back in the women's camp. Yes, it will be all right." She got up quickly. "Now let us go back and tell the others."

It was Joey Long who cried.

Shortly after dawn Joey's woebegone face became wreathed in delighted smiles; Sergeant Thomas Smyth appeared to inform him that he would be going to Norfolk Island on Golden Grove, so get his things together and be at the eastern jetty for embarkation at four that afternoon—and no farewelling crowd, either.

His own few things were packed more quickly than Richard's, for they mostly fitted into his box. What Richard had to do was to sort out which books he would take with him and which he would leave in Port Jackson for Will, Bill, Neddy, Tommy Crowder and Aaron Davis. The collection had grown amazingly, mostly thanks to Stephen Donovan's efforts in gathering those books the marine officers and enlisted men had left behind in Sirius. Finally he selected the ones he thought would be of most practical use plus those Cousin James-of-the-clergy had given him. What he needed was *Encyclopaedia Britannica,* but that would have to wait until he wrote home to beg for it, as would Jethro Tull's book about farming, published fifty-five years ago but still every cultivating man's bible. One day he *must* write home! Only not yet. Not yet.

Golden Grove's longboat was waiting at the hastily constructed little jetty, companion to a second on the western shore of Sydney Cove; there were 19 other convicts to go on board, some of whom Richard knew well from Alexander. Willy Dring and Joe Robinson from Hull! John Allen and his beloved violin—there would be good music at Norfolk Island. Bill Blackall, a rather moody individual from the starboard side. Len Dyer, a Cockney who had lived forward, truculent and given to violent outbursts. Will Francis, who went back to Ceres as well as Alexander, a constant nuisance to those in authority. Jim Richardson, also from Ceres as well as Alexander, another moody individual; he and Dyer had been up a deck among the Londoners on Ceres. The rest were strangers come on other ships from other hulks.

There is, thought Richard as he got himself, Joey Long and MacGregor settled in the bow, a solution to this human equation which time will give to me. When I see which women the Governor has personally chosen, the answer will grow clearer.

As Golden Grove was a storeship she owned no slaver-style accommodation; the men were led to the after hatch and found themselves in a lower deck devoid of anything save hammocks. A two-decker, this ship's remaining cargo, for Norfolk Island, was stored further below. He left Joey Long and MacGregor to guard their belongings and went up on deck.

"We meet again," said Stephen Donovan.

Wordless, Richard gaped.

"How nice to see ye without an answer," Donovan purred, taking his companion by one arm and drawing him forward. "Johnny, this is Richard Morgan. Richard, this is my friend Johnny Livingstone."

One glance was enough to make the attraction understandable; Johnny Livingstone was slight, graceful, owned a mop of golden curls and large, soulful greenish eyes fringed with very long, black lashes. Extremely pretty and probably a very nice fellow doomed, if he had followed the sea as a profession from childhood, to be the plaything of a succession of naval officers. He had the look of a ship's boy, of whom there had been three on Alexander, all the property of Trimmings the steward, who would have been neither gentle nor compassionate.

"I cannot shake your hand, Mr. Livingstone," said Richard with a smile, "but I am very glad to meet you." He moved to the rail to put distance between himself and the free pair because other convicts were back on deck again, gazing curiously. "I thought ye were with Sirius."

"And off to the Cape of Good Hope around Cape Horn," Donovan said, nodding. "The trouble is that we are not needed as badly aboard Sirius as we are at Norfolk Island. His Excellency is very short of free men to act as supervisors of convicts because Major Ross has let it be known very loudly that the Marine Corps is not about to extend guard duty to supervisory duties. So the Crown has deputed me to act as supervisor of convicts at Norfolk Island." He dropped his voice, wriggling his brows expressively. "I suspect Captain Hunter decided he would like a nice long cruise alone with Johnny, and personally nominated me to the Governor. But, alas, Johnny elected to go to Norfolk Island too. Captain Hunter has retired cursing, but no doubt will live to seek a return bout."

"What will you do at Norfolk Island, Mr. Livingstone?" asked Richard, resigning himself to being identified by his fellow convicts as friendly with two free men who were a little—free.

Mr. Livingstone made no attempt to answer for himself; he was, as Richard discovered, extremely shy and self-conscious.

"Johnny has a great talent for the woodworking lathe, one of which—it is probably the only one, knowing London—is aboard for use at Norfolk Island. The wood at Port Jackson cannot be worked on a lathe, whereas the pine can be. That His Excellency was eager to accommodate Johnny in the matter of his desire to leave Sirius lies in the new Government House's balusters—he will turn them at the source of the timber. Also many other useful wooden objects His Excellency lacks."

"Surely a job better done at Port Jackson?"

"There is not room for the raw timber aboard ships plying back and forth between the two settlements—every ship will be loaded to the gunwales with sawn timber to get the bachelor marines and convicts into better houses."

"Of course. I should have thought of that."

"And here," Donovan announced blithely, "are the ladies."

There were eleven women in the longboat. Richard knew most of them by sight thanks to Lizzie, though none by acquaintance. Mary Gamble, who had told Captain Sever to kiss her cunt and had cut a swathe through those men who prided their masculinity by demeaning it in any way her barbed tongue could; her back would scarcely have time to heal before she was lashed again. Ann Dutton, who loved rum and marines, and would go after the latter to obtain the former. Rachel Early, a slattern who would pick a fight with an iron post. Elizabeth Cole, who had married a fellow convict shortly after reaching Port Jackson and been so shockingly beaten by him that Major Ross had stepped in and put her in the women's camp as a laundress. If the other seven were like these, then His Excellency was ridding himself of nuisances, though obviously Elizabeth Cole was being sent 1,100 miles from her husband as an act of pure compassion.

"What a jolly voyage this is going to be," Richard sighed, watching the women being herded to the forward hatch.

Golden Grove sailed at dawn on the 2nd of October, 1788, in company with Sirius until the two ships shook free of the Heads; then Golden Grove tacked to find a wind to bear her northeast while Sirius took advantage of the south-flowing coastal current and headed away to find her eastings for Cape Horn, 4,000 miles to the east.

By the time that the ship drew close to Lord Howe Island five days later, Richard had solved his equation. As he suspected, the Governor was ridding himself of nuisances. Not necessarily because they were disciplinary problems like Mary Gamble and Will Francis. No, the majority were less fortunate than that: they had been adjudged mildly mad. Only four of the men could pass muster as what the ship's manifest purported them to be—young, strong, unattached and sea crazy. They were to man the fishing coble at Norfolk Island. For himself, he was not sure quite why he had been chosen—a sawyer he was not, yet that was what he was listed as. Did Major Ross somehow sense that Morgan was tired of Port Jackson? And if he had, what was so different about that? Everybody was tired of Port Jackson, even the Governor. At the core of him he had a feeling that Major Ross was banking him like money—tucking him away for future use. Well, maybe. . . .

Men like poor, timid John Allen and Sam Hussey were distinctly peculiar, twitched or muttered or stayed too long in one position. The real villains were outstanding ones—Will Francis, Josh Peck, Len Dyer and Sam Pickett. Some were married and had been allowed to bring their wives, in every case because one or the other or both were odd—John Anderson and Liz Bruce; the fanatical Catholics John Bryant and Ann Coombes; John Price and Rachel Early; James Davis and Martha Burkitt.

Sergeant Thomas Smyth, Corporal John Gowen and four privates of marines made up the guard detachment, though guard on Golden Grove was so relaxed a business that Private Sammy King was able to commence a touching and passionate affair with Mary Rolt, one of the peculiarities (she conducted whole conversations with herself). A temporary aberration, it seemed, for after she and the Private became lovers her imaginary dialogues stopped completely. A sea voyage, Richard mused, could indeed be highly beneficial.

For him it had commenced badly; Len Dyer and Tom Jones lay in wait for him below to teach him how they felt about convicts who not only hob-nobbed with free men but with Miss Molly free men into the bargain.

"Oh, grow up!" he said wearily, not backing down. "I can take both of ye with one hand tied behind me."

"How about six of us?" asked Dyer, beckoning.

Suddenly there was MacGregor, snapping and snarling; Dyer aimed a foot at him, caught him on the hind leg just as Golden Grove heeled hard over. The rest of it happened very quickly as Joey Long hurled himself into the fray and three of the six attackers lost interest in anything but their rising gorges. Richard put a shod toe into Dyer's backside right behind his testicles, Joey climbed on Jones's back and started biting and scratching, and MacGregor, uninjured, sank his teeth into Josh Peck's heel tendon. Francis, Pickett and Richardson were busy vomiting, which came in very handy; Richard finished the fight by rubbing Dyer's face in spattered deck and putting all his weight into kicking Jones and Peck in the groin.

"I fight dirty," he said, panting, "so do not lie in wait for me again. Otherwise ye'll never sire children."

It was politic, however, he decided after making sure that Joey and MacGregor were all right, to shift themselves and their stuff up on deck. If it rained they would shelter under a boat.

"I hope," he said to Stephen Donovan later, "that ye can handle yourself, Mr. Donovan. Tom Jones and Len Dyer do not care for Miss Mollies. Ye'll be supervising them, not to mention Peck, Pickett and Francis. Though the last man is their leader, he let Dyer do the job. Therefore he is dangerous."

"I thank ye for the warning, Richard." Donovan studied him thoughtfully. "No black eyes or bruises that I can see."

"I kicked them in the balls. Seasickness," Richard grinned, "was a great help. My luck held, you see. Just as they rushed me Golden Grove found a wind and some of the stomachs revolted."

" 'Tis true, Richard, ye do have luck. It seems odd to say that of a man unlucky enough to have gone down for something he did not do, yet ye do have luck."

"Morgan's run," said Richard, nodding. "Luck runs."

"Ye have had your runs of bad luck too."

"In Bristol, aye. As a convict I have had very good luck."

Lord Howe Island marked a kind of halfway point, and save for the day they spent in its vicinity the weather was glorious. That meant the ship's company never saw this magical island of turtles, palm trees and soaring peaks, 500 miles east of the coast of New South Wales. They ploughed onward, another 600 miles to go.

This was Richard's first venture into the mightiest of all seas, the Pacific, which he had thought to find no different from the King's herring pond, or that unnamed monster of an ocean south of whatever lay between New Holland and Van Diemen's Land. But the Pacific was different; it must, he decided, leaning for hour after hour over the rail looking into illimitable distances, be unfathomably deep. Seen close up as the tremendous yet tranquil swell cradled Golden Grove, its waves were a luminous ultramarine shot with pure purple. Of fish they caught none, though of denizens there were plenty—huge turtles skimmed along, porpoises leaped. Massive sharks cruised by scornfully ignoring the baited lines, their dorsal fins three feet clear of the water, their length terrifying. A sea of giant sharks rather than whales. Until the day when they were surrounded by leviathans, voyaging south to summer while Golden Grove, inexplicable marine creature, surged northeast. Strange. He had never really felt lonely on the way to New South Wales, but now he was perpetually conscious of his loneliness. The sense of belonging a year ago probably lay in the fact that there were always ten sets of sail in sight. Here no ship ventured except Golden Grove.

At some time during the eleventh night he became aware that he was not lifting and falling gently; Golden Grove had backed her sails and was standing. *We are here.*

The deck was absolutely quiet because the sailors had nothing to do and the helmsman, out in the open on the quarterdeck, had only to keep the tiller steady. The night was still, the sky cloudless save for that haunting wilderness of numberless stars, no moon to dim them as they wheeled in some incalculable cycle across the heavens. Anything so thinly and ethereally brilliant, he felt, ought to be audible: what privileged ear could hear the music of the spheres? His ear heard naught but the creaks and washes of a ship standing in an easy sea, and the shadow-sounds of night birds flitting like ghosts. Land is there, invisible. Yet another shape to my fate. I am going to a tiny isle in the midst of utter nowhere, so remote that even men have not dwelled in it until we English came. Counting us, there will be about sixty Englishmen and Englishwomen.

One thing is certain. This place can never be home. I come alone through a lonely sea, and I will leave alone through a lonely sea. Nothing so far away can have substance, for I have reached that point on the globe where I begin to swallow my own tail.

PART SIX

From
October of 1788
until
May of 1791

The women were ordered to ftay below, but at dawn all the men had their belongings on deck and waited for morning to reveal Norfolk Island. Light came in the midst of a stunning sunrise, high billows and wisps of rainless cloud turning slowly from purple-shot plum through fiery scarlet to the glory of pure gold.

"Why does sunrise feel so strange?" Joey Long asked as he stood with Richard at the rail, MacGregor panting at his feet.

"I think because it is the reverse of sunset," said Richard. "The colors go from dark to light until the clouds are white and the sky is blue."

MacGregor barked to be picked up; Joey obliged. The dog was on a homemade leash his master had manufactured out of tiny scraps of leather even Lieutenant Furzer could not find a use for; more accustomed to freedom, MacGregor disliked the leash but wore it with resignation. The voyage had provided him with plenty of pickings, and Captain William Sharp had been delighted to let the little terrier have the run of the holds. The ship's cat (MacGregor had no patience with cats) had retired to the forecastle in a huff and left the field to this impertinent intruder.

Having lain some miles off during the night, they were under sail again. Captain Sharp had never been to the island before, and was taking no chances. Getting in would be no trouble, as Harry Ball of Supply had lent him Supply's sailing master, Lieutenant David Blackburn, who knew every kink in the reefs and every rock and shoal offshore.

Because the sun shone in the eyes until it climbed higher into the vault, all that could be seen of the island—three miles by five miles in extent, Donovan had informed Richard—was a dark, disappointingly low mass. No Teneriffe, this. Then, it seemed in a second, its bulk filled up with light. The green of it was blackish and the 300-foot-high cliffs were either dull orange or charcoal. Therefore the place should have looked ominous, brooding; that it did not lay in the sea, shading from purple-blue out where Golden Grove was trying to find a wind to a glowing aquamarine around its coast. That gradually paling water made the island seem as if it grew there as part of some gigantic marine plan, as natural as inevitable.

They were sailing from west to east in catspaws of breathy breeze which came from the southwest, then from the northeast. Two other isles attended the big one: a tiny low isle close in shore bristling with pine trees, and a larger isle perhaps four miles to the south, craggily tall and vividly green save for a few clumps of dark pines. White waves broke at the base of all the cliffs and against some sort of bar in the direction they were heading, but the ocean was quiet and calm.

Golden Grove anchored some distance off the reef where the surf broke in placid flurries; beyond it a lagoon glittered almost more green than blue, and having two beaches, the western one straight, the eastern one semi-circular. The sand was apricot-yellow and merged at its back right into the pines, thinned out by men, and the tallest, biggest trees Richard had ever seen. Amid them along the straight beach lay a small collection of wooden huts.

A large blue flag with a yellow plus was flying limply from a staff very close to the straight beach, on which people were busy manning two tiny boats. Golden Grove's jollyboat went over the side and across to the reef to meet them; the tide had flooded in sufficiently for the jollyboat to cross the reef into the lagoon, where it would remain. The longboats, said Lieutenant Blackburn firmly, would go no farther than the outside of the coral, there to transfer cargo to the smaller boats for the run to the sand.

One of the two tiny boats approached the ship, a man clad in white, dark blue and gold braid standing in its bow, his powdered wig and hat on his head, his sword at his side. He came aboard, shook Captain Sharp warmly by the hand, and Blackburn, and Donovan, and Livingstone. This was the Commandant, Lieutenant Philip Gidley King, whom Richard had never really seen before. A well-made man of medium height, King had sparkling hazel eyes in a tanned face which was neither plain nor handsome; it owned a firm, good-natured mouth and a large, though not beaky, nose.

The pleasantries over, King turned to the convicts. "Who among ye are the sawyers?" he asked.

Richard and Bill Blackall shrinkingly held up their hands.

King's face fell. "Is that all?" He toured the ranks of the 21 men, pausing before Henry Humphreys, a big man. "Step out," he said, and continued touring until he found Will Marriner, another strong-looking man. "You step out too."

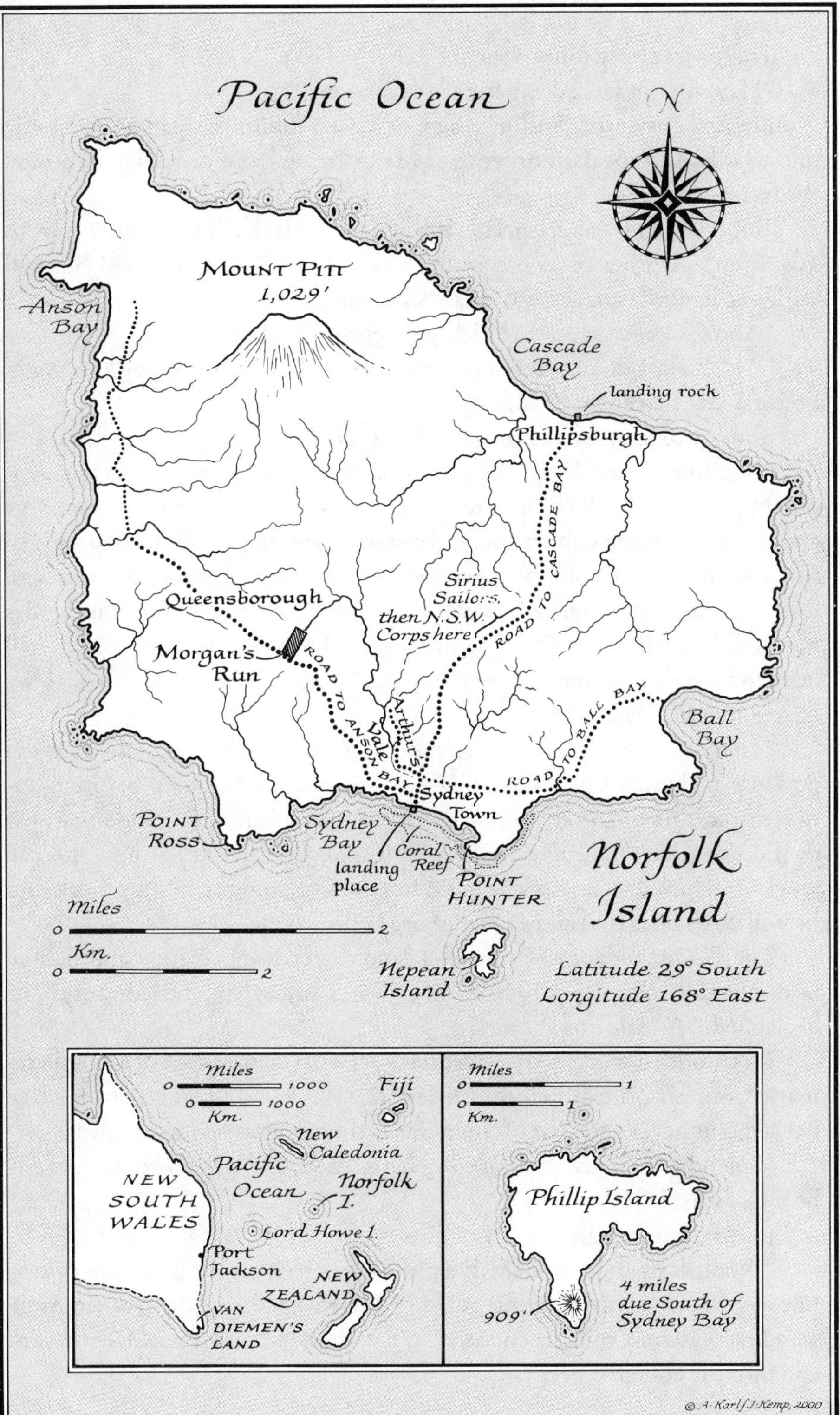
Pacific Ocean
N
Mount Pitt
1,029′
Anson Bay
Cascade Bay
landing rock
Phillipsburgh
Road to Cascade Bay
Sirius Sailors, then N.S.W. Corps here
Queensborough
Morgan's Run
Road to Anson Bay
Arthur's Vale
Road to Ball Bay
Ball Bay
Sydney Town
Point Ross
Sydney Bay
landing place
Coral Reef
Point Hunter
Norfolk Island
Miles
0
2
Km.
0
2
Nepean Island
Latitude 29° South
Longitude 168° East
Miles
0
1000
0
1000
Km.
Fiji
New Caledonia
Pacific Ocean
Norfolk I.
New South Wales
Lord Howe I.
Port Jackson
New Zealand
Van Diemen's Land
Miles
0
1
0
1
Km.
Phillip Island
4 miles due South of Sydney Bay
909′
© A. Karl/J. Kemp, 2000

There were now four of them.

"Have any of ye had experience as sawyers?"

No one answered. Stifling a sigh, Richard found himself, as usual, the one who had to speak in order to save the group from official irritation in the face of silence.

"None of us is experienced, sir," he said. "Blackall and I know how to saw, though neither of us has worked as a sawyer." He indicated Blackall with one hand. "I am actually a saw sharpener."

"And," Donovan put in quickly, "a gunsmith, Lieutenant."

"Ah! Well, I do not have enough work for a gunsmith, but I certainly do for a saw sharpener. Names, please."

They gave their names and convict numbers.

"Numbers," said King, "are unnecessary in a place owning so few people. Morgan, Blackall, ye'll head the sawpit—go ashore with Humphreys and Marriner in the coble at once. To start work, not sit about. We have to fill Golden Grove's holds with timber for Port Jackson before she sails, and losing my only experienced sawyer in a boating accident has meant there is not near enough done. The saws are nigh as blunt as a Scotchman, so ye'll have to start sharpening this very minute, Morgan. Have ye any tools? We have only two files."

"I have plenty of tools, sir," said Richard, and proceeded to do what experience had taught him was politic: ask for what he wanted before ignorance or misinformation burdened him with people he either did not know or did not trust. "Sir, may I take yon Joseph Long? I know him and can work with him. He has not the build for a sawyer and his wits are weak, but he will do as he is told and can be of use at the sawpit."

The Commandant of Norfolk Island's eyes went to Joey and lighted upon the dog, clasped in Joey's arms. "Oh, I say, what a little beauty!" he exclaimed. "A male dog, Long?"

Joey nodded wordlessly, never having been the recipient of a simple remark from an official before. Orders he had heard aplenty, snapped or barked, but never the kind of thing one ordinary man said to another.

"Splendid! We have but one dog here, a spaniel bitch. Does he rat? *Say* he rats, please?"

Joey nodded again.

"What dashed good luck! Delphinia rats too, so we will have ratting pups—oh, do we *need* ratting pups!" King realized that the five were still standing watching him, fascinated. "What are ye waiting for? Over the side and into the coble!"

"I always heard that the Navy was mad," said Bill Blackall as the boat pulled away.

"Well," said Richard, uncomfortably aware that the two oarsmen, both strangers, could overhear, "ye must not forget that there are but few people here. The Commandant and they must be very used to each other by now. They are probably short on ceremony."

"Aye, we are short on ceremony, but very glad to see some new faces," said one of the rowers, a man in his fifties with a Devon drawl in his voice. "John Mortimer, late Charlotte." He tilted his head at his opposite number. "My son, Noah."

They did not look a bit like father and son. John Mortimer was a tall, fair, placid-looking man, whereas Noah Mortimer was short and dark—and rather self-opinionated, if his expression was anything to go by. It is a wise man knows his own father.

The coble, so called because it was clinker-built in the manner of a Scotch fishing dinghy, very flat-bottomed, glided across the reef without grazing itself and stroked the mere 150 yards across the lagoon to the straight beach, where some of the surviving members of the community stood waiting: six women, one—the oldest—big with child, and five men whose ages, if their faces reflected their years, varied between shaveling young and grizzled old.

"Nathaniel Lucas, carpenter," said a man of thirty-odd, "and my wife, Olivia."

An attractive and intelligent-looking couple.

"Eddy Garth and my wife, Susan," said another fellow.

"I am Ann Innet, Lieutenant King's housekeeper," said the eldest female, one hand a little defensively on her swollen belly.

"Elizabeth Colley, Surgeon Jamison's housekeeper."

"Eliza Hipsley, farmer," said a handsome, strapping girl, her arm protectively about another girl of the same age. "This is my best friend, Liz Lee. She farms too."

Good, thought Richard, I know where I stand with that pair, as must any man of perception. Eliza Hipsley is terrified at the advent of so many new men, which means that she is not sure of Liz Lee. And Len Dyer, Tom Jones and their like will be hard on them. So he smiled at them in a way which told them that they had an ally. Oh, names! Out of the seventeen women Norfolk Island would now own, five were Elizabeths, three Anns, and two Marys.

Like several of the other men, the lone marine had not bothered to introduce himself. "Lieutenant King has ordered us to work now," said Richard to him. "Could I trouble you to show us the sawpit?"

Lieutenant King's residence, somewhat larger than the others, stood on a small knoll directly behind the blue-and-yellow landing flag; a Union flag on a second staff closer to the house lay with equal limpness down its mast. The gubernatorial mansion probably contained three small rooms and one attic; no doubt the shed at its rear was its kitchen. There seemed to be a communal oven and cooking area, a smithy, a few buildings which looked as if they stored supplies, each about ten feet by eight, if that. On another rise to the east were extensive cultivated gardens to which all the women, including Ann Innet, were hurrying. And between the two hillocks, among the pines, stood fourteen huts of wooden planks, each very well thatched with some kind of tough, strappy plant; the walls facing the ocean were blank, indicating that their doors looked inland.

The sawpit was close to the beach at the end of a cleared path free of stumps which ran back into the pines; the area around it had also been cleared to make room for dozens of twelve-foot logs, the smallest five feet in diameter. Though he badly wanted to stop to inspect these gargantuan trees he was supposed to reduce to beams and boards, Richard dared not; King's orders were specific and the marine, who had grudgingly admitted that his name was Heritage, did not look the kind to be nice to felons.

Somehow he and his inexperienced little band had to produce enough sawn timber to fill Golden Grove's holds, he presumed within the space of ten to fourteen days. Two small mast logs and what appeared to be a spar had already been prepared and lay to one side, together with a stack of planks. The mast logs and the spar were probably for one of the ships left at Port Jackson.

The sawpit itself was lined with boards to prevent its walls crumbling; it was seven feet deep, eight feet wide and fifteen feet long. Two squared-off beams were mounted across it at five-foot intervals, with rocky rubble banked against the ends of the beams to form sloping ramps. A log minus bark had already been rolled up onto the beams, lying wedged and supported on them lengthwise above the pit, but no one was working and he could see no one in attendance. He found five pit saws varying between eight and fourteen feet in length lying in the bottom of the pit covered with an old sail.

Along came Nathaniel Lucas.

"This is the worst air for iron and steel tools I have ever encountered," he said, dropping into the pit as Richard uncovered the saws. "We cannot keep the wretched things free of rust."

"They are also horribly blunted," said Richard, running the ball of his thumb along one large, wickedly notched tooth. He grimaced. "Whoever sharpened this saw seems to think that the blade bevel goes in the same direction from tooth to tooth instead of in opposite directions. Christ! It will take hours and hours to rectify that, let alone get an edge on the thing. Is there anybody here can teach Blackall, Humphreys and Marriner how to saw?"

"I can teach," said Lucas, a very slight and small man, "but I have not the strength for the pull. I understand what you are saying—you will have to sharpen because that must be done first."

Richard found a ten-foot saw with reasonably sharp teeth. "This is the best of a bad lot—Nat, or Nathaniel?"

"Nat. Are you Richard or Dick?"

"Richard." He looked up at the sun. "We will have to get a shelter over the pit as soon as possible. The sun is much stronger here than in Port Jackson."

"It is more overhead by four degrees of latitude."

"However, a shelter will have to wait until after Golden Grove departs." Richard sighed. "That means hats and a good supply of drinking water. Is there some place Joey can take our belongings before we start? I had best stay here and start sharpening." He sat himself down in the bottom of the sawpit against its eastern edge, still shaded, crossed his legs under him and pulled a twelve-foot saw onto his lap. "Joey, pass down my tool box and then go with Nat, like a good fellow. You others put your things away too, then straight back here."

All of which means that I am once more a head man in charge of men who cannot function without constant direction.

The most popular saw was obviously the twelve-footer; staring up at the log, over five feet in diameter, Richard fully understood why. There were two twelve-footers, one fourteen-footer, one ten-footer and an eight-footer. In another pile beneath the old canvas lay a dozen hand saws also in desperate need of sharpening.

He wrapped his right hand in a bandage of rags, picked up a coarse, flat file wider than the tooth, laid it against the metal at the slight angle necessary to "set" the cutting bevel and drew it downward, always stroking toward the edge of the blade. After the coarse filing of the first section of saw was done, he fine-filed it, then shifted the saw along his lap to come at the next section. When it was all done he would have to remove the rust.

Above him, a little later, he could hear Nat Lucas explaining the saw to Bill Blackall, deputed to work on top of the log, and Willy Marriner, who was to be the bottom man.

"Each tooth is angled in the opposite direction," Nat was saying, "so that the cut is wide enough to allow the body of the blade to pass easily through the timber. If the teeth were all angled the same way, the body of the blade would be wider and would jam. In due time ye'll learn to saw by eye, but to begin with I'll give ye a cord line to saw against. Norfolk pine has to be debarked because the bark oozes resin and would stick the saw in the cut better than glue after two rips. For your first cut ye start on the outside of the log at one side, making your second cut the outside of the log on the other side. Then, alternating sides, ye work inward an inch at a time to make inch-thick sheets until ye get to the heartwood, which ye'll saw for two-inch-wide scantlings at first, then four inches wide and finally six inches wide for beams. 'Tis only on the pull upward—the rip—that the saw cuts, and the man on top is in control. Because he bends and pulls from a crouch upward some two feet—more if he is really strong—his is harder work. On the other hand, the man underneath in the pit gets a face full of sawdust. He returns the saw down by pulling from chest level to groin, farther if the man on top is one of those strong enough to rip up on a three-foot pull."

Marriner appeared in the pit at the far end of the log, where the pair would begin, and gave Richard a wry look.

Nat Lucas was still talking, now to Bill Blackall. "There is a knack in standing, and I recommend bare feet. If ye get your foot in the path of the saw 'twill rip through a shoe like butter, so shoes afford no protection. Ye're standing on a slight curve, one foot either side of the saw, so 'tis easier to balance and hang on firm in bare feet. Ye pull equally with both hands—rip! A pit saw is designed for cutting down the grain, so it is not as hard as cutting across the grain. Since no one in London put in any big two-ended cross grain saws, we use axes to fell and then use a rip saw to cut the logs into twelve-foot lengths, which is hideous hard work."

"Can ye do without the eight-footer?" Richard called.

"Aye, if we have to. Why, Richard?"

"It will take a long time, but I have the instruments to turn a rip saw into a cross cut saw of a sort."

"Oh, God bless ye!" came the fervent reply. Nat's voice went back to Bill Blackall. "Sawing is a thinking man's job," he said. "If ye learn from how it happens, ye'll learn to get the most result from the least effort. Only big men have the strength for this, and I warn ye, for the first few days 'twill kill ye."

"What happens when I get to the support beam?" Blackall asked.

"Ye get help to shift the whole log farther down, which is fairly easy to do once the wedges come off. Then ye wedge it again to keep the sawn section together. And by the time this becomes too hard, ye finish the cut by splitting the rest of the log with a steel wedge and hammer—'tis as straight as a die."

A good man, Nat Lucas, was Richard's verdict, patiently filing.

Lucas, who used a hand saw to cut the inch-thick sheets of timber into ten-inch-wide planks and trim the rounded edges off the outside boards, had set himself up with his saw horses beneath the shade of a pine on the margin of the clearing, and was supervising a large number of other men doing the same thing, including Johnny Livingstone and a dozen off Golden Grove. Lieutenant King's orders were that every possible available person was to lend a hand until Golden Grove's holds were full, and that made the sawpit the center of all activity for the following fourteen days.

Fourteen days during which Richard saw very little beyond saws, files and the sawdust-smothered figure of the bottom man. At first he had hoped to take a turn on the saw itself, but the pace of work meant that he was always sharpening, hand saws as well as pit saws. How, he wondered, was this relative handful of saws to last until more came from England? Every time a tooth was filed, it lost some of its substance.

He had worked until dusk on that first day, when Joey came to find him and tell him there was food. They all ate around a big fire of pine offcuts, for the moment the sun went down a chill greater than that in Port Jackson at this time of year descended. They were served salt meat and fresh-baked bread (it was only six days old—Norfolk Island had been given no hard bread, only flour) and—wonder of wonders!—uncooked green beans and lettuce. Richard ate ravenously, noticing that the loaves of bread were larger and the portions of salt meat less shriveled than what he would have been served in Port Jackson.

"The Commandant is very fair," Eddy Garth explained, "so we get the full ration. In Port Jackson the marines short cut the convicts to give themselves more to eat. As on Scarborough."

"And Alexander." Richard heaved a sigh of happiness. "I had heard, however, that there were no vegetables here—that the grubs had eaten every last leaf and shoot."

Garth put an arm around his wife, who leaned against him with obvious content. " 'Tis true that the grubs eat a great deal, but not everything. The Commandant keeps the women in the patches all day picking the grubs off, and poisons the rats with his port bottles ground to powder in oatmeal—handy for the parrots too." He put a finger to the side of his nose and grinned. "A great port bibber, Mr. King. Gets through several bottles in a day, so we are never short of ground glass. And the grubs come and go. Here a month or six weeks, gone a month or six weeks. There are two sorts. One likes wet conditions, one likes dry conditions. So whatever the weather does, we have grubs. Malign creatures." He cleared his throat. "I do not suppose ye have any books?" he asked casually.

"I do indeed, and ye're welcome to borrow them provided that ye look after them and return them," said Richard. "I wonder how my belly will take greens after so long? Where are the privies?"

"Quite a distance away, so do not leave your run too late. Mr. King is fussy, insisted they be dug where they cannot contaminate the ground water. Our drinking water comes from up the vale, and it is perfect. No one is allowed to wash in it above the spot from which the water is taken, and the penalty for urinating in the stream is a dozen lashes."

"Why should one need to urinate in it? There are trees."

Joey Long, who had eaten earlier because he had to introduce MacGregor to Delphinia, came to show Richard to the privies and then lead him to their house, all by the light of a short piece of pine which ended in a thick knot: the ideal torch.

Richard stared at the interior of the house in amazement.

"It is all ours, yours and mine," said Joey contentedly. "See? It has a window at either end that can be closed by a shutter. See? The wood is pegged into place. But we only put these shutters up if there is a blow—Nat says it is rare for rain to beat in from east or west. Most rain comes from the north."

The floor was a carpet of peculiar—twigs? leaves? They looked for all the world like scaly tails about twelve or fifteen inches long, and felt firm yet yielding underfoot. Beneath them was a thin layer of sand, beneath that was bedrock. Against the windowless wall facing the lagoon stood two low wooden double beds furnished with fat mattresses and fat pillows.

"A double bed all to myself, Joey?" Richard lifted the fat mattress to discover that the bed had a lattice of rope supporting it, then realized that both mattress and pillows were stuffed with feathers. "Feathers!" he exclaimed, laughing. "I have died and gone to heaven."

"This is the sawyer's house," Joey explained, delighted to be the fount of knowledge. "The sawyer was a seaman off Sirius and he shared this house with another seaman off Sirius. They were both drowned in the same accident on the reef almost three months ago, so Nat said. As free men they had the time to go out to the little island and kill some sort of bird to stuff their bedding—it takes a thousand birds to fill one mattress and two pillows, so Nat said. We have inherited the house and the beds." Suddenly he looked downcast. "Though Nat did say that we would have to give them up to Mr. Donovan and Mr. Livingstone as soon as a house is built for Mr. Donovan and Mr. Livingstone. That will happen after Golden Grove sails. For the time being they are staying with Mr. King in Government House. This one is only ten by eight, but Mr. Donovan's house is to be ten by fifteen. Nat has been the head carpenter, but he is a convict, so Mr. Livingstone will be the head carpenter from now on."

"I care not if I have this mattress and pillows for one night," said Richard, "I intend to enjoy them. But first I am going down to the beach to bathe the sweat away. Come on, Joey, you too."

But Joey dug his heels in and refused to budge, terrified at the idea of venturing even knee-deep into water full of invisible monsters waiting to devour him and MacGregor. Richard went alone.

The sky was cloudless, the stars fantastic. Clothes left on the sand, Richard walked into surprisingly cold water and stood enchanted; every ripple he made created shimmers and tremors of light, so that it seemed he bathed in liquid silver. Oh, what a sea! How many wonders did it hold? On fire from within, for what reason he had no idea. All he could do was enjoy it, watch the water slide off his arms in luminous runnels, shake his hair free of glittering droplets. Beautiful! So beautiful. He felt filled with strength, as if this living sea transmitted its energies into his body through a natural magic.

When he turned to emerge he saw that the island was deceptively low from out in the roads; now that he was on it, its hills reared steeply behind this flat saucer of seashore, and everywhere against the starry sky their contours were outlined in spiky pines. Thousands upon thousands of them.

Once dried off and the sticking sand brushed away, he returned to his house and that big feather bed. Where he lay sybaritically, so comfortable that he could not sleep for many hours. Such still air, so few sounds—a sighing rustle, the occasional squealing cry of a sea bird, the soft whoosh of waves advancing and retreating on the reef. Joey did not snore, nor did MacGregor; at this time just over four years ago he had entered the Bristol Newgate, and not a night since had passed without a symphony of snores, even when he had lain alone with Lizzie Lock, for the snores of the men next door penetrated the sapling wall as if through paper. Until tonight. And he could not sleep for the sheer pleasure of it.

One of King's original party, Ned Westlake, had sawn with the drowned Westbrook, so there were two teams to spell each other: Blackall and Marriner, Westlake and Humphreys. The record to date, said Westlake, was 898 superficial feet* of timber in five days, but there had been only the one team to saw. Though he was not a free man like the drowned Westbrook, Richard had—mostly by residence in the sawyer's house, saved for Westbrook's replacement (whom King had assumed would be another free man)—become the head sawyer. His first decision was not popular, but was obeyed; he refused to allow the two teams their elected preference, which was that each team should saw on alternate days.

"If ye do that your muscles will seize up and the pain will be worse," he said. "Bill Blackall and Will Marriner in the mornings, Ned Westlake and Harry Humphreys in the afternoons. Five hours in any one day are enough in a sawpit. Each of the four of ye will take turns to sharpen with me. In time that will give us all a chance to saw and all a chance to sharpen. Whoever is not sharpening or sawing will take an axe and help Joey strip the bark off the logs. The better we get and the faster we get better, the more privileges we will enjoy. To have a craft or trade is far preferable to being at the beck and call of general labor. If I read Lieutenant King aright, on your days off ye'll be allowed to saw timber to put up your own houses. Think of that pleasure! A roof and walls ye can call your own."

By the end of the third day of sawing the pace began to build; by the end of the first week they were sawing 500 superficial feet in a single day, and by the end of the second week that figure had crept to 750. Joey Long was the permanent hand stripping the bark off the logs.

"Well done, everybody!" said Lieutenant King cheerfully to the sawyer teams after Golden Grove sailed on the 28th. "Now we get on and build more houses, as I am informed there will be a great many more people here soon. Sixty at the moment, two hundred by the end of next year—and many more the year after that. His Excellency wants Norfolk Island and Port Jackson to be of equal size."

King paced from one end of the sawpit to the other, then back to the six

* In square, not linear or cubic measure. Thus it represented 30 x 30 feet of cut timber.

assembled men. "I owe ye time off. On Norfolk Island we work Monday to Friday for the Government. Saturdays ye work for yourselves, Sundays ye rest—*after* divine service, which I take and is compulsory for every last soul here, is that understood? While Golden Grove was loading ye've worked for the Government on two Saturdays and two Sundays. Today being Tuesday, no one will work for the Government until next Monday. I advise ye to use some of this time to saw for your own houses—just continue the row eastward. The land behind each house down to the swamp the occupants of that house will use as private vegetable gardens. Cresses grow wonderful well in the swampier bits and the worms cannot eat it, so grow cress, no matter what else ye fancy growing and Stores can give ye."

His eye lighted on Richard, his head sawyer who was not a free man. "Morgan, I need a report. Walk with me, an ye please."

He really does have good manners, thought Richard as he strode alongside the Commandant down the pathway which led from the sawpit to Government House and the storage sheds, one of which, he noted, held the coble and an even smaller boat made from the pieces of the old coble which had foundered on the reef and drowned four men. Willy Dring, Joe Robinson, Neddy Smith and Tom Watson—the four young, strong, unattached, sea-mad men—were to man the coble to fish whenever possible.

"I discovered that my house is not situate in the deep soil that abounds here, so I was able to excavate a sort of soft bedrock and make a nice dry cellar. I did the same under Surgeon Jamison's house, which is now a storehouse—I have shifted him into the vale. The nature of the shore accounts for the fact that all the houses straggle east on this rocky eminence between the straight beach and the swamp—we could fix the support posts in rock," said Lieutenant King as they passed Government House. "D'ye like fish?" he asked, changing the subject with one of those tangential shifts of thought Richard fancied typical of him.

"Aye, sir."

"Ye'd think the buggers would be right glad of fresh fish in lieu of salt meat, but most resent it when I issue fresh fish or turtle instead of salt meat. Baffles me, it really does." He gave a shrug. "So if they are too obstreperous, I lash 'em. Sounds as if I'll not be lashing you, Morgan."

Richard grinned. "I would far rather fish than cat, sir. I have not so far been lashed since I was convicted."

"Aye, that is true of many of ye, I have noted it. Ye did well with the division of labor. One team of sawyers was not enough. What size logs d'ye think the best, given what tools we have?"

"Six-foot diameter at the most, sir, until we are provided with longer pit saws. 'Twould be a help to have a cross cut saw big enough to need two men on it, so I am turning our only eight-foot rip saw into something that will cut across the grain better than the pit saws," said Richard, very comfortable with this man.

He is as different from Major Ross as chalk is from cheese, yet I managed to get on well with Major Ross too. This man is very paternal and regards us as his family, and that is not in the Major's nature. But coming to Norfolk Island has served to show me how much the marines in Port Jackson reduced our rations to supplement their own. For which I cannot blame them. The marines are hungry too. Neither Governor Phillip nor Major Ross ever witnessed what Furzer did in Stores, which only goes to show that the bigger Government is, the less Government knows what goes on at the bottom.

Lieutenant King is scrupulous, keeps the weights himself and checks their weight against his standard set. We have had a meal of fresh turtle and several meals of the most delicious fish I have ever tasted. After the first meal of fresh flesh we all felt a thousand times better. Not to mention that there are always greens to eat. No scurvy in Norfolk Island, despite the grubs and the rats. But I can understand the aversion of some men to marine meals—they did not grow up eating fish and deem meat the only acceptable diet. There is also the need in us for salt. According to Cousin James-the-druggist, the more a man sweats, the more he needs salt.

Yes, I am very content to be here. It is kinder than Port Jackson, and there are no natives to fear if one ventures into the wilds. Though the stories around the camp-fire say that the growth of trees and vines is so dense that even Lieutenant King has been hopelessly lost.

"What have ye to report, Morgan?" King asked as they set off across the swamp on a rickety bridge mounted on piers above felled pine logs sunk into the morass, evidently not a very deep morass.

"Only that the sawpit needs a shelter to keep the sawyers out of the sun as well as the rain, and that if ye want to build something needs longer beams than twelve feet without joining, ye'll have to dig a second pit and make it longer, Mr. King."

"There was a shelter over the sawpit, but it blew down in a winter gale—they are fierce, I can tell ye. I used its relics to shore up the cellar under my house, but I do realize that we will have to build a new shelter, and quickly. The strength in the sun grows every day."

They had crossed the swamp to the far shore of a small stream which seemed to terminate in the swamp rather than run through it; King turned left and began to walk up a path through a meandering valley wider in its bottom than any of the clefts between the steep hills coming down to what King had named Sydney Town.

"What of the saws?" King asked.

"I came just in time," said Richard simply.

"Hmmm. Better then that Major Ross sent you rather than a true sawyer. There was no one here knew more than the rudiments of sharpening. 'Tis cheering to know that ye can convert the eight-footer into a cross cut saw. That will further increase the supply of logs—I note ye've gone through the logs already hauled to the pit."

He stopped just before the vale took a little turn around a bluff coming down from the north. "I call this Arthur's Vale, for His Excellency's Christian name. The big island to the south bears his surname—Phillip Island. Cultivation of plants is gradually being shifted from Sydney Town to here because here affords some protection from the south and west winds, and I hope from the east wind as well on the far side of this bluff. Yon hill to the south between Arthur's Vale and the sea is Mount George, and we are slowly clearing it to plant grain, as also on the hills to the north. We have some wheat and Indian corn in already, and there is barley in the bottom. The new sawpit should go up hereabouts. The present one is too far away, but it can continue to handle twelve-foot logs taken from the hills behind and within Sydney Town itself."

They had rounded the bluff and looked more or less westward; the ground of the vale descended about twenty feet abruptly, the stream tumbling in a thin cascade down the slope. The Commandant pointed to it. "I intend to dam the stream on that incline, Morgan. There is enough hollow ground above the slope to make a capacious pond of water which we can let out through a sluice to irrigate the Government gardens, which will lie not far below it. One day I hope to install a water-wheel on my dam. At the moment we are confined to hand querns for grinding our grain, but we do possess a proper millstone against the day when we have the power to turn it. Did we have oxen or mules we could turn it now. We could also use men to turn it, but of men we have not sufficient either. One day, one day!" He laughed, waved his arms about. "The granary, as ye saw, is just about finished, but I plan to build a big barn and a yard for the animals here on the south bank of the stream. The salt winds, Morgan, the salt winds! They stunt every sort of living thing save pines, flax and the local trees which grow in their lee. I did find the flax—those fools in Port Jackson did not describe the plant properly, was all. It makes excellent thatch, but we have not managed to make canvas out of it."

He laughed again, went back to discussing Arthur's Vale. "Yes, the salt winds. We have to find a better place for the vegetables than a mound looking straight at Phillip Island. I have tried fences to shelter the plants, but they don't help a bit. Therefore the vegetables will be moved into the vale."

Then off he went upon some urgent business apparently suddenly recollected, leaving Richard alone halfway up Arthur's Vale.

The weather was thick and rain threatened; much though he yearned to walk farther up and explore, Richard decided that it was probably prudent to walk back to Sydney Town. In the nick of time: he had no sooner entered his house than it began to pour. Joey came in from their garden in a rush, MacGregor at his heels, and Richard wondered for the first time how he would pass the hours on rainy days until the sawpit received a new roof. Reading was all very well, yet he was getting enough food now to want to expend physical energy. But the rain was warm; he abandoned the hut to Joey, perfectly content to lie on his bed, cuddle the dog and hum tunelessly.

He walked along the hard strand, shoes on—he had been warned that the rock rubble was as sharp as a razor, and had lamed many. The half-circle of Turtle Bay looked as alluring in the rain as it did in the sun, its bottom pure sand, its water crystal, the pines pressing down as far as nurture permitted. He peeled off his drenched clothes and went in to swim, finding the water much warmer in the rain than it was in the sun. Finished, he donned his canvas trowsers together with his shoes, slung his shirt around his shoulders and turned to see if there was any place he might shelter to watch the sea, getting up.

Stephen Donovan had had the same idea; Richard found him in the lee of an outcrop on Point Hunter, where few pines grew, looking down the length of the reef toward the distant out-thrust of Point Ross in the west.

"Did you ever see anything so beautiful?" Stephen asked.

Richard put his shirt on the rock as a cushion and sat with his arms linked about his knees. The rain had cleared for the moment and the wind had veered northward. A great surf thundered in upon the reef, its waves curling over like satin candy rolled around a stick before exploding into walls of white foam. And the wind, blowing briskly in the counter direction, caught the spume and sent it flying backward across the waves in trailing plumes and veils.

"Nay, I do not think I ever have," he said.

"I keep watching to see Aphrodite born."

The sky cleared in the south and west just enough to let the sinking sun turn those drifts of spume to gold, then the rain fell again, but gently.

"I am ravished by this place," said Stephen, sighing.

"Whereas I have spent my time in the bottom of the sawpit with a saw across my knees," said Richard wryly. "How goes it with you?"

"As superintendent of convict labor, ye mean?"

"Aye."

" 'Tis not a wonderful job, Richard. D'ye remember Len Dyer?"

"How could I forget that weasel?"

"He brought things to a head three days ago when he informed me that he was not about to take orders from a shirt-lifting Rome mort turd pusher, and that when he took over the island I would be the first man he would kill. Next to go would be my fancy blond doll, Miss Molly Livingstone. He likes the sound of 'Rome mort' best, it seems—he used it more often than he did 'Miss Molly.' "

"He is a Londoner, 'tis the phrase they use most." Richard turned to stare at him, but Donovan gazed straight ahead. "What happened next, Mr. Donovan?"

"Oh, I wish ye'd call me Stephen! The only one who does is Johnny." The shoulders lifted, his head hunched into them. "I ordered forty-eight lashes and made Private Heritage lay it on. Luckily for me, Dyer had not endeared himself to Heritage either, so he laid it on hard with the meanest cat. There were mutters from Francis, Peck, Pickett and a few others, but after they saw Dyer's back they shut up." His eyes finally slewed to look at Richard, their expression hard. "Ye'd think they would realize a man's preferring his own gender does not indicate that he is soft or timid, would ye not? But no! Well, I have survived over fifteen years at sea and gained respect, so I am not about to take cheek from the likes of a Len Dyer. As he now understands."

"I would watch my back if I were you," said Richard. "The pity of it is that I scarcely know what is going on among those not concerned with the sawpit, but Golden Grove told me that there was something ominous in the air. Just what, I do not know. Nothing was said or done in my vicinity, since I'd kicked them in the cods. Perhaps Dyer was testing the temperature of the water in your vicinity when he spoke insolently. If that was the case, then he now has ye down in his book as"—Richard grinned—"no simpering Rome mort. Sincerely, watch your back."

Stephen rose to his feet. "Dinner time," he said, extending a hand to pull Richard up. "If ye hear anything at all, tell me."

* * *

The carpenters were busy building a shelter for the sawpit the next morning, so as soon as he had eaten his leftover bread and a few mouthfuls of cress, Richard set off up Arthur's Vale, keeping to the north side of the stream. Close to where Lieutenant King had indicated that he intended to build a large barn, a group of convicts were beginning to dig a new sawpit long enough to take a thirty-foot log. All the malcontents were on the job save the temporarily ruined Dyer, Stephen supervising—with two of the new marines off Golden Grove as guards, Richard was pleased to see.

Stephen does not wish more ardently than I do that I could call him by his name, Richard thought as he gave Donovan a wave. But I am a felon and he a free man. It is not fitting.

He continued around the north bluff to where the brook gushed down that slope where King wanted a dam. Standing on top of the rise, he could see why the Commandant considered a dam feasible, for there was indeed a big depression in the ground before the vale widened yet again.

Clearing of the trees had progressed some distance farther on and was creeping up the lower slopes of the hills, quite as steep as those along the back of Sydney Town. When he saw the plantains he recognized them for what they were from drawings in his books, and marveled at their height and maturity—such growth in a mere eight months? No, that was not possible. King had gotten into the vale only recently, which meant that the plantain grew in Norfolk Island naturally. A gift from God: the long bunches of a little green banana were already formed, so in months to come there would be fruit to eat—filling fruit at that.

As the vale narrowed again the clearing stopped abruptly, though a track continued into the forest alongside the stream, which here was some feet deep in places and so clear that Richard could see tiny, almost transparent shrimp swimming in it. Around the dinner camp-fire they had talked of large eels, but these he did not glimpse.

Brilliant green parrots flashed overhead and a weeny fantail fluttered twittering only inches from his face, as if trying to tell him something; it kept him company for at least a hundred yards, still trying to communicate. He thought he saw a quail, and then stumbled upon the most beautiful dove in the world, soft pink-brown and iridescent emerald green. So tame! It simply glanced at him and waddled off, head bobbing, quite indifferently. There were other birds too, one of which looked to be a blackbird save that its head was grey. The air was full of song unlike any he had heard in Port Jackson. Melodic except for the parrots, which screeched.

At no time since his arrival had he been able to stand back and take in the sight of a Norfolk pine, for the simplest of reasons: a lone Norfolk pine did not exist, and King's clearing technique so far was to denude an area of every tree rather than to leave an odd one standing. He had discovered that the tails carpeting the floor of his hut were the leaves of the pine, if leaves they could be called. On either side of the track was the forest, an impenetrable wilderness he was not tempted to enter, though it bore no resemblance to what his reading had led him to believe was a jungle. Small plants did not exist, starved out by the pines, which grew very close together and must surely produce but few young; some were fifteen and more feet in diameter, most were about the size of the logs he had been sharpening the saws to cut, and a very few only were slender. Their roughish bark was brown with purple in it and they grew amazingly tall before they gave out branches. Occasional leafy green trees were sprinkled among them, but most of the space was taken up by a climbing vine the like of no vine anywhere. Its major trunks were as thick as a man's thigh, and twisted, turned, ran back upon themselves, soared upward in gnarled humps and knees, were entangled in the thinner parts of the vine's chaotic randomness. When it encountered a tree small enough to throttle, it did so, or else bent the hapless thing sideways and compelled it to continue its upward course feet from the place where its trunk left the ground.

The valley broadened a little to reveal more plantains having bunches of green fruit and showed him yet another bizarre tree which, like the plantains, confined itself to the watercourse area. This new plant had a round trunk a little like a palm's—they were there too, with stiff, erect fronds rather than graceful ones—but plated with sharp-ended knobs; at the very top spread a canopy of what could only be fern leaves. A giant fern! A fern that grew as a forty-foot tree!

More birds arrived, among them a small kingfisher in cream, brown and a brilliant, iridescent blue-green exactly the color of the lagoon. The most mysterious bird he did not see until it moved, for it looked like a continuation of the mossy stump upon which it perched. The movement was sudden and startling: Richard jumped involuntarily. The thing was an enormous parrot.

"Hello," he said. "How are you today?"

It cocked its head to one side and stalked toward him, but he had the wisdom not to hold his hand out; that huge, wicked black beak was powerful enough to take a finger off. Then, it seemed deciding that he was beneath contempt, it disappeared into the ferny or broad-leafed undergrowth along the banks of the brook.

On the way back he noticed a shrub which seemed able to compete with the forest giants, its trunk very smooth and rosy, its leafy branches loaded with bright red berries the size of small plums. Will I, or won't I? Some weeks before he drowned, the unfortunate sawyer, Westbrook, had eaten a local fruit he mistook for a Windsor bean and nearly died. Richard pressed one of the berries to find it hard and unyielding; whatever it was, it was certainly not yet ripe. Later, he promised himself, I will try just one. I do not believe that eating one of anything can kill.

The sun was westering as he retraced his steps and emerged into Arthur's Vale; time to join the others and eat. This place is unique, not to be compared with New South Wales in any way whatsoever. Different trees, different soil, different hills, different rocks, and not one single blade of any kind of grass. Perhaps this was God's first attempt to create land out of the sea? Or perhaps it was His last attempt? If His last, then He gave it no people. Which might lead a man like Jem Thistlethwaite to say that God had come to the conclusion that Man was not a desirable addition to His menagerie.

"Are there any snakes?" he asked Nat Lucas, whom he liked very much, as he did old Dick Widdicombe, full seventy years old—*why* had London sent aged men to hew out a new place?

"If there are, they have remained invisible," Nat said. "No one has seen a lizard, a frog or a leech either. Ground animals seem to be absent save for the rat, though it does not look like our rats. The Norfolk Island one is a soft grey with a white belly and is not enormously large."

"But it eats anything," said Ned Westlake. "A rat is a rat."

At dawn on the morrow Richard turned his footsteps eastward, choosing to walk along the sand of Turtle Bay before scrambling up and over to yet another lovely beach, this one unprotected by a reef; here the sand had spread inland upon a raft of petrified logs, and beyond this beach some distance around the shore reared a massive cliff. Yet more pine forest; it truly was everywhere, and always impenetrable. The only way he could proceed was to hug the rocks, a dangerous alternative in the face of a heavy sea. Today, however, was perfect weather, and the brisk breeze blew from the northwest. The tide was on the ebb, so he must make sure that he returned before it reached half-flood. Two little brooks joined forces in a small flat area beyond which the water glowed an ethereal aquamarine. For a short while he tried to climb up the cleft which led to that mighty headland, but gave it up. Not sensible.

So he returned to Turtle Bay to discover two men he had not seen before heaving a gigantic turtle onto its back, where it lay, flippers waving, utterly helpless.

They had to be brothers, and they did not wear the look of men who had spent time in an English prison. Both spare, young, decent-looking; brown of skin, brown of hair, brown of eye.

"Ahah! Ye must be Morgan," said one. "I am Robert Webb and this is my brother, Thomas. We go by our full names. Help us to tether this beauty—there will be turtle for dinner tomorrow."

Richard helped tie a rope firmly around the creature's chest where its flippers would prevent the rope's sliding off.

"We are the gardeners," said Robert, who, if he were not the elder, was certainly the spokesman. "I thank ye for bringing us women. Thomas is not keen for a woman, but I was desperate."

"Whom did ye choose?" asked Richard, wondering why he was to be thanked.

"Beth Henderson, a good woman. Which means Thomas and I have come to the parting of the ways," said Robert cheerfully, while his brother grimaced. "He has gone to live with Mr. Altree in Arthur's Vale, where there is much planting going on."

The turtle was hauled into the water and towed, the men knee-deep, around the point of Turtle Bay. Richard helped the Webbs bring it up the straight beach near the landing place, then left them to return to his hut.

"Lieutenant King was looking for you," said Joey.

So off Richard went again; he found the Commandant at the site of the second sawpit, excavated in soil and so needing to be shored up with timber.

"There is turtle, sir," said Richard, saluting.

"Oh, splendid! Dashed good!" King turned to walk off a little way and faced his head sawyer. "I do not allow many turtle to be turned, otherwise there will end in being none," he said. "Nor do I permit the eggs to be dug out. 'Tis not as turtle-populous as Lord Howe Island to begin with, so why ruin a good thing?"

"Aye, sir."

Lieutenant King then demonstrated one of the more exasperating facets of his nature: he clean forgot what he had said two days ago when he congratulated his sawing teams and gave them time off until Monday. "Ye'll be back sawing tomorrow," he announced, "and I intend to build a third sawpit farther up the vale beyond where the dam will be. That means more sawyers. I understand enough about the work to know that it is exceeding hard and cannot be done by weak men, but I leave it to you to pick out the men ye want, Morgan. Ye can have your choice of any provided they are not carpenters. The old pit's shelter is up, so ye'll start sawing there tomorrow—planks for the granary ceiling. And ye'll continue to do this on Saturday, even though by rights the day should be yours. I need the granary finished, there are crops close to harvesting." He prepared to go. "Think about whom ye want, Morgan, and let me know on Monday."

"Aye, sir," said Richard woodenly.

Two sawpits meant four teams: three sawpits meant six teams. Christ, he would never have a chance to saw! Ned Westlake, Bill Blackall and Harry Humphreys could not seem to learn to use a file properly. The only man who had shown any kind of aptitude was Will Marriner, who would have to be left at the old sawpit to sharpen while he hied himself to Arthur's Vale. The saws needed touching up every ten to twelve feet along a cut. But who would be willing to saw? Men hated it, did it grudgingly. Weasels like Len Dyer, Tom Jones, Josh Peck and Sam Pickett were impossible. John Rice, one of the originals, had the build for it, but he was the ropemaker and therefore unavailable. John Mortimer and Dick Widdicombe were too old, and Noah Mortimer was an idler, always in trouble for not pulling his weight. If a man disliked physical labor, he was not capable of doing any work without being driven to it, and that was Noah. The very young original, Charlie McClellan, was another such.

Who then off Golden Grove? John Anderson, yes. Sam Hussey, yes. Jim Richardson, yes. Willy Thompson, yes. But that was the end of the supply. Richardson, who had taken up with Susannah Trippett, would manage the job with equanimity, if not enthusiasm. Hussey and Thompson were peculiarities, already busy building themselves huts of their own because they could not bear company; they both reminded Richard of Taffy Edmunds. As for Anderson—he was an unknown quantity. At divine service on Sunday at eleven in the morning, Richard thanked God for his convict status: it would never be in his province to order a man flogged. He had to find other ways to ensure that his sawyers worked, chiefly by pairing one good man with one doubtful one. Never two doubtfuls together.

"Four teams are as many as I can scrape up," he informed Stephen when they met at Turtle Bay for a swim on Sunday evening. "I am doomed to sharpen forever, it seems. Such a simple job, ye'd think, Mr. Donovan, and yet most men lack the—the *idea* of it. They take no care to set the teeth at the right bevel, nor do they have the eyes in the tips of their fingers a man must have. Oh, I wish I had Taffy Edmunds! Not only can he sharpen as well as I, but he would like it here."

"More are coming, so I understand, though Supply cannot carry many at once. And, since they are finding some trees they can cut in Port Jackson, I fear ye won't see Taffy landed here in a hurry. Richardson is a good, strong fellow, he will work out, I think. Who knows? Perhaps one of this second four will turn out to have a talent for sharpening. Though why, Richard, ye should want to saw yourself baffles me," said Stephen.

"Because to the men who saw, my job is child's play. I sit cross-legged like a tailor and appear to be doing nothing. One reason why I put them all to it, and will go on putting them to it. Each of them knows that if he should prove good at sharpening, he has a comfortable job. When they fail, at least they know that sharpening is a job of patience and skill."

Stephen lay back on the sand and stretched voluptuously. "Ye would think," he said, "that Johnny, being a seaman, would be down here with us. But no, he would rather be outside our house, planing or polishing some fancy piece of wood. He will have finished the balusters for Port Jackson's Government House by the time Supply returns, whenever that might be. How isolated we are! More than a thousand miles across an empty ocean to the only other place an Englishman can be found. I feel it every time I look at the horizon. This isle is a gigantic ship at anchor in the midst of a nowhere, surrounded by infinity. It is completely its own entity."

Richard rolled over to dry his back. "I do not feel that this isle is small, though I agree about the isolation. To me, Norfolk Island seems quite as large as New South Wales. Here lies a certain privacy. I do not feel as if I am a prisoner, whereas everything at Port Jackson reminded me I was a prisoner."

"More officials," said Stephen dryly.

"Is your Johnny getting on with the carpenters?"

"Oh, yes. Mostly thanks to the fact that he sticks to his lathe and has more sense than to tell Nat Lucas how to do his job or how to make sure the others do their jobs. 'Tis I suffer."

"Just watch your back—I have a feeling."

"D'ye want me to pull your four new sawyers out of the gang?"

"It has to be either you or Lieutenant King. Whoever."

"I will do it. King is a will o' the wisp—he darts here, there and everywhere. Always starting new things before the old are done, and never stopping to remember that he has too few hands to do what has been started, let alone deal with new work as well. That is why I insisted that he finish the granary before he lifts a finger to build the barn or the dam. In the midst of which he wants more houses built, if you please! But then, he has never served on any but big ships, wherein more hands run around than are necessary save in a battle or a blow."

"Which reminds me, Mr. Donovan. Joey and I are sleeping in double beds with feather mattresses and feather pillows. By rights they belong to you and Mr. Livingstone."

That provoked gales of laughter. "Keep them, ye hedonists! Neither Johnny nor I would sleep in anything other than a hammock." He looked at Richard with a derisive gleam in his fine blue eyes. "When men make love, Richard, they do not need to have a big bed. 'Tis women like comfort."

Richard took Ned Westlake and Harry Humphreys with him to the new sawpit in Arthur's Vale together with Jim Richardson and Juno Anderson, as this John called himself.

Naturally the pace slowed greatly, much to Lieutenant King's displeasure. "It has taken ye five days to produce but seven hundred and ninety-one feet of timber!" he said to Richard indignantly.

"I know, sir, but two of the four teams are new to the work and the other two are busy instructing," Richard explained respectfully but firmly. "Ye must expect less wood for a while." He drew a deep breath and decided to say it all. "Also, sir, ye cannot expect the sawing teams or me to strip bark as well. The old sawpit has Joseph Long permanently stripping and one of the others assisting him, whereas the new sawpit has no regular hand preparing the logs. I am sharpening, and I have no time to do aught else because I have to do the big sets for Marriner as well as keep my men going here. Is it not possible for those who fell the trees to debark them the moment they are down? The longer the bark stays on, the more risk there is of the beetle which eats the wood getting into it. And there should be one man felling who has the skill to look at each tree before it is felled to assess its sawing worth. Half the logs we receive are of no use, but by the time we can look at them ourselves, the men who have hauled them to the sawpit have vanished. So we have to waste our valuable time shifting them to the burning heap."

Oh, the Lieutenant did not like that speech! His face was frowning direfully before half of it was said. In which case, thought Richard, holding those angry hazel eyes without flinching, I am in for a flogging for insolence. Yet better now than later, when the situation grows worse because he decides on a third pit, leaving us with only one spare saw now that I have amended the eight-footer into a cross-cut tool.

"We shall see," said King eventually, and marched off in the direction of the carpenters and his new granary. Every inch of his retreating form radiated offended feelings.

"What," asked King of Stephen Donovan over lunch in Government House, "d'ye make of the supervisor of sawyers?"

The very pregnant Ann Innet did not sit with them to eat, just brought the food and disappeared. The port decanter was half-empty and would be a marine before lunch was over; the Commandant was always more mellow in the afternoons than in the mornings, a fact Richard Morgan was unaware of. Port was King's besetting sin; never a day went by that he did not get through at least two bottles of it. No keg port for Philip Gidley King! He liked the best, which came already bottled and was laid down carefully for at least a month before he personally decanted each bottle.

"Richard Morgan, ye mean?"

"Aye, Morgan. Major Ross said he would be an asset, but I am not so sure. The fellow had the effrontery to stand up to me this morning—virtually told me I am going about things the wrong way!"

"Yes, Morgan has the sinew to do that—but not, I hazard a guess, in an insolent fashion. He was on Alexander and proved of great service in the matter of Alexander's bilge pumps—d'ye not remember coming aboard her shortly before we reached Rio? 'Twas Morgan said flatly that only chain pumps could remedy the problem."

"Gammon!" snapped King, blinking in amazement. "Utter gammon! *I* recommended chain pumps!"

"Ye did indeed, sir, but Morgan was before ye. Had Morgan not convinced Major Ross and Surgeon-General White that hard measures were necessary, ye would never have been summoned to Alexander," said Stephen valiantly.

"Oh. Oh, I see. But that does not alter the fact that Morgan exceeded his authority this morning," King maintained stubbornly. "It is not his place to criticize my arrangements. I ought to have him flogged."

"Why flog a useful and hardworking man because he has a head on his shoulders?" Stephen asked, leaning back easily and declining the port. Another glass of it and King would be more malleable. "Ye know he has a head on his shoulders, Mr. King. His intention was not insolent—he is a man cares about his work, is all. He wants to produce more," Stephen labored.

The Commandant looked unconvinced.

"Sir, be fair! If I had suggested the changes—what precisely were they, may I ask?"

"That no one is inspecting the trees before they are hauled to the pits—that no one is stripping the logs of their bark—that stripping ought to be done when the trees are felled—that the sawyers waste too much time dragging unusable logs to the burning heap—and so on, and so forth."

Sip away, Lieutenant King, sip away. Stephen said nothing as his superior sipped away. Finally, one glass of port later, he held out his hand and looked imploring. "Mr. King, if I had said what Morgan did, would ye not have listened?"

"The simple fact is, Mr. Donovan, that ye did not."

"Because I am elsewhere and ye have a supervisor of sawyers—*Morgan!* They are all sensible observations and all designed to see more timber sawn. Why put wagon harness on your saddle horses, sir? Ye have an excellent team of woodworkers and carpenters, and I note ye display no aversion to listening to whatever Nat Lucas has to say. Well, in Richard Morgan ye have another Nat Lucas. If I were you, I would use his talents. His sentence finishes in two years. Were he to develop a fondness for this place, ye'd have some continuance, as with Lucas."

And that, Stephen Donovan decided, was enough on the subject. The petulance was leaving King's face, and he did have many good qualities. A pity that he so disliked being told where he had gone wrong by a convict.

By the end of November the humidity was such that the hours of labor were changed. Work commenced at dawn and continued until half past seven, when everyone had half an hour for breakfast; at eleven in the morning work ceased and did not resume until half past two, then ended at sunset. And the first harvest came in, an acre of barley which yielded 80 gallons of valuable seed despite the grubs and rats. This was followed by 3 quarts of wheat from the 260 ears the grubs and rats had not destroyed; could the pests only be controlled, this magnificent soil could grow anything.

The little red plums—cherry guavas—had ripened and were so delicious that the temptation to eat too many was hard to resist; resigned to gluttony, Surgeon Jamison declared that no free man or felon would be let off work because of diarrhoea. The bananas were ripe too. Catches of fish came in on occasions Richard looked forward to very much. In this taste he had few companions—and quite a lot more fish than he was entitled to. He had discovered that the fish lasted another day if it were submerged in a cold and shady current of salt water, so was happy to trade his next day's ration of salt meat for someone else's despised fish. Such *delicious* fish! Not unlike a snapper, it could be grilled in a fire and eaten down to the very few bones. Shark was good eating, so too were the hundred-pound ugly monsters which lurked in reef crannies, and a local kingfish that grew to a length of eight feet. The only trouble was that the fish were capricious; on some days the coble would come in with a hundred, on other days with none.

Toward Christmas, Lieutenant King decided to send Assistant Surgeon John Turnpenny Altree, Thomas Webb and Juno Anderson to live permanently at Ball Bay, a stony beach on the eastern side of the island wherein Supply was occasionally forced to anchor. His intention was that the three men should clear and keep clear a channel through the round, kettle-sized rocks so that a ship's boat could land; the basalt boulders stove a boat's keel in. This decision of King's was one which provoked covert winks and smirks all round. Altree, a strange and ineffectual man who had not been able to face doctoring the female convicts of Lady Penrhyn, avoided women as if they carried plague. Wherever he went, so too would Thomas Webb go, eased out of his brother's life by Beth Henderson and fled to Altree for succor. Delighted at the prospect of abandoning his wife and his job as a sawyer, Juno Anderson went to dance attendance on the two free custodians of Ball Bay. It was no more than a mile away, but was so cut off by the forest that Joe Robinson, trying to find his way back to Sydney Town, was lost for two nights. A path to Ball Bay was therefore mandatory, though no trees were felled to make it. The massively thick, strangulating vine between the pines was easily severed by one blow from an axe, and its bark, the path hewers discovered, made quite good twine provided the lengths were kept short.

Richard was now down two sawyers, and of prospective sawyers there were none until Supply returned—if Supply ever did. Jim Richardson had ventured out on a Sunday in quest of bananas and broken his leg so badly that it would be months healing; he would never saw again. And Juno Anderson was no loss, a sentiment his wife echoed heartily.

This meant that Richard would have to saw himself; the three-and-a-half-hour midday break would have to be spent sharpening, as would every other second of spare time. But who as a partner?

"Needs must," said the Commandant, having long since recovered from his miff at Morgan's presumption. "I shall ask Private Wigfall if he would care to make an additional wage as a sawyer. He has the body and stature of a boxer."

"A good choice, sir," said Richard, then pretended to be horrified. "What if Private Wigfall cannot saw straight and has to be the bottom man? It is not seemly for a convict to give a marine free man a face full of sawdust."

"He can wear a hat," said King blithely, and hurried off.

Luckily Private William Wigfall was a typical large and burly fellow: habitually phlegmatic, impossible to rile. He hailed from Sheffield and owned no close friends among his tiny detachment.

"My friends all remained at Port Jackson," he said to Richard. "Honestly, I am right glad for the chance to get away from this lot, not to mention that I will earn more for sawing than I do for being a marine. I will be able to retire earlier. 'Tis my ambition to buy an acre of good ground with a nice little cottage on it somewhere near Sheffield. If I work my passage home as a sailor I will have even more money."

"D'ye mind if I try being the man on top of the log first?" asked Richard. "My eye is very straight, so I am curious to see if that holds true when I am sawing. Besides, being bottom man is easier on the muscles. Unfortunately ye will not be able to wear a hat—ye have to stand too close to the saw. I will yell as I begin my pull to give ye the chance to look down."

His eye proved straight; Wigfall's did not. The work was every bit as grueling as Richard had thought, but Wigfall turned out to be a magnificent partner, capable of a tremendous pull downward. But I could never have done this in Port Jackson on those miserable rations. Here, between the fish, the occasional turtle and the masses of green vegetables and turnips—not to mention the better bread—I can saw without losing more weight than I can afford. For a man of forty, I am in far better condition than Lieutenant King is at a mere thirty.

At Christmastide the Commandant killed a large pig just for his convict family, so on that dark and windy day the porker was spitted over a fire of smoldering coals and roasted until its skin crackled and bubbled up crisply; each man and woman got a double portion, there were scarce potatoes to go with it, and a half-pint of rum to wash the meal down. This was the first roast meat that Richard had eaten since his days at the Cooper's Arms—incredibly delicious! As were the potatoes. Dear Lord, he prayed that night as he tumbled into his feather bed, I am so very grateful. Only those who have truly wanted can ever enjoy simple plenty.

For the next few days it rained and blew too hard for outside work, though, as both sawpits were sheltered, the sawyers continued to cut logs into planks, scantlings and beams; Government House was receiving some additions, Stephen Donovan was getting a new house in close proximity to the Commandant's, and all the sawyers were allowed to cut timber to build themselves private dwellings. Nor was Richard, already possessed of a good house, unwilling to saw for his teams' houses.

New Year of 1789 dawned clear and fine; the convicts were given a half-day off work and a quarter-pint of rum. Thanks to the subtle and unobtrusive exertions of his supervisors, Lieutenant King was settling into something vaguely like a routine—please, sir, if we finish what we have started, it will mean we can devote all our attention to the new work in its turn. . . .

King's joy overflowed when his healthy son by Ann Innet was born eight days into 1789. As the only person who conducted religious worship, King baptized the boy himself and christened him "Norfolk."

"Norfolk King has a pleasing sound," said Stephen to Richard on the sand at Turtle Bay. "I am delighted for him. He needs to have a family, though 'twill not help his naval career to marry Mistress Innet. But a more doting father would be hard to imagine. Things will go hard for him when comes the time he must leave for England—what to do with a much-loved bastard, not to mention the mother? He is very fond of her."

"He will solve all his dilemmas," said Richard tranquilly. "A flightier commanding officer would be hard to find, but he lacks neither honor nor a sense of responsibility. There are some things he cannot deal with happily—routine, for one—and he has a hot temper. Witness Mary Gamble."

Mary Gamble provoked that hot temper when she threw an axe at a boar and severely wounded it. Furious at the near-demise of this immensely valuable animal, King refused to listen to her frenzied explanation that the boar had charged her and she had thrown the axe in self-defense. Before his temper cooled he levied the atrocious number of a dozen-dozen lashes at the cart's tail upon her. Once calm returned, he was aghast—strip that gallant creature to the waist before men like Dyer and give her 144 licks of the cat, even the kindest cat among the assortment? Oh, Christ, he could not do it! What if the boar had indeed charged her? The axe she had by right, as she was one of the women deputed to debark pine logs. Oh, Jesus! He had never ordered half that many lashes for a man! What a pickle! So he summoned Mary Gamble to Government House and announced in lordly tones that he forgave her.

His conduct of this debacle told a few of the convicts that he was stupid, soft-hearted and weak; certain plans already in train were advanced in time because it was so obvious that King had neither the stomach nor the kidney for harsh action.

Robert Webb the gardener came to see him urgently. "Sir, there is a plot afoot," he said.

"A plot?" King asked blankly.

"Aye, sir. A great many of the felons plan to take you, Mr. Donovan, the other free men and all the marines prisoner. They are then going to wait for the next ship, take her, and sail her to Otaheite."

The Commandant's face paled from brown to dirty white; he stared at Webb incredulously. "Jesus Christ! Who, Robert, who?"

"From what I was told, sir, all but three of the convicts off Golden Grove, and"—he swallowed, blinked away tears—"a few of our original party."

"How quickly the rot sets in, Robert," King said slowly. "If just one fresh intake of felons has caused this, what is going to happen when His Excellency sends hundreds more?" He passed his hand across his eyes to brush away moisture. "Oh, I am *hurt!* A few of our originals. . . . How could they be so foolish? Noah Mortimer and that silly youth Charlie McClellan are the originals, I imagine." He set his shoulders and squared his jaw. "How did ye discover this?"

"My woman told me, sir—Beth Henderson. William Francis got her on her own and asked her to see if I would be in it. She pretended to agree to persuade me to be in it, then told me."

The sweat was running into his eyes; high summer at these latitudes made the uniform of a naval lieutenant—and a commandant at that, doomed always to be in uniform—a torment to wear. "Who off Golden Grove are the three not involved?" he asked, voice thin.

"The Catholic, John Bryant. The sawyer Richard Morgan and his simple hut companion, Joseph Long," said Webb.

"Well, of the latter pair, one is too busy at the sawpits and the other, as ye say, is a simpleton. 'Tis the Catholic Bryant I will learn from, he works with them. Go to his hut from here and fetch him to me as quietly as ye can, Robert. This being a Saturday, Sydney Town is fairly deserted—they all like to think I do not notice that they have vanished into Arthur's Vale. Also ask Mr. Donovan to report to me immediately."

Lieutenant King's talents shone at full brilliance in dealing with concrete peril; it was all over and done with before one of the ringleaders knew he had been detected.

Armed with their rusted muskets, the marines took the dangerous men into custody—William Francis, Samuel Pickett, Joshua Peck, Thomas Watson, Leonard Dyer, James Davis, Noah Mortimer and Charles McClellan. Exhaustive examination winnowed out the real villains; though almost every convict on the island had indicated a wish to be in the coup provided it succeeded, only a handful were actively involved. Francis and Pickett were put into double irons and confined in the stoutest storehouse; Watson and Mortimer were fettered and released until Monday's full enquiry brought the whole story out.

A startled Richard Morgan was told to walk at once to Ball Bay and fetch its three custodians into the Sydney Town fold, while King arranged his scant supply of free men and marines around his end of the beach and the convicts were ordered on pain of being shot to remain in their huts.

"And as if that were not enough," said King to Donovan in huge indignation, "Corporal Gowen found Thompson pilfering Indian corn in the vale! From which, given what Robert and Bryant have told me, I gather that men like Thompson thought the island would be taken over by Francis before I could flog him for theft. He is mistaken."

"They should have waited until Supply was in the roads and our attention was taken up in that direction," said Stephen thoughtfully, too tactful to add that King's conduct in the Mary Gamble business was the reason for the plot's advancement in time. "What of the women, sir?"

King shrugged. "Women are women. They are neither the cause nor the trouble."

"Whom will ye punish?"

"As few as I can," King said, looking worried. "Otherwise I stand no hope to keep control of Norfolk Island, ye must surely see that, Mr. Donovan. Hardly a musket fires and there are many more of them than of us. But most of them are sheep, they need leaders. That is our salvation provided that I do not punish the sheep. I will have to wait until Supply comes, send word to Port Jackson on her, and then wait for her to return before I will be able to ship the ringleaders to stand trial in Port Jackson."

"Why," asked Stephen dreamily, "do I have a feeling that ye'll not solve Norfolk Island's difficulties by shipping them to Port Jackson and the Governor's justice?"

King's eyes flashed angrily. "Because," he said grimly, "I am well aware that most of those on Golden Grove were sent here to rid Port Jackson of them. His Excellency will not want them back, especially branded as mutineers. He would have to hang them, and he is not a man likes to see others at the end of a rope. If he is forced to hang, he would rather that the crime was committed under the gaze of those around him, not a thousand miles away in a place he has been using as an example of felicitous success. Norfolk Island is too isolated to prosper under a system which delegates the real authority to men who are not here, to men who are more than a thousand miles away. The Government in Norfolk Island ought to have authority over Norfolk Island's affairs. But I am strapped. I must first wait months, then no doubt will not get answers which improve Norfolk Island's lot."

"Just so," sighed Stephen. "It is a cleft stick." He leaned forward eagerly. "Sir, ye have a master gunsmith right here in the island who was not implicated in the plot—Morgan the sawyer. May I humbly request that ye set him at once to fixing our firearms? Then on every Saturday morning the free men, marines and Morgan will shoot for two hours. I will undertake to set up a proving butt beyond the eastern end of Sydney Town, and also undertake the supervision of firing practice. Provided that ye give me Morgan."

"An excellent idea! See to it, Mr. Donovan." The Commandant grunted. "If, as I expect, His Excellency does not want any of our mutineers sent to trial in Port Jackson, then he will have to send me a bigger detachment of marines under the command of a proper officer, not a mere sergeant. And I want some cannons. Plus powder, shot and cartridges aplenty for the muskets." He looked brisk. "I shall draft a letter this instant. And from now on, Superintendent of Convicts, ye will see a stricter discipline enforced. If flogging is what they want, then flogging is what they will get. *I am hurt!* Wounded to the quick! My happy little family has serpents in its midst, with many more serpents to come."

It was John Bryant the fanatically devout Catholic who bore the brunt of convict resentment once the hearing of testimony was over. His evidence was all the more damning because he also told of a plan aboard Golden Grove to take her over—a plan foiled when he informed Captain Sharp. The blame for the Norfolk Island revolt fell upon William Francis and Samuel Pickett, who were to be kept permanently in double irons and permanently locked up. Noah Mortimer and Thomas Watson were put in light fetters at the Commandant's pleasure, and the rest of those questioned were dismissed.

The most tragic consequence of the January plot concerned the beauty of tiny Sydney Town, graced by the presence of tall pines and leafy "white oaks." Lieutenant King took every last tree away, even cleared lower vegetation; a marine could stand at either end of the settlement and see any coming and going between the huts, even after dark. Tom Jones, an intimate of Len Dyer's, received 36 lashes from the meanest cat for contemptuous sexual references aimed at Stephen Donovan and Surgeon Thomas Jamison.

"The climate has changed," said Richard to Stephen as they dealt with muskets preparatory to the first shooting practice, "and it saddens me. I like this little place, could be happy here were it not for other men. But I do not want to live in this village any longer. The trees are gone and so is the privacy—a man cannot piss without a dozen others watching. I want to be somewhere on my own so that I can mind my own business and confine my contacts with my fellow convicts to the sawpits."

Stephen blinked. "D'ye dislike them so much, Richard?"

"I like some of them very well. It is the villains always spoil things—and for what? Can they never learn? Take poor Bryant. They have vowed to get him, you know, and they will."

"As Superintendent of Convicts I will exert every effort to make sure they do not get him. Bryant has a very nice little wife and they love each other madly. Were anything to happen to him, she would become a lost soul."

1789 was not coming in well. There had been intermittent rain and gales which ruined the rest of the barley, spoiled some casks of flour, made fishing impossible on most days, and life in the denuded collection of wooden huts a jeremiad of wet clothes, damp bedding, mold on precious books and precious shoes, summer colds, sick headaches and painful bones. Halfway through February the Commandant released Francis and Pickett from their storehouse and returned them to their huts free of manacles but heavily ironed on their legs. Of Supply there was no sign; the last ship to call had been Golden Grove, and that was now four months ago. Were they never going to see another ship? Had something happened to Supply? To Port Jackson?

Everybody was grumpy thanks to the foul weather, none grumpier than the Commandant, who was engineer enough to realize that he did not dare commence building a dam in the midst of such downpours, and had a crying baby in the house. Most of the work had to be postponed and too many people had little to do beyond grumble. The only truly happy persons were the three men at Ball Bay, snug under the pine trees in a good house, well provisioned, and able to rock fish no matter how hard it rained.

Even so, the 26th of February came as a mighty shock. Dawn arrived with high winds just to the south of east and seas so high that the surf broke all the way into the beaches of the lagoon. To Stephen and Richard, who walked as far out on Point Hunter as they dared, the sight of the coastline to the west was a terrifying vista of white water crashing down so hard and high against the cliffs that the spray soared up over 300 feet and blew inland as far as the mountain four miles away.

"God help us, we are in for the father of all gales!" Stephen shouted. "We had best be sure they are battening down the hatches!"

By the time they fought their way around Turtle Bay and turned to look back, not only had lofty Phillip Island disappeared; so also had Nepean Island, close in shore. The world was a seething mass of waves as big as those in the southern ocean on the voyage from the Cape of Good Hope, and the wind continued to rise even as it swung to the southeast, throwing the whole force of sea and sky straight at the settlement. Bent double in the blast, people were shooing pigs and poultry into the storehouses and huts, piling logs against their doors and climbing inside through their windows.

So huge were the noises of howling wind and thundering water that neither Richard nor Stephen noticed the shrieking groan of a 180-foot pine behind Turtle Bay as it lifted itself piecemeal out of the ground; they simply saw it fly, its massive roots and tapering top giving it the look of an arrow, thirty feet up in the air back toward the hills. More pines followed it, the bombardment of a fortress by an army of giants, the wind their bows, the pine trees their arrows, the white oaks their grapples.

Stephen struggled on down the row of huts making sure that all the hatches were battened; finding his own house door already bolstered by a pine log, Richard elected to stay outside, thankful that Joey and MacGregor were safe. As far as his own skin was concerned, he would far rather be out than in, blinded to his fate—horrifying thought! He sat on the ground with his back to the lee wall and the log to witness the cataclysm, massive pines and huge old white oaks flying to crash into the swamp, the hillsides, the lashing spray.

Then the rain came, so horizontal that Richard remained dry even as he looked upon the deluge. Thatched roofs farther down were lifting to blow away like umbrellas, but the vastest winds seemed to be thirty feet above the ground, which was what saved the settlement. That, and its lack of trees. Had Lieutenant King not ordered total visibility, the huts, store sheds and houses would have been buried together with those inside them.

It started at eight in the morning; it began to blow itself out at four in the afternoon. The huts in this middle section where Richard and Joey lived kept their roofs, as did the bigger houses, all shingled rather than thatched with flax.

But not until the next day—innocently balmy, the breeze a zephyr—did the sixty-four people of Norfolk Island see what havoc the hurricane had wreaked. Where the swamp had been was a tumbling river lapping around the flanks of the old garden hill; the ground everywhere was feet deep in pine branches, pine tails, bushes, sand, coral chunks, leaves; and the windward sides of the buildings were smothered in debris so blasted into the wood that it needed great effort to pull the debris off. There were literal fields of felled pines, their root systems so mighty, their tap roots so long, that imagination foundered at gauging the strength of those winds. Where they had grown were craters many feet deep, and looking up to where the forest had not yet been touched by any axe, the pine casualties were as numerous. Many hundreds of trees had come down just within sight of Sydney Town; three acres of recently cleared ground on the far side of the swamp were solidly covered with pines. Not fifty men cutting down trees every day for a month could have produced so much timber.

"This cannot be anything but a true freak of nature," Lieutenant King said cheerily to his assembled family, even its serpents in a chastened mood. "Nowhere that I have been on this island have I seen any evidence that a hurricane like this has ever struck before, at least in the however many hundreds of years it takes for the pines to grow to two hundred feet. It has simply never happened." His expression changed to something approaching a Wesleyan preacher in full fire-and-brimstone spate. "Why did it happen in this year? Those of ye who have transgressed should examine your souls. This is God's work! *God's work!* And if it is God's work, ask yourselves why He has sent this visitation upon the first men ever to inhabit one of His most precious jewels? Pray for forgiveness, and do not transgress again! Next time God might choose to open up the earth and swallow ye whole!"

Brave words which actually sank in for several weeks after the event; then, as is the wont of men, the lesson was forgotten.

Lieutenant King had cause to wonder if perhaps his own hot temper was a contributing factor toward God's tantrum; a tree killed his privately owned sow and her litter of piglets.

That the devastation was island-wide was evident in the logs and branches which dammed up the stream in Arthur's Vale, carried down from the hills during the torrents of rain. Spring cleaning took days for the men, weeks for the women, who bore the brunt of it, and it was a full month before the lagoon turned from the red of washed-away soil to its customary aquamarine.

But when Supply arrived in the roads on the 2nd of March, Richard and his sawyers went back to work in the sawpits. The New South Wales settlement was still hungry for planks, scantlings and beams, not to mention ship's spars. At least no one had to ply an axe; the timber was already on the ground, though of course much of it was old and rotten.

Among others, Supply brought an experienced sawyer, William Holmes—*why* did they have to be Williams? After the trees at Port Jackson, Holmes said, Norfolk Island's pines were a mere nothing.

Aware that the Commandant was lusting after a third sawpit, Richard told Holmes to find three other men from among Supply's new infusion of convict blood and take over the sawpit on the beach. A good man; he brought his wife, Rebecca, with him, and the pair settled quickly into community life. That left Bill Blackall and Will Marriner in charge of the Arthur's Vale sawpit; while I, said Richard to himself with iron determination, take Private Wigfall, Sam Hussey and Harry Humphreys to the new third pit farther up the vale. It will be far more peaceful and I will ask Lieutenant King if I may build myself a good house nearby. Joey Long must fend for himself. All I will take are my books, my bed and feather bedding, half of our blankets and my own belongings. And one of MacGregor's pups, since Mr. King is allowing Joey to take two of Delphinia's five, the males. A good ratter up the vale will be a blessing.

All of these resolutions came to pass. They were a grief to Stephen Donovan only, who did not see as much of Richard as he had when it was a simple matter of calling in at his door on the way to Turtle Bay for a swim.

Lieutenant John Cresswell and a detachment of 14 more marines arrived with winter; the work force was now formidable enough and the policing of it strict enough to see the bulk of the Commandant's most cherished schemes come to pass, including his dam. Richard's house was several hundred yards above it, almost at the point where the forest commenced. *Peaceful.*

Paths suddenly loomed high on Lieutenant King's agenda. One such path was cut all the way across the island—three miles—to the leeward side at Cascade Bay, so called because the most spectacular of the many small waterfalls tumbled down a cliff there to cascade into the sea. A jagged but platformish outcrop of rock just offshore made landing there feasible when

Sydney Bay's prevailing winds prevented any thought of landing across the reef. The Cascade path was also necessary because most of the best flax grew around Cascade, and Lieutenant King resolved to set up his canvas-from-flax industry in a tiny new settlement not far above the landing place he would call Phillipburgh.

Richard went into Sydney Town but rarely, for it was rapidly mushrooming into an actual street of huts and houses. Save for attending divine service each Sunday and collecting his rations, he had no need to visit the place. MacTavish was every bit as good a watchdog as his father, and all the company Richard wanted save for Stephen, who had become so firmly "Stephen" in his mind that it was increasingly hard to remember that he was "Mr. Donovan."

His house was ten by fifteen feet, had several big window apertures to let in plenty of light, and Johnny Livingstone had made him a table and two chairs. His roof was thatched with flax, but he had been promised shingles before the end of the year. It had a wooden floor some inches off the ground and foundations of round pine logs; the pine rotted quickly once embedded in soil, so this method of construction enabled him to ease out a rotting foundation post without dismantling the house, which was lined with thin pine boards of the most attractive kind because the Commandant had inexplicably taken against this particular grain—the wood owned a rippling pattern which reminded Richard of sunlight on calm water. Privately he wondered whether the ripples were evidence of the way the pine compensated for the perpetual winds; no one knew of any other tree anywhere which could grow absolutely straight in the teeth of a high prevailing wind, yet the Norfolk pine did, even on the most exposed clifftops. After that colossal hurricane all the young trees had bent over to touch the ground or snapped their tops off, but within two months the bent ones were ramrod straight again and the snapped ones sprouting two separate tops.

Burglaries had increased now that the population stood at 100 souls, but thieves left Richard Morgan severely alone. Anyone who had watched him pull the fourteen-foot saw through three full feet, the muscles of his naked back and chest moving beneath the brown skin, decided that he was not a man to offend. He was, besides, a notorious loner. The community's loners, of whom there were a number, were viewed with a superstitious shiver of fear; there had to be something mentally wrong with a man who preferred his own company, who did not need to see himself reflected in somebody else's eyes or hear himself praised, drawn into an entity larger than he was. Which suited Richard perfectly. If people thought him dangerously strange, all the better. What surprised him was that more men did not elect to become loners after years of being jammed cheek by jowl with others. Solitude was not only bliss, it was also a healing process.

The hard core of January's mutineers got John Bryant at last midway through winter. Francis, Pickett, Watson, Peck and others off Golden Grove were cutting timber on Mount George when—who knew how, who knew why?—Bryant stumbled into the path of a falling pine. His head crushed, he died two hours later and was buried on the same day. Half crazed with grief, his widow wandered Sydney Town keening and moaning like an Irishwoman who spoke no English.

"The mood is very nasty," Stephen said as he walked back to Richard's house after the funeral.

"It had to happen" was all Richard said.

"That poor, wretched woman! And no priest to bury him."

"God will not care."

"God *does* not care!" Stephen snapped savagely. He entered the house without needing to bend, noting its scrupulous tidiness, the lined walls and ceiling, and the fact that Richard was slowly polishing them. "Christ," he said, sagging onto a chair, "this is one of the very rare days in my life when I could do with a beaker of rum. I feel as if I am to blame for Bryant's death."

"It had to happen," Richard repeated.

MacTavish, in whom the Scotch terrier line had run true, leaped into Richard's arms without making a nuisance of himself in the usual manner of a young dog; he has trained it, Stephen thought, with the same thoroughness he devotes to everything. How does he manage to look exactly as he did when I first met him? Why have the rest of us aged and hardened while he has preserved intact every iota that he always was? Only more so. Much more so.

"If ye get me a few stalks of the sugar cane running riot," said Richard, gently thumping the dog's lower spine with the flat of his hand, "in two years I will give ye all the rum ye can drink."

"*What?*"

"Oh, plus two copper kettles, some copper sheet, a few lengths of copper tubing and some casks cut in half," Richard went on with a smile. "I can distill, Mr. Donovan. 'Tis another of my hidden talents."

"Christ, Richard, ye're a commandant's dream! And for the love of God, will you please call me Stephen? I am so tired of this lopsided friendship! Surely after so many years it is time ye gave in, convict though ye may still be? 'Tis that Bristol prudishness, and I hate it!"

"Sorry, Stephen," said Richard, eyes twinkling.

"Begorrah! Victory at last!" Tremendously pleased at hearing his name come from Richard's lips, Stephen concealed his joy by frowning. "The marines are boiling because there is never enough rum to give them their full ration—Lieutenant Cresswell is at his wits' end. Nor does he do any better. King does not care, of course, as long as his port does not run out. Cresswell would far rather drink rum. Port Jackson has little rum either. I warrant that a rum distillery in Norfolk Island would receive full sanction from His Excellency. 'Twould cost far less to make rum than to bring it out on storeships, for even the most idealistic official understands that rum is as necessary as bread and salt meat."

"Well, there is certainly nothing to stop my growing my own patch of sugar cane. This soil loves it, and the grubs hate it. Though despite the rats and the grubs, we will harvest both wheat and Indian corn this summer, I am sure of it."

"I hope so, for all our sakes. Harry Ball of Supply says that there are many more to be shipped here soon. In Port Jackson things are much worse, despite the lack of grubs." Stephen shivered. "I do not think, even including the hurricane, that I have ever been so terrified as when the whole vale was one heaving mass of grubs. Not one million but millions upon millions, an army on the move that left Attila's hordes looking minuscule. Maybe 'twas my Irish blood, but I swear I thought that the Devil had cursed us. Brr!" Shivering again, he changed the subject. "Tell me, Richard, who is attacking the Government sows? One dead and one maimed."

Richard studied Stephen's face with an affection bordering on love. That he felt he could not call what he experienced "love" was not because of its lack of a sexual element; it was because "love" was an emotion he associated with William Henry, with little Mary, with Peg. Whom he had kept below the level of all thought for what had piled up into years.

Yet now their names fell inside his mind as clear and limpid as the brook farther up across a pattern of stones, as distant as the stars, as close as MacTavish on his lap. It was Stephen, it was calling Stephen by his name. The other names came rushing up, rang on a peal of memories not all the time and all the things that had happened to him could tarnish, diminish, expunge. William Henry, little Mary, Peg. . . . Gone forever, yet not gone at all. I am a vessel filled with their light, and somewhere, sometime, I will know that love again. Not in an after life. Here. Here in Norfolk Island. I am awake again. I am alive. So alive! I will not waste my essence in a thankless exile. I will not belong to that segment of this place who would ruin it for sheer spite. Peg, little Mary, William Henry. They are here. They are waiting to be with me. And they will be with me.

This had occurred in the silence between two beats of a heart, yet Stephen understood that some enormous change in Richard had just come about. As if he had sloughed off a skin and stood forth in all the splendor of new raiment. What did I say? What brought it to pass? And why did the privilege of seeing it fall to me?

Richard answered Stephen's question about the sows. "That is easy," he said. "Len Dyer."

"Why Len Dyer?"

"He fancies Mary Gamble, who will not give herself to anyone. When he solicited her attentions, he did so as any weasel would—without respect or acknowledgment of her humanity. You know what I mean: 'Hey, Gamble, how about a fuck?' So she told him in no uncertain terms what he could do with his tossle—*if* he could find it. In front of his cronies." Richard looked grim. "He is a weasel, and needs to be revenged. Mary threw an axe at a boar and was almost lashed for it. So why not attack some of the swine? Mary is bound to be blamed."

"Not now she will not be." Stephen got to his feet and blew Richard an impudent kiss. "I know how to deal with Dyer. Call me Stephen again, please."

"Stephen," said Richard, laughing. "Now leave me to get on with my polishing."

Lieutenant King had discovered an easily quarried rock underlying all the land between the old garden hillock and Point Hunter at the far end of Turtle Bay, and also found that it burned to make excellent lime, though his primary purpose had been to use it for stone chimneys and ovens.

When Supply arrived in December with enough convicts to bring the population up to 132, she bore orders from Governor Phillip that rations were to go down to two-thirds, as they were already at Port Jackson. For the growing Norfolk Island this news was not so calamitous; though the millions of grubs had eaten every leafed thing they crawled on, the wheat crop off eleven acres came in splendidly and the rain held off right through its harvesting. The Indian corn did even better, the pigs were multiplying quickly—as were the ducks and chickens—and it was banana season. For those who would eat fish, there was fish.

Endurance and tenacity had turned Richard Morgan into one of the more privileged convicts, for no other reasons than that he gave absolutely no trouble, worked indefatigably and was never sick. So to Richard went enough of this new stone and mortar to build himself a decent chimney. All the sawpits were sawing flat out—what more could a commandant ask of his supervisor of sawyers? Luckily more saws arrived from Port Jackson on Supply; Governor Phillip, planning to more than triple Norfolk Island's population, had decided that Port Jackson needed saws less than Norfolk Island did. A decision he would find reinforced when Supply returned bearing the first consignment of splendid clean lime.

When Supply also brought more women than Lieutenant King could find a use for, Richard had a brilliant inspiration: he put six of them to sharpening saws. It was, he admitted to himself ruefully, an alternative he should have thought of long before. The work suited females of a certain temperament—it could be done sitting down in the shade, it was not exhausting, it required fine attention to detail and yet could be pursued in a spirit of camaraderie. As one woman was needed at each pit to touch up the saws halfway through each cut and yet more women were put to stripping logs of bark, romances developed between those who were unattached. Though a woman soon learned that Richard Morgan was married already and not interested in amorous intrigues.

Two-thirds rations were a symptom of the fact that two years had gone by without a single ship from England; the long-awaited Guardian storeship which carried so much marine private property as well as tons of flour, salt meat, other provisions and animals had never arrived, and no one knew why. Every day on top of South Head at the entrance to Port Jackson the sentinel on watch gazed out to sea with painful urgency, had been doing so for a year; a whale spout was a sail, a water spout was a sail, a little low white cloud was a sail. But none of them was a sail. The foods that Sirius had fetched back from the Cape of Good Hope in May of 1789 were running out, and still no ship came. The only ray of hope Governor Phillip had was Norfolk Island, where at least some things grew, other things could be caught, and there were no marauding natives to worry about.

Conditions in Port Jackson were appalling, the latest arrivals off Supply vowed; people there were literally starving to death, looked like skeletons.

Rose Hill showed some promise, as did other areas to the north and west of Port Jackson like Toongabbe and the Boundary Farms, but though they were now producing a few vegetables, a decent crop of grain was still years off.

Nothing for it, Governor Phillip decided after Supply returned to Port Jackson with lime and timber; he would have to send Sirius somewhere to obtain food in vast quantities. The Cape of Good Hope, he realized now, was simply not a large enough community to furnish adequate flour and salt meat, nor even sufficient animals. It sold its surpluses to the Dutch, English and other East Indiamen making port there, a matter of provisions for crews between 20 and 50 in number. To feed a thousand-plus mouths even for a mere twelvemonth was not in Cape Town's power; Sirius had returned half-empty.

Therefore Sirius would have to sail to Cathay, where rice and smoked meats were abundant—not to mention tea and sugar, both of which would sweeten a convict's lot, albeit the nourishment in them was slight. In Wampoa the Governor also hoped to purchase rum off the European emporiums. 1790 was off to a worse start than 1789, though he had not thought that possible.

And in the night marches Phillip wondered if perhaps there had been a massive political upheaval in England—if Mr. Pitt had tumbled—if a Royal decision had been made not to continue with the Botany Bay experiment—and just forget about those already at Botany Bay. Not knowing was terrible, especially as the months dragged by with his nightmares still unappeased. It really did begin to look as if they were as marooned as Robinson Crusoe.

Before Sirius could be readied for a long sea voyage, Supply had time to make yet another round trip to Norfolk Island with more convicts, swelling its population to 149 all told. The Governor then planned that Sirius (on her way to the Orient) and Supply would sail together to Norfolk Island, bearing 116 male convicts, 67 female convicts, 28 children, 8 marine officers and 56 troops. Which would inflate the island's population overnight to 424 souls—tripled within a month, quadrupled within four months.

The gentle, cultivated little governor knew some of his people very well indeed, particularly Lieutenant Philip Gidley King, who had served with him on Ariadne and Europe before joining Sirius for the voyage to New South Wales. Every time Supply returned to Port Jackson she bore despatches from King, all of which reinforced His Excellency's reservations about leaving King to govern a populace suddenly numerous enough to render most faces anonymous. King was a patriarch, wildly devoted to his son by Ann Innet—*Norfolk!* Really! If that name did not indicate King's innate romanticism, nothing could. And Norfolk Island was about to become a place ill suited to government by a romantic.

His Excellency had other considerations besides, principally two: one, that Major Robert Ross was a carping Scotch thorn in his side; the other, that he desperately needed to send someone he could trust—a romantic someone—back to England in a tearing hurry. This envoy would have to find out what had gone wrong, and eloquently persuade whoever was in power that New South Wales had enormous potential, yet could not possibly realize that potential unless a little capital was invested in it. Less than £50,000 was ridiculous considering that the Honourable East India Company spent more than that per annum in bribes. King the Governor trusted, Ross he did not. Nor, for that matter, did he trust Captain John Hunter of Sirius, another possible candidate—and another Scotchman, croaking harbingers of doom that all Scotchmen were. Ross and Hunter were sour about New South Wales, saw no potential in it whatsoever, and were more likely to recommend to the Crown that the whole experiment be forthwith canceled. Therefore Phillip knew he could not send either Ross or Hunter to England as his envoy. He *knew* his judgment was correct. New South Wales would thrive. But not yet. It needed time and money.

So when Supply sailed for Norfolk Island with the complement of convicts which would bring its population up to 149, she bore a letter for Lieutenant King commanding him to return to Port Jackson with Mistress Innet and Master Norfolk King, there to be drilled in the details of his vital mission to England. To take his place at Norfolk Island, Phillip would send a full Lieutenant-Governor rather than a mere Commandant—Major Robert Ross. Thus killing lots of birds with the same stone, for with Sirius going on from Norfolk Island to Cathay, he would also be rid of Captain John Hunter for months. And there would be 424 people at Norfolk Island, leaving only 591 people in Port Jackson.

Sirius and Supply arrived together on Saturday the 13th of March, 1790. Landing on Norfolk Island had to commence on the leeward side at Cascade; after that wet, storm-tossed summer, the equinoctial gales and rains had arrived with a vengeance. The track across the island was hideous enough, but at Cascade itself matters were even worse, as the hills plunged straight into the ocean. The only way up to the crest of them was through a precipitous valley adjacent to the landing rock. This cleft ascended over 200 feet so steeply that the women convicts could not climb it without assistance, especially with water tumbling down it and the ground slippery as ice from mud.

Sawyers and carpenters excepted, every convict was sent across the island to help get the new arrivals and the baggage up the cleft to the top and then across the island to Sydney Town, Major Ross in the vanguard.

"I felt exceeding sorry for the poor bastard," said Stephen to Richard over a lunch of cold, unsweetened rice pudding mixed with a morsel of salt pork and a handful of parsley. They were sitting together in Richard's house watching the rain pelt down through the unshuttered lee window. Stephen had contributed the flour and the salt pork, Richard the rice and parsley.

"Major Ross, you mean?"

"Aye, the same. He and Hunter loathe each other, so Hunter made sure he sent Ross off Sirius in a longboat loaded to the gunwales with chickens, turkeys, crates, kegs—Ross's calf muscles were so cramped that he had terrible trouble jumping from thc boat to the landing rock, couldn't stand when he got there. And no one helped him—Hunter's men to the core. I think they fancied the sight of the Major swimming for his life, but he ain't Major Ross for naught, fucked 'em good by getting ashore as dry as the rain permitted. They ought by rights to have sent his stuff off with him, but 'tis still on Sirius and no doubt will be the last cargo unloaded. I met him and tried to help him up that deathly haul to the top, but would he let me? Not he! Marched up it soaked to the skin with his chin in the air and his mouth the double of a staple. And marched straight across the island on that horror of a track with me floundering in his wake like a seal on a beach. The image of a horse's rear end he might be, but ah, he is a lovely man!"

Richard was grinning from ear to ear by the end of this tale, but got up without comment to put the dishes outside the door in the rain, then tidied the table. Of course the whole community had known within hours of Supply's last visit that Lieutenant King was to go and Major Ross was to come, news greeted wellnigh universally with groans and curses. The holiday had come to an end, Major Ross would see to that. To the Dyers and Francises, an awful prospect. But to Richard Morgan, a not unattractive prospect. Oh, Lieutenant King had been a good commandant, but even 149 people were too many for his style. All King could do was pluck at his wig and set men to cutting timber, sawing it, and building huts out of it. Norfolk Island was less than ten thousand acres in extent, but surely Sydney Town was not the only spot where this enormous new influx of people could be accommodated? Phillipburgh and the flax was King's only attempt at putting people elsewhere; the truth was that he liked to see the members of his extended family all gathered in the tiny sea-level shelf around Sydney Town. When Robert Webb and Beth Henderson emigrated along the track to Cascade, King had been quite distracted; Richard Phillimore off Scarborough was anxious to be gone around the eastern corner of the far beach to farm a small valley he fancied, but King did not want to let him go.

Whereas Richard thought the most sensible thing to do with Norfolk Island was to open it up, settle people anywhere in it that they fancied. What he dreaded was to see the Sydney Town settlement advance up to the head of Arthur's Vale, where he enjoyed the fact that there were no abodes near him, and could call the privy he had dug into the hillside entirely his own. His bath lay along the stream in the midst of the fern tree forest, a bywater he had cut and dug out so that his body did not foul the main course of water—if a healthy body could, which he doubted. But under King, he could see the day coming when Sydney Town would reach him. Not that he hoped for more wisdom from Major Ross; only that Ross was a very different kind of man and might therefore have different solutions for this relatively monstrous and sudden growth in population.

"I take it, then, that the Major is already drying his coat in Government House?" Richard asked as they walked, heedless of the rain, back down the stream toward the pond and dam.

"Oh, nothing surer. Poor Mr. King! Half of him is in raptures over this huge mission he is to undertake for the Governor, while the other half is beside itself at the thought of what Major Ross will do to Norfolk Island."

Private Wigfall, who had lunched with some of the new marines—among them were several of his Port Jackson friends—saw Richard coming and dashed for the pit. They were halfway through a 30-foot log and down to the heartwood—scantling time, after which would come beams. Stephen Donovan continued in the direction of the first of his dozen gangs, engaged in making sluices for the dam wall of basalt boulders, pounded limestone and piled earth. Even in this rain the dam was holding, which had surprised everybody; the rain had been drumming down for days and days.

Within the space of four days the population of Norfolk Island swelled from 149 to 424; more extra people had arrived on Sirius and Supply than had ever lived there before March of 1790. Both ships also carried additional provisions of everything from flour to rum.

"But not nearly enough!" cried Lieutenant King to Major Ross distractedly. "How am I to feed everybody?"

"That will not be your concern," said the Major bluntly. "Ye're Commandant only until Supply sails, which will not be long once the seas abate and she can land her stores on this side of the island. Until ye go, I will defer to your judgments. But feeding this lot devolves upon me. As does housing it." He put his arm about his ten-year-old son, Alexander John, who had been appointed a second lieutenant in the Marine Corps after the death of Captain John Shea resulted in an upward movement of the officers and created a vacancy right at the bottom. Little John, as he was known to all, was a quiet child who knew better than to make his father's life more complicated than it already was; he bore his lot with resignation, knowing full well that this unorthodox promotion did not endear him to his fellow officers. His father, standing atop the eminence upon which humble Government House was built, gazed across the sea-level shelf at the same kind of chaos had ensued after the landing at Port Jackson.

People were wandering about aimlessly, including the 56 new marines, minus a barracks. Their officers had commandeered eight-by-ten huts from the old convict residents, who contributed to the confusion by joining the ranks of the newly arrived homeless.

"I hope," said Ross grimly, "that ye have a good crowd of men sawing, Mr. King?"

"Aye, as far as it goes." King's distraction increased, as did his sudden anxiety to quit Norfolk Island. "There are three sawpits, but I will have to find more men to saw—and that, as ye know, Major Ross, is not easily done."

"There are Port Jackson sawyers among the new convicts."

"And more saws, I hope?"

"His Excellency has sent all but three pit saws, as well as a hundred hand saws." Ross dropped his arm from his son's shoulders. "Is Richard Morgan sawing?"

King's face lit up. "I could not do without him," he said, "any more than I could do without Nat Lucas, my head of carpenters, or Tom Crowder, my clerk."

"I told ye Morgan was a good man. Where is he?"

"Sawing while ever there is daylight."

"Not sharpening?"

King grinned. "He puts women to sharpening, and it answers exceeding fine. His sawing partner is Private Wigfall—well, we ran out of suitable convicts. 'Tis an unenviable job, but Wigfall seems to thrive on it, as do Morgan and a few others. They enjoy rude health, probably thanks to the hard labor and good food."

"And they have to be kept well fed, no matter who else goes hungry. The first thing," said Ross, temporarily forgetting that King was still nominally in charge, "is to build barracks for my marines. Living under canvas is Hell—if and when Hunter gets off his royal arse to unload the tents." He added, though not by way of an apology, "D'ye have any idea whereabouts the barracks ought to go?"

"Over there on the far side of the swamp," said King, nobly swallowing his displeasure. "The land along the base of the hills behind Sydney Town is free of water, though I must tell ye that the Norfolk pine rots quickly if put in the ground. 'Twould be best to use stone for the foundations—did any stonemasons come?"

"Several, and a few stone chisels. Port Jackson is not in need of new buildings at the moment, whereas His Excellency knows Norfolk Island will need them desperately. He was, incidentally, delighted to get the lime—we have not found one pebble of limestone on our travels through Cumberland County."

"Then when I see him I can tell him not to worry. We can produce a hundred bushels of lime a day if pushed to it," said King, longing for a glass of port and acutely aware that the Major did not approve of more than a daily half-pint of anything intoxicating. He caught sight of Ann in the doorway of the house and decided to leave the Major to his own devices; after all, Ann was carrying a second child and might be in distress. "Must go!" he said, and bolted.

Along came the delicate figure of Second Lieutenant Ralph Clark, whom Ross had despised until he realized that the mawkish, immature Clark had a rare touch with children, actually seemed pleased to take care of Little John. Useless as a marine, but a wonderful nursemaid.

"I will be dashed glad, sir," said Clark politely, smiling at Little John, "to have a clean shirt to put on my back. As, I am sure, will you. They might at least have sent our baggage ashore."

"I doubt Sirius will ever manage to unload," said Ross dourly, "though I note that Supply makes light enough work of it."

"Supply has Ball and Blackburn, sir. They know the place."

While Hunter of Sirius, said Ross to himself, is a crotchety fool. Aloud he said, "Take charge of Little John, Lieutenant. I need to do some walking."

The scars of the mighty hurricane were still visible more than a year after it had happened, though the usable trees had been stripped of their bark and reduced to appropriate lengths. Those too large for the pit saws and those already rotten had been disposed of in various ways: their branches were lopped off to be made into torches and firewood, their trunks lopped into sections and dropped into craters for burning or heaped into piles for burning. The settlement was still, King had explained, sawing timber felled by the wind, though clearing of the hills around the vale and Sydney Town was continuing and that timber was being stockpiled. In winter, thought Ross, I will have a bonfire every night. Too much precious flat land is being wasted on pine detritus.

To Ross, the island was even worse than Port Jackson; how it could support more than 400 people in some degree of comfort he did not yet know. Of vegetables there were plenty despite the grub armies, but humankind could not live on vegetables alone if they were required to labor hard—people needed flesh and bread as well. The size of the wheat crop in the granary had astonished him, as did the amount of Indian corn. Only the constant presence of some of MacGregor's and Delphinia's offspring around the granary kept the rats at bay, King had explained, but with the new arrivals had come a dozen more dogs and two dozen cats to help control the rodent hordes. The pigs here were thriving far better than at Port Jackson. They dined on Indian corn, mangel-wurzel, fish scraps and whatever else was fed them, including the pith of the palm and tree fern. They also dined off some sort of sea bird which came in to nest in burrows on Mount George between November and March.

"A fool of a thing," King had said, "that gets lost and cannot find its burrow. Waaaah! Waaaah! It howls like a ghost all night when it is here, frightens the living daylights out of newcomers. Take a torch and ye can catch it easily. The pigs just scamper up on top of Mount George and feast. We tried to eat 'em because they are so nearby, but they are fearsome fatty and fishy—ugh!"

Therefore, thought Ross as he walked, porkers will loom large in my calculations.

The wheat, good crop though it was, would never feed 424 people until the next harvest came in; sowing happened in May or June, reaping in November or December. According to King, Indian corn grew all year round. His technique in dealing with the rats and grubs was to plant wheat just at the conclusion of a grub wave and Indian corn continuously. Wheat in ear was too frail for rats to climb, whereas corn was a ladder. But the ripe ears of both were ravaged by the green parrots, which came out of the skies in vast flocks. Taming Nature, the Major reflected, was a constant war.

He toured the sea-level shelf from end to end and front to back, thinking, thinking. No more people up Arthur's Vale; that was clearly where the produce flourished best, must be reserved for cultivation. Therefore Sydney Town would have to house everybody for the time being—but only for the time being. He would have to visit Robert Webb and his woman and the time-elapsed convict Robert Jones, who had taken up land halfway between Sydney Town and Cascade. Oh, Cascade—what a place to have to come ashore! And how Hunter must have sniggered as he watched the new Lieutenant-Governor, baggageless, in a longboat full of poultry. Ross glowered, concentrated all his energies upon ill-wishing Captain John Hunter of Sirius; practical and down-to-earth Scotchman though he was, the Major believed that a curse held great power. Hunter would not prosper. Hunter would come to grief. Hunter would fall. A murrain on him, a murrain on him, a murrain on him. . . .

Feeling much better, he paused on the far side of the causeway and turned to look east down the cleared but unoccupied land which ended at the sea along the beach beyond Turtle Bay. This end plus the road down to the landing place, he decided, would accommodate the marines and their officers, thus effectively cutting off the convicts from access to Arthur's Vale and the food, which was now stored in King's huge barn and the mezzanine of the granary. He would house the convicts eastward of the troops, ten to a hut, and bugger the Reverend Johnson's strictures about keeping male and female felons from fornicating. In Ross's opinion, freedom to fornicate meant a certain degree of content. God would forgive them, for God had sent them many other trials.

Those convicts possessed of huts along the beach who had been evicted in favor of his officers would have to be returned to their dwellings; hard he was, but just he was. Those who had labored here—very few, when all was said and done—must have some sort of thanks for their efforts. They would go back to their huts as soon as his officers were properly housed, and they would also be the first convicts to receive land. For that, he had already concluded, was the only answer: break open the interior of this speck in the midst of an infinity of ocean and people it. Give those who were willing to work an incentive to work by dowering them with land—some around Sydney Town, a very few in Arthur's Vale, and the big majority in the virgin bulk of the island. No more tracks: a proper road to Ball Bay, to Cascade, to Anson Bay. Once there were roads, people could move out and away. If there was one asset he owned, it was a huge laboring force.

Those resolutions tucked away, he turned then westward into Arthur's Vale, grudgingly admitting to himself that, considering the tiny size of his work force, Lieutenant King had not loafed during the two years he had occupied Norfolk Island. The granary and the barn were gradually having their wooden foundations replaced by the lime-producing stone (it was not limestone, but calcarenite) King had discovered around the cemetery, the stockyard attached to the barn was roomy, and the dam was an inspiration. He found the second sawpit, sheltered from the sun, its men working frantically; gazed sourly at the gaggle of women under a roof busy sharpening saws; and passed on up the vale beyond the dam, where the hillsides were being cleared in preparation for yet more wheat and Indian corn. Here he located the third sawpit, and Richard Morgan atop a gigantic log. Far too sensible to attract the sawyer's attention to him while that lethal instrument ripped inches at a time through the six-foot girth—he was down to heartwood and big beams—Major Ross stood quietly watching.

The air was humid, the weather finer than any since he had landed four days ago, and the men at the sawpit worked clad only in worn, tattered canvas trowsers. It is not right, thought Ross. Not one of them has the luxury of underdrawers, that I know from Port Jackson, where the last convict underdrawers fell apart a full twelvemonth ago. So they do this work with the rough seams of their trowsers chafing at their groins. Though I detest convicts, I have to admit that a fair proportion of them are good men, and some are superlative. King may rave about the likes of a Tom Crowder—a useful lickspittle—but I prefer the likes of Richard Morgan, who never opens his mouth save to voice common sense. And Nat Lucas, the little carpenter. Crowder will work indefatigably for himself; Morgan and Lucas simply work for the pleasure of a job well done. How strange are the machinations of God, Who makes some men and women genuinely industrious, and others lazy to the very marrow. . . .

The cut finished, Ross spoke. "Hard at it, Morgan, I see."

Not troubling to conceal his delight, Richard turned on the log, leaped from it onto solid ground, and walked over. His hand went out automatically, but he caught the gesture in time to turn it into a salute. "Major Ross, welcome," he said, smiling.

"Have ye been evicted from your hut?"

"Not yet, sir, but I expect I will be."

"Where d'ye live, that it has not happened?"

"Farther up, right at the end of the vale."

"Show me."

On stone piers now and with its roof shingled, the house—it could not be called a hut—lay under the eaves of the forest. Ross noted that it had a stone chimney, as did some of the convict huts and houses on the shore; a sign that King thought Richard Morgan worthy of reward. Below it but up the hillside was a privy. A lush-looking vegetable garden surrounded it save for a path of basalt rocks to the door, and beyond the garden sugar cane waved. A few plantains flourished and the slope around the privy was planted with a bushy small tree that bore pinkening berries.

Entering, Major Ross thought the house a remarkably professional piece of work for a man not a carpenter; it was *finished*. The walls, ceiling and floor had actually been dully polished. Of course! Gunsmiths worked with wood too. An impressive collection of books stood on a shelf on one wall, another shelf held what looked suspiciously like a dripstone, the bed was sheeted with Alexander-issue blankets, and a very nice table and two chairs stood in the middle of the floor. The window apertures had been equipped with proper shutters.

"Ye've made a home," said Ross, occupying one chair. "Sit down, Morgan, otherwise I will not be comfortable."

Richard sat rather rigidly. "I am glad to see ye, sir."

"So your face betrayed. One of the very few."

"Well, folk dislike change of any kind."

"Especially when the change is named Robert Ross. No, no, Morgan, there is no need to look squalmy! Ye're a convict, but ye're not a felon. There is a difference. For instance, I do not see Lucas as a felon either. What did he go down for, d'ye know? I am gathering evidence for a theory I have conceived."

"Lucas lived in a London boarding house, in a room he was not allowed to lock because he was obliged to share it at a moment's notice. Two other lodgers were a father and daughter. The father found some of his daughter's property beneath Lucas's mattress—some muslin aprons and the like. Not items a perverted man would steal. Lucas denied he had put them there, but the girl and her father prosecuted him."

"What d'ye think the truth was?" asked the Major, interested.

"That the girl coveted Lucas himself. When she could not have him, she chose revenge. His trial lasted not ten minutes and his master neglected to appear for him, so he had no one to speak for his character. But I gather that the London courts are such a mass of people and confusion that his master could well have been there, either lost or refused entrance. The magistrate questioned him and he denied the charges, but it was his word against two people. He went down for seven years."

"Yet one more confirmation of my theory," said Ross, leaning back in the chair until its front legs left the floor. "Such tales are fairly common. Though some of ye are recognizably villains, I have noted that most of ye keep out of trouble. 'Tis the few who make it difficult for all. For every convict flogged, there are three or four who are never flogged, and those who are flogged inevitably get flogged again and again. Mind you, some of ye are neither decent nor villainous—the ones who are averse to hard work. What the English trial boils down to is someone's word against someone else's word. Evidence is rarely presented."

"And many," said Richard, "commit their crimes sodden drunk."

"Is that what happened to you?"

"Not exactly, though rum contributed. An excise fraud hinged upon my testimony, therefore it was expedient that I not be able to testify. It took place in Bristol, but I was removed to trial in Gloucester, where I knew no one." Richard drew a breath. "But in all fairness, sir, I blame no one except myself."

Ross thought he looked like a Celtic Welshman—dark hair, dark skin, light eyes, fine-boned face. The height he must have inherited from English forebears, and the musculature was the result of hard labor. Sawyers, stonemasons, smiths and axemen who threw their hearts into their work always had splendid bodies. Provided they had enough to eat, and clearly those in Norfolk Island had enough to eat. Whether they would in the future was not so sure.

"Ye look the picture of health," Ross said, "but then, ye never were sick, were ye?"

"I managed to preserve my health, mostly thanks to my dripstone." Richard indicated it affectionately. "I have also been fortunate, sir. The times when I have not had enough to eat have either been short enough or idle enough not to cause bone-deep illness. Had I remained in Port Jackson, who knows? But ye sent me here sixteen months ago." His eyes twinkled. "I like fish, and there are many who do not, so I have had more than my share of flesh."

MacTavish erupted through the open door and made a flying leap onto Richard's lap, panting.

"Good lord! Is that Wallace? 'Tis not MacGregor."

"Nay, sir. This is Wallace's grandson out of the Government spaniel, Delphinia. His name is MacTavish and he eats rat."

Ross got up. "I congratulate ye on this house, Morgan, 'tis a comfortable dwelling. Cool in summer thanks to the trees, warm in winter thanks to the fireplace."

"It is at your disposal, sir," said Richard dutifully.

"Were it closer to civilization, Morgan, I would grab it, make no mistake. Your canniness is worthy of a man from north of the border, to build at the far end of the vale. None of my officers would relish the walk save Lieutenant Clark, and I need him close to me." It is too isolated to make safe officer housing, Ross said to himself—who knows what the bastard who occupied it might get up to? "However," he added, going to the door, "in time I will oblige ye to share it."

Richard walked with him as far as the sawpit, where Sam Hussey and Harry Humphreys were attacking a new log.

"I am supervisor of sawyers, sir, so as soon as ye have the time, I would discuss the sawing with ye," he said.

"There is no time like the present, Morgan. Talk now."

They visited each of the sawpits in turn, Richard explaining his system, the worthiness of using women to sharpen and strip bark, the sites where more sawpits could be dug, the kind of men he needed to saw, the desirability of letting the sawyers cut timber for their own houses in their spare time, the need to convert some of the extra pit saws into cross cut saws.

"But that," he ended as they stood on the edge of the sawpit on the beach, "is work I dare not trust to anyone save myself. Unless ye've brought William Edmunds?" he asked, sure that Major Ross would know the names of all his immigrants, free or felon.

"Aye, he is among the throng somewhere. He is yours."

And, thought Richard in great content, I have made this transition painlessly. How friendless Major Ross must be, to talk to a convict as to a colleague. Is that why he banked me here?

On Friday the 19th of March, the sea fair, the day fine, Sirius stood in to Sydney Bay to unload her cargo. She lay to under the lee of Nepean Island and prepared to hoist her boats into the water, but when her commanders realized that she was drifting too close to the rocks of Point Hunter they made sail to get her farther out; she missed stays and lay immobile. Sailing master Keltie decided to wear her by tacking with the wind around her stern at the very moment when it gusted from a breeze to a gale. Sirius missed her stays again. Just as the noon bell rang a wave plucked her out of a trough and flung her broadside on the reef. Armed with axes, her sailors lopped the masts through at deck level, stoving in her boats and smothering her in a welter of spars and canvas. Boats flew from the beach and from Supply in the roads, but had no hope of reaching her; the treacherous surf was suddenly high enough to soar over her chess tree, a piece of oak where the curve of the bow straightened to run aft as the rail. While the sailors worked in a frenzy to clear the decks of the felled rigging, a seven-inch-circumference hawser was towed ashore and fixed high on a surviving pine; those people who could be spared aboard were dragged in clinging to the hawser through the flooding afternoon tide. As the hawser bowed in its middle exactly where the surf broke, Captain John Hunter, the first man winched ashore, arrived bruised, cut and battered enough to assure Major Ross that his curse had worked a treat. There would be far worse to come for Hunter, who had lost his ship and would have to stand trial for it in England.

Other officers followed him before someone thought to rig the hawser with a traveler, a piece of grating upon which the men could perch and at least save their legs and bottoms from the coral. Only when the surf went down would they be able to put a tripod under the bow in the hawser, and there was no chance of that at the moment.

Some of Sirius's crew, on shore leave, swam back and forth to the wreck, as did Stephen Donovan, very angry that no one on Sirius had asked him about the local winds and currents. Christ, she was a big ship, and *someone* ought to have realized that Nepean Island did strange things with wind! Why hadn't Hunter utilized David Blackburn or Harry Ball, if he was too haughty to ask a mere sailor of the merchant service?

The news reached the sawpits as quickly as bad news always does; Richard went the rounds and forbade his teams to stop work unless orders came that they were needed. There were several hundred people to house, especially given that the crew of Sirius was now marooned on Norfolk Island as well—an extra hundred souls. If Sirius could not sail to Cathay, Supply would have to go, and that meant months and months without relief. Or so Richard reasoned—as it turned out, correctly.

Dawn of Saturday revealed Sirius still intact; her back was broken but her stern had swung off the reef, where she lay at an angle. Landing conditions were terrible. The wind had risen to a minor gale and clouds threatened rain, but the work of getting her provisions off went on all day; by four that afternoon the last of the men had come ashore, having emptied Sirius's holds and put her cargo on the cleared decks for easier removal.

But at nine on that Saturday morning King, deferring to Major Ross, called a meeting of all the commissioned officers belonging to Sirius and the Marine Corps. Ross conducted it.

"Lieutenant King, as is proper in this emergency, has formally handed command to me as Lieutenant-Governor," said Ross, whose pale eyes bore the same steely gloss as a highland loch. "It is necessary to make decisions that will ensure the peace, order and good government of this place. I am informed that Supply will be able to take about twenty members of Sirius's crew as well as Mr. King, his lady, and child, and it is imperative that Supply sails for Port Jackson as quickly as possible. His Excellency must be apprised of this disaster forthwith."

"It was not my fault!" gasped Hunter, face cut, skin so white that he looked about to faint. "We could not keep her in stays, we could not! The moment the wind shifted, the sails backed—it all happened so fast—so fast!"

"I have not convened this meeting to apportion blame, Captain Hunter," said Ross crisply; he was in control, and for once the Royal Navy would have to bow to a member of a corps did not have the right to call itself "Royal." "What we are here to discuss is the fact that a settlement which six days ago held one hundred and forty-nine people will now contain more than five hundred people, including over three hundred convicts and eighty-odd men off Sirius. The latter will not, as seamen, be of much use either in governing convicts or working land. Mr. King, d'ye expect that Governor Phillip will send Supply back here from Port Jackson?"

King's expression was a compound of shock and bewilderment, but he shook his head emphatically. "No, Major Ross, ye cannot count on Supply's returning. As I understand it, Port Jackson is starving and His Excellency very much fears that England has—for what reason no one knows—forgotten us. With Sirius gone, Supply is the only link he has with other places. She will have to go either to Cape Town or Batavia for provisions, and my bet is that His Excellency will choose Batavia because 'twill be an easier voyage for such an old, fair-weather ship. His chief concern is that somebody *must* get home to remind the Crown that conditions in both settlements are appalling. Unless, that is, a storeship should arrive. But that, gentlemen, grows less rather than more likely."

"We cannot count on anything except the worst, Mr. King, so we will not entertain the hope of a storeship. There is wheat and Indian corn in the granary but planting is still at least two months off and harvesting eight or nine months off. If we manage to get all the provisions off Sirius before she sinks"—he ignored the look on Hunter's face—"I estimate that we can feed everybody for three months at most. Fishing will have to be continuous, and whatever edible birds we find we will also consume."

Brightening, King said eagerly, "I told ye of the summer bird wails like a ghost, but there is also a winter bird. It is a fat and tasty sea bird arrives about April and remains until August. It uses the mountain, which is why we have never bothered to try to eat it in any quantity—the walk is long and perilous without any paths. However, it is so tame that a man can walk straight up to it and grab it. There are thousands upon thousands of them. They fish out to sea all day and come in on dusk to their burrows, the same as the summer ghost birds. If things become desperate, they are a source of food. All ye'd have to do is cut paths."

"I thank ye for that information, Mr. King." Ross cleared his throat. "Be that as it may, what worries me most is mutiny." He glared at his marine officers. "I do not necessarily mean a convict mutiny. Many of my enlisted men are ruffians who must be kept supplied with rum. And when I said that we have provisions enough to last three months, I include rum in that estimate. I must conserve enough rum for my officers, which will cut rations for the enlisted men. Not to mention that Captain Hunter's seamen will also expect their rum—is that not so, Captain?"

Hunter swallowed. "Aye, Major Ross, I fear so."

"Then," said Ross, "there is only one solution. Law Martial. Theft of anything by any man, free or felon, will be punishable by death without trial. And, gentlemen, I will enforce it, have no doubts about that."

This announcement was greeted with a profound silence. The noises of those toiling outside to retrieve men and supplies from Sirius percolated through the walls of Government House, a reminder of prevailing chaos.

"On Monday," said Ross, "the entire complement of those on this island will assemble at eight o'clock beneath the Union flagstaff, when I will inform them of the new state of affairs. Until then, gentlemen, button your mouths as tight as a fish's arsehole. I mean that. If news of Law Martial leaks out before Monday morning, I will have the offender flogged no matter how exalted his rank. Ye are at liberty to go."

Property and provisions continued to come off Sirius; the stock—pigs and goats—were simply thrown overboard and herded by boats and swimmers in the direction of the beaches, with surprisingly few casualties. Though her back was broken, the vessel showed no sign of coming apart or sinking; casks, barrels, kegs and sacks were ferried ashore. She lay sometimes stern off the reef, sometimes stern on, always pinioned by her midships and remorselessly pounded by gale-whipped seas, but somehow as each day passed she never seemed to look worse.

At eight on Monday morning every single soul was herded into position at the Union flagstaff, the marines and seamen lined up on the right, the convicts on the left, with the officers in the center right below the flag.

"As commandant of this English colony, I hereby declare that the Law Martial will come into effect as of this moment!" shouted Major Ross, his stentorian voice assisted by a wind west of southwest. "Until God and His Britannic Majesty send relief we are thrown upon our own resources. If we are to survive, then every last man, woman and child will have to work with two goals in mind—to build shelter from the elements and produce food. On my count, there are five hundred and four persons who will be remaining here after Supply sails—over triple the number a week ago! I am not about to disguise the fact that starvation stares us in the face, but of one thing I can assure ye—no one here—*no one!*—will have a scrap more to eat than all have to eat. God is trying us as He tried the Israelites in the desert, but we can lay no claim to the virtue of that ancient and admirable people. What happens to us rests squarely upon our own resourcefulness—our will to work hard, our will to behave with the interests of all at heart, our will to survive in the teeth of terrible adversity!"

He paused, and those near enough could see the bitter look on his face. "Ye are no Israelites, I repeat that! Among ye are the scum of the earth, the dregs of humanity, and I will deal with ye accordingly. For those who bear their misfortunes with grace and unselfishness, there will be rewards. For those who steal food from the mouths of others, the penalty is death. For those who steal to barter, to have more comfort, to get drunk, or for any other reason, I will flay ye until the bones show from neck to ankles! Man or woman makes no difference, nor will children be let off lightly. The Law is Martial, which means that I am your judge, jury and executioner. I care not if ye fornicate, I care not if ye work in your own time to grow a little more or house yourselves, but I will not countenance the slightest infringement of the general public good! For the first six weeks every single vegetable and fruit will go to Government Stores, but I expect that all men and women commence this very moment to grow vegetables and fruit to augment the Government supply, which means that at the end of those six weeks all with productive gardens will contribute only two-thirds of what they grow to Government Stores. My motto is productiveness through labor, and that applies as much to the free as to the convicted."

His lip lifted in a snarl. "I am Major Robert Ross, and my reputation precedes me! I am Lieutenant-Governor of Norfolk Island, and what I say is no less the Law than if it issued from the King's own mouth! Now I will have three cheers for His Royal Majesty King George, and make them loud! Hip-hip!"

"Hurrah!" everybody bellowed, and twice more.

"And three cheers for Lieutenant King, who has worked wonders! Mr. King, I salute ye and wish ye Godspeed. Hip-hip!"

The cheers for King were louder than those for the King, and their King stood dazed, beaming, immensely gratified. For a minute he actually loved Major Ross.

"I now require that every last one of ye pass beneath the Union and bow the head as affirmation of your oath of loyalty!"

The crowd filed past, awed into fearful solemnity.

Though Richard stood at the head of his sawyers and closer to the Union than the new convict arrivals, he had spotted many faces he knew, some with delight: Will Connelly, Neddy Perrott and Taffy Edmunds; Tommy Kidner, Aaron Davis, Mikey Dennison, Steve Martin, George Guest and his boon companion, Ed Risby; George Whitacre. Among the new marines he saw his gunsmith apprentice, Daniel Stanfield, and two privates from Alexander days, Elias Bishop and Joe McCaldren. No doubt the convicts would come rushing to greet him—how to explain that Major Ross meant every word he said, and would not appreciate his head sawyer dallying to chat with old friends? Then Major Ross solved his dilemma by shouting his name.

"Yes, sir?" he asked as the crowd melted away.

"I will depute Private Stanfield to find Edmunds. Will ye be at the third sawpit?"

"Aye, sir."

"I am sending ye John Lawrell to live with ye and do whatever ye require of him. A good enough fellow, but a little slow in the noggin. Have him tend your garden. For the first six weeks Tom Crowder will collect everything as it ripens, after that he will take only two-thirds."

"Aye, sir," said Richard, saluted and departed in haste. John Lawrell. . . . He had been at Norfolk Island for a year and Richard knew him slightly; a good-natured, rather shambling Cornishman off Dunkirk hulk and Scarborough, and part of the general labor pool operated by Stephen. What *was* Major Ross up to? In effect, he had just endowed Richard with a servant to tend his unofficial block.

By the time he reached the third sawpit to find Sam Hussey and Harry Humphreys sawing, he had seen the Major's reason: with so many new people on the island, those old residents who owned good vegetable gardens were at risk of losing their produce to thieves, Law Martial or no Law Martial. Ross had given him a guard to make sure his produce was not pilfered, and he would be doing the same to all those with decent gardens. And trust Ross to select guards from among the ranks of the unoffending dimwitted. Stifling a sigh, Richard vowed that during his time off he would be sawing to build Lawrell his own hut. The thought of sharing a house was far more repugnant than the thought of too little food.

"I am off to see to the new pits, Billy," he said to Private Wigfall, whom he counted a good friend. He winked, laughed. "*And* make sure we don't get any fucken Williams as sawyers." He thought of something else. "If a Welshman named Taffy Edmunds reports in, sit him down in the shade—not with the women!—and tell him to wait until I get back. He will be our master sharpener. A pity he does not like women, but he will have to learn to."

Three of the new pits lay beyond the limits of Sydney Town to the east, where the hillsides were still heavily forested. Somehow Ross had already managed to find time to think out what he wanted, and issued instructions that trees were to be felled in a strip twenty feet wide from Turtle Bay to Ball Bay as the start of a proper road. Those on the slopes leading to Turtle Bay would be laid lengthwise and slid downhill; once the tilt switched to Ball Bay, another sawpit would be dug at Ball Bay to deal with that timber. It was going to be impossible for one man to keep an eye on so many pits so far apart, which meant that he would have to make sure he picked a head sawyer for each pit who would not slacken the pace because the supervisor was elsewhere. Nor was this the only road: a strip twenty feet wide was to be cleared to Cascade, and a third, the longest, westward to Anson Bay. Sawpits and more sawpits, those were the Major's orders.

On the way back he skirted the unnamed beach which seemed to act as a net to catch any pines which tumbled down the cliffs into the water, piling them up while the sea pushed them inland to form a raft of logs so ancient that they had turned to a kind of stone. And there, washing back and forth in the water—the wind was too far west to lash up a heavy surf—was a convoluted heap of canvas sail off Sirius. Useful, he understood immediately, quickening his pace. The tide was just beginning to come in, so it was unlikely that the sail would wash out to sea again, but he thought the find too important to risk losing by dawdling.

The first man in authority he saw was Stephen, deputed to the stone quarry these days.

Wreathed in smiles, Stephen promptly abandoned his workers. "Plague take this huge influx! I've hardly seen ye in a week." His face changed. "Oh,

Richard, the shame of it!" he cried. "To lose Sirius—what evil forces are conniving against us?"

"I know not. Nor do I think I want to know."

"What brings ye down here?"

"New sawpits, what else? With Major Ross as commandant, we are to go from the idealism of Marcus Aurelius to the pragmatism of Augustus. I do not say the Major will leave Norfolk Island marble, as he did not find it brick, but he will certainly give it roads—a hint, I am sure, that he is going to send people elsewhere than Sydney Town." He looked brisk. "Can ye spare some time and men?"

"If the reason be good enough. What's amiss?"

"Nothing for a change," grinned Richard. "In fact, I am the bearer of good news. There is a huge mass of Sirius's sail lying in the far beach, and more may come around the point with the tide on the flood. It will serve as canopies for those untented. Once people are properly housed it can be cut into hammocks, sheets for the officers' beds—a thousand and one things. I imagine that quite a lot of the officers' property will be spirited away by the likes of Francis and Peck."

"God bless ye, Richard!" Stephen ran off, shouting and waving to his men.

That evening, armed with a pine-knot torch to find his way back up the vale in the darkness (curfew was set for eight o'clock), Richard ventured into Sydney Town in search of the faces he had seen amid the assembly. Tents were pitched behind the row of huts on the beachfront, but many of the convicts were doomed to sleep in the open, Sirius's crew taking precedence in the matter of tents. By tomorrow, he hoped, Sirius's sails would roof them over.

A big fire of pine scraps burned where the shelterless would lie down their heads. Though he had been on the island for sixteen months, it still amazed Richard how suddenly the air chilled once the sun went down, no matter how hot the day had been; only when humidity descended did this cooling off not happen, and so far 1790 had not been at all sultry. A sign, he thought, that the weather this year would be drier, though how he came to that conclusion he did not know. Instinct arising from some Druid ancestor?

About a hundred people were huddled together around the tall blaze, belongings strewn about them. Unlike the marines and their officers, the convicts had been disembarked together with all they owned, including their precious blankets and buckets. Feet were universally bare; shoes had run out months ago, nor did Norfolk Island have any. He prayed that it would not rain that night; much of the island's rain fell at night, and out of what had been a clear sky moments before. The convicts had all been landed in downpours, had not had sufficient fine weather yet to dry out completely. There would be an epidemic of chills and fevers, and perhaps the island's record would be broken: not one person in it had died of natural causes or disease since Lieutenant King and his original 23 companions had come ashore over two years ago. Whatever else Norfolk Island might or might not be, its climate engendered splendid health.

Sirius wallowed on the reef, a mournful sight. The grapevine had already informed Richard that Willy Dring and James Branagan—the latter a man he did not know—had volunteered to swim out to the wreck, toss the remaining poultry, dogs and cats over the side, and heave floatable kegs and casks into the water. Dring was not the right man for this; the Yorkshireman and his crony Joe Robinson, once steady fellows, seemed to have deteriorated.

He spied Will Connelly and Neddy Perrott sitting with women who must be theirs—that was a good sign!—and began to pick his way through the crowd.

"Richard! Oh, Richard my love, Richard my love!"

Lizzie Lock threw herself upon him, twined her arms about his neck and covered his face with kisses, crooning, weeping, mumbling.

His reaction was utterly instinctive, over and done before he could think of suppressing it, of waiting until some more private opportunity arrived to tell her that he could not share any part of himself with her, wife though she was. No one had told him that she was here, and he had not thought of her once since that magical day when William Henry, little Mary and Peg had returned to live in his soul. Before he could control them, his hands had gone to fasten about Lizzie's arms and wrench her away.

Flesh crawling, hair on end, he stared at her as if she were a visitation from Hell. "Don't touch me!" he cried, white-faced. "Don't *touch* me!"

And she, poor creature, staggered plummeting from ecstatic joy to horror, to bewilderment, to a pain so great that she clutched at her meager chest and looked at him out of eyes blinded to everything but his revulsion. Breath gone, her mouth opened and closed without a sound; she fell to her knees, powerless.

The moment she had uttered his name the whole group turned to look, and those in it who knew him, who had so eagerly anticipated this reunion, gasped, gaped, murmured.

"I am your wife!" she screamed thinly from her knees. "Richard, I am your wife!"

His eyes were clearing, took in the sight of her at his feet, took in the growing anger and outrage on the faces of his friends, took in the greed of the uninvolved to eat up as much of this show as its participants were willing to enact. What to do? What to say? Even as one part of him asked these unanswerable questions, a second part of him was noting the onlookers, and a third part of him was shrinking in horror—she was going to touch him! The visceral part won: he backed away, out of her reach.

The die was cast. Better then to finish it the way it had started, by the glaring light of a public bonfire in the midst of a collection of people who would—and rightly so—condemn him as a heartless wretch in sore need of a flogging.

"I am very sorry, Lizzie," he managed, "but I cannot take up with you again. I—just—cannot." His hands lifted, fell. "I want no wife, I—"

He could find nothing else to say, and having nothing else to say, turned and left.

The next day, Tuesday, he met Stephen as usual at Point Hunter to watch the sunset. It was one of those cloudless evenings when the massive red disc had slid into the sea with what Richard always fancied should be a boiling sizzle, and as the light died out of the sky and the vault darkened to indigo, the vanished sun seemed to bend its rays back through the vast depths of the water to endow it with a pale, milky-blue luminousness far brighter than the heavens.

"This is a wondrous place," said Stephen, who must surely have heard what the whole settlement was saying, but chose not to mention it. "Here is where the Garden of Eden was, I am convinced of it. It ravishes me, it calls to me like a siren. And I do not know why, only that it is unearthly. No parallel anywhere. But now that men are here, they will ruin it. 'Twas Man ruined Eden."

"No, they will merely try to ruin it, mistaking it for other earth they have ruined. This place looks after itself because it is beloved of God."

"There are ghosts here, you know," Stephen remarked idly. "I saw one as clear as day—it was day, as a matter of fact. A giant of a fellow with huge calf muscles, golden skin, naked save for a piece of papery cloth marked in brown across his loins. His face was sternly beautiful, patrician, and both his thighs were tattooed in a pattern of curliqued stripes. A kind of man I have never set eyes upon, could not have imagined in my dreams. He came down the beach toward me, then, when I might almost have touched him, he turned and walked straight through the wall of Nat Lucas's house. Olivia began to scream the place down."

"Then I am glad I live up the vale. Though Billy Wigfall told me recently that he saw John Bryant on the hillside where the tree killed him. One moment he was standing there, the next moment he was gone. As if, said Billy, he was startled at being discovered."

The surf was pounding in; Supply had sailed from the roads, was working her way around to Cascade. Embarkation would not be easy for Mr. King's pregnant lady, forced to leap from that rock into a heaving longboat.

"Is it true that Dring and Branagan got into the rum last night aboard Sirius and set fire to her?" Richard asked.

"Aye. Private John Escott—he is Ross's servant—spotted the flames after dark from Government House's eminence and volunteered to swim out. Ross agreed because the man is very strong in the water. Escott found Dring and Branagan almost insensible from rum, busy warming themselves at the fire. He threw them into the sea, put out the conflagration—it had burned right through the gun deck—and stayed on Sirius until this morning, when they got him off together with the rum. Dring and Branagan have been clapped in irons and put in Lieutenant King's new guardhouse. The Major is livid, having left the rum aboard Sirius thinking 'twould be much safer there than ashore. I suspect that as soon as the old commandant has sailed on Supply, the new commandant will administer either capital punishment or five hundred lashes. He cannot afford to ignore this first infringement of his Law Martial."

Very dark in the failing light, Stephen's eyes turned to Richard, sitting coiled as tensely as a steel spring. "I hear that ye had a visit from the Major early today?"

Richard smiled wryly. "Major Ross's ears belong to a bat. How or from whom I cannot hazard a guess, but he heard what went on last night at the bonfire. Well, ye know him. Waited until I went home for breakfast, barged in, sat himself down and looked at me very much as he might have inspected a new sort of grub. 'I hear that ye publicly repudiated your wife,' he said. I answered with a yes and he grunted. Then he said, 'Not what I might have expected from ye, Morgan, but I daresay ye have your reasons, ye usually do.' "

Stephen chuckled. "He really does have a way with words!"

"He then proceeded to ask me if I thought my wife would make a suitable housekeeper for an officer! I told him she was clean, tidy, an excellent mender and darner of clothes, a good cook, and—as far as I knew—a virgin. Whereupon he slapped his hands on his knees and stood up. 'Does she like children?' he asked. I said I thought so, judging from her behavior with the children in Gloucester Gaol. 'And ye're sure she is not a temptress?' he asked. I said I was absolutely positive about that. 'Then she will suit me down to the ground,' he said, and marched out looking as pleased as the cat that got to the cream."

Stephen doubled up with laughter. "I swear, Richard," he said when he was able, "that ye cannot put a foot wrong with Major Ross. For some reason quite beyond me he likes you enormously."

"He likes me, " said Richard, "because I am not a bit afraid of him and I tell him the truth, not what I think he wants to hear. Which is why he will never esteem Tommy Crowder the way King did. When I stood up to King he had half a mind to flog me, whereas I have never needed to stand up to Major Ross."

"King is an English King," said Stephen rather tangentially, "not an Irish King. The Celt in him is pure Cornish, far more akin to the Welsh. Which means he is touchy and moody. And Royal Navy down to his marrow. Ross is your classical Scotchman with but one mood—dour. His roots lie in a cold, bleak land that either makes or breaks." He rose to his feet and held out his hand to help Richard up. "I am glad that he has solved the problem of what was going to happen to your repudiated wife."

"Well, ye told me not to marry her," said Richard with a sigh. "Had I known she was here I would have been prepared, but it was a bolt from the blue. My eyes were on Will Connelly when suddenly she was hanging around my neck smothering me in wet kisses. I—I smelled her and felt her, Stephen. She was far too close to see. As long as I have known her there have been other smells, and none of them nice. Port Jackson stank, just as the old castle stank. But the rank smell of woman in my nostrils—I have been alone too long, and things smell sweet away from the sawpits and Sydney Town. 'Tis not that she actually stinks, she does not, only that I could not bear how she smelled. My reasons are not very reasonable, even to myself, and God knows I am not proud of what I did. All I was conscious of at the time was revulsion—as if I had walked after dark straight into a spider's web. My gut reacted, I struck out blindly. And after that it was too late to mend any of my fences, so I tore them out of the ground."

"I can understand," said Stephen gently. "What I do not begin to understand is how ye could have forgotten she was likely to be here with the rest."

"Nor do I, looking back on it."

"My fault too. I should have said something."

"Ye were too busy with Sirius and the consequences. But there is another thing torments me—she was ashore for days and she knew I was here—why did she wait?"

They had reached Stephen's house; he slipped inside without answering, then watched through the window as Richard's torch went away up the vale and winked from sight. Why did she wait, Richard? Because in her heart of hearts she knew that were she to approach you in private, you would do what you ended in doing anyway—rejecting her. Or perhaps, being a woman, she longed for you to seek her out and claim her. Poor Lizzie Lock. . . . He has been entirely alone for six months up there in his solitary house with only his dog for company, and he is very content. I do not know what goes on in his mind, except that until fairly recently he had put his emotions to sleep like a bear through winter. His marriage to Lizzie was a thing done in that sleep, from which I think he did not expect to awaken. Then suddenly he did—I saw him do it.

Time was getting on. Stephen looked at his watch, pressed his lips together and debated about whether he was hungry enough to bother heating broth to go with his bread supper. Captain John Hunter was in residence at Government House, and Johnny—oh, well. Heat the soup, Stephen, it is chill enough for a fire.

"All I want," said Richard, erupting into the room as Stephen blew on the reluctant flames, "is to be left alone with my books and my dog! To have a meed of privacy!"

"Then what are ye doing here?" Stephen asked, sitting back on his heels. "The meed of privacy is up yon vale."

"Aye, but—but—" said Richard, floundering.

"Why not simply admit to yourself, Richard," Stephen said, in no mood to put up with megrims, "that ye's consumed with guilt over what ye did—all right, *had* to do!—to Lizzie Lock? Ye're not a man finds it easy to live with a you who did not come up to expectations. In fact, I never saw anybody with such high standards of self-conduct—ye're a fucken Protestant martyr!"

"Oh, don't fucken preach!" Richard snapped. "Your trouble is that ye're never sure whether to be a Catholic or a Protestant anything, let alone martyr! Why not simply admit to yourself that ye're lovesick for Johnny and want to wallop Hunter?"

Blue eyes blazed at eyes gone absolutely grey for a full minute; neither man moved a muscle. Then both mouths started to quiver at the same instant; they howled with laughter.

"It clears the air," Stephen said, mopping his face on a rag.

"Aye, that it does," gasped Richard, borrowing it.

"Ye'd better eat Johnny's share of the soup now that ye're here—why did ye come back?"

"I think because you didn't answer my question, to which I no longer require an answer. Ye're right, Stephen. Lizzie is something I have to suffer through, including not liking myself."

John Lawrell moved in, and moved out again so quickly that the poor fellow's weak head spun; Richard had a comfortable hut up for him within a month, erected at the far end of his little acre with its door and window apertures facing away from his own house. If Lawrell snored after that, Richard was too far away to hear. With regard to his duties he proved excellent, but he had one flaw: he loved to play card games and had to be restrained from gambling away his scant rations.

Sydney Town was mushrooming into veritable streets of small wooden huts, banged together by Nat Lucas and his carpenters as fast as Richard's sawpits could feed him planks and beams. With neither the time nor the equipment to put a shiplap or dovetail on the boards to join them in a finished way, thin battens were nailed down the gaps—a style not unattractive if, like the interior of Richard's house, the wood was sanded to a dull polish. Government House, enlarged by King to a size permitting him to entertain half a dozen dinner guests in better days, finally sported sheet glass in its small-paned windows, courtesy of Governor Phillip. Every other residence, including those commodious enough to satisfy the naval and marine officers, had to make do with shutters or naked apertures. One pit was put to sawing the basis for creating shingles; all the roofs would eventually be shingled, though the timber had first to be seasoned in sea-water for six weeks before it could be split. This meant temporary roofs of flax thatch; the task of venturing far and wide in search of flax was handed over to Sirius's sailors, whom Ross flatly refused to let do nothing.

Liberated from the need to supply Port Jackson with lime, at least for the present, the deposits of calcarenite stone were worked for foundations and chimneys. Having found a good local hardwood the shingle sawpit also cut, the four coopers the island now possessed began to make barrels. Ross had set women to grinding King's crop of wheat in hand querns, deeming barrels of flour safer from rats than loose grain. Aaron Davis, who had ended in working as a baker at Port Jackson, was appointed community baker. Not that bread was something the community saw every day; Sundays and Wednesdays were bread, Mondays and Thursdays were rice, Saturdays were pease, and Tuesdays and Fridays a porridge of Indian corn mixed with oatmeal.

Eyeing his rapidly proliferating swine, Ross built a small hearth and furnace and started producing salt. What parts of the beast not suitable for salting down were minced and became sausages sheathed in intestine.

"The best thing about a pig," Major Ross was heard to say, "is that the only inedible part of it is the oink." As he was known to possess absolutely no sense of humor, the general assumption was that he had spoken seriously.

Sirius, which continued to lie with her stern on and off the reef, was gradually stripped of every salvageable item, from some of her six-pounder guns to the last of the many kegs of nails His Excellency had sent from his settlement, turning to brick and stone, to this settlement of perpetual wood. Saddest loss was the scrap iron Sirius had carried for Norfolk Island's smithy, still down in her holds and too risky to go after. Almost all the canvas she flew had washed ashore tangled in lines and spars, and her cutter had survived together with its oars; lopping down the masts had wrecked every other boat she owned.

Among the last things to come off her were several casks of tobacco and some crates of cheap Bristol soap. Though the soap did go into Government Stores for general distribution, the tobacco never saw the interior of a pipe bowl—much to the disgust of the seamen, who deemed a puff only slightly less desirable than a swig of rum. George Guest and Henry Hatheway, both from rural parts, went to Major Ross and informed him that in Gloucester gardens wives dealt with slugs, caterpillars and grubs by plundering their husbands' tobacco. They steeped the leaves in boiling water, then sudsed the liquid with soap and sprinkled the concoction upon their vegetables. The first rain washed it away, but until that fell, wriggly pests turned up their noses and refused to eat such horrid-tasting food.

From that moment on, no one was allowed to throw away a single drop of soapy water. A small group of women was put to stewing the tobacco, which, experience revealed, retained its potency through several infusions.

As for soap—why, it could be made just as it was made in poor farmhouses and cottages from one end of the British Isles to the other: fat and lye. Lard was the fat of the pig, and the settlement had plenty of it. To obtain lye was easy: soak the thoroughly burned ashes of unwanted potato, carrot, turnip and beet leaves, boil the mess down a little, and strain. The liquid part was lye. Watering cans were scarce, but a woman armed with a bucket of sudsed tobacco solution and a pewter dipper with holes punched in its bottom sprinkled the growing vegetables—and crops!—quite efficiently enough. To be ready for the next wave, the grub poison was stockpiled in empty rum pipes.

In such practical matters the Commandant shone. His mind had progressed from manufacturing salt, sausages and grub poison to whether he might use some of the sawdust in smokehouses instead of turning it all into the soil. What could not be salted down might perhaps be smoked, including fish. Owning a large work force, Ross was determined no member of it would be idle. The first step was to produce as much food as possible; the second step was to get as many of his charges as possible maintaining themselves without consuming Government food. This latter step was clearly the only justification for the whole Botany Bay experiment—what was the point of dumping thousands of convicts and guards at the far ends of the earth if the Government had to keep feeding them ad infinitum?

At which moment, Supply having gone two weeks earlier to bear the dreadful news about Sirius to His Excellency, the birds arrived on Mt. Pitt, a 1,000-foot sprawl at the northwestern end of the island. A very few days verified King's report on these big petrels; they came in from the day's fishing on dusk to waddle to their burrows, equipped with so little brain and so much ignorance of the ways of men that they allowed themselves to be captured without flight or resistance.

Paths were cut through the vine (coming to be called "Samson's sinew" from its immense girth) up the flanks of the mountain from the new Cascade road, and work was finished in time for the bird catchers to set out in daylight of the first day, armed with sacks. Salt meat rations were cut to three pounds a week and the quantities of bread, rice, pease and oatmeal were halved. The Mt. Pitt bird would have to fill up the ration gaps.

Rum was reduced to a half-pint of very watery grog a day even for the officers, which did not worry Lieutenant Ralph Clark in the least; he was still able to trade his share of it for badly needed shirts, underdrawers, stockings and the like; hardly any of his property off Sirius had reached him, though he caught glimpses of it on some convict's back. Nor had Major Ross got his property off Sirius, but he bore his losses with a great deal less whinging than Clark, a natural complainer.

Potatoes were issued whenever they were dug at the rate of a few between each dozen people, and harvested vegetables were shared equally. Perhaps because green vegetables owned so little substance—and especially because scurvy was nonexistent—there were always more than enough of them to go around; people would rather eat anything (except fish) than a huge bowl of spinach or runner beans.

It was going to be a long, desperate business. Supply, the Major knew, would not return. The thirty-four-year-old Channel tender would have to sail to the East Indies for food, else those at Port Jackson would certainly starve to death; those at Norfolk Island would probably not, but would be reduced to scratching a primitive living. And the great experiment would fail.

Robert Ross believed as ardently as Arthur Phillip that whatever perils and privations the future might hold, those people in his charge must not be permitted to sink below the Christian standards of any British community anywhere. Somehow morality, decency, literacy, technocracy and all the other virtues of proper European civilization *must* be preserved. Were they not, then those who did not actually die would be nothings. Where Ross differed from Phillip lay in the more abstract virtues of optimism and faith. Phillip was determined that the great experiment would succeed. Ross simply knew that all of it—the time, the money, the property, the pain—was utterly wasted, sucked into the maw of ignominy to leave no trace behind. Which conviction, rooted though it was, did not deter him in the slightest from exerting his every effort to deal with matters those posturing fools in London had not even taken into account while they listened to Sir Joseph Banks and Mr. James Maria Matra and drew up their fine Heads of a Plan. How easy it was to move human pawns on a global chessboard when the chair was comfortable, the stomach full, the fire warm and the port decanter bottomless.

The diet of Mt. Pitt bird brought no protests from anyone. Its flesh was dark and tasted slightly but not offensively fishy, it oozed very little fat when spitted or stewed, and at the beginning of this winter breeding every female bird carried an egg inside her. Once the feathers—easily plucked out—were removed, the body was not large, so one bird fed a child, two a woman, three a man, and four or five a glutton. The official catchers were instructed to bring down enough birds for smoking too. At first Ross tried to limit both the number of birds and the number of people let walk up the mountain in search of them. When Law Martial and the sight of Dring and Branagan after 500 lashes (administered in increments) did not deter people from venturing after this fantastic change from salt meat, fish and vegetables, Ross shrugged his shoulders and ceased trying to put a curb on bird-getting. Lieutenant Ralph Clark, head of Government Stores, began to record the figures as best he knew them: the catch crept up from 147 birds a day shortly into April to 1,890 a day one month later. Of these some were smoked, but the vast majority were thrown away uneaten; what all the bird catchers wanted to eat were the unlaid eggs and only the unlaid eggs. Clark himself was an unabashed egg fancier and great bird gatherer.

For Richard, who walked the five-mile round journey every other day and enjoyed his Mt. Pitt poultry very much, the arrival of the bird led to the temporary loss of his garden guard. John Lawrell was apprehended by the Law Martial patrol after curfew dragging a sack; when told to halt he tried to flee, got a musket butt on the head and was thrown into the guardhouse. A week later he was released, still nursing his aching pate, and given a dozen lashes with a medium cat.

"What on earth possessed ye, John?" Richard demanded at Turtle Bay, whence he had marched the moaning Lawrell as soon as his day's work at the sawpits was done. "*Sixty-eight* birds!" He threw a dipper of salt water onto Lawrell's back unsympathetically. "Will ye stand still, damn it? I would not need to do this if ye'd just get up the gumption to walk farther into the water and duck down."

"Cards!" gasped Lawrell, teeth chattering; the wind was due south and very cold.

"Cards." Richard led him out of the water and patted his welts dry with a rag. "Ye'll live," he said then. "Jimmy Richardson did not lay it on hard, ye're not bleeding much. Were ye a woman, ye'd not have fared so well. And what do cards have to do with it?"

"Lost," said Lawrell simply, following Richard down the road past the outermost row of houses. "Had to pay somehow. Josh Peck said I could save them a walk and get their birds for them. But I did not know how heavy the sack would be, so I was too slow to get back before curfew."

"Then learn from this lesson, John, *please.* If ye must play cards, play with decent men, not cheats and liars like that lot. Now go on up the vale to bed."

After several moves, Stephen Donovan now had a very good house just to the east of the Cascade road, and Nat Lucas an equally good house on an acre of flat ground beyond him. The swamp did not encroach on this area, but Major Ross was busy trying to drain the swamp by digging an outlet to Turtle Bay. Flat land was arable land, and all the tiny brooks which fed the Arthur's Vale stream could not contribute enough water to force an exit to the sea; the swamp was a terminus using up growing space.

"Come!" Stephen called when Richard knocked.

"I have just sent my erring guard to bed," said Richard, sitting down with a sigh. "Peck and the rest called in his card debts by making him bring them birds. Oh, he is a nodcock!"

"But useful. Here, share my fish. The coble got out today and Johnny is dancing attendance on Captain Hunter, so I have his share too. A welcome change from Mt. Pitt birds."

"I would rather eat fish any day," said Richard, tucking in, "and why the craze for female birds gravid with egg I do not know. I will repay this kindness by digging ye a handful of potatoes tomorrow. Mine are coming on nicely, one reason why I am glad to have Lawrell back on duty now I can keep a third of my produce."

"Is anybody speaking to you yet?" Stephen asked when they were done, the dishes washed, the chessboard set up.

"Not among those who have sided with my wife—Connelly, Perrott and a few others from Ceres and Alexander days. Oddly enough, the group who knew her in Gloucester Gaol before my time there—Guest, Risby, Hatheway—have sided with me." He looked disgusted. "As if there are sides to take. Ridiculous. Lizzie is very satisfied with her lot, up there on the Government House knoll clucking and fussing over Little John, though she don't try it with the Major."

"She is in love with you, Richard, and scorned," Stephen said, thinking that enough time had gone by to bring this aspect up.

Richard stared in astonishment. "Rubbish! There was never love between us. I know you hoped that marrying her might lead to love, but it did not."

"She loves you."

Troubled, Richard said nothing for a while, moved and lost a pawn, essayed a knight. If Lizzie loved him, then her hurt was far greater than he had thought. Remembering what she had said about Lady Penrhyn and the stripping of women's pride, that was how he had seen the worst aspect of his crime against her—as a public humiliation of unpardonable kind. She had never said she loved him, never indicated that by word or look. . . . He lost his knight.

"How goes it between the Marine Corps and the Navy?" he asked.

"Very touchy. Hunter has never liked Major Ross, but his exile here only serves to enhance his loathing. So far they have managed not to have an actual falling out, but that is definitely coming. Limited to Sirius's cutter, he can undertake no long sea excursions, so he spends most of his time rowing around his nemesis, Nepean Island—looking, I suspect, for navigational evidence to bolster his defense when he comes to court martial in England. Once he has sounded every inch of the bottom and compiled his chart, he will do the same sort of thing everywhere on these coasts."

"Why has Johnny half-returned to him, if that is not an intrusion into your private world?"

Shrugging, Stephen turned the corners of his mouth down. "No, I will answer. 'Tis very hard for a seaman to resist the authority of the captain unless he is of mutinous make, and that Johnny is not. Johnny is Royal Navy and Hunter next to God."

"I also heard that Lieutenant William Bradley, Royal Navy, has quit the naval officers' quarters and moved himself out along the road to Ball Bay."

"Ye deduced that, no doubt, from sawing timber for his new house. Aye, he has gone, and no one mourns the fact. A very strange man, Bradley—talks to himself, which is why he needs no company other than himself. As I understand it, the Major has put him to rough surveying of the interior. A great affront to Hunter, who is adamant that naval persons of any rank ought not to toil on land."

Ignominiously beaten, Richard rose to kindle a pine knot in Stephen's fire. "I would like my revenge, but if I do not go now I will be caught out after curfew. D'ye care to walk to the mountain with me tomorrow for another lot of birds?"

"Since we ate all the fish, gladly."

Stephen waved him off down the vale, trying to imagine the expression on Richard's face when he entered his house. Sirius's sail had been released from duty as shelter and had been divided up among the free men for use as mattresses or hammocks; thanks to King's wheat crop as well as the fact that the settlement owned neither horses nor cattle, there was ample straw for stuffing. To Stephen, officially the captor of the sail, went as much as he wanted, so he had taken enough for his own needs and Richard's. Long weathering and a few soapy washes in fresh water softened the canvas sufficiently to turn it into reasonable sheets, not to mention stout trowsers. Parties of women skilled with a needle were sewing away to produce new trowsers for the enlisted marines and sailors, who were obliged to give up a pair of old trowsers to a convict in return for a pair of new ones. No one truly appreciated the amount of sail a ship the size of Sirius carried until it was liberated for other uses.

"I cannot thank you enough for the canvas," Richard said when he met Stephen on the Cascade road at sundown on the following day. "Using blankets as a bottom sheet on one's bed wears them out in no time. The canvas will last for years."

"I suspect it may have to."

They climbed up the farthest path, which was the least popular one as it involved the longest walk, and gathered a half-dozen birds each high on the mountain, where the creatures still thronged in countless numbers. All that was necessary was to reach down and pick one up; a quick wring of its neck, and into the sack. The eggs were laid now, though the amount of birds being caught had not diminished; Clark's tally was growing into many thousands, and took account only of birds handed over to Government Stores plus whatever he and his fellow officers collected.

On the way back they passed through a vast clearing where the timber was already felled—some acres of it—on the flattish crest of the hills which divided the direction of the streams from those flowing north to Cascade Bay, those flowing east to Ball Bay, and those flowing south to the swamp or what was becoming known as Phillimore's stream, around the corner from the far beach. Here in this clearing—what *was* Major Ross's purpose?—it was possible to look north at the mountain.

Cloudless darkness had fallen, the stars so dense and brilliant that a man could fancy there must be an intensely glowing white layer behind the darkness of the sky, and that God had pricked the heavens to let some of that silver firmament shine through. Where the bulk of the mountain should have loomed as a black shadow, what looked like streamers of darting fireflies flickered in and out of the gloom, shifting and sparkling rivers of flame; the torches of hundreds of men coming down the slopes.

"Beautiful!" breathed Richard, stunned.

"How could a man tire of this place?"

They remained watching until the lights died away and then resumed their walk amid dozens of panting, sack-laden predators, torches all around them.

* * *

Winter came, drier and colder than last year's; the wheat and Indian corn were planted over many more acres than King's eleven, but were slow to come up until a welcome day of squally rain followed by a day of sun saw the vale and hillsides turn magically from blood-red soil to vividly green grass.

The official tally of Mt. Pitt birds rose to over 170,000—an average of 340 birds per person over 100 days. The island was still under Law Martial; Major Ross cut salt meat entirely from everybody's rations, aware that the thousands of petrels remaining on the mountain would fly away once their chicks were strong enough to take wing. There had been plenty of heavy floggings administered by Jim Richardson, whom Richard had used as a sawyer until he broke his leg. To wield his assortment of cats put no strain on the afflicted member, and he quite liked this exclusive occupation. The odium in which he was regarded by almost all of his fellows, free as well as felon, worried him not in the slightest.

There had also been some hangings. Not of convicts: of sailors. Captain Hunter's servants, assisted by Ross's servant the noble Escott of Sirius fame, pillaged the Major's scanty supply of rum, drank some of it and sold the rest. In his role of judge, jury and executioner, Lieutenant-Governor Ross hanged three of the offenders, though not Escott and not Hunter's chief minion, Elliott. Escott's other punishment was to be stripped of his Sirius valor; Ross gave the official credit for swimming out to the wreck to a convict named John Arscott. Escott and Elliott were let off with 500 lashes from the meanest cat, a punishment which, as the Major had promised in his address at the beginning of Law Martial, laid them bare to the bone from neck to ankles. This total was administered in a series of five floggings of 100 lashes each, 100 lashes being considered the most any man could bear at one time. The flogger started at the shoulders and moved slowly down the body over back, buttocks and thighs to finish at the calves. Murmurs of mutiny arose among the sailors, but in the face of this terrible crime against the free, rum-drinking community Captain Hunter was unable to support his men's cause, while the furious marines looked only too happy to shoot a mob of sailors down. Thanks to Private Daniel Stanfield their muskets were in excellent condition and they kept their cartridges dry; musket practice under Stephen and Richard still happened on Saturday mornings.

Major Ross arrived at Richard's house in the aftermath of the rum-stealing disaster, face even grimmer than usual.

This task is killing him, thought Richard, ushering the Major to a chair; he has aged ten years since arriving here.

"Mr. Donovan," Ross announced, "imparted some interesting facts about ye to me, Morgan. He says ye can distill rum."

"Aye, sir—given the equipment and the ingredients. Though I cannot promise that it will taste any better than the stuff produced in Rio de Janeiro, from reports of that. Like all spirits, rum should be aged in the cask before being drunk, but if ye want what I think ye want, there is not the time. The results will be raw and nasty."

"Beggars cannot be choosers." Ross snapped his fingers at the dog, which bustled over to be patted. "How are ye, MacTavish?"

MacTavish wagged his undocked tail and looked adorable.

"I was a victualler in Bristol, sir, among other things," said Richard, throwing a log onto his fire, "so I understand better than most how big are the horns of this dilemma. Men who are used to rum or gin every day cannot live happily without it. That can be as true of women. Only the Law Martial and lack of equipment has prevented construction of a still here already. I will gladly build ye the still and work it, but. . . ."

Hands out to the fire, Ross grunted. "I know what ye're implying. The moment 'tis known a still exists, there will be those who will not be content with a half-pint a day and others who will see profit in it."

"Aye, sir."

"Ye have a fine crop of sugar cane, as does the Government."

Richard grinned. "I thought it might come in handy."

"Are ye a drinker yourself these days, Morgan?"

"Nay. On that I give you my word, Major Ross."

"I have one abstemious officer, Lieutenant Clark, so to him I will apportion supervision of this project. And tear my ranks apart looking for privates. Stanfield, Hayes and James Redman I can trust neither to imbibe nor to sell, and Captain Hunter"—his face twisted, was disciplined—"recommends his quarter gunner Drummond, his bosun's mate Mitchell, and his seaman Hibbs. That gives ye a total of six men and one officer."

"Ye cannot site it in the vale, sir," said Richard strongly.

"I agree. Have ye any suggestions?"

"Nay, sir. I travel only as far afield as my sawpits."

"Let me think about it, Morgan," said Ross, rising with some reluctance. "In the meantime, have Lawrell cut your sugar cane."

"Aye, sir. But I will tell him that ye've ordered me to start refining sugar to sweeten the officers' tea."

Off went the Major, nodding in satisfaction, to supervise the final installation of his grindstone. When the wheat came in, hand querns would not cope with it. Therefore the full-sized millstone would have to be turned by the only labor he had, that of men. A useful adjunct to floggings, which Ross tolerated but privately detested—not because of scruples, rather because the lash only deterred crime when it was administered in very large doses, and those rendered the victims partially crippled for the rest of their lives. To chain a man to the grindstone for a week or a month and make him push it like a sailor a capstan was *good* punishment, hideous but not ruinous.

The roads to Ball Bay and Cascade were finished. Hacking a road westward to Anson Bay began at the beginning of June, and yielded a delightful surprise; about a hundred acres of rolling hills and vales halfway between Sydney Town and Anson Bay were discovered utterly free of pine forest—for what reason, no one could fathom. Accepting this as a gift like unto the manna of the Mt. Pitt bird, Major Ross immediately decided to establish a new settlement there. The ground he had cleared at the middle of the Cascade road was intended as a place of banishment for the Sirius sailors; Phillipburgh, at the Cascade end of the road, was still trying to turn flax into canvas.

The settlement in the direction of Anson Bay was called after Her Majesty Queen Charlotte—Charlotte Field. Why was Richard not surprised when none other than Lieutenant Ralph Clark was deputed to establish Charlotte Field? In company with Privates Stanfield, Hayes and James Redman? The still would be tucked somewhere along the way between Sydney Town and Charlotte Field, he was sure of it.

Rightly so. Soon after, he was summoned to walk out in that direction to site a new sawpit for Charlotte Field. A nice area. The pineless ground was densely covered with a creeper Clark fancied resembled English cow-itch; the creeper came out of the ground easily and was found useful in the construction of fences when mixed with a bush sporting thorns two inches long—not a fence a pig would tackle, enterprising though pigs were.

Major Ross had chosen a site for the distillery down a track off the Anson Bay road well before Charlotte Field; a stream arose from a spring below the crest and flowed down with other tributaries to join a creek which entered Sydney Bay not far from its western promontory, Point Ross. On additional pay, the three marines and three sailors set to with a will to clear enough ground for a small wooden building and a woodheap of white oak, the same local tree which fueled both the salt house and the lime kiln because it burned to scant ash. The stone blocks which would make the hearth and furnace were hauled by convicts from Sydney Town, ostensibly destined for Charlotte Field later on; Richard and his six men took them from the road to the distillery themselves after dark. They also had to erect the shed. Ross furnished copper kettles, a few stopcocks and valves, copper pipe and vats made from barrels sawn in half. Richard managed the welding and assembling himself. Secrecy was maintained, rather to his surprise; the cut cane and some ears of Indian corn simply vanished to presses and hand querns at the distillery.

Four weeks later he was able to produce his first distillate. The Lieutenant-Governor sipped at it cautiously, grimaced, had another sip, then drank the rest of his quarter-pint down; he liked his rum as much as any other man.

"It tastes dreadful, Morgan, but it has the right effect," he said, actually smiling. "Ye may well have saved us from mutiny and murder. 'Twould be much smoother if it were aged, but that is for the future. Who knows? We may yet supply Port Jackson with rum as well as lime and timber."

"An it please ye, sir, I would now appreciate it if I could return to my sawpits," said Richard, to whom the sight of a still brought no happy memories. " 'Tis necessary to keep up the mash and the fire, not to mention the water, but I do not see the need to be here myself. Stanfield can take one shift and Drummond the other. If ye've any drop of good rum in store, we can put a bit of the raw distillate in an oak cask with a mite of the good stuff and see how it goes."

"Ye can share the task of supervision with Lieutenant Clark, Morgan, but 'tis a waste of your talents to keep ye here feeding the apparatus and the furnace, ye're right about that." He strolled off, smacking his lips, obviously permeated with a feeling of well-being. "Walk with me back to Sydney Town." Then he remembered the rest of the team, and paused to clap each man on the shoulder. "Guard and tend this well, boys," he said with startling affability, still smiling. " 'Twill earn each of ye an extra twenty pounds a year."

The road through the pines followed the crest down across the top of Mount George, where the views were glorious—the ocean, the whole of Sydney Town and its lagoons, the surf, Phillip and Neapean Islands. Stopping to gaze, Major Ross spoke.

"I have it in mind, Morgan, to free ye," he said. "I cannot give ye an absolute pardon, but I can give a conditional one until time and altered circumstances make it possible for me to petition a full pardon from His

Excellency in Port Jackson. I think ye've earned a better status as a free man than simple emancipation by virtue of having served out your sentence—which, as I remember, ye said expires in March of ninety-two?"

Richard's throat worked convulsively, his eyes overflowed with tears; he tried to speak, could not, nodded as he brushed at the torrent with his palms. Free. *Free.*

The Major continued to stare at Phillip Island. "There are others I am freeing as well—Lucas, Phillimore, Rice, the elder Mortimer, et cetera. Ye should all have the chance to take up land and make something of yourselves, for all of ye have behaved like decent men for as long as I have known ye. 'Tis thanks to your sort that Norfolk Island has managed to survive and I have been able to govern—not to mention Lieutenant King before me. As of now, Morgan, ye're a free man, which means that as supervisor of sawyers ye'll be paid a wage of twenty-five pounds a year. I will also pay ye an emolument for supervising the distillery—five pounds a year—and a sum of twenty for building it. None can be paid in coin of the realm—that His Majesty's Government did not give us. 'Twill be accorded to ye in notes of hand which will be properly entered in the Government's accounts. Ye can use it to transact business with the Stores or with private vendors. On the subject of the distillery I want complete silence, and I warn ye that I may close it down—this is an experiment only, which I am performing because I do not want to see any naval individuals go into the distilling business for themselves. My conscience gnaws, I suffer doubts," he ended, mood flattening. "Lieutenant Clark I can trust not to breathe a word, even to his journal. Its contents—as he well knows—must reflect not only his virtues, but mine also. Oh, I acquit him of the desire to publish, but sometimes journals fall into the wrong hands."

The speech was long enough to allow Richard to compose himself. "I am your man, Major Ross. That is the only way I can thank ye for all your many kindnesses." A smile lit his eyes, turning them very blue. "Though I have a favor to ask. Would ye let me make my first act as a free man the honor of shaking your hand?"

Ross extended his hand willingly. "I am for town," he said, "but I am afraid, Morgan, that ye must return to the distillery and fetch me enough of that horrible brew to water down my little remaining good stuff at dinner this evening." He grimaced. "I am as tired of Mt. Pitt bird as the next man, but I doubt there will be any complaints if there is a jug of spirits to wash it down."

Free! He was free! And *pardoned* free, which meant everything. All men were free once their sentences expired, but they were mere emancipists. A pardoned man had a reference. He was vindicated.

On the 4th of August a sail was sighted from Sydney Town; the entire community forgot work, discipline, illness, good sense. Lieutenant Clark and Captain George Johnston ascended Mount George and verified that the sail was real, but the ship passed serenely onward. Landing at Sydney Bay was impossible in the teeth of a strong southerly gale, so Captain Johnston and Captain Hunter walked to Cascade in the expectation of a landing there, where the water was as quiet as a millpond. But the ship passed serenely on, and by dusk she had disappeared northward. The mood that night in the town and vale, even in Charlotte Field and Phillipburgh, was despairing. To see a ship and be ignored! Oh, what worse disappointment could there be?

The next day Major Ross sent a party to the top of Mt. Pitt to watch, but in vain; the ship was definitely gone.

Then on the 7th of August people in Sydney Town were woken at dawn by screams of a ship on the far southern horizon.

The wind against her, she had not worked much farther in by late afternoon, but she had been joined by a second set of sails. This time it was real, this time they would not be ignored!

Unable to make contact with the first of the two sighted ships, Lieutenant Clark in the coble headed for the second one and managed to board her. She was Surprize, captained out of London by Nicholas Anstis, who had been first mate on Lady Penrhyn and had an interest in the slaving business. Surprize, he informed Clark, carried 204 convicts—but very few stores—for Norfolk Island. Before Clark could have a conniption fit, Anstis added that the other ship was Justinian, carrying no convicts but lots of provisions. Port Jackson no longer starved, and nor would Norfolk Island, where less than three weeks' rations of salt meat and flour remained.

"Which vessel was it ignored our signals?" Clark demanded.

"Lady Juliana. She carried a cargo of women felons to Port Jackson, but was leaking so badly that she sailed straight for Wampoa empty. She is to pick up a cargo of tea there, but first she needs dry docking," said Anstis. "Justinian and I are going on to Wampoa as soon as we have dropped our loads here."

Even men like Len Dyer and William Francis worked energetically to pile Surprize and Justinian longboats with vegetables for the greens-starved crews; neither was able to land any cargo, human or food. Letters came ashore from England and Port Jackson, together with some ships' officers of a mind to stretch their legs. Unloading would have to wait, happen if necessary at Cascade. The delighted Lieutenant Clark received no less than four fulsome missives from his beloved Betsy, learned that she and baby Ralphie were very well, and felt less anxious.

Governor Phillip explained to Major Ross on paper that Supply had been sent to Batavia, there to pick up whatever food her tiny holds could carry, if possible charter a Dutch vessel to follow her back to Port Jackson with more food, and drop off Lieutenant Philip Gidley King; His Excellency hoped that King would be able to board a Dutch East Indiaman from Batavia at least as far as Cape Town on his long journey of petition to London. As soon as Supply had returned to Port Jackson and was shipshape, she would be sent to Norfolk Island to pick up Captain John Hunter and his Sirius sailors—an event Phillip did not think likely to happen until well into 1791. But, said Phillip firmly, now that sufficient provisions had arrived, Major Ross had no excuse to continue governing under the Law Martial. That would have to be repealed *immediately.* Oh, bugger ye, King! thought the Major savagely. This is your doing, no one else's. How am I to get any work out of Hunter's sailors if I cannot hang them?

There was other bad news from Port Jackson as well. Storeship Guardian, en route from England laden with food, had purchased every beast Cape Town had to spare and set off on the last leg to Botany Bay. On Christmas Eve of 1789 she was 1,000 miles out of the Cape and proceeding placidly through reasonable seas when she sighted a summer iceberg. Her captain had not counted on how much water cattle could drink in one day, so he decided to take advantage of his good fortune and send a few boats to chip off some of the ice, thus replenishing his water. This was done expeditiously, and Guardian made sail away from the ice island. Captain Riou, a happy man, saw for himself that Guardian was well clear and went below to enjoy a good dinner. Fifteen minutes later the ship struck by the stern, wrenched her rudder off and stove in her round tucks. She made water slowly enough for Captain Riou to think that he stood a good chance of getting her back to Cape Town; every last animal was thrown over the side and five boats were launched with the majority of the crew and some very choice artisan convicts in them. But the sailors had broached the rum to deaden the pain of dying in a sea cold enough to harbor ice; the five boats reeled away loaded to the gunwales with drunken men. Only one of them reached land. Guardian reached land too, after limping in aimless spirals all over the south Indian Ocean for weeks. She beached not far from Cape Town, hardly any of her cargo worth salvaging. What could be saved was put aboard Lady Juliana, the first Botany Bay ship to arrive at the Cape of Good Hope after the disaster. But of animals Cape Town had absolutely none to sell Justinian a few days later; they had all been lost off Guardian. As had the personal effects of Governor Phillip, Major Ross, Captain David Collins and others among the senior marine officers. Ross for one never recovered from the magnitude of his financial losses when Guardian foundered, for by proxy he had bought a great many animals for his own use and breeding.

Good news perhaps to learn that starvation was postponed, but repeal of Law Martial and news of Guardian made the Major wish he was a genuine drinking man.

Some stores off Justinian and Surprize were landed over the next days, but none of the convicts—47 men and 157 women. The women were all off Lady Juliana; she had been the first of five ships to make Port Jackson during June. Naturally Phillip had expected a storeship. To find instead that this first vessel to reach them after so long held nothing more useful than women and clothing was appalling. Then storeship Justinian had sailed in, to be followed at the end of the month by Surprize, Neptune and none other than Scarborough, on a second venture to New South Wales.

"Oh, what a shock!" said Surgeon Murray of Justinian to a big audience of marine and stranded naval Norfolk Island officers. His face paled at the memory, he drew a long breath. "Surprize, Neptune and Scarborough brought an additional thousand convicts to Port Jackson, but two hundred and sixty-seven of them had died during the passage. They landed only seven hundred and fifty-nine, of whom nearly five hundred were gravely ill. It was—I thought that His Excellency the Governor was going to faint, and no one blamed him. You can have no idea, no idea . . ." Murray gagged. "The Home Department had changed contractors, so the victualler of the three ships was a slaving firm, paid in advance for each convict with no stipulation that he be landed alive and well. In fact, it was to the contractor's financial advantage if the convicts died early in the voyage. So the poor wretches were not—fed. And they were confined for the whole length of the voyage in the old kind of slave fetters—you know, a foot-long, rigid iron bar welded between the ankle cuffs? Even had they been allowed on deck—they were not—they could not have gotten up to the deck. They could not walk. Hard enough on negroes for a six or eight weeks' passage, but ye can imagine what the fetters did to men incarcerated below deck for nigh a year?"

"I daresay," said Stephen Donovan through his teeth, "that they died in hideous misery and pain. God rot all slavers!"

When no one else offered a comment, Murray continued. "The worst was Neptune, though Scarborough was not much better—she had near sixty extra men in less space than on her first voyage. Surprize was the best of the three, she lost but thirty-six of her two hundred and fifty-four on the way out. We wept when we were not vomiting, I tell ye frankly. They were living skeletons, all of them, and they kept on dying as they were helped from the holds—*the stench!* They died on the decks, they died as they were put into boats, died as they were carried ashore. Those who were still alive as they got near to the hospital had to be treated outside until their vermin were dealt with—they seethed with thousands upon thousands of lice, and I do not exaggerate—do I, Mr. Wentworth?"

"Not one iota," said the other visitor to the officers' mess, a tall, fair, handsome fellow named D'arcy Wentworth, who had been posted to Norfolk Island as an assistant surgeon. "Neptune was the ship from Hell. I sailed on her as a surgeon from Portsmouth, but never once was I asked to go below during the voyage—in fact, I was forbidden access to the prison. The smell of the prison was in our nostrils the whole way, but when I went down into the orlop at Port Jackson to help—Christ! There are no words to describe what it was like. A sea of maggots, rotting bodies, cockroaches, rats, fleas, flies, lice—but some men were still alive, can ye imagine it? We surgeons expect that any who do manage to survive will emerge raving mad."

Knowing more merchant masters than the navy men, Stephen asked, "Who is the captain of Neptune?"

"A beast named Donald Trail," said Wentworth. "He could not understand what all the fuss was about, which made us wonder how many live slaves he delivers to Jamaica. The only thing interested him—or Anstis, for that matter—was selling goods to those in Port Jackson at such exorbitant prices only his rum was bought."

"I have heard of Trail," said Stephen, looking sick. "He can keep a negro alive because he can sell the live ones only. To give him a contract that was tacit permission to murder *is* murder. God rot the whole Home Department!"

"He did not even treat his free paying passengers well, is the mystery,"

Wentworth said, shaking his head. "Ye'd think he would at least be conscious enough of his own skin to pander just a little to them, but he did not. Neptune carried some of the officers and men of a new army regiment recruited solely to do duty in New South Wales. Captain John MacArthur of the New South Wales Corps, his wife and babe, their son and servants were jammed into a tiny cabin and forbidden access to the great cabin or the deck save through a corridor filled with women convicts and overflowing buckets of excrement. The babe died, MacArthur quarreled fiercely with Trail and his sailing master and transferred in Cape Town to Scarborough, but not before the squalor had made him quite gravely ill. I understand that the son is seedy too."

"How did you fare, Mr. Wentworth?" asked Major Ross, who had listened without a word.

"Unpleasantly, but at least I could get up on deck. After the MacArthurs left I was able to put my woman in their cabin—a vast improvement for her." He looked suddenly nasty. "I have important relatives in England, and I have written to demand that Trail be made to answer for his crimes when Neptune gets home."

"Do not hope for it," said Captain George Johnston. "Lord Penrhyn and the slaving group carry more weight in the parliament than a dozen dukes and earls."

"Tell me more about what happened to these poor wretches at Port Jackson, Mr. Murray," Major Ross commanded.

"His Excellency the Governor ordered a huge pit dug well out of town," Murray went on, "and there the dead were placed for Mr. Johnson to conduct a funeral service. A dear man, Mr. Johnson—he was very good to those who still lived, brave in going below Neptune's deck to fetch men out, and tender in his last rites. But the pit cannot be closed. The corpses have been piled over with rocks so that the natives' dogs cannot get at them—they will scavenge anything—and bodies were still going into it when Surprize sailed for Norfolk Island. Men were still dying by the score. Governor Phillip is beside himself with grief and anger. We carry a letter from him to Lord Sydney, but I fear 'twill not reach the Home Department before the next lot of convicts are sent—under the same slave contractors and on the same terms. Paid in advance to deliver corpses to Port Jackson."

"Trail liked to see everybody die early," said Wentworth. "Neptune lost soldiers too."

"I take it that most of the thousand-odd aboard Neptune, Surprize and Scarborough were male convicts?" asked Ross.

"Aye, there were but a handful of women, in Neptune, in that filthy corridor. The women were sent earlier in Lady Juliana."

"What was their fate?" asked Ross grimly, seeing in his mind's eye 157 walking skeletons being landed at perilous Cascade.

"Oh," said Surgeon Murray, brightening, "they fared very well! Mr. Richards—he who contracted for your fleet—victualled Lady Juliana. The worst one can say about that ship is that her crew—she carried no troops—had as good a time as they would have in a rum distillery. A cargo of women? Little wonder that her passage out was exceeding slow."

"We can be thankful for small mercies, it seems," said Ross. "No doubt our midwives will shortly be busy."

"Aye, some are with child. Some already have babes."

"What of the forty-seven men? Are they old Port Jackson men, or are they off these ships from Hell?"

"New arrivals, but the very best of them. Which is not saying much. But at least none is mad and all can keep food down."

The local rum was in evidence, but from the beginning canny Robert Ross had disguised it by mixing it with better spirit and calling it "Rio rum." He was also stockpiling Richard's product in empty oaken casks adulterated by some good Bristol rum off Justinian to see what happened when it aged a little. This cache he, Lieutenant Clark and Richard had hidden in a dry place where no one would find it. The still would continue until he had 2,000 gallons—by which time, he estimated, both the supply of sugar-cane and casks would be exhausted. Then he would dismantle the apparatus and give it to Morgan to hide. Conscience appeased, he made a mental resolution to use the bit of barley the island managed to grow to make small beer; Justinian had brought hops among its cargo. That way even the convicts would occasionally get something better than water to drink.

Jesus Christ, what kind of trade was this one in convicted men and women? Handed by the King's own government to worms and snakes. He had hanged men and he had flogged men, but he had fed them and cared for them too. Does Arthur Phillip realize yet that the wickedness of slavers has saved him from starvation a second time within a twelvemonth? What would have happened if all the 1,200 convicts who arrived in June had been landed in as good a condition as those off our own fleet? Minus Guardian, what food Justinian carried would have lasted scant weeks. God has saved New South Wales through the agency of soulless slavers. But who, when God calls this debt in, will be asked to pay?

* * *

On the morning of August 10th before any convicts had been landed from Surprize, Major Ross assembled every member of his community under the Union flag and addressed them.

"Our critical situation has been alleviated by the arrival of sufficient supplies to last us for some time!" he roared. "I hereby announce that the Law Martial is repealed! Which does not mean that I grant any of ye license to run amok! I may not be able to hang, but I can still flog ye within an inch of your lives—and flog ye I will! Our population is about to increase to seven hundred and eighteen persons, and that is not a prospect can be viewed with complacency! Especially given that the new convicts are mostly women, while the few men among them are sick. Therefore the new mouths we have to feed are not attached to bodies which can do hard labor. Every hut and house will have to take one additional person, for I am not about to build a barracks for women. Only those who will act as superintendents of convicts—Mr. Donovan and Mr. Wentworth—are given dispensation in this respect. Be ye sailors, marines outside the barracks, pardoned convicts or convicts still under sentence, ye will take charge of at least one woman. Officers may participate or not, according to their choice. But I warn ye, so hear me well! I will have no woman beaten or disgraced by becoming the plaything of a number of men. I cannot stop fornication, but I will not condone conduct that brands ye as savages. Rape and other sorts of physical abuse of the women will earn ye five hundred lashes from Richardson's meanest cat, and that goes as much for marines and sailors as it does felons."

He paused to frown direfully at the silent ranks, eyes resting on Captain John Hunter's smug countenance; there was one who fully understood that His Excellency's abolition of the Law Martial gave him a great deal more latitude in defiance.

"Excluding those naval persons who do not wish to remain here and settle once Supply arrives to take them off the island, from now on I am going to thin Sydney Town out by putting as many of ye as I can onto one-acre lots, provided that ye are supporting a new man or a woman. The contents of your lots will not be subject to any Government garnish, but rather must serve to lessen your need for the Government's stores of food. Ye are, however, at liberty to sell any surplus to the Government, and ye will be paid for all such surpluses, be ye free or felon. Those of convict status who work hard, clear their lots and sell to the Government will be freed as soon as they demonstrate their worth, just as I have already freed some of ye for good work. The Government will dower each occupant of a one-acre lot with a breeding sow and provide the services of a boar. I cannot extend this to poultry, but those of ye who can afford to purchase turkeys, chickens or ducks will be let do so as soon as poultry numbers permit."

There were low murmurs in the crowd; some faces beamed, others glowered. Not everybody liked the idea of hard work, even in his own interests.

The Major continued. "Richard Phillimore, ye may take up one acre of the lot ye fancy around the corner to the east. Nathaniel Lucas, ye may regard the one acre behind Sydney Town whereon ye presently live as yours. John Rice, ye may take up one acre above Nat Lucas fronting on the stream which flows between the marine barracks and the inner row of houses. John Mortimer and Thomas Crowder, ye'll go to the same locality as Rice. Richard Morgan, ye will remain on your present piece at the head of the vale. I will be notifying others as soon as Mr. Bradley gives me his plan. The crew of Sirius will go to the big clearing midway along the Cascade road. The flax workers, including the retters and weavers I believe have come in Surprize, will settle at Phillipburgh and establish a proper canvas factory there."

Run out of things to say, he simply stopped. "Get ye gone!"

Richard returned to his sawpit up the vale, his mood a blend of exhilaration and gloom. Ross had given him his own acre right where his house stood—a wonderful boon, as it was already cleared and growing. Nat Lucas and Richard Phillimore had been similarly gifted, whereas Crowder, Rice and Mortimer would have to fell trees. His gloom revolved around his solitude, which Ross definitely intended should end. Though Lawrell might occupy his own hut, Richard knew that he could not so banish a woman, any more than he could hand her over to Lawrell. Lawrell was decent enough, but would certainly expect to enjoy her body whether she wished it or not. No, the wretched creature would have to live in his house, just one largish room. That canceled his plans for the coming weekend, which had consisted of fishing with a hand-line from the rocks west of the landing place and taking a long walk with Stephen. Instead, he would have to start adding a new room onto his house for the female. Johnny Livingstone, wise enough not to ask why he needed one, had built him a sled on smooth runners to which he could attach himself by canvas harness and draw like a horse. He had needed it to cart the ingredients for mash to the distillery, deeming that a task only he should perform, and under darkness. It held about as much as a good big handcart, and it was invaluable. Now he would have to use it to lump stone from the quarry for more foundation piers. Damn all women!

This being winter, the senior officers messed together at one o'clock for the hot main meal of their day, and did so with Major Ross in the dining room of Government House. Mrs. Morgan, as Lizzie Lock insisted upon being called, was a superb cook now she had a few ingredients. Today she served roast pork in honor of the arrival of Surprize and Justinian, though no officers from either ship had been invited to eat it any more than had Messrs. Donovan, Wentworth and Murray. Lieutenant Ralph Clark was not present either; he had taken Little John to dine with Messrs. Donovan, Wentworth and Murray. His own table was notoriously meager, had been ever since the voyage from England. When it came to spending his own money, Clark, whose circumstances were financially shortened, was extremely frugal. Nor was Lieutenant Robert Kellow present; he was still in Coventry after fighting a ridiculous duel with Lieutenant Faddy.

Present were Major Robert Ross, Captain John Hunter, Captain George Johnston, Lieutenant John Johnstone and, alas, that shocking gossip, Lieutenant William Faddy.

The Major served a before-dinner drink of "Rio rum," reserving the bottle of port Captain Maitland of Justinian had given him for an after-dinner tipple. The meal was a little long in coming; the Major served a second before-dinner drink. So when they sat down to do justice to Mrs. Morgan's haunch of pork, its skin beautifully crackled, the gravy delicious and the roast potatoes perfectly crusted with meat juices, the five men were a little too light-headed to banish the effects of the rum by eating; a situation not helped because more rum accompanied the feast.

"I see ye've replaced Clark as head of Government Stores," said Hunter, finishing off the last of his baked rice pudding, swimming in treacle.

"Lieutenant Clark has better things to do than count up numbers on his fingers," said Ross, chin shining with crackling fat. "His Excellency sent me Freeman to be of use, and I will use him thus. I need Clark to superintend the building of Charlotte Field."

Hunter stiffened. "Which reminds me," he said, voice quiet, "that during your memorable address this morning, ye implied that my seamen are to be moved out of Sydney Town—along the Cascade road, I think ye put it."

"I did." Ross wiped his chin with one of the napkins dear Mrs. Morgan had hemmed out of an old linen tablecloth—a gem of a woman! What had possessed Richard Morgan to repudiate her, Ross could not guess with certainty, but he suspected it had to do with activities in bed, for Morgan had been right: she was definitely not a temptress. Folding the napkin, Ross looked straight at Hunter, sitting at the far end of the table.

"What of it?" he asked.

"Ye're not the Lord High Executioner any longer, Ross, so what gives ye the right to make decisions about my crew?"

"I am still the Lieutenant-Governor, I believe. Therefore it is my right to shift pillars to posts and the Royal Navy to the Cascade road. With a half plus one hundred women about to descend upon us, I do not want Sydney Town crawling with ruffians who will not work yet expect to be fed."

Hunter shoved his pudding plate aside with a force that toppled his empty rum mug and leaned forward, the bases of his palms against the edge of the table. "I have had enough!" he shouted, lifted one hand and banged it down. "Ye're a perfidious dictator, Ross, and so I will inform the Governor when I return to Port Jackson! Ye've hanged my men, ye've flogged my men, and I curse ye for it! Ye've made seamen of the Royal Navy work at tasks I'd not give to Judas Iscariot—gathering flax, risking their lives moving stones on the reef"—he rose to his feet, glaring at Ross with teeth bared—"and what is more, ye've enjoyed every minute of your Law Martial!"

"I have indeed," said Ross with deceptive affability. " 'Tis wonderful good for my liver and lights to watch the Navy *work* for a change."

"I tell ye now, Major Ross, ye'll not banish my men!"

"Fuck I won't!" Ross got up, eyes blazing. "I have suffered ye and your privileged lot for five months—and from the sound of it, I have to keep suffering ye for the next six months! Well, not at close quarters! You Royal Navy bastards think ye're the lords of creation, but ye're not! Not here, at any rate. Here ye're a pack of leeches sucking blood out of other persons. But here there is a marine in charge—*this* marine! Ye'll do as ye're told, Hunter, and that is the end of it! I care not if ye bugger every ship's boy silly, but ye'll not continue to do it close enough to me to smell the farts! Go and push your turds on the Cascade road!"

"I'll have ye court martialed, Ross! I'll have ye recalled to Port Jackson in disgrace and sent home on the first ship!"

"Try, ye pathetic old shirt-lifter! But remember that *I* am not the one lost his command! And if ye've hied me to England for court martial, I will be there to testify that ye took no notice of those present in this island who could have told ye how not to lose your ship!" roared Ross. "The truth is, Hunter, that ye could not navigate a barge between Woolwich and Tilbury if ye were being towed!"

Face purple, Hunter sucked the flecks of foam from the corners of his mouth with a hiss. "Pistols," he said, "tomorrow at dawn."

The Major burst into laughter. "In a pig's eye!" he said. "I would not so demean the Marine Corps! Fight a duel with a Miss Molly granny has one foot in the grave already? Piss off! Go on, piss off, and don't show your face in Sydney Town while I am still Lieutenant-Governor of Norfolk Island!"

Captain Hunter turned on his heel and left.

The three witnesses looked at each other across the table, Faddy itching to make his excuses and rush off to tell Ralph Clark, John Johnstone feeling sick to his stomach, and the rapacious George Johnston conscious of a delicious well-being not entirely due to rum or Mrs. Morgan's food. *That* was telling the Navy! He heartily concurred with Ross's opinion of the Sirius crew; besides which, it devolved upon him, the only captain, to keep the enlisted marines from the seamen's throats. Not an easy task. And how very clever the Major was, to shift a part of his problem out of Sydney Town before 157 women arrived in it.

"Faddy," said the Major, sitting down with a sigh of satisfaction, "keep your arse on your chair. I will not order ye to keep your mouth shut because not even God Himself could do that unless He struck ye dumb. George, do the honors with the port. I'll not let this truly memorable dinner conclude before we have drunk a loyal toast to His Majesty and the Marine Corps, which one day will be the *Royal* Marine Corps. Then we will have equal rank with the Navy."

On Friday the 13th, a day so inauspicious that the entire community shivered with superstitious fear, the female convicts began to be disembarked from Surprize at Cascade, for the wind stubbornly refused to shift out of the south.

Though he had ten sawpits working these days and Ralph Clark wanted one at Charlotte Field together with a team of carpenters—Ross was anxious to get the settlement there up and running to have yet more land to grow grain—Richard still sawed himself, and still with Private Billy Wigfall. But early on Friday the 13th he was obliged to report to Major Ross that he could not persuade one man to saw on such an unlucky day.

"The thing is, sir, that were I to summon Richardson and his cat they would work, but in such a pother that there would be accidents. I cannot run the risk of having men incapacitated by injuries when we have to saw timber for so many new settlements," Richard explained.

"Some things," said Ross, a trifle fearful of the omens himself, "cannot be resisted. I shall give everybody the day off. They will have to work tomorrow instead. Incidentally, I have forbidden all convicts to walk to Cascade today in search of likely women." He grinned mirthlessly. "I also told them that if they defied me and did try, they would be bound to pick the wrong ones on Friday the thirteenth. However, the useless creatures will have to be helped ashore and up to the top of the climb, and as I have also ordered my marines to stay away, that leaves the field to Sirius's sailors." This put a little genuine amusement into his smile. "However, I want someone there to report back to me on the conduct of Sirius's sailors, most of whom came into the world without benefit of father or mother. Ye can accompany Mr. Donovan and Mr. Wentworth, Morgan."

The three men set off at eight in the morning, in the best of spirits despite the date. Stephen and D'arcy Wentworth got on together famously; like Richard, Wentworth was too sensible a man to condemn a man for being a Miss Molly. The pair also shared certain characteristics, particularly a zest for new places and adventures, and both were very well read. The sea had provided an outlet for Stephen's desire for action, whereas Wentworth had experienced the call of the road and been apprehended and tried on several occasions for highway robbery. Only those important relatives had gotten him off, but even family patience can eventually erode; having dabbled in medicine when he was not holding up coaches, Wentworth was told to take himself off to New South Wales and never come back. The lure was a small income payable only in New South Wales.

Stephen still wore his black hair in long, luxuriant curls, but Wentworth had gone to what he said was starting to be the new fashion—cropped hair like Richard's, though his was not as short. The three of them walking abreast down the road looked striking: handsome, tall, lithe, with Wentworth, the tallest and the only fair one, between the two dark-headed ones.

They scrambled down the steep cleft which emerged 100 yards from the landing place to find Surprize fairly close in shore and the sea calm. The tide was turning to the flood, and Captain Anstis had been instructed two days ago by Mr. Donovan as to how to manage the business of getting people safely onto dry land. Advice he, a merchant master, was sensible enough to heed.

"Anstis is an awful man," said Stephen, sitting down on a rock. "I am told that in Port Jackson he sold paper for a penny a sheet, ink for a pound the small bottle, and cheap unbleached calico for ten shillings the ell.* Surgeon Murray says he had nowhere near as many customers as he had expected, so we shall see how he does when he sets up a stall here."

Remembering Lizzie Lock—Morgan, Richard, *Morgan!*—and what she had told him about Lady Penrhyn's lack of rags for bleeding women, Richard decided that, much though he loathed enriching the likes of a man who starved other men to death for profit, he would be at that stall to buy some ells of unbleached calico for the woman he would be obliged to shelter under the Ross Plan. Perhaps Lady Juliana's complement had been provided with rags, but he doubted it. If the behavior of Lady Penrhyn's sexually satiated crew was anything to go on, the sailors would not have been sympathetic no matter how many women they plundered. He would certainly have to provide a bed for her, which meant a mattress, pillow, sheets and maybe a blanket, clothing. Johnny Livingstone had promised to make him the bed and some more chairs, but his unwelcome guest was going to prove expensive. He still had his gold coins in his box and in the heels of Ike Rogers's boots. Interesting to see what Nicholas Anstis had for sale. Emery powder? He hoped so; his supply was almost exhausted. Sandpaper he made himself from Turtle Bay sand, fish-glue he made himself from fish scraps, but emery powder he could not duplicate.

Shortly after ten o'clock the first longboat struck for shore to a cheer from about fifty of Sirius's seamen, waiting eagerly; other longboats in the water alongside Surprize were filling with more women. The conditions were nothing like as wet or as rough as when Major Ross had landed from Sirius, but when the first boat maneuvered itself near the landing rock, its oarsmen poised to shove off in a hurry if a wave larger than the rest came rushing in, the women shrieked, struggled, refused to make the leap. One Sirius sailor advanced to the edge of the rock and held out his hands; when the boat came in a second time the two sailors aboard it threw a screaming woman at him, followed her up with others. No one fell in, and the bundles of personal property landed safely in their wake. Another boat succeeded the first, the process was repeated; soon the whole of the very little negotiable ground in the vicinity of the landing place was milling with Sirius seamen and women. There were, however, no offensive liberties; most of the

* One ell equals 45 inches.

women were led off, each by the man who apparently fancied her, to make the climb to the crest 200 feet above.

"Wait," said Stephen, "until the news reaches town that Sirius has made off with the best women. The marines will be fit to be tied, since Ross forbade them to come over."

"Did he do that deliberately?" asked Wentworth curiously.

"Aye, but not for the reason ye might think," said Richard. "Which is worse? To let those of his marines not on duty take first pick, or let Sirius take first pick? Since there is bound to be contention, the Major would rather it lay between marines and sailors than marines and other marines."

"Anyway," Stephen smiled, "there has been little picking. I imagine Medusa the Gorgon would look good to them after so long. I have counted a mere fifty-three women, which means, my friends, that we will have to get up off our arses and down to the rock. The helpers from Sirius have disappeared."

Like Stephen Donovan and Richard Morgan—but for very different reasons—D'arcy Wentworth was not tempted to find himself a woman from among those who landed after the three men took over on the landing rock, encouraging the terrified creatures to leap ashore. His own convict mistress, a beautiful red-haired girl named Catherine Crowley, was pledged not to be landed at Cascade; she and their baby son, William Charles, would wait until Sydney Bay calmed down. Wentworth had fallen in love with her at first sight and defiantly moved her out of the filthy corridor on Neptune; in the cabin which had belonged to the MacArthurs, Catherine bore her baby shortly before Neptune reached Port Jackson. Both a sweet joy and a sore sadness. Little William Charles, with his mother's copper curls and the promise of his father's stature, had a badly crossed eye and would never see very well.

Having landed almost seventy of her female and all her male convicts, Surprize signaled as the tide reached half-ebb that she would not be sending more. The women were a sorry-looking lot; though Lady Juliana might have treated them well, they had made the voyage to Norfolk Island on a "wet" ship, damp and leaky, on a deck which had contained men on the long journey out and still contained filth, decay and excrement.

But the 47 men landed were in an appalling way. Were *these* the fittest who had been delivered to Port Jackson? Wentworth had to jump into each boat as it arrived—the Surprize seamen were not interested—and pick the poor wretches up, throw them bodily to Richard and Stephen, for they could not have jumped an inch. Of flesh they had none, eyes sunk into their sockets like shriveled gooseberries in paper rings, teeth gone, hair gone, nails rotted. Full of scurvy, lice and dysentery. Richard, the fleetest, ran to Sydney Town and demanded marine or convict helpers—the last of the women, unclaimed by Sirius, were straggling along the road hampered by the weight of their bundles as he returned at a run, Sergeant Tom Smyth urging the recruits in his wake. Few men were as strong as a top sawyer, even one about to turn forty-two. Neither he nor Smyth saw one of the convict volunteers, Tom Jones Two, sneak off before the group reached the cleft at Cascade; there were still women trying to walk to Sydney Town.

But by dusk the last of the work was done, all the landed convicts safe in Sydney Town, where fresh choices were made for the women and the emaciated, terribly ill men were put into the small hospital and a hastily converted store shed. Olivia Lucas, Eliza Anderson, John Bryant's widow, and the Commandant's housekeeper, Mrs. Richard Morgan, ministered to the sick and despaired of their ever getting well again. And these were the best from among 1,000 men? That was what everybody could not get over.

As Surprize was still at Cascade the next day, Stephen, D'arcy Wentworth and Richard returned to help again, having scrubbed themselves raw last night to remove the dirt and vermin handling those men and women had produced. Then the wind got up, Surprize signaled that she was finished, Stephen and D'arcy took charge of the last party of women and jollied them along, showing them how to carry their burdens easier, taking whatever they could carry themselves, assuring the terrified creatures that they were going to like life in Norfolk Island, which was a better place by far than Port Jackson.

Deputed to make sure that Surprize did not change her mind and suddenly launch another longboat, Richard was some minutes behind them in leaving Cascade. At the top of the crest he turned to look along that coast, a less familiar sight than Sydney Bay's fabulous reef, lagoon, beaches and offshore islands. But no less hauntingly beautiful, Richard thought, between the waterfalls, the outcrops of rock in the water, a great blowhole to the north sending a jet of foam higher and higher as the sea rose.

What interesting trees were the Norfolk pines! Those felled to make the road had been cut off right at ground level with a cross saw and were already crumbling, sinking slowly beneath the surface. In two years, with a little rubble to fill the craters in, no one would ever know that pines had once occupied every inch. Aware that the sun was lower than he had counted on, he quickened his pace as he walked through the clearing around Phillipburgh, where Ross was heroically following in King's footsteps by attempting to establish a canvas-from-flax industry, and set off into the forested section that led to the fairly flat crest to which the Lieutenant-Governor had banished the men off Sirius. Captain Hunter had declined to join them; he had elected to move in with Lieutenant William Bradley at what was beginning to be known as Phillimore's Run, from the strength of the stream which ran through Dick Phillimore's land.

Well, he was safe for yet another day. None of the women had taken a fancy to him, none had lacked eager takers acceptable to them—though all had fancied Stephen best, the devil. With any luck, Richard thought as he strode along, I will wriggle out of having to care for anybody save John Lawrell, even if that does mean I will not qualify for a sow.

Something mewed. Richard stopped, frowning. The settlers had a few cats brought on Sirius, but they were greatly prized as pets and ratters and did not need to wander this far in search of food. Sirius's crew had cats too, but loved them, so it was hardly likely to belong to the sailors. Unless it had strayed, climbed a tree and could not get down.

"Here, kitty, kitty!" he called, ear tilted for a response.

Another mew, but less catlike. Skin prickling, he left the road and entered the realm of vine-choked pine buttresses. Once off the cleared ground the darkness increased dramatically; he paused long enough to allow his eyes to accustom themselves to the gloom, then started off again, suddenly sure that the sound was a human one. What a pity. He had hoped for a cat, longing to be able to gift Stephen with a replacement for his beloved Rodney, which, as ship's cat, had remained behind on Alexander when Stephen moved to Sirius and Johnny Livingstone's arms.

"Where are ye?" he asked in an ordinary but loud voice. "Sing out to me, then I can find ye."

Silence save for the creaking of the pines, the sound of the wind high up in them, the flutters of birds.

"Come, it is all right, I want to help ye. Sing out!"

A faint mew, some distance farther in. Richard looked back to fix his landmarks, then ventured toward the sound.

"Sing out," he said at normal volume. "Let me find you."

"Help me!"

After that it was no trouble to find her, crouched inside the cavity time and perpetually gnawing beetles had carved out of an enormous pine; a refugee might have made a dwelling out of it, which lent credence to the stories of the occasional convict who absconded into the wilderness, only to reappear in Sydney Town weeks later, starving.

A little girl, or so at first she seemed. Then he saw that it was a woman's breast showed amid a great tear in her dress. Crouched on his heels, he smiled and held out his hand.

"Come, it is all right. I will not hurt you. We must leave this place or it will be too dark to see the way back to the road. Come, take my hand."

She put her fingers into his palm and let him draw her out, shivering with cold and terror.

"Where are your things?" he asked, careful to touch no more of her than those trembling fingers.

"The man took them," she whispered.

Mouth compressed to a thin line, he led her to the road, there to look at her in the dying light. No taller than his shoulder, very thin, with what might have been fair hair, though it was too dirty to tell. Her eyes, however, were—were—his breath caught. No, sunshine would give the lie to them, had to! William Henry's eyes had belonged to him alone, they had no like on the face of the globe.

"Are ye able to walk?" he asked, wanting to give her his shirt but afraid of frightening her into running off.

"I think so."

"At the next clearing I will get a torch. After that we can take our time."

She flinched, shuddered.

"No, no, it is all right! We have three more miles to get home, and we will need to see our way." He held her hand strongly and began to move onward. "My name is Richard Morgan, and I am a free man." How wonderful to be able to say that! "I am the supervisor of sawyers."

Though she did not reply, she walked with him more confidently until they reached the Sirius settlement. The sailors were living in tents until the carpenters could erect proper barracks and huts, and a few men were moving about in the distance. A big fire burned adjacent to the road, but no one sat at it. They were probably all drunk on rum. So no one saw him pick up a torch and kindle it, nor saw the waif still clinging for dear life to his hand.

"What is your name?" he asked as they set off again into the pines, more exposed to the south and beginning to roar now that the full force of the wind struck into them like a hammer into thin copper sheeting—boom, boom, boom.

"Catherine Clark."

"Kitty," he said instantly. "Kitty."

She jumped. "How did you know that?"

"I did not," he said, surprised. "It is just that when I first heard ye, I thought I heard a kitten. Ye're off Lady Juliana?"

"Yes."

Sensing that she was foundering but afraid to carry her for fear of frightening her—who was the cur had attacked her?—he said, "We will not waste our time or breath on talking, Kitty. The most important thing is to get ye home."

Home. **The** most beautiful word in the world. He uttered it as if it genuinely meant something to him, as if he promised her all the things she had not known in so long. Since years before she was convicted and sent briefly to the London Newgate, then sent to Lady Juliana on the Thames to wait for months before the ship finally sailed for Botany Bay all alone. That had not been utter horror because no sailor had lusted after her; with 204 women to choose from, why should a mere 30 men select any but the strapping girls with hips, breasts, nicely rounded bellies? A few of the men were given to prowling, not satisfied with one conquest, but Mr. Nicol had made sure no girl was raped. Most of the crew had behaved like potential buyers at a horse fair and fastened upon just one "wife," as he called her. Like a hundred others on board, Catherine Clark had never attracted male attention. In Port Jackson they had not been landed, had remained upon Lady Juliana until 157 of them were picked at random to transfer to Surprize for the voyage to Norfolk Island, a place she had never, never heard of. Nor had she heard of Port Jackson: all she had known was "Botany Bay," a petrifying name.

Surprize had been far worse than Lady Juliana. Seasick even in the Thames, desperately ill for most of Lady Juliana's leisurely progress, Catherine had descended into a nightmare only terrible seasickness had rendered endurable without madness. The place where they were put crawled with vermin, slopped with a noisome fluid the nature of which no one dared to guess, stank so badly that the nose never got used to it, and there was no fresh air, no deck privilege.

To be rowed ashore and flung like a doll onto the rock had terrified her, but a handsome man with a beautiful smile and the bluest eyes had caught her, reassured her, given her a gentle push and asked her if she could manage to climb that awful crevice. Wanting to please him, she had nodded and set off, her bundle and her bedding serving as props while she toiled upward. By some quirk of fate she had not set eyes upon Richard Morgan, who had come down on a more precipitous track at the moment she was crawling into the cleft. At the top she paused to catch her breath, then set off along the road, realizing that so much seasickness and so little food for the past year and more had not equipped her for this walk, however far it might be, wherever its termination might be. A group of men passed her by at a run, took no notice of her.

Not far into the forest her legs could carry her no farther; she set her bundle and her bedding on the ground and sat upon them, her head between her knees, wheezing.

"Well, what have we here?" a voice asked.

She looked up to see a corn-gold fellow clad only in a pair of tattered canvas trowsers staring at her. Then he smiled to reveal that he had two mouths: both front teeth in upper and lower jaw were missing, creating a sinister black hole. But she was very tired, so when he held out his hand to her she took it, expecting him to help her to her feet. Instead he jerked her into his arms and tried to cover her mouth with that awful aperture in his face. Struggling weakly, she resisted, felt her thin convict slops dress rip as he grabbed cruelly at her breasts.

Someone in the distance spoke. His grip relaxed immediately; she tore herself away from him and ran into the trees. For a moment he stood, clearly debating whether to follow her, then several more voices spoke. He shrugged, picked up her bundle and her bedding, and set off in the direction she had been pointed. The noises of conversation grew closer. Panicking, she ran farther into the forest until she had no idea where she was, whereabouts the road was. Something flew in her face, but she did not scream. She fainted, struck her head on a root.

When she came to, moaning and retching, darkness had fallen. Scurries, thin keeking shrieks, the mighty groans of mighty trees moving, a night so black she could see nothing—she crawled on hands and knees to the hollow in a tree so large she could not see around it, and there huddled until a wan morning light let her discover where she was. Surrounded by these gigantic trees and penned into her prison by a creeper as big around as her waist.

All that day she had heard the confused sounds of people far off but had not cried out, terrified that the man with two mouths was lurking. Why, with the light fading, she had suddenly tried to shout, she never knew. Only that she had, and had been answered: "Here, Kitty, Kitty!" Whoever it was called her name, and she thought of the wonderful man who had helped her ashore.

Her finder was very like that man, but not he; his hair was cut off, his eyes were greyer. His smile was beautiful too, teeth as white as snow and not one missing. It was too dim to see more, but when he extended his hand she took it and held on to it, associating him with the one who brought her ashore and still lived in her memory vividly. Once on the road, her eyes cleared enough to see that he was older than her hero of the rock, as brown of skin and dark of hair; they might have been brothers. This conclusion was what prompted her to trust him, to walk with him.

"You are cold," he said now. "I beg ye, let me give ye my shirt. I mean no insult, but I must touch ye to put it on, Kitty."

Even had he meant to insult her she was too exhausted to resist, so she stood docilely while he peeled his shirt off and slid her arms into its sleeves, then left her to tie its ends together in a knot about her waist.

"Warmer?"

"Yes."

Somehow she managed to force her legs to keep moving until they reached the last section of road, which plunged steeply down a hill to a different darkness, lit with pinpoints of flame and, far out, a white flurry. She tripped and fell heavily.

"That settles it," said Richard, abandoning the torch. He plucked her up, draped her around his shoulders with her wrists pinioned by one hand, her legs by the other, and set off, as sure-footed as if he walked by day. Near the bottom stood a house. He marched up to it and thumped on its door.

"Stephen!" he called.

"Christ, Richard, abducting females?" asked the man from the rock, eyes dancing with unmalicious mockery.

"The poor child spent last night in the Cascade woods. Some bastard attacked her and stole her things. Light me home, please."

"Let me carry her," said Stephen. "Ye must be worn out."

Yes, oh yes, please carry me! she cried silently. But Richard Morgan shook his head.

"Nay, I've carried her down the hill, no more. She has lice. Just see me home."

"What do lice matter? Bring her in," Stephen commanded, holding the door wide. "Ye have no fire lit, and since ye planned to eat with me, ye have no food prepared. Bring her in, man! I have seen my share of vermin these past two days." His heart twisted at the look on Richard's face. Who knows why a man loves, or whom he will love? He has crossed the deck to his fate, just as I did on Alexander. "I have fish-chowder. She will be able to tolerate the broth."

"Lice first, else she'll sicken. What she needs most is a bath and clean clothes. Have ye ample hot water on the hob? D'ye need cold? I am off to Olivia Lucas to borrow."

"I have water enough, but no bath and no louse comb. See if Olivia can oblige."

Off went Richard, leaving Stephen alone with the scrap, who had recovered sufficiently to stare at him with worshipful eyes—the most extraordinary eyes he had ever seen, an ale color speckled with dark brown dots, and fringed by thick lashes so fair that only their crystal gleam in the candlelight betrayed their presence. Thinner by far than probably God had intended her to be, owning an oval face and no beauty save for those eyes; she had a typically large English nose and prominent English chin.

He put a chair in the middle of the floor and sat her on it. "I am Stephen Donovan," he said, ladling liquid off the top of the chowder and setting it aside in a bowl to cool. "Who are you?"

"Catherine Clark. Kitty," she answered, smiling to reveal a trace of dimple in her left cheek and regular, discolored teeth. A sign, thought the experienced sailor, of perpetual seasickness and lack of nourishment.

"You helped me onto the rock," she said.

"Along with half a hundred others, so indeed I did. Now tell me about the man and your night in the woods, Kitty."

She explained, composure growing with every passing minute, taking in the neat parlor-cum-kitchen with its table, several nice chairs, kitchen bench, another table which apparently served him as a desk, the sanded walls adorned with three sets of enormous fanged jaws; a chessboard and men sat on the desk together with an inkwell, quills and papers, and the table was set for two.

"A man with yellow hair and four missing front teeth."

"Yes."

"Tom Jones Two, for sure." He gave her the bowl. "Drink."

When she sipped gingerly at the broth an expression of bliss came over her face; she drank it down greedily and held out the empty bowl. "Please may I have some more, Mr. Donovan?"

"Stephen. Ye may have more in a little while, Kitty. Let that lot settle first. Have ye been seasick often?"

"Forever," she said simply.

"Well, starting tomorrow, scrub your teeth every day with some ashes from the fire. If ye do not, ye'll lose them. Bringing up bile for months on end eats them away to nothing."

"I am sorry for bringing lice into your house," she said.

"Pish and tush, child! Richard will fetch ye new clothes and we will burn these. But I think ye should cut off your hair, if ye can bear to. Not to the scalp, just short."

She flinched, but nodded obediently.

Richard returned bearing a small tin bathtub with clothes in it. "Olivia Lucas is a treasure," he said, dumping the bath down and removing its contents. "Has Kitty told ye what happened?"

"Aye. Her attacker was Tom Jones Two. Unmistakable."

The two men half-filled the baby's bath with a mixture of hot and cold water, working, thought the dazed Kitty, as if they truly were brothers.

"Are ye accustomed to bathing, Kitty?" Richard asked. It was the most delicate way he could think to put the question; she may never have washed in her life, judging from her appearance.

"Oh, yes. I cannot thank you enough, Mr. Morgan. I have not been able to wash properly since I left Lady Juliana. Aboard her, we managed to keep clean and free of lice. If you give me a pair of scissors I will cut off my hair," she said, her speech polite but faintly Londonish—Surrey or Kent, perhaps.

Richard looked horrified. "Let us not cut off the hair yet! I have a fine-toothed comb and we will keep using it until your hair is free, even of nits. My name is Richard, not Mr. Morgan. Where are ye from, Kitty?"

"Faversham in Kent. Then the girls' workhouse in Canterbury, then the manor at St. Paul Deptford as a kitchen servant. I was tried at Maidstone and sentenced to seven years' transportation," she recited humbly. "I stole some muslin from a shop. I think."

"How old are ye?" Stephen asked.

"Twenty last month."

"Time for that bath." Richard bent and picked up the tub as if it weighed a feather. "Ye can have the bedroom and the candle, and *scrub.* Give me your shoes and throw your dirty clothes through the window onto the ground outside. Stephen, carry her new clothes, soap and a brush—look useful, do! Wash your hair, child, scrub your scalp and then comb the hair as if your life depended upon it." He laughed softly. "The fate of your hair certainly does."

"Now to Tom Jones Two," said Richard when they had left her to her own devices. "How do we go about that?"

"Leave it to me." Stephen lit a candle from the fire, then ladled chowder into two big bowls and broke a loaf of bread into pieces. "I do not think it politic to bother the Major, as Mrs. Morgan is his housekeeper. The news that ye've picked up a stray will reach her soon enough as it is. What good fortune that her surname is Clark! I shall go to our Lieutenant Ralphie darling and recount the tale, emphasizing that the girl is not one of his 'damned whores.' With a name like Clark, he will be disposed to believe me. Besides, he loathes the second Thomas Jones, in which matter he displays excellent taste. But I fear we will never see her bedding or her property—Jones will already have bestowed them upon some damned whore in return for her favors."

Picking up her shoes, Richard exchanged a glance with Stephen and grimaced. "They smell worse than Alexander's bilges," he said, throwing them into the fire. He washed his hands thoroughly at Stephen's bench. "See if ye can charm our Lieutenant Ralphie darling into donating her a new pair of shoes now that Stores has some." He sat down to consume bread and chowder hungrily. "I thought she was a cat," he said out of the blue.

"Eh?"

"She mewed from the forest. It sounded like cat. I went in hoping to find ye a new Rodney."

Face softening, Stephen looked at him across the table. If that was not just like him! Did he never think of himself first? And now this girl of wretched circumstances, no more a criminal than the Virgin Mary. Some poor little bumpkin out of a workhouse. What had possessed him to fall in love with her? He was hooked, sad fish. But why *her?* He had helped dozens ashore, girls and women of great good looks, some of them clearly educated, some of them sprightly, witty, refined even. Not every female convict was a damned whore. So why Catherine Clark? Pinched and plain, fair and foolish. An everyday nobody, devoid of charm, brain, beauty.

"Bless ye for the thought," Stephen said, "but Olivia has promised me one of her kittens, a marmalade male with no white on him. He already has a name—Tobias." Chowder finished, he rose to make sure there was enough in the pot to yield them more, yet still leave a bit for the Kitty. "Did ye ever see such eyes?" he asked as he went to the hob.

Because he turned away he missed the sight of Richard's spasm; by the time he swung back the pain was vanishing, though enough of it lingered to shock him.

"Yes," said Richard steadily, "I have seen such eyes. In my son, William Henry."

"Did ye have just the one son, Richard?"

"Just William Henry. His sister died of the smallpox before he was born. His mother died as if felled by a fist when he was eight. He—he disappeared not long before his tenth birthday. People thought he drowned in the Avon, though I did not think so. Or perhaps it is more honest to say that I did not want to think so. He was with a master from Colston's School. The master shot himself—left a note saying he *caused* William Henry's death, which only compounded the confusion. The whole of Bristol searched for a week, but William Henry's body was never found. I kept on with the search. The worst agony was the doubt—if he died, how did he die? The only one who might have told me was dead by his own hand."

The wonder of it, thought Stephen, is that he could make a brother out of me, an unashamed Miss Molly. The master—what a fabulous profession for a child molester!—did *something.* On that I would stake my life, and Richard knows it too. Yet never once has he identified me with that man because of what I am. "Go on, Richard," he said gently.

"After that I cared not whether I lived or died. I have told ye of the excise fraud and the swindlers who ridded themselves of me by sending me to trial in Gloucester." His head tilted, he looked down at the tabletop with lashes lowered, face contemplative and smooth. "But now I understand that William Henry *is* dead. Her eyes are God's message. They have answered much."

Stephen wept. Part of his grief was for Richard's loss, but part was for his own, though he had never hoped, simply attended like an acolyte a priest, waiting for the divine communion to begin. Thinking that, in the absence of love, at least there was the exquisite comfort of knowing that Richard belonged to no one else. But of course he belonged: to his dead family, and most of all to William Henry. Whom he had lost forever. Until God sent Catherine-Kitty Clark to stare at him out of his son's eyes. A benediction. And that is how it happens. A look, a laugh, a word, a gesture, meaningless to others because meaning lies in the absolutely unique and personal. Time and torment.

"If ye rest easier, I rejoice," Stephen said.

The inner door opened; both men turned.

To Richard she looked so beautiful, scrubbed clean from baby-floss hair to pearly toenails, smiling as gravely as a child on its first independent errand. Enchanting. So lovable. His own little Kitty, whom he would care for until he died.

To Stephen she simply looked a more palatable version of what she had been dirty—pinched and plain, fair and foolish. The smile? Ordinary, a trifle mawkish. Oh, the machinations of fate! To give this humdrum girl the one thing in all the world could catch and hold Richard Morgan fast.

"Ye need a shirt before we brave Sydney Town's August wind," said Stephen, tossing one to Richard. "Kitty, your shoes were so filthy we had to burn them. I will get ye more as soon as maybe, but ye'll have to let us chair ye to Richard's house."

"Could I not stay here?" she asked.

"In a house with naught but hammocks? Besides, I may have a visitor later. Ready?"

Outside he extended his hand to Richard, who gripped it. Kitty hopped onto their linked arms, one of her own arms about Richard's neck, the other about Stephen's. Each with a torch in his free hand, the two men bore her down the vale, up beyond King's dam and pond, to where Richard's house stood on the edge of the forest.

The fire was set, wood piled alongside the hearth. Stephen saluted Richard, bowed lavishly to Kitty, and left them to their own devices. There was housework to do in his own home and work with the convicts started at dawn. No, it did not! Tomorrow, he remembered, was Sunday.

Richard carried her to his privy, worried that her tender feet would not tolerate the path, then carried her back. "If ye need it in the night, wake me," he said, tucking her into his feather bed.

"Where will you sleep?" she asked.

"On the floor."

Her lips parted to say something else, but sleep claimed her with the words unsaid, and Richard knew that no amount of noise or movement would wake her. So he stripped off his clothes, put them in a bucket and carried it outside before walking to his pool, there to make sure he harbored no louse. Shivering with cold, he returned to warm by the fire, donned a pair of old trowsers, made a bed of Sirius canvas on the floor and lay down in perfect content. His eyes closed and he slept immediately.

To wake before dawn to the sound of John Lawrell's rooster crowing. The fire was embers but retrievable; he piled wood on it and inspected the contents of his larder, no better stocked than any other Norfolk Island larder. Most of the provisions were still to come ashore. As usual, what had already come ashore consisted of rum and clothing, the two least useful items in his opinion. But he had a loaf of Aaron Davis's corn bread, made with just enough precious wheat flour to render it edible, and the garden was full of good things—cabbages, cauliflowers, cress down by the stream, broad beans—parsley and lettuce, which grew all year round.

Dawn came, then sunrise. He walked across to his bed to look down at Kitty, who seemed not to have moved. Lying on her back in the modified man's shirt Olivia Lucas had donated, arms and chest uncovered. With her eyelids down, he could study her more dispassionately than when she gazed at him through William Henry's eyes. Fair, fine straight hair that could not be called either gold or flaxen; fair brows and lashes; white skin gone only a little pink, which led him to assume she had not gone on deck very often; a rather big and bumpy nose; a sweet pink mouth which reminded him of Mary's; a prominent chin above a long, slender neck; fine hands with tapering fingers.

Major Ross held divine service at eight, and, like King (a later riser), would tolerate no absentees; Richard would have to go, though she, not yet on the island's register, would not be missed. Expose her to Lizzie Lock unprepared? Never! So he went up the brook to his bath, donned his only pair of carefully preserved breeches and stockings, his coat, greatcoat and tricorn, one of his two remaining pairs of shoes. She slumbered on. He debated whether to leave her a note, then concluded that she probably could not read or write. So in the end he departed in the hope that she would not wake until he returned in an hour and a half.

"How is Kitty?" Stephen asked, joining him after the service.

"Asleep."

"Johnny will bring ye a second bed this afternoon, but I am afraid ye'll have to stuff its mattress and pillow with straw."

"Ye're very good." He whistled up MacTavish, who had accepted the presence of a stranger in his house by retreating outside before she could see him.

"I will try to get ye some extra stores, but they may have to wait until the morrow. Ralphie darling does not have the keys anymore, and Freeman is a cold bastard, not prone to put himself out."

"Well I know it. I had best be off."

Stephen cuffed him affectionately on the shoulder. "Richard, ye're as clucky as an old hen."

"I have a chick," grinned Richard. "Come, MacTavish!"

Morning had apparently generated a change of heart in the dog, which bounded through the door and leaped onto Richard's bed, there to lick Kitty's arm, flung across the pillows. She woke with a start, stared into a whiskery canine face, and smiled.

"That," said Richard, removing his hat, "is MacTavish. Are ye well, Kitty?"

"Very," she said, struggling to a sitting position. "Is it so late? You have been out already."

"Divine service," he explained. "Get out of bed and I will take ye to my bath. The ground is fairly soft, ye'll not hurt your feet. Tomorrow ye'll probably have shoes."

She visited the privy, then followed him to the small pool in the forest, alongside which he had put soap and a rag towel.

"The water is cold, but ye'll enjoy it once ye're in. 'Tis very Roman—deep enough to submerge ye, not deep enough to drown in. When ye're done, come back to the house and I will give ye breakfast, such as it is. Mrs. Lucas will visit later to talk to ye about your needs, though I fear ye'll have naught but convict slops to wear, and horrible shoes—no heels or buckles. Did ye have nice things in your bundle?"

"No, just slops." She hesitated. "I had a bath last night. Must I have another this morning?"

Now was the time to get some things straight. Richard looked stern. "This climate is not England's and this place is not England. Ye'll have to work in the garden, care for a sow, find food for it with a hatchet or carry cobs of Indian corn from the granary for it. Ye'll sweat, just as I sweat. Therefore ye'll bathe every evening after the work is done. Today ye can have *two* baths—ye'll not wash the last of Surprize away with one scrub, particularly your hair. If ye're to share my house, I require that your person be as clean as my house and my own person."

She blanched. "But this is open! I might be seen!"

"No one ventures into *my* domain, and this is my domain. I am not a man others take liberties with."

He left her then, sorry to be hard on her, but determined that she would understand the rules.

The pool was peculiarly constructed, with a channel from it to the stream blocked off by a wooden sluice; another channel, similarly blocked, led off downhill to his vegetables. The reason for this arrangement escaped her, not because she lacked the mental acuity to plumb its purpose, but rather because of the hideously narrow existence she had lived.

Having been given the rules and made aware that Richard was not a person to be disobeyed, she pulled off the shirt and jumped into the water before any man spying on her from the undergrowth could glimpse much. The coldness made her gasp, but within a short while it vanished; the sensation of being immersed to her neck was very pleasant. She could dunk her head to get all the soap out of her hair, scrub her scalp properly, her armpits and groin. When she used the fine-toothed comb, eyes watering at the pain, it came out virtually clean.

Getting out was not difficult; there was a block of stone on the pool's bottom to use as a step. The ground about it was thick with cress to keep the feet clean until they dried and the rag was capacious, hid her until she was dry enough to don her shift and convict-issue slops dress, donated it seemed by Mrs. Lucas, who, with the rest of these people, had been at the far ends of the earth for over two and a half years.

Now that she was at the far ends of the earth too, she had no idea whereabouts the far ends of the earth were; all she knew was that it had taken nearly a year to sail to them, calling in at a series of ports she hardly saw. Kitty had been one of those who hid, did not go on deck much, always tried to avoid being noticed by a member of Lady Juliana's crew. Her plight had not broken her heart the way it had the poor little Scotch girl who died of shame before the ship had left the shelter of the Thames; Kitty had no parents to grieve and disgrace, and that, the Scotch girl's fate had taught her, was a mercy. Illness had isolated her too; no sailor could be bothered philandering with a retching girl, even if he had fancied her because of her eyes. Those, she knew, were her sole claim to beauty.

Safely clothed and secure in the knowledge that Richard's house was within hailing distance, she stared about her in wonder. Norfolk Island bore no more resemblance to Kent than had Port Jackson.

When Lady Juliana had arrived in Port Jackson she was so heavy and sluggish that she had been towed from the Heads by longboats and moored well off the shore. A very strange place, so frightening! Naked black people had paddled a bark canoe alongside and jabbered, pointed, brandished spears just as she had found the courage to go up on deck; she had fled back below and hardly ventured out again. Some of the convict women—oh, how much she admired them!—had dressed in the finery Captain Aitken had stored for them during the voyage and strutted about the deck preening, sure of their reception once ashore. What courage they had! One could not live for eighteen months among them, no matter how cowed and seasick, without understanding that Lady Juliana's 204 women were as different as chalk was from cheese, and that even the hardened madams owned a kind of dignity and self-respect. More by far than she did.

Norfolk Island had begun in terror too; terror over and done with only if she did not offend Richard Morgan and Stephen Donovan, both of whom reminded her a little of Mr. Nicol, Lady Juliana's steward, innately compassionate. Richard, she had sensed already, owned more power than Stephen. Both had said they were free men, both were supervisors. Yet it was Richard intimidated her, Stephen who drew her. And though she had no inkling of what her fate was to be—how this place worked or who made it work—somehow she knew that the decisions about her rested with Richard rather than with Stephen.

The trees overwhelmed her, she could see no beauty in them. Heaving a big sigh, she set her bare feet upon the path to the house, matted with scaly tails that felt crisp, more uncomfortable than hurtful. As she emerged from the pines she saw Richard working at building something on the far side of his garden, the dog cavorting around him; clad only in a pair of canvas trowsers, mortaring a row of stones set into the ground. His arms and shoulders were massive, the smooth brown skin of his back moved like a river. Her experience of partially naked men was minimal; Captain Aitken had insisted his seamen wear shirts, no matter how hot or becalmed the air was. A godfearing man, Aitken, who had cared for his female prisoners with Christian impartiality, though too sensible a man to forbid his crew—or himself—access to the cargo. Listening to the brasher and bawdier women had acquainted her with male anatomy; they gleefully discussed the attributes and amorous talents of their lovers and despised the Catherine Clarks and Annie Bryants as missish mice. The London Newgate she had blotted from her memory, her disgrace too recent then to have banished shock and fright. She had simply huddled in a corner and hidden her face, fed only because Betty Riley had brought her food and water. In Port Jackson came her first sight of men stripped to the waist, some of them with terribly scarred backs. And though Richard Morgan had been shirtless last night, she had not noticed him because of Stephen.

The sight of Richard now awed her without arousing any tender or feminine yearnings; what she saw reinforced her impression that he was a man to be respected and obeyed. He was also old. Not in the least wrinkled or crabbed, just—*old.* On the inside rather than on the outside. His outside she thought very strong, very handsome, very graceful. But she had seen Stephen Donovan first, and could see no further.

Stephen. He was like a dream—very strong, very handsome, very graceful—and also youthful, carefree, brilliant of eye and smile, appreciative of the feminine attention he attracted. After landing her, he had bantered saucily with some of the more forward women, yet managed to turn their hints and open remarks aside without offending them. It never occurred to Kitty that these knowing women took one look at him and knew him for what he was, for she had no idea that some folk liked their own sex. A Church of England workhouse in Canterbury, cradle of the Church of England, did not teach the facts of life. It preferred to badger and beat good work habits into its children, use them to best effect while they were young enough, then send them out to find a living as meanly paid servants obsessed with their own worthlessness and utterly ignorant of what went on in the big wide world. Illiterate, innumerate, insignificant. Of course Kitty had heard words like Rome mort and Miss Molly in both her prisons, but they held no meaning for her and went right over her head. That some of the folk who liked their own sex were women, and that they had lived alongside her in Lady Juliana, had also not sunk in.

Stephen, Stephen, Stephen. . . . Oh, why had he not been the one to find her? Why was it not his house sheltered her? And what did Richard want of her?

Richard straightened and pulled on a shirt. "Was the bath very bad?" he asked, letting her precede him through the door, his eyes, had she only possessed the courage to look, twinkling.

"No, sir, it was very pleasant."

"Richard. Ye must call me plain Richard."

"It goes against the grain," she said. "You are old enough to be my father."

For the first time she experienced a quality in Richard she was to find over and over again; no alteration in expression of the face, no inappropriate movement of hands or body, no change in his eyes, yet *something* was happening, some kind of mysterious, invisible reaction.

"I am indeed old enough to be your father, but I am plain Richard nonetheless. We do not keep up appearances here, we have more important things to occupy us. I am not one of your gaolers, Kitty. I am a free man, yes, but until recently I was a convict just like you. Only good work and good fortune pardoned me." He sat her down at the table and gave her corn bread, lettuce and cress to eat, water to drink.

"Was Stephen a convict too?" she mumbled, ravenous.

"Nay, never. Stephen is a master mariner."

"Have you been friends for long?"

"For at least one span of eternity." Tucking his shirt into his trowsers, he sat down and ran his finger through his cropped hair rather nervously. "D'ye know why ye were sent here?"

"What is there to know?" she asked, bewildered. "I will be set to work until I serve out my sentence. At least, that is what the judge said at my trial. No one has mentioned it since."

"Have ye not wondered why you and two hundred other women were put on board a ship and sent seventeen thousand miles to serve out your sentences? Does that not seem strange, to send ye to a place devoid of workhouses and factories?"

In the act of reaching for another piece of bread, her hand fell limply into her lap; her eyes widened, revealing that they were only partially William Henry's eyes—his had been set in with a sooty thumb, hers with a crystal one. "Of course," she said slowly. "Of course. Oh, how idiotic I am! Except that I was so sick, and before that, so shocked and confused. There are no workhouses or factories at the far ends of the earth. No gentlemen's waistcoats to embroider. . . . That is what I did at the Canterbury workhouse. You mean that we have been sent here as wives for the convicts?"

His lips set. " 'Tis more honest to say that ye've been sent here as conveniences. I do not pretend to know the official reasons why this experiment had been put into practice, save that a great many men have been removed from England who might otherwise have become a population to be reckoned with. Mutinies have happened, men with nothing to lose have escaped into the English countryside. Whereas at the far ends of the earth it matters not to England if men mutiny or escape. They do not threaten England. The only folk who have to be protected are their gaolers and their gaolers' wives, children." He paused to fix her gaze. "Men without women sink to the level of beasts. Therefore women are a necessary part of the great experiment, which is to turn the far ends of the earth into a vast English prison. Or so *I* have come to believe."

Frowning, she listened to this and tried to assimilate it: he was saying that the only reason she had been transported was to be a pacifier of men. "We are your whores," she said. "Is *that* why Lady Juliana's crew called us whores? I thought it was because they thought we had all been convicted of prostitution, and I wondered at that. Most of us were convicted of stealing, or having stolen goods, or attacking someone with a knife. It is not a crime to be a prostitute, some of the women insisted—they used to grow angry when they were called whores. But what the sailors meant was that we were *future* whores. Is that it?"

He rolled his eyes at the ceiling, sighed. "Well," he said finally, smiling at her wryly, "if my daughter were alive, she would be about your age. Just as ignorant—as a good father I would have made sure of that. What are your circumstances, Kitty? Who were your parents?"

"My father was a tenant farmer at Faversham," she said proudly, lifting her chin. "My mother died when I was two, and my father had a housekeeper to look after me. He died when I was five. His farm went back to the manor because he had no heir. I was given to the parish, and the parish sent me to Canterbury."

"Ye were the only child?"

"Yes. Had Papa lived, I would have been taught to read and write, and been brought up to marry a farmer."

"But instead ye were sent to the poorhouse and ye never did learn to read or write," said Richard gently.

"That is so. My fingers are nimble and my eyes keen, so they put me to embroidering. But it does not last forever. The work is too fine for hands that are grown. I was kept until after I turned seventeen, when suddenly I grew. So I was sent to the manor at St. Paul Deptford as cook's maid."

"How long were ye there?"

"Until I—I was arrested. Three months."

"How did ye come to be arrested?"

"The manor had four below-stairs maidservants—Betty, Annie, Mary and me. Mary and I were the same age, Annie was sixteen, and Betty five-and-twenty. The master and mistress were called up to London very suddenly and Mr. and Mrs. Hobson got drunk on the port. Cook locked herself in her garret. It was Betty's birthday, and she said we should all walk to the shops for an outing. I had never been to the shops before."

Oh, this was awful! He sat there like the Master at the workhouse, a figure of age and authority, listening to this silly story with no expression on his face. It *was* a silly story—too silly to tell at the Kent assizes, had anybody asked. No one had.

"Did ye never go abroad from the workhouse, Kitty?"

"No, never."

"Surely ye had a day off sometimes at the St. Paul Deptford manor?"

"I had a half-day once a week, but never with one of the other girls, so I used to walk into the fields. I would rather have gone to the fields on Betty's birthday, but she mocked me for a rustic because I had never been into a shop, so I went with them."

"Were ye tempted in a shop? Is that it?"

"I suppose it must have been like that," she said doubtfully. "Betty brought a bottle of gin with her and we drank it as we went along. I do not remember the shops, or going into them—just men shouting, the bailiffs locking us up."

"What did ye steal?"

"Muslin in one shop, they said at the trial, and checkered linen in another. I do not know why we stole either—the dresses we wore were of the same sort of stuff. Four and sixpence the ten yards of muslin, the jury determined, though the shopkeeper kept roaring that it was worth three guineas. They did not charge us with the theft of the linen."

"Were ye in the habit of drinking gin?"

"No, I had never tasted it before. Nor had Mary or Annie." She shuddered. "I will never drink it again, that I know."

"Did ye all get transported?"

"Yes, for seven years. We were all on Lady Juliana almost as soon as the assizes were over. I suppose the others are here somewhere. It is just that I was so seasick—everybody loses patience with me, so they did not wait. And it was dark in Surprize."

He got up abruptly and walked around the table, put his hand on her shoulder and rubbed it. " 'Tis all right, Kitty, we will not speak of it again. Ye're a child, as only English parish charity can make a child out of a young woman."

MacTavish bounced in, having breakfasted on two juicy young rats. Giving her a final pat, Richard did the same to the dog, and sat down again. "The time has come to grow up, Catherine Clark. Not to lose your innocence, but to preserve it. There are no manors or workhouses here, ye know that. Had ye stayed at Port Jackson ye would have gone to the women's camp, but Norfolk Island's commandant, Major Robert Ross, is not willing to segregate the women. He is right, it only leads to worse trouble. Each of ye who came on Surprize is to be taken in by a man having a hut or house, though some will go to homes like that of Mrs. Lucas to help with the chores and children, and some will go as servants and conveniences to the officers and enlisted marines, yet others to Sirius men."

Her skin paled. "I am yours," she said.

His smile was very reassuring. "I am no rapist, Kitty, nor do I intend to plague ye with hints or wooing. I will keep ye as my servant. As soon as maybe, I will build a room onto this house to give each of us a meed of privacy. All I ask in return is that ye do whatever work ye're capable of. Yon structure I am building is a sty for the sow Major Ross will give me, and one of your responsibilities will be to look after the sow. As well as the house, the chickens when they come, and the vegetable garden. I have a man, John Lawrell, who looks after my grain and does the heavy work. The community will regard ye as mine, which is all the protection ye need."

"Have I no choice?" she asked.

"If ye had, where would ye rather be?"

"I would be Stephen's servant," she said simply.

Neither face nor eyes changed, though she knew that something happened inside him. All he said was, tone ordinary, "That is not possible, Kitty. Do not dream of Stephen."

The rest of the day passed with bewildering swiftness; Mrs. Lucas came to visit, puffing a little.

"I fall," she announced, flopping into a chair, "as soon as my Nat hangs his trowsers on their peg. Two so far, and a third well on the way."

"Are the two boys or girls?" Kitty asked, happier with this kind of conversation than the serious subjects Richard chose.

"Twin girls a year old—Mary and Sarah. I am carrying this one differently, so I expect it will be a boy." She fanned herself with her homemade shady hat. "Richard says ye mentioned a young girl named Annie who is here somewhere, or about to be landed. I am of a mind to take her in as help if I can get to her first—if, that is, ye think she would be happier in the bosom of a family than with a man."

"Of that I am sure, Mrs. Lucas. Annie is like me."

The large brown eyes narrowed. So, Richard, that is how things stand, is it? Stephen said ye'd fallen head over ears, and today I thought to find ye happy at last. What woman would be fool enough to spurn a man like you? But here she is, not a woman at all—a silly girl and a virgin to boot. Ye'd think gaol and transportation would make them grow up in a hurry, but I have seen Kitty's like before. Somehow they escape the taint, largely by being mice. In Port Jackson they are the first ones to die, but in Norfolk Island they live to learn what neither gaol nor transportation has managed to teach them: that the most a convict woman can hope for is a good, kind, decent man. Like my Nat. And like Richard Morgan.

Smothering these thoughts, Olivia Lucas proceeded to instruct Kitty in women's matters and how she should conduct herself in this place of too many men.

The conversation broke up with the arrival of Stephen and Johnny Livingstone carrying a bed; Olivia squawked and hurried home, leaving the three men and Kitty to eat Sunday dinner, a makeshift affair of pooled resources—pease cooked with a little salt pork, a dish of rice and onions, corn bread and a dessert of bananas from Richard's palms, several of which had the peculiar habit of bearing different-looking fruit early.

Kitty sat and listened to the men talk, realizing that in all her life she had not been exposed to masculine talk or the company of men. Half an hour of it humbled her; she knew so little! Well, to listen and remember was to learn, and she was determined to learn. They did not gossip in the manner of women, though they could laugh heartily over a story Johnny—how *beautiful* he was!—recounted about Major Ross and Captain Hunter, who apparently had fallen out very badly. Most of the talk revolved around problems of construction, discipline, timber, stone, lime, grubs, tools, the growing of grain.

Stephen, she noticed, was a toucher. If he passed by Richard or Johnny he would rest his hand on a shoulder or back, and once he jokingly rumpled Richard's short hair in exactly the same way he rumpled MacTavish's coat. But if he passed her by he was very careful to steer a wide berth around her chair, and never drew her into the conversation. Nor, for that matter, did the other two.

I think I am forgotten. Not one of them looks at me as I would have Stephen look at me, with fond love. If they do look at me, their eyes move immediately away. Why is that?

It was always Stephen who drove the talk, never allowing a silence to develop; Richard, she fancied, normally contributed more to the discussions than he did today. Today he spoke only when spoken to, and then sometimes absently. When they got up to move outside for an inspection of the pigsty, Kitty started clearing away the few dishes and tidying what she thought she would not get into trouble for moving. Only then did she understand that it was her presence had inhibited them, and that this was particularly true of Richard.

The Commandant's insistence that we be taken in by men with a house or hut has spoiled Richard's leisure—probably Stephen's too, since they are such good friends. I do not matter. I am a nuisance. In future I must find excuses to leave them alone.

That night Richard had a bed to sleep in, constructed in the same way hers was, a wooden frame connecting a lattice of rope, but when he ordered her to bed shortly after dusk he took a candle to the table he used as a desk, propped a book on a lectern and started to read. Whatever crime he committed, she thought drowsily, he has been schooled and brought up as a gentleman. The master of the St. Paul Deptford manor did not own such fine manners.

* * *

On the morrow, Monday, she saw little of Richard, who was off shortly after dawn to his work in the sawpits, came home for a hasty lunch of something cold with a pair of shoes for her, and spent most of his break at the pigsty, growing rapidly. It was about twenty feet on each side and consisted of wooden palings atop a course of stone.

"Pigs root," Richard explained as he labored, "so they cannot be confined as sheep or cattle are, within a simple fence. And they must be shaded from the sun because they overheat and die. Their excrement stinks, but they are tidy creatures and always choose a corner only of the sty as their privy. That makes it easy to gather for manure—it is very rich manure."

"Will I have to gather the manure?" she asked.

"Yes." He lifted his head to give her a grin. "Ye'll find that baths are very necessary."

In the evening he did not come home. Her rations were hers to do with as she pleased, he told her; he was used to caring for himself and usually ate with Stephen, who was a stern bachelor and did not care for women in his house. They played chess, he explained, so she was to go to bed upon darkness without waiting for him or expecting to see him. Naive though she was, this seemed odd to Kitty. Stephen did not behave like a stern bachelor. Though, come to think of it, she had little idea how a stern bachelor behaved. However, that Sunday dinner had taught her that men liked the company of men and were hampered by the presence of women.

On Tuesday a marine private appeared to summon her to Sydney Town, where she was required to identify the man who had molested and robbed her. The view from Richard's house was limited; Arthur's Vale, opening out and out, astonished her. Green wheat and Indian corn grew up the slopes of the hills on either side, waved in the vale itself; there were occasional houses perched at the edges, several barns and sheds, a pond harboring ducks. Then all of a sudden she emerged from the vale into a large collection of wooden houses and huts arranged in proper treeless streets, an expanse of vividly green swamp separating them from bigger structures at the bottom of the hills; she passed by Stephen Donovan's house without recognizing it.

Two military officers—she did not know a marine from a land soldier—waited for her outside a big, two-storeyed building she found out later was the marine barracks. A motley group of male convicts had been lined up nearby, and the officers were correctly dressed down to wigs, swords and cocked hats. The convicts all wore shirts.

"Mistress Clark?" asked the older officer, piercing her to the soul with a pair of pale grey eyes.

"Yes, sir," she whispered.

"A man accosted ye on the road from Cascade on the day of the thirteenth of August?"

"Yes, sir."

"He tried to force himself upon ye and tore your dress?"

"Yes, sir."

"Ye ran into the woods to escape?"

"Yes, sir."

"What did the man do then?"

Cheeks burning, striking eyes wide, she said, "He seemed at first to think of chasing me, then came voices. He picked up my bundle and bedding and walked in this direction."

"Ye spent the night in the woods, is that so?"

"Yes, sir."

Major Ross turned to Lieutenant Ralph Clark, who, having heard the story from Stephen Donovan and verified it from Richard Morgan, was curious to discover what his namesake looked like. Not a whore, he was relieved to see; as gentle and refined as Mistress Mary Branham, taken advantage of by a Lady Penrhyn seaman and delivered of a son in Port Jackson. She and the infant had been sent to Norfolk Island aboard Sirius; Clark had become interested in her after she was put to work in the officers' mess. Adorably pretty, much in the mold of his beloved Betsy. Now that he knew Betsy and little Ralphie were safe and well in England—and especially now that he had his own comfortable house—it might be easier for Mary to look after just one officer and one house; her little boy was walking now and making rather a nuisance of himself. Yes, to take Mary Branham in would be doing her a good turn. Of course he would not mention this arrangement in his journal, which was written for darling Betsy's eyes and could contain nothing might shock or perturb her. Slighting references upon damned whores were permissible, but *approval* of any convict woman was definitely not permissible.

Good, good! His mind made up on the future of Mary Branham and himself, he looked at the Major enquiringly.

"Lieutenant Clark, pray conduct Mistress Clark down the line to see if the villain is among this lot," said Ross, who had rounded up every convict ever punished.

Talking to her kindly as they went, the Lieutenant led Kitty along the row of sullen men, then took her back to his superior.

"Is he there?" barked Ross.

"Yes, sir."

"Where?"

She pointed to the man with two mouths. Both officers nodded.

"Thank ye, Mistress Clark. The private will escort ye home."

And that was that. Kitty fled.

"Tom Jones Two," said the private.

"That is who Mr. Donovan said it would be."

"Ain't none of them Mr. Donovan don't know."

"He is a very nice man," she said sadly.

"Aye, he ain't bad for a Miss Molly. Not one of your pretty field flowers. I watched him take a man apart with his fists—a bigger man than him too. Nasty when he are annoyed, Mr. Donovan."

"Quite," she agreed placidly.

And so went home with the private, Tom Jones Two forgotten.

Richard continued to absent himself in the evenings—not always, she learned, to play chess with Stephen. He was friends with the Lucases, someone called George Guest, a marine private Daniel Stanfield, others. What hurt Kitty most was that none of these friends ever asked her to accompany him, a reinforcement of his statement that she was his servant. It would be nice to have a friend or two, but of Betty and Mary she knew nothing, and Annie had indeed gone to the Lucases. Meeting Richard's other helper, John Lawrell, had been an ordeal; he had glared at her and told her not to fiddle with his poultry or the grain patch.

So when she noticed a female figure tittuping up the path between the vegetables, Kitty was ready to greet the visitor with her best smile and curtsey. On Lady Juliana the woman would have been apostrophized as a quiz, for she was very grand in a vulgar sort of way—red-and-black striped dress, a red shawl with a long fringe proclaiming its silkness, shoes with high heels and glittering buckles, and a monstrous black velvet hat on her head nodding red ostrich plumes.

"Good day, madam," said Kitty.

"And good day in return, Mistress Clark, for so I believe you are called," said the visitor, sweeping inside. There she looked about with some awe. "He does do good work, don't he?" she asked. "And more books than ever. Read, read, read! That is Richard."

"Do sit down," said Kitty, indicating a handsome chair.

"As fine as the Major's," said the red-and-black person. "I am always amazed at Richard's run of good luck. He is like a cat, falls on his feet every time." Her little black eyes looked Kitty up and down, straight, thick black brows frowning across her nose. "I never thought I was anything to look at," she said, inspection finished, "but at least I can *dress.* You are as plain as a pikestaff, my girl."

Jaw dropped, Kitty stared. "I beg your pardon?"

"You heard me. Plain as a pikestaff."

"Who *are* you?"

"*I* am Mrs. Richard Morgan, what do you think about that?"

"Nothing very much," said Kitty when she got her breath back. "I am pleased to meet you, Mrs. Morgan."

"Christ!" Mrs. Morgan said. "Jeeesus! What *is* Richard up to?"

As Kitty did not know what he was up to, she said nothing.

"You ain't his mistress?"

"Oh! Oh, of course!" Kitty shook her head in vexation. "I am so silly—I never thought—"

"Aye, silly is right enough. You ain't his mistress?"

Kitty put her chin in the air. "I am his servant."

"Hoo hoo! Hoity-toity!"

"If you are Mrs. Richard Morgan," said Kitty, growing braver in the face of her visitor's derision, "why are you not living in this house? If you were, he would have no need for a servant girl."

"I am not living here because I do not want to live here," Mrs. Richard Morgan said loftily. "*I* am Major Ross's housekeeper."

"Then I need not detain you. I am sure you are very busy."

The visitor got up immediately. "Plain as a pikestaff!" she said, mincing to the door.

"I may be plain, Mrs. Morgan, but at least I am not beyond my last prayers! Unless you are also the Major's mistress?"

"Fucken bitch!"

And off down the path she went, feathers bouncing.

Once the shock wore off—at her own temerity rather than at Mrs. Morgan's conduct and language—Kitty reviewed this encounter more dispassionately. Well on the wrong side of thirty, and, under the outrageous apparel, quite as plain as she had professed to know herself. And not, if she had read Major Ross aright at her only meeting with him, his mistress. That was a very fastidious man. So why had Mrs. Richard Morgan come—and, more importantly, why had Mrs. Richard Morgan gone in the first place? Closing her eyes, Kitty conjured up a picture of her, saw things that sheer amazement had veiled in the flesh. Much pain, sadness, anger. Knowing herself a pathetic figure, Mrs. Richard Morgan had presented herself to her supplanter with a great show of haughty aggression that overlay grief and abandonment. How do I know that? But I do, I do. . . . It was not her left him. *He* left her! Nothing else answers. Oh, poor woman!

Pleased with her deductive powers, she sat up in her bed in her convict-issue slops shift and waited by the dying light of the fire for Richard to come home. Where *does* he go?

His torch came flickering up the path two hours after night had fallen; he had, as on most evenings, eaten quickly at the pit and hied himself off to the distillery to make sure all was well and personally measure the amount of rum, enter it in his book. Time shortly to close it down. Casks and sugar were running low. All told, the installation would have produced about 5,000 gallons.

"Why are you awake?" he demanded, closing the door and tossing logs on the fire. "And what was the door doing open?"

"I had a visitor today," she said in meaningful tones.

"Did ye now?"

He was not going to ask who, which rather spoiled things.

"Mrs. Richard Morgan," she said, looking like a naughty child.

"I was wondering when she would appear" was all he said.

"Do you not want to know what happened?"

"No. Now lie down and go to sleep."

She subsided in the bed, quenched, and tired enough that lying flat out induced immediate torpor. "You left her, I know it," she said drowsily. "Poor woman, poor woman."

Richard waited until he was sure she was asleep, then changed into his makeshift nightshirt. The timber for her room was piling up, and he would begin to pull stones for its piers home on his sled this coming Saturday. A month from now he would be rid of her, at least from the room where he slept. She could have her own door to the outside as well, and he would cozen a bolt out of Freeman for his side of the communicating door. Then he could return to the freedom of sleeping naked and feeling as if he owned some part of himself. Kitty. Born in 1770, the same year as little Mary. I am an old fool, and she a young one. Even admitting this, the last thing he saw before weariness turned into sleep was the lump she made in his bed, silent and unmoving. Kitty did not snore.

"What," she asked the next day when he came home for a hot midday dinner, "is a Miss Molly?"

The bolus of bread in his mouth was in the act of sliding down his throat; he choked, coughed, had to be banged on the back and given water. "Sorry," he gasped, eyes tearing. "Ask again."

"What is a Miss Molly?"

"I have absolutely no idea. Why d'ye ask? Was it something Lizzie Lock said? Was it?" His expression boded ill.

"Lizzie Lock?"

"Mrs. Richard Morgan."

"Is *that* her name? What an odd combination. Lizzie Lock. It was you left her, is that not so?"

"I was never with her in the first place," he said, deflecting her attention from Miss Mollies.

The eyes were bright and sparkling, fascinated. "But you did marry her."

"Aye, in Port Jackson. 'Twas a chivalrous impulse I have since regretted bitterly."

"I understand," she said, sounding as if she actually did. "I think you suffer from chivalrous impulses you later regret. Like me."

"Why should ye think I regret you, Kitty?"

"I have cramped your style," she said candidly. "I do not truly believe that you wanted a maidservant, but Major Ross said you must take one of us in. I happened by, so you took me." Something in his eyes gave her pause; she put her head on one side and regarded him speculatively. "Your house was complete without me," she said then, voice wobbly. "Your life was complete without me."

In answer he got up to put his bowl and spoon on the bench beside the fireplace. "No," he said, turning with a smile that tugged at her heart, "life is never complete until it is over. Nor do I refuse gifts when God offers them to me."

"What time will you be home?" she called to his retreating back.

"Early, and with Stephen," he shouted, "so dig potatoes."

And that was life: digging potatoes.

In fact she loved the garden and was busy in it whenever the wretched sow gave her a spare moment. Augusta had arrived already pregnant by the Government boar, and had the most voracious appetite. If Kitty had preserved sufficient sense to wonder what serving out her sentence might entail before Richard had enlightened her—but she had not preserved sufficient sense—she would never have guessed that it would be spent waiting upon a four-trottered, mean-spirited glutton like Augusta. Since Richard was always absent, she had to learn the hard way how to take an axe and chop down cabbage palms and tree ferns, chip their skins off and feed the pith to Augusta, guzzling away; she carted baskets of Indian corn from the granary; she recited Kentish farmer's spells over their own Indian corn, coming on nicely. If Augusta was bottomless now, what would she be like when she was nursing a dozen piglets?

Those three months attending Cook in the kitchen of the manor at St. Paul Deptford had proven invaluable, for though she had not been allowed to cook anything, Kitty had watched with interest, and found now that she was quite capable of preparing the simple fare Norfolk Island provided. With no cows and only enough goats for babies and children, of milk there was none; fresh meat was rare now that the Mt. Pitt bird had gone (though Kitty had merely heard of it, came too late to taste it); vegetables varied from green beans to, in winter, cabbages and cauliflowers; Richard had harvested a fine crop of calavances—chickpeas; and, with the arrival of Justinian, there was bread of some kind every day. What she missed most was a cup of tea. Lady Juliana had provided both tea and sugar for its women convicts; though some of them preferred wheedling rum out of the seamen, most enjoyed sweetened tea more than anything else. It had been almost the only thing the seasick Kitty had been able to keep down, and now she missed it badly.

So when Richard and Stephen arrived she had a meal of boiled potatoes and boiled salt beef ready to put upon the table together with a loaf of wheaten bread.

They trooped in laden with pots and boxes.

"Captain Anstis had a stall on the beach today," said Richard, "and everything I wanted to buy was on it. Open kettles, a spouted kettle for boiling water, frying pans, little pots, tin dishes and tubs, pewter plates and mugs, knives and spoons, unbleached calico—even, when I asked for it, emery powder. Look, Kitty! I bought a pound of Malabar peppercorns and a mortar and pestle for grinding them." He dumped a wooden box a foot cubed down on the desk. "And here is a chest of hyson tea just for you."

Her hands to her cheeks, she stared at him tearily. "Oh! You thought of *me?*"

"Why should I not?" he asked, surprised. "I knew ye missed a cup of tea. I bought a teapot too. Sweetening it will not be hard. I will cut ye a stalk of sugar cane and chop it into short bits. All ye'll have to do is crush it with a hammer and boil it to make syrup."

"But this cost money!" she cried, appalled.

"Richard is a warm man, girl," Stephen said, beginning to take articles off Richard as he handed them up from the sled. "I must say ye did amazing well, my friend, considering who ye dealt with. Nick Anstis is hard-headed."

"I slapped gold coin on the board," said Richard, coming inside again. "Anstis has to wait for money when it is tendered in notes of hand, whereas gold is gold. He was happy to quarter his prices for coins of the realm."

"Just how much gold have ye got?" Stephen asked, curious.

"Enough," said Richard tranquilly. "You see, I inherited from Ike Rogers as well."

Stephen gaped, thunderstruck. "Is *that* why Richardson would not lay it on when Lieutenant King sentenced Joey Long to a hundred lashes for losing his best pair of Royal Navy shoes? Christ, ye're close, Richard! Ye must have paid a little something to Jamison as well for insisting that Joey's mental condition was too frail to sustain the whole flogging—Christ!"

"Joey looked after Ike. Now I look after Joey."

They sat down at the table to do justice to the food, all three too active to scorn a diet banal and repetitive in the extreme.

"I gather that ye spent today at Charlotte Field, so ye may not have heard what happened to Kitty's assailant," Stephen said to Richard when they were done and Kitty stood happily washing their bowls and spoons in a new tin dish—no more bucket!

"Ye're right, I have not heard. Tell me."

"Tommy Two did not like being chained to the grindstone in the least, so last night he picked the locks on his irons and absconded into the forest, no doubt to join Gray."

"With the birds gone, they will starve."

"Aye, so I think. They will end up back on the grindstone."

Richard rose, so did Stephen; Richard threw his arm about Stephen's shoulders and steered him doorward, out of earshot. "Ye might," he said quietly, "inform the Major that there may be a small conspiracy going on. Dyer, Francis, Peck and Pickett apparently have some purloined sugar cane growing somewhere off the track, and all four were sniffing around Anstis's stall enquiring after things like copper kettles and copper pipe."

"Why not tell the Major yourself? 'Tis you who is involved in that sort of activity."

"Exactly why I would rather not be the one to tell the Major. In that respect, Stephen, I walk very carefully. Were I the one to speak of it, the Major might—should illicit spirits appear among the convicts and private marines—think I had concocted the tale to cover my own guilt."

What are they muttering about? wondered Kitty, drying the bowls and spoons with a rag and putting them on their shelf before starting to wash the new pewter plates, mugs and eating utensils. Oh dear, I truly do cramp their style!

Though her world still consisted of Richard's acre, Kitty was too busy to think of exploring; her only trip to Sydney Town apart from divine service had been to identify her attacker, neither an occasion to take notice of her surroundings. All her farmer's bones were asserting themselves; Richard could not have picked a better kind of woman than Kitty for the kind of life she was called upon to lead.

She kept hearing about "the grubs," and on the 18th of October she experienced them at first hand. The wheat on Richard's acre was in ear and thriving, but the Government wheat in the more open parts of the vale had been hit by high, salty winds and blighted, though by no means all of it was ruined. The year was a dry one, the crops saved only by an occasional night of heavy rain which had vanished by the morning. Perhaps for this reason, the grubs had not come during winter. Then suddenly it seemed as if every growing thing was covered with a heaving green blanket—the caterpillars were bright green, about an inch long, and thin. Again Richard was lucky, for Kitty had no fear of wrigglers, crawlies and bugs. She was able to pick the creatures off without revulsion, though the solution of tobacco and soap was more effective. Every woman on the island save those who danced attendance on the marines and the sawpits was put to picking and sprinkling. Within three weeks they were gone. There would be a harvest, very soon for the Indian corn, early in December for the wheat. Though under Major Ross's new scheme everything the freed Richard grew was his, he was very scrupulous about sending excess produce to Stores, for which he accumulated more notes of hand. What he kept was either eaten by the humans or Augusta, or saved for seed.

The weather in Norfolk Island, she occasionally thought as she toiled with her hoe or got down on hands and knees to weed, was truly delightful—balmy, warm, never hot out of the sun. And just when things began to wilt from lack of water, one of those nights of solid rain would roll in, disappear at dawn. The soil, blood-red and very friable, grew anything. No, Norfolk Island could not compete with Kent in her affections, yet it did have a magical quality. Rainy nights, sunny days—that was the stuff of fairies.

Some of those she had known on Lady Juliana had fallen to the lot of

Richard's friends. Aaron Davis, the community baker, had taken Mary Walker and her child. George Guest had taken eighteen-year-old Mary Bateman, whom Kitty had known very well, had liked, but yet sensed a strangeness, as of madness yet to come. Edward Risby and Ann Gibson were happily together and planning to marry as soon as a person empowered to marry visited the island. These women and Olivia Lucas visited—how delightful it was to be able to offer them a mug of tea with sugar in it! Mary Bateman and Ann Gibson were both expecting babies; Mary Walker, whose child Sarah Lee was toddling, was also expecting her first by Aaron Davis. The only barren one was Kitty Clark.

Of fish there were none. Sirius's cutter, which might have ventured well outside the lagoon to fish, was smashed to pieces trying to land six women convicts off Surprize, one with a child. The oarsmen drowned, as did a man swimming to their rescue; one of the three women who survived was the drowned child's mother. So the very occasional catches of fish the coble managed all went to the officers and marines; neither Sirius's seamen nor freed convicts received a share. But Justinian had carried plants, including bamboo, and Richard was given one small piece of it from which to grow a clump of potential fishing poles. Hand-lines caught nothing fishing off rocks.

There was a panic at Charlotte Field, where the paddocks were hedged in by a mixture of creeper skeleton and a very thorny bush; one of the fences accidentally caught fire and the flames spread into ripe Indian corn. At first Sydney Town heard that all the corn had been burned to the ground, but Lieutenant Clark, speeding there at a run, reported back to the distraught Major Ross that only two acres had perished thanks to the great exertions of the convicts, who beat the fire out. So grateful was Lieutenant Clark to the damned whores of Charlotte Field that he gave each of them a new pair of shoes from the Government supplies.

D'arcy Wentworth was deputed to move to Charlotte Field with his mistress Catherine Crowley and little William Charles as soon as a house could be built for him; he was to be superintendent of convicts and also Charlotte Field's surgeon. The duties of this latter position varied from midwifing to deciding when a convict being flogged could bear no more strokes. If the culprit were a woman, Wentworth tended to be lenient, whereas Lieutenant Clark, who despised the women of Charlotte Field, would of choice have had Richardson lay a meaner cat on harder.

Much to Kitty's pleasure, the variety of food increased. She now had a wonderful cooking area because Richard had fixed an iron shelf across two-thirds of the big fireplace and a rod over the naked flames of the other third. She had covered kettles for braising, open ones for stewing or boiling, pans for frying and a spouted kettle she kept perpetually simmering on a coolish back corner of the shelf so that she could make herself or her visitors a pot of tea, tip a dollop of hot water into her washing-up dish. Richard had even made her what he called a soap-saver: a wire basket attached to a wire handle in which she could put a chunk of soap and swish it through the water without losing the soap.

Richard told John Lawrell firmly that he must give up some of his chickens and ducks, so Kitty added to her living charges and was able on special occasions to put eggs on the menu. Augusta farrowed twelve piglets and only twice rolled over to squash them; she was considerate enough to leave all six females alive as well as two males Richard intended would be roast suckling pig at Christmas. The pig produce was entirely theirs. If any successful breeder wished to sell pork to the Stores, he or she (Ross had made no sexual distinctions) was paid for it; if anyone wished to salt pork down, he or she was given the salt and a barrel to do so. Ross's objective was, as he had said at the outset, to take as many convicts as possible off Government Stores. Folk like Aaron Davis, Dick Phillimore, Nat Lucas, George Guest, John Mortimer, Ed Risby and Richard Morgan demonstrated that Ross's scheme could work, given time.

The Major's chief troubles rested with the marines and Sirius's sailors, who refused to soil their hands by growing vegetables and other fresh produce, demanding that Stores supply them. When Stores could not, they were prone to steal vegetables, melons and poultry from the convicts, a transgression Ross punished as severely as if the larceny were the other way around. The grumbles and dark looks among these free people increased; they all believed absolutely that no convicted felon ought to be able to keep the fruits of his or her labors, that every morsel the convicts grew belonged to them and must feed them ahead of any and all convicts. Why should they labor in a garden when so many convicts were growing enough to feed them? Convicts were the property of His Majesty the King, they could own nothing, keep nothing. *Convicts had no rights,* so who exactly did Major Robert Ross think he was? The fact that Major Ross levied two-thirds of the produce of convicts for Stores was conveniently overlooked; only freed men kept everything.

Christmas Day, a Saturday, dawned fine and clear, though the wind was in the south and a huge sea thundered into Sydney Bay. Richard killed his two boar piglets, Nat Lucas two geese, George Guest three fat ducks, Ed Risby four chickens, and Aaron Davis baked full wheaten bread from flour ground out of grain all of them had grown surplus to Government requirements. They picnicked under the shade and shelter of the pines on Point Hunter with Stephen Donovan, Johnny Livingstone and D'arcy Wentworth and his family, the pork and poultry turning on spits D'arcy had commandeered from the smithy. Stephen and Johnny contributed ten bottles of port, enough for both men and women to enjoy half a pint each.

The Major had publicly proclaimed that this was to be a dry Christmas for the convicts apart from small beer, and the marines were ordered to consume their half-pints away from any convict eyes; King had always given the convicts rum on festive occasions, whereas Ross, especially in the aftermath of discovering what Dyer, Francis and company were planning to do with their sugar cane, had no intention of doing the same.

For Kitty, the day was the happiest she had known since her father died. Sirius canvas was spread out for the women to sit on, pillows provided to ease the awkwardness of the pregnant ones. The pines broke the force of the wind, fathers took their toddlers down onto Turtle Bay to paddle and build sand castles, mothers gossiped comfortably. Kitty had brought her kettle to make tea for her friends, setting it on its own fire. The men, once duty at the water's edge was over, moved off a little way to squat on their haunches and talk together, while the women attended to the spits, prepared bowls of lettuce, celery, raw onion and raw beans, buried potatoes in the embers. About two in the afternoon they sat down to feast, then the men joined the women in a toast to His Britannic Majesty and afterward lay flat out for a postprandial nap, toddlers cuddled against them.

They are all so easy together, thought Kitty. Because of shared experiences and hardships, she had grown up sufficiently to realize. We are a new sort of English people, and what we make of ourselves will always be influenced by the fact that we were sent here as unwanted by our betters. Betters who are not betters at all, but rather people who do not see beyond their own noses. Out of the blue, it seemed, she suddenly had a feeling that none of these convicted people would return to England. They have lost respect for England. This has become home.

What about herself? Never having been to the shore, she sat with her arms wrapped about her knees and propped her chin on them to look along the reef, invisible under billows of foam and tendrils of spray. Though its spectacular beauty was not lost on her, it did not draw her either. In her mind's eye true beauty was Faversham, a good big stone house with bullioned casement windows and tumbles of pink and white roses—snapdragons, stocks, columbines, pansies, foxgloves, snowdrops, daffodils—apple orchards, yews, oaks—grassy green meadows, fluffy white sheep, birches and beeches. Oh, the perfume of her father's flower garden! The placid, dreaming quality which overlay all human activity and endeavor. This Norfolk Island kind of beauty was too alien, too untamable. This humbled and crushed people. Whereas home enhanced people.

She looked up to find Stephen's eyes upon her, and blushed crimson. Clearly startled, he transferred his gaze at once to the reef. Oh, Stephen! Why will you not love me? Did you love me, Richard would let me go—I know he would. I am not the center of his life. He has put me in my own room and he bolts the door between us, not because I tempt him—if I did, the bolt would be on my side of the door. To shut me out of his home. To pretend that I am not there. Stephen, why will you not love me when I love you? I want to cover your dear face in kisses, take it between my hands and smile into your eyes, see my love shining in their blueness like the sun in a Norfolk Island sky. *Why* will you not love me?

As soon as the strength went out of the sun and the toddlers became tired enough to grizzle, everybody started packing up. Families dropping off as they went, Richard and Kitty walked home with their share of the leftovers, Nat and Olivia Lucas the last to leave them. Olivia's tiny son, William, was but recently born, and her twin girls were extremely proud of him. What nice folk!

"Did ye like your first antipodean Christmas?" Richard asked.

"What sort of Christmas? But I did, I did, truly!"

"Antipodean. That is the correct name for the ends of the earth—the Antipodes. It comes from the Greek, and means something like 'feet at the opposite end.' "

The sun had gone behind the hills to the west, Richard's acre was plunged into deep cold shadow.

"Would ye like a fire?"

"No, I would sooner go to bed," she said rather mournfully, her mind occupied with Stephen, the way he had turned from her in rejection. Of course she did know why: she was as plain as a pikestaff despite the weight she was so delighted at gaining, fancying that her breasts were now quite as nice as most, her waist as small, her hips as properly hippy.

"Close your eyes and hold out your hand, Kitty."

Obeying, she felt something small and square put into her palm, and opened her eyes. A box. Fingers trembling, she prised its lid off to see that it held a necklet of gold. "Richard!"

"Merry Christmas," he said, smiling.

She flung her arms about his neck and pressed her cheek to his, then, in an ecstasy of gratitude and pleasure, kissed him on the mouth. For a moment he stayed very still, then put his hands upon her waist and returned her kiss, which transformed it from a thank you to something very different. Far too intelligent to mistake her response for anything other than what it was, he contented himself with savoring her deliciously soft lips. She neither fled nor made a protest; instead she nestled against him and let the kiss go on. Vibrant warmth kindled inside her, she forgot herself and Stephen to follow where his mouth led, thinking with what remained of her to think that this first real kiss of her life was a very exotic and wonderful experience, and that Richard Morgan was more interesting by far than she had realized.

He released her abruptly and went outside; the sound of the axe came immediately after. Kitty stood, immersed in an afterglow, then remembered Stephen and was consumed with guilt. How *could* she have enjoyed being kissed by Richard when it was Stephen she loved? Tears brimming over, she retreated to her own room and sat on the edge of her bed to weep silently.

The box with the gold necklet in it had somehow stayed in her hand; when her tears dried she took it out and clasped it around her neck, resolved that before next she bathed, she would look at her reflection in the pool. How kind of him! And why did some of her keep wishing that Richard had not let her go?

On the 6th of February 1791, the tender Supply finally arrived in the roads, bearing a letter from Governor Phillip instructing all Sirius personnel to board her for Port Jackson, but promising that those who wanted to take up land and settle in Norfolk Island would be granted 60 acres each and be returned on Supply's next voyage. Captain John Hunter's eleven-month exile was over, and not a moment too soon. He had conceived a hatred of Norfolk Island that was never to leave him—and was to bias much of his conduct later in his career. He had also conceived a hatred of Major Robert Ross and every fucken marine in the world. With him Captain Hunter took Johnny Livingstone, back in the fold at last.

Storeship Gorgon from England, which had been expected in New South Wales for months, had not arrived. Nor had any other ship save Supply on the 19th of November last from Batavia with a piddling amount of flour and a great deal of everybody's least favorite food, rice. The chartered vessel Waaksamheid had followed in her wake from Batavia to reach Port Jackson on the 17th of December, loaded with tons more rice, plus tea, sugar and Dutch gin for the officers; the salt meat she carried proved to be a putrid mess of mostly bones.

According to Lieutenant Harry Ball of Supply, His Excellency was going to hire Waaksamheid to carry Captain Hunter and the crew of Sirius to England. In a hurry to get back to Port Jackson, Supply sailed on the 11th of February. Among those who went on her but intended to return as settlers were the three Sirius men who had helped guard and run Major Ross's distillery, now closed, the contents of its kegs nicely maturing in a secret place. John Drummond had fallen in love with Ann Read off Lady Penrhyn. She was living with Neddy Perrott; though Drummond understood that *he* could not have her, he could not bear to sail to England either. William Mitchell had taken up with Susannah Hunt off Lady Juliana and they planned to stay in this part of the world. Peter Hibbs was caught in the toils of another girl off Lady Juliana, Mary Pardoe, who had been a sailor's "wife" and borne a little girl toward the end of the voyage, whereupon the wretch had abandoned her, left her to be transferred to Norfolk Island.

On the 15th of April Supply was back again. Her first cargo ashore was a detachment of the New South Wales Corps, specially commissioned in London to police the great experiment and free up the marines to go home, though any marine on finishing his three-year term was at liberty to join the New South Wales Corps rather than go home. Captain William Hill, Lieutenant Abbott, Ensign Prentice and 21 soldiers were to replace the same number of marines, save that four marine officers were to leave: three were intentional, the fourth an evil necessity. Captain George Johnston was taking his convict mistress Esther Abrahams and their son, George, to Port Jackson; the affable Lieutenant Cresswell, discoverer of pineless Charlotte Field, went as he had come, alone; Lieutenant Kellow, so odious to his fellow officers, departed with his convict mistress Catherine Hart and her two sons, the younger belonging to him; and Lieutenant John Johnstone was carried on board Supply desperately ill. Of the old brigade, only Major Ross, First Lieutenant Clark and Second Lieutenant Faddy were left. And Second Lieutenant Little John Ross, of course.

Ominously, Supply brought two more surgeons: Thomas Jamison, after a vacation in Port Jackson; and James Callam off Sirius. As D'arcy Wentworth and Denis Considen were already on the island, that brought the medical complement up to four—four to treat a population reduced by over 70 persons?

"This tells me," said Major Ross grimly to Richard Morgan, "that as soon as more convict transports arrive from England, we are to receive many of their tenants. His Excellency has also given me to understand that he intends to ship some of his multiple offenders here. In Port Jackson, he says, they escape to kill the natives, plunder the outlying settlements, and rape women left alone. In this much smaller place he feels they will be easier to control. I must therefore build a stouter gaol than the old guardhouse, and I will have to start it now—no one knows when the next transports will arrive, only that they will arrive. It seems London cares more to be rid of England's felons than London cares whether or not they will survive here. So keep sawing, Morgan, as hard and fast as ye can, and do not even think of such whimsies as closing down a pit."

"How seem the men of the New South Wales Corps?" Richard asked.

"I see little difference between their enlisted men and my own—a rascally lot who by accident escaped the attention of the English courts. The officers are a cut above them, but I am not inspired to rave about their efficiency. What I would not give for a decent surveyor! Here I am to allocate sixty-acre grants to Sirius men like Drummond and Hibbs as well as some of my own time-expired marines, yet I have no surveyor. Bradley was pathetic, Altree even worse." His eyes gleamed. "I do not suppose, Morgan, that amongst your many hidden talents is surveying?"

Richard laughed. "Nay, sir, nay!"

The yield of Indian corn from Charlotte Field had been huge; dozens of convict women were put to husking and scraping the grain off thousands upon thousands of cobs, and the wheat harvest had also come in much bigger than the blighting winds and gnawing grubs had promised. But Port Jackson was back on two-thirds rations, which meant that Norfolk Island was ordered to follow suit. Luckily when she sailed on the 9th of May, Supply had been so laden with departing people that she had no room for a cargo of grain. What Norfolk Island had, it would keep—for the time being, at any rate. A commodious house of young pine logs had been built at Charlotte Field for D'arcy Wentworth and his family, who were sorely missed in Sydney Town. Though this western village was no longer named Charlotte Field; on Saturday the 30th of April, Major Ross officially announced that it was to be called Queensborough, and that Phillipburgh would become properly possessive as Phillipsburgh.

Sufficient time had elapsed since the arrival of Surprize to enable the 700-odd people of Norfolk Island to get to know each other. The entire island hummed with gossip; Lieutenant Ralph Clark snipped the first two bunches of grapes ever to form in the Antipodes, but the gossip grapevine was much longer and stronger than the real thing, bore bigger fruit. Mrs. Richard Morgan was not averse to disseminating interesting tidbits garnered in the Lieutenant-Governor's house; Mistress Mary Branham in Lieutenant Ralph Clark's house also contributed her mite. From highest to lowest, the doings of everyone were examined, speculated upon, and judged. If a convict abandoned his Lady Penrhyn woman in favor of a newer, younger female off Lady Juliana, it was known; if a marine secretly philandered with a convict's wife, it was known; if private marines Escott, Mee, Bailey and Fishbourn were brewing beer from island barley and Justinian hops, it was known; if Little John Ross was off color, it was known; and everybody knew the identity of the third man who broke into Stores and tried to steal saleable items. Mr. Freeman's servant John Gault and convict Charles Strong were sentenced to 300 lashes each from the meanest cat: 100 in Sydney Town, then, upon recovery, 100 in Queensborough, then, upon recovery, 100 in Phillipsburgh. Even in the face of this terrible punishment—it would partially cripple them for life—they would not divulge the name of the third man. But everybody knew.

Despite the intermeshing relationships established between those who guarded and those who were guarded, the camps were very much divided when it came to totting up grievances. This meant that when rations were reduced and his enlisted marines looked like mutinying, Major Ross held no fears that the convicts would take advantage of a suddenly perilous situation. Led, as always, by men like Mee, Plyer and Fishbourn, the marines refused to take their rations from the Stores, complaining that their flour supply was already eroded because they had to use some of it to barter for fresh produce from the convicts. The insurrection was short-lived and unsuccessful; Major Ross, confronted, told them that they were a fucken lazy lot of fucken scum for whom he had neither time nor pity. If they wanted to keep the flour ration intact, then they ought to grow their own fresh produce. They had more leisure and more fish than the convicts, so what was stopping them? Ross's ex-servant Escott and a group of other privates crumbled; the threat of mutiny faded. Shortly afterward, a daily allowance of a good mug of rum was issued again. If nothing else would pacify them, rum would. How could he deprive half his marines of their muskets? Ross asked himself. The answer was that he could not. Therefore keep them sedated and the hell with conscience.

Naturally the departure of Johnny Livingstone was noted. All eyes became riveted upon Stephen Donovan to see who Johnny's replacement was going to be. Nobody permanent and nobody from among the convicts; since Donovan carried on superintending his gangs in the same cheerfully ruthless way, the final assumption was that Johnny had not mattered much.

Another interesting situation was that between Richard Morgan and his house girl, Kitty Clark, who was locked out of that strange man's bed. *Locked* out!

"Fitting," said Mrs. Richard Morgan, whose maiden name was Lock.

Richard was famously friendly with Stephen Donovan, but those who knew him from Ceres and Alexander days swore that he had no Miss Molly leanings; though Will Connelly and Neddy Perrott continued to ostracize him, they could not be brought to admit that he lifted Donovan's shirt. If anyone peeked furtively through Donovan's unshuttered windows, all the inquisitive individual saw was the pair of them bent over a chessboard, or sitting companionably side by side at the fire, or eating at the table. Never with Kitty Clark there. She stayed home, guarded by Lawrell and MacTavish.

Stephen had been in a quandary ever since he had seen Kitty blush on Christmas Day of 1790. Eyes opened, he noticed after that how her attention was always fixed upon him, though her attitude to Richard had subtly changed. Before that picnic he had utterly intimidated her—she was a natural mouse, and not a very bright mouse either. Very sweet, very humble, very dull. Had she not owned William Henry's eyes, Stephen was sure that Richard would have passed her by without a glance. Therefore Richard's strength, his intelligence and his reticent nature made him appear in her eyes as a God the Father kind of person, immensely old and the fount of all authority. Fear and obey. After the picnic Kitty had definitely lost a little of her terror of him, Stephen presumed because of the gold necklet she never left off—how women adored sparkling gewgaws! Or was it that sparkling gewgaws cost precious money, and were thus an indication of esteem? But it was he, Stephen, who fueled her dreams of love. That was unmistakable. Precisely why he had no idea, though he was used to attracting women. Probably, he thought, I give off emanations of unattainability; women inevitably want what they cannot have. Though it has not occurred to Kitty that Richard is hers for the lifting of a finger, so there must be more to it than that.

What to do for the best? How to channel her feelings away from himself and toward Richard?

Tobias, curled in his lap, got up, stretched, repositioned himself. A weeny marmalade bundle with gigantic paws that promised he would one day be a lion. What a cat Olivia had given him! Brilliantly clever, scheming, tough, stubborn, and irresistibly charming when he wanted to be worshiped and fussed over. The kittens he might have sired! But Stephen, wanting a pet which slept alongside him in his hammock rather than roamed abroad in search of sexual conquests, had castrated him without qualm or regret.

The answer to his quandary had not yet appeared when Supply sailed for Sydney in May. May of 1791 already! Where did the years go? Over four years since he had met Richard Morgan.

Stephen had been put to surveying, since he knew the rudiments of the art; those who had returned on Supply to take up land were anxious to do so, and Major Ross wanted them out of town post-haste. The Sirius seamen would probably last the distance, Stephen thought, but the marines were not so enthusiastic. Men like Elias Bishop and Joseph McCaldren—incorrigible troublemakers in their day—were principally interested in being deeded their land, then selling it. Having gotten what they could out of Norfolk Island, they would then return to Port Jackson and apply for land there, also to sell. They wanted hard money, not hard labor. And in the meantime they lolled around Sydney Town making mischief with those marines not yet due to retire. Poor Major Ross! An enormous kettle of trouble was brewing for him in Port Jackson and England. With backbiters like George Johnston and John Hunter—not to mention that mental-case Bradley—whispering in Governor Phillip's receptive ear, Ross would see little thanks for his work. Stephen respected him as much as Richard did, and for the same reasons. Faced with a virtually insoluble predicament, Ross had proceeded without fear or favor. Always a dangerous thing to do.

"The trouble is," Stephen said to Richard over a mess of fried chicken and rice Kitty had flavored splendidly with sage and onion from her garden and pepper from her pestle, "that one has to have a line of sight to survey, and Norfolk Island is a dense forest of trees which all look the same. I can survey wherever there is cleared ground, but a lot of these sixty-acre blocks will not be on cleared ground. I can put Elias Bishop at Queensborough, but Joe McCaldren refuses to go so far out of Sydney Town, and Peter Hibbs and James Proctor want adjoining pieces right in the middle of the island. Danny Stanfield and John Drummond want to be near Phillipsburgh. By the time I am through, I swear I will need to be confined in a strait-waistcoat and chained to a gun in the shade. Supervising the likes of Len Dyer is a holiday compared to this."

"Is Danny Stanfield coming back, then?"

"Aye. He went off to marry Alice Harmsworth. A good man."

"The best of all the marines."

"With Juno Hayes and Jem Redman, aye," Stephen agreed.

Kitty interrupted. "Is the supper tasty?" she asked anxiously.

"Magnificently so!" Stephen responded, wishing he could snub rather than encourage her, but too fair to do so. "Such a change from eternal Mt. Pitt bird too! I admit they save our salt meat—I admit that the Major's pessimism about how many future mouths we will be feeding is well founded—but I confess that when I heard the birds had flown in to nest in apparently unreduced numbers, I was near sick to my stomach. However," he said blandly, "Tobias is very partial to Mt. Pitt bird."

"Oh, dear! I thought it was forbidden to give them to our pets," said Kitty, looking frightened. "Please do not get into trouble, Stephen!"

Richard went into God the Father mode. "The wastage of Mt. Pitt birds," he said ponderously, "is shameful. Stephen has no need to catch any to feed Tobias, Kitty. All he needs is to pick up carcasses strewn along the tracks. The greedy ingrates pillage the poor females of their eggs, then throw the rest away."

"Oh, yes, quite!" squeaked Kitty, retreating in confusion.

"Richard," said Stephen after she disappeared through the door with an empty bucket and a flustered explanation that she needed to fetch water from the stream, "sometimes ye're an absolute looby!"

"Eh?" asked Richard, startled.

"When the poor little creature ventures a remark, ye squash her flat with logic and good sense! She makes us a delicious repast—out of fucken rice, of all things!—yet how d'ye thank her? By donning the snowy vestments of God the Father!"

Mouth open, Richard sat stunned. *"God the Father?"*

"That is what I call you these days. You know—as in God the Father, God the Son, and God the Holy Ghost? God the Father is the one sits on the throne and dispenses whatever-it-is He deems just reward or punishment, though it seems to me that He is quite as blind as every other judge in or out of Christendom. Kitty is the most harmless of all His creatures—for a man in love, Richard, ye're as inept as a hobbledehoy! If you want her, why in fucken Hell d'ye not act as if you want her?" Stephen demanded, his exasperation fanned because of his own predicament with her.

Face a study might have made Stephen laugh were the situation different, Richard heard this diatribe through, then said flatly, "I am too old. Ye're right—she thinks of me as a father, which is not unreasonable. My daughter would be her age."

Stephen saw an even brighter shade of red. "Then make her think of you otherwise, you fool!" he cried, shaking with rage. "Damn you, Richard, ye're one of the most beautiful men I have ever seen! There is no flaw—I know, because I have searched for one. I have been in love with you since before I was born and I will be in love with you until long after I die. The fact that I am a Miss Molly and you are not is irrelevant—no one *chooses* whom to love. It simply happens. Somehow you and I have managed to cope with our different preferences and forge a friendship too strong ever to break. Yes, I know the silly child thinks she is in love with me, so shut your mouth and stop looking noble! Just as well for her that she does fancy herself in love with me. Did she not, she would come to you a complete child—and that no man in his right mind wants!" He ran down, hiccoughed, looked spent.

"But you said it, Stephen. No one chooses whom to love, it simply happens. And she has chosen you, not me."

"No, no, you miss the point! Jesus, Richard, where Kitty is concerned ye're an ass! To her, I am the transition between child and woman—I am her first girlish passion, unrequited because they always are. She is a plum ripe for the picking, man! I saw her walking down the vale to Stores the other day, dangling an empty basket. The wind was blowing straight in her face and plastered her shapeless slops against her—were I a man for women, I would have snatched her away that instant. And do not think that other men did not notice! Apart from her eyes, her face does not have much to recommend it, but in the body she is Venus. Long shapely legs, swelling hips, tiny waist and superb breasts—*Venus!* If ye do not lay claim to her, Richard, someone else will in spite of his fear that ye'll tear him in half."

Stephen got to his feet. "Now I am going home to Tobias before she returns from her errand. Tell her that I remembered some urgent business." He went to the door. "Ye're too patient, Richard. 'Tis an admirable virtue, but while the cat crouches for an hour watching the mouse, a hawk may swoop down from the sky and steal it."

* * *

Kitty shrank into the shadows beneath the unshuttered window, but Stephen Donovan looked neither to left nor to right; he strode off down the path between the vegetables and disappeared into the darkness. The moment he vanished, she crept back to the stream. Why was it not deep enough to drown in? Stephen's calling Richard an absolute looby had stilled her footsteps, aroused her curiosity; forgetting adages about eavesdroppers, she placed herself beneath the window and listened.

How was that possible? How could Stephen say he was *in love* with Richard? Mind reeling, she could not get beyond that. Stephen, a man, was in love with—desired—another man. Richard. And he had called *her* love a girlish passion. He had called her a child. Spoken of her with tender sympathy but no love whatsoever. Could recount the details of her figure with the same sort of remote admiration she felt for Richard. Who, Stephen had said, was in love with her. But Richard was her father's age! *He* had said it! She fell to her knees and rocked back and forth, tearless. I want to die, I want to die. . . .

Richard crouched beside her. "You heard."

"Yes."

"Well, better to hear it that way than from my wife," he said, put an arm about her shoulders and hauled her upright with himself. "You were bound to find out sooner or later. Come, off to bed. 'Tis cold out here."

She suffered herself to be led inside, then looked at him out of a wan white face and William Henry's eyes.

"Go to bed," he said firmly, face impassive.

Without a word she turned and went to her room. He was right, it was cold; shivering, she got into her night shift and climbed into that warm soft feather bed, there to lie sleepless, going over and over what she remembered of their—no, not conversation. Nor argument. What she had heard was an exchange of feelings and impressions between two very old friends, friends who could not truly offend each other no matter what had to be said. From the little her life had shown her, a rare occurrence. The word "maturity" came from somewhere, and it suited them. Why were they what they were? Why did Stephen choose to love a man? And why was that man Richard? Why had he called Richard "God the Father"? Oh, she thought, squeezing her hands together in pain and bewilderment, I know nothing about either of them! Nothing!

The wish to die faded, died. Nor, she discovered, was she shattered beyond hope of mending. That Stephen did not love her was a grief, but she had never thought he loved her; that was an old disappointment. The shape of her sorrow melted, burned away by yet more questions. Perhaps, she thought, I do have the brain to learn, though what the lesson is I do not know. Only that I have spent my life hiding, and I cannot go on hiding. Those who hide are never seen. With that enlightenment, she fell asleep.

When she woke in the morning, Richard had gone. The dishes were washed, the stove top tidy, the kettle steamed, the fire lay in embers, and a plate of cold chicken and rice lay on the table.

She made herself tea in the sturdy baked clay pot warming on the hearth and sat to pick at the food, looking back on last night as if from a great distance. The memories were all firmly embedded, but the intensity of feeling had gone. Feeling. . . . Surely there was a better word than that?

Richard walked in with his usual easy smile. As if nothing had happened. "You look very thoughtful," he said.

The comment was a signal, she divined that: he did not wish to discuss last night. So she said, rather feebly, "No work?"

"Today is Saturday."

"Oh, of course. Some tea?"

"That would be nice."

She poured him a mug and cooled it down with cold sugar syrup, then sat down again to go on toying with her food. Finally she put the spoon down on the pewter plate with a clang and glared at him. "If I cannot talk to you," she burst out, "who is there?"

"Try Stephen," he said, sipping appreciatively. "Now that is one could talk the leg off an iron pot."

"I do not understand you!"

"You do, Kitty, you do. 'Tis yourself you do not understand, and where is the wonder in that? Ye've not had much of a life," he said gently.

She stared across the table straight into his eyes, something she had never had the courage to do before. Wide, the color of the sea beyond the lagoon on a squally day, and deep enough to drown in. Without, it seemed, the slightest effort, he took her inside himself and swept her away on a tide of—of— Gasping, she leaped to her feet, both hands clutching at her chest. "Where is Stephen?"

"Fishing at Point Hunter, I imagine."

She fled through the door and into the vale as if Satan's hounds bayed at her heels, slowing down only when she realized that he was not following her. How had he done that? How?

By the time she negotiated the perils of walking unescorted through Sydney Town—a matter of running from one group of women to the next—Kitty had regained a little composure and was able to smile and wave at Stephen, who rolled in his line, strolled to meet her, then shepherded her away from the vicinity of half a dozen other men also fishing. He seemed ignorant of what had happened; that eventuality had not occurred to her, she had automatically assumed that Richard would have gone to tell him. Did Richard discuss nothing with anyone?

"They are not biting," he said breezily. "What brings ye here? No Richard in your wake?"

"I overheard what passed between you last night," she said, and gulped audibly. "I know I ought not to have listened, but I did. I am sorry!"

"Bad child. Here, we can sit on this rock and look at the wonder of yon isles in the midst of such a smother, and the wind will blow our words away."

"I am indeed a child," she said miserably.

"Aye, and that I find the strangest part of it," he said. "Ye've been through the London Newgate, Lady Juliana and Surprize as if none of it touched you. But it must have, Kitty."

"Yes, of course it did. But there were others like me, you know. If we did not die of shame—one poor girl did—we managed not to be seen. Among so many, that is not as difficult as you might think. The crowds—the fighting, spitting, snarling, prowling—stepped over us as if we did not exist. Everybody was so drunk, or else after someone—to rob or fuck or beat upon. We were thin, poor, plain. Not worth going after for any reason."

"So ye became a hedgehog curled into a ball." His profile against the pines of Nepean Island was pure and serene. "And the only word ye know for the act of love is 'fuck.' That is the saddest thing of all. Did ye see people fucking?"

"Not really. Just clothes and jumping about. We used to shut our eyes when we realized it was going to happen near us."

" 'Tis one way to keep the world at a distance. What about Lady Juliana? Were ye not pecked at by the brazen madams?"

"Mr. Nicol was very good, so were some of the older women. They would not let the mean ones peck at us for spite. And I was always seasick."

" 'Tis a wonder ye lived. But ye came through it all to land here, and land none other than Richard Morgan. That, Mistress Kitty, is the most remarkable thing of all. I doubt there is a woman or a Miss Molly has not—well, perhaps tried is too strong a word, but at least wondered if it would be possible." He turned his head to laugh at her.

How strange. His eyes were much bluer than Richard's, so blue that they reflected the sky as if making a barrier of it. Not water to be engulfed by but a wall to come up against.

"I have fallen out of love with you," she said in tones of wonder.

"And into love with Richard."

"No, I do not think so. There is *something*, but it is not love. All I know is that it is different."

"Oh, very different!"

"Tell me about him, please."

"Nay, I'll not do that. Ye'll just have to stay with him and find things out for yourself. Not an easy task with our close-mouthed Richard, but ye're a woman, and ye're curious. I am sure," he said, pulling her up, "that ye'll give it your best try." Leaning down, he put his cheek against her hair and whispered, "Whenever ye find something out, tell me."

Tears sprang to her eyes, she was not sure why, except that a spasm of grief clutched at her heart. Grief for him rather than because of him, and not because she had taken anything away from him. I wish, she thought, that the world was better ordered. I am not in love with this man, but I love him dearly.

"Tobias and I," he said, taking her hand and swinging it as they walked, "will make excellent uncles."

At the head of Arthur's Vale he released her hand and stopped. "This is as far as I go," he said.

"Please come with me!"

"Oh, no. Ye must go alone."

The house was empty; Richard had gone out, but the fireplace had been cleaned and fresh kindling stacked in it, her water buckets were full, four of the six chairs Richard had accumulated were tucked neatly beneath the table. Disappointed and bewildered—why had he not waited to see what Stephen had said to her?—she wandered about aimlessly, then went into the garden and began to dig, hoping that one day sufficient plenty arrived to allow her to waste ground outside the house upon flowers. Time passed; John Lawrell arrived with six Mt. Pitt birds he had cleaned and plucked, which solved dinner, served in the middle of the day now that winter approached.

By the time that Richard returned the birds had been browned in a pan and were braising, stuffed with herbed bread, in a covered pot with onions and potatoes.

"What," she asked for something to say, "are the tiny green trees growing in a sunny spot below the privy?"

"Ah, you found them."

"Ages ago, but I never remember to ask."

"Oranges and lemons grown from seed I saved in Rio de Janeiro. In two or three years' time we will see fruit during winter. A lot of my seeds came up, so I gave some of the plants to Nat Lucas, some to Major Ross, some to Stephen and some to a few others. The climate here should be perfect for citrus, there is no frost." One brow lifted quizzically. "Did ye find Stephen?"

"Yes," she said, pricking a potato with a knife to see if it was cooked.

"And he answered all your questions?"

Blinking in surprise, she paused. "Do you know, I do not believe I had time to ask any? He was too busy asking me questions."

"What about?"

"Gaol and transports, mostly." She began to transfer pieces of bird, onions and potatoes onto two plates, spooning juice over them. "There is a salad of lettuce, chives and parsley."

"Ye're a very good cook, Kitty," he said, tucking in.

"I am improving. We almost support ourselves, Richard, do we not? Everything on our plates we either grew or found."

"Aye. This is good soil and there is mostly enough rain to keep things going. My first year here was very wet, then it became dry. But the stream never ceases to flow, which means that it must originate in a spring. I would like to find the source."

"Why?"

"That would be the best place to put a house."

"But you already have a house."

"Too close to Sydney Town," he said, carefully scooping juice onto his spoon with the last of his potato.

"More?" she asked, getting up.

"If there is any, please."

"It is close to Sydney Town in one way," she said, sitting down again, "but we are quite isolated."

"I suspect that when the next lot of convicts arrive, we will not be so isolated. Major Ross believes that His Excellency intends to push the number of people here up beyond a thousand."

"A thousand? How many is that?"

"I forgot, ye cannot do sums. Remember last Sunday at divine service, Kitty?"

"Of course."

"There were seven hundred present. Cut that crowd in half, then add your half to all who were there. That is over a thousand."

"So many!" she breathed, awed. "Where will they go?"

"Some to Queensborough, some to Phillipsburgh, some to the place where the Sirius sailors were, though I believe that the Major might end in putting the New South Wales Corps soldiers there."

"They do not get on with his marines," she said, nodding.

"Exactly. But the vale will blossom with houses at this end, where the land is not in Government cultivation. So I would rather pick up and move farther away." He leaned back in his chair and patted his belly, smiling. "At the rate ye feed me, I will have to work harder or grow fat."

"You will not grow fat because you do not drink," she said.

"None of us drinks."

"Gammon, Richard! I am not as green as all that! The marines drink, so do the soldiers—and so do many convicts. If they have to, they make their own rum and beer."

His brows flew up, he grinned. "I should lend ye to the Major as an adviser. How did ye pick that up?"

"At the Stores." She took their empty plates and carried them to the counter beside the fireplace. "I had heard that you do not care for company," she said, getting out her dish and soap whisk, "and in a way I understand. But moving from here would mean that you would have to start all over again. A terrible burden."

"No amount of work is a burden if it means my children are protected," he said in a steely voice. "I would have them grow up untainted, and they will not do that in close proximity to Sydney Town. There are many good people here, but there are also many bad people. Why d'ye think the Major racks his brains to devise punishments that might deter violence, drunkenness, robbery and all the other vices which spring up where people are too close together? D'ye think that Ross takes pleasure in sending men like Willy Dring to Nepean Island for six weeks with two weeks' rations? Did he, I would not respect him, and I do respect him."

The first part of this (for Richard) long speech sent her mind whirling, but she chose to answer the second. "Perhaps, did we understand better how folk think, we might find a way. So much trouble happens in drink. Look at me."

"Aye, look at you. Growing in leaps and bounds."

"I could grow more if I could read and write and do sums."

"I will school you if you want."

"Oh, would you? Richard, how wonderful!" She stood with the soap whisk in her hand, motionless, the same look in her eyes William Henry had borne after his first day at Colston's School. "God the Father! I know now what Stephen meant. You need people to depend upon you as children do upon their father. You are very strong and very wise. So is Stephen, but he is not a father in his mind. I will always be your child."

"In one way, yes. In another way, I want to father children of you. I am not God—Stephen spoke in jest, not in blasphemy. He was simply trying, as Stephen must, to put me under a title in his mental library."

"You have a wife," she said. "I cannot be your wife."

"Lizzie Lock is entered in the Reverend Johnson's register as my wife, but she has never been my wife. In England, I could have the marriage annulled, but the far ends of the earth do not run to bishops and ecclesiastical courts. You are my wife, Kitty, and I do not believe for one moment that God does not understand. God gave you to me, I knew it when I looked into your eyes. I will introduce you to people as my wife, and call you my wife. My other self."

A silence fell, neither moved for what seemed an eternity. Her gaze was fixed in his, all the consent and communion necessary.

"What happens now?" she asked, a little breathlessly.

"Nothing until after curfew," he said, preparing to depart. "I do not intend to be disturbed by visitors, wife. Dig in your garden, but bearing in mind that a lot of seedlings will end in being transplanted elsewhere. I am going up the stream to seek its sources. Ye may have been next door to a skeleton, but nine months of Norfolk Island sun and air and food have made a new woman of you. One I do not want gardening alone so close to Sydney Town."

The pressure of work had left no time to explore farther up the stream than his bath, nor had curiosity prompted him until the truth about Kitty had dazzled him. How long might he have been prepared to wait if Stephen had not lost his temper? Loving her had been an idea; his gift from God was too precious to defile by behaving as most men would, by cozening and coaxing her into something she knew the wrong things about. Gloucester Gaol had shown him what the London Newgate must have been like, copulating couples everywhere. He did not believe for a moment that she had been the victim of any man's lust, but lust she must have seen through every day and night she spent there. Luckily not long, yet quite long enough. Her attraction to Stephen had blasted his hopes apart without actually destroying them; he knew too well that Stephen was impossible. What he had decided upon was another long wait, patiently standing to one side caring for her while she came to terms with the fact that the object of her affections was incapable of returning them.

He did not think she loved him, but that he had never hoped for anyway. Close to twenty-three years lay between them, and youth called to youth. Yet when she had stared across the table at him this morning he felt his body stir and unveiled his very core to her. She had fled to Stephen, but not unmoved and not in fright. That revelation of himself had kindled emotions in her that were entirely new and entirely his. The fact that he had such power had filled him with elation. Never a man to spend his leisure looking into the depths of his own being, he had not understood until he worked that power upon Kitty why he was what he was: God the Father, as Stephen had put it. All men and women needed to see and touch someone of their own kind who yet appeared to be more than they were. A king, a prime minister, a head man. He had taken on the care of others reluctantly, as a last resort because he witnessed their floundering and could not bear to have them sink. And slowly this skin of calm strength and purpose had infiltrated him to the marrow; what had once been done with an internal sigh of resignation had become an automatic assumption of authority. The germ must always have lain there in his spirit, but had he lived out his life in Bristol, it would never have awakened. We are born owning many qualities; some we may never know we possess. It all depends what kind of run God gives us.

After twenty minutes of walking barelegged up the muddy-bottomed brook he came to its first tributary, which led down from heights to the northeast. An amphitheatrical dell stuffed with tree ferns and plantains tempted him, but it was still too close to Arthur's Vale, so he continued up the main course, which bent and wove its way through more tree ferns, palms and plantains until it branched again at the base of a flat expanse he thought the ages had deposited there during heavy rains. The western fork, which he followed first, was too short. The southwestern branch was clearly the principal source of the water in Arthur's Vale, running deep and strong from somewhere up a fairly steep cleft. Wading on, he climbed higher and higher until, almost at the top of a crest, he found the spring gushing out between mossy, lichen-covered rocks smothered in ferns of more kinds than he had known existed—frilly, feathered, fluffed, fishtailed.

Squinting at the sun, sliding down the sky, he gained his perspective and entered the pine forest of the crest, which he soon discovered was quite flat and broad. To his amazement, he emerged not long afterward on the Queensborough road not very far from the track which led off its opposite side down to the distillery. Ah, that was interesting! Richard was visited with an idea. He went back to the spring and stood looking down the cleft. Not far below the spring on the western slope was a shelf wide enough and deep enough to hold a good big house and a few fruit trees; the ground beneath would serve as a vegetable garden.

His next stop was Stephen Donovan, who had frittered away the hours since he had left Kitty by playing chess against himself.

"Why," he asked when Richard came through the door, "does my right hand win every game?"

"Because ye're right-handed?" Richard asked, subsiding into a chair with a deep sigh.

"Ye look more like a man who has been trying to walk on water than one making love."

"I have not been making love, I have been trying to walk on water. And I have an idea."

"Pray enlighten me."

"We both know that Joe McCaldren wants land on the way to Queensborough, yet not that far out. And we both know that what Joe McCaldren really wants is to sell his land the moment it is surveyed and deeded to him. Not so?"

"Absolutely so. Have a glass of port and continue."

"Would ye do me a very great favor by surveying McCaldren's land next? I know the ideal piece to give him," said Richard, accepting the wine.

"Ye want to get Kitty away before the next convicts come, of course. But have ye the money to buy sixty acres, Richard? Joe McCaldren will ask ten shillings the acre," said Stephen, frowning.

"I have at least thirty pounds in notes of hand, but he will want coin of the realm. Besides, I do not need or want sixty acres, which are too many for one man to farm. Is it true, what ye told me, that every sixty-acre lot will make contact with a stream of water?"

"Aye, so I have suggested to the Major, who agrees."

"Does the Major object to a sixty-acre portion's being split up after it is deeded?"

"Once the sixty acres are handed over, Richard, the Major would not care if they flew away with the Mt. Pitt birds. But he also intends to give ten- and twelve-acre grants to those convicts like yourself who have been pardoned or emancipated. Why not save your money and get your land for nothing?"

"Two reasons. The first is that the free settlers have to be served first. That is going to take a year, a year in which we all expect to see well over a thousand people here. Some of the new convicts will be men His Excellency deems too depraved to be safely held in Port Jackson. The second is that when our grants do come to pass, they will be side by side. The nature of the streams here will dictate that each block be long and narrow, and all the houses must be built close to the water—in a row. Yes, separated by many yards, yet still in a row. I do not want to live like that, Stephen. So I want my twelve acres to be surrounded by sixty-acre blocks and I want my house on a run of water no one else will be close to."

"Morgan's run."

"Exactly. *Morgan's* run. I have found the place. It is the main tributary of Arthur's Vale stream and it arises from a strong spring at the top of a narrow valley. Above it lies the flat land which abuts onto the Queensborough road in the same region as the track to the Major's distillery. A mere thirty-minute walk from Sydney Town, which will please McCaldren, and on good water. But I want the survey to take in both sides of the stream, because the best place to build is on the western slope. If ye make the block to the west of McCaldren's another sixty-acre one, 'twill extend to water courses flowing west through Queensborough itself."

Stephen stared at Richard in complete admiration. "Ye've solved all your problems, haven't ye?" He shrugged, slapped his hands on his knees. "Well, I am going in that direction, having proceeded from the Cascade side. There I alternated sixty-acre lots with twenty-acre ones—big lot, hard land, small lot, easy land—which evens out the selling price, ye may say. At the moment I am up to James Proctor and Peter Hibbs. Not so far away. So I will proceed to the Queensborough road and start moving from it northward until I get back to Proctor and Hibbs. And I will make sure that I enclose Morgan's Run within McCaldren's sixty in such a way that ye have the head of the stream all to yourself."

"Just twelve acres of it, Stephen, that is enough. Up the valley on both sides and through to the Queensborough road. What McCaldren does with the other forty-eight acres I care not," said Richard with a grin. "However, if ye make my block more of a square, the rest of the piece could connect to my stream well below me. I can pay as much as twenty-five pounds in gold."

"Let me lend ye the price of all sixty in gold, Richard."

"Nay, it is not possible."

"Between brothers anything is possible."

"We shall see" was as far as Richard was prepared to go. He put the wine glass on the counter and bent to pick up Tobias, mewing around his feet with heartbreaking plaintiveness. "Ye're a fraud, Tobias. Ye sound like the saddest orphan in the world, but I happen to know that ye live like a king."

"Have a good night!" Stephen called after him, then scooped up the cat. "You and I, pussykins, are about to dine off Mt. Pitt bird. Why is it that dogs and cats are happy to eat the same thing each and every day of their lives, while we humans grow sated and sick after a week of monotony?"

Night had come creeping into the vale as Richard walked up the path, MacTavish rushing to greet him with somersaults of joy. The dog would much rather have spent his time with Richard, but was resigned to the fact that Richard expected him to guard Kitty, who luckily loved all animals save what she called the "dross"—her vocabulary's more unusual words were either biblical or the result of gaol and Lady Juliana.

He stepped into the house to find Kitty at the counter, apparently able to see sufficiently in the dimness to prepare a meal. Though he had told her that she might, she never would use one of his precious candles for her own purposes. Smiling, she turned her head; he crossed the room to kiss her lips as if she had been his wife forever.

"I am for a bath," he said, and disappeared again.

It seemed to take a long time; when he returned he looked at the stove. "Is there still hot water?"

"Of course."

"Good. 'Tis easier to shave."

She watched him with interest as he plied the ivory-handled razor quickly, deftly. But then, she had never seen him make a clumsy or unsure movement. Such beautiful hands, male yet graceful; they inspired confidence. "I do not understand," she said, "how you can shave without a mirror. You never cut yourself."

"Long years of practice," he mumbled, mouth contorted. "In warm water with a bit of soap, easy. On Alexander I shaved dry."

Finished, he rinsed the razor, folded it and laid it in its case before washing and drying his face. That done, he looked aimless, glanced at the fire and decided that it needed a part-burned log pushing back. No, it was still dangerous; he added a log as a prop, stood back, adjusted it. He lifted the lid of the spouted kettle, seemed disappointed that it did not need more water, walked over to his books, just about invisible.

"Richard," she said gently, "if you are truly trying to find something to do, we can eat. That will fill in a few more minutes while you summon your courage to start giving me children."

His eyes flew to hers, astonished, then he threw back his head and laughed until the tears came. "No, wife." His tone growled down to a caress. "Suddenly I am not hungry for food."

She smiled at him sidelong and walked through her door. "Do close the shutters," she said as she went. Her voice floated back out of the darkness. "And put MacTavish out for the night."

They will always, thought Richard, lead us when they want to. Ours is an illusion of power. Theirs is as old as creation.

His clothes he left behind him, halting inside her room until he could see shadows within shadows, the vague outline of her upon the bed, sitting bolt upright.

"No, not where I cannot see you. In the firelight, and as God made you. Come," he said, holding out his hand.

The rustle as she shed her night shift, the feel of warm and trusting fingers. He took her back and left her standing near the hearth to pluck the straw mattress from his bed, then threw it on the floor between them and looked at her. So beautiful! Like Venus, made for love. And it would be naked skin from the beginning, he wanted this to bear no resemblance to clothed convulsive couplings on the flags of the London Newgate. Sacred, an act dedicated to God, Who had made it possible. This is what we suffer for, one divine spark that turns the blackness of the pit to the brilliance of the sun. In this is true immortality. In this we fly free.

So he folded her into his arms and let her feel the satin of skin, the play of muscle, the strength and the tenderness, all the love for which he had found no outlet in years upon years. And she seemed in their wordless mingling to sense the timeless pattern of it, to know how and where and why. Always why. If he hurt her, it was only for a moment, after which there was no tomorrow, no more than her and this for all eternity. Pour forth your love, Richard Morgan, hold nothing back! Give her everything that you are and do not count the cost. That is the only reason for love, and she, my gift from God, knows and feels and accepts my pain.

PART SEVEN

From
June of 1791
until
February of 1793

"Peg," ſaid Richard, for once in a mood to volunteer emotional information, "was first love. Annemarie Latour was purely sex. Kitty is last love."

Eyes twinkling, Stephen contemplated him, wondering how he had managed to turn what ought to be infatuation into what would undoubtedly be an enduring passion. Or is it perhaps that he has gone so far for so long that whatever he feels is magnified a thousandfold?

"Ye're living proof of the fact that there's no fool like an old fool. But ye're wrong about one thing, Richard. Kitty is love *and* sex rolled up in the same parcel. For you, at any rate. For myself—I used to think that sex was—well, if not the most important, certainly the most urgent, the one I had to satisfy. But ye've taught me a great many things, one of which is the art of going without sex." He grinned. "As long, that is, that no one absolutely delectable comes along. Then I am all to pieces. But it passes, and so does he."

"Like every man, ye need both."

"I have both. Just not rolled up in the same parcel. Which, I have come to realize, suits me very well. I certainly do not repine," he said with genuine cheerfulness, jumping up. "Out of my stint on Norfolk Island I am going to get a commission in the Royal Navy, I am determined upon it. Then I will strut around a quarterdeck in my white, gold and Navy blue with a spyglass tucked under my arm and forty-four guns at my command."

They had paused for a drink of water and a brief rest from digging the foundations of Richard's new house. Joseph McCaldren had been granted his 60 acres and happily parted with the best 12 of them for the sum of £24; he drove a hard bargain. Then D'arcy Wentworth bought the other 48 acres as well as a part of Elias Bishop's 60 acres at Queensborough. Major Ross had endorsed the transfer of deeds with great good will.

"I am very pleased ye'll occupy McCaldren's land," he said to Richard. "Ye'll have it cleared and under cultivation in no time, and that is what the island needs. More wheat, more Indian corn."

There were only four lots in Norfolk Island which incorporated both sides of a stream in them; they immediately became known as "runs," prefixed by the name of the owner. Which gave Norfolk Island four new landmarks to add to Sydney Town, Phillipsburgh, Cascade and Queensborough: Drummond's Run, Phillimore's Run, Proctor's Run and Morgan's Run.

Unfortunately the sawpits left Richard little time to get on with building his new house. Barracks had to be constructed in Sydney Town and reasonable huts for the New South Wales Corps at the place the Sirius seamen had occupied; a proper gaol had to be finished, more civilian officials' houses—Major Ross's list seemed endless. Nat Lucas, who had over fifty carpenters toiling under his command, was frantic.

"I cannot guarantee the quality of the work anymore," he said to Richard over Sunday dinner in Richard's domain at the head of the vale. "Some of the buildings are downright shoddy, hammered together without thought or care, and I cannot divide myself into enough of me to keep an eye on Queensborough, Phillipsburgh *and* all the rest. I run, run, run, Lieutenant Clark yapping at my heels about the western settlement, Captain Hill rudely poking my shoulder because the New South Wales Corps huts are leaky, or drafty, or—truly, Richard, I am at my wits' end."

"Ye can do no more than ye're able to, Nat. Has the Major himself complained?"

"Nay, he is too great a realist." Nat looked a little worried. "I heard this morning that Lieutenant Clark had been deputed to take divine service because the Major is not well. Not well at all, according to Lizzie Lock." None of Richard's close friends ever called the Major's housekeeper "Mrs. Richard Morgan."

The food had been delicious. Kitty had killed two fat ducks and roasted them in her big oven-kettle with potatoes, pumpkins and onions around them; she had taken Olivia and the twins outside to look at Augusta and her rapidly growing female offspring, soon either to be killed and sold to the Stores or sent with their mother to a different Government boar. Thank God Richard had built a large sty!

"When your foundations are in, Richard," said Nat, changing the subject, "George and I have organized a working bee for two weekends in a row to put up your house, and I have secured the Major's permission to absent ourselves from Sunday service. That way, with any luck ye'll be able to move from here before the next transport arrives. 'Twill be rudimentary but livable, and ye can continue with the finishing unaided. Have ye enough timber?"

"Aye, from my own land. I put a sawpit on it and Billy Wigfall, God bless him, saws with me. Harry Humphreys and Sam Hussey turn up on some Saturdays, while Joey Long debarks the logs. I thought I may as well start clearing my own land rather than use trees from other locations."

He is, thought Nat, a very happy man, and I am so glad for him. When Olivia told me that he was keeping Kitty as a friend—oh, and he was so much in love with her!—I prayed that the girl would grow some sense and see her luck. Olivia insists that most women swoon away at the mere sight of him, but women are very queer cattle. To me, he appears a fine-looking man who happens to be a decent man. I am even more pleased that Kitty is no minx.

The women came inside laughing and talking rather feverishly, Kitty holding baby William with such a glow in her eyes that Nat blinked, wondering why he had ever considered her plain. Little Mary and Sarah remained outside to play with an utterly bewildered MacTavish; whether he looked to his left or to his right, he saw an identical child.

"I am very fond of all your friends and their wives, Richard, but I confess I like the Lucases best," said Kitty after they had gone, coming to stand behind his chair and draw his head against her belly. Eyes closed, he rested there contentedly.

Her world had opened up beyond imagination, in so many different directions. That first night of love had been a dazzling dream; she called it so because dreams to her were far nicer than life. In dreams, magical and impossible things happened, like farmhouses in Faversham surrounded by flower gardens. Yet the night had been a reality that continued into the following night, and all the nights thereafter. The hands she had thought beautiful to look at had moved upon her body with the cool smoothness of silk velvet.

"Why are your hands not hard and calloused?" she had asked at some moment, stretching and flexing under their rhythmic caress.

"Because I am a master gunsmith by craft, so I value them. Every corn and scar destroys a part of the sensitivity a gunsmith cannot work without. I wrap them in rags whenever I cannot find gloves," he had explained.

And that had answered one of her questions. The trouble was that the majority of them he refused to answer, like what sort of life had he lived in

Bristol? What were the details of his conviction? How many wives had he had? Did he have living children in Bristol? How had the daughter who would be her age die? His reply was always a smile, after which he would turn her queries aside firmly but kindly. So she had ceased to plague him. If and when he was ready to tell her, he would. Perhaps he was never going to be ready.

Oh, how he could make love! Though she had listened to literally hundreds of conversations between women about the sexual importunities of men, the nuisance it was to have to oblige them, Kitty looked forward to her nights. They were the greatest pleasure she had ever known. If she felt him reach for her in the early hours she turned to him in delight, roused by a kiss on her breast, his mouth against the side of her neck. Nor was she a passive recipient; Kitty adored learning how to rouse and please him.

But she did not believe that she was in love with him. Yes, she loved him; *that* was true. His immense age, she had concluded, served only to make him a better lover, a better companion. Yet simply looking at him did not arouse desire in her, nor did her heart flutter, her breath vanish. Only when he touched her or she touched him did the warmth and want begin. Every day he would tell her as naturally and spontaneously as a child that he loved her, that she was the beginning and the end of his world. And she would pay attention, flattered that he said such gratifying things, body and soul unmoved.

Today, however, was special. For once she initiated a demonstration of affection by cradling his head against her.

"Richard?" she asked, gazing down at his cropped dark hair and wishing that he would grow it; it had the potential to curl.

"Mmmmm?"

"I am with child."

At first he stilled absolutely, then looked up at her with a face transfigured by joy. Leaping to his feet, he whirled her off the ground and kissed her and kissed her. "Oh, Kitty! My love, my angel!" The exaltation faded, he looked afraid. "Ye're sure?"

"Olivia says I have fallen, though I was already sure."

"When?

"Late February or early March, we think. Olivia says that you quickened me at once, just like Nat. She says that means we will be fruitful, that there will be as many children as we wish."

He took her hand and kissed it reverently. "Ye're well?"

"Very, all considered. I have had no courses since you took me. I am a little sick sometimes, but nothing like being at sea."

"Are ye pleased, Kitty? It is very soon."

"Oh, Richard, it is a dream! I am"—she found a new word—"ecstatic. Truly ecstatic! My own baby!"

On Monday morning Richard heard through the grapevine that Major Robert Ross was gravely ill. On Tuesday morning he was summoned by Private Bailey to wait upon the Major at once.

Ross had been put upstairs in the large room he usually used as a study because one floor up insulated him from importunate visitors. When Richard followed Mrs. Richard Morgan—very anxious and subdued—up the stairs and entered the room, he was shocked. The Major's face was greyer than his eyes, sunken glazed into black sockets; he lay as rigid as a board with his arms by his sides, their hands curiously expectant.

"Sir?"

"Morgan? Good. Stand where I can see ye. Mrs. Morgan, ye can go. Surgeon Callam will be here soon," Ross said steadily.

Suddenly his body spasmed dreadfully and his lips drew back in a rictus from his teeth; fight though he did to remain silent, he emitted a groan that Richard knew in any other man would have emerged a scream. He suffered through the bout, groaning, hands clenched into the counterpane like claws; this was what they had expected, must be ready for. Richard waited quietly, understanding that Ross wanted neither sympathy nor assistance. Finally his agony retreated to leave his face drenched in sweat.

"Better for a while," he said then. " 'Tis a kidney stone, Callam says. Wentworth agrees. Considen and Jamison disagree."

"I would believe Callam and Wentworth, sir."

"Aye, I do. Jamison could not castrate a cat and Considen is a wonder at drawing teeth."

"Do not waste your energies, sir. What can I do?"

"Be aware that I may die. Callam is giving me something he says relaxes the tube between kidney and bladder in the hope that I may pass the stone. To do so is my only salvation."

"I will pray for ye, sir," said Richard, meaning it.

" 'Twill help more than Callam's medicaments, I suspect."

Another spasm came on, was endured.

"If I die before a ship comes," he said when it was over, "this place will be in parlous condition. Captain Hill is a fucken fool and Ralph Clark is mentally about the same age as my son. Faddy is a simpleton as well as a child. War will break out between my marines and the soldiers of the New South Wales Corps, with every felon villain from Francis to Peck enlisting with Hill. It will be a bloodbath, which is why I intend to pass this fucken stone no matter what. No matter what."

"Ye'll pass it, sir. The stone does not exist can break *you,*" said Richard with a smile. "Is there anything else I can do?"

"Aye. I have already seen Mr. Donovan and some others, and authorized the issue of muskets. Ye'll be given one too, Morgan. At least the marine muskets fire, thanks to ye. The New South Wales Corps take no care of their weapons and I have not volunteered your services to Hill. Keep in touch with Donovan—and do not trust Andrew Hume, who has sided with Hill and participates in his felonies. Hume is a fraud, Morgan, he knows no more about flax processing than I do, but he sits there in Phillipsburgh like a spider fancying that between himself and Hill, they control half of this island."

"Concentrate upon passing your stone, sir. We will not let Hill and his New South Wales Corps take over."

"Oh, here it comes again! Go, Morgan, and stay wide awake."

Mind whirling, Richard stood outside on the landing trying to visualize Norfolk Island without Major Ross. It was boiling already, thanks to marine private Henry Wright. Wright had been caught in the act of raping Elizabeth Gregory, a ten-year-old Queensborough girl. To make matters worse, this was Wright's second offense; he had been sentenced to death in Port Jackson two years earlier for raping a nine-year-old girl, but His Excellency had reprieved him on the condition that he spend the rest of his life at Norfolk Island. Thereby transferring his problem to Major Ross. Wright's wife and toddling daughter had come with him, but in the aftermath of Elizabeth Gregory the wife had petitioned to take her daughter back to Port Jackson on the next ship. Ross had agreed. He had sentenced Wright to run the gauntlet three times: first at Sydney Town, then at Queensborough, and then at Phillipsburgh. The Sydney Town gauntlet had happened the very day Major Ross fell ill; stripped to breeches, Wright had been made to run between two lines of people from all walks, thirsting for his blood and armed with hoes, hatchets, cudgels, whips.

The child rape had destroyed the reputation of the marines, even among many of the law-abiding convicts, though the whole of the old Norfolk Island community was equally angered by Governor Phillip's developing tendency to rid himself of his troublemakers at Norfolk Island's expense.

Ross was absolutely right, Richard thought. If he dies, there will be war.

But, being Major Ross, he did not die. His life hung in the balance for a week during which Richard, Stephen and their cohorts prowled regularly, then the pain began to diminish. Whether he had passed the stone or whether it had retreated back into the kidney Surgeon Callam had no idea, for the pain did not lift in an instant; it dwindled away gradually. Two weeks after the onslaught he was able to go downstairs, and a week after that he was the same brisk, snarling, caustic Major Ross everybody knew and either loved or feared or loathed.

The balance tipped more in favor of the New South Wales Corps when Mary Ann arrived midway through August of 1791, the first ship since Supply in April, and the first transport in a year. She brought 11 more soldiers with 3 wives and 9 children belonging to the New South Wales Corps, and 133 felons—131 men, a woman and a child. By the time she had unloaded her human cargo, the population of Norfolk Island had risen to 875. Mary Ann was supposed to have nine months' supplies aboard for the contingent she brought, but, as usual, whoever determined how much the newcomers would eat had grossly erred. Five months' supplies, more like.

The fresh influx consisted of 32 intractables who had long plagued Governor Phillip and 99 sick, half-starved wretches off another ship which had arrived in Port Jackson, Matilda. Matilda and Mary Ann were the first two of ten ships sailed from England around the end of March, which meant that vessels were making the journey faster with fewer and shorter ports of call along the way. Matilda had made the run in four months and five days without stopping at all, Mary Ann almost as swiftly. The brevity of the passage was what saved the convicts they carried, for the same slave contractors had victualled 1791's transports: Messrs. Camden, Calvert & King. Only the Royal Navy storeship, Gorgon, would be delayed by a long port of call; she was to stay in Cape Town and buy as many animals as possible. As Gorgon carried most of the mail and parcels, the old inhabitants of Norfolk Island settled in with a sigh to wait several more months for news. Oh, the frustration of never knowing what was happening in the rest of the world! Added to which, Mary Ann's captain, Mark Monroe, was so ignorant of world events that he could contribute nothing.

He did, however, set up a stall on the straight beach.

"Stephen," said Richard, "I am going to call in a brother's promise. Will ye lend me gold? I can pay ye for it in notes of hand with interest."

"I will gladly lend ye the gold, Richard, but I will wait for repayment until ye can give me gold," said Stephen craftily. "How much d'ye require?"

"Twenty pounds."

"A trifle!"

"Ye're *sure?*"

"Like you, brother, I have plenty of credit with Government. Two or three hundred pounds by now, I expect—I never can bother asking Freeman to tot it up. My wants are simple and not usually to be assuaged by gold or notes of hand. Whereas you have a wife and family to provide for, not to mention a new and much bigger house of two storeys." Closing all the shutters, he reached into the skeletal maw of a shark he had caught on Alexander and fiddled until a catch sprang, revealing a small door in the wall. The purse he removed was a fat one.

"Twenty pounds," he said, dropping them into Richard's palm. "As ye see, I am not skint because of the loan."

"What if someone fancies a pair of shark jaws?"

"Luckily I deem them last on a thief's list." He shut the door and adjusted his trophy. "Let us go, or some other hoarder of gold will beat us to the best bargains."

Richard bought several lengths of sprigged muslin, well aware that Kitty had told him a small lie; servant maids wore wool, and ten yards of muslin *were* worth three guineas. The jury had felt sorry for the weeping, devastated girls. As well the jury might. He also bought cheap cotton calico which would make everyday dresses for dealing with pigs and poultry, sewing thread, needles, scissors, some yard rules and trowels for himself, and an iron stove with a fire grate and ashpan in its base surmounted by an oven with a flat top and a hole for a chimney. Captain Monroe had sections of thin steel chimney pipe of the kind installed on ships; they cost more than the stove. What pounds were left he spent on thick napped cotton cloth he knew would make excellent diapers, and dark red woolen serge to make winter coats for Kitty and the baby.

"Ye've just spent almost as much as ye did on twelve good acres," said Stephen, testing the rope binding the goods to the sled. "Monroe is a robber."

"Land requires labor, and that I give free," said Richard. "I would have my wife and children as comfortable as Norfolk Island life permits. This is no climate for woolen or canvas slops, and the clothing already made up falls apart on first washing. We are swindled by London over and over again. Kitty sews even better than she cooks, so she can make things to last." He eased his shoulders into the sled harness and buckled it across his chest. The sled moved off effortlessly, though its contents weighed over 300 pounds. "Ye're welcome to come up the vale for supper this evening, Stephen."

"Thankee, but nay. Tobias and I are celebrating the departure of the fucken Mt. Pitt bird by eating two splendid snappers I caught on the reef this morning."

"Christ, ye'll be killed doing that!"

"Not I! I can smell the big wave coming a mile away."

Which he probably could, reflected Richard; Stephen's gift for wind, weather, current and waves was uncanny, and no one knew more about Norfolk Island's conditions than he.

Wanting to drop the stove off at the site of the new house first, Richard commenced to toil up the steep slope of Mount George on the Queensborough road. This one-mile slog was nothing new; he had dragged the sled laden with calcarenite stone up the hill time and time again. Wheels would have made the pull even harder, for the sled moved in smooth tracks its runners had worn when the road was muddy. Not a frequent occurrence this year, a dry one. Only an occasional night of heavy rain was bringing the wheat and Indian corn on superbly.

It had become a temptation to skimp his Government work—a temptation others also felt, wanting to get their own land cleared and bearing, but Richard had sufficient sense to resist such urges. Poor George Guest had succumbed before he was out of his sentence—so ambitious!—and been flogged for it.

The lash ruled more and more as Major Ross and Lieutenant Clark—and Captain William Hill of the New South Wales Corps—struggled to maintain some kind of control over a people existing without solidarity or rhythm. They flew in a hundred directions according to their origins, their limited experiences and their ideas of what constituted a happy life. All too often the idea of a happy life was an idle life. In England most of them would never have rubbed shoulders, and that fact was as true of the marines and soldiers as it was of the convicts. Exacerbated by a further fact: that almost everybody in military command was Scotch, yet of Scotch felons or enlisted troops there were virtually none.

We are ruled by the lash, exile to Nepean Island and being chained to the grindstone because not a soul in English government can see any other way to rule than to punish mercilessly. There must be another way, there *must* be! But what it is, I do not know. How does one make a better marine out of the likes of Francis Mee or Elias Bishop? How does one make a better man out of the likes of Len Dyer or Sam Pickett? They are lazy, greedy weasels who derive their chief pleasure from making mischief and creating chaos. Punishment does not transform the Mees, Bishops, Dyers and Picketts into hardworking, responsible citizens. But then again, nor did the relatively benign rule of Lieutenant King in days when this place held less than a hundred souls. His kindness was repaid by mutinies and plots, contempt and defiance. And when toward the last his domain grew to near a hundred and fifty souls, Lieutenant King too resorted to the lash with greater severity and ever greater frequency. When their backs are to the wall, they flog. There is no answer, but oh, how I wish there were! So that my Kitty and I could rear our children in a clean and better ordered world.

In such manner did Richard render the ordeal of pulling his sled up the terrible hill of Mount George endurable; he put his back to the work and his mind to conundrums beyond his understanding.

Once atop the mount it was much easier; the road went up and down somewhat, but never so dreadfully. Morgan's Run came into sight and he turned off the road down a track into the trees, many of them reduced to stumps already. His intention was to leave a border of pines fifty feet deep all around the perimeter and clear the middle of the flat section entirely. There he would plant his wheat, a delicate crop, protected from the mighty salt-bearing winds which blew from every point of the compass; the island was not large enough to render any wind free of salt. The less steep slopes of the cleft wherein the run of water originated he would put to Indian corn for his multiplying pigs.

At the top of the cleft he undid his harness, though he had made a good clear track down to the shelf where the house was going up. Strong though he was, he knew he could not hold the sled downhill with all that iron upon it. He unloaded all but the stove itself, then transferred himself and his harness to the back of the sled, digging in his heels as he and the sled gathered momentum, sled in front, he behind. The distance was almost too great; the sled ran up a banked slope he had installed as a brake, overshot it slightly, and came to a halt with a thump that had Kitty up from her garden in a hurry.

"Richard!" she squawked, arriving at a run. "You are mad!"

Too out of breath to refute this accusation, he sat upon the ground and panted; she brought him a beaker of cool water and sat beside him, worried that he had done himself an injury.

"Are you all right?"

He gulped the water down, nodded, grinned. "I have a stove for ye, Kitty, with a baking oven."

"Captain Monroe had his stall!" She got to her feet and inspected the new arrival eagerly. "Richard, I will be able to bake my own bread! And make cakes when I have enough crumbs and egg whites. And roast meat properly—oh, it is wonderful! Thank you, thank you!"

A hoist was rigged on one of the roof beams, so getting the big stove off the sled was not as difficult as had been keeping it from whizzing off the end of the brake slope into the valley below. He and Kitty walked together to the crest, where she found all the fabrics, threads, sewing apparatus.

"Richard, you are too good to me."

"Nay, that is not possible. Ye're carrying my child." He began to load the sled for another trip down the slope with the chimney, which of course Kitty had dismissed as uninteresting. That delivered, they walked home down the Queensborough road with Richard pulling a much lighter sled.

Robert Ross, standing outside Government House to appreciate a magnificent sunset, watched them get the sled down Mount George. He had seen Richard expending his Saturday hauling it up that cruel hill several hours ago, marveling at the stamina of the man. So clever! He was a Bristolian, of course. A city of sledges. If ye cannot have wheels, have runners. I doubt a mule has more pure strength, and he with only two legs. I am but eight years older than he, but I could not have done that at twenty. The girl, he decided, was Morgan's indulgence. A sweet wee mite, and oddly genteel. A workhouse brat, Mrs. Morgan had informed him, sniffing. But then, workhouse brats from strict Church of England workhouses like the girls' in Canterbury (he had her papers) usually were genteel. Morgan himself was an educated man from the middling classes, so a workhouse brat was a comedown. But not, thought the Major cynically as he turned away, as big a comedown as his legal wife was.

Richard and Kitty moved house on Saturday and Sunday the 27th and 28th of August, 1791. The several working bees had gotten beams, scantlings and cladding up, shingles on the roof and a path from the front doorstep down to the spring; for the time being they would finish only the ground floor, deal with upstairs when an upstairs was necessary. There was a long way to go before his new home looked as nice as the old, but Richard did not care.

They had several tables, a kitchen bench, six fine chairs, two fine beds (one with a feather mattress and pillows), shelving for all Richard's bits and pieces, and a stone chimney with a big hearth. The iron stove sat within the fireplace, its steel smokestack thrust up into the chimney's maw; from now on they would have no open fire, which would darken the interior after nightfall, but was much safer.

Housewarming presents were tendered from folk who had little to give save plants or poultry. Richard and Kitty accepted them with full hearts, knowing their real value. Nat and Olivia Lucas gave them a female tortoiseshell kitten, Joey Long another dog. The two more prosperous members of the Morgan circle were typically generous: Stephen donated an oak kitchen cabinet that he had bought from Surgeon Jamison, and the Wentworths a cradle. The cat they named Tibby and the new female pup Charlotte because it looked like a King Charles spaniel. MacTavish approved of both; he remained the sole male animal.

The pigsty and privy were difficult to site until Richard thought of a way to determine the course of the underground stream which fed the spring; nothing must contaminate it. Remembering what Peg's brother had done when he had needed to dig a new well, Richard cut a forked rod from a sappy green shrub, held on to each fork with a hand, and attempted to divine. The sensation was curious when it happened, as if suddenly the wood shivered into life and fought him gently. Yet Kitty could not make the tip stir any more than could Stephen.

"It is our skin," said Stephen, ruefully eyeing his palms. "Hard, dry and calloused. Your skin, Richard, is soft and moist. I think the diviner's skin completes the water chain."

Whatever lay at the root of the magic in it, Richard had no choice other than to site both pigsty and privy north of the house; there were underground streams everywhere south of it.

The saddest consequence of the move no one could have predicted, though Richard blamed himself for not foreseeing it. On the very Sunday that they said an unregretful farewell to the acre at the head of Arthur's Vale, John Lawrell was caught by a married marine corporal playing cards with William Robinson Two in his hut. Major Ross had told the marine that he might shift himself and his family into the vacated house for the last few months of his duty, and the fellow had eagerly rushed to see it. Fervently religious, he was scandalized by what he saw as he peered through Lawrell's hut door. *Playing cards on Sunday!* Lawrell and Robinson were sentenced to 100 lashes each for gambling on a Sunday.

"Oh, it is too bad!" Richard cried to Stephen. "They meant no harm to God or men. It never occurred to me that there was anything wrong in it, they are simply friends who spend Sunday afternoons with a deck of cards. Not gambling, just amusing themselves. If I spoke to the Major—"

"No, you cannot," said Stephen firmly. "Richard, leave it go! Since his near-mortal illness the Major has had a bee in his bonnet about God and our lack of a chaplain here. He is now quite convinced that the rising incidence of local crime is thanks to godlessness and improper observance of Sundays. Well, he is a Scotchman, and much influenced by that pitiless Presbyterian ethic. Lawrell is no longer under your protection—nothing ye could say will alter the Major's decision. In an odd way it reflects well on you, or so the Major sees it. You depart, Lawrell sins."

"I want no approbation at the cost of another man's flesh," said Richard bitterly. "Sometimes I hate God!"

" 'Tis not God ye hate, Richard. 'Tis the fools of men who call themselves God's servants ye really hate."

Salamander arrived on the 16th of September carrying 200 male convicts and more men of the New South Wales Corps. By the time she sailed the population of Norfolk Island had risen to 1,115. Both deaths and floggings had soared since Mary Ann; the first death from illness or natural causes had not occurred until the end of 1790, when John Price, a convict off Surprize, had expired from the after-effects of his awful voyage.

Now the ratio of males to females increased dramatically in favor of males, but not strong, healthy males. Many of the new arrivals were so sick that they would eventually die, while some of the less enfeebled ones preyed constantly upon gardens or tried to rob the Stores, after anything to make life more comfortable. Governor Phillip's intractables gravitated immediately into the Francis-Peck-Dyer-Pickett camp, joined by scarred and disillusioned men like Willy Dring, whom Richard remembered from Alexander as not a bad sort of young fellow. Fierce quarrels broke out every day and the gaol was always full, the grindstone fully powered. The sight of ironed men, even an occasional ironed woman, became more common. Sydney Town, Queensborough and Phillipsburgh were good places to be out of. Nat Lucas, closest to Sydney Town among Richard's friends, had commenced to clear the upper slopes of his increased

Arthur's Vale portion and was building a new house as far from the flat as he could.

Of course Richard had brought cuttings and small offshoots of his bamboo and sugar cane, having removed enough of the grown bamboo to provide himself with several fishing poles. He no longer went to Point Hunter to fish with a hand-line; Stephen had also abandoned that site. Too many used it, and it necessitated a walk through Sydney Town besides. More and more Sydney Town looked as Richard fancied Port Jackson must, except that the buildings were wood. Norfolk Island lime had gone back to His Excellency in Port Jackson aboard Mary Ann and Salamander to provide mortar for bricks and sandstone blocks; Port Jackson, more usually called "Sydney" these days, was also expanding.

Now that Richard lived on Morgan's Run, he and Stephen had taken to fishing from the rocks near a small, sandy beach between Sydney Bay's landing place and its western headland, Point Ross. The walk was no longer than that to Point Hunter, the eastern headland, and having poles to fish with greatly helped their chances of kingfish and other large denizens of surface waters.

"What d'ye think of these rumors that a huge revolution has happened in France?" Stephen asked as they cleaned a six-foot kingfish under the shade of an overhanging rock.

"It happened in the American colonies, so why not? I wish that Mary Ann or Salamander had carried gazettes from London, but I think we will have to wait until Gorgon arrives in Port Jackson before we find out what actually has happened. Gorgon will also carry more than personal letters from wives to men like Ross and Ralphie darling."

"Have ye ever written home, Richard?"

"Nay, never. I want to have something to say before I do."

Stephen gazed at him in wonder. Something to say? What was Alexander? What was Port Jackson? What was Norfolk Island?

"I see no point in writing sad letters," Richard explained. "When I write, I want to be able to tell my family and friends in England that I have survived and even prospered a little. That my life in the Antipodes is not an empty vessel."

"Yes, I understand. Then ye'll be writing soon. If, that is, ye have not forgotten how to form the alphabet."

"I do that as well as ever. I do not write letters, but if I am not too tired, I transcribe notes upon whatever I am reading."

They walked back to Morgan's Run the long way to give some of the magnificently meaty fish to Olivia Lucas, met D'arcy in town and gave him some, then waded upstream past Richard's old house and climbed the cleft.

Kitty was beginning to look a little pregnant, and had shown that she was an ideal wife for a Norfolk Island settler by learning to ply a hammer, cope with minor emergencies like one of Augusta's daughters in the vegetable patch, sand and polish interior walls as Richard put them up, chop down quite large trees, deal with the firewood, carry water, wash, cook, clean, and sew. In her spare time, she informed Richard gravely, she was unraveling some linen cloth and weaving the strands into what she hoped would form wicks. Then she would make tallow out of the hard back fat when Richard killed a pig, and dip candles. That way they would not have to purchase tallow candles from Stores, which charged a penny each.

"Ye're doing too much," Stephen chided her as they sat to eat the kingfish, baked in the oven wrapped in plantain leaves.

"Stephen, do not start!" she said dangerously, eating with gusto all the while. "Richard is always at me about it. Truly I am well, strong and full of vim. And I have discovered that I am happiest when doing things. Especially because this is *my* house, I have been with Richard since before its beginning."

"When I find a man I can trust, Kitty, I will pay the Government for his labors and put him to the tasks ye'll not be able to do once ye become heavy."

"That is where George Guest went wrong," said Stephen. "If he had waited until he was out of his sentence and then come to an arrangement with Major Ross about hiring two laborers, neither he nor they would have been flogged."

"George is a good fellow, but *too* keen to get on. He thought to get the work done cheaper by hiring two marines directly rather than paying the Government to hire on his behalf. That is not how English government works. I deplore English government, but I see no sense in trying to hoodwink it. I will get my man for ten pounds a year, which I can afford. After, that is," he said with a smile, "I have paid my debts."

"Ye work too hard yourself, Richard."

"I do not believe so. Rock fishing on a Saturday morning is a wonderful rest, so is gardening and mucking out the pigsty after Sunday service. Luckily the Major's objections to Sunday activities do not extend to things which might eventually arrive in the Stores. His shibboleths are limited to drinking and gambling."

"On the subject of drinking, the New South Wales Corps men have set up a very nice still with Francis Mee and Elias Bishop."

"Well, that had to happen, especially after the Major grew so religious. Besides, he shipped a good deal of what we made to Port Jackson on Supply last February. 'Tis amazing how the total soars when ye have a humble little pair of kettles going day and night—*and* on Sundays," Richard said, laughing.

After Stephen left, Richard and Kitty worked side by side in the garden until supper time, eaten just before night fell. The small citrus trees had survived transplanting, as had almost everything. The year had been a fairly grubless one and dry enough that the Government wheat in Arthur's Vale and the Government corn at Queensborough looked like yielding bumper crops. Of course there had been salt winds galore, but luckily most had been accompanied by squally showers, which reduced their blighting effect. There had been just enough rain to keep the grain coming on. Even with 1,115 inhabitants, Norfolk Island seemed likely to provide its own bread and surplus pork to salt for Port Jackson.

In Sydney Town, Queensborough and Phillipsburgh the same old squabbles recurred between industrious convict gardeners and lazy marines and soldiers. There were now a great many very sick convicts who literally could not work; some died, and some were subject to the kind of thing rife in Port Jackson—the strong robbed the weak of sustenance and clothing. Those upon whom devolved the burden of feeding the indigent-through-illness men grew sour about having to do so. Especially if they were not yet pardoned or emancipated, and therefore free to keep what they grew on their own blocks or sell to Stores.

Hunger still stalked on the Phillipsburgh-Cascade side of the island; only three miles away by road, it may as well have been as far as Port Jackson, so isolated was it. Phillipsburgh grew less edibles in order to cultivate flax, and importation of edibles from the south side of the island was the responsibility of Mr. Andrew Hume, the superintendent. He did a brisk trade in the acquisition of convict slops and constantly incurred Major Ross's wrath by short-rationing his workers in order to sell to the New South Wales Corps soldiers, living somewhat closer than the middle of the Cascade road. As almost all the Lieutenant-Governor's troops were now New South Wales Corps soldiers, Ross found it impossible to police Phillipsburgh and the alliance between Hume and Captain Hill. One starving flax worker ate a forest plant he mistook for cabbage, and died; even then Hume continued in his peculations and frauds, abetted by Hill and his soldiers.

The growing evil was the act of growing food, and the chasm between those who grew plenty and ate well and those who grew nothing widened every day to the whistles and screams of floggings, floggings, floggings. A surgeon was required to witness the application of the cat, so Callum, Wentworth, Considen and Jamison entered into a conspiracy; whichever one was deputed to watch would call a halt after somewhere between 15 and 50 of the total number had been laid on, then make sure that the next installment was not administered before healing was complete. It could take a long time for a convict to receive all 200 lashes, and what usually happened was that Major Ross forgave the culprit the rest before too much damage had been done.

Courts martial also increased as the differences of opinion and resentments arising out of rank and precedence rubbed rawly at abraded military feelings, real or (all too often) imagined. Most of the marines and soldiers, including their officers, were uneducated, narrow, impressionable, hot-tempered, appallingly immature, and prone to believe whatever they were told. A fancied slight became inflated into an unpardonable insult before it had finished traveling the gossip grapevine, as efficient and widespread among the free as among the felon.

The indefatigable Lieutenant Ralph Clark endeared himself even more to Major Ross by (snooping just a little) detecting the presence of an illicit letter from the Major's clerk, Francis Folks, to the Judge Advocate in Port Jackson, Captain David Collins. The document accused Ross of extreme cruelty, oppression, depriving the free as well as the felon of rations, and so on, and so forth. Included with it were supporting papers and some opinions on the Lieutenant-Governor's conduct of Norfolk Island's affairs which depicted him as a mixture of Ivan the Terrible and Torquemada. Ross's response was to clap Folks in irons, confiscate the letter, papers and opinions as concrete evidence, and order Folks tried at Port Jackson by the addressee, Collins. Who, though a marine officer, loathed Robert Ross passionately. Even as he acted, the Major knew whom Collins would believe. No matter. The protocols were specific, and Law Martial was a thing of the past. Alas.

Atlantic arrived on the 2nd of November with news that came as a bolt from the blue to all save Major Ross himself. She brought the mail and parcels Gorgon had carried from Portsmouth: yes, Gorgon had finally arrived. Atlantic also brought a new Lieutenant-Governor for Norfolk Island, Commander Philip Gidley King, who had returned from England on Gorgon and brought his bride, Anna Josepha, with him. By the time they quit Atlantic at Norfolk Island she was in the last stages of pregnancy, coddled and cossetted by young William Neate Chapman, King's protégé and (officially) his surveyor. To a community used by now to the reign of Major Ross, it was hard to tell which of the two, Anna Josepha or Willy Chapman, was the sillier; they called themselves "brother" and "sister," giggled a lot, eyed each other archly, and drew everybody's attention to the similarity of their facial features. King's two boys by Ann Innet did not come, though rumor said that Norfolk, the elder, was being cared for—in England—by Mrs. Philip Gidley King's parents. King's own parents were more rigid, which led some to speculate that Anna Josepha's family was more accustomed to bastards, so perhaps Anna Josepha and Willy Chapman *were*. . . .

Also disembarked from Atlantic were Captain William Paterson of the New South Wales Corps and his wife—Scotch, of course—and the Reverend Richard Johnson, who had come to bless, marry, and also to baptize 31 Norfolk Island babies. Some of the visitors were staying a short time only. Queen, newly arrived in Port Jackson, was to bring the island yet more convicts—genuinely Irish convicts this time, embarked in Cork.

All of which spelled an end to the marine presence. Major Ross, Lieutenants Clark, Faddy and Ross Junior, and the last of the enlisted marines were to depart the island on Queen. They would spend time in Port Jackson to await the return of Gorgon from a food voyage to Bengalese Calcutta, the home of a sturdy, hardy kind of cattle. The years had gone by in Port Jackson, but of that vanished Government herd no sign had ever been seen.

So confusing! So upsetting! It all seemed to happen in the twinkling of an eye—ships and commandants coming and going, yet more mouths to feed. The old inhabitants of the island walked around in a daze, and wondered whereabouts it was all going to end.

Commander King was horrified at what he saw in his beloved Norfolk Island. Dammit, the place was no better than a wooden version of that den of iniquity, Port Jackson! As for Government House—! How could he ask a new bride to live in such a run down, ramshackle, hideously small residence? *And* under the aegis of a vulgar trollop like Mrs. Richard Morgan, who had donned all her finery to greet him and usher him through the premises? She would have to go, the sooner the better.

King's mood was not improved by the knowledge that the large supply of livestock that he had acquired on his own initiative at Çape Town had not thrived during Gorgon's onward passage; a tiny remnant only came with him on Atlantic—a few sickly sheep, goats and turkeys, not a cow left alive.

Oh, the whole place was so dilapidated and slipshod! How *had* Major Ross allowed his jewel in the ocean to sink to this? Yet what else could one expect from a boorish Scotch marine? A trifle full of his own importance and with the Celtic side of him uppermost for the moment, King itched to do great things even as he despaired of Norfolk Island's ability to give him the opportunity. Ever the romantic, he had genuinely expected a settlement of more than 1,300 people to look exactly like a settlement of 149 people. The only cheering fact apart from his darling little Anna Josepha was that his supply of port was wellnigh infinite.

He and Major Ross, thrown together for a number of days at least, eyed each other as warily as two dogs debating which would win a possible fight. With characteristic bluntness the Major made neither excuses nor apologies for the awful condition of the island, merely confined himself to clipped summaries of what his papers and records said at more length. What might have developed into a brawl over dinner in the sadly overcrowded Government House did not, thanks to the tact of the Reverend Johnson, the presence of the twinned Anna Josepha and Willy Chapman, the delicious food served by Mrs. Richard Morgan, and a number of bottles of port.

Captain William Hill of the New South Wales Corps did his level best to ruin the departing Major Ross's reputation by having selected convicts examined on oath before the Reverend Johnson and Mr. William Balmain, surgeon, arriving to take the place of Denis Considen. Hill and Andrew Hume threw a great deal of dirt, but the Major fought back, establishing without much difficulty that the convicts were perjurious villains and Hill and Hume not far behind. The battle was bound to continue in Port Jackson, but for the time being the combatants declared a cessation in hostilities and set about packing or unpacking trunks and bags.

Richard remained carefully out of the way, very sorry that Major Ross was going, and not at all sure whether he wanted to see Lieutenant—oops, Commander—King take the Major's place. Whatever Ross was or was not, he was first and foremost a realist.

The official changeover occurred on Sunday, the 13th of November, after the Reverend Johnson had taken divine service. The entire huge population was assembled in front of Government House and Commander King's commission read out. Atlantic was making sail and Queen was retreating to Cascade, the two ships passing in the morning. Major Ross requested of the new Lieutenant-Governor that all the convicts in detention or under sentence of punishment be forgiven; Commander King graciously acquiesced.

"We did all save kiss," said the Major to Richard as the big crowd dispersed. "Walk a little way with me, Morgan, but send your wife ahead with Long."

My luck persists, thought Richard, nodding to Kitty that she and Joey should proceed without him. His transaction with Ross to secure the services of Joseph Long, a fourteen-year man, as his laborer and general hand for the sum of £10 per annum had only recently been signed into effect. For after considering a number of men, he had decided that simple, faithful Joey Long was preferable to any other. As several of the recent arrivals were cobblers, Major Ross had been willing to let Joey go. This change of employment was as well for Joey too; Commander King was not likely to have forgotten the loss of his best pair of shoes.

"I am glad of the opportunity to wish ye well, sir," said Richard, dawdling. "I will miss ye greatly."

"I cannot return the compliment in exactly the way ye mean yours, but I can tell ye, Morgan, that I never minded the sight of your face nor the words that came from your lips. I hate this place every bit as much as I hate Port Jackson, or Sydney, or whatever they are calling it these days. I hate convicts. I hate marines. And I hate the fucken Royal Navy. I am obligated to ye for the services of your wife, who has been precisely what ye said—an excellent housekeeper but no temptress. And I am obligated to ye for both wood and rum." He paused to think, then added, "I also hate the fucken New South Wales Corps. There will be a reckoning, never doubt it. Those idealistic Navy fools will let a pack of wolves loose in this quadrant of the globe, wolves who masquerade as soldiers of the New South Wales Corps, which I gather marine wolves like fucken George Johnston intend to join. They care as little for convicts or these penal settlements as I do, but I will return to England a poor man, whereas they will return fatter by every carcass they can sink their teeth into. And rum will be a very large part of it, mark my words. Enrichment at the expense of duty, honor, King and country. *Mark my words, Morgan!* So it will be."

"I do not doubt ye, sir."

"I see your wife is with child."

"Aye, sir."

"Ye're better off out of Arthur's Vale, but ye were wise enough to see that for yourself. There will be no trouble for ye with Mr. King, who has little choice other than to honor those transactions I have negotiated as His Majesty's legally appointed Lieutenant-Governor. Of course your pardon ultimately rests with His Excellency, but ye're out of your sentence in a few months anyway, and I cannot see why ye will not get your full pardon." Ross stopped. "If this benighted isle ever succeeds, 'twill be because of men like you and Nat Lucas." He held out his hand. "Goodbye, Morgan."

Blinking back tears, Richard gripped the hand and wrung it. "Goodbye, Major Ross. I wish ye well."

And that, thought the desperately sorry Richard as he hurried after Kitty and Joey, is one half of the work done. I have yet to deal with the other half.

It happened as Queen discharged cargo and convicts first at Cascade and then at Sydney Bay; Richard was sawing with a new man because Billy Wigfall was going, and was too busy shouting instructions to his partner below to bother looking up. When the cut was done he noticed the figure in its Royal Navy uniform aglitter with gold braid, unwrapped the rags from around his hands and walked across to salute Commander King.

"Should the supervisor of sawyers actually saw himself?" King asked, staring at Richard's chest and shoulders with some awe.

"I like to keep my hand in, sir, and it informs my men that I am still better at it than they are. The pits are all working well at the moment and each has a good man at the helm. This one—your third pit, sir, d'ye remember?—is where I saw myself when I do saw."

"I swear ye're in far finer body than ye were when I left, Morgan. I understand ye're a free man by virtue of pardon?"

"Aye, sir."

His mouth pursing, King tapped his fingers a little peevishly against his brilliantly white-clad thigh. "I daresay I cannot blame the sawpits for the shockingly bad buildings," he said.

The gulf yawned, but had to be leaped. Richard set his jaw and looked straight into King's eyes, more aware these days that he possessed a certain power. Thank you, Kitty. "I hope, sir, that ye're not about to blame Nat Lucas."

King jumped, looked horrified. "No, no, Morgan, of course not! Blame my own original head carpenter? Acquit me of such idiocy. No, 'tis Major Ross I blame."

"Ye cannot do that either, sir," said Richard steadily. "Ye left this place twenty months ago, a week or two after the people in it had jumped from a hundred and forty-nine to more than five hundred. During the time ye've been away, the population has gone to over thirteen hundred. After Queen, more, and Irish Irish at that—they'll not even speak English, most of them. 'Tis simply not the place ye left, Commander King. Then, we enjoyed good health—we lived hard, but we managed. Now, at least a third of the mouths we are feeding are sick ones, and we have besides Port Jackson's leavings when it comes to utter villains. I am sure," he swept on, ignoring King's mounting indignation and annoyance, "that while ye were in Port Jackson ye discussed with His Excellency the terrible difficulties His Excellency is suffering. Well, it has been no different here, is all. My sawpits have produced thousands upon thousands of superficial feet over the last twenty months. Much of it ought to have been seasoned for longer than it did because the new arrivals kept coming and coming. Ye might say that Major Ross, Nat Lucas, I and many others here have been caught in the middle. But that was nobody's fault. At least not on this side of the globe."

Eyes still fixed on King's, he waited calmly. No servility, but not a trace of impudence or presumption either. If this man is to survive, he thought, then he must take notice of what I have said. Otherwise he will not succeed, and the New South Wales Corps will end in ruling Norfolk Island.

The mercurial Celt struggled with the coolheaded Englishman for perhaps a minute, then King's shoulders slumped. "I hear what ye're saying clearly. But it cannot continue thus, is what I meant to say. I insist that whatever is built is constructed properly, even if that means some have to live under canvas for however long it takes." His mood changed. "Major Ross informs me that the harvest will come in magnificently, both here and at Queensborough. Many acres and none spoiled. I admit that is an achievement. Yet we have to put men on the grindstone." He gazed at his dam, still holding up very well. "We need a water-wheel, and Nat Lucas says he can build one."

"I am sure he can. His only enemies are time and lack of materials. Give him the latter and he will find the former."

"Aye, so I think too." His face assumed a conspiratorial look as he moved completely out of earshot. "Major Ross also told me that ye distilled rum for him during a time of crisis. That rum also saved Port Jackson from mutiny between March and August of this year, with no rum and no ships."

"I did distill, sir."

"D'ye possess the apparatus?"

"Aye, sir, very well hidden. It does not belong to me, it is the property of the Government. That I am its custodian lies in the fact that Major Ross trusted me."

"The pity of it is that those wretched transport captains have not been above selling distillation apparatus to private individuals. I hear that the New South Wales Corps and some of the worst convicts are distilling illicit spirits. At least Port Jackson can grow no sugar cane, but here it grows like a weed. Norfolk Island is potentially a source of rum. What the Governor of New South Wales has to decide is whether to continue importing rum from thousands of miles away at great expense, or to start distilling here."

"I doubt His Excellency Governor Phillip would consent."

"Aye, but he will not be governor forever." King looked very worried. "His health is breaking down."

"Sir, there is no point in fretting about events which still lie very much in the future," Richard said, relaxing. He had leaped the chasm, things would be all right between him and King.

"True, true," said the new Lieutenant-Governor, and hied himself off to spend an hour or two in his office, with perhaps a *tiny* drop of port to palliate the monotony.

"Ye've a box at Stores," said Stephen not long after this encounter. "What is it, Richard? Ye look exhausted for someone who thinks nothing of ripping a dozen gigantic logs apart."

"I have just spoken my mind to Commander King."

"Ooooo-aaa! Well, ye're a free man, so he cannot have ye flogged without trial and conviction."

"Oh, I survived. I always do, it seems."

"Do not tempt fate!"

Richard bent and knocked on wood. "This time, anyway," he amended. "He had the sense to see I spoke naught but the truth."

"Then there is hope for him. Did you hear the first thing I said, Richard?"

"No, what?"

"There is a box for you at Stores. It came on Queen. Too heavy to carry, so fetch your sled."

"Dinner this evening? Then ye can help me explore the box."

"I will be there."

He collected his sled at midday and was led to the box by Tom Crowder, taken under Mr. King's patronage at once. Someone had broken into it—no one here in Stores, he decided. On Queen or in Port Jackson. Whoever had inspected it had had the courtesy to hammer the lid back on. Pushing at the box, he decided from its weight that little had been confiscated, from which he assumed it contained books. A great many books, since it was bigger than a tea chest and made of stronger wood. When he bent to pick it up and heft it onto the sled, Crowder squealed.

"Ye cannot do that alone, Richard! I will find ye a man."

"I am a man, Tommy, but thankee for the offer."

RICHARD MORGAN • CONVICT OFF ALEXANDER had been lettered large on every one of the box's six sides, but there was no shipper's name.

That afternoon he pulled it home. There were still some hours of daylight left; the nature of the work meant that the sawpits closed earlier than common labor. He was, besides, a free man, at liberty to go home early once in a while.

"You bloom more beautiful each time I see you, wife," he said to Kitty when she came skipping down the steps to greet him.

They kissed lingeringly, her lips promising lovemaking that night; physically, he knew, he enchanted her. Fearing harm to the baby, he had wanted to stop, but she had looked amazed.

"How can anything so lovely hurt our baby?" she had asked in genuine puzzlement. "You are not a hell-for-leather rammer, Richard."

His mouth had tugged into a smile at her choice of words, which occasionally reflected that long sojourn aboard Lady Juliana.

"What is inside?" she asked now as he removed the box from the sled.

"As I have not yet opened it, I do not know."

"Then do so, please! I am dying!"

"It came on Queen rather than Atlantic from Port Jackson, but on Gorgon from England. The delay in Port Jackson is a mystery. Maybe someone wanted to know the name of the shipper." Richard used a claw hammer to prise the lid off—too easily. Without a doubt the box had been opened and its contents examined.

As he suspected, books. On top of the books and deprived of whatever had surrounded it as packing—clothes, probably—sat a hat box. Jem Thistlethwaite. He untied the tapes and took out the hat to end all hats, of scarlet silk-covered straw with a huge, warped brim and a profusion of black, white and scarlet ostrich feathers fixed under a preposterous black-and-white striped satin bow. It tied under the chin with similarly striped satin ribbons.

"Ohhhhh!" said Kitty as he lifted it up, her mouth sagging.

"Alas, wife, 'tis not for you," he said before she could get any ideas. " 'Tis for Mrs. Richard Morgan."

"I am so glad! It is very grand, but I have not the height or the face—or the clothes—to wear it. Besides," she confided, "I think people like Mrs. King and Mrs. Paterson would deem it dreadfully vulgar."

"I love you, Kitty. I love you very, very much."

To which she returned no answer; she never did.

Stifling a sigh, Richard discovered that the hat box also held a few small items wrapped in screws of paper, all of which had been opened, then closed again. How odd! Who had opened the box, and why? The hat could have bought the least attractive male in Port Jackson a year with that place's best whore, yet the hat had not been appropriated. Nor the objects wrapped in paper. Unrolling one, he found a brass seal attached to a short wooden handle; when he mentally mirrored its emblem he saw that it consisted of the initials RM entwined with unmistakable fetters or manacles. The other six papers contained sticks of crimson sealing wax. A hint.

On the bottom of the hatbox sat a fat letter, its JT-and-quill seal definitely unbroken, though fingerprints upon its outside said that it had been carefully felt and squeezed. At which moment he understood why his box had been opened, and by whom. In Government Stores at Port Jackson, by a high official in search of gold coin. Had any been found, it would have gone into the Government coffers, very short of gold. Richard knew that the box did contain gold, though he very much doubted from its condition that gold had been found. High officials did not have much imagination.

He found Jethro Tull's book on horticulture and a set of the second edition of *Encyclopaedia Britannica;* three-volume novels by the dozen, a whole collection of *Felix Farley's Bristol Journal* and several London gazettes, the works of John Donne, Robert Herrick, Alexander Pope, Richard Dryden, Oliver Goldsmith, more of Edward Gibbon's masterwork on Rome; some parliamentary reports, a ream of best paper, more steel pens, bottles of ink, laudanum, tonics, tinctures, laxatives and an emetic; several jars of ointments and salves; and a dozen good candle molds.

Kitty hopped from one foot to the other, a little disappointed that the box held books rather than a dinner service by Josiah Wedgwood, but very pleased because Richard was pleased. "Who is it from?"

"A very old friend, Jem Thistlethwaite. With inclusions from my family in Bristol," said Richard, the letter in his hand. "Now, if ye will excuse me, Kitty, I am going to sit down on the doorstep and read Jem's letter. Stephen is coming for dinner, then I will tell both of ye all my news."

Kitty had planned on bread and salad for dinner that day, but rose to the occasion by producing a salt pork stew with peppered dumplings; the meat was excellent and newly done, for it was their own produce.

When Stephen saw the hat he roared with laughter, insisted upon setting it on Kitty's head and artistically tying its ribbons. "I fear," he said, still chuckling, "that the hat wears you, not you the hat."

"I am aware of that," she said loftily.

"How are your family?" Stephen asked then, replacing the hat.

"All very well, save for Cousin James-the-druggist," Richard said sadly. "His eyesight has almost failed, so his sons have taken over the business and he has retired to a very nice mansion outside Bath with his wife and two spinster daughters. My father has removed to the Bell Tavern around the corner because the Corporation is in the throes of another building orgy and has pulled the Cooper's Arms down. My brother's oldest boy is with them—a great comfort. And Cousin James-of-the-clergy has been awarded a canon's stall at the Cathedral, much to his joy. My sisters are thriving too." A shadow crossed his face. "The only death among those I knew is that of John Trevillian Ceely Trevillian, who died of a surfeit—what sort of surfeit is a mystery."

"Soporifics and ecstatics, most likely," said Stephen, who knew the story in its entirety. "I rejoice."

"There is a lot of general news, and many flimsies to plump the news out. France did indeed have a revolution and abolished its monarchy, though the King and Queen are still alive. Much to Jem's surprise, the United States of America continues to be an entity, is drafting a radical kind of written constitution and fast regaining its moneys." Richard grinned. "According to Jem, the only reason the Frogs revolted was because of Benjamin Franklin's fur hat. What does Jem write?" Richard shuffled the pages. "Ah! 'Unlike the Americans, who have scientifically calibrated a system of parliamentary checks and balances, the French have decided to institute none. Logic will perforce have to do what the Law does not allow to be done. As the French have no logic, I predict that republican government in France will not last.' "

"He is right about that."

Kitty sat with her eyes going from one face to the other, not really following very much, but delighted that Richard and Stephen were so absorbed in things at the right ends of the earth.

"The King was very ill in 1788 and certain elements tried to have the Prince of Wales installed as regent, but the King recovered and Georgy-Porgy failed to lift himself out of his mire of debt. He still refuses to marry suitably, and Roman Catholic Mrs. Maria Fitzherbert is still his great love."

"Religion and religious differences," Stephen said with a sigh, "are the greatest curses of mankind. Why cannot we live and let live? Look at Johnson. Insisted the convicts marry each other but gave them no opportunity to get to know each other first because fornicating is a part of knowing. Pah!" He suppressed the flash of temper and changed the subject. "What of England?"

"Mr. Pitt reigns supreme. Taxation has absolutely soared. There is even a tax on news sheets, gazettes and magazines, and those who advertise in them must pay a tax of two-and-sixpence irrespective of the size of the advertisement. Jem says that is forcing small shops and businesses out of advertising their wares, leaving the field to the big fellows."

"Does Jem have anything to add to the fact that the first mate and some of the crew of Bounty mutinied and put Lieutenant Bligh in a longboat? 'Tis the mutiny on Bounty everybody is talking about, not the French Revolution," Stephen asked.

"Oh, *I* think interest in Bounty arises from the fact that the crew preferred luscious Otaheitian maidens to breadfruit."

"Undoubtedly. But what does Jem say? 'Tis a huge scandal and controvery in England, apparently. Bligh, they say, is not blameless by any means."

"His best snippet concerns the genesis of the expedition to Otaheite to bring back the breadfruit, which I gather was intended as cheap food for the West Indian negro slaves," said Richard, hunting through pages again. "Here we are. . . . Jem's style is inimitable, so 'tis best to hear it direct from him. 'A naval lieutenant named William Bligh is married to a Manxwoman whose uncle happens to be Duncan Campbell, proprietor of the prison hulks. The convolutions are tortuous, but probably through Mr. Campbell, Bligh was introduced to Sir Joseph Banks, very occupied with the mooted breadfruit pilgrimage to Otaheite.

" 'What fascinated me was the incestuous nature of the final outcome of the expeditionary marriage between the Royal Navy and the Royal Society. Campbell sold one of his own ships, Bethea, to the Navy. The Navy changed her name to Bounty and appointed Campbell's niece's husband,

Bligh, commander *and purser* of Bounty. With Bligh sailed one Fletcher Christian of a Manx family related by blood to Bligh's wife and Campbell's niece. Christian was the second-in-command but had no naval commission. He and Bligh had sailed together previously, and were as close as a couple of Miss Mollies.' Say no more, Jem, say no more!"

"That," said Stephen when he could for laughing, "just about sums England up! Nepotism reigns, even including incest."

"What is incest?" asked Kitty, well aware of Miss Mollies.

"Sexual congress between people very closely related by blood," said Richard. "Usually parents and children, brothers and sisters, uncles or aunts and nieces or nephews."

"Ugh!" Kitty exclaimed, shuddering. "But I do not exactly see how the Bounty mutiny fits in."

" 'Tis a literary device called irony, Kitty," said Stephen. "What else does Jem write?"

"Ye can have the letter to read at your leisure," Richard said, "though there is another thought in it worth airing ahead of that. Jem thinks that Mr. Pitt and the Parliament are very afraid that an English revolution might follow the American and French ones, and now deem a Botany Bay place a necessity for the preservation of the realm. There is huge trouble brewing in Ireland, and both the Welsh and the Scotch are discontented. So Pitt may add rebels and demagogues to his transportation list."

He did not discuss Mr. Thistlethwaite's personal news, which was excellent. The purveyor of three-volume novels to literate ladies had become so adept at the art that he could produce two a year, and money flowed into his coffers so copiously that he had bought a big house in Wimpole Street, had twelve servants, a carriage drawn by four matched horses, and a duchess for a mistress.

After Stephen left carrying Mr. Thistlethwaite's letter and the dishes were washed up, Kitty ventured another remark; to do so no longer terrified her, for Richard tried very hard to restrain his God the Father tendencies.

"Jem must be very grand," she said.

"Jem? Grand?" Richard laughed at the idea, remembering that burly, bulky figure with the red-tinged, pale blue eyes and the horse pistols protruding from his greatcoat pockets. "Nay, Kitty, Jem is very down-to-earth. A bit of a bibber—he was one of my father's most faithful customers in his

Bristol days. Now he lives in London and has made a fortune for himself. While I was aboard Ceres hulk he enabled me to safeguard both my health and my reason. I will love him for it all of my life."

"Then I will too. If it were not for you, Richard, I would be far worse off than I am," she said, thinking to please him.

His face twisted. "Can ye not love me at all?"

The eyes turned up to his were very earnest; they no longer seemed the image of William Henry's eyes, but rather had become her own, and equally—nay, *more*—loved.

"Can ye not love me at all, Kitty?" he repeated.

"I do love you, Richard. I always have. But it is not what I believe is *true* love."

"You mean I am not the be-all and end-all of your existence."

"You are, such as my existence is." Her eloquence was a thing of gesture, expression, look—her words, alas, fell down badly; she had not the knack of finding the right ones to explain what was going on in her brain. "That sounds ungrateful, I know, but I am not ungrateful, truly I am not. It is just that sometimes I wonder what might have happened to me had I not been convicted and sent to this—this place so far from home. And I wonder if there was not someone for me in England, someone I will never have the chance to meet now. Someone who is my *true* love." Seeing his face, she hurried on in a fluster. "I am very happy, and I like working in the garden and around the house. It is a great joy to be with child. But. . . . Oh, I wish I knew what I have missed!"

How to answer that? "Ye do not pine for Stephen anymore?"

"No." It came out confidently. "He was right, it was a girlish passion. I look at him now and marvel at myself."

"What d'ye see when ye look at me?"

Her body hunched and she squirmed like a small, guilty child; he knew the signs and wished he had not asked, provoked her into being obliged to lie. As if he could see into it, he knew that her mind was racing in circles to find an answer that would satisfy him yet not compromise herself, and he waited, feeling a twinge of amusement, to hear what would emerge. That of course was *true* love. To understand that the beloved was flawed, imperfect, yet still to love completely. Her idea of *true* love was a phantom, a knight in shining armor who would ride off with her across his saddle bow. Would she ever attain the kind of maturity that saw love for what it was? He doubted it, then decided it was better that she did not. Two hoary-headed sages in a family were one too many. He had enough love for both of them.

Her answer was honest: she was learning. "I truly do not know, Richard. You are not a bit like my father, so it is not in—incest. . . . I like to see you, always. . . . That I am carrying *your* child thrills me, for you will be a wonderful father."

Suddenly he realized that there was one question he had never asked her. "D'ye want a girl or a boy?"

"A boy," she said without hesitation. "No woman wants a girl."

"What if it should be a girl?"

"I will love her very much, but not with hope for her."

"Ye mean that the world belongs to men."

"I think so, yes."

"Ye'll not be *too* disappointed if it is a girl?"

"No! We will have others, and some will be boys."

"I can tell you a secret," he whispered.

She leaned into him. "What?"

" 'Tis better if the first child is a girl. Girls grow up much faster than boys, so when the first little man comes along, he will have at least two mothers—one close enough to his own age to grab him by an ear, take him to a quiet place, and drub the daylights out of him. His real mother will not be so ruthless."

She giggled. "That sounds like experience."

"It is. I have two elder sisters." He stretched like a cat, elongating every fiber. "I am very glad that they are all well in Bristol, though my cousin James's sight is a grief. Like Jem Thistlethwaite, he was the saving of me. I never suffered the illnesses most convicts do, especially in a gaol or on board a transport. That is why, at three-and-forty, I can labor like a much younger man. *And* make love to you like a much younger man. I have kept my health and vigor."

"But you went as hungry as the rest, surely."

"Aye, but hunger does no harm until it chews away a man's muscles beyond repair, and my muscles I suppose had more substance than most. Besides, the hunger never lasted quite long enough. There were oranges and fresh meat in Rio—meals on a Thames dredge—an occasional bowl of fish-chowder—a man named Stephen Donovan who fed me fresh buttered rolls stuffed with Captain Hunter's cress. That is luck, Kitty," Richard said, smiling, his eyes half-closed. Today seemed to be a day for memories.

"I cannot agree," she said. "I would rather call it some quality many men do not possess, but you do. So does Stephen. And I always fancied Major Ross had it too, from listening to you and Stephen talk. Nat and

Olivia Lucas both have it. I do not. That is why I am glad 'tis you is the father of my children. They have a chance of inheriting more than I am."

He picked up her hand and kissed it. "That is a very pretty compliment, wife. Perhaps ye do love me just a little."

She huffed a sound of exasperation and turned to look at the tables and chairs, strewn with books. One chair held the hat box. "When will you deliver Lizzie's hat?" she asked.

"I think you should deliver it and heal the breach."

"I could not!"

"I will not."

The question of the hat was still undecided when they went to bed, Kitty so tired that she fell asleep before she could make overtures of love.

Richard dozed for two hours, his half-dreams a parade of old faces transformed and distorted by the years between. Then he woke and slid out of the bed, donned trowsers and stepped outside softly. Tibby had been joined by Fatima and Charlotte by Flora; the two pups and two kittens stirred until Richard hushed them. They were curled together inside a piece of hollow pine Richard had thought an ideal kennel; more dogs and cats having the run of the house would discourage them from ratting. MacTavish was a law unto himself, too late to change his habits now. And he was still the sole male, ruler of the roost.

The moon was full and rising into the eastern sky, snuffing out the blazing stars as its cold pale brilliance poured upward; one could read by it easily when it was overhead. Not a cloud in the sky and the only sounds the gurgle and gush of the spring, water pelting away downhill, a great murmur from pines, the skreek-skreek-skreek of a pair of white fairy terns in black silhouette against the silvered heavens. He lifted his head and inhaled the night, the clean purity of it, the comfort in its loneliness, the distance, the utter peace.

On Sunday after divine service he would write to his father, to the Cousins James and Jem Thistlethwaite to tell them that he had managed to make a home for himself in this southern immensity. He had hewn a niche, helped by a little gold, for which he had to thank them. But gold or no gold, he had hewn it with his own hands and his own will. Norfolk Island was home now.

In the meantime there was a box to examine before Kitty and Joey Long took it into their heads to chop it up for kindling or use it to hold mulch for the garden. Rather than walk up the cleft, he walked down it; Joey's tiny house was just inside the Queensborough road boundary of Morgan's Run along the edge of the track down to the main house. Joey and MacGregor were his sentinels, his first line of defense in case of predators. Not that he expected any yet. But who knew how many and what kind of convicts His Excellency would send here as his task over there in New South Wales grew ever harder?

Having found a cleared patch in the moonlight he began to attack the box with a chisel and a small hammer, tapping quietly; sure enough, once the heavy border was removed, the space between inside and outside skins sprang into sight as white lint wadding. Not many minutes later the box was in pieces and he had amassed £100 in gold. Removing his trowsers, he piled the coins into their middle, gathered up the fragments of wood, put the trowsers on top of the pile, and walked back to his house. Kitty had said it was not luck. For himself, he was never sure whether he had luck or the grace of God. Though was there any difference?

When building his house he had thought of this eventuality; around the back and against the western slope he had randomly chosen one stone pier and constructed it with a hollow center. No one knew, and no one would know. Retaining twenty of the coins, he put the other eighty into his hiding place, then padded silently inside and into bed. Kitty murmured, purred; MacTavish's tail thumped against the blanket. Richard patted the dog and folded Kitty's back into his front, stroked her flank and closed his eyes.

The hat box was still on the chair when Richard went to work in the morning; it sat reproaching Kitty as she moved about the room, dusting, washing, tidying books, preparing the ingredients for a cold lunch; too hot to eat the main meal in the heat of the day, and perhaps if she took Joey and walked into Sydney Town she could find Stephen, persuade him to join them for a hot supper.

Oh, how thoughtful Richard was! The remains of the box were stacked in the kindling heap to one side of the front door, chopped to precisely the right size to start the stove fire—too hot to light it now, she would wait until mid afternoon, then bake bread. This typical kindness from him gave her pause; already outside, she turned back to look into the room and at the hat box. Sighing, she went back to pick it up and started the walk to the Queensborough road. Joey was chopping pines; Richard was determined that he would clear enough of Morgan's Run to plant several acres of wheat and Indian corn next June, and though Joey could not saw, he could fell timber competently. MacGregor warned him of her advent—no danger of dropping a tree in the wrong place with MacGregor on duty!

"Joey, do you mind walking me to Sydney Town?"

Puffing, the simple soul looked at her with adoration and mutely shook his head. He snatched his shirt off a nearby branch and donned it eagerly, then the pair of them set off toward Mount George, MacGregor and MacTavish frisking around them.

"My own errand is to Government House," she said, "and while I do that, Joey, find Mr. Donovan and ask him to come to supper this evening. I will meet you here. Do *not* dawdle!"

Government House was in the throes of huge alterations and additions. Men were crawling all over it, Nat Lucas was barking instructions and the others were very quick to obey. It was a stupid convict took his time over work for the Commandant himself, and surprisingly few convicts were stupid. These renovations were of a temporary nature; Commander King had still not made up his mind whether Government House should remain on its present knoll or move to the other knoll where Richard said the original gardens had been. Never having been to Government House, Kitty did not know whether as a convict she ought to find a back door, or whether all traffic went to the front door, facing the sea.

"Who are ye looking for, Kit-kat?" Nat Lucas asked.

"Mrs. Richard Morgan."

"In the kitchen house. Around there," he said, pointing and giving her a wink.

She walked along the side of the main house to the separate building which housed the kitchen.

"Mrs. Morgan?"

The stiff, dark-clad figure hovering over the stove turned, the black eyes widened; a young convict girl peeling potatoes at the work table laid down her knife and stared with mouth adenoidally agape. Staggering a little, which seemed peculiar to Kitty, Lizzie walked to the table and gave the girl a thump. "Take that outside and do it!" she snapped. Then, to Kitty, "What d'ye want, madam?"

"I have brought you a hat."

"A hat?"

"Yes. Would you not like to see? It is very splendid."

Kitty looked absolutely blooming, belly protruding a little, fair skin shaded by a wide sun hat made of a local strappy grass (the convict transports had contained far more milliners than farmers), fair hair straggling in fetching wisps from beneath its brim, fair lashes and brows giving her face a slightly bald look that somehow managed not to be a disfigurement. Plain she was, but plain she definitely was not. Gossip had told Lizzie that Kitty Clark was beautifully shaped these days, was far from the thin scrawn she had been when Mrs. Richard Morgan had marched up the garden path. Well, now she could see for herself, which was no comfort. Nor was that bulging belly. Waves of sorrow and disappointment swept over her—where was that bottle of medicine?

"Sit down," Lizzie said curtly, then gulped furtively from a medicine bottle, its contents catching her breath.

Kitty held out the hat box, smiling gravely. "Please take it."

Taking it, Lizzie sat on a chair, untied the tapes, lifted the lid. "Ohhhh!" she sighed, exactly as Kitty had. "Ohhhh!" Out it came to be examined, held, gazed at raptly. Then, so unexpectedly that Kitty jumped, Lizzie Lock burst into noisy tears.

Calming her took some time; in an odd way she reminded Kitty of Betty Riley, the tough older servant girl who had led all four of them to disaster. "It is all right, Lizzie, it is all right," she crooned as she stroked and patted.

There was a small spouted kettle on the hob and an old china teapot on the table. Tea. That was what Lizzie needed, tea. A search unearthed a jar of tea and a jar containing a huge rock of sugar together with a sugar hammer; Kitty made the tea, let it steep, chopped off some sugar, then poured the steaming liquid into a china cup and saucer—how well equipped Government House was! China cups and saucers in the *kitchen!* Kitty had not seen a cup and saucer since she had been arrested, now here were two cups and two saucers—*matching!*—in a mere kitchen. What sort of treasures did Government House itself contain? How many servants were there to wait on Mr. and Mrs. King? Was there tea on demand without fear of its running out, were there china bowls and plates and soup tureens? Pictures on the walls? Chamber pots?

"I have just been given my notice," Lizzie managed to say through hiccoughs and tears. "Mr. King has just told me."

"Here, drink your tea. Come, 'twill make you feel much more the thing, truly," coaxed Kitty, stroking the black hair.

Lizzie mopped her eyes with her apron and stared at her nemesis ruefully. "Ye're really a nice little girl," she said, the tea beginning to warm the other contents of her stomach.

"I hope I am," said Kitty, sipping daintily. Why did tea taste so wonderful sipped from a china cup? "Do you like your hat?"

"As ye said, it is a very splendid hat. Major Ross would have whistled and told me I looked like a queen in it, but Mrs. King will only *try* to be complimentary. She is a very pleasant person with excellent manners, so I cannot say she is to blame for my going. Commander King is responsible. And that Chapman fellow, the crafty booby! An eye to the main chance, that one! Already scheming how to make money out of the place. Brings out the worst in Mrs. King too—which the Commander is starting to realize, let me tell you! I predict that Willy Chapman will shortly be packed off to Queensborough or Phillipsburgh. But Commander King don't like me, Kitty, and that is a fact I cannot get around. Too vulgar for the likes of Mrs. King, is how he put it. Vulgar! *Me?* He don't know what vulgar is! Said he don't want his children to hear me—sometimes I forget myself and out pops a fuck or two. But never a cunt, Kitty, never a cunt, I swear! It ain't my fault—blame gaol. Never used to swear and curse."

"I understand *completely,*" said Kitty fervently.

"Anyway, he cannot just throw me out, he will have to do the decent thing by me," growled Lizzie, thrusting out her chin. "I am a free woman, not a convict. And d'ye know who he is going to put in my place?" she demanded, outraged.

"No, who?"

"Mary Rolt. *Mary Rolt!* Says cunt as well as fuck, I do assure you! Huh! 'Tis all because Mary Rolt fucks Sam King the marine, and he is settling here, and all that. King. Same name, y'see. Makes anyone better in the Commandant's eyes. Huh!" She sipped a little more tea and stared at the hat. "I wish I had a mirror."

"Mrs. King must have one."

"Oh, she does, a big one in her bedroom."

"Then ask her if you may look. If she has excellent manners and is kind, then she will not say no."

"It *is* a fine hat, ain't it?"

"The finest I have ever seen. Mr. Thistlethwaite said in his letter that it is all the crack—exactly what duchesses and other high ladies are wearing. He says you cannot tell high-born women from whores these days—" She broke off, horrified at where her tongue had led her, but Lizzie was staring fixedly at the medicine bottle. "Perhaps," Kitty rushed on, "the Kings might keep you on as cook? Richard told me that Major Ross said your cooking was the best he had ever tasted."

"*I,*" said Lizzie haughtily, "have other ideas."

Kitty's heart soared; some of it was rawness, some of it was shock, but underneath both Lizzie Lock was already springing back. Of course she was! So do we all, we convict women. We have not come this far and survived without being able to spring back. Lizzie is tough. Not hard, just tough. She has had to be. No doubt everybody free will prate their admiration for Mrs. King's courage in coming so far and putting up with inconveniences, but Mrs. King has never been a convict woman and Mrs. King will never be as admirable in my eyes as Lizzie Lock. Or Mary Rolt. Or Kitty Clark. So there, Mrs. King! said Kitty to herself. Drink your tea from your fine china cups after the convict servant girl has made it and served it to you! Pin on your course clouts after the convict servant girl has washed your blood from them and hung them out to dry! You may be everything a prison commandant's wife should be, but you are not *our* equal.

"What ideas do you have?" she asked.

"I have gotten over hating ye for stealing Richard," Lizzie said, getting up to refill the pot, chip off a bit more sugar, pour more tea.

"Truly I did not steal him!"

"I know *that!* He stole you, more like. Peculiar, ain't they? Men, I mean. As far as most of them are concerned, keep the belly and what hangs off it well fed, and they are happy. But Richard was always different, right from when he stalked into Gloucester Gaol like a prince of the blood—you know, sort of cool and royal and quiet. Never needed to raise his voice. Mind you, he is a big man, ha ha ha! Eh, Kitty? Ain't that right?"

"Yes," said Kitty, blushing.

"Took on Ike Rogers—an even bigger man—without the blink of an eye. Faced him down. Yet I heard that later on they was real good friends. That is Richard. I am in love with him, but he was never in love with me. No hope. No hope." Voice teary, Mrs. Richard Morgan got up again to tip the contents of the medicine bottle into her tea. "There! That will ginger it up a treat. Like some?"

"No, thank you. What are your plans, Lizzie?" Kitty realized that whatever Lizzie had gurgled into her tea had been sipped at for some time, probably since the moment Mr. King had walked out after giving her her notice.

"I am thinking of Thomas Sculley, a marine just arrived back to take up land here. Not far from Morgan's Run. Quiet sort of man, a bit like Richard in that respect. Don't want no children, but. He ain't got a woman, and he made me an offer after tasting my banana fritters in rum. I turned him down, but now that the Commandant says I have to go, I may as well move in with Sculley."

"It will be nice to have you as a neighbor," Kitty said with sincerity, preparing to take her leave.

"When is the baby due?"

"About another two and a half months."

"Thankee for bringing the hat. Mr. Thistlethwaite, ye said?"

"Yes, Mr. James Thistlethwaite."

A great deal more at peace, Kitty pattered off to find Joey and the two dogs waiting for her at the foot of Mount George.

"You were quite right to insist that I take the hat," she said to Richard as she sliced their own salt pork thinly, spooned gravy over it made with lots of onions, and piled potatoes and fresh beans onto the pewter platters. "Lizzie and I will become friends." She giggled. "The two Mrs. Richard Morgans." She put a plate in front of Stephen and another in front of Richard, then carried her own to the table and sat down. "Commander King gave the poor thing her notice this morning."

"I was afraid of that," said Stephen, cutting busily with his knife until everything could be scooped up with the spoon. How good it would be to have a fork! "King is a strict husband, wants to shelter his wife from all undignified or sordid phenomena, and Lizzie Lock is definitely an undignified phenomenon. A pity, really. Mrs. King is a tall, gangling sort of creature who does not present as particularly prudish, especially when Willy Chapman is with her." He pulled a face. "Now there's a sordid phenomenon, William Neate Chapman. A natural leech."

"They have china cups and saucers," said Kitty, busy eating for two, "and I drank my tea out of one. Since there are china cups and saucers even in the kitchen, I think that Mrs. King must be *very* genteel."

"I would gladly give ye china cups and saucers of your own, Kitty," said Richard, "but it is more than a question of money."

Attention caught, Stephen looked up. "Exactly," he agreed. "For a long time to come, I suspect, the closest thing Norfolk Island will have to a shop is a stall set up on the straight beach by some ship's captain. Unfortunately such stalls do not contain fribbles like china tea sets and silver forks. 'Tis always the same kettles, stoves, calico, cheap paper, ink."

"We need kettles, stoves and calico more than fribbles," said Richard, God the Fathering. "There are clothes occasionally."

"Aye, but I notice they never appeal to the women," Stephen objected.

"That is because men chose them," said Kitty, smiling. "They always think women would rather buy clothes than china or window curtains, then they choose the wrong clothes anyway."

"Ye'd rather have window curtains?" Stephen asked, wondering to himself why Kitty seemed not to care that she couldn't marry Richard. "The two Mrs. Richard Morgans"—said without a qualm.

"Oh, yes." Kitty put her spoon down to gaze about the living room, which was coming on; the interior walls were all up and most of them were polished, there were now several shelves of books one beneath the other, and she had found a flowering plant to put in a battered mug. "I love my home best. Rugs and curtains would be truly wonderful, and vases, and pictures on the walls. If I had embroidery silks, I could work tapestry cushions for the chairs and samplers for the walls."

"One day," Richard promised. "One day. We will just have to hope that one day a more enterprising ship's captain comes along to sell lamps and oil, embroidery silks, china teasets and vases. Government Stores are not very imaginative. Slops, shoes, wooden bowls, pewter spoons and mugs, blankets, dippers and tallow candles."

After the meal was done the men settled to talk of what the flimsies and gazettes said, then drifted to more important things like wheat, clearing, sawing, lime, and the changes Commander King was implementing.

"For all his fine talk, he has not managed to cut punishments down," said Richard. "*Eight hundred* lashes, for pity's sake! Far kinder to hang a man. The most Major Ross ever levied were five hundred, the bulk forgiven, and I note that the surgeons are not allowed to intervene as freely as they used to."

"Be fair, Richard. The fault lies with the New South Wales Corps, who are brutes commanded by brutes. I wish they would not single out the poor Irish, but they do."

"Well, the Irish come from outside the Pale and few of them speak English. The soldiers insist that they do, but will not admit it. How can they work when they do not understand their instructions? Yet I have found one man among them with whom it is a pleasure to saw—the best partner since Billy Wigfall. Cheerful, obliging—does not understand a word I say to him any more than I him. Put a rip saw between us, and we are in utter communion."

"What is his name?"

"I have no idea. Flippety O'Flappety, it may as well be. I call him Paddy, and give him a good lunch of bread and vegetables at the sawpit. Cold meat too. A man cannot saw without plenty of food, I will have to reinforce that with Mr. King."

Suddenly Kitty laughed and clapped her hands. "Oh, Richard, do stop talking about your sawpits! Stephen has big news."

Richard stared. "*Do* you? Tell us!"

"King summoned me this morning and informed me that I am to be the official pilot for Norfolk Island. I think he and Major Ross must have had a talk about the number of longboats, cutters and jollyboats which have been wrecked coming across the reef against orders and signals not to attempt to land. Or even defying advice not to return to their ships from the beach. So from now on I and I alone have the ordering of it, no matter what any ship's master might have to say on the subject. My word is law—and that includes a ship in the roads—when she may bear in, or go to Cascade, or Ball Bay. *I am pilot!* Had I been pilot when Sirius was here, she would never have gone on the reef."

"Stephen, that is truly splendid!" cried Kitty, eyes shining.

Richard wrung his hand. "That is not all, is it?"

"There is more, I admit." He looked lit from within, a fine man not many years past thirty with a whole new world spread before him. "I am in the Royal Navy with a temporary rank of midshipman, but as soon as Commander King can get permission from His Excellency I am to be commissioned a lieutenant—for rank, probably to some ship permanently in Portsmouth harbor. I will be staying here, however, so do not panic. When a genuine lieutenancy comes up, then I am afraid I will have to go. Not an immediate prospect. Meanwhile I am pilot, shortly ye'll have to address me as Lieutenant Donovan, and in my spare time I have been placed in charge of men clearing forest on Mount George, so I am out of that wretched stone quarry."

"This calls for a small celebration," said Richard, rising to dig behind a bookshelf. Out came a bottle. " 'Tis my own rum—Morgan's special blend. Major Ross gave me a good supply of it when he left, but I have not tasted it. So you and I will see what the local rum is like after it has aged a while in a cask with some decent Bristol spirits to help it along."

"Here is to you, Richard." Stephen lifted his mug and sipped, expecting to flinch or at least grimace. Surprise spread over his face, he took a full mouth of it. "Richard, not bad at all!" The mug was tipped in Kitty's direction. "And here is to Kitty and the baby, whose godfather I demand to be. May she be a girl and may ye call her Kate."

"Why Kate?" asked Kitty.

"Because in this part of the world 'tis better to be a shrew than a mouse." Stephen grinned. "Do not blanch so, little mother! Some man will tame her."

"What if it is a boy?" the little mother enquired.

Richard answered. "My first boy will be William Henry, and he will always be called all of it. William Henry."

"William Henry. . . . I like it," said Kitty, pleased.

Head bent over his mug, Stephen concealed a sigh. So she did not know. Would she ever know? Richard, *tell* her! Admit her as an equal, I beg you!

"I have news too, Lieutenant—and may ye be an Admiral of the Blue one day," Richard announced, toasting Stephen. "Tommy Crowder has been ordered by Mr. King to start a register of land and land owners. I am to go down in it as Richard Morgan—free man—possessed of twelve acres in his own right and not by power of the Crown. I am also to have ten acres at Queensborough on part of the treeless area. That will come next June or thereabouts as a grant from the Crown. So I will grow wheat on Morgan's Run and Indian corn at Queensborough to feed my pigs." He lifted his mug. "I drink a second toast to ye, Lieutenant Donovan, for all your many kindnesses through the years. May ye command a hundred guns in a big sea battle against the French before ye become an Admiral of the Blue. Kitty, turn your back and do not peek."

The twenty gold coins were slipped into Stephen's palm; he raised his brows, then put them into the pockets of his canvas jacket. When Kitty was told that she could look, she found them laughing, for what reason she did not know.

1792 came in dry, though there had been the usual rain around Christmas, luckily just after reaping had ended. Kitty grew heavier, but she was not one of those women who looked as if they might burst; she carried small and could keep busy without too much extra effort.

"You know, Richard, it truly ought to be you having this poor baby!" she said to him, exasperated. "You fuss and cluck so!"

"I do think that ye ought to go into Arthur's Vale and stay with Olivia Lucas," he said anxiously. "Morgan's Run is isolated."

"I am not going to stay with Olivia Lucas!"

"What if the baby comes earlier than ye expect?"

"Richard, I have had a long talk with Olivia—*I know all about it!* Believe me, I will have plenty of time to let Joey know and let you know and let Olivia know. This is a first baby. They do not come in a hurry," she said firmly.

"You are sure?"

"Truly," she said in the voice of a dying martyr, walked to a chair lithely, sat down without making a difficulty of it, and looked at him very seriously. "I have some questions to ask you, Richard, and I insist upon some answers," she said.

An air of authority surrounded her; fascinated, Richard could not take his eyes off her. "Then ask," he said, sitting down where his face was on full display to her. "Go ahead, ask."

"Richard, shortly I am to have your child, but I know next to nothing about your life. What little I know is thanks to Lizzie Lock. What she told me amounts to a pinpoint, and I think I am entitled to know *more* than Lizzie Lock. Tell me about the daughter who would be my age now."

"Her name was Mary, and she is buried next to her mother in the burying ground of St. James's, Bristol. She died of the smallpox when she was three. One reason why I would rather my children grew up here. The worst we have to worry about is dysentery."

"Did you have other children?"

"A son, William Henry. He drowned."

Her face crumpled. "Oh, Richard!"

"Do not grieve, Kitty. It was all a very long time ago, and in a different country. My children will not grow up with the same sort of risks."

"There are risks here, and drowning is the most common one."

"Believe me, the way my son drowned could not happen here. His was a death happens in cities, not on small islands where we all know each other. There are bad folk here and we do not mix with them, but when a school is organized, we parents will know a great deal more about the schoolmasters than Bristol parents do. William Henry died because of a schoolmaster." Head to one side, he looked at her quizzically. "Any more questions?"

"How did your Bristol wife die?"

"Of an apoplexy, luckily before William Henry went. She did not suffer at all."

"Oh, Richard!"

"There is no need to be sad, my love. *You* are why it happened, I am sure of it. In that I was not meant to know the joy of a real family in Bristol, where I never knew the joy of living in my own house. All I ask from you is that ye keep a small corner of your heart for me as the father of your children. That and the children will be enough."

Her mouth parted, she almost said that he had more than a small corner of her heart, but she closed it with the words unspoken. To say them would be a promise, a commitment that she was not sure she would be able to honor. She liked him enormously, and, liking him, did not think it decent to imply that he was more than he truly was. No music in her heart, no wings on her soul. Did he give her those, it might be different. Did he give her those, she would be able to call him "my love."

February was blowy and wild, hurricanes lurking. At least the crops were all in and the grain under shelter; a harvest big enough to feed every person in Norfolk Island, though there would be none to spare for New South Wales. Just a lot of lime, a little timber.

On the 15th of February, Richard hurried home, late and very anxious because the Lieutenant-Governor had delayed him with more questions than Kitty could think of in a week. Kitty was not yet due, but the head had engaged, so Olivia Lucas had told him, and Joey Long was nobody's idea of a midwife. Comforted by Olivia's and Kitty's assurances that first babies did not come in a hurry, he headed down the track to the house. No smoke issued from the tall stone chimney; his pace quickened. Even at almost nine months, she still insisted upon baking her own bread.

Not a sound.

"Kitty!" he called, bounding up the three steps to the door.

"I am here," came a small voice.

Heart drumming a tattoo against his rib cage, Richard burst through the door, taking in the room with a single glance. Not a sign of her. In the bedroom—Christ! It had begun!

She was sitting on the bed propped against two pillows, her face turned toward him with a beatific smile. "Richard, meet your daughter," she said. "Say good evening to Kate."

His knees sagged but he managed to reach the bed, sit on its edge heavily. *"Kitty!"*

"Look at her, Richard. Is she not beautiful?"

A pair of work-scarred hands offered him a tightly wrapped bundle—oh, it was not fair that his hands should be better cared for by far than hers! He took the bundle and delicately pushed the swaddling away from a tiny folded face, its mouth a perfect O, its puffy eyelids shut, its skin too dark to be red, surmounted by a shock of thick black hair. The ocean of love opened and swallowed him whole; he sank without a protest back into that magical realm, leaned forward to kiss the weeny creature upon her forehead, felt the tears come.

"I do not understand! Ye were so well when I left for the afternoon. Ye said nothing."

"There was nothing to say. I was truly well. It happened all in a muddle, I had no warning. My water broke, I had a gripey pain, and then I felt her head. So I spread a clean sheet on the floor, squatted down and had her. The whole did not take above a quarter of an hour. As soon as the afterbirth came I found some thread, tied the cord and cut it with my scissors. She was screaming—oh, what a voice! I cleaned her, tidied up the floor, put the sheet in to soak, and bathed myself." Bursting with pride, she beamed complacently. "I truly do not know what all the fuss is about." She pushed her calico house shift aside and displayed one exquisite breast, its dark red nipple beaded. "My milk has come in already too, though Olivia said to wait a while before giving suck. Am I not clever, Richard?"

Careful not to squash the bundle, Richard leaned forward to kiss her reverently upon the lips. His eyes worshiping her, he brushed the tears from his face and smiled shakily. "Very, very clever, wife. Ye did it as if ye'd done it twenty times."

"I have no scales so I cannot weigh her, but she seems to be a good size—quite long too. She looks a Morgan, not a Clark."

He squinted at Kate's face and tried to verify this, but could not. "She is very beautiful, wife, that is all I can see." After that he looked more closely at Kitty. She seemed a little tired, but glowed so radiantly that he could not believe she stood in any danger. "Ye're well? Honestly?"

"Truly. Just weary. She slipped out so easily that I am not even uncomfortable. Olivia recommended that I squat. That is the natural way, she says." Kitty took Kate back to look at her again. "Richard!" she exclaimed, her tone reproachful. "She is your image—how can you not see it?"

"Are ye happy to call her Catherine, like yourself?"

"Yes. Two Catherines—one Kitty, one Kate. We will call our next girl Mary."

He could not help it; he wept until Kitty put the baby down and took him into her arms.

"I love you, Kitty. I love you more than life itself."

Again her lips parted to say something offering him herself. Then Kate yelled lustily. So instead she asked, "Will you listen to that? I think Stephen is right, we have a shrew to rear. And that settles it. I am going to give her suck."

She slid both arms out of the shift and let it drop to her waist, unwrapped the little creature and held her naked against her own skin with a sensuous pleasure that devastated Richard. The O of mouth fastened around the nipple offered it; Kitty emitted a huge sigh of utter pleasure. "Oh, Kate, this makes you truly mine!"

It had never occurred to Kitty to doubt one fact: that Richard would be a wonderful father. What surprised her was his complete surrender to fatherhood. So many of her women friends and acquaintances complained that their men were wary of being seen as unmanning themselves if they had too much to do with the children or domestic chores. To carry a tired child was permissible, to kiss and cuddle a small one was permissible, but nothing to what they deemed excess. Whereas Richard simply did not care what any of his men friends thought of him. If one was visiting, he would cheerfully change Kate's dirty clouts, did not even care if he was discovered washing them or hanging them out to dry. And apparently his masculine image did not suffer in their eyes. Or if it did, he never noticed. Or if he noticed, he did not consider such opinions worth valuing. In one respect he was lucky: he did not look like a milksop. Had he, things might have been different for him.

He worked too hard because he tried to fit more into less time, always eager to be off home to see Kitty and Kate. When Kitty timidly suggested that perhaps he could do less sawing and more farming, he looked horrified—no, no! His job as supervisor of sawyers was well paid, and every note of hand he accumulated on the Government books was an insurance against the future of his children. He would manage to saw *and* farm, he was not dead yet.

Kate was six months old at the moment when Tommy Crowder came to the second sawpit looking for Richard, enquiring when Richard intended putting baby Kate on the Government Stores list.

"I can keep my wife and child off the Stores," said Richard with dignity.

"Commander King insists that they be on the Stores. Come to my office and we will do it now." Off trotted Crowder, not pausing to see if Richard followed.

"I do not see why my wife and child should be on the Stores," said Richard stubbornly in Crowder's tiny office. "I am the head of the family."

"That is just it, Richard. Ye're not the head of a family. Kitty is a convict woman and a spinster. That is why she is still on the Stores list and her baby must go on it too. I simply need ye here as a witness," Crowder explained.

Richard's eyes had gone completely grey and dark. "Kitty is my wife. Kate is my daughter."

"Catherine Clark, spinster. . . . Yes, here she is," Crowder burbled on, finding the right line on the right page in his big register. He picked up a quill, dipped it in his inkwell and added, speaking aloud as he wrote, "Catherine Clark, child." He looked up brightly. "There! That is done and ye've seen me do it. Thank you, Richard." He put the quill down.

"The child's name is Catherine *Morgan.* I acknowledge her."

"No, 'tis Clark."

"Morgan."

Tommy Crowder was not a very perceptive man; he spent too much of himself upon becoming invaluable to people who could help him get ahead. But suddenly, looking up into eyes as stormy as Sydney Bay during a squall, he felt the blood leave his face. "Do not blame me, Richard," he stammered. "I am not your judge, I am merely a servant of the Norfolk Island Government. Commander King wants everything"—he simpered—"shipshape and Bristol fashion. As a Bristolian, ye should be pleased." He was babbling now, could not stop babbling. "I have to put the baby on my lists, and I have to ask ye to witness the fact that I have. Her name is Clark."

"It is not fair!" Richard said to Stephen later, fists clenched. "That trained monkey in Government service wrote my daughter's name in his fucken register as Catherine Clark. And rubbed my nose in it by making me watch."

Stephen eyed the muscles tensing under the skin of Richard's arms and shivered involuntarily. "For God's sake, Richard, hold your temper! It is not Crowder's fault, nor is it King's fault. I agree that it is not fair, but there is nothing ye can do about it. Kitty is not your wife. Kitty cannot be your wife. She still has some years of her sentence left to serve, which means that the Government is entitled to do what it wills with her. And Kate's surname officially is Clark."

"There is one thing I can do," said Richard through his teeth. "I can murder Lizzie Lock."

"Ye're not capable of that, so stop talking as if ye are."

"While Lizzie lives, my daughter is a bastard. So will the other children I sire on Kitty be bastards."

"Look at it this way," Stephen coaxed, "Lizzie Lock is well settled with Tom Sculley, but Tom Sculley is learning fast that he is not a farmer, hence his move from grain to poultry. Sooner or later he will sell out and quit the island. From what the marine free settler gossip tells me, he says he wants to visit Cathay and Bengal before he is too old. D'ye think for one moment that he will sail for the Orient without Lizzie Lock on his arm?"

Closing his eyes, Richard slumped despondently. "I am trying to look at it your way. Ye mean that if Lizzie departs for the Orient, I can wait a while and then pretend I am a single man."

"Exactly. If necessary, I will pay some furtive forger in a London alley to use some Wampoa merchant's address and write a touching letter to the Gentlemen Sheriffs of Gloucester explaining that Mrs. Richard Morgan, née Elizabeth Lock, has passed away in Macao, and does Gloucester know of any relatives? That will prove that she is dead, after which ye can marry Kitty."

"Sometimes, Stephen, ye're the bitter end." But the ploy worked; Richard opened his eyes and managed a laugh. "Does this fine consoling speech containing references to London alleys mean that ye're leaving us soon?"

"I have had no word beyond the lieutenancy, but 'twill happen."

"I will miss ye something terrible."

"And I you." Stephen threw his arm about Richard's shoulders and propelled him gently in the direction of home. Good, his rage had cooled. Superficially at least. God rot the Reverend Johnson!

"It affects him far more than it does me," said Kitty when Stephen related what had happened. Richard had gone off to the bath pool he had made, there to wash himself clean of the sawpits and Thomas Restell Crowder. "I am sorry that Kate's name is not Morgan, but who could deny that she is a Morgan? What is marriage anyway? At least half of us convict women are not officially married, but that does not make us any less wives. I do not repine, Stephen, truly I do not."

"Richard is a churchgoing believer in God, Kitty, and thus he finds it extremely difficult to deal with the fact that his progeny are bastards in the eyes of the Church of England."

"They will not be bastards after Lizzie dies, and she is old," said Kitty comfortably.

How to explain to her that marriage later could never remove the slur? Stephen decided not to bother trying. Instead he grabbed at Kate. "Hello, my peach! My darling angel!"

"Kate is not an angel—she is exactly what you called her, a shrew. Strong willed! Goodness, Stephen, she is but six months old and already she rules us with a rod of iron."

"Nay," said Stephen, holding the mite's serious stare with smiling eyes, then kissing her on both plump cheeks, "she needs no rod of iron to rule Richard. A wisp of thread or a feather would do equally well. Is that not so, my Kate? Where is your Petruchio, I wonder? In what guise will he come?" He handed Kate back.

"Petruchio?"

"The Shakespearean gentleman who tamed Kate the shrew. Take no notice, 'tis just my whimsy."

A silence fell. Stephen contented himself with contemplating this Norfolk Island madonna, a study in rag-quality calico. No matter where her life may have led her, Kitty would always have been best at this, mothering a child. Here was this powerful baby who ought to be filled with thundering rages, yet with Kitty for a mother she was a peach, an angel. Good tabbies have good kittens. A good tabby is our Kitty.

What else was she? Not intellectually brilliant, but not stupid by any means. The mouse who had hidden in the forest had long gone. During the two years she had lived with Richard Morgan she had blossomed into a plain-faced, fabulously seductive woman. The trouble was, did Richard have her love? Stephen was never sure because he fancied she was never sure herself. What she feels for Richard is sexual enchantment. That binds her to him, as babies do, but still. . . . She does not see any allure in him—why, I will never know. Is it his years? Surely not! He carries them with as little effort as he saws.

"D'ye love Richard?" he asked.

Those ale-and-pepper eyes looked sad. "I do not know, Stephen. I wish I did, but I do not. I am not educated enough to make those sorts of judgments. I mean, how do you know that you love him?"

"I just do. He fills my eyes and my mind."

"He does not do that to me."

"Do not hurt him, Kitty, please!"

"I will not hurt him," she said, jigging Kate on her knee, then smiled and patted his hand. "I will stick to Richard through thick and thin, Stephen. I owe it to him, and I pay my debts. That is what transportation is supposed to teach us, and I have learned all my lessons. Except that somehow I never get around to reading and writing. House and babies come first."

When Kitty told him she was with child again, Richard was appalled. "Ye cannot be! It is too soon!"

"Not really. There will be fourteen months between them," she said placidly. "They will fare better if they are close in age."

"The work, Kitty! Ye'll be old before your time!"

That made her laugh. "Gammon, Richard! I am very well, I am young, and I am looking forward to the arrival of William Henry."

"Kitty, I was happy to wait, truly—oh, damn that word, I am picking up the habit of it!"

"Do not be angry," she pleaded. "Olivia said that I would not fall while ever I gave Kate the breast."

"An old wives' tale! I should have waited."

"Why?"

"Because another one will be too much for you."

"*I* say another one will not be too much for me." She handed Kate to Richard and picked up an empty bucket. "I am off to get water for the house."

"Let me get it."

Her teeth showed, her eyes blazed. "For the hundredth time, Richard Morgan, will you stop fussing and clucking? Why do you never want to give me the credit I deserve? I am the one grows the babies! I am the one says when that will be! I am the one lives in this house for all of my days and nights! I am the one decides what is too much for me and what is not! Leave me alone! Stop making all my decisions for me! Let me do as I want without forever plaguing me—this is too much, that is too little, why did I not ask you to do it—I have had enough! I am not an orphan child anymore, I am grown up enough to have babies! And if I want another one, I will have another one! You are not my lord and master, His Majesty the King is!"

She marched off with the bucket, radiating rage.

Richard sat down on the top step with Kate on his knee, both of them silenced.

"I think, daughter, that I have just been put in my place."

Kate sat bolt upright, unsupported, and looked at her father out of speckled eyes neither William Henry's nor Kitty's; hers were a fawnish grey which tended to disguise the presence of the dark dots peppering them. Those who found them had looked deeply. Her beauty was manifest, though perhaps it was simply the beauty of babyhood, but her coloring, like Richard's two dead children's, was striking—masses of black curls, finely marked black brows, thick black lashes around those widely opened storm-hued eyes, a full red mouth and Richard's flawless brown skin. Kitty was right, she was definitely a Morgan. A Morgan named Clark.

He writhed, cursed himself for the millionth time. All his children would be born bastards; Lizzie Lock was not going to oblige him by dying in a hurry. Of course he could not murder her, but there was no one save God to say that he was not allowed to *wish* her dead.

Why can we never seem to keep the threads which weave into the pattern of our lives untangled? I did not think when I went into marriage with Lizzie Lock. Or rather, I did not think of myself or the future. I pitied her, I fancied I owed her a debt—I thought like a head man and I still think like a head man. Stephen warned me, I seem to remember that, but I did not listen. The people I have harmed are my own children—the dear soul who is my heart's wife is dismissed as my "woman." They never even say "mistress." The term is "woman." A word which suggests that she has no identity, absolutely no status of any kind. A simple convenience. I can, as some men are already doing, throw her to one side without any kind of compensation to her. Sentences are up, those who have hoarded enough gold are buying their passages to England, or Cathay, or anywhere else that takes their fancy. Old faces like Joe Robinson's are disappearing. But so many of them are leaving their women here to fend for themselves. As well that, like Major Ross, Commander King is as willing to grant a lone woman land as a lone man. These sad abandoned creatures do not need to hawk their favors around the barracks of the New South Wales Corps soldiers. What we do to women is unforgivable. They are not whores by nature. We force them to it.

Kate gurgled, smiled, revealed that she was cutting teeth. My firstborn, my daughter. My bastard. Hugging her, Richard put his lips to the unbelievable sleekness of her skin, inhaled the fresh clean smell of it, aware that Kate adored to be adored.

"Kate," he said to her, turning her within his hands so that she faced him and could give him seductive glances—in that she took after her mother—and he could talk to her as if she understood what he was saying. "My Kate, what is to become of you? How can I ensure that ye're never reduced to the sort of life God inflicted upon your mother? How can I turn ye from the bastard child of two convict parents into a well-schooled young lady with her pick of every young man in this part of the world?" He kissed her tiny hand, felt its fingers curl strongly around one of his. Then he snuggled her into the crook of his arm, tucked her head beneath his chin and looked into the distance, his mind filled with the dilemma of her fate.

* * *

Kitty took a long time to fetch one bucket of unneeded water. First she sat beside the spring and smoldered for a while, then held the bucket beneath the main fall to fill it, after which she set it on the ground and sat down again. Her outburst had caught her unaware, she had not realized that these resentments simmered so near the surface; her days were too busy to permit the luxury of self-examinations. The reason why her feelings had come tumbling out today was manifest: Richard did not want a second child so soon—if he wanted one at all. But these were not things in his province! God had made her to procreate and she loved procreating. The words of workhouse days and workhouse sermons rattled off as fingers were busy embroidering held meaning now. Adam may have been the first person on earth, but until Eve appeared he was an—an—an *exhibit!* Eve was more important than Adam. Eve made the children and a house a home.

Richard could not have it entirely for himself because he won their bread. She *baked* their bread! And in future, she vowed, jumping up and lifting the twenty-pound bucket with ease, he was going to have to take notice of *her* wishes. I am not a mouse and I am not a boot-scraper. I am a person of consequence.

The picture he presented as she walked up the path through the vegetables from the spring was, she admitted, softening, truly heart-warming. Her heart warmed. Unnoticed, she stood still to watch him with the baby, turn her to face him, talk solemn words to her, kiss her hand and gaze down on it with a face filled by love and wonder. The way he cuddled her then. The way he stared over her head into nothing.

Move, Richard, move! Kitty stood willing him to move, but he would not. The sun always set behind the house and its front lay in shadows, yet the light was absolutely clear, fell on father and child as if they had been petrified, stilled to stone. A very old memory came surging up from the depths, of the Master at the workhouse presiding over the Sunday service, sitting in his chair of state looking into nothing while the chaplain preached the sins of a flesh none of his listeners comprehended. The Master continued to stare vacantly; the chaplain ended, the orphan audience remained without stirring, the stiff and bitter spinster mistresses let their eyes patrol the ranks to make sure no girl wore an unchurchlike expression; and the Master sat gazing into the distance as if he saw a vision neither pleasant nor unpleasant. It was only when the chaplain took him timidly by the shoulder that he moved. Moved to fall forward out of the chair onto the chapel flags and lie there as shapeless as the stockings half-full of sand with which the inmates were beaten so that the marks did not show.

Move, Richard, move! But he did not, while time flowed on and the child in his arm slept obliviously. Suddenly she knew that he was dead. It broke on her in an instant and drove her to her knees, the bucket falling, water cascading, the world a thing of utter silence. Even then he did not move. He was dead! He was dead!

"Richard!" she screamed, scrambling up, running.

Her cry dragged him out of his abstraction, but not in time to catch her. She was upon him in the same moment, weeping and keening, her hands plucking at his shoulders, his chest.

"Kitty! What is it, my love? What is the matter?"

She wailed and howled, tears streaming down her face, lost to all reason. When Kate joined her mother to bawl in her own key, Richard got to his feet with two demented female creatures clinging to him as to a lifeline, his head spinning. Kate he dumped in her cradle unceremoniously, where she yelled in outrage at being so cavalierly discarded; Kitty he sat in the armchair by the stove, where she sobbed as if her heart were broken. Out came the rum; fussing and clucking, he forced Kitty to drink.

"Oh, Richard, I thought you were dead!" she moaned, choking, looking up at him with eyes and nose running. "I thought you dead! I thought you dead!" She flung her arms about his hips and pushed her face against him, weeping afresh.

"Kitty, I am *not* dead." He disengaged her hands, picked her out of the chair and sat down in it with her on his lap. The hem of her calico dress was the only available rag, so he took it and wiped her eyes, her nose, her cheeks, her chin, her throat—the spate of tears had even soaked into the yoke of her dress. "My dearest love, I am not dead. See?" he asked, smiling tenderly. "Corpses cannot deal with fits of the vapors. Though it is nice," he added, heart full, "to know that I am so desperately mourned. Here, have another sip of rum."

Kate's tantrum in the bedroom was increasing in volume, but she would get over it faster than Kitty would get over her shock, so he turned his head and shouted sternly, "Kate, hush your roars! Go to sleep!" Much to his surprise, his daughter's howls subsided into blessed silence.

"Oh, Richard, I thought you were dead like the Master, and I could not bear it! You were dead—and you had loved me so much—and I had never understood—and I had hurt you and spurned you—and then it was too late to tell you that I love you. I love you the way you love me, more than life itself. I thought you were dead, and I did not know how to live in a world without you! I love you, Richard, I love you!"

He pushed her hair off her face, did some more work with his makeshift rag. "All my Christmases have come at once," he said. "I know there have been a lot of tears, but why are ye so wet?"

"I lost the bucket of water, I think. Kiss me, Richard! Oh, kiss me with love and let me kiss you with love."

Love reciprocated, they both discovered, turned lips into the thinnest possible of skins between body and spirit. From now on, thought Richard, there need be no secrets. I can tell her anything. Kitty simply knew the bliss of music in her heart and wings on her soul. Love had been there all along.

Stephen came out to see them on Kate's first birthday, the 15th of February, 1793, bearing an amazing gift.

But it was not the gift which caused Richard, Kitty and the child to stare: Lieutenant Donovan was clad in the full glory of his Royal Navy rank—black shoes, white stockings, white breeches and waistcoat, ruffled shirt, cutaway Navy coat, a few touches of gold braid, sword by his side, wig on his head, hat tucked beneath his arm. Not merely strikingly handsome—also strikingly impressive.

"You are going!" said Kitty, eyes filling with tears.

"What a figure ye cut!" said Richard, concealing his grief with a laugh.

"The uniform came from Port Jackson—not a bad fit," said Stephen, preening, "though the coat needs work about the shoulders. Mine are too broad."

"Broad enough for command. Congratulations." Richard held out his hand. "I knew there was some significance in the name of this wretched ship just arrived."

"Aye. Kitty. I wore the uniform in honor of young Kate, I do not go immediately. Kitty will not sail for at least a week, so we still have a little time." He pulled the wig off to reveal that he had imitated Richard and cropped his hair. "Christ, these things are hot! Meant for the English Channel, not Norfolk Island in humid Februaries."

"Stephen, your beautiful hair!" Kitty cried, looking closer to weeping. "Oh, I loved it! I keep trying to persuade Richard to grow his, but he says it is a nuisance."

"He is absolutely right. Since I cut mine I feel as free as a bird—except when I have to put the wig on." He went to Kate, sitting in a high chair Richard had made, and put his parcel on its tray. "Happy birthday, dearest little godchild."

"Ta," she said, smiling and reaching out to touch his face. "Stevie." She looked beyond him to Richard and beamed. "Dadda!"

Stephen kissed her and removed the parcel, which did not upset her in the least; while her father was in the same room she saw little beyond him.

"Put it away for her," Stephen said, giving the parcel to Kitty. " 'Twill be some years before she can appreciate it."

Curious, Kitty undid the wrappings and stared in awe. "Oh, Stephen! It is beautiful!"

"I bought it from Kitty's captain. Her name is Stephanie."

She was a doll with a delicately painted porcelain face, eyes which had properly striped irises, minutely drawn lashes, a mop of yellow hair made from strands of silk, and she was dressed like a lady of thirty years ago in a panniered pink silk gown.

"Ye return to Port Jackson in Kitty, I gather?" Richard asked.

"Aye, and then on her to Portsmouth in June."

They ate roast pork and then a birthday cake Kitty had managed to make feather-light on a rising ingredient no more substantial than white-of-egg beaten in a copper bowl with a whisk Richard had made her out of copper wire. He was so good with his hands, could make her anything she asked for.

The sporadic visits of ships had provided tea, real sugar, various small luxuries including Kitty's pride and joy, a frail porcelain teaset. The unglazed windows fluttered green Bengalese cotton curtains, but pictures and forks still eluded her. Never mind, never mind. William Henry was perhaps three months from his birth; she knew he was William Henry. Mary would have to wait until the next time—not as long a wait as Richard would choose, but never mind, never mind. Children were all she had to give him. There could never be too many; Norfolk Island had its dangers too. Last year poor Nat Lucas, chopping down a pine, watched in horror as it fell with a monstrous roar upon Olivia, baby William in her arms and her twin girls clinging to her skirts. Olivia and William had escaped almost unharmed, but Mary and Sarah died instantly. Yes, of children there must be many. One mourned their passing dreadfully, yet thanked God for those still living.

Her life was filled with happiness, for no better reason than that she loved and was loved, that her daughter was bursting with good health and the son growing inside her drove her mad with his incessant kicking. Oh, she would miss Stephen! Though not, she knew, one-tenth as much as Richard would. Still, these things happened. Nothing remained the same, everything kept marching to somewhere else that was a mystery until it arrived on the doorstep. Stephen was sailing in *her* all the way to England, and that meant much. Kitty would keep him safe, Kitty would skim the waves like a petrel.

"May we have Tobias?" she asked.

The mobile brows flew up, the vivid blue eyes twinkled. "Part from Tobias? Not likely, Kitty. Tobias is a Navy cat, he sails with me wherever I go. I have trained him to think of me as his place."

"Will you visit Major Ross?"

"Definitely."

Richard waited to ask his burning question until he strolled up the cleft with Stephen toward the Queensborough road. "Will ye do me a favor, Stephen?"

"Anything, ye know that. Would ye like me to see your father, Cousin James-the-druggist?"

"If ye've time, not otherwise. I want ye to carry a letter from me to Jem Thistlethwaite in Wimpole Street, London, and give it to him in person. I will never see him again, but I would like someone who knows *this* Richard Morgan to vouch for him."

"It shall be done." At the white boundary stone Stephen took the wig and clapped it on with a rueful look at the grinning Richard. "Ye have a week to write your letter. Kitty is in the roads until I say otherwise."

With the advent of the Reverend Mr. Bain as resident chaplain in Norfolk Island, the pressure to attend Sunday service had eased a little. Commander King insisted that every felon be present, so if all the free came as well, the crush was dreadful. Felons were deemed to need God's attention more than did the free.

Knowing therefore that his face would not be missed if he missed service on the morrow, Richard warned Kitty that he would be up late on Saturday night writing a letter to Mr. Thistlethwaite, and would sleep on when morning came. Delighted that he would gain a few extra hours of rest (writing a letter was not like sawing a log, after all), Kitty took herself off to bed.

Richard lifted the oil lamp off its shelf with great care; it had been bought at the same stall as the teaset, and cost more because it was accompanied by a fifty-gallon keg of whale oil. His use of it was sparing—sheer weariness did not permit nightly reading—but possessing it had meant that he could pore over the treasure trove of books Jem Thistlethwaite had sent in the only leisure activity did not make him feel a traitor to his family. Kitty, he understood now, would never learn to read and write because neither was important to her. The sole fount of knowledge in their house was he, therefore he had to read.

Paper bathed in a golden glow from the two-wicked lamp, he dipped one of his steel pens into the inkwell and began to write with scant hesitation; what he wanted to say had already been rehearsed in his mind over and over again.

> "Jem, this letter is borne by the best man I have ever known, and the only consolation I have in losing him is that you will come to know and love him. Somehow we have trodden the same path through all the years since Alexander sat in the Thames, from ship to ship and place to place. He a free man, I a convict. Always friends. Did I not have Kitty and my children, losing him would be a mortal blow.
>
> "What I write of on these pages is different from the letter I sent after your box came. That one went by any official hand it encountered, at the mercy of prying eyes and prurient minds. The miracle is that our letters ever do reach their destination, but the trickle of replies which arrived during 1792 (and on Bellona and Kitty so far this year) tells us that those who bear our letters to England pity us enough to make good their promises. Some of us, however, never do receive word from the place most of us still call 'home.' I am unsure whether that is accidental or on purpose. This one will never leave Stephen's care. I can say anything, and, knowing Stephen, he will sit in silence to let ye read this before he speaks, and that frees me too.
>
> "This year, 1793, I will turn five-and-forty. How I look and how I have physically weathered this span Stephen will relate better than I, for we lack mirrors in Norfolk Island. Save that I have kept my health and can probably work harder for longer now than ever I could when a young man in England.
>
> "As I sit here in the night the only sounds which reach my ears are of mighty trees moving in a rising wind, and the only smells which assail my nostrils are sweetly resinous or indefinable relics of the rain which fell a few hours ago and wetted the soil.
>
> "I will never return to England, which is a place I no longer

think of as, or call, 'home.' Home is here in Norfolk Island and always will be here. The truth is, Jem, that I want no truck with the country sent me to Botany Bay jammed aboard a slaver for just over twelve months amid misery and suffering still haunt my dreams.

"There were good times and good moments, none of them given us by those who shipped us off—greedy contractors, indifferent shufflers of paper, port-swilling barons and admirals. And we on the first fleet which sailed for Botany Bay enjoyed luxury compared to the horrors those who follow us must endure—ask Stephen to tell you what they found aboard Neptune when she anchored in Port Jackson.

"To be the first for Botany Bay was at once the best and the worst of it. *No one* knew what to do, Jem, not even the sad and desperate little governor, Phillip. It was neither planned nor decently equipped. Not one person in Whitehall worked out the logistics, and the contractors cheated on both the quality and the quantity of the clothing, tools and other essentials that were sent with us. I keep imagining the look on Julius Caesar's face did he know of our shambles.

"Yet somehow we have survived the first five years of this ill-conceived, misshapen experiment in men's and women's lives. I am not sure how this has happened, except that it is perhaps evidence of the persistence and perseverance of men and women. It would be wrong to say that England offered us a second chance here. We were not offered *any* chance, first or last. Rather, we behaved according to our natures. Some of us simply vowed to survive and, having survived, then hurried 'home' or still skulk about. And some of us, having survived, were determined to begin again as best we can with what we have. I put myself in the second group, and say of it that while we were convicts we worked hard, we incurred no official displeasure, we were not lashed or ironed, we effaced ourselves in some situations and made ourselves useful in others. After being freed by pardon or emancipation, we have taken up land and begun the alien business of farming.

"How much of England has England wasted! The intelligence, the ingenuity, the resourcefulness, the hardiness. A list of assets I could make pages long. And all of the owners had sat in English gaols and hulks utterly wasted. What is wrong with England, that England is blind enough to throw such assets away as worthless rubbish?

"It is fair to say that very few of us had any idea what sort of stuff we were made of. I know that I did not. The old tranquil, patient Richard Morgan who could not even bring himself to care about the loss of £3,000 has died, Jem. He was passive, content, unambitious and *small.* His griefs were the griefs of all men—loss of what he loved. His vices were the vices of all men—self-absorption and self-indulgence. His joys were the joys of all men—taking his pleasure in what he loved. His virtues were the virtues of all men—belief in God and country.

"Richard Morgan was resurrected in the midst of a sea of pain, and finds the pain of others more unbearable than his own. He takes nothing for granted, he speaks out when necessary, he guards his loved ones and his fortune with his very life, he trusts hardly anybody, and he relies on one person only—himself.

"The tragedy of it, Jem, is that despite these new beginnings we have dragged the worst of England with us—coldhearted arrogance from those who govern us or hold sway over us, the unwritten laws which make some men better than others by virtue of rank or wealth, the stigmata of poverty and despicable origins, the mistaken creed that Crown and Church can do no wrong, the ignominy of bastardy.

"So I fear for my children, who must carry the burden of my sins as well as their own. Yet I hope for them in a way I could never have hoped for my Bristol children. There is room here for them to fly, Jem. There is room here for them to matter. And when all is said and done, what more could I ask of God than that?

"I had thought to write at much greater length, but I find that I have said my piece. Look after yourself—have a care for Stephen, who brings my love with him—and write soon. Ships from England now make the voyage in under six months, and Norfolk Island is a watering place for vessels sailing to Cathay, Nootka Sound or Otaheite. With any luck, I will be able to reply to your answer before too many more children have been born. I cannot get Kitty out of the habit of conceiving, and I am too weak to say no when she throws her leg over.

"By the grace of God and the kindness of others, I have had a fine run."

He signed it, folded the pages so that their corners met in the middle, melted wax and applied his seal. RM in chains. Then, leaving the letter to lie on his table, he leaned to blow out the lamp and went to Kitty.

Finis

Author's Afterword

The saga of Richard Morgan is not ended; he was to live for many years to come and experience yet more adventures, disasters and upheavals. I hope to continue with his family's story.

The American War of Independence upset the European applecart profoundly, and in ways the people of the time could not have envisioned. Until then, a nation's constitution was generally accepted as embodied in its laws; until then, the concept of a people's existing without a monarch at the top of the social pyramid had become virtually unimaginable; until then, the rights of individuals of moderate or low status had not been considered as equal to the rights of those with rank, property and/or wealth.

One of the less well-known results of American independence was the establishment of the British colony of New South Wales and its almost immediately synchronous offshoot at Norfolk Island. There are strong differences of opinion between modern historians as to the British Crown's reasons for colonizing a quadrant of the globe scarcely known, even including its geophysical dimensions. Some experts in the field think New South Wales was conceived and carried out purely to have somewhere to dump the hapless victims of a penal legal system by far the harshest in western Europe. Whereas others insist that higher ideals and philosophies were also involved.

I do not pretend to sufficient erudition to clarify this debate. I say only that with the closure of the thirteen American colonies to the shipment of convicts there as indentured servants, the British Crown understood that it had to find *somewhere* to send its convicted felons, and that that somewhere had to be at least an ocean's breadth away from home. The occurrence of the French Revolution and growing unrest not only in Ireland but also in Scotland and Wales provided additional impetus to ensure that this penal experiment at the far ends of the earth should succeed. The story of the early decades of New South Wales and Norfolk Island contains few evidences of ultimate wealth or even the beginnings of a positive gross national product; it does, however, contain many evidences that, whatever the higher ideals and philosophies of the British Crown might have been, the place was eminently suited to the quarantine of convicts, rebels, political demagogues and free ne'er-do-wells. They could scratch a living there without representing a danger to "home."

To me, the two most fascinating aspects of the great transportation experiment are, first, the blithe assumption on the part of the British Crown that all one had to do was *do it,* and, secondly, the character of its guinea pigs, the convicts. That it succeeded rests far more with the character of its guinea pigs, the convicts, than with anything else. Which is why I chose to write this novel about the genesis of the much later Commonwealth of Australia (1901) from the convict point of view.

Why were these people convicted in the first place? What in fact were the circumstances of their crimes? How did English justice work? What rights did the accused felon have at law? What were their backgrounds? How did they rub along together? Why, having been landed in an utterly alien place of no milk or honey, did they persevere? Why, having served out their sentences and in a lot of instances made enough money to buy passage home, did so relatively few choose to return home? What did they cling to to sustain their spirits? How did they cope with the brutal, soulless punitive regimes of the time? How did they view freedom when it came, and what did they think of England?

More of the latter part of this book takes place at Norfolk Island than at New South Wales. This unique speck in the midst of the Pacific Ocean has a rich and varied history all of its own.

There have been three separate attempts by the British Crown to colonize it, the first two of which were terminated and the island depopulated: the so-called First and Second Settlements. It is the hideous Second Settlement (1825–1855) which most people think of when it comes to unconscionable cruelty; the First Settlement (1788–1813), despite its horrors, was much kinder.

The third attempt was yet another experiment in transportation. The descendants of the Bounty mutineers and their Tahitian women were uplifted in totality from Pitcairn Island in 1856 and given the larger and more fertile Norfolk Island as a new homeland. Some of the Pitcairners, disillusioned by broken promises, returned from Norfolk to Pitcairn after 1856, and it is their descendants who today form the minute Second Settlement on Pitcairn Island.

The so-called Third Settlement was a success, I think because the Pitcairners were already an island people in the true sense. Island peoples can cope with extremely limited landmasses, which require a very different attitude to life—and governmental style—than vast landmasses. Though since 1979 Norfolk Island has had a limited form of self-government incorporating federal powers (an odd arrangement reflecting the Australian uncertainty), it remains at the mercy of a colonial overlord from across the seas. In 1914 it passed from being a dependent territory of the British Crown to a dependent territory of the Commonwealth of Australia; successive Australian governments and their unelected public "servants" have displayed exactly the same arrogance and insensitivity to the special nature of Norfolk Island and its Pitcairn people as did the British Crown. So one wonders what Australia, long a victim of colonialism itself, has actually learned about the phenomenon of colonialism, as the peoples of its equally remote Indian Ocean dependencies suffer even more than does vocal, mutineer-ridden Norfolk Island.

The sources for research are very rich, but often (as in the case of the Public Records Office at Kew in London) dauntingly haphazard and confused due to inexcusable lack of funding. As in my Roman research, I tend to lean far more on original sources than on modern treatises and works of scholarship. It is necessary for any student of any period of history to go back to the sources in order to formulate opinions, deductions and ideas of one's own.

I have not included a bibliography for the simple reason that it would run to many pages and contain as many documents as books. However, if anyone is interested in obtaining a bibliography of the published material, please write to me care of my publishers.

I must thank many people for help and information.

Chief among them is my beloved stepdaughter, Melinda, who went off to brave Kew, Bristol, Gloucester, Portsmouth and other English places, and also invaded repositories of history in Sydney, Hobart and Canberra. The materials she brought back have proven invaluable.

I must also specially thank Helen Reddy, another many-times-great-grandchild of Richard Morgan. When not singing and acting, she pursued the career of Richard Morgan to the top of her formidable bent, and furnished me with some terrific documentation.

My heartfelt thanks go to Mr. Les Brown, whose grasp of the history of Norfolk Island far exceeds anyone else's, no matter which of the three separate settlements one is interested in. Les has been an unsung historian hero, but I now sing his praises loud and long for all to hear. What a library, what documents!

How can I forget my perennially loyal and devoted staff? Pam Crisp, my personal assistant, Kaye Pendleton and Karen Quintal in the office, the ubiquitous master-of-all-trades, Joe Nobbs, Ria Howell and Fran Johnston in the house, Dallas Crisp, Phil Billman and Louise Donald outside. It is only due to their strenuous exertions that I find the time to write at such a pace. I love you all, and thank you. Thanks also to my mother-in-law, May, who kitty-sits Poindexter the cat whenever we are away. To Jan Nobbs. To Brother John and Greg Quintal for firsthand descriptions of sawing Norfolk pine the old way, in a pit with a rip saw.

My husband, Ric, is a tower of strength as well as my best friend. He is the four-times-great-grandson of both Richard Morgan the convict, and Fletcher Christian the Bounty mutineer. How strange are the workings of fate, that the one bloodline should meet the other in 1860 on a three-by-five-mile dot in the midst of an ocean and find that on Richard Morgan's side, that link with Norfolk Island goes back to a three-times-great-grandmother (Kate) born there in 1792. This is also true of Joe Nobbs.

In conclusion, I have not forgotten that there are still two volumes left to write in the Masters of Rome series. They will come, God willing, but it is necessary that I take a holiday from Rome, rather than yet another Roman holiday.

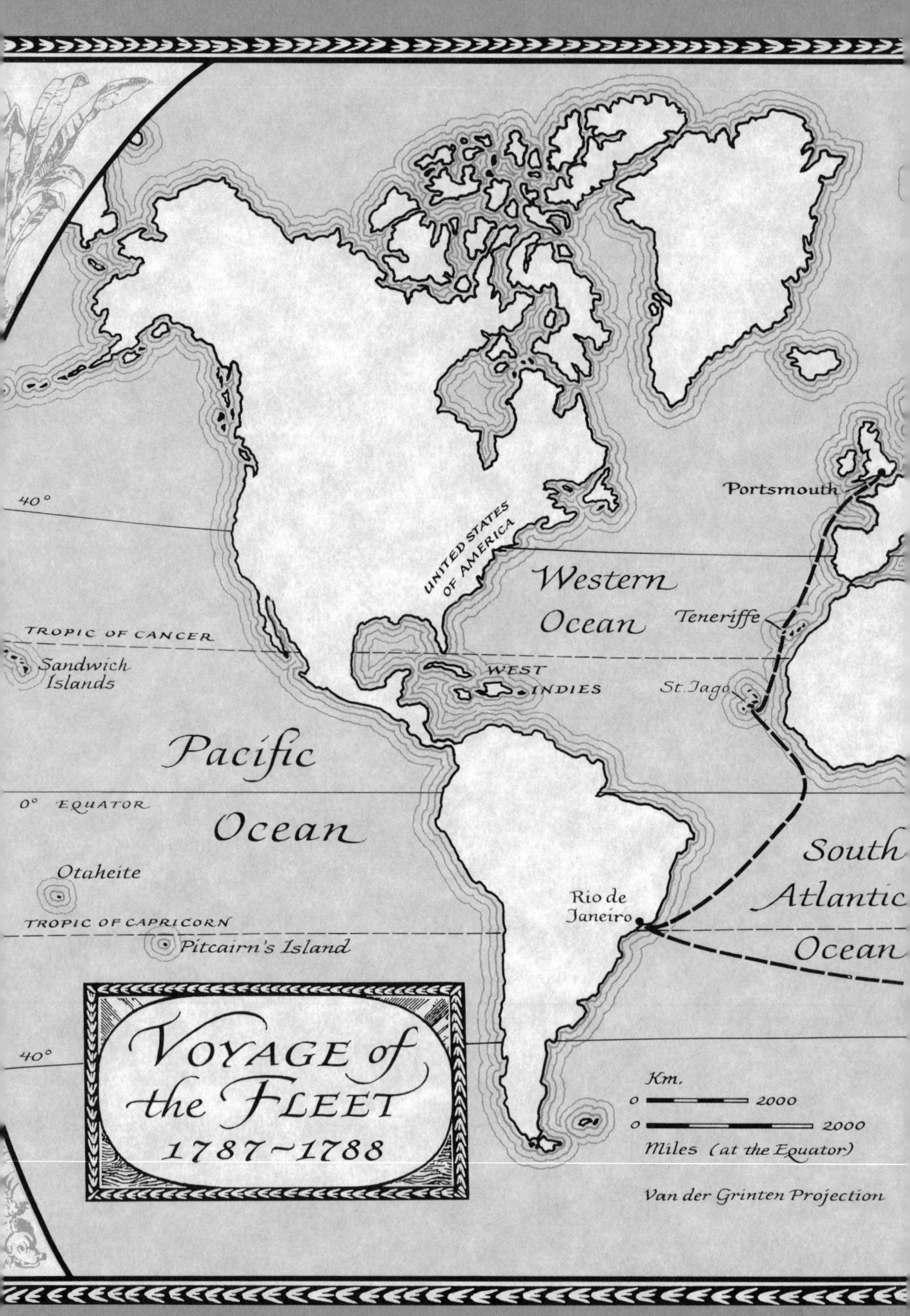
Voyage of the Fleet
1787~1788
Pacific
Ocean
Western
Ocean
South
Atlantic
Ocean
UNITED STATES
OF AMERICA
WEST
INDIES
Portsmouth
Teneriffe
St. Jago
Rio de
Janeiro
Sandwich
Islands
Otaheite
Pitcairn's Island
40°
TROPIC OF CANCER
0° EQUATOR
TROPIC OF CAPRICORN
40°
Km.
0 2000
0 2000
Miles (at the Equator)
Van der Grinten Projection